NEW YORK REVIEW BOOKS
CLASSICS

THE UNCOLLECTED STORIES OF MAVIS GALLANT

MAVIS GALLANT (1922–2014) was born in Montreal and worked as a journalist at the *Montreal Standard* before moving to Europe to devote herself to writing fiction. In 1960, after traveling extensively she settled in Paris, where she would remain for the rest of her life. Over the course of her career Gallant published more than one hundred stories and dispatches in *The New Yorker.* In 2002 she received the Rea Award for the Short Story and in 2004, the PEN/Nabokov Award for lifetime achievement.

GARTH RISK HALLBERG is the author of the novels *The Second Coming* and *City on Fire* and the novella *A Field Guide to the North American Family.* His stories have been anthologized in *Best New American Voices* and *Granta*'s *Best of Young American Novelists.*

THE UNCOLLECTED STORIES

of Mavis Gallant

Edited by

GARTH RISK HALLBERG

NEW YORK REVIEW BOOKS

New York

THIS IS A NEW YORK REVIEW BOOK
PUBLISHED BY THE NEW YORK REVIEW OF BOOKS
207 East 32nd Street, New York, NY 10016
www.nyrb.com

Library of Congress Cataloging-in-Publication Data
Names: Gallant, Mavis, author. | Hallberg, Garth Risk, editor.
Title: The uncollected stories of Mavis Gallant / by Mavis Gallant ; edited with
  an introduction by Garth Risk Hallberg.
Description: New York : New York Review Books, [2024] | Series: New York
  Review Books classics
Identifiers: LCCN 2024007871 (print) | LCCN 2024007872 (ebook) | ISBN
  9781681378749 (paperback) | ISBN 9781681378756 (ebook)
Subjects: LCSH: Short stories, Canadian. | Canadian fiction—20th century. |
  Canadian fiction—Women authors.
Classification: LCC PR9199.3.G26 A6 2024 (print) | LCC PR9199.3.G26
  (ebook) | DDC 813/.54—dc23/eng/20240529
LC record available at https://lccn.loc.gov/2024007871
LC ebook record available at https://lccn.loc.gov/2024007872

ISBN 978-1-68137-874-9
Available as an electronic book; ISBN 978-1-68137-875-6

Printed in the United States of America on acid-free paper.
10 9 8 7 6 5 4 3 2 1

Think where man's glory most begins and ends
And say my glory was I had such friends.

—W.B. YEATS

Marta Dvorak
John and Evie Flint
Alison Harris
Phyllis Springer Sipahioglu

CONTENTS

STORIES OF SOUTHERN EUROPE

STORIES OF PARIS AND BEYOND

APPENDIX: THREE EARLY STORIES

INTRODUCTION
Make Me Happy, Send Me A Story

I

THE ARCHIVES of *The New Yorker* consist of thousands upon thousands of letters and memos and cablegrams and onionskin-thin carbon copies—enough that, by the mid-1980s, a vertical stack of them might have reached the height of the Chrysler Building. Instead, more sensibly, the archivists have opted for boxes. These can be found a few blocks down Forty-Second Street, in the catacombs of the New York Public Library. The filing system, like the magazine itself, retains a whiff of midcentury punctilio: a "whichy thicket" regimented by date and rubric'ed by genre and only then, almost as an afterthought, subdivided by author's last name. Still, given a margin of time and a taste for digging, any fool with a library card can enter the third-floor rare books room and scrutinize the editorial correspondence of a Nabokov or a Cheever, a John Updike or an Alice Munro.

In the autumn of 2023, I was that fool. What had drawn me to the NYPL was an artist less well known than the foregoing, but, I'd come to feel, every inch their equal: the late Canadian short-story writer Mavis Gallant. I'd first encountered her work back in 2017, a period when, for complicated reasons, I'd begun to despair of the whole enterprise of prose fiction. In some sense, Gallant had been my cure. Reeled in by a late-1970s picaresque called "Speck's Idea," I spent the winter hopscotching my way through her *Paris Stories*. The following winter, I devoured a Montreal-themed companion volume, *Varieties of Exile*, wondering anew at each story's complexity, its beauty, its independent life. By spring, I'd ordered a used hardcover of Gallant's magnum opus, *The Collected Stories*, and resolved to parcel out whatever remained, one piece per day, like a kid rationing Halloween candy.

For weeks after the big book arrived, I spent the daylight hours plotting for the moment when my own kids would be in bed and I could return to the vivid dream that was my reading. It wasn't always easy to stop. Nonetheless, I remember looking up from the page a half-dozen times ("The Remission," "Across the Bridge," "Potter," "In the Tunnel," "The Pegnitz Junction") and thinking, blasphemously, "This is the greatest short story ever written."

And I remember a note of melancholy setting in as the pages dwindled. I started poking around to see whether, in the long decades of her working life, any further Gallant stories might have slipped through the cracks. What I found was the paradox that eventually sent me to her letters. On the page, Gallant had been exacting, consummate, but her history in book form fell so eccentrically between mercenary and haphazard that it was hard to say how many books she'd even written. A collection published under the same title in the United States and abroad might turn out to share only 80 percent of the same contents. Or two collections published under different titles might be 50 percent the same. A cluster of stories from *The New Yorker* might appear in one book in the States, only to resurface a few years later in Canada with new and different neighbors. There were times when a single story was available in as many as four editions at once. Yet amid this restless shuffling and reshuffling, a few stories never made it past the serial-publication stage, and dozens more ultimately fell out of print.

I decided to excavate a couple. From the serials, "Crossing France" (published in 1961 in *The Critic*): by turns droll, dreamy, casually devastating—pure-D Mavis. From the out-of-print books (namely 1964's *My Heart Is Broken*), "Its Image on the Mirror": a barbed and intricate masterpiece of nearly novelistic proportions. Were *these* the lost pieces Gallant had deemed "not worth reprinting," as she'd written in the mid-1990s . . . and if so, had she made a mistake? Or were they simply among the many stories she'd cut from *The Collected Stories* for length,

3

It is almost impossible to overstate the allure this would have held for any writer, let alone one as starved for sustenance, figurative and literal, as Gallant was in the early 1950s. In the decades that followed, as she seemed to gratify Maxwell's wish to see her in the fiction pages "every other week," the bond between writer and magazine grew correspondingly strong. The identification would persist in the monumental *Collected Stories*, whose acknowledgments inform us that, with three exceptions, "all of the stories in this work ... were originally published in *The New Yorker*." The dedication was to Maxwell, who edited her until 1975, and to Daniel Menaker, who succeeded him.

There's a certain modish brand of criticism that might use these details, along with a full accounting of Gallant's years in the wilderness, to stage an institutional *Pygmalion*—as if the writer, before winning favor for her submissions, had to first submit to the strictures of "the *New Yorker* story." The great obstacle to this is of course Gallant herself, who in art as in life bent the knee to exactly no one. A benefit of this new edition, then, is to clarify the lines of influence, and to underscore her blazing independence of mind.

One way it does so is by presenting a dozen pieces first published in other magazines—a larger portion than in any of her previous collections. This isn't to say that Gallant took the judgment of her *New Yorker* editors lightly, allowing second-tier work to slip into print. In fact, the opposite. No one was harder on a story, or less inclined to settle for "good enough," than Gallant. As she posited to an interviewer in 1988, the essence of her art was an unceasing vigilance: "In a successful short story, you are standing on your toes the whole time. You don't dare let down for a second." Even after her 1952 breakthrough, the correspondence is studded with the titles of manuscripts she must have agreed fell short of this "extremely high standard": "The Elephant's Funeral," "The Dancing Hour," "And Planted Firm Britannia's Flag." If the picnic hamper in Montreal had given way to a linen closet near Montparnasse (where manuscripts got stashed "between bath mats and towels") the work she deemed truly "not worth reprinting" ended up in the same old place: the wastebasket, "torn to shreds."

But on those occasions when Gallant shook off a rejection from Maxwell & Co. and pursued another home in print, *The Uncollected Stories* shows her to have been almost invariably right. The one exception might be "The Flowers of Spring," from 1950—the first full-length story she ever published, now returned to print after seventy-five years. When she passed the manuscript to *Northern Review*, Canada's leading literary magazine, she may still have been out to prove that she could escape Montreal. At any rate, "The Flowers of Spring" can be seen to form a missing link between her three early sketches (reprinted here as an appendix) and the mature work. There are moments of illumination—the hospitalized veterans wheeled into the sun "like plums to be ripened," the visiting wife's idea that certain feelings "photographed badly"—and also a quality of estrangement that Mildred Wood had singled out as "too cryptic." Far from avoiding this quality in future stories, however, Gallant would redouble her efforts to turn it to account. And by the time of "The Old Place," eight years later, physical and existential dislocation—the state she called being "set afloat"—would be revealed as her great subject, deployed not to seal us off from character but to deliver it to us in all its fathomlessness.

This story, last seen in the spring 1958 issue of *Texas Quarterly*, also marks one of her first attempts to render what Francine Prose has called "an entire existence and a whole world, a milieu precisely situated in time and on the map." It concerns a college-age American named Dennis Arnheim whose suffocating mother has been killed in a car crash a few years after his father's death at war. She is survived by Dennis's unloved stepfather, a colorful immigrant named Dr. Rudolf Meyer, and a question of inheritance—"what to tell his stepfather about the house"—pulls the two men into closer propinquity. Gallant was only eight years removed from newspaper work when "The Old Place" appeared, but her mastery of her chosen medium is almost alarming. She introduces the stepfather in swift sure strokes, even as she probes the limits of such economy:

> He said he was Russian, but he also said he was Viennese . . . He said that his mother was Hungarian and that his first wife had been the most beautiful woman in Central Europe . . . He had

been in a concentration camp: his number was tattooed just above his right wrist. However, and this was typical, he said he had been in no fewer than six: Auschwitz, Ravensbruck, Belsen, Dachau, Mauthausen, and Buchenwald. He was huge and tall and well-muscled, and said he had been fencing champion of Vienna and amateur boxing champion of Austria. Gray curly hair stood straight up all over his head like a tangled wire wreath. He wore double-focus spectacles, which fit badly, so that he had to throw back his head to get a good view through the lower half-circle.

We, too, are being given double vision here: The more the jumble of particulars piles up, the less (and more) we know about the man. And rather than smooth away the discontinuities—trivial, world-historical—Gallant lets them strike suggestive sparks. For the stepson is likewise built from scraps, just on a different scale, and as the story goes on, other doublings jostle to the fore. If, like his stepfather, Dennis can "appear haughty," it is only because he is continually throwing himself back to an objective distance from the world, as though refusing to have feelings about the story he's in might protect him from the fact that it's a tragedy.

The emotional climax comes overseas, where Dr. Meyer has taken "the extraordinary notion of revisiting the concentration camps"—and, not incidentally, of introducing his new family to his adult daughter, Charlotte. Now living in neutral Switzerland, she "had been through too much and had no heart left," the doctor says. "The truth is she has no natural feelings." In other words, Charlotte is Dennis seen through a glass darkly, and he returns from the encounter "with the same half-hearted despair he had felt coming away; a mirror image of himself in limbo."

So vivid is the writing here, so forcefully sketched the inner conflict, so deft the movement through time, that it is easy to forget that the moment, like the rest of the story's long second act, occurs in the fictional past, while Dennis's mother is still alive. One can almost lose sight, that is, of the "question of disposal" on which Dennis's memories now hang. But in the end, the story will wind its way back to Dr. Meyer's urgent entreaties—"I have little money to leave and I must think of my poor Charlotte." And as he holds out to Dennis the photographs he's taken on their trip, "the empty barracks, the disused railway sidings . . . as if he were holding squares of silence in his hands," a buried trip wire comes, just barely, into view. Dennis is being asked not only to sell the house but to offer up the proceeds to his fellow survivors. It's a choice that anticipates Gallant's great German stories of *The Pegnitz Junction*, fifteen years later, which muster even more dazzling temporal structures to evoke the double bind of history. What claim does Dennis have on "the old place"? What claims does it have on him? And in the face of such claims, acknowledged or suppressed, can a person ever become as free, or even as biographically coherent, as he longs to be? Or are we consigned to live like Dr. Meyer, "his past life float[ing] over their heads, tantalizing and brilliant, like a cluster of escaped balloons"?

"Crossing France," finished around the same time, shows some of this same mastery, as does a comparably constructed story, "Paola and Renata," from a few years later. Superficially less weighty, they belong to a decade's worth of glittering comedies inspired by Gallant's sojourns in southern Europe (see also "The Moabitess," "Jeux d'Été," and the superb "Better Times"). *The New Yorker*'s rejection of these two stories involved much behind-the-scenes gnashing of teeth. Of "Crossing France," for example, Maxwell fretted to a colleague that its boys-on-bicycles *donné* was simply too close to a Harold Brodkey story recently published in the magazine. And "Paola and Renata," he remarks, accurately, "is so well written that it seems a crime to be sending it back." Gallant might have been heartened to hear such misgivings. As things stood, she had the good sense to send the two pieces on to the sterling little magazines where each would find a home.

Still, the standout among her non–*New Yorker* pieces is the novella "Its Image on the Mirror," whose length foreclosed any appearance in the magazine. Unusually for Gallant, it centers not on an ad hoc ménage but on an intact nuclear family—specifically, on the fraught relationship between two sisters, Jean and Isobel Duncan. The story is also notable for its sustained and virtuosic use of dramatic monologue, where Gallant had previously reserved the first-person voice for memoiristic recollection. One can almost feel her gathering breath to record, from within the armor of imposture, everything she has to say about parents and marriage and womanhood and Canada and "the common inheritance, the family walls." As if to create further deniability, Gallant places the more glamorous sister, Isobel, center stage. But the entire story lives in plainer Jean, who narrates their lives ostensibly from the wings.

It is difficult to hear Jean talk of Isobel and her lovers without thinking of the narrative structure of *The Great Gatsby*, a novel Gallant held "without peer": "They were the lighted window, I was the watcher on the street." But Gallant takes us deeper. Trapped in her own staid marriage, Jean does not attempt to hide her jealousy of Isobel, or persuade us of her comparative innocence: "My nights were long and uneasy and full of ugly thoughts." Nor, in the privacy of retrospect, does she spare other characters her lacerating candor. Her dismissal of one of Isobel's children—"He was a detestable little boy"—rivals Hemingway for how much meaning it squeezes into six words. But Jean is also capable of plangent evocations of life in the 1940s, charged with hardship and destruction ("the harsh wartime paper of letters from overseas, the ends of cigarettes . . . smoked with a stranger"), and of a lyricism that touches poetry, as when she sums up the drumbeat of overseas postings and deaths: "The men we knew dissolved in a foreign rain."

Particularly in America, particularly now, we prefer a more Calvinist shade of empathy: bestowed reflexively, but only on the obvious good guys. Gallant's version is both more implacable and more universal, and seems to me closer to the God's honest truth. Her "unsentimental compassion," in Alberto Manguel's fine phrase, is not a commodity to be granted or withheld, but an unfolding that sees people in all their messiness and refuses to flinch. Wounded, rebarbative, brilliant, at a loss, Jean Duncan is an extraordinary act of commitment on Gallant's part. The character may be what admirers (often male) mean when they call Gallant "daunting" or speak of her as a writer's writer (or even that loneliest of creatures, a writer's writer's writer). But "Its Image on the Mirror" asks less of a reader's intellect than it does of her heart, and if you can commit to Jean the way Gallant does, she will carry you through the temporal twists and eddies to a resolution you won't soon forget.

And then there is "With a Capital T," which Gallant gave to *Canadian Fiction Magazine*'s 1978 festschrift in her honor, rather than to *The New Yorker*. In final decisions over what to include in *The Collected Stories*, not having passed through the usual channels may have told against it, considering the other Linnet Muir pieces appear in the book in sequence. But to skip the last, the capstone, story, is to be deprived of their novelistic patterning, a Proustian full circle wherein the prohibitions of childhood ("not to say, do, touch") become the adult's pursuit of freedom . . . and wherein the rival who threatened to snatch Linnet's father in "Voices Lost in Snow" reappears in a new light. I mean not just Linnet's feckless godmother, Georgie, but also something like time itself:

> Her life seemed silent and slow and choked with wrack, while mine moved all in a rush, dislodging every obstacle it encountered. Then mine slowed too; stopped flooding its banks. The noise of it abated and I could hear the past.

4

A thoroughgoing perfectionist, Gallant often arranged her collections thematically, as if to soft-pedal any diachronic shift in approach. (As she said years later when asked if her storytelling had changed, "I don't compare . . . It's just a straight line to me.") *The Uncollected Stories* follows Gallant's practice, adapting the loose geographic structure of her 1981 collection *Home Truths*. But because its continental divisions also track a broad evolution in her subject matter—from North Americans to exiles to Europeans at home—the stories follow a rough chronology as well. The net effect is another windfall: a portrait of Gallant's development over time.

This can be seen most clearly in the thirty-odd stories first printed in *The New Yorker*, which cover the waterfront from the early 1950s to the mid-1980s. They reveal Gallant to have been not only a student of her form, an admirer of Chekhov and Eudora Welty, but also a fearless experimenter, interrogating every formal assumption and discarding those that might stand in her way. She liked to claim of William Maxwell, "He made no attempt to influence his writers," but this seems wishful, if not hagiographic. Their editorial exchanges read at times like the best writer's workshop ever conducted, at others like a literary sparring session; what matters is that Gallant gave as good as she got, or better. It may be fair to say that, apart from the inexhaustible Updike, no contributor from this period was more closely associated with "*New Yorker* fiction." But it is equally true that no writer, not even Donald Barthelme, did more to broaden its vocabulary. Three stories, early, middle, and late, suffice to illustrate the point.

First, "Thank You for the Lovely Tea," published in 1956. She later chose it as the leadoff piece for *Home Truths*—an honor preserved here, and likely for the same reasons. The opening in particular shows the same deft touch with place that "The Old Place" did with time. We are at a girls' boarding school in Canada, where

> It was the last lap of term, the dead period between the end of exams and the start of freedom. Handicrafts and extra art classes were improvised to keep them busy, but it was hopeless; glooming over their desks, they quarreled, dreamed of summer, wrote plaintive letters home.

Seemingly leisurely, this description is quickened by purpose: It soon alights on Ruth Cook, the smart, bored, contemptuous girl who, ignoring the drone of her art teacher, writes "Life is Hell" on the top of her desk, "hoping that someone would see it and that there would be a row." An antagonist comes blundering up the walk outside: "untidy" Mrs. Holland, her widowed father's new "friend," arrived to take Ruth and two classmates to tea. Just like that, Ruth is cemented as our protagonist—the figure who, by the force of her desire, will fulfill in some surprising way the teacher's prophecy: "It is a year of change." And this is all in keeping with Maxwell's amiable gloss on Aristotle: "By convention, at least, there has to be—oh, nothing so vulgar as a moral ... but something stated or unstated that the reader takes to be the reason the author wrote this story instead of some other."

But where we are braced for climax—change, recognition—Gallant proceeds to mount her own bravura lesson in "Perspective as well as Proportion," an ironic roundelay that sends us in stages through Mrs. Holland's head and the headmistress's and the two classmates'. By the time we return to Ruth in act three, we'll have glimpsed not only what each character wants—the story of which she might be the center—but also what each is missing about the others . . . the failures of generosity that freeze them in place. A prophecy has been fulfilled: Life is hell, if not in the religious sense, then in the more ordinary sense of everyday unhappiness. Whose story is this, then, really? Who might walk out of it different than they came in? The answer appears to be the narrator herself, hedged by retrospect from the story's first lines—perhaps a Ruth given heart by time and distance, or someone very much like her.

"Bonaventure," from 1966, is of another order of ambition altogether, expanding the aperture to take in music and sex and Freud and the Brothers Grimm and thirty years of history. Yet even as the story goes wide, Gallant's pursuit of subjectivity intensifies, with sometimes disorienting effects. Instead of the stately merry-go-round of "Thank You for the Lovely Tea," we are plunged into the protagonist's turbulent interior: "He was besieged, he was invaded, by his mother's account of the day he was conceived. . . . Before he *was*—Douglas Ramsay—the world was covered with mist, palm fronds, and vegetarian reptiles." Eventually the mists clear and we find ourselves in Switzerland, where Ramsay, a young composer, has come to stay as the guest of a maestro's widow, and perhaps to sleep in his bed. A neat setup, a cousin to "Goldilocks," yet we remain so close to consciousness that the tale keeps folding in on itself, as if there has been "a mistake in time." Ramsay slips from a present predicament, one of my favorite in Gallant's work—"it was a June day, he was recently twenty, and he had to get rid of chocolate wrappers"—to a reverie about his hostess, to a memory of a girlfriend in Berlin, then back to the hostess . . . but is she now standing before him, or is she still simply a figment of memory (or imagination)? The question remains unanswerable for pages.

The story is also, like much of Gallant, very funny, not least because of these distortions. An endearing childishness undercuts Ramsay's heroic self-image, leaving room for our sympathies to steal in. We watch him go from denying the very existence of his parents to crying at the thought of a letter received from his father during a hospital stay. And we may think, Who wasn't asinine at twenty?... at least until Ramsay, spellbound, watches himself take the step that will either exile him from this fairy tale or seal him permanently in. "There they were, Anne cold and excited, her heart like a machine under his hand, and Ramsay the vivisectionist, and poor Peggy, who had been in love." Even here at the turning point, a sense of traumatic repetition undercuts the realism, furthering the feeling of a midsummer night's dream, or sex comedy, or nightmare. Or perhaps of Gallant's proprietary genre, the "squashed novel." This well after Maxwell had cautioned her, "you know you have a tendency to get the hook in firmly... by telling something fairly far—too far, maybe—into the story, and then shuttling back and forth, instead of sticking to chronology." But *The New Yorker* had by the mid-1960s accepted who would be the maestro and who the pupil. According to a note from Maxwell, William Shawn, the editor in chief of *The New Yorker*, thought "Bonaventure" "one of your best."

In "Dédé" (1987), previously anthologized in *The Best American Short Stories of the Eighties*, we can see the final fruits of Gallant's experiments with structure, language, and interiority: a sense of freedom brought under calm control. The story returns once more to a child on the cusp of adulthood, a perspective Gallant loved. But her present-tense opening anchors us so securely in the mind of fourteen-year-old Pascal Brouet that she can depart from it for almost the entire remainder of the story, leaving us to fill in his reactions. "Going round and round," as Maxwell might say, she loops through memories of Pascal's daft uncle Dédé and a dinner party he will ultimately ruin, and rescue. It is as if the sturdily circular structure of "The Old Place," the point-of-view shifts of "Thank You for the Lovely Tea," and the poetic bursts of "Bonaventure" had been chiseled away to yield a Gothic illumination. But what is being illuminated here? On one level, the manners and morals of the Parisian bourgeoisie two decades after a failed revolution. On another, in the person of Dédé, the persistence of something anarchic, contrary, ungovernable—yet also imaginative, and pure, and kind. In a conversation with *The New Yorker*'s Deborah Treisman, Ann Beattie chooses the image of the dragonfly—fierce but gossamer—to capture the grace with which Gallant flits through her beautifully rendered scene. It's a flight that will end, characteristically,* with Pascal himself up in the air. He could follow in the steps of his father, the Argus-eyed magistrate who (when he is not half asleep) is said to see everything—"a steady look, neither hot nor cold." But Pascal seems to sense, as Gallant does throughout her work, that for a truly just life something more is needed than a commitment, however unblinking, to "Truth with a Capital T." We require a compound vision that, even if it "never miss[es] a turning"—even if it is the very soul of toughness—never loses sight of human fragility or forgets the human heart.

5

We read Gallant today, in other words, not because she accepted the parameters of the story or the world that were handed to her but because she dared to go her own way—and in so doing redefined, as every great writer must, what the story and the world can be. To put it another way, where most writers aim for mastery, Gallant never stopped chasing mystery. In my view, her *Collected Stories* is one of the great works of fiction of the last century; it has the burnished perfection Linnet Muir aspires to: "seamless, and as smooth as brass." But that doesn't mean its author has nothing else to say.

Late in the preparation of this volume, flipping back through the Canadian editions of Gallant's previous works, I happened across the Editor's Note to *Going Ashore*. In it, Douglas Gibson, her publisher in Canada since the 1970s, recounted a transatlantic phone conversa-

---

*Wood had signaled early on that Gallant's open endings might not be to *The New Yorker*'s taste, writing of one of her submissions: "At the end, though one is finished with the story, one is not finished with the people [...] We kept it so long because we like it," she added, but Gallant seized on the gravamen, writing contemporaneously to her friend William Weintraub, "This isn't sour grapes, but I don't consider that valid. The point of a short story is just that: that you should be quite through with the story, but the people should have continuity." As for the editorial tactic of using praise to soften the critique, Gallant observed: "Fine words butter no croissants."

tion from the last decade of her life: "Mavis Gallant remarked to me that it was unfortunate that so many of her stories were out of print, or had never appeared in a book." It turns out that in the 1990s, hundreds of pages had been cut from *The Collected Stories* for reasons more commercial than aesthetic. The publisher's absolute limit seemed to be 900 pages, beyond which, as Gallant pointed out in interviews, "You wouldn't be able to pick it up." But she regretted not having those pages available elsewhere, and further tempted Gibson on the phone with talk of stories "that had never appeared in a book." When he promised to publish the missing stories, he says, Gallant was "delighted, and asked—in a typically direct way—if I could bring the book out before she died."

Their joint attempt to fashion a sequel to *The Collected Stories* was interrupted by a health crisis, whose repercussions would dog her last five years. But we can take some satisfaction that *The Uncollected Stories* completes a project conceived by Gallant herself, at both ends of a singular life: first as a vision of the artist she might become; later as a summing up of the one she always was.

With this publication, the entirety of Mavis Gallant's fiction is restored to print. Her oft-quoted injunction from *The Collected Stories* remains in force: "Stories are not chapters of novels. They should not be read one after the other, as if they were meant to follow along. Read one. Shut the book. Read something else. Come back later. Stories can wait." Some of these have had to wait longer than others; any one of them is a good place to start. But I'm struck, looking back at "Orphans' Progress," at "Virus X," at "An Autobiography," at "The Statues Taken Down," at "His Mother," by the recurrence of a word not always associated with uncompromising artists: love. In "Its Image on the Mirror," Gallant writes, arrestingly, "We would rather say adore: it is so exaggerated it can't be true. Adore equals like, but love is compromising, eternal."

So are these stories, this incomparable body of work. I do not adore them; I love them. Here's hoping you will, too.

—GARTH RISK HALLBERG

STORIES OF NORTH AMERICA

THANK YOU FOR THE LOVELY TEA

THAT YEAR, it began to rain on the twenty-fourth of May—a holiday still called, some thirty years after her death, Queen Victoria's Birthday. It rained—this was Canada—until the middle of June. The girls, kept indoors, exercising listlessly in the gym, quarreled over nothing, and complained of headache. Between showers they walked along spongy gravel paths, knocking against spiraea bushes that suddenly spattered them with water and white. It was the last lap of term, the dead period between the end of exams and the start of freedom. Handicrafts and extra art classes were improvised to keep them busy, but it was hopeless; glooming over their desks, they quarreled, dreamed of summer, wrote plaintive letters home. Their raincoats were suddenly hot and heavy, their long black stockings scratchy and damp.

"Life is Hell," Ruth Cook wrote on the lid of a desk, hoping that someone would see it and that there would be a row. It was the slow time of day—four o'clock. Yawning over a drawing of flowerpots during art class, she looked despairingly out the streaked window and saw Mrs. Holland coming up the walk. Mrs. Holland looked smart, from that distance. Her umbrella was furled. On her head was a small hat, tilted to one side, circled with a feather. She looked smart but smudged, as if paint had spilled over the outline of a drawing. Ruth took her in coldly, leaning on a plump, grubby hand. Mrs. Holland was untidy—she had heard people say so. She was emotional. This, too, Ruth had overheard, always said with disapproval. Emotion meant "being American"; it meant placing yourself unarmed in the hands of the enemy. Emotion meant not getting one's lipstick on straight, a marcel wave coming apart in wild strands. It accounted for Mrs. Holland's anxious blue eyes, for the button missing on a blouse, the odds and ends forever

3

falling out of purse or pocket. Emotion was worse than bad taste; it was calamitous. Ruth had only to look at Mrs. Holland to see what it led to. Mrs. Holland passed up the front steps and out of sight. Ruth went back to her bold lettering: "Life is Hell." Any other girl in the room, she thought with satisfaction, would have gone importantly up to the desk and whispered that a lady had come to take her to tea, and could she please go and get ready now? But Ruth knew that things happened in their own good time. She looked at her drawing, admired it, and added more flowerpots, diminishing to a fixed point at the center of the page.

"Well done," said Miss Fischer, the art teacher, falsely, strolling between the ranks of desks. If she saw "Life is Hell," she failed to comment. They were all cowards; there was no one to fight. "Your horizon line is too low," said Miss Fischer. "Look at the blackboard; see how I have shown Proportion."

Indicating patience and self-control, Ruth looked at the blackboard, over it, around it. The blackboard was filled with receding lines, the lesson having dealt with Perspective as well as Proportion. Over it hung a photograph of the King—the late King, that is. He had died that year, and so had Kipling (although far less fuss was made about him), and the girls had to get used to calling Kipling "our late beloved poet" and the Prince of Wales "King Edward." It was hopeless where the Prince was concerned, for there hung the real King still, with his stiff, elegant Queen by his side. He had died on a cold January day. They had prayed for him in chapel. His picture was in their prayer books because he was head of the Church—something like that. "It is a year of change," the headmistress had said, announcing his death.

"It's a year of change, all right," Ruth said softly, imitating the headmistress's English accent. Even the term "headmistress" was new; the old girl, who had retired to a cottage and a faithful spinster friend, had been content with "principal." But the new one, blond, breathless, pink-cheeked, was fresh from England, full of notions, and felt that the place wanted stirring up. "I'm afraid I am progress-minded," she told the stone-faced, wary girls. "We must learn never to fear change, provided it is for the best." But they did fear it; they were shocked when the tinted image of George V was taken down from the dining-room wall and the famous picture of the Prince of Wales inspecting the front during the Great War put in its place. The Prince in the photo was a handsome boy, blond, fresh, pink-cheeked—much like the new head-mistress, in fact. "A year of change," the headmistress repeated, as if to impress it forever on their minds.

Scrubbing at her flowerpots with artgum, Ruth thought it over and decided there had been no real change. She had never met the King and didn't care for poetry. She was still in school. Her mother had gone to live abroad, but then she had never been around much. The only difference was that her father had met unfortunate Mrs. Holland.

Coming into the flagged entrance hall, Mrs. Holland was daunted by the chilly gloom. She stared at the row of raincoats hanging from pegs, the somber portraits of businessmen and clergymen on the walls. Governess-trained, she considered herself hopelessly untutored, and attached to the smell of drying coats an atmosphere of learning. Some-one came, and went off to fetch the headmistress. Mrs. Holland sat down on a carved bench that looked like a pew. Irreligious but fond of saying she would believe in something if only she could, she gazed with respectful interest at the oil portrait of the school's chief financial rock, a fruit importer who had abandoned Presbyterianism for the Church of England when a sudden rise in wealth and status demanded the change. Although he wore a gay checked suit and looked every inch himself, a small-town Presbyterian go-getter, Mrs. Holland felt he must, surely, be some sort of Anglican dignitary; his portrait was so much larger than the rest; besides, the hall was so hushed and damp that religion had to come into it somewhere. She recalled a story she had been told—that the school had been a Bernardine abbey, trans-ported from England to Canada stone by stone. The lightless corridors, the smell of damp rot emanating from the linen cupboards, the drafts, the cunning Gothic windows with Tudor panes, the dark classrooms and sweating walls, the chill, the cold, the damp, the discomfort, wist-fully British, staunchly religious, all suggested this might indeed have been the case. How nice for the girls, Mrs. Holland thought, vaguely but sincerely.

In point of fact, the school had never been an abbey. Each of its clammy stones had been quarried in North America, and the architectural ragout was deliberate; it was intended to provide the pupils with character and background otherwise lacking in a new continent. As for the fruit importer, the size of his portrait had to do only with the size of his endowment. The endowment had been enormous; the school was so superlatively uncomfortable that it cost a fortune to run. The fruit importer's family had been—still were—exceedingly annoyed. They wished he would take up golf and quit meddling in church affairs. He could not help meddling. Presbyterianism had left its scar. Still, he felt uneasy, he was bound to admit, if there were nuns about, or too much incense. Hence his only injunction, most difficult to follow: The school should be neither too High nor too Low. Every regime had interpreted this differently. The retiring principal, to avoid the vulgarity of being Low, had brought in candles and Evensong. The new headmistress, for her part, found things disturbingly High, almost Romish. The white veils the girls wore to chapel distressed her. They were so long that they made the girls look like Carmelite nuns, at least from the waist up. From the waist down, they looked like circus riders, with their black-stockinged legs exposed to garter level. The pleated serge tunics were worn so short, in fact, that the older girls, plump with adolescence, could not sit down without baring a pink inch between tunic and stocking top. The modernism she had threatened took form. She issued an order: lengthen the tunics, shorten the veils. Modernism met with a mulish and unaccountable resistance. Who would have believed that young girls, children of a New World, would so obstinately defend tradition? Modernism, broadmindedness foundered. The headmistress gave up the fight, though not her claim to the qualities in which she took greatest pride.

It was broadmindedness now that compelled her to welcome Mrs. Holland briskly and cordially, ignoring Mrs. Holland's slightly clouded glance and the cigarette stain on the hand she extended. Ruth's father had rung up about tea, so it was quite in order to let Ruth go; still, Mrs. Holland was a family friend, not a parent—a distinction that carried its own procedure. It meant that she need not be received in the private sitting room and given cake but must wait in the office. It meant that

Ruth was not to go alone but must be accompanied by a classmate. Waved into the office, Mrs. Holland sat down once more. She propped her umbrella against her chair, offered the headmistress a cigarette. The umbrella slid and fell with a clatter. The cigarette was refused. Reaching for her umbrella, Mrs. Holland tipped her case upside down, and cigarettes rolled everywhere. The headmistress, smiling, helped collect them, marveling at the variety of experience inherent in teaching, at the personal tolerance that permitted her contact with a woman of Mrs. Holland's sort.

"My hair's all undone, too," said Mrs. Holland, wretchedly, clutching her properties. And, really, watching her, one felt she had too much for any one woman to handle—purse, umbrella, and gloves.

The headmistress retrieved the last cigarette and furtively dropped it in the wastebasket. "With all this rain, one can hardly cope with one's hair," she said, almost as cordially as if Mrs. Holland were a parent. Resolved to be lenient, she remembered that Ruth's father's money did, after all, lend the situation a certain amount of social decency. The headmistress had heard, soon after her arrival, this wayward story of divorce and confusion—Ruth's parents divorced; Ruth's mother, who had behaved badly, gone abroad; the sudden emergence of Mrs. Holland—and she had decided that Ruth ought to be watched. There might be tendencies—what someone less broadminded might have called bad blood. But Ruth was a placid girl, to all appearances—plump, lazy, rather Latin in looks, with glossy blue-black hair, which she brushed into drooping ringlets. In spite of the laziness, one could detect a nascent sense of leadership; she was quite bossy, in fact. The headmistress was satisfied; like the school, the imitation abbey, Ruth was almost the real thing.

Summoned, Ruth came in her own good time. Conversation between the two women had frozen, and they turned to the door with relief. Ruth was trailing not one friend but two, May Watson and Helen McDonnell. The three girls stood, berets on their heads, carrying raincoats. Their long black legs looked more absurd than ever. They shook hands with Mrs. Holland, mumbling courteously. For some reason, they gave the appearance of glowering, rather like the portraits in the hall.

"What time do we have to be back, please?" said Ruth.

"I expect Mrs. Holland will want to bring you back soon after tea," said the headmistress. She made a nervous movement toward Mrs. Holland, who, however, was collecting her belongings without difficulty. The girls were being taken to the tearoom of a department store, Mrs. Holland said. "I *am* pleased," said the headmistress, too enthusiastically. The girls glanced at her with suspicion. But her pleasure was authentic; she had feared that they might be going to Ruth's house, where Mrs. Holland, the family friend, might seem too much at home. Mrs. Holland pressed on the headmistress a warm, frantic farewell and followed the girls out. It had begun to rain again, the slow warm rain of June. Mrs. Holland, distracted, stopped to admire the Tudor-Gothic façade of the school, feeling that this was expected, and was recalled by the fidgeting of her charges. There was more fumbling, this time for car keys, and, at last, they were settled—Ruth in front, as a matter of course (the car was her father's), and Helen and May in back.

"Out of jail," said Ruth, pulling off her beret and shaking out her hair.

"Is it jail, dear? Do you hate it?" said Mrs. Holland. She drove carefully away from the curb, mindful of her responsibilities. "Would you rather—"

"Oh, Ruth," Helen protested, from the back. "You don't mean it."

"Jail," said Ruth, but without much interest. She groped in the side pocket on the door and said, "I left a chocolate bar here last time I was out. Who ate it?"

"Perhaps your father," said Mrs. Holland, wishing Helen had not interrupted that most promising lead about hating school.

"He hates chocolate. You know that. He'd be the last person to eat it. But honestly," she said, placid again, "just listen to me. As if it even mattered."

Situations like this were Mrs. Holland's undoing. The absence of the chocolate bar, Ruth's young, averted profile, made her feel anxious and guilty. The young, to her, were exigent, full of mystery, to be wooed and placated. "Shall we stop somewhere and get another chocolate bar?" she said. "Would you like that?"

It was terrible to see a grown woman so on the defensive, made uneasy by someone like Ruth. Helen McDonnell, taller than the others, blond, ill at ease, repeated her eternal prayer that she might never grow up and be made unhappy. As far as she knew, there were no happy adults, other than teachers. She looked at May, to see if she had noticed and if she minded, but May had turned away and was staring at her pale, freckled reflection in the window, thrown back from the dark of the rainy streets. She knew that May was grieving for an identical face, that of her twin, who this year had been sent to another school, across the continent. Driving through thicket suburbs and into town now, they passed May's house, a white house set back on a lawn.

"There's your house, May," Ruth said, twisting around on the front seat. "How come you're a boarder when you are right near?"

"How about you?" said May, angrily.

Ruth twisted a curl and said, "Haven't got a mother at home, that's why."

"Would you like to live at home?" said Mrs. Holland eagerly, and Ruth stiffened. Oh, if only she could teach herself not to be so spontaneous! Instead of drawing the child toward her, she drove her away.

"It's much better to board," said Helen, before Ruth could reply. "I mean, you learn more, and they make you a lady."

"Don't be so stupid," said Ruth, and May said, "Who cares about that?"

Helen, reminded that these two would grow up ladies in any case, colored. But then, she thought, seeing the three of us together, no one could tell. They wore the same uniform, and who was to guess that Ruth's father was rich and May's clever? As long as she had the uniform, everything was all right. Pious, Helen repeated another prayer—that God might miraculously give her different parents.

Furious with Helen for having again interrupted, Mrs. Holland clamped and relaxed her gloved hands on the wheel. Traffic lights came at her through a blur of rain. If only she and Ruth were alone. If only Ruth, with the candor Ruth's father was so proud of, would turn to her and say, "Are you and Daddy getting married?" Then Mrs. Holland might say, "That depends on you, dear. You see, your father feels, and I quite agree…" Or if Ruth were hostile, openly hating her, if it were a question of winning her confidence, of replacing the mother, of being a sister, a companion, a friend ... But the girl was closed, indifferent. She seemed unable to grasp the importance of Mrs. Holland in her father's life. There was an innocence, a lack of prudence, in her references to the situation; she said things that made shame and caution fill Mrs. Holland's heart. She was able to remark, casually, to Helen and May, "My father and Mrs. Holland drove all the way to California in this car," reducing the trip (undertaken with many doubts, with fear, with a feeling that hotel clerks were looking through and through her) to a simple, unimportant outing involving two elderly people, long past love.

They crawled into the center of town, in the wake of streetcars. Mrs. Holland, afraid for her charges, drove so slowly that she was a traffic hazard. An irritated policeman waved them by.

"Is the store all right?" Mrs. Holland said to Ruth. "Would you rather go somewhere else?" She had circled the block twice, looking for a parking space.

Ruth, annoyed by all this caution, said, "Don't ask me. It's up to the girls. They're the guests."

But neither of the girls could choose. Helen was shy, May absorbed. Mrs. Holland found a parking place at last, and they filed into the store.

"I used to come here all the time with my sister," May said, suddenly coming to as they stood, jammed, in the elevator. "We came for birthdays and for treats. We had our birthdays two days in a row, because we're twins and otherwise it wouldn't be fair. We wore the same clothes and hardly anybody could tell us apart. But now," she said, echoing a parental phrase, "we have different clothes and we go to different schools, because we have to develop separate personalities."

"Well," said Mrs. Holland, unable to take this in. "Have you a sister?" she said to Helen.

There was a silence; then Helen blurted out, "We're seven at home."

"How nice," said Mrs. Holland. But Helen knew that people said this just to be polite, and that being seven at home was just about the most shameful thing imaginable.

"Are your sisters at school with you?" Mrs. Holland asked.

Everyone in the elevator was listening. Helen hung her head. She had been sent to school by an uncle who was also her godfather and who had taken his duties seriously. Having promised to renounce Satan and all his works in Helen's name, he uprooted her, aged six, from her warm, rowdy, half-literate family and packed her off to school. In school, Helen had been told, she would learn to renounce Satan for herself and, more important, learn to be a lady. Some of the teachers still remembered her arriving, mute and frightened, quite as frightened as if the advantages of superior schooling had never been pointed out. There were only three boarders Helen's age. They were put in the care of an elderly house-keeper, who filled a middle role, neither staff nor servant. After lessons they were sent to sit with her, in her red-papered, motto-spangled room. She taught them hymns; the caterwauling got on her nerves, but at least they sat still while singing.

She supervised their rushed baths and murderously washed their hair. Sometimes some of the staff wondered if more should not be done for the little creatures, for although they were clean and good and no trouble, the hand that dressed them was thorough but unaffectionate, and they never lost the wild-eyed hopelessly untidy look of unloved children. Helen now remembered very little of this, nor could she imagine life away from school. Her uncle-godfather conscientiously sent her home each summer, to what seemed to her a common, clamorous, poverty-stricken family. "They're so loud," she would confide to the now quite elderly person who had once taught her hymns. "Their voices are so loud. And they drink, and everything." She had grown up to be a tall, quiet girl, much taller than most girls her own age. In spite of her height she wore her short, ridiculous tunic unselfconsciously. Her dearest wish was to wear this uniform as long as she could, to stay on at the school forever, to melt, with no intervening gap, from the students' dining hall to the staff sitting room. Change disturbed her; she was hostile to new girls, could scarcely bear it when old girls came back to be married from the school chapel. Hanging over the stairs with the rest of the girls, watching the exit of the wedding party from chapel to street, she would wonder how the bride could bear to go off this way, with a man no one knew, having seen school again, having glimpsed the girls on the stairs. When the headmistress said, in chapel, confusing two esteemed poets, "The old order changeth, girls. The Captains and Kings depart. Our King has gone, and now our beloved

Kipling has left us," Helen burst into tears. She did not wish the picture of George V to leave the walls; she did not want Kipling to be "the late." For a few days afterward, the girls amused themselves by saying, "Helen, listen. The Captains and Kings depart," so that they could be rewarded, and slightly horrified, by her astonishing grief. But then they stopped, for her shame and silence after such outbursts were disconcerting. It never became a joke, and so had to be abandoned.

Mrs. Holland and her guests settled into an oval tearoom newly done up with chrome and onyx, stuffed with shoppers, smelling of tea, wet coats, and steam heating. Helen looked covertly at Mrs. Holland, fearing another question. None came. The waitress had handed them each a giant, tasseled menu. "I'll have whatever the rest of them have," Helen said, not looking at hers.

"Well," said Ruth, "*I'll* have chocolate ice cream with marshmallow. No, wait. Strawberry with pineapple."

May forgot her sister. The choice before her was insupportable. "The same as Ruth," she said, at last, agonized and uncertain.

Mrs. Holland, who loathed sweets, ordered a sundae, as a friendly gesture, unaware that in the eyes of the girls she had erred. Mothers and their substitutes were expected to drink tea and nibble at flabby pâté sandwiches.

As soon as their ice cream was before them, Ruth began again about the chocolate bar. "My father never eats chocolate," she said, quite suddenly. "And he knew it was mine. He'd never touch anything that wasn't his. It would be stealing."

"Maybe it got thrown away," said May.

"That'd be the same as stealing," said Ruth.

Mrs. Holland said, "Ruth, I do not know what became of your bit of chocolate."

Ruth turned to Mrs. Holland her calm brown eyes. "Goodness!" she said. "I never meant to say you took it. Anyway, even if you did make a mistake and eat it up sometime when you were driving around— Well, I mean, who cares? It was only a little piece, half a Cadbury bar in blue paper."

"I seldom eat chocolate," said Mrs. Holland. "If I had seen it, let alone eaten it, I should certainly have remembered."

"Then he must have had somebody else with him," said Ruth. The matter appeared to be settled. She went on eating, savoring every mouthful.

Mrs. Holland put down her spoon. The trend of this outing, she realized now, could lead only to tears. It was one of the situations in her life—and they were frequent—climaxed by a breakdown. The breakdown would certainly be her own: she wept easily. Ruth, whose character so belied her stormy Latin looks, had rarely wept since baby-hood. May, the thin, freckled one, appeared quite strung up about something, but held in by training, by discipline. I lack both, Mrs. Holland thought. As for the big girl, Helen, Mrs. Holland had already dismissed her as cold and stupid. Mrs. Holland said softly, "*Les larmes d'un adolescent.*" But it doesn't apply to cold little Canadians, she thought.

"I know what that means," said Ruth. She licked her spoon on both sides.

Mrs. Holland's phrase, the image it evoked, came from the outer circle of experience. Disturbed, the girls moved uneasily in their chairs, feeling that nothing more should be said.

"Don't you girls *ever* cry?" said Mrs. Holland, almost with hostility.

"Never," said Ruth, settling that.

"My sister cried," said May. She turned her light-lashed gaze to Helen and said, "And Helen cries."

"I don't," said Helen. She drew in, physically, with the first appre-hension of being baited. "I do not."

"Oh, Helen, you do," said May. She turned to Ruth for confirma-tion, but Ruth, indifferent, having spoken for herself, was scooping up the liquid dregs of her ice cream. "Do you want to see Helen cry?" said May. Like Mrs. Holland, she seemed to have accepted the idea that one of them was going to break down and disgrace them; it might as well be Helen. Or perhaps the remark went deeper than that. Mrs. Holland, who could barely follow Ruth's mental and emotional spirals, felt unable, and disinclined, to cope with this one. May leaned forward, facing Helen. Mrs. Holland suddenly answered "No," too late, for May was saying, in a pretty, piping voice, "Hey, Helen, listen. The King has left us, and Kipling is dead."

Helen failed to reward her. She stared, stolid, as if the words had been in a foreign language. But there remained about the table the knowledge that an attempt had been made, and Mrs. Holland and Helen, both natural victims, could not look away from May, or at each other. Ruth had finished eating. She sighed, stretched, began to tug on her coat. She said to Mrs. Holland, "Thankyouverymuchforalovelytea. I mean, if our darling new headmistress asks did we thank you, well, we did. I was afraid I might forget to say it later on."

"Thanks for a lovely tea," said May. She had been afraid to speak, in case the effort of forming words should release the tight little knot of tears she felt in her throat. It was so much more difficult to be cruel than to be hurt.

"Thank you," said Helen, as if asleep.

"I can only hope they thanked you," the headmistress said when Mrs. Holland delivered them, safe, half an hour later. "Girls are apt to forget."

"They thanked me," said Mrs. Holland. The three girls had curtsied, muttering some final ritual phrase, and vanished into an area of dim, shrill sound.

"Study hall," said the headmistress. "Their studies are over for the term, but they respect the discipline."

"Yes, I suppose they do."

"It was kind of you to take them out," said the headmistress. She laid her cold pink hand on Mrs. Holland's for a moment, then withdrew it, perplexed by the wince, the recoil. "One forgets how much it can mean at that age, a treat on a rainy day."

"Perhaps that's the answer," Mrs. Holland said.

The headmistress sensed that things were out of hand, but she had no desire to be involved; perhaps the three had been noisy, had overeaten. She smiled with such vague good manners that Mrs. Holland was released and could go.

From an upstairs window, Ruth watched Mrs. Holland make her way to the car. May and Helen were not speaking. Helen was ready to forgive, but to May, who had been unkind, the victim was odious, and she avoided her with a kind of prudishness impossible to explain to anyone, let alone herself. They had all made mistakes, Ruth thought. She wondered if she would ever care enough about anyone to make all the mistakes those around her had made during the rainy-day tea with Mrs. Holland. She breathed on the window, idly drew a heart, smiled placidly, let it fade.

JORINDA AND JORINDEL

A SUMMER night: all night someone has been learning the Charleston. "I've got it!" the dancer cries. "I've got it, everybody. Watch me, now!" But no one is watching. The dancer is alone in the dining room, clinging to the handle of the door; the rest of the party is in the living room, across the hall. "Watch me!" travels unheard over the quiet lawn and the silent lake, and then dissolves.

The walls of the summer house are thin. The doors have been thrown back and the windows pushed as high as they will go. Young Irmgard wakes up with her braids undone and her thumb in her mouth. She has been dreaming about her cousin Bradley; about an old sidewalk with ribbon grass growing in the cracks. "I've got it," cried the witch who had captured Jorinda, and she reached out so as to catch Jorindel and change him into a bird.

Poor Mrs. Bloodworth is learning to dance. She holds the handle of the dining-room door and swivels her feet in satin shoes, but when she lets go the handle, she falls down flat on her behind and stays that way, sitting, her hair all over her face, her feet pointing upward in her new shoes. Earlier, Mrs. Bloodworth was sitting that way, alone, when, squinting through her hair, she saw Irmgard sitting in her nightgown on the stairs. "Are you watching the fun?" she said in a tragic voice. "Is it really you, my sweet pet?" And she got to her feet and crawled up the stairs on her hands and knees to kiss Irmgard with ginny breath.

There is prohibition where Mrs. Bloodworth comes from. She has come up to Canada for a party; she came up for just one weekend and never went away. The party began as a wedding in Montreal, but it has been days since anyone mentioned the bride and groom. The party began in Montreal, came down to the lake, and now has dwindled to five: Irmgard's mother and father, Mrs. Bloodworth, Mrs. Bloodworth's friend Bill, and the best man, who came up for the wedding from Buffalo. "Darling pet, may I always stay?" said Mrs. Bloodworth, sobbing, her arms around Irmgard's mother's neck. Why she was sobbing this way nobody knows; she is always crying, dancing, embracing her friends.

In the morning Mrs. Bloodworth will be found in the hammock outside. The hammock smells of fish, the pillow is stuffed with straw; but Mrs. Bloodworth can never be made to go to bed. Irmgard inspects her up and down, from left to right. It isn't every morning of the year that you find a large person helplessly asleep. She is still wearing her satin shoes. Her eyeballs are covered with red nets. When she wakes up she seems still asleep, until she says stickily, "I'm having a rotten time, I don't care what anybody says." Irmgard backs off and then turns and runs along the gallery—the veranda, Mrs. Bloodworth would say—and up the side of the house and into the big kitchen, where behind screen doors Mrs. Queen and Germaine are drinking tea. They are drinking it in silence, for Germaine does not understand one word of English and Mrs. Queen is certainly not going to learn any French.

Germaine is Irmgard's *bonne d'enfant*. They have been together about a century, and have a history stuffed with pageants, dangers, near escapes. Germaine has been saving Irmgard for years and years; but now Irmgard is nearly eight, and there isn't much Germaine can do except iron her summer dresses and braid her hair. They know a separation is near; and Irmgard is cheeky now, as she never was in the past; and Germaine pretends there have been other children she has liked just as well. She sips her tea. Irmgard drops heavily on her lap, joggling the cup. She will never be given anything even approaching Germaine's unmeasured love again. She leans heavily on her and makes her spill her tea. Germaine is mild and simple, a little dull. You can be rude and impertinent if necessary, but she must never be teased.

Germaine remembers the day Irmgard was kidnapped. When she sees a warm August morning like this one, she remembers that thrilling day. There was a man in a motorcar who wanted to buy Irmgard ice cream. She got in the car and it started moving, and suddenly there came Germaine running behind, with her mouth open and her arms wide, and Molly, the collie they had in those days, running with her ears back and her eyes slits. "Stop for Molly!" Irmgard suddenly screamed, and she turned and threw up all over the man's coat. "*Le matin du kidnap*," Germaine begins softly. It is a good thing she is here to recall the event, because the truth is that Irmgard remembers nothing about that morning at all.

Mrs. Queen is standing up beside the stove. She never sits down to eat, because she wants them to see how she hasn't a minute to waste; she is on the alert every second. Mrs. Queen is not happy down at the lake. It is not what she expected by "a country place." When she worked for Lady Partridge things were otherwise; you knew what to expect by "a country place." Mrs. Queen came out to Canada with Lady Partridge. The wages were low, and she had no stomach for travel, but she was devoted to Lady P. and to Ty-Ty and Buffy, the two cairns. The cairns died, because of the change of air, and after Lady P. had buried them, she went out to her daughter in California, leaving Mrs. Queen to look after the graves. But Mrs. Queen has never taken to Canada. She can't get used to it. She cannot get used to a place where the railway engines are that size and make that kind of noise, and where the working people are as tall as anyone else. When Mrs. Queen was interviewing Irmgard's mother, to see if Irmgard's mother would do, she said she had never taken to the place and couldn't promise a thing. The fancy might take her any minute to turn straight around and go back to England. She had told Lady Partridge the same thing. "When was that, Mrs. Queen?" "In nineteen ten, in the spring." She has never felt at home, and never wants to, and never will. If you ask her why she is unhappy, she says it is because of Ty-Ty and Buffy, the cairns; and because this is a paltry rented house and a paltry kitchen; and she is glad that Ty-Ty and Buffy are peacefully in their graves.

The party last night kept Mrs. Queen awake. She had to get up out of her uncomfortable bed and let the collies out of the garage. They knew there was a party somewhere, and were barking like fools. She let them out, she says, and then spent some time on the gallery, looking in the living-room window. It was a hot, airless night. (She happens to have the only stuffy room in the house.) The party was singing "Little Joe." Apparently, she did not see Mrs. Bloodworth dancing and falling down; at least she doesn't mention it.

Mrs. Queen is not going to clean up the mess in the living room. It is not her line of country. She is sick, sore, and weary. Germaine will, if asked, but just now she is braiding Irmgard's hair. Eating toast, Irmgard leans comfortably against Germaine. They are perfectly comfortable with each other, but Mrs. Queen is crying over by the stove.

Irmgard's cousin Bradley went back to Boston yesterday. She should be missing him, but he has vanished, fallen out of summer like a stone. He got on the train covered with bits of tape and lotion, and with a patch on one eye. Bradley had a terrible summer. He got poison ivy, in July, before coming here. In August, he grew a sty, which became infected, and then he strained his right arm. "I don't know what your mother will say," Irmgard's mother said. At this, after a whole summer of being without them, Bradley suddenly remembered he had a father and mother, and started to cry. Bradley is ten, but tall as eleven. He and Irmgard have the same look—healthy and stubborn, like well-fed, intelligent mice. They often stare in the mirror, side by side, positively blown up with admiration. But Bradley is superior to Irmgard in every way. When you ask him what he wants to be, he says straight off, "A mechanical and electrical engineer," whereas Irmgard is still hesitating between a veterinary and a nun.

"Have you dropped Freddy now that Bradley is here?" It seems that she was asked that a number of times.

"Oh, I still like Freddy, but Bradley's my cousin and everything." This is a good answer. She has others, such as, "I'm English-Canadian only I can talk French and I'm German descent on one side." (Bradley is not required to think of answers; he is American, and that does. But in Canada you have to keep saying what you are.) Irmgard's answer—about Freddy—lies on the lawn like an old skipping rope, waiting to catch her up. "Watch me," poor Mrs. Bloodworth said, but nobody cared, and the cry dissolved. "I like Freddy," Irmgard said, and was heard, and the statement is there, underfoot. For if she still likes Freddy, why isn't he here?

Freddy's real name is Alfred Marcel Dufresne. He has nine sisters and brothers, but doesn't know where they are. In winter he lives in an orphanage in Montreal. He used to live there all the year round, but now that he is over seven, old enough to work, he spends the summer with his uncle, who has a farm about two miles back from the lake. Freddy is nearly Irmgard's age, but smaller, lighter on his feet. He looks a tiny six. When he comes to lunch with Irmgard, which they have out in the kitchen with Germaine, everything has to be cut on his plate. He has never eaten with anything but a spoon. His chin rests on the edge of the table. When he is eating, you see nothing except his blue eyes, his curly dirty hair, and his hand around the bowl of the spoon. Once, Germaine said calmly, uncritically, "You eat just like a pig," and Freddy repeated in the tone she had used, "*comme un cochon*," as if it were astonishing that someone had, at last, discovered the right words.

Freddy cannot eat, or read, or write, or sing, or swim. He has never seen paints and books, except Irmgard's; he has never been an imaginary person, never played. It was Irmgard who taught him how to swim. He crosses himself before he goes in the water, and looks down at his wet feet, frowning—a worried mosquito—but he does everything she says. The point of their friendship is that she doesn't have to say much. They can read each other's thoughts. When Freddy wants to speak, Irmgard tells him what he wants to say, and Freddy stands there, mute as an animal, grave, nodding, at ease. He does not know the names of flowers, and does not distinguish between the colors green and blue. The apparitions of the Virgin, which are commonplace, take place against a heaven he says is "*vert*."

Now, Bradley has never had a vision, and if he did he wouldn't know what it was. He has no trouble explaining anything. He says, "Well, this is the way it is," and then says. He counts eight beats when he swims, and once saved Irmgard's life—at least he says he did. He says he held on to her braids until someone came by in a boat. No one remembers it but Bradley; it is a myth now, like the *matin du kidnap*. This year, Bradley arrived at the beginning of August. He had spent July in Vermont, where he took tennis lessons and got poison ivy. He was even taller than the year before, and he got down from the train with pink lotion all over his sores and, under his arm, a tennis racket in a press. "What a little stockbroker Bradley is," Irmgard heard her mother say later on; but Mrs. Queen declared that his manners left nothing wanting.

Bradley put all his own things away and set out his toothbrush in a Mickey Mouse glass he traveled with. Then he came down, ready to swim, with his hair water-combed. Irmgard was there, on the gallery, and so was Freddy, hanging on the outside of the railings, his face poked into the morning-glory vines. He thrusts his face between the leaves, and grins, and shows the gaps in his teeth. "How small he is! Do you play with him?" says Bradley, neutrally. Bradley is after information. He needs to know the rules. But if he had been sure about Freddy, if he had seen right away that they could play with Freddy, he would never have asked. And Irmgard replies, "No, I don't," and turns her back. Just so, on her bicycle, coasting downhill, she has lost control and closed her eyes to avoid seeing her own disaster. Dizzily, she says, "No, I don't," and hopes Freddy will disappear. But Freddy continues to hang on, his face thrust among the leaves, until Bradley, quite puzzled now, says, "Well, is he a friend of yours, or what?" and Irmgard again says, "No."

Eventually, that day or the next day, or one day of August, she notices Freddy has gone. Freddy has vanished; but Bradley gives her a poor return. He has the tennis racket, and does nothing except practice against the house. Irmgard has to chase the balls. He practices until his arm is sore, and then he is pleased and says he has tennis arm. Everybody bothers him. The dogs go after the balls and have to be shut up in the garage. "Call the dogs!" he implores. This is Bradley's voice, over the lake, across the shrinking afternoons. "Please, somebody, call the dogs!"

Freddy is forgotten, but Irmgard thinks she has left something in Montreal. She goes over the things in her personal suitcase. Once, she got up in the night to see if her paintbox was there—if that hadn't been left in Montreal. But the paintbox was there. Something else must be missing. She goes over the list again.

"The fact is," Bradley said, a few days ago, dabbing pink lotion on his poison ivy, "I don't really play with any girls now. So unless you get a brother or something, I probably won't come again." Even with lotion all over his legs he looks splendid. He and Irmgard stand side by side in front of the bathroom looking glass, and admire. She sucks in her cheeks. He peers at his sty. "My mother said you were a stockbroker," Irmgard confides. But Bradley is raised in a different political climate down there in Boston and does not recognize "stockbroker" as a term of abuse. He smiles fatly, and moves his sore tennis arm in a new movement he has now.

During August Freddy no longer existed; she had got in the habit of not seeing him there. But after Bradley's train pulled out, as she sat alone on the dock, kicking the lake, she thought, What'll I do now?, and remembered Freddy. She knows what took place the day she said "No" and, even more, what it meant when she said "Oh, I still like Freddy." But she has forgotten. All she knows now is that when she finds Freddy—in his uncle's muddy farmyard—she understands she hadn't left a paintbox or anything else in Montreal; Freddy was missing, that was all. But Freddy looks old and serious. He hangs his head. He has been forbidden to play with her now, he says. His uncle never wanted him to go there in the first place; it was a waste of time. He only allowed it because they were summer people from Montreal. Wondering where to look, both look at their shoes. Their meeting is made up of Freddy's feet in torn shoes, her sandals, the trampled mud of the yard. Irmgard sees blackberries, not quite ripe. Dumb as Freddy, having lost the power to read his thoughts, she picks blackberries, hard and greenish, and puts them in her mouth.

Freddy's uncle comes out of the foul stable and says something so obscene that the two stand frozen, ashamed—Irmgard, who does not know what the words mean, and Freddy, who does. Then Freddy says he will come with her for just one swim, and not to Irmgard's dock but to a public beach below the village, where Irmgard is forbidden to go; the water is said to be polluted there.

Germaine has her own way of doing braids. She holds the middle strand of hair in her teeth until she has a good grip on the other two. Then she pulls until Irmgard can feel her scalp lifted from her head. Germaine crosses hands, lets go the middle strand, and is away, breathing heavily. The plaits she makes are glossy and fat, and stay woven in water. She works steadily, breathing on Irmgard's neck.

Mrs. Queen says, "I'll wager you went to see poor Freddy the instant that Bradley was out of sight."

"Mmm."

"Don't 'Mmm' me. I hope he sent you packing."

"We went for a swim."

"I never saw a thing like it. That wretched boy was nothing but a slave to you all summer until Bradley came. It was Freddy do this, come here, go there. That charming English Mrs. Bustard who was here in July remarked the same thing. 'Irmgard is her mother all over again,' Mrs. Bustard said. 'All over again, Mrs. Queen.'"

"*Mrs. Bustard est une espèce de vache*," says Germaine gently, who cannot understand a word of English.

"Irmgard requires someone with an iron hand. 'A hand of iron,' Mrs. Bustard said."

Irmgard was afraid to tell Freddy, "But we haven't got our bathing suits or any towels." He was silent, and she could no longer read his mind. The sun had gone in. She was uneasy, because she was swimming in a forbidden place, and frightened by the water spiders. There had been other bathers; they had left their candy wrappers behind and a single canvas shoe. The lake was ruffled, brown. She suggested, "It's awfully cold," but Freddy began undressing, and Irmgard, not sure of her ground, began to unbuckle her sandals. They turned their backs, in the usual manner. Irmgard had never seen anybody undressed, and no one had ever seen her, except Germaine. Her back to Freddy, she pulled off her cotton dress, but kept on her bloomers. When she turned again, Freddy was naked. It was not a mistake; she had not turned around too soon. He stood composedly, with one hand on his skinny ribs. She said only, "The water's dirty here," and again, "It's cold." There were tin cans in the lake, half sunk in mud, and the water spiders. When they came out, Irmgard stood goosefleshed, blue-lipped. Freddy had not said a word. Trembling, wet, they put on their clothes. Irmgard felt water running into her shoes. She said miserably, "I think my mother wants me now," and edged one foot behind the other, and turned, and went away. There was nothing they could say, and nothing they could play any longer. He had discovered that he could live without her. None of the old games would do.

Germaine knows. This is what Germaine said yesterday afternoon; she was simple and calm, and said, "*Oui, c'est comme ça. C'est bien malheureux. Tu sais, ma p'tite fille, je crois qu'un homme, c'est une déformation.*"

Irmgard leans against Germaine. They seem to be consoling each other, because of what they both know. Mrs. Queen says, "Freddy goes back to an orphan asylum. I knew from the beginning the way it would end. It was not a kindness, allowing him to come here. It was no kindness at all." She would say more, but they have come down and want their breakfast. After keeping her up all night with noise, they want their breakfast now.

Mrs. Bloodworth looks distressed and unwashed. Her friend has asked for beer instead of coffee. Pleasure followed by gloom is a regular pattern here. But no matter how they feel, Irmgard's parents get up and come down for breakfast, and they judge their guests by the way they behave not in pleasure but in remorse. The man who has asked for beer as medicine and not for enjoyment, and who described the condition of his stomach and the roots of his hair, will never be invited again. Irmgard stands by her mother's chair; for the mother is the mirror, and everything is reflected or darkened, given life or dismissed, in the picture her mother returns. The lake, the house, the summer, the reason for doing one thing instead of another are reflected here, explained, clarified. If the mirror breaks, everything will break, too.

They are talking quietly at the breakfast table. The day began in fine shape, but now it is going to be cloudy again. They think they will all go to Montreal. It is nearly Labor Day. The pity of parties is that they end.

"Are you sad, too, now that your little boy friend has left you?" says Mrs. Bloodworth, fixing Irmgard with her still-sleeping eyes. She means Bradley; she thought he and Irmgard were perfectly sweet.

Now, this is just the way they don't like Irmgard spoken to, and Irmgard knows they will not invite Mrs. Bloodworth again, either.

They weigh and measure and sift everything people say, and Irmgard's father looks cold and bored, and her mother gives a waking tiger's look his way, smiles. They act together, and read each other's thoughts—just as Freddy and Irmgard did. But, large, and old, and powerful, they have greater powers: they see through walls, and hear whispered conversations miles away. Irmgard's father looks cold, and Irmgard, without knowing it, imitates his look.

"Bradley is Irmgard's cousin," her mother says.

Now Irmgard, who cannot remember anything, who looked for a paintbox when Freddy had gone, who doesn't remember that she was kidnapped and that Bradley once saved her life—now Irmgard remembers something. It seems that Freddy was sent on an errand. He went off down the sidewalk, which was heaving, cracked, edged with ribbon grass; and when he came to a certain place he was no longer there. Something was waiting for him there, and when they came looking for him, only Irmgard knew that whatever had been waiting for Freddy was the disaster, the worst thing. Irmgard's mother said, "Imagine sending a child near the woods at this time of day!" Sure enough, there were trees nearby. And only Irmgard knew that whatever had been waiting for Freddy had come out of the woods. It was the worst thing; and it could not be helped. But she does not know exactly what it was. And then, was it Freddy? It might have been Bradley, or even herself.

Naturally, no child should go near a strange forest. There are chances of getting lost. There is the witch who changes children into birds.

Irmgard grows red in the face and says loudly, "I remember my dream. Freddy went on a message and got lost."

"Oh, no dreams at breakfast, please," her father says.

"Nothing is as dreary as a dream," her mother says, agreeing. "I think we might make a rule on that: no dreams at breakfast. Otherwise it gets to be a habit."

Her father cheers up. Nothing cheers them up so fast as a new rule, for when it comes to making rules, they are as bad as children. You should see them at croquet.

THE DECEPTIONS OF MARIE-BLANCHE

MARIE-BLANCHE wrote from Canada a few days ago to say that she was engaged again. Her letter was, for one betrothed, uncommonly cynical. "This one seems all right," it said, "but I'm not buying my trousseau or anything else until the last minute. This one is a widower. He has a little bakery, and behind it *un joli logement*. He has kept the hair of his first wife. Little plaster doves standing in a circle hold the hair in their beaks so that it forms *un cordon*. In the middle are paper roses, and over it all is a glass cover. It stands on the dining-room table. *C'est un homme de sentiment.*"

For the sake of Marie-Blanche, I hope that he is a man of sentiment. I also hope that he isn't paying for anyone's music lessons and that he doesn't own a horse and that he isn't too attached to one of his own cousins. The reminder of her engagement is, for me, only a reminder of her deceptions. When I lived with Marie-Blanche and her mother in Montreal during the war, I saw the rise and fall of three love affairs in a very short time. Marie-Blanche is deception-prone the way some people keep bumping their heads or spraining their ankles. For nearly twenty-five years her married sister and her cousins have been drawing on their reservoirs of eligible men, funneling them one after the other into the Dumards' front parlor. Marie-Blanche loves them all, without favor; but something always goes wrong.

The parting scene is always very beautiful. Usually she cries, and so does her mother, Madame Dumard, who is never far away. "You're too good for me," the departing suitor says, misty-voiced. He presses her hand and calls her a saint or a little white flower. Sometimes he asks for a keepsake and Marie-Blanche cuts off a lock of her hair and gives it to him. This is a nuisance for her. It breaks the symmetry of her headdress, and a neighboring curl must be divided, like the fission of an amoeba, to replace the missing one.

There are thirty-one curls on Marie-Blanche's head, and the number is no accident. Many years ago, when she saw Shirley Temple in the cinema for the first time, she wrote to a French-language newspaper that ran a questions column and asked for specific instructions on how to make Shirley Temple curls. Shirley Temple has long outgrown these little corkscrews, but Marie-Blanche is faithful forever. When I knew her, the curls bounced over her ears and on her forehead. Sometimes she held them in check with two enamel hairpins shaped like pansies. When her hair, which was a light fluffy yellow, had been washed, the curls would swell to the size of Polish sausages and the effect was truly striking. Between the curls, her face peeped out, alert and inquisitive. Her eyes were blue and innocent, and her cheeks were like a Baroque baby's. She was inordinately proud of the size and shape of her mouth, which was so small that she frequently called attention to it by eating blueberries one at a time.

I have seen a picture of Marie-Blanche taken when she was nineteen, before Shirley Temple was born. Most of her hair then was hidden under a deep cloche hat, but the trusting, anticipatory expression is still the same. "That was the happiest year of my life," Marie-Blanche would often say, putting the picture in a tin box that also contained handkerchiefs and a rosary. "It was the year of my first love and my first deception." The first deceiver was an Irish boy called Georgie O'Ryan. The Dumard family pronounce it Georgie Rhine, with a stress on every other syllable so that the final effect is nearly that of a yodel. Georgie Rhine courted Marie-Blanche for nearly six months, at the end of which he left, bearing a lock of her hair and assuring her that any man would be lucky to have her. A few months later he married an Irish girl from his own parish. Marie-Blanche never knew why, but Madame Dumard had an explanation that she provided for all the friends and relations indiscreet enough to ask. "*Il avait un grand défaut,*" she would say. "So great that we never speak of it." This statement, Machiavellian in its cunning, removed from Marie-Blanche all suspicion of having been rejected and implied, indeed, that she had been mercifully saved from something too grave to mention.

Actually, Georgie may have been discouraged, as were subsequent suitors, by the courting protocol laid down by Madame Dumard. Marie-Blanche's admirers, once the first minuet of introduction was over, were expected to call one evening a week. The evening was Friday and the hour was half past seven. By that time, the supper dishes were put away and Marie-Blanche and her mother dressed and ready. The suitor was received in the parlor, a small, icy room at the end of their long flat. The walls of the room were papered in brown with a creeping pattern of flowers. An imitation fireplace filled most of one wall, and over it hung a colored picture of the San Francisco earthquake. There were also pictures of saints, rendered cross-eyed by a faulty printing process, of Swiss mountains, of the Pope, and of Queen Elizabeth as a baby, all cut from magazines.

Marie-Blanche's suitor would sit on one of the plum-covered upholstered chairs. At his side was a small table covered with a white doily and on the doily was a small brass ash tray, the only one in the house. It bore the trademark of a brand of good Canadian beer. Across the room, side by side on the sofa, sat Marie-Blanche and her mother. Their hands were folded in their laps and their ankles were crossed. Madame Dumard wore black: she had many cousins, and she was in perpetual mourning for one or more of them. Her ears were pierced and through them drawn the thin gold earrings that had been hung there in childhood to ward off eye infections. Marie-Blanche, her hair a triumphant monument to Shirley Temple, wore crepe in some electric shade.

Every light in the room was turned on, from the hanging chandelier with its cluster of orange lampshades to the modern bridge lamp that looked like a traffic signal in the world of the future. Behind the sofa, a curtain tied back with ball fringe revealed an extra bedroom. This room was never used, but because of its exposed position it contained the family's most elegant furniture: a high, polished imitation-oak bedstead, a pink satin chair on which no one sat, a Pierrot doll, and a fluffy dressing table with a three-way mirror. The bedroom opened onto a small balcony, and here the three—Madame Dumard, Marie-Blanche, and the suitor—would sit when the weather was fine.

There was nothing more entertaining than to sit on the balcony and watch the cars and bicycles going by. Up and down the street ran rows of red brick flats with winding outside staircases on which the children of the neighborhood played and from which they frequently fell. They were hearty children, nourished on jam, bread and mayonnaise, and a sickly imitation cola drink on which they had been weaned as infants. There was not a tree on the street, not a bird, not a blade of grass. The Dumards felt sorry for people who had to live in the country, and sometimes, when they visited relatives who lived on farms, they were bored and unhappy and hurried back to Montreal.

Next door to the Dumards, in a low two-story building, lived a large family in whose rickety garage was conducted what Marie-Blanche called "*un beau grand* crap game." On summer evenings it was pleasant to see the big cars pull up at the curb, their well-fed occupants stopping to pat the neighbors' little children on the head before they proceeded inside. It was Marie-Blanche who first pointed out to me that successful gamblers wear black knit ties while *les petits bon-à-riens* wear the hand-painted ones. On this street a French-Canadian parish merged with a Jewish district, full of kosher meat markets and dingy shops. In her peripatetic career as a salesgirl, Marie-Blanche had often worked for Jews and as a result she spoke a singular kind of English, with a French-Canadian accent and a Yiddish lilt. She also used many Yiddish words, believing them to be English, and some of her accounts of clashes and tiny bargains between clerk and customer were exceedingly funny.

However, none of this was ever related to her suitor, which was probably a pity. Conversation during the courting evenings was polite and circumspect, never ruffled by anything so coarse as humor. The suitor was expected to express many sentiments of a noble nature about one's mother, earning money, and marriage. During this preliminary, or prologue stage of the drama he was said to be "frequenting" Marie-Blanche. If the courtship went well the verb was used reflexively and they were said to be frequenting each other.

After a few months, if the noble young man had not dropped out of the race, he was permitted to call on an additional evening, every Tuesday. "That's enough for the first year," Madame Dumard would say. She liked to describe her own courtship, which had taken place in the years 1894 and 1895, and how her husband had held her hand for the first time as they were leaving the church after the wedding.

Georgie Rhine had been the first to sound the knell that what would pass as courting in Madame Dumard's day served only to dishearten Marie-Blanche's admirers. But whenever Marie-Blanche tried to point this out, her mother would remind her of what a good marriage her sister, Agnès, had made, omitting the lucky accident of history that had rushed Agnès to the altar.

Agnès had been married very quickly one day in 1940 when it was announced on the radio that young men not married by a certain date in June would be considered bachelors thereafter for the purposes of military service. To the Dumards, the war came and went like a distant, murmuring stream, but they were alive to such irritants as rationing and military service. Agnès was married at once in a borrowed dress. They had great difficulty finding a ring; all the jewelry shops in the area were sold out. I lived with the Dumards for a period of several months that included Pearl Harbor, the fall of Hong Kong and Singapore, and the blunder of Dieppe, but I do not recall that the war was ever discussed except as a perplexing nuisance conducted for the pleasure and profit of muddle-headed Anglo-Saxons.

That winter, Marie-Blanche was being frequented by a suitor called Wilfrid. Wilfrid's attendance was then in its second year and Marie-Blanche, who had never until now received so much encouragement, had assembled a trousseau of pillowcases and towels embroidered with bowknots. He was a big, blond hulk of a man, with manicured hands and a boneless handshake. His conversation was filled with meaningless curlicues that Madame Dumard considered real *politesse*. Every Friday he brought Marie-Blanche a corsage of tinted carnations, tortured onto wire stems and embalmed in prickly greenery. For Madame there was a box of chocolates, each piece wrapped in colored tinfoil. On the cover of the box was a young person, dressed as Columbine, looking at the moon. Wilfrid talked a great deal about his own mother, who had died, and as he spoke tears coursed down his round cheeks, and there were answering tears in Madame's eyes and sympathetic sounds from Marie-Blanche. After they had cried for a while they put away their handkerchiefs and moved solemnly into the dining room, where they drank scalding tea and ate éclairs and creamy pastries called *religieuses* because their shape resembles little nuns.

Wilfrid did not appear disturbed by the courting rules of the house. He sat in perfect ease and happiness two nights a week and talked about his dead mother. He had once begun preparation for holy orders but had decided in time he lacked the true vocation; however, he had acquired (or had been born with) many characteristics of an urban priest in a sound, prosperous parish, where the parishioners want to hear good things said about private property. He pressed the tips of his fingers together when he talked, and he pursed his mouth and closed his eyes when he listened. He moved quietly and slowly, and it took him ten minutes to say "Good morning," or "How do you do?" so beautifully did he phrase the message.

Madame Dumard was enchanted with him. She permitted him to take Marie-Blanche to the cinema, where they were chaperoned by a young friend of Wilfrid's called Jean-Jacques. Jean-Jacques was a sweet, nervous young man with the smile of a pious child. He was a singer by profession, and sang on the radio many songs about love, joy, or frustration in Paris. He sounded exactly like Tino Rossi. When he sang he tilted his head and turned his eyes to Heaven, as if he were posing for a picture on the occasion of his First Communion. Madame Dumard liked him almost as well as Wilfrid and he often sang, just for her, her two favorite songs, *"Hirondelle"* and *"J'ai Deux Amours."*

One Sunday, as Marie-Blanche was leaving church after eleven o'clock Mass, she was surprised to see Jean-Jacques waiting for her on the steps with what she later described as an agitated air. He begged her to accompany him to a drug store, where they could talk. He guided her into a booth and ordered ice cream for them both. When it came, a tear formed in his eye and fell in the dish.

"I'm very fond of Wilfrid," he said. It is difficult to report this conversation, because Marie-Blanche's histrionic talents later got in the way of her giving a straight account. But she held firm on a few of Jean-Jacques' declarations.

"Wilfrid pays for my singing lessons," he said next. He stirred his ice cream to soup while Marie-Blanche privately decided she would soon put a stop to *that* once she and Wilfrid were married.

"When Wilfrid marries, I will be alone in the world," said Jean-Jacques. "He is my only friend."

"Have you no maman?" said Marie-Blanche. She was beginning to think that Jean-Jacques asked a great deal in the name of friendship.

Jean-Jacques shook his head. "Wilfrid often speaks of getting married," he said. "And then, he's so fond of your mother. This time, I think he's serious." He lifted his heavy-lashed eyes and looked straight across the table. She later described his expression as sinister, but it was probably only stagily tragic and third-rate tragedy at that. "Why can't we go on just as we are?" he said. "All going to the cinema together once a week, and Wilfrid calling on your mother? We would be so happy and have such fun."

Marie-Blanche remarked that it didn't seem like much fun to her, at which Jean-Jacques pronounced: "If you marry Wilfrid you will be unhappy all your life." He paid for the ice cream and departed, leaving Marie-Blanche to run home with the exciting news.

The family spent an agreeable though tiring day trying to decide what Jean-Jacques meant. Marie-Blanche thought it meant another wife, but Madame Dumard was all for some congenital ailment, like having fits. On Tuesday, when Wilfrid came to call, they told him what had happened, chattering like a pair of squirrels. Wilfrid turned red, then he looked blank, then he sat down and remained so silent and depressed for the rest of the evening that Marie-Blanche assured him she would never, never mention the distressing incident again. Her promise was just, for that was the last time she saw him. He wrote a poetic letter in decorated handwriting. He said Jean-Jacques' singing lessons were so expensive he felt he couldn't support a wife. He called Marie-Blanche his never-to-be-forgotten little white flower.

None of the Dumards, nor any of their friends, knew what to make of it. Their parish priest, whom they consulted, solicited a small sum for prayers of gratitude that Marie-Blanche had been spared, which confused them more than ever. They began to read something criminal and vicious into the behavior of these immature and silly men. Although I was often asked for one, I never contributed a solution because I much preferred Madame Dumard's summing up. She often told the story to callers, from beginning to end, concluding with these words: "*Il avait un grand défaut,* but we don't know what it was and so we never speak of it."

Later they heard that Wilfrid was engaged again and moving in a more elevated society: she was the daughter of a city councilor. Wilfrid and the fiancée and Jean-Jacques were frequently seen at the cinema together, and the Dumards, when they were told of this, indulgently decided that it was just Wilfrid's way.

It was hard for Marie-Blanche to get used to the ordinary cut of man after someone so *raffiné*, but a few weeks later, in the spring, a cousin introduced her to a new cavalier and she began to perk up. The new one was called Télèsphore Ouimette, and he was a tailor. Madame Dumard, still brokenhearted over Wilfrid's defection, looked upon him with immediate dislike. He had a head of rich, black, glossy waves that he combed every few minutes, lovingly pushing the ridges into shape. When he came to call, he would stop in the hall and comb his hair in the mirror with a swan painted on it. Then, in the parlor, he would peer from time to time into the beveled looking glass that was covered with etched grapes. The haircombings punctuated the bantering wit that was his mating cry to Marie-Blanche.

Madame Dumard disliked him so much that she could not sit in the same room. She would rock fiercely by the kitchen stove, observing him (for the sake of decorum) down the hall through the two opened doors, muttering to herself. Télèsphore called her Mémère, as if she were a country grandmother, and this infuriated her almost more than anything else he might have done. After Wilfrid's splendid French, Télèsphore's ripe local accent fell harshly on her ears, and she often pretended not to know what he was saying. Of this he seemed unaware. He would saunter into the kitchen and comb his hair in the only mirror he could find, which was part of the stove. The stove was glossy and black. It supported a panel of creamy tiles decorated with pink roses, and over the tiles was the warming oven, whose curving nickel-plated front, which Madame Dumard kept at a fevered state of polish, formed an excellent looking glass. Here Télèsphore would comb and comb, unmindful of the bread she was toasting on top of the stove.

Being a tailor was evidently profitable, for he was the only one of Marie-Blanche's suitors who owned a car. It was a Ford convertible of dusky red, and sometimes, on warm spring nights, Marie-Blanche was permitted to drive with him. The problem of a duenna was difficult at this period. Agnès was launched on the second of her many pregnancies, and Madame Dumard would as soon have been caught in a downtown bar as a red convertible. One day she asked me, rather shyly, if I would chaperone the two on their Friday night sorties. Marie-Blanche was, biologically at least, old enough to be my mother, and Télèsphore was already launched on a fattish middle-age; but no one seemed to find my presence silly or incongruous, and even Télèsphore seemed to take it for granted that I would come along.

The order of the evening was that we drove at a pace that was almost a standstill through the streets of the quarter, so that Marie-Blanche could be seen and admired by one and all. Then we drove west along Sherbrooke Street, picking up speed, out to the west-end suburbs, where he would weave in and out of innumerable chintzy crescents, drives, and circles, while Marie-Blanche stared solemnly at the attitudes of suburbia on a spring night. This was evidently an accepted form of outing, like going to the zoo; and it was clear that the customs of suburban dwellers were as foreign to her as the life of the penguin. After the monotonous colonial houses and limitation Tudor had been fully appreciated, he drove a short distance out of the city to a curb-service restaurant and bought us potato chips and a soft drink. Then we drove home.

During the drives, their conversation floated back to me on the warm spring air. It was as innocent as that of the Babes in the Woods. Rendered in English it amounted, in effect, to two lines: "You don't really like me," and "Oh, you don't mean that." Back at the house, I always tried to hurry up the stairs so that they could be alone for at least a second. Their courtship was, to say the least of it, blameless, although he sometimes would give her a pat on her soundly armored behind as he helped her into the car. Télèsphore tailored all his own clothes, of course, and I particularly remember a brown suit with stripes in a lighter tone, and a long green jacket with magnificent shoulders. Marie-Blanche began to recover from Wilfrid's *grande déception*, and what with the potato chips and drives through the suburbs and the little pats, she became quite cheerful and began to put on weight.

Early in the summer, Télèsphore began missing Fridays; and one night he took Marie-Blanche's hand in his and said he was not the marrying kind. When she replied tearfully that *no* man was the marrying kind, but that she would wait if he thought he ever could be, he said she was a saint and better off without him. A few weeks later, having obtained a hurried dispensation to do so, he married his third cousin. Marie-Blanche attended the wedding, her head high. She wore a new hat decorated with blue and pink velvet *choux*. There was no need to mention a *grand défaut*; the condition of the bride, inadequately concealed under tucks, drapes, and flowing panels of white, spoke of it eloquently. I was surprised at Marie-Blanche's lack of restraint in discussing the wedding; she was indignant, but not really shocked. It was simply another drama, like the story of Wilfrid, an example of the inexplicable ways of men. I also realized, gradually, that she had only the haziest notion of how the situation had come about; her information was pieced together from romantic magazine stories, the prudishly censored confidences of her married sister, and the unprudish stories of salesmen in the shops where she worked. Madame Dumard, of course, would rather have died on the spot than utter one enlightening word to an unmarried daughter; and even had she chosen to do so, at Marie-Blanche's age it would have seemed rather silly.

After Télèsphore came many smaller deceptions, men who frequented for a few Fridays and fell away. It is difficult to remember the minor suitors who emerged that year, as distinct from those who have happened since. There had been men named for flowers, for saints, and for martyred heroes. There have been men whose names were a euphonious stringing together of syllables, meaning nothing, and impossible on the Anglo-Saxon tongue. There were suitors who drove buses and streetcars, who sold aspirin and band-aids, who dealt in false teeth and in shoes. She would, of course, have married any one of them, had he not disappeared after his fellows, unequivocally labeled with a *grand défaut*; however, like most women she aspired to a marriage above her station. She looked upward (in vain) to the plateau on which dwelt dentists, notaries and radio announcers. There were still more euphoric heights, peopled with doctors and lawyers and civil engineers—in the Dumards' circle one still said *"Madame Docteur Tremblay"* or *"Madame l'Avocat Arsenault."* But Marie-Blanche knew better than to sour her disposition by dreaming of that.

Once, and only once, was she courted by someone socially beneath herself, and that was at the end of the terrible year that began with Wilfrid and Télèsphore. In the autumn, disillusioned into a devil-may-care attitude, she permitted herself to be frequented by a farmer. Sylvestre Dancereau fell in love with Marie-Blanche one Sunday afternoon when, as she was visiting cousins thirty miles outside the city, he saw her posing for a snapshot. She was wearing white eyelet and had ribbons in her hair. Marie-Blanche usually poses by wetting her lips and parting them in a curly half-smile. Sometimes she rests her head on one hand or, again, looks beyond the camera as if she had just been surprised by a rainbow. Sylvestre, who lived nearby and had come over for some sociable purpose, spoke of his feelings almost at once. Everyone was pleased and astonished; he was nearly forty, and had never in his life courted anyone. Marie-Blanche's cousins broke their necks bringing the two together and the Dumards accepted the new suppliant with a tolerant air. The superiority of city over country people was too established to require pointing out; they would wait and see.

Early in October Sylvestre began calling in town. He arrived a little later than the accustomed hour—he had a complicated schedule that involved changing buses twice—and he left at nine to avoid missing any link in his chain of transport. The Dumards were relieved. His visits were a terrible strain. He was a thin, gangling man who dressed as all farmers do when they come to the city. He sat with one hand on each of his knees and unless someone spoke to him directly he hung his head and looked at the carpet. He was shy and miserable and terrified of committing a social blunder. He even left the parlor when he had to blow his nose. And, although they spread out for him their usual tea and pastry, he could not bring himself to eat in their presence. Sometimes he drank a little tea, with the spoon firmly held between two fingers so that it would not hit him in the eye.

In November, he asked Marie-Blanche's cousins to ask her if she would marry him, and she wrote a gracious note of acceptance. The cousins, now awhirl with intrigue and message-bearing, were asked to point out to Sylvestre that she would not, of course, be expected to live on the farm. Sylvestre would have to come into town and get a job. The cousins could see the point: a girl with Marie-Blanche's knowledge of

English, her intimacy with the business world and all aspects of city life, including the mores of crap shooters, could not be expected to cook over an iron range or pump her own water in the country. Sylvestre was made to see this; his father and his brother could easily carry on.

Marie-Blanche's brother-in-law, who was a milkman, was commissioned to find Sylvestre a job. He exerted his influence for several weeks and finally turned up a job for Sylvestre in the bottling department. The plant was out of town and work began at seven in the morning, but everyone agreed that Sylvestre was accustomed to early rising. His starting salary was twenty-two dollars and fifty cents a week. Sylvestre put off the move as long as possible. He muttered excuses that were connected with the farm and frequently said there was someone he didn't like to leave. Marie-Blanche knew there was no woman in his life other than herself and guessed that he meant his mother. She approved of this, for it was often repeated in the Dumards' circle that men who loved their mothers made excellent husbands.

On New Year's Day, the most festive day of their calendar, Sylvestre was required to desert his home and spend the day with his fiancée's assembled family. He was to present Marie-Blanche with a ring (he had already given her, for Christmas, a heart-shaped locket with an imitation pearl at its center) and their engagement would be acknowledged before the eyes of all. Marie-Blanche wept the morning of New Year's Day because, the previous year, it had been Wilfrid who had sat at her Aunt Elzema's table, nibbling turkey with delicate bites, modestly refusing a glass of wine with an upturned hand. When Madame Dumard reproached her for weeping, she dried her eyes and said somberly, "*Dieu me comprend*." Then they went off together down the snowy street, two little cocoons of wool, overshoes, veils and something black with furry accretions wrapped over it all.

I had spent the day somewhere else and arrived back about an hour before the Dumards. They entered the flat in silence, shaking the snow from their coats without a word. Still wearing their hats and overshoes they proceeded to the kitchen, that lap of comfort, without a word. Madame Dumard shook the fire down and put some wood on it and put the kettle on for tea. I wandered in and sat down and we looked at each other. "Le Sylvestre," said Marie-Blanche at last, as if she were pronouncing the name of a brother drowned at sea. "Wait till I tell you. Some guy."

"*Parle donc français*," said her mother sharply. She was in a terrible mood. Marie-Blanche sighed and removed her hat. The imprisoned curls expanded. She placed the hat on the kitchen table and Madame Dumard said at once: "Haven't we had enough bad luck for one day?" She brushed the hat onto a chair. She looked at me and drew a long breath. "Try to imagine the scene," she said, and both women settled back for a good dramatic account.

There had been thirty-five people at Aunt Elzema's, but good humor had prevailed and they had eaten in shifts. It had been *un diner* extra, with seven kinds of dessert, including a huge *bûche*, a cake shaped like a log with little sugar rosebuds all over it. And wine. "For the men, of course," Madame said hastily.

"And Sylvestre?" It was one of those accounts that requires a shove from time to time.

"Sylvestre. *Ah, ça.*" First of all, there had been his table manners. There had been a little side dish of green peas that he had tried to eat with a fork instead of the teaspoon so clearly provided for the purpose. He had picked up his dainty glass of tomato juice and said audibly: "*Qu'est-ce que c'est donc, cette affaire, donc, donc,*" the additions of "*doncs*" being the cadence of his unfortunate country speech. Unlike Wilfrid, he had not, smilingly, demurred when offered wine. He drained not one glass but many and then, flushed with alcohol and love, had risen on his trembling legs and made a little speech. He was coming into the city, he said, for the sake of the one he loved; and here he had leered in the direction of his betrothed. But on this festive day, he went on, he wanted to show them a few snapshots, to show what this move meant to him. He had drawn out his wallet; Marie-Blanche had looked modestly at the tablecloth, remembering the autumn day, the eyelet frock and the hair ribbons. But Sylvestre produced a handful of pictures, and they were not of Marie-Blanche. They were of a horse.

"Victorine," said Sylvestre. Victorine was so clever she could almost talk. She understood everything one said. Grace, beauty, fidelity, intelligence; tribute after tribute fell from his lips. Many of the photos included Sylvestre, of course. There was Sylvestre in a cowboy suit, waving his hat in a dashing manner; Sylvestre offering Victorine a lump of sugar; Sylvestre negligently rolling a cigarette with the bridle lying slack. He told them his chaps and gauntlets were hand-made by Indians out west.

"I thought 'e'd never shut up about the damned 'orse," Marie-Blanche told me, in English.

The pictures had gone round the table silently, and then producing increasing hilarity. One of the cousins began to sing "Joe, le Cowboy," and from there they went on to "Le Cowboy des Western Plains," "Le Cowboy Canadian," and finally united in many rolicking choruses of "Dans Les Plains du Fa-ar West." Sylvestre led the singing while Marie-Blanche and her mother sat, mortified but stonyfaced. Marie-Blanche held the pictures in her hand. There was not one of her. Sylvestre was so happy and excited that he forgot all about the ring. It was still in his pocket when the Dumards left, swept out on the sympathetic clucking of their female relatives. The males were still singing. "It's a terrible thing to marry a drunk," one of her aunts remarked.

Marie-Blanche spoke only once to Sylvestre, a memorable parting line. She returned to him his packet of snapshots before the eyes of all and, addressing him in her perfect English, said: "To heach 'is own, Monsieur Dancereau."

"Ah, well," Madame Dumard sighed, beginning to make the tea. "It's just as well we know now what he is. *Il a un grand défaut...*" She would have said more, but Marie-Blanche slammed her hand down on the table with exasperation.

"*Défaut* be damned," she said. "He's just like the rest of them, nothing but a big schlemiel."

WING'S CHIPS

OFTEN, since I grew up, I have tried to remember the name of the French-Canadian town where I lived for a summer with my father when I was a little girl of seven or eight. Sometimes, passing through a town, I have thought I recognized it, but some detail is always wrong, or at least fails to fit the picture in my memory. It was a town like many others in the St. Lawrence Valley—old, but with a curious atmosphere of harshness, as if the whole area were still frontier and had not been settled and cultivated for three hundred years. There were rows of temporary-looking frame and stucco houses, a post office in somebody's living room, a Chinese fish-and-chip store, and, on the lawn of the imposing Catholic church, a statue of Jesus, arms extended, crowned with a wreath of electric lights. Running straight through the center of town was a narrow river; a few leaky rowboats were tied up along its banks, and on Sunday afternoons hot, church-dressed young men would go to work on them with rusty bailing tins. The girls who clustered giggling on shore and watched them wore pastel stockings, lacy summer hats, and voile dresses that dipped down in back and were decorated low on one hip with sprays of artificial lilac. For additional Sunday divertissement, there was the cinema, in an old barn near the railway station. The pictures had no sound track; airs from "My Maryland" and "The Student Prince" were played on a piano and there was the occasional toot of the suburban train from Montreal while on the screen ladies with untidy hair and men in riding boots engaged in agitated, soundless conversation, opening and closing their mouths like fish.

Though I have forgotten the name of this town, I do remember with remarkable clarity the house my father took for that summer. It was white clapboard, and surrounded by shade trees and an untended garden, in which only sunflowers and a few perennials survived. It had been rented furnished and bore the imprint of Quebec rural taste, running largely to ball fringes and sea-shell-encrusted religious art. My father, who was a painter, used one room as a studio—or, rather, storage place, since he worked mostly out-of-doors—slept in another, and ignored the remaining seven, which was probably just as well, though order of a sort was kept by a fierce-looking local girl called Pauline, who had a pronounced mustache and was so ill-tempered that her nickname was *P'tit-Loup*—Little Wolf.

Pauline cooked abominably, cleaned according to her mood, and asked me questions. My father had told her that my mother was in a nursing home in Montreal, but Pauline wanted to know more. How ill was my mother? Very ill? Dying? Was it true that my parents were separated? Was my father *really* my father? *"Drôle de père,"* said Pauline. She was perplexed by his painting, his animals (that summer his menagerie included two German shepherds, a parrot, and a marmoset, which later bit the finger of a man teasing it and had to be given away to Montreal's ratty little zoo, where it moped itself to death), and his total indifference to the way the house was run. Why didn't he work, like other men, said Pauline.

I could understand her bewilderment, for the question of my father's working was beginning to worry me for the first time. All of the French-Canadian fathers in the town worked. They delivered milk, they farmed, they owned rival hardware stores, they drew up one another's wills. Nor were they the only busy ones. Across the river, in a faithful reproduction of a suburb of Glasgow or Manchester, lived a small colony of English-speaking summer residents from Montreal. Their children were called Al, Lily, Winnie, or Mac, and they were distinguished by their popping blue eyes, their excessive devotion to the Royal Family, and their contempt for anything even vaguely queer or Gallic. Like the French-Canadians, the fathers of Lily and Winnie and the others worked. Every one of them had a job. When they were not taking the train to Montreal to attend to their jobs, they were crouched in their gardens, caps on their heads, tying up tomato plants or painting stones to make gay multicolored borders for the nasturtium beds. Saturday night, they trooped into the town bar-and-grill and drank as much

Molson's ale as could be poured into the stomach before closing time. Then, awash with ale and nostalgia, they sang about the maid in the clogs and shawl, and something else that went, "Let's all go down to the Strand, and 'ave a ba-na-ar-na!"

My father, I believed, was wrong in not establishing some immediate liaison with this group. Like them, he was English—a real cabbage, said Pauline when she learned that he had been in Canada only eight or nine years. Indeed, one of his very few topics of conversation with me was the England of his boyhood, before the First World War. It sounded green, sunny, and silent—a sort of vast lawn rising and falling beside the sea; the sun was smaller and higher than the sun in Canada, looking something like a coin; the trees were leafy and round, and looked like cushions. This was probably not at all what he said, but it was the image I retained—a landscape flickering and flooded with light, like the old silents at the cinema. The parents of Lily and Winnie had, presumably, also come out of this landscape, yet it was a bond my father appeared to ignore. It seemed to me that he was unaware of how much we had lost caste, and what grievous social errors we had committed, by being too much identified with the French. He had chosen a house on the wrong side of the river. Instead of avoiding the French language, or noisily making fun of it, he spoke it whenever he was dealing with anyone who could not understand English. He did not attend the English church, and he looked just as sloppy on Sundays as he did the rest of the week.

"You people Carthlic?" one of the fathers from over the river asked me once, as if that would explain a lot.

Mercifully, I was able to say no. I knew we were not Catholic because at the Pensionnat Saint-Louis de Gonzague, in Montreal, which I attended, I had passed the age at which children usually took the First Communion. For a year and more, my classmates had been attending morning chapel in white veils, while I still wore a plain, stiff, pre-Communion black veil that smelled of convent parlors, and marked me as one outside the limits of grace.

"Then why's your dad always around the frogs?" asked the English father.

Drôle de père indeed. I had to agree with Pauline. He was not like any father I had met or read about. He was not Elsie's Mr. Dinsmore, stern but swayed by tears. Nor did he in the least resemble Mr. Bobbsey, of the Bobbsey Twins books, or Mr. Bunker, of the Six Little Bunkers. I was never scolded, or rebuked, or reminded to brush my teeth or say my prayers. My father was perfectly content to live his own summer and let me live mine, which did not please me in the least. If, at meals, I failed to drink my milk, it was I who had to mention this omission. When I came home from swimming with my hair wet, it was I who had to remind him that, because of some ear trouble that was a hangover of scarlet fever, I was supposed to wear a bathing cap. When Lon Chaney in *The Hunchback of Notre Dame* finally arrived at the cinema, he did not say a word about my not going, even though Lily and Winnie and many of the French-Canadian children were not allowed to attend, and boasted about the restriction.

Oddly, he did have one or two notions about the correct upbringing of children, which were, to me, just as exasperating as his omissions. Somewhere in the back of his mind lingered a recollection that all little girls were taught French and music. I don't know where the little girls of the England of his childhood were sent to learn their French—presumably to France—but I was placed, one month after my fourth birthday, in the Pensionnat, where for two years I had the petted privilege of being the youngest boarder in the history of the school. My piano lessons had also begun at four, but lasted only a short time, for, as the nun in charge of music explained, I could not remember or sit still, and my hand was too small to span an octave. Music had then been dropped as one of my accomplishments until that summer, when, persuaded by someone who obviously had my welfare at heart, my father dispatched me twice a week to study piano with a Madame Tessier, the convent-educated wife of a farmer, whose parlor was furnished entirely with wicker and over whose household hung a faint smell of dung, owing to the proximity of the outbuildings and the intense humidity of summer weather in the St. Lawrence Valley. Together, Madame Tessier and I sweated it out, plodding away against my lack of talent, my absence of interest, and my strong but unspoken desire to be somewhere else.

"*Cette enfant ne fera jamais rien,*" I once heard her say in despair.

We had been at it four or five weeks before she discovered at least part of the trouble; it was simply that there was no piano at home, so I never practiced. After every lesson, she had marked with care the scales I was to master, yet, week after week, I produced only those jerky, hesitant sounds that are such agony for music teachers and the people in the next room.

"You might as well tell your father there's no use carrying on unless you have a piano," she said.

I was only too happy, and told him that afternoon, at lunch.

"You mean you want me to get you a *piano*?" he said, looking around the dining room as if I had insisted it be installed, then and there, between the window and the mirrored china cabinet. How unreasonable I was!

"But you make me take the lessons," I said. How unreasonable *he* was!

A friend of my father's said to me, years later, "He never had the faintest idea what to do with you." But it was equally true that I never had the faintest idea what to do with him. We did not, of course, get a piano, and Madame Tessier's view was that because my father had no employment to speak of (she called him a *flâneur*), we simply couldn't afford one—the depth of shame in a town where even the milkman's daughters could play duets.

No one took my father's painting seriously as a daily round of work, least of all I. At one point during that summer, my father agreed to do a pastel portrait of the daughter of a Madame Gravelle, who lived in Montreal. (This was in the late twenties, when pastel drawings of children hung in every other sitting room.) The daughter, Liliane, who was my age or younger, was to be shown in her First Communion dress and veil. Madame Gravelle and Liliane drove out from Montreal, and while Liliane posed with docility, her mother hung about helpfully commenting. Here my father was neglecting to show in detail the pattern of the lace veil; there he had the wrong shade of blue for Liliane's eyes; again, it was the matter of Liliane's diamond cross. The cross, which hung from her neck, contained four diamonds on the horizontal segment and six on the vertical, and this treasure he had reduced to two unimpressive strokes.

My father suggested that Madame Gravelle might be just as happy with a tinted photograph. No, said Madame Gravelle, she would not. Well, then, he suggested, how about a miniature? He knew of a miniaturist who worked from photographs, eliminating sittings, and whose fee was about four times his own. Madame Gravelle bore Liliane, her cross, and her veil back to Montreal, and my father went back to painting around the countryside and going out with his dogs.

His failure weighed heavily on me, particularly after someone, possibly Pauline, told me that he was forever painting people who didn't pay him a cent for doing it. He painted Pauline, mustache and all; he painted some of the French-Canadian children who came to play in our garden, and from whom I was learning a savory French vocabulary not taught at Pensionnat Saint-Louis de Gonzague; he very often sketched the little Wing children, whose family owned the village fish-and-chip store.

The Wing children were solemn little Chinese, close in age and so tangled in lineage that it was impossible to sort them out as sisters, brothers, and cousins. Some of the adult Wings—brothers, and cousins—ran the fish-and-chip shop, and were said to own many similar establishments throughout Quebec and to be (although no one would have guessed it to see them) by far the richest people in the area. The interior of their store smelled wonderfully of frying grease and vinegar, and the walls were a mosaic of brightly painted tin signs advertising Player's Mild, Orange Crush, Sweet Marie chocolate bars, and ginger ale. The smaller Wings, in the winter months, attended Anglican boarding schools in the west, at a discreet distance from the source of income. Their English was excellent and their French-Canadian idiom without flaw. Those nearest my age were Florence, Marjorie, Ronald, and Hugh. The older set of brothers and cousins—those of my father's generation—had abrupt, utilitarian names: Tommy, Jimmy, George. The still older people—most of whom seldom came out from the rooms behind the shop—used their Chinese names. There was even a great-grandmother, who sat, shrunken and silent, by the great iron range where the chips swam in a bath of boiling fat.

As the Wings had no garden, and were not permitted to play by the river, lest they fall in and drown, it was most often at my house that we played. If my father was out, we would stand at the door of his studio and peer in at the fascinating disorder.

"What does he do?" Florence or Marjorie would say. "What does your father do?"

"He paints!" Pauline would cry from the kitchen. She might, herself, consider him loony, but the privilege was hers. She worked there, not a pack of Chinese.

It was late in the summer, in August, when, one afternoon, Florence and Marjorie and Ronald and Hugh came up from the gate escorting, like a convoy, one of the older Wings. They looked anxious and important. "Is your father here?" said the grown-up Wing.

I ran to fetch my father, who had just started out for a walk. When we returned, Pauline and the older Wing, who turned out to be Jimmy, were arguing in French, she at the top of her voice, he almost inaudibly.

"The kids talk about you a lot," said Jimmy Wing to my father. "They said you were a painter. We're enlarging the store, and we want a new sign."

"A sign?"

"I told you!" shrieked Pauline from the dining-room door, to which she had retreated. "*Ce n'est pas un peintre comme ça.*"

"*Un peintre, c'est un peintre,*" said Jimmy Wing, imperturbable.

My father looked at the little Wings, who were all looking up at him, and said, "Exactly. *Un peintre, c'est un peintre.* What sort of sign would you like?"

The Wings didn't know; they all began to talk at once. Something artistic, said Jimmy Wing, with the lettering fat and thin, imitation Chinese. Did my father know what he meant? Oh, yes. My father knew exactly.

"Just 'Wing's Chips'?" my father asked. "Or would you like it in French—'*Les Chips de Wing*'?"

"Oh, *English,*" said all the Wings, almost together. My father said later that the Chinese were terrible snobs.

He painted the sign the next Sunday afternoon, not in the studio but out in the back garden, sitting on the wide kitchen steps. He lacquered it black, and painted—in red-and-gold characters, fat and thin—WING'S CHIPS, and under this he put the name of the town and two curly little letters, P.Q., for "Province of Quebec."

Tommy and Jimmy Wing and all the little ones came to fetch the sign the next day. The two men looked at it for a long time, while the little ones looked anxiously at them to see if they liked it. Finally, Jimmy Wing said, "It's the most beautiful thing I ever saw."

The two men bore it away, the little Wings trailing behind, and hung it on a horizontal pole over the street in front of their shop, where it rocked in the hot, damp breeze from the river. I was hysterically proud of the sign and, for quite the first time, of my father. Everyone stopped before the shop and examined it. The French-Canadians admitted that it was *pas mal, pas mal du tout*, while the English adults said approvingly that he must have been paid a fine penny for it. I could not bring down our new stature by admitting that he had painted it as a favor, and that it was only after Jimmy and Tommy had insisted that he had said they could, if they liked, pay for the gold paint, since he had had to go to Montreal for it. Nor did I tell anyone how the Wings, burdened with gratitude, kept bringing us chips and ice cream.

"Oh, yes, he was paid an awful lot," I assured them all.

Every day, I went to look at the sign, and I hung around the shop in case anyone wanted to ask me questions about it. There it was, WING'S CHIPS, proof that my father was an ordinary workingman just like anybody else, and I pointed it out to as many people as I could, both English and French, until the summer ended and we went away.

THE LEGACY

LATE IN the afternoon after Mrs. Boldescu's funeral, her four children returned to the shop on St. Eulalie Street, in Montreal, where they had lived when they were growing up. Victor, the youngest, drove quickly ahead, leaving, like an unfriendly country, the trampled grass of the cemetery and the sorrowing marble angels. Several blocks behind came Marina and the two older boys, Carol and Georgie, side by side in the long black car that had been hired for the day. Emptied of flowers, it still enclosed a sickly smell of lilies and of Carol's violet horseshoe, that had borne on a taffeta ribbon the words "Good Luck to You, Mama."

These three sat in silence, collapsed against the prickling plush of the cushions. Marina was thankful that Victor had driven up from Bloomfield, New Jersey, in his own three-year-old Buick. It would have been too much at this moment to have shared the drive with his American wife, Peggy Ann, hearing her voice carried out on the hot city air as she exclaimed over the slummy landscape and congratulated her husband on his plucky triumph over environment. Glancing at Carol and Georgie, Marina decided they might not have cared. Their triumph had been of a different nature. They stared out of the car at brick façades, seemingly neither moved nor offended by the stunning ugliness of the streets that had held their childhood. Sometimes one of them sighed, the comfortable respiration of one who has wept.

Remembering the funeral, Marina bent her head and traced a seam of her black linen suit where the dye had taken badly. Her brothers had cried with such abandon that they had commended themselves forever to Father Patenaude and every neighborhood woman at church. "Those bad pennies," Marina had heard Father Patenaude say. "Bad pennies they were, but they loved their mother. They did all of this, you know."

By "all of this," he meant the first-class funeral, the giant wreaths, the large plot they had purchased *in perpetuum*, to which their father's coffin, until now at rest in a less imposing cemetery, had been removed. There was space in the new plot for them all, including Victor's wife, who would, Marina thought, be grateful to know that thanks to her brothers-in-law's foresight her bones need not be turned out, for lack of burial space, until the Day of Judgment. A smaller tract, spattered with the delicate shadow of a weeping willow, had been set aside for Victor's children. He was the only one of her brothers who had married, and his as-yet-unconceived offspring were doomed to early extinction if one considered the space reserved for their remains. Marina could only imagine the vision of small crosses, sleeping babies, and praying cherubs that had been painted for Carol and Georgie. At the same time, she wondered what Victor felt about his brothers' prescience. His expression at the funeral had been one of controlled alarm, perhaps because of his wife, whose fidgetings and whisperings had disturbed even the rolling tide of Carol's and Georgie's grief. These two had stared hard at Peggy Ann on the edge of the grave, and Georgie had remarked that nothing worthy of life or death was likely to come out of that blond, skinny drink of water—which Marina took to be a reference to the babies' plot.

The way they had been grouped at the funeral—Marina unwillingly pressed between her weeping brothers, Victor a little apart—had seemed to her prophetic. The strain of her mother's long illness had made her superstitious. Visiting her mother at the hospital toward the end, she had seen an omen in every cloud, a message in a maple leaf that, on a treeless street, unexpectedly fell at her feet. Sometimes she felt that all of them had combined to kill their mother—Victor by behaving too well, the others by behaving badly, herself through the old-maidish asperity that had lately begun to creep through her conversation like an ink-stain. She had even blamed Father Patenaude, remembering, in her mother's last moments, the cold comfort her mother had brought home from the confession box. Watching the final office of death, Marina waited for him to speak the words of reassurance her mother wanted; but nothing came, and Mrs. Boldescu was permitted to die without once being told that the mores of St. Eulalie Street and not her own inadequacies had permitted Victor's escape into a Protestant marriage, and Georgie's and Carol's being led away again and again by the police.

Marina had quarreled with Father Patenaude, right then and there in the hospital, where all the nurses could hear. The priest's thin face had been pink with annoyance, and the embarrassment of Carol and Georgie caused them, later on, to press upon him a quite unnecessary check. His sins of omission—they had possibly been caused, she now realized, through nothing sterner than lack of imagination—were for God and not Marina to judge, Father Patenaude said.

Mrs. Boldescu had only by courtesy been attached to his flock. She belonged by birth and breeding to the Greek Catholic Church, that easy resting place between Byzantium and Rome. The Father was French-Canadian, with the peasant distrust of all his race for the exotic. Perhaps, Marina thought, he had detected her mother's contempt for the pretty, pallid Western saints, each with his crown of electric lights. In the soaring exaltation of her self-reproach, Father Patenaude must have sensed the richness of past devotions, seen the bearded priest, the masculine saints, the gold walls glittering behind the spears of candlelight, the hanging ruby lamp swaying in the thick incense-laden air. Victor's marriage had probably offended him most. Even Georgie and Carol, for all their cosmic indifference to the affairs of their sister and brother, had been offended.

However Mrs. Boldescu might deplore the deviation of her youngest son, she trusted his good business sense. It was to Victor that the shop had been left. Now, driving back to it for the final conference, Marina could not have said if Carol and Georgie minded. Their feelings toward each other as children had been so perfunctory that jealousy, then, would have struck any one of them as much too familiar to be comfortable. Of course, Carol and Georgie might have changed; meeting over their mother's bed, after a separation of years, they had had no time to sift their memories, even had they chosen to do anything so out of character. Their greeting had been in the matter-of-fact tones of consanguinity, and Marina had retired at once to a flower-banked corner of the hospital room, so that her brothers might have scope and space for their emotions.

The two had scarcely glanced at her again. Pale and tired, graced with only the ghost of a racial bloom they had long disavowed and now failed to recognize, Marina appeared to satisfy their image of a sister. To her, however, the first few moments had been webbed in strangeness, and she had watched her brothers as if they came from an alien land. They knelt by the bed, barred with the shadow of the hospital shade, their glossy, brilliantined heads bowed on clasped hands. Disliking their rings, their neckties, their easy tears, she remembered what had formed them, and saw behind her brothers a tunnel of moldering corridors, the gray and stifling walls of reformatories named for saints. Summoning this image, like a repeated apology, she was able to pardon the violet horseshoe, the scene of distracted remorse on the brink of the grave. Their strangeness vanished; boredom took its place. She remembered at last what her brothers were like—not the somber criminal of sociological texts, denied roller skates at a crucial age; still less the hero-villain of films; but simply men whose moments of megalomaniacal audacity were less depressing than their lack of common sense and taste. It was for their pleasure, she thought, that people manufactured ash trays shaped like little outhouses, that curly-haired little girls in sailor suits were taught to tap-dance, and night-club singers gave voice to "Mother Machree" and "Eli, Eli."

Still, she thought, neither of them would have married into apostasy like Victor, nor flustered poor Father Patenaude by listening to his sermons as if analyzing them for truth and intellectual content, as she herself did every week. The Father was horrified that the shop had been left to Victor instead of to them. "It might have been their redemption," Marina had heard him say after the funeral, as she threaded her way out between the elaborate graves. "And they were so good to her; they loved their mother."

Certainly, their periodic descents on St. Eulalie Street had been more impressive than Victor's monthly check and letter, or Marina's faithful presence at Sunday dinner. Carol and Georgie, awash in the warm sea of Mother's Day, had left in their wake a refrigerator for the shop that could hold fifteen cases of beer, a radio inlaid with wood in a waterfall pattern, a silver brush and mirror with Old English initials, a shrine containing a Madonna with blue glass eyes, a pearl-and-diamond pin shaped like a daisy, a Persian lamb coat with summer storage prepaid for ten years, two porcelain lamps of shepherd and shepherdess persuasion, and finally the gift that for some reason appealed most strongly to Carol and Georgie—a sherry decanter and ten tiny glasses, each of which sounded a note of gratifying purity when struck with a knife.

The coat, the pin, the shrine, and the brush and mirror had been left to Marina, who, luckily, bore the same initials. Carol and Georgie, awarded similar tokens, had been warm in their assurances that neither of them wanted the shop. No one, they said, was more suited to shop-keeping than Victor—a remark that offended Victor's wife into speech-lessness for half an hour.

She and Victor were standing on the sidewalk in front of the shop when the hired car drew up to the curb. Peggy Ann, when she saw them, made exaggerated gestures of melting away in the sun, and then incomprehensible ones of laying her head on a pillow, which drew an unflattering remark from Georgie.

"Home," Carol said, evidently without sarcasm, looking up and down the shadeless chasm of brick, here and there enlivened by Pepsi-Cola signs. A few children, sticky with popsicles, examined the New Jersey license of Victor's Buick and then the shining splendor of the rented limousine. Not recognizing it, they turned back to the Buick and then suddenly scattered into the street, where Georgie had thrown a handful of quarters. Some of the children, Marina's pupils at a paro-chial school named for Saint Valerie the Martyr, glanced at her shyly.

"They look scared of you," Georgie said. "What do you do, beat them?"

"I'd like to," Marina said.

"I'm sure she doesn't mean that," Peggy Ann said, smiling.

A wide ribbon of crepe hung on the shop door, and green shades were pulled at door and window, bearing in shadow the semicircle of words on the glass, RUMANIA FANCY GROCERIES, and then in smaller letters, MRS. MARIA BOLDESCU.

"How many times did I get up on a ladder and wash that window!" Georgie said, as if the memory were enchanting.

"Victor, too?" said Peggy Ann. "I'll bet he was an old lazy."

No one replied, and Victor fitted the key into the padlock while

Carol, restless, hummed and executed a little dance step. The smell of the shut-up store moved out to meet them. Carol, with a look of concern, went at once to the cash register, but Marina had forestalled him. "I took it all out when Mama took sick," she said.

"Good idea," said Georgie, approving.

"You were awfully clever to think of everything," Peggy Ann said. "Although it seems to me that, with crepe on the door and everything, no one would break in." She stopped, as if she had uttered an indelicate thought, and went on rapidly, "Oh, Victor, do look! What a sweet little store. Look at all the salami and my goodness, all the beer! Cases and cases!"

"We bought Mama the beer license," Carol said. He walked around, rattling change in his pocket.

"She must have been pleased," said Peggy Ann. "Victor, look at all the things—all the tins of soup, and the spaghetti."

Marina, parting the blue chintz curtains at the end of the counter, moved into the kitchen behind the shop. She lifted her hand and, without glancing up, caught the string of an overhead light. Two doors, varnished to simulate oak, led off to the bedrooms—the one she had shared with her mother, until, at twenty-three, she had overcome her mother's objections to her having a place of her own, and the other room in which had slept, singly or together, the three boys. The kitchen window looked out on a fenced-in yard where Mrs. Boldescu had tried to grow vegetables and a few flowers, finally managing a tough and spiky grass. Marina opened the window and pushed back the shutters, admitting a shifting layer of soot. Weeds grew as high as the sill, and wild rhubarb, uncontrolled in this summer of illness, flourished along the fence. A breath of city air entered the room, and an old calendar bearing a picture of the shrine at St. Anne de Beaupré suddenly flapped on its pin. She straightened it, and then, from some remembered prudence, turned out the light.

Carol, who had come in behind her, glanced at the calendar and then at her. Then he said, "Now that we're alone, tell me just one thing. Was that a nice funeral or wasn't it?"

"It was charming," she said. "It was nice that you and Georgie were both free for it at once."

Carol laughed; evidently he expected this sour, womanly reprimand, and now that their mother was dead he would expect it still more from Marina. "You ought to get married," he said.

"Thanks. The boys I grew up with were all so charming." She sat down, tipping her chair against the wall in a way her mother had disliked. She and Carol were alone as they had seldom been in childhood, able now to take stock of each other. Twenty, fifteen years before they had avoided each other like uncongenial castaways, each pursuing some elusive path that led away from St. Eulalie Street. Considering the way they had lived, crowded as peas in a pod, their privacy, she now thought, must have been a powerful act of will. In the darkening room, she saw herself ironing her middy blouse, the only one she owned, a book propped insecurely on the ironing board. Georgie and Carol came and went like cats, and Victor shouted outside in a game of kick-the-can. Again, she did her homework under the overhead light while Georgie and Carol, shut in their room for punishment, climbed out the window and were fetched home by the police. At last, her memory alighted on one shining summer with both the older boys "away" (this was the only word Mrs. Boldescu had ever used) and Marina, afloat with happiness, saying to every customer in the shop, "I'm going to France; have you heard? I'm going to France."

"I'm *talking* to you," said Carol. "Don't judge all the boys you knew by me. Look at old Victor."

"The pride of the street," said Marina, remembering that summer.

"*Was* he?" said Peggy Ann. She stood in the doorway, holding back the curtains with either hand. "I never get a thing out of him, about the store, or his childhood, or anything. Victor, do look at this room! It's just like a farmhouse kitchen! And the adorable shrine ... Did your mother bring it from Rumania?"

"I bought that," said Carol. He looked at it, troubled. "Does it look foreign or something?" he said to Marina. "It came from Boston."

"I would have said Rumania," said Peggy Ann. She sat down and smiled at the coal-and-wood stove.

"Well," Victor said, smiling at them all. "Well, the old place." He dropped his cigarette on the floor and stepped on it.

"It's all yours now," Georgie said. He sat down at the round table under the light, Carol beside him. Victor, after glancing about uncertainly, sat opposite, so that they appeared to face him like inquisitors. "Yours," Georgie repeated with finality.

"I wouldn't say that," Victor said, unnecessarily straightening his necktie. "I mean to say, I think Mama meant me to have it in trust, for the rest of you. My idea was—"

"We ought to have a drink," Georgie said. He looked at Marina, who was sitting a little apart, as if to confound the prophecy of the graveyard that they would someday all lie together. "Would it be all right, today I mean?"

"You're old enough to know if you want a drink," Marina said. She had no intention of becoming the new matriarch of the family; but the others still waited, uncertain, and she finally found in a cupboard a bottle and the glasses that were her brothers' special pride. "Mama's brandy," she said. "Let's drink to Victor, the heir."

"No," said Victor, "honestly, now, I keep trying to tell you. I'm not exactly the heir in the way you mean." He was still talking as the others picked up their glasses and drank. Marina filled the glasses again and then sat away from the table, tipping her chair against the wall. The kitchen was cool after the flat glare of the cemetery and the stuffiness of the drive home. Sounds filtered through the shop from the street; a cat dropped from the fence and sniffed the wild rhubarb plants. The calendar, its shrine surrounded by a painted garland of leaves, stared at her from the opposite wall.

Her brothers talked on, Victor with some sustained and baffling delicacy retreating from the idea of his inheritance. Opening her eyes, Marina saw the calendar again and remembered the summer—the calendar bore its date—when she had looked at the room and thought, Soon I'll never have to see any of this again unless I want to.

"... would care to live here again," Peggy Ann's high voice cut into a silence. Carol refilled the glasses, and the conversation rose. Peggy Ann leaned toward Marina and repeated, "I was saying, we think we should keep the store and all, but I don't think Victor would care to live here again."

"I can't imagine why not," Marina said, looking thoughtfully at the torn linoleum. "Mama thought it was Heaven. Where she grew up, they all lived in one room, along with a goat."

"I know," Peggy Ann said, distracted. "It would make a difference in your point of view, wouldn't it? But you know, Victor left so young."

"You might say that all of my brothers left young, one way or another," said Marina. "You might even say I was the patsy." She handed her glass to Carol, who filled it, frowning a little; he did not like women to drink. "You might even say," Marina went on, "that it was Victor's fault."

"I don't see how it could be *Victor's* fault," Peggy Ann said. "He was so different from the rest, don't you think?" She folded her hands and regarded them primly. "I mean to say, he's a C.P.A. now, and awfully well thought of. And we own our own home."

"A triumph of education," said Marina. "The boy who went to college." She finished her brandy and extended the glass, this time to Georgie.

"*You're* educated," said Peggy Ann graciously. "Victor's awfully proud of you. He tells everyone how you teach in the very same school you went to! It must be wonderful for those children, having someone from the same—who understands the sort of home background. I mean it must help you a lot, too, to have come from the same—" She sighed and looked about the room for succor. "You must have liked your school," she said at last. "Victor hated his. Somebody beat him with a snow shovel or something."

"I loved mine," Marina said. She looked into the depths of her glass. "*Loved* it. I had a medal every week that said on it 'Perfection.' Just the same, I was ungrateful. I used to say to myself, Well, all told, I don't give a goddamn if I never see these dark green walls again … But then, as you say, the home background helps a lot. I look at my pupils, and I see nine little Carols for every little Victor. I don't see myself anywhere, though, so I guess there's nothing much between the Victors and the Carols."

"Yes, I see what you mean," said Peggy Ann. She slid back her white organdie cuff and glanced at her watch. "The boys do talk on, don't they? Of course, they haven't seen each other for so long…There's something we wanted to talk to you about, but I guess Victor's just never going to get around to it." She smiled at Marina, wide-eyed, and went on. "We wondered if you wouldn't want to have this little apartment for your own."

"My own?"

"To live in," Peggy Ann said. "We thought it was such a good idea. You'd be right near your school, and you wouldn't have to pay any rent—only the heat and gas. If there *is* heat or gas," she said uncertainly, glancing around. "It was Victor's idea. He thinks the store belongs to the family and you should all get something out of it. Victor says you really deserve something, because you always took such good care of your mother, and you made so many sacrifices and everything."

"Live here?" said Marina. She straightened her chair suddenly and put down her glass. "Courtesy of Victor?" She looked across the table at her brother, and then, rising, unhooked the calendar from its pin. "Victor—" she said, cutting through a remark of Carol's—"dear, sweet little Victor. Now that you're proprietor of Rumania Fancy Groceries, there's a keepsake I want you to take home. You might like to frame it." She placed the calendar carefully before him on the table.

"I was just coming to that," said Carol. "I was just going to say—"

"Well, I said it," said Marina, "so shut up."

"What a memory," Georgie said. "God—women and elephants!" He pulled the calendar toward him and read aloud, "Nineteen thirty-seven."

"The year I did not go to France," said Marina. "The year I had the scholarship to Grenoble."

"I remember," Victor said, smiling a little but glancing uneasily at his wife.

"You should," his sister said. "You damn well should remember."

"Victor, what *is* it?" said Peggy Ann. "You know, we should start back before dark." She looked appealingly at Marina standing over the table.

Turning the calendar over, Georgie read, "Sergeant-detectives Callahan and Vronsky, and two phone numbers. You ought to know them by heart, Vic."

"Not exactly," Victor said. He shook his head, amused and rueful. "I'd rather just forget it."

"We haven't," Carol said. He pushed the calendar back toward his brother, staring at him.

"It's a long time ago now," Victor said, relaxing in his chair as if the effort of leaving were hopeless. "You sort of started it all, as I remember."

"I started it," said Marina. She moved around the table to stand between Carol and Georgie, the better to face Victor. "I had the scholarship in France and Mama had the money to send me."

"What has that—" Carol began, annoyed, glancing up at her.

"Women," Georgie said. "They always have to be first in the act. It was Carol started it."

"Your brother-in-law, Carol," said Marina to Peggy Ann, "was arrested for some schoolboy prank one Sunday morning as the Boldescu family returned from church. Brother Georgie was 'away,' and after Carol's departure, amid the tears of his sister and mother—"

"Peggy Ann doesn't want to hear this," Victor said.

"—a gun was discovered on a shelf in the shop, between two tins of chocolate empire biscuits," said Marina. "Which our mother took and with a rich Rumanian curse—"

"That part's a lie," said Georgie, shouting.

"—flung as far as she could out the kitchen window. I guess her arm wasn't too good, because it fell in the snow by the fence."

"She never swore in her life," said Georgie. "That's a lousy thing to say the day of her funeral." His voice went hoarse, brandy having failed to restore the ravages of weeping.

"Since when do you drink so much, too?" Carol asked her. "I'd like Mama to see you." Virtuously, he pushed her empty glass out of her reach.

"In the spring," said Marina, "after the snow melted some, little brother Victor wandered out in the yard—"

"I was a kid," Victor told his wife, who wore a faint, puzzled smile, as if the end of this could only be a wonderful joke.

"A stripling," Marina said. "Full of admiration for the pranks of his older brothers."

"Tell the story or shut up," said Carol.

"Found the little gun," said Marina, "all wet and rusty. Was it, Vic?

I've forgotten that part. Anyway he took it to school and after making sure that every boy in class had admired it—"

"The dumb little bastard," said Carol, looking moodily at the floor.

"—took it to a pawnshop that can be seen from the front door here, and, instead of pawning it, poked it into the stomach of a Mr. Levinson. It was noon—"

"Twelve o'clock noon," said Carol. "Jesus."

"I don't believe this," said Peggy Ann. Her eyebrows drew together, fumbling in her handbag, she found a handkerchief with a rolled tiny black border. "I don't believe it."

"As I said, it was noon," said Marina. She clutched the back of Carol's chair, looking straight at Victor. "Little children were passing by. Mr. Levinson called out to them—small girls in convent dresses, I think they were. Victor must have been nervous, because he took one look at the little girls and cut for home, running down the street waving the gun like a flag."

"It isn't true," said Peggy Ann, mopping her eyes. "Anyway, if he ever did do anything wrong, he had plenty of example. I name no names."

"Don't cry," Victor told her. "Marina's acting crazy. You heard what Carol said; she's an old maid. She always took sides against me, even though I never gave Mama half the trouble—"

"We know," Georgie said, smiling. "Mama knew it. That's why she left you the store. See?" He tapped Victor affectionately on the arm, and Victor jumped.

"I never took sides," Marina said. "I never knew any of you were even alive." She brushed lint from her dyed suit and glanced across at Peggy Ann's fragile and costly black summer frock. "Do I finish this story, or not?"

"Tell it, tell it," said Georgie. "You don't have to make it a speech. Callahan and Vronsky came and told Mama for six hundred there'd be no charge. So Mama paid it, so that's the end."

"They looked at Mama's bankbook," Marina said. "Vronsky had a girl my age at home, he said, just eighteen, so that meant he had to pat my behind. Mama had just the six, so they said that would do."

"Six," Georgie said. The injustice of the sum appeared to overwhelm him anew. "For a first offense. They would have settled for one-fifty each in those days."

"You weren't around to advise us," Marina said. "The nice thing was that we had it to give. As I said before, that was the year I didn't go any place."

"For Christ's sake stop harping on that," Victor said. "Sure, Mama did it for me. Why wouldn't she want to keep me out of trouble? Any mother would've done it."

"Any," said Peggy Ann, looking around the table. "Any mother."

"You keep your snotty face out of this," Carol said. He stood up, shouting. "Do you know what she had to do to get six hundred, how many bottles of milk and pounds of butter and cans of soup she had to sell?" He leaned over the table, tipping a glass of brandy. It dripped on Peggy Ann's dress, and she began once more to cry.

Marina sat down, exhausted. "It was Victor's insurance policy," she said. "We looked at it that way. They wrote their names on the back of the calendar. They told Mama if he ever got in trouble again she should call them."

"It was the only thing I ever did," Victor told his wife, who pushed away his consoling hand. "The only thing in my whole life."

"Then we paid the money for nothing," said Marina. "It was your immunity. You should have kept on doing things, just for the hell of it. That's why Mama kept the calendar: insurance for Heaven on the front and on the back for this earth. She told Father Patenaude about it afterward, but he never saw the joke."

"Never mind all that," said Carol, impatient. "Let's get this the hell over with. You got the store, Vic; now we want to know what you're going to do about this," and he pointed again to the calendar.

"What can I do?" Victor said. "What do you want me to do, turn myself in?" Gaining confidence, he pushed back his chair. "It's crazy to even talk about it. We came back here to talk about the store. I thought that was settled."

"Well, it isn't," said Georgie. "Mama left it to you, but there's a couple of guys who owe you six. You ought to collect it."

"Collect it?" Victor said. He looked at Marina. "Are you in this, too? You want me to go out and beat up a couple of middle-aged cops, old men? Make a lot of trouble? And for what? You know we'd never get that money back."

"For Mama," Carol said, sitting down.

"I never heard anything so crazy," Peggy Ann said. "Why should Victor get mixed up in all these old things?"

"If Mama had wanted it, she'd have said so in her lifetime," Victor said.

"She left you the shop," Georgie said, "and the calendar along with it."

"How about it?" Victor asked Marina once more. "Did you plan this together, to show me up in front of my wife? Or are you so jealous because Mama left it to me? Do you think I ought to make a lot of trouble for Mama's sake?"

"For mine," Marina said, twisting her fingers. She did not look up.

"She's crazy," Georgie said. "Listen," he told her, "you'd better get married or something. Or something."

"Honestly, Victor," said Peggy Ann. "It's too awful."

"I know." He stood up. "Look," he said, "this damn place is no good to me. I only wanted it to keep it in the family for Mama's sake. But I give up. Wherever she is, she sees me now, and she knows I'm acting for the best."

"You better not talk about where she is," Carol said, glancing at the ceiling. "Unless you do something before you die," and he glanced at Peggy Ann.

"The hell with this," Victor said. He drew the key to the shop from his pocket and placed it quietly on the table. "We can't work anything out. You're all so jealous and—"

"And awful," said Peggy Ann. "Just awful."

"Melodramatic," Victor said firmly. "As for Marina, she gets crazier every time I see her, crazier by the year. If she was so damn crazy to study in France, she could have taken a job and saved some money. She blames me because I got out and she never had the guts. You could have gone next year, or the next," he told her.

"There was the war," she said, still looking away.

"So I started the war," Victor said. "I sent Mama money every month.

I never gave her trouble, only that once. The hell with it; I'm going. Come on," he told his wife, who stumbled after him between the curtains, adjusting her hat.

"I'm sorry I met you under such circumstances," she paused to say to Marina. "I imagine at heart you're a very fine person."

"Come on," Victor said, and in a moment the front door slammed behind them.

Peggy Ann had left her handkerchief on the table. Carol looked at it and grunted. "He deserves her," he remarked.

Marina looked around the room, now nearly dark. Carol pulled the light cord, and the sickly ring of yellow swayed back and forth on the walls. Marina clutched the edge of her chair, in a sudden impulse to run after Victor and away; but Carol, who had picked up the key, now held it out to her.

"It's yours now," he said. "Yours, and in the family." He was smiling, and Georgie, a little behind him, smiling, too.

"What for?" Marina said. She put her hands behind her. "What am I supposed to do with it?"

"Keep it," Carol said. "Run the business. With the beer license it's a nice little business now. If you want to fix up this place behind it, we'll kick in."

"We figured it out," Georgie said. "Mama would have wanted it. Victor's a rat. He doesn't deserve it. Look at what he wouldn't do for Mama. He's only a rat. But what about you? You can't teach forever, and it doesn't look like you're going to get married. So we set the thing up for you."

"For *me*?" Marina said. For *me*?" Carol took her hand and pressed the key into it.

"If you're still so crazy to go to France," he said, indulgent at the thought of her feminine whim, "you could make enough in a year to close it up for a month next summer, maybe. Anyway, it's a hell of a lot more than you'll make as a teacher."

He started to say something else, but Marina flung out her arm, almost striking him as she threw the key away. "For me?" she cried again. "I'm to live here?" She looked around as if to find, once more, the path away from St. Eulalie Street, the shifting and treacherous path that described a circle, and if her brothers, after the first movement, had not held her fast, she would have wrecked the room, thrown her chair out the window, pulled the shrine from the wall, the plates from their shelves, wrenched the curtains from the nails that held them, and smashed every one of the ten tiny glasses that were her brothers' pride.

ITS IMAGE ON THE MIRROR

What is love itself,
Even though it be the lightest of light love,
But dreams that hurry from beyond the world
To make low laughter more than meat and drink,
Though it but set us sighing? Fellow-wanderer,
Could we but mix ourselves into a dream
Not in its image on the mirror!

from "The Shadowy Waters"
William Butler Yeats

I

MY LAST sight of the house at Allenton is a tableau of gesticulating people stopped in their tracks, as in those crowded religious paintings that tell a story. Usually everyone points, and there are gross signs of doom and dismal virtue: Judas counts his money, Daniel indicates the wall, the Prodigal and his father are applauded by cheerful servants. Our picture, on the afternoon of a July day in 1955, was this: my mother sat beside me in my car, the back of which was filled with sweaters and winter coats, the overflow of the moving. Behind us, at the wheel of my parents' old Chevrolet, my father looked grim and aggrieved. He had been asked by my mother to keep an eye on her precious Staffordshire figurines. Across the street, the driver of a vanload of furniture bound for storage in Montreal slammed the doors. Half a dozen French-Canadian children straggled along the sidewalk. They are the new tide. French-Canada flows in when English-Canada pulls away.

The faces of the unknown children, like ours, are turned to the house. On the west lawn, where the copper beech has shed a few leaves, a tall priest in black points. We can see, through the trunk of the tree gone transparent, the statue of St. Therese of Lisieux that will stand in its place very soon.

Mr. Braddock, the real estate agent, opens the front door for a cleaning woman. We have never seen her before.

A gardener kneels before a row of stones, painting them white. Nearby is the pile of gravel with which the new owners of the house intend to kill the grass.

My mother says I saw nothing of the kind. She says the priest had called in the morning, but was nowhere around when we left. She says she remarked: "I suppose they'll have the typical institutional garden, phlox with white stones," and that I imagined the gardener because of that. As for Mr. Braddock and the cleaning woman, my mother had simply observed that the house was clean, and she hoped all those priests would find it clean enough.

Nothing remains now in Allenton to remind me of the past. I have been told that a bright aluminum-painted fence surrounds what used to be the lawn. The tree is down, and the gravel trodden into the dead grass. I do not have to see to remember the murmuring seminarists and their pale tormented faces. The windows of our house are shut tight in all seasons. Glassy white curtains cover the panes. On summer nights an unshaded light shines on the front porch, where the older priests sit in a row. They have kept the custom of the towns they come from, and they sit and rock and watch the cars passing by.

To be truthful, from home to institution wasn't an abrupt change. Even before the house was sold, before it became the dormitory annex of a seminary, it began to die. Three of the bedrooms were anonymous and empty, used as storage places. Ghosts moved in the deserted rooms, opening drawers, tweaking curtains aside. We never saw the ghosts, but we knew they were there. We were unable to account for them: no one had lived here but our family, and none of us had died in Allenton. The house was built for my parents, when they married, in 1913.

It resembled the other Allenton houses of that period, with the two porches screened in summer and double-glassed in winter, and the lightning rod on the roof, and the Virginia creeper surrounding the windows, pressing behind the shutters. A hedge parted the lawn and vegetable garden. The house next behind ours was a farm, and our garden backed into a cornfield. Now the field is a development of bungalows, and I doubt if the farmhouse exists. Some of the bungalows are in Quebec and some stray over the border to Vermont, but nearly everyone in the development speaks French. When my sister and my brother and I were children we thought there was a difference in physical substance between people who spoke English exactly as we did, and the rest of mankind. I think my parents still believe it, for nothing else can explain the expression of honest dumbfoundedness that comes over my father's face when he meets someone decent, moderate, conservative and polite, and discovers that this acceptable person is not English or Scottish or Protestant—all that one can be; and I feel sorry for my father when this happens, for it seems hard to have your views shared by everyone around you all your life and then confounded in your old age.

My mother lived much as she ever had in the expiring house. There were flowers in the rooms, and a fresh book from the library beside her chair. She would never have tolerated the unmade bed, the picnic supper taken with television, the jam jar and mustard pot astray on the dining room table; but the ghosts moved on the stairs, and she knew that her existence was a draft of air too feeble to blow them away. When I visited my parents for a weekend, a ghost in my old bedroom watched me watching myself in the glass. It was not mischievous, but simply attentive, and its invisible prying seemed improper rather than frightening. My mother must have felt that way too. The ghosts outnumbered the survivors. Nothing could bring back Frank, my brother, killed in the last war, or Isobel, my sister, married, and in Venezuela, and equally lost.

My mother's selling the house to a religious order was a gesture of total renunciation. She pushed our past and our memories of Allenton as an Anglo-Scottish town over a cliff. It meant she would never be tempted to go back.

If she had been challenged about it, she would have said that it was a quick sale, and that since Allenton is all Catholic and all French-speaking now, what is one more dormitory, one more sleeping place for embryo priests? Once the sale was arranged we had to find an apartment for my parents in Montreal. My mother, unexpectedly old and trying, said she wanted to be near stores but away from traffic. She wanted sun, but preferred the ground floor. She did not want windows on a busy street and she did not want windows on a court. Before discovering this marvel, my husband and I had to invite my parents to live with us, and they had to refuse. My mother then sent Isobel a cordial note, explaining that the old house was sold, and asking if Isobel wanted any of the furniture, carpets, curtains, china or silver before they vanished, perhaps forever, into a storage warehouse.

My mother knew perfectly well that Isobel wanted nothing from Allenton, but the letter had one unexpected result: Isobel answered. She said nothing about spoons or teacups. Her vain and immature handwriting covered four sheets of paper. She talked about her two children, and her husband, and on the last page said that her husband was attending a medical conference in Boston in August, that she and the two boys were coming with him, and that we would all meet at my parents' lakeside cottage on Labor Day weekend.

There was something touching and innocent in Isobel's assumption that our parents still lived on a rhythm of school holidays, with Labor Day weekend at the lake the last episode of summer. My mother seemed bemused by the letter. She said it had been written with a cheap ball point pen, and that the paper didn't match the envelope. That was all she found to say about a letter from a daughter she had not seen, and scarcely heard from, in six years. Isobel is married to an Italian doctor none of us had then set eyes on. She seemed young when she left us, but now—I counted—must be all of thirty-three. My mother says "poor Isobel" when she mentions her just as she says of our dead brother "poor Frank."

When I say that Isobel's marriage was unfortunate, or that my mother was distressed by it, it is only because I am shy before words like "calamity," or "catastrophe" or "disgrace." Isobel had been married once before, and we had lavished our fund of disapproval on the first husband—the bumptious, the unspeakable Davy Sullivan. We were too worn out to insult Alfredo, even in secret. Nothing in Mother's experience could account for that second marriage. She said she guessed Isobel had married an Italian because she wanted to live abroad; but if she wanted to travel all that much, my mother said, why not marry someone we could be proud of—an attaché of some kind? She could have been photographed with him and their normal-looking children on a Canadian-looking lawn, no matter where the government sent them. There was also the question of Isobel's happiness; I think my mother did care about it, and truly believed that only a Canadian—and not just any Canadian—was good enough. Look at the miserable girls who married Polish officers after the last war, my mother commanded! Were those girls happy now, with the husbands drunk as owls every night of the week in the White Eagle of Pilsudski Club? Look at the girls who fell in love with the Free French and the Free Norwegians! Free was the word: every one of them had a wife back home. It wasn't just that Isobel had deceived her family, which never paid, but she had probably made herself wretched as well.

What my mother did not say aloud was that Isobel had tricked us by not dying. She had been dying of a kidney infection and we were told to pay our last visits. Her face was smooth and round and babyish on the pillow. Between puffed lids her eyes were slits. She had gone well away from us by then and seemed amused at something too personal to share. I thought she was telling me, "You think you've always known all about me, but you don't know this; you can't follow me here." Once I thought that when Isobel died I would surely die too. I would kill her cat, Barney, because no one else would look after him for her, and I would sit in an armchair and close my eyes and rest my hands on my lap and never move again. This thought lasted no longer than the time it takes to see the weather in the sky; for, in the space of the same thought, cloud into cloud, I knew that Isobel's death would end the problem of my sister forever, and that if she died I had every reason to live. Her death would remove the ungovernable daughter for my parents and the unattainable for my husband. Dead-and-buried Isobel, under a heap of snow, or a rectangle of grass, would be harmless Isobel, the pretty Duncan sister, taken too soon to her Maker. We cried, all of us, when we thought she was lost. We spoke of feelings for her and for each other we have certainly never mentioned since: and then Isobel recovered, and left us all looking like fools.

She had met Alfredo in the hospital. He had nothing to do with her case, and no business in her room. On a gray June day we drove her to Allenton for her convalescence. She was docile and sweet, then, only half returned from dying. She lay in a garden chair, and ate what was put before her, and looked at the books my mother placed in her hands. For a short time my mother had the submissive daughter she had always dreamed of. Then Isobel began taking short trips to Montreal to visit me, and at the end of August, during one of those journeys, she married Alfredo in the sacristy of St. Patrick's Church. She left for Caracas by plane the same day, after ringing and asking me, in a light fluty voice, if I would mind telling our mother she was married. I was pregnant with my second child then, and stupid with heat and summer; I said, "Alfredo who?" It was the fourth summer after the end of the war. It seemed to me I had waited years for life to begin and that the false start of after-war was all there had been to wait for. The shape of life was pressed on stones in the form of ferns and snails, immutable. Yesterday, tomorrow: stones had picked up the pattern and there was nothing I could change. Isobel had broken a stone. She was married (so was I), but she was leaving for Caracas: I was here.

"Well, at least she didn't turn Catholic," my mother has said since. My mother went to St. Patrick's to inquire, and thanked God for a small favor. There must have been a fair amount of messing round with priests, all the same; that was my father's contribution.

My mother was upset because Isobel must have been married in the clothes she had worn for her shopping trip to Montreal—shopping had been the pretext for the journey, and the lying girl had said she was meeting me. She was last seen wearing a green and white cotton frock and open sandals. She was carrying a straw bag. Her legs and head were bare.

"She wasn't wearing stockings," my mother said. "She wasn't even wearing a hat." She reflected on it, and then said, rather pathetically I thought, "Do you think Isa had just brains enough to get some stockings and buy herself a hat?"

"I can't imagine her wearing a hat," I said.

"Oh, that child!" my mother burst out. "As if Davy Sullivan wasn't enough to put us through."

Yes, I thought, and Alec Campbell, and Tom. It has so often been in my power to destroy my sister—to destroy, that is, an idea people might have about her—but something has held back my hand. I think it is the instinct that tells me Isobel will betray herself; there will always be the hurt face of her admirer turning slowly to me, as if to tell me, So you were the good one, after all. And then, because Isobel is my sister, there is the other restraint, for the vision of my sister delivered, my sister undone, is totally repugnant. When she flew off to Caracas I thought, Well, she will never want to see any of us again, but instead of rejoicing I felt as though my own life drained away with her. I was left face down on a beach with no one to get me to my feet but a muddling trio of husband, mother, infant son. Isobel was in romantic Caracas, which I began to construct, feverishly, as a paradise of coral islands. I could not have found it on a map, and confused it with Bermuda.

Six years later, when the Allenton house was sold, and my mother asked me to spend a weekend with her so as to help with the packing, my husband said, "Your mother ought to leave you alone. She's always after you for something." I answered meekly, "I know, but she only has one daughter now. There's only me." He could not know that her bothering me was a victory. I was the only daughter: I had won.

Tom was right; that weekend was a bother. There were the children to be left, and the long drive on crowded roads. Trust my mother to summon me on a weekend, with her wonderful certitude that life outside the family never matters, even if all life is just where you want to be—thronging the highways and beaches and eating-places. I found her in panic, for she had dawdled all summer as if the sale weren't taking place, and the need for moving unreal: now she had to pack and be out in three days. I kissed her, a bird peck on the cheek, and we began to work in silence. As I grow older I see that our gestures are alike. It touches me to notice a movement of hands repeated—a manner of folding a newspaper, or laying down a comb. I glance sharply behind me and I know I am reproducing my mother's quick turn of head. Our voices are alike, we have the flat voice of our part of the country; our *r*'s fall like stones. I am pleased to be like her. There is no one I admire more.

We took down and folded green rep curtains bleached white in streaks. We rolled carpets that showed frayed bars straight through the weave. Removing pictures, we saw what the walls had been like. A breath would have crumpled the rooms. My father rescued rubbish as we threw it away. He made a private store of pots and pans, and the Elsie Dinsmore books, and a vegetable dish so cracked it could never be used for anything. "It will do for the church," he said. There are only a handful of Protestants in Allenton now, and most of the Old Presbyterians went into the United Church of Canada years ago. "Don't bother Father," said my mother sharply when I saw him walking resolutely out and toward the Old Presbyterian Church with an oil painting of a child feeding ducks under his arm. "He thinks that picture was a wedding present from his side of the family. Let him give it to the minister, if he wants to."

That weekend of packing must have been anguish for her. She was leaving the house she had lived in forty-two years, and the town where she had spent her life. She said not a word about it, and expected no embarrassing behavior from me. When it was over, and the vans were loaded, and two of them gone, she stood out on the porch, before the locked door, and handed the keys to Mr. Braddock.

She was small, commanding, and permitted no backchat. My mother has lived every day of her life as if it were preparation for some kind of crisis. You could look straight through her and find not a sand-grain of weakness or compassion or pity: nothing to start up emotional rot. She looked calmly past Mr. Braddock to the French-Canadian children loitering on the sidewalk.

"I don't know these children's names, and I don't know who their parents are," she said. "That's what Allenton has become. At least in Montreal I shall *expect* people to be strangers."

I wanted to put my arms around her, but even without Mr. Braddock she would have hated it, and it would have been wrong: it would have been an attempt to put myself in her place, think for her, sense what she ought to feel. This was the house of my childhood, but not my home. Here, I might have spent my life, creeping in my mother's small shadow, welcomed as companion and errand girl, despised as a sexual failure, if marriage, the only rescue possible, had not taken me away. I was twenty-four when it happened. It was a late marriage, in our terms. My husband thinks he married too young, but too young for him was almost too late for me. Twenty-one was the limit for girls, and my mother must have spent many anxious seasons wondering what would become of me. Isobel married Davy Sullivan when she was eighteen.

I brought out of our common past two dozen fish knives and forks my mother insisted I have, and a pile of children's books. In one of the books was a snapshot of Frank and Isobel and me sitting on the lawn, all three in dark woolen bathing suits. It must have been taken the summer of 1926. We look happy enough; I am thankful to say we look unremarkable. "Happy families are all alike," Davy Sullivan used to say, unpleasantly, because he thought we weren't happy, but pretending. "All's well with the Duncans" was one more of his taunts. I sometimes heard his voice, like a record, repeating, "Happy families are all alike, and all's well with the Duncans," and I thought Davy odious but clever until I opened Isobel's *Anna Karenina*. "Happy families are all alike" came from there. It is just at the beginning, first thing on the first page. Davy wasn't clever about anything.

In the snapshot Isobel is chubby, flaxen-haired, the baby of the family. She was three years younger than Frank (grave and skinny here, aged about seven) and five younger than me. Even her baby face is secretive, although no one would think that except me. I pick up a book with her autograph inside, or a striped towel with her boarding school name tape, and I remember that she was evasive and stealthy, and that I used to imagine she knew something she was too careless or indifferent to tell. I believed that one day she would speak, and part of my character hidden from everyone but her would be revealed. She might have spoken, but our dialogue was cut short. Our family is open, blameless, and plain. Anything she cares to say, now, would be spiteful but harmless. Perhaps she has been silent because she respects us. I can't believe she is afraid.

"You people are going to haunt this house," said Mr. Braddock, as the advance guard of new occupants fanned out on the lawn. They were a priest, a gardener with a paintbrush and bucket of white paint, and a boy with a barrow of gravel.

"The house is full of ghosts as it is," my mother said pleasantly. "There wouldn't be room for ours."

The gardener began painting stones, and the boy spilled his barrow of gravel on the lawn. He raked the gravel into swirls and scrolls. How long did it take them to kill the grass? (My mother says I did not see this.)

The rector of the seminary climbed three front steps, paying his courtesy call. He stared with a cold suspicion my father fully rendered. My mother addressed the rector in unstressed French, and he replied in their curious English. This exchange in opposing languages was the extreme limit of mutual politeness and contempt. "Quebec Highlander," muttered my father, giving the old wartime invective for a priest. I was grown before I realized that the difference between my parents was apparent in the use of a phrase like this. My mother would never have said it.

"He's going to have the beech down," my mother remarked, as we were leaving. She sat in the car beside me and said, "The priest told me. He said so this morning. He says the leaves make a mess and the place is neater without trees." She began to speak about something else. I have seen her cry twice, once when Frank was little and said something dreadful about sex, and once when Isobel was dying. She wept as I imagine a doll could, with a still face, and a slow gathering of moisture on an eye so wide it might have been painted. She was dry-eyed, now, and scornful, holding her shabby alligator purse. We drove down the main street of Allenton, strange and bustling and full of people whose names my mother didn't know, hot in the hot afternoon, and presently she said, "We won't be getting down to the lake much anymore." Now, at this I felt a shock of real nostalgic panic. We had spent all our summers there. We went to the lake every summer—every summer for years and years. "If Tom wants to buy it," my mother went on, "he can have first choice. Do you think he'd be interested?"

"He might be." I knew better. He was deeply attached to his family's summer house in Muskoka. He wanted a repetition of his childhood summers for his own children.

"He ought to have another look at the cottage," my mother said. "A buyer's look. He can think about it when you come down on Labor Day. We'll talk about it then. Tom can take his time. There is no great rush."

"Isa will be there," I said.

"Oh, yes, of course. Naturally Isobel will be there," said my mother, as if my sister came every year.

A car hooted behind me, wanting to pass, and I thought if that car has a Texas license Tom will buy the cottage. It had a Texas license, and I burst out laughing. I felt gay and light-headed. I said, "I'm just laughing at myself."

"I like to think you weren't laughing at me," my mother said.

We had lost my father miles back. He was driving like a snail because he was being careful with the figurines. I could imagine his plaintive face over the wheel. My mother suddenly said she had been trying to imagine the best thing in the world and it had taken the form of a dry martini. We stopped at the next place we saw and waited for my father. We were tired, and silly and innocent as girls. Those were the good times with my mother. They were rare, but when they occurred we were so close, so similar, that I would think, Life with her could have been all right; and I would remember everything I had done to make my marriage happen; just so that I could get away. My father caught up, and we three sat down at a shaky table covered with beer rings.

In my father's family women do not drink in public and men drink their beer at home. I could tell that he was wondering how it was that a woman as irreproachable as my mother could sit in this filthy atmosphere and ask her married daughter (another decent woman) if she thought the martinis would be fit to drink. We chose beer, and my father and mother suddenly fell silent and stared straight before them in a way I hope observers didn't consider too dramatic. For the first time in my life, I saw my parents holding hands. My father's hand lay on the table, and my mother placed her small freckled hand over his. It was the singularity of the gesture that made me uneasy. Their tenderness seemed a sign of their defeat. Searching for an excuse—why should they hold hands here?—all I could think was, All's well with the Duncans. Happy families are all alike. Frank was dead and Isobel gone and the house sold. I had been called Price for many years. I was Jean Price. I had four children, and although I wasn't tough enough to control them as Mother had hers, they were mine. They were the Price children, another clan. I got up from the table and looked at postcards. When I turned back to my parents they were still staring straight before them. The public handholding had not been a mistake or an illusion: their hands were now palm to palm. No one was looking at them: I cast a quick glance about to make sure. I was cold with shame, and I remember saying to myself, I'm not like either of them, really. My children will be different too.

"Isobel wouldn't like this place. She wouldn't think anything of it," I heard my mother say. She stared round and back at me, the old mad-woman, and said, "She would never have brought me to live here."

2

On Labor Day weekend we drove to the lake with our usual accoutre-ments. The car looked as if we had lived, eaten and slept in it all our lives. In the back seat, three of the children devoured an emergency picnic, while Hughie, the youngest, proud of his reputation for being carsick, tried his best to vomit into a plastic pot. My parents had gone down to the cottage a few days earlier, and Isobel and her family had been with them overnight. We made poor time because of the holiday traffic. I rang my mother from a filling station when we were still an hour away. "Don't hurry," she said pleasantly, as if we could.

At half-past one, with my children uproariously hungry again, we turned off the lake road onto our gravel drive. Beds of perennial flow-ers were picked out in thick colored wool. The sun striking off the lake made me blink. Parked so that we could not get by it was a caramel Chrysler with foreign license plates—Isobel's! We abandoned our own car behind it and the next thing I saw was a pair of child's underpants drying on a bush. Then Isobel came towards me leading a little boy who wore nothing but a shirt. I have forgotten what she said. Her tone was childish and light, and the brush of her cheek against mine like a whisper. We tried to introduce our children, but they were shy as animals. Suddenly shy as well, I looked down at her baby, and her thin hand.

My mother, following Isobel down the drive, walked in a strange way, as if she were wandering on spongy ground. Isobel's elder boy clung to her.

"This is Claud," said my mother firmly.

"Claudio," said my sister, making *Cloudio* of it.

The half-naked baby was Franco. I supposed he had been named for our dead brother, Frank. Claudio, who had evidently taken a fancy to my mother, strained up at her, gabbling incomprehensibly, and then fell into a hostile silence, sulking and hanging his head. He was a detestable little boy. Franco, all belly under his shirt, trotted close to my sister as he ran about, clad in his shirt, urinating with pride on the steps or in the flowers. My three elder children found this unbelievably funny. I expected Isobel to put a stop to it, but she was the mother one might have expected.

My mother wore an expression that might have been suitable if lightning had got in the house. When Alfredo appeared she could not speak. She could not as much as say our names. A gesture was all she could manage: here he is. I shook hands with the dashing doctor from Caracas who had carried my sister away. He was a shad fly of a man, dressed for a hot summer day in town. At lunch, he fretted about mosquitoes, and declared that he liked comfort and air-conditioning. In his opinion, the only places worth living in were Caracas, Rome, Mexico City, and New York. My mother had now lost any power to react normally. I think she smiled and nodded happily, as I certainly did. It is difficult to explain why, but an admission that one really liked New York was all of a piece with his towny shoes. We smiled and said we agreed with him, perfectly.

My children, sitting at their table across the room, sensed that something had gone wrong. The eldest boy, Jamie, stared thoughtfully at his bantam uncle-by-marriage. He knew, already, that Alfredo was something one must never become. Jamie then looked at me, to see if I agreed, and we had a moment of complicity before I told him sharply to turn around and get on with his food. My mother finally selected a tone. She asked Alfredo tenderly if Caracas was a social sort of place. Alfredo said it might well be, for all he knew, but that he was busy with his medical practice. "I am a busy man," he said, with a perhaps foreign emphasis on the "I." He had been at a university in the States—I think in California. His accent was not one my mother would like, but I doubt if he would have cared.

Franco and Claudio had refused to eat with the children. One sobbed, the other screamed, and their parents seemed to take it for granted we wanted them with us. An extra chair was squeezed in so that Claudio could sit next to my mother, while Franco sat on my sister's lap and picked bits from her plate with his fingers. He was now wearing the damp underpants I had seen drying in the bush. I wondered if the child had made the journey from Caracas in his underclothes. From across the room my Jamie began taking an interest again.

"Do you like sailing?" he asked Alfredo.

"Not on your lake," said Alfredo. "Too many speedboats."

"Do you like swimming?"

"Jamie, that's enough," I said.

"I like to swim where the water is clean and not too cold," said Alfredo. "I don't *object* to swimming if I have the conditions I want. Your lake is full of sewage because the land around is overdeveloped. Not only is the water here disgusting," Alfredo continued, addressing himself only to the child, "but the lake is too far north and too cold."

"I think so too," said Jamie, who had never been south of this cottage. He sounded like Tom. "But if you won't sail and you won't swim there's nothing to do around here."

"Jamie, do you want to leave the table?" I said. Tom and I both detest pert, precocious children; also, I was hurt to realize that Jamie was bored at the cottage. Our complicity vanished; I saw him in league with Tom, who would not buy the place. That "nothing to do" carried a familiar whine.

My sister said softly, "And so in the end he did nothing at all, but sit on the shingle wrapped up in a shawl." She was smiling to herself, as if alone in the room except for the unruly baby on her lap.

"Don't let that child eat all your lunch," my mother said to her. The ex-family favorite glanced at my mother, still smiling. She had become accustomed to the unshared reference, the solitary joke. I had not dared to look at Isobel until now. She was dry and frail as a leaf.

Alfredo and Isobel did not exchange a word or a glance. It occurred to me that the only contact in the room had been between Jamie and Alfredo.

Alfredo's eyes now went to the screen door. Outside the door, sitting on the floor of the porch, was Poppy Duncan, my dead brother's daughter. She was neither child nor grownup and, because we had tried to make her sit at the children's table, she had decided not to eat. She appeared to be wearing a hideous wig, for she had dyed her hair that summer and then cut most of it off. Alfredo was obviously the source of his sons' table manners: he held a slice of bread flat on his hand and buttered it as if he were painting it, and then, without asking my mother's opinion, carried this bread outside and offered it to Poppy. He sat down beside her on the floor of the porch. I had a view of their two heads. Poppy's was rusty-orange and slightly larger than his.

My mother said swiftly, "He might have taken it for granted we know Poppy better than he does."

"He likes girls," said my sister, smiling, eyes down.

My mother was less shocked by the meaning of the remark than astonished that anyone could find Poppy likable.

After lunch my father removed his hearing aid and went to sleep. My mother lay back in a deck chair, and my husband and I sat at her feet. My youngest child had been put to bed, and the others, united for once instead of wrangling and quarreling, sat in a ring with the neighbor's children, the MacBains. They were charming, there, in the porch, playing jacks. The harmony wouldn't last an hour, but it made a pretty picture.

From the house came a crash and a roar: the Shostakovich Fifth.

"Turn it down, Poppy," said my mother, unheard. Poppy has always been a trial to us all. She has been a trial since her conception. When she came to Canada, a little thing of seven months, Frank was already dead, and Poppy's mother a war widow. The child's name is unfortunate, but she was christened in England. Her mother remarried years ago and went back there. Poppy used to think of her mother as a fairy princess. She would threaten to run away and join her. "Go, by all means," my mother would reply. "Go, if you think you will be welcome." My mother was always fair. She would fetch pen and paper and let Poppy sit at her desk. "Write and tell your mother when to expect you," she would say, and leave Poppy to it. Poppy must have thought she would not be welcome, for her letters were only of the "Dear Mother, I am fine" sort. When she ran away from camp or school, it was always back to my mother.

Poppy's mother gave her up when Poppy was still an infant. She talked to me about it and while she was talking she stabbed a pen in her hand. "There's nothing I can do," I remember her saying. "She's strong and I'm weak." She meant that my mother was strong. We stared at the blue hole below the cushion of her thumb, where the point of the pen had gone in. Poppy's mother hadn't a cent of her own, and was an incompetent girl. My mother had done the only thing possible.

Right or wrong, my mother has had the worst of it, for Poppy has been more scandal and strain than her three children put together. I saw next to nothing of her when she was growing up. She was at camp in summer and in boarding school all winter. There were stray periods when she had run away and we were looking for another school, and of course we had her about at Easter and Christmas. She is unlike any of us. At eleven she wore orange lipstick. Once, banished to a school in Vancouver, she was found by the police in Detroit. On this Labor Day weekend she was between camp and school. She spent the last days of summer mooning around, all dyed hair and bangle bracelets, playing Shostakovich and Sibelius and writing us up in her diary.

I felt, that afternoon, the closest feeling I have to happiness. It is a sensation of contentment because everyone round me is doing the right thing. The pattern is whole. Even Poppy, with her music and her vague adolescent longings and hates, seemed correct. I was proud of my children and pleased with my mother and husband. The Sunday papers lay on the grass. There was the slightly sad atmosphere that hangs in the air between summer and autumn. This may be our last weekend here, unless Tom buys the cottage. All at once my gaze fell on my sister, whom I had forgotten. She sat apart from the rest of us, on the dock, with her husband and her two monkey-babies. The husband had changed to swimming trunks; his clothes were neatly folded beside him, as if he were in a dubious hotel and could not trust the staff. He was a stray animal here. Daunted by our family likeness, our solidarity, he kept his things nearby. He lay prone, his face on his folded arms. One of the boys sat on Isobel's lap, the other in a moored rowboat.

My sister was straggly and unkempt—the aging bohemian. Her dress was saffron colored; she wore with it a belt that belonged to some other frock. On her feet were elaborate sandals with high heels. She seemed washed-out, rather than fair, and gaunt instead of slim. Isobel had never cared for her untidiness. My mother had dressed her until she rebelled, and I suspected that Alfredo chose her dresses now. He must have dressed her with another woman in mind: her dress and her shoes would have suited someone Latin, plump, and jeweled. She wore her hair just as she had at eighteen—long and straight, with a band to hold it back from her forehead. When she was young, she had reminded everyone of a Tenniel Alice. From the lawn, against the luminous yellow haze on the lake, she looked thin and sallow and all of a color with her saffron dress. As for her sons, curly-haired, eyes too liquid, eyebrows too dark, they might have been adopted. She and her family were isolated and lost, and although I could not help comparing her children with mine, and Alfredo with Tom, I was so filled with pity for her and her children that the pity was a physical pain; I started up from the grass and went toward her, pushed by the old feeling that she might want me and need me. As I drew near, walking softly on the long grass, her shad-fly husband rolled on his back, sat up, and began to speak. Isobel laughed, shrugged, examined her sandals, kissed the monkey-boy on her lap. Everything about her spoke of wretchedness. She could laugh all she liked, but I knew my sister: her tense shoulders were eloquent. It was incredible that Isa, blessed at the cradle, should be unhappy.

I was intensely conscious of my appearance as I advanced, composing in my mind's eyes the picture they would have of me. As my mother had been saying for some time, I was nearer forty than thirty, but the signs of aging that had begun so young with me stopped when Isobel married. My hair had grown no grayer than it had been when I was thirty-two; I had the same faint cobweb lines from eye to temple I had noticed in my twenties. I wore a blue denim skirt with zippered pockets, a white cotton shirt, and tennis shoes. I wore a watch with a plain strap, and if there was an aura around me it was of Yardley talcum powder. I knew that my expression was kindly and my waist slim. I looked like any other woman of my age and my condition. I was part of my mother and father, and my children were part of me. I had succeeded in that, and Isa had failed.

Isobel and her family looked like excursionists from a factory town in New England, plumped down on our dock by mistake. They looked like forlorn picnickers, hating the countryside, littering the lakeshore with beer cans, wishing they had gone to a movie instead. I would never have sought revenge for myself, for the past, but I had it now through my children, who would never be mistaken for anything except themselves; and that was true justice, or vindication—call it whatever it is. I was near enough now to hear Alfredo say "Why didn't you warn me about the food?" I heard Isobel's laughter, but not her reply. She saw me. The laughter stopped, her eyes darkened, and then I remembered how she had looked when she was dying. She summed me up. Her total tallied with mine, but failed to daunt her. My pride in my children was suddenly nothing. I was part of a wall of cordial family faces, and Isobel was not hurt by her failure, or impressed by my success, but thankful she had escaped. I approached; we spoke. Alfredo complained about the towel he had been lying on. He said it was too rough for his skin.

They left that afternoon. I think Alfredo had had enough. My mother made a mild suggestion he leave Isa and the children for a bit, but that brought on a puffed chest and the statement that Venezuelans do not abandon their wives. Heaven knows who or what that was aimed at. Everyone seemed to have a private perplexity, to judge from our expressions. We stood in a knot near the caramel Chrysler. Isobel was going, and had said nothing to me. She had not spoken at all. There was no limit to the size of the world and we would never find each other in it again. Their car vanished, and the world contracted. Left behind, the rest of us were a family again. The children began to rush about and quarrel as if released, and I heard Poppy accuse someone of reading her diary. No one answered. We had all read it, often.

"Funny little guy," said my husband, casually, as we walked back.

I was tempted to repeat what Alfredo had said about the food, but the realization that Isobel would expect nothing better of me—would expect me to gossip—kept me still. Besides, I knew what Alfredo had meant. At lunch, our parents had sat at opposite ends of the table. My mother, presiding over covered vegetable dishes, received the passed-along plate on which my father had placed a dry slice of salmon loaf. The vegetable dish covers were removed to reveal creamed carrots, and mashed potatoes piled like a volcano, with a pat of salty butter melting inside the crater. The ritual of mealtime mattered to us more than food. None of the women in our family could cook, and we felt that women who worried about what they were to eat or serve were wanting in character: I did bother about it, once, and even took a Cordon Bleu course, but then I had Jamie and lost interest in cooking. Nothing on a plate seems attractive after you have fed children and tried to push into their reluctant mouths puréed spinach and sieved yolk of egg. "Food" came to mean the soggy remnants of their cornflakes, or the sliced apple gone yellow. I had the habit of spooning up their leftovers— fruit salad from which they had carefully picked out with their fingers the slices of banana and maraschino cherries.

The day had turned cold, and we went indoors. The children were given their tea, tea moved into our Sunday night supper. My husband built a fire in the fireplace and after the children were asleep we sat round it.

"Do you think Isa is happy?" I ventured. She and Alfredo had not been spoken of since Tom's remark.

"I should think so," said my mother. "Why wouldn't she be?"

"I suppose she is, as much as most people," said Tom. There was a depth of satisfaction under his voice. I think he has what he wanted in life. He wanted children, and he has them. He sees his own boyhood, which he says was happy, in our children's lives: the same kind of house, the same schools, the summer in the country. He has repeated his parents' cycle—family into family: the interlocking circles. I see the circles too, for happy families are all the same, and only the unhappy families seem different.

My mother said nothing for a minute or two. She frowned and stared into the fire. Then she told us that Alfredo was maniacally jealous of Isobel. Their servant had orders to report the telephone calls that came to the house when he was away. If a strange man looked at Isa on the street, Alfredo made a scene that went on all day. If Isa had to shop, or pay a bill, or take the children to the dentist, Alfredo went with her and waited for her in the car. As I had suspected, he chose Isobel's clothes.

"Did Isobel tell you that?" I asked.

"Not *she*," said my mother with pride. She was proud of Isa for keeping her secrets. No, an Allenton neighbor had gone to Caracas to visit her son. The son, who had known Isobel as a child, had tried to meet Isa and Alfredo, but Alfredo was impossible, he said. As for Isobel, she was so sloppy and untidy that she could not be invited anywhere. By a stroke of fortune, they had hired a cook whose last employer had been Alfredo. The cook had told all this, and it came back to Allenton and my mother. The most astonishing thing was not the story itself, which I might almost have put together without help, but that my mother had waited two years before telling it. "I thought it might have been just gossip," she said. "I knew some day I'd be able to judge for myself. Poor old Isa," said my mother quietly.

"She ought to put her foot down," said Tom. "She used to be tough enough."

"Maybe she doesn't mind," I said. "Maybe that's why she married him, so she'd have somebody to think for her, and make all the decisions for her," but everyone laughed at that, and my mother said, "Don't complicate a simple situation." If we are to assume that Isobel likes having her dresses chosen by Alfredo and keeping servants who spy, then we get to what my mother calls "the unnecessary side of life." My husband probably agrees. He would never be the one to complicate a simple situation, either. "Bad things don't happen to decent people," he once said to me, seriously, when we were both of us much younger.

"Funny little guy," said Tom again, vaguely, perhaps bored with it now.

"He's not little," said dreadful Poppy, suddenly speaking up from a couch, where, lying on her stomach, she was reading the comics spread on the floor. It was odd how one forgot that child, then suddenly there she was—loud as life, saying her piece. "He's taller than Aunt Isobel, and she's tall."

"I didn't mean that the gentleman was short," said Tom, who always talked to Poppy in a mocking pedantic way. "Alfredo is quick, nervous, and thin, and his constant hopping around gives him a grasshopper look that—"

"He's better looking than you," said Poppy, turning a page.

"Poppy, you are a horror," I said. "Besides, it isn't true."

"Thanks," said my husband.

"Anyway, that's what I'm going to be when I grow up," said Poppy.

"Handsome?" my husband said.

"No," said Poppy, swinging round and sitting up on the couch. "Married to some person like Alfredo."

"I don't doubt that," my mother said.

"But first I'll fall in love," said Poppy.

We all laughed as if it were a fate we were fortunate to have escaped. I tried to meet my husband's eyes, to see what it had been for him to have Isobel here again; but he was already thinking about something else. He was probably trying to find the right words with which to refuse the cottage. When the words came, finally, they were Alfredo's. "I think the place is overdeveloped now," he said. "And the water's not too clean."

"We're all still alive," my mother answered.

I blame Alfredo unfairly. Tom would have turned it down in any case. Every inch of shore is built on now. The lake is criss-crossed with speedboats, radios scream, there is a shoddy camp for children at the far end of the lake; although none of that was mentioned, I knew Tom thought the value of the place was dropping every year, and that something should be knocked off the price for a son-in-law. He didn't say so. Nothing was said, after that day. The less said the better, always; and, as my mother had pointed out, we were still alive.

3

When our father caught Frank reading *The Yellow Fairy Book* down at the lake one Sunday, long ago, he snatched the book and threw it in the water. Frank must have been ten or eleven then. He was the only boy, and our father was afraid he would become girlish under the influence of two sisters. My brother had been a pretty baby with yellow curls, our mother's pet, but when he was three she suddenly relinquished him, saying she knew nothing about the upbringing of sons. His curls were shorn, and our father took him over. He said Frank had got off to a bad start, but that he, our father, was going to make a man of him. Frank must have had a miserable time. He was an undistinguished little boy, slow in his reactions, rather dull. Although suspicious of Isobel and me, he was a born dupe, and we teased him wickedly.

Our father had only a short period in which to admire the product of his training. Frank was killed young. I suppose he was manly enough to please our father, but during the very few years he had of life as a man he seemed to me severe rather than strong. There was something disapproving and spinsterish in his behavior. He was on the side of discipline and hanging and all the rest of that—not brutally, but as disappointed elderly women sometimes are. When he was angry his voice became tight and sharp. Far from resenting the past, and our father's heavy hand, he seemed to be grateful. I often heard him boast about his upbringing, and describe broken promises, the supperless nights, the frequent beatings, with self-satisfaction, as if they had made him the excellent person he was.

Those beatings, so alarming in retrospect, never disturbed our family life. Like *The Yellow Fairy Book* they sank below the surface. Hearing Frank catching it in an upstairs room, I never pitied him, but was simply glad I was not a boy. His punishments were a masculine ritual, like a religious mystery. I remember our father going round the house, closing the windows so that the neighbors wouldn't hear, while Frank, crying before he was touched, howled incoherent tear-laden promises from cellar to attic. He never tried to run away and never tried to hide. I wish I could say that compassion or loyalty had kept Isobel and me from tormenting and betraying him, but his nervous rages made us laugh, and Isobel was particularly skillful at making him lose control. He was the weeper in our dry household. "The more you cry the less you'll pee," said our beautiful sister in her elegant voice. That was because no amount of punishment could make him stop wetting his bed.

Isobel ruled Frank. She was three years younger than he, but twice as quick. She spent her pocket money on herself, and then appropriated his. In Frank's books you will find Isobel's name. She went through a period of signing in a round back-slanting hand, never using capital letters, and drawing globes instead of dotting her *i*'s. That was a sign of vanity, our mother said. She never failed to point out some flaw in her best-looking child, but her tone was complacent. Now she implied that Isobel could afford to be vain. Vain or not, she was persistent: in one of Frank's old books I found curly lower-case "isobel duncan" twenty-seven times.

It was our mother who used to buy those Christmas albums from England—the boys' stories that were supposed to make a man of Frank, and the boarding school tales for Isobel and me. The girls' books, solemnly read by Frank, contained stories of plucky children named Gillian and Monica. The illustrations had them rushing in a half crouch with field-hockey sticks in their hands and cantaloupe hats on their innocent heads. They were honest girls, if plain, and they had our brother's entire approval. He may have wanted his sisters to be more like Gillian and Monica—wholesome and fair instead of annoying and rude. Years later when I met Frank's bride, Poppy's mother, I remembered the girls in the books, their speech, their spines, their upper lips, and saw he had carried his old admiration on into love. What fascinated Isobel in the English stories was the unfamiliar slang, which seemed to us pallid and coy, and the obsession with eating. "They must be half starved over there," she said, with sympathy. Nothing less than national famine could account for the delight in jelly and custard and little pieces of cake.

I don't know why our mother wanted us to steep in books so removed from Canadian life. She may have been trying to counteract the comics and the radio—the American influence. As long as I can remember there has been a preoccupation with that. Also, in those days being English-minded was respectable. In my Allenton public school I sang:

Oh dearest island far away
Beyond the ocean wide
Our hearts are true to thee alway'
Whatever may betide.
We love our own dear native land
Home of the brave and free
But we are part of England
The ruler of the sea.

Anything from England was elegant. The newspaper photograph of the chaste engagement kiss exchanged by the Duke of Kent and Princess Marina was shown to Isobel and me and compared with those disgusting creatures embracing in Hollywood. When the time came for us to marry, our mother implied, we would know how to behave. My mother may have had more fantasy in her nature than I suspect, all the same, for she did buy us the fairy books. When Isobel asked her point-blank, once, if mermaids existed, she replied without hesitating that they certainly did, but not in Canada. I believed it briefly, and Isobel believed it for years. She was confident it was only a matter of finding the right country. Isobel and I must have been dumb little girls. My children would never have asked the question, or accepted my mother's reply. There is no special country, and they were born knowing it. They inherited from me the assurance that there are no magic solutions. They were not to inherit the house at Allenton, or the cottage at the lake, but I did give them that.

It was when I brought our old books out of Allenton that I thought of all this. I remembered, for instance, that I had once believed that planets were small and cold, and melted like ice cubes. An instant later I knew I had never thought anything of the kind, but that *Isobel* had. The truth was I had preferred the Monica-Gillian stories and scarcely ever finished reading a fairy tale in my life. A prince of a country: what country? Which castle? I never understood; I was always putting myself in my sister's place, adopting her credulousness, and even her memories, I saw, could be made mine. It was Isobel I imagined as the eternal heroine—never myself. I substituted her feelings for my own, and her face for any face described. Whatever the author's intentions, the heroine was my sister. She was the little Mermaid, she was Heidi; later she was Gatsby's Daisy. She was Anna Karenina with the velvet dress and the little crown of pansies on her head.

"isobel duncan," twenty-seven times: what a vain, silly child she must have been! Yet when I traced her signature with my finger I felt the old unquietness, as if I must run after her into infinity, saying, "Wait, I am not the person you think at all." Even if I were to catch her, the meeting would be incomplete, like the Labor Day disaster at the lake. Even when we were young I silenced her. She would catch my eye (the hopeful, watching, censor's eye) and become silent, "behaving," as our family called it, and nothing could bring her back except my departure. People said I was a heavy presence for Isa to support. She was another person when I wasn't there. I don't know why. I loved her.

My children fell on Isobel's books (we might as well call them hers, since her name is everywhere). We went through an old-book period until the children were bored. I read aloud, and that was good for me. Addressing my audience of small, intent faces, I lost Isobel's perception and held onto my own. Mine told us that fairy stories are stupid and a bore. My children liked a few. They liked best a story about a woman surpassingly beautiful (Isobel again) married to a man wretchedly poor. The husband, downcast because he cannot give his wife the gowns and jewels her beauty deserves, meets an old man in a magic shop in one of those unexplained forests. The old man offers him a purse that can never be emptied of gold in exchange for the husband's sense of beauty and the wife's sense of humor. The husband accepts. He can buy his wife the most exquisite dresses imaginable, but her absence of humor permits her to go about like a peacock, while the husband, who now lacks all feeling for beauty, finds her only absurd. At last they take the purse back to the forest, reclaim their lost senses, and live happily ever after.

"Did they keep the jewels, though?" Jamie asked.

Was it only the humorless woman that made me think of Isobel? The husband was surely a man I had known. That man would have kept the purse. He was mean to the marrow; and if I had been in the story I would have advised him to keep the purse, because my sister had little humor to lose or regain. It is one of the things we can say about people whose characters differ from ours: they have no sense of humor, they don't know what it is to worry, they have never been unselfish. I said all of that about her, once. I remember saying, "She can't have much sense of humor, or she wouldn't keep falling in love." I was the humorless one then; I can see myself, glum-faced, apprehensive, barely in sight of my sister's secrets, creeping round the edge of her life. She never asked me to worry about her. Except once, she never asked anything of me except to be let alone.

Her humorless love was for Alec Campbell. He would have kept the purse. I can see him any day of the year, for he lives not far away and is assistant headmaster of Hughie's school. Sometimes he drives by, and I catch a glimpse of his failed poet's face concave with discontent, and the Macintosh scarf above the collar of his coat. (His mother must have been a Macintosh; he would always be punctilious about details like that.)

Last autumn he and I had an interview about Hughie. The school sent for me. Why should a child with plenty of pocket money steal?

We talked about Hughie as if we had never met. Gradually our tone changed, as if the room had been filled with witnesses, and the witnesses were disappearing, leaving us free to speak. He tried to set a tone of comradeship: we are modern, we are not stuffy. He is modern in the doom-laden manner of the 'thirties. To him the Spanish war is going on. *Ash-Wednesday* was published recently, and Spender and his friends are mischievous leftwing sprites. Years ago his Englishness in Montreal was an asset. He assumed a cultural superiority I am certain he felt. He was politically important: if he had not actually fought in the Spanish war, he had surely thought about it. I am positive he was somewhere near the Spanish frontier part of the time. I expect he wouldn't want his old Spanish feelings known, now. He is assistant headmaster of a conservative school. He has a pinched, bewildered look, as if the apple had been snatched away. I don't pity him. He must have wanted everything he has—this desk, and this room, and the colored picture of the Queen in full fig on the wall, and the black-and-white picture of the founder of the school. Above Alec's head is a framed text of the school founder's moral code: "Let me do my duty always for I shall pass through this world but once." Seeing Alec sitting between the Queen and the Founder I saw Isa defeated, Isa betrayed, and I thought, Be unhappy, you deserve it, you built your unhappiness—the little worms gnawing the closed box.

"How are your kids?" he said.

"Growing," I said. "As for Hugh, you seem to know more than I do."

"It's funny," he said, "how quiet the town is now. The city's cleaned up. This mayor's made a difference. The men with the big cigars have gone back to the States. I'm just as glad," said my sister's love, suddenly one with the creed of the Founder. His children are grown. At least one must be in college.

"Kids are quieter now," I said, meaning people in their twenties.

He smiled the rueful smile of the tamed rebel. He was well in his middle-life when Isa loved him, but I expect he thinks she was part of an extreme and heedless youth. "*You* weren't noisy," he said. He may have wanted to lead the talk on to Isobel, but I had to get away. I know something I could tell him, because I know what she became. I saw her on Labor Day weekend, 1955. Why should I tell Alec anything? He never confided in me. Besides, think of the absurdity of our conversation, if we'd tried having one: a failed poet and a middle-aged matron on the subject of love.

Once I followed Isobel down a busy street during the noon rush hour. It was a hot April day, I think in 1944. I remember the moist heat, the snow melted and rushing in the gutters, and the winter clothes weighing pounds on one's back. My sister wore a belted raincoat. Her ankles were thin and her shoes fitted badly. She stumbled along in her careless way as if she had never been shown how to walk. I remember that a man turned to stare at her. It shocked me to have him look at my sister, for I shared the Allenton belief that the purity of a decent girl showed in her demeanor, and that no man, however ill-mannered, could make a mistake. Isobel had our family features, after all, even though she had come out of the mold better than Frank or me. Why should a man look at her and not at her sister?—not that I wanted him to! Isobel seemed childish, younger than her age. She was a child in grownup clothes—a corrupt, untidy child. Men who knew her slightly found her enchanting. Her love for Alec Campbell was known, but because he was older than Isobel he was blamed. Corrupted innocence had a quality of attraction I could not understand, believing, as I did, that only prostitutes and movie stars provoked desire. She told me once that men sometimes spoke to her on the street. It was never the compliment she might have heard in a Latin country, but a puritan insult, or an obscenity, as if the attraction of her child's face aroused resentment and hate. That day, she stopped and turned and saw me. It should have been easy to smile and talk. I could have said, "I've been trying to catch up with you," but she would have known the truth, which was "I am trying to catch you." "Come on," she said, that day, and we walked on together, Isa the besieged, I the sister-pest.

It should have been easy, but I *was* her sister, and that was the barrier. There was between us a wall of family knowledge. No people are ever as divided as those of the same blood; yet we were alike, and our sameness was stamped on our faces and spoke in our breath: Eastern Canadian. Protestant, Anglo-Scot. The seed of our characters came from another continent. Like the imported daisies and dandelions, it was larger than the parent plant. Flowering in us was the dark bloom of the Old Country—the mistrust of pity, the contempt for weakness, the fear of the open heart.

In those days, Isobel and I lived in Montreal. It was wartime and our husbands—Tom, and Davy Sullivan—were overseas. We could have lived the life our mother, in Allenton, suggested when she said, "The girls are up in Montreal with war jobs." It could have meant sharing an apartment, attending the same Red Cross meetings, and baking cakes together to send our husbands. To our mother, war was a good occasion for everyone's keeping busy. For Isobel and me it was an excuse to leave home, and for Isa to get away from home and husband and me. If I think the word now—war—it is just emptiness, empty streets. War is an old house with the furniture out and the hangings down and the women left to click their heels along the floor. The day I followed Isobel was the day of my twenty-seventh birthday. I thought she might say something about it, but I suppose she forgot. That night I saw a spider's web of lines take form at the corner of my eyes. I saw it growing. I got up to take aspirin because I had a headache, and I leaned my head against the mirror of the medicine chest. I drew back, looked at my face, and I saw, spreading, the indelible web.

Was it that night or another I knew that news of my husband's death would be a release? That any news would do, providing it put a stop to the emptiness of the city, the passage of time, the length of winter? My nights were long and uneasy and full of ugly thoughts. Daytimes I was busy and sensible as my mother would have wished. I worked in the industrial research office of a railway. I painted sewers and waterworks on maps of cities. It was fine detailed work that strained my eyes, and must have been responsible for my headaches at night. Apart from my work, I had a busy life. Twice a week I went to meetings of my war-work committee. There, I often sat near Alec Campbell's wife. My sister's lover's wife: those two possessives terminated in the person of Bitsy Campbell, short and merry, with a head of sheared curls, like a wig of Persian lamb. She was named Bitsy because she had been unable to say Elizabeth as a child: I can't think how many times she explained it, or how important she seemed to consider the explanation. She had been one of the dimpled girls of the 'thirties. Her mouth was a narrow bow, and her eyes blinking and bright. Bitsy Campbell and I wrapped each other up in bandages (what to do after the air raids) and once we collected salvage in her car. While we drove up and down wintry streets collecting newspaper and old pots and pans, my sister was somewhere with Bitsy's husband. I was swollen with my secret: I knew. I realize now that Bitsy knew too. She must have known. She may not have realized the enemy was my sister, but her nails were bitten to the skin and her dimpled face was frozen and hard. She had dignity, all the same; she collected salvage and got ready for air raids and kept her troubles to herself.

I wrote to my husband every Sunday, Tuesday and Thursday. Saturdays I sent him either a box of candy or five hundred cigarettes. Sometimes he wrote asking me to post parcels to Dutch or English families who had been kind to him. I was conscientious about this. I washed my clothes and shampooed and set my hair twice a week. I spent one weekend a month at Allenton, and dined with my husband's married sister every two weeks. Sometimes I was invited to a party by a girl named Suzanne Moreau, the only friend in the world Isobel and I had in common. Suzanne was even stranger to me than my sister, but as there was no blood tie between us I expected her to be odd. She accepted me as she thought I was, whereas Isobel (turning and finding me behind her on the street) never laid eyes on me without wishing I were someone else. At Suzanne's parties I would see my own sister in the room, among strangers, and she would treat me as if I were just anyone. I would go up to her then and insist on talking about home, giving her news of Frank, forcing her to recognize me as kindred if she would not let me into her life. I wanted her to say, You and I are alike, and we are not like any other person in this room. But, of course, she never did.

I wish I could say I had spent those years, when I had time and a vacant mind and freedom to do what I liked, learning something useful. I think with astonishment that I complained I had time on my hands. No matter how busy I was, I still had time. I could have learned a foreign language: Suzanne and Isobel both tried Russian, and at Suzanne's I met a Red Army officer who was later arrested in his own country—an event that made us feel close to history. I could have attended evening classes in world literature. It would have improved my mind. Unlike my sister and brother I had not been sent to college, and I was ignorant. I might have read the newspaper and mapped the progress of the war with colored thumbtacks. None of it interested me. In those days I had one pursuit, and that was my sister's life. No mystery could have drawn me as much as the mystery of the plain rooms she lived in. No romantic story of my own (if ever I'd had one) tormented me as much as her story with Alec Campbell. Her denial of me was as entire as she could make it without an open breach. I know what she thought of me, and even now, knowing I have succeeded and she has failed, I am still troubled. She was wrong about me, but this is what she thought: she thought I was flat-minded, emptily optimistic, and thoroughly pleased with myself. She despised my safe marriage to a man my mother liked, and my war work, and even my job. I was the pattern of life discarded, the route struck off the map, the possible future. She walled herself away from me. There were gaps through which I could come in; there were times when, shameless, I forced my way. When she was ill, for instance, in the depths of one of her winter bouts of tonsillitis, I would hear about it in a letter from Allenton. I would remember that Isobel had always doctored her colds with a special honey from a shop in the East End of the city. I would spend my lunch hour traveling to and from the shop by tram. I would stop off and buy her a magazine, and arrive, finally, my hands cramped with cold, bearing the honey and the magazine as an excuse for my presence. Isobel might be up, smoking (the worst thing in the world for her throat, and I would tell her so), wearing a flowered crêpe dressing gown too short for her long legs. Most of her clothes looked as if they had belonged to someone else first, like the cut-down dinner dresses and ratty fur bits women passed on to their maids. The very sight of me, cold and sniffling, seemed a reproach. She would say, in a kind of comic despair, "Oh, why do you bother? It isn't a command, if I once say I like something." Her voice was nervous and rapid, and a little hoarse because of her bad throat. She would laugh, but her laughter was false. I think she knew it, then. She must have sensed it. I had to bother. I warmed my hands at her life. I cherished any reason for visiting her apartment, staring at the Matisse drawing torn from a magazine and pinned to the wall, seeing the envelopes of letters, the harsh wartime paper of letters from overseas, the ends of cigarettes she had smoked with a stranger, the four yellow tulips drooping in a milk bottle on the window sill. In illness she was weak. She had been delicate as a child—she and Frank were what our old Allenton doctor called TB types—and she gave up easily. Feverish, depressed, she could not prevent my changing the water in the milk bottle, emptying the ashtray, rinsing the sticky beer-smelling glasses I found in the kitchen. She must have sensed that I was drawn, curious, although I made it seem so ordinary—one sister visiting another.

"Are you moving again soon, or do you think you'll stay for a while?" I asked, keeping busy, chattering.

"I don't know. It depends."

She worked for a real-estate firm with one foot outside the law. She changed apartments often—it was part of her job. Isobel signed the lease, and the firm then sublet the apartment, furnished. Moving was easy for her. She owned nothing except a coffee pot and a cat named Barney. Barney owned more than she did: he had a cushion, a tennis ball, a cake tin, a plate, a teacup, and pieces of string to which Isobel had tied buttons. When she moved, she took Barney and Barney's possessions and the coffee pot and her clothes, and left everything else behind. She left magazines, books, cups, plates, can openers, paper napkins, bottles, hand lotion, Kleenex, needles and thread, shoe polish, scissors, and ashtrays. She did not keep or collect the odds and ends that seem to me, now, the symbol of women: I mean the chocolate box containing lipstick brushes, hair curlers, imitation pearls, lighters without wicks, a glove, a stamp from Finland. She did not keep buttons, or match folders with something scribbled inside. I had all of that then, and have it now. I cannot throw away the single earring for fear I might afterward discover its mate. I am sure that the left-hand blue suede glove will be returned to the Lost and Found department of the store where I think I left it three years ago. Well, she and I were very different. Our friends were different too.

When I remember all the foreigners Isobel knew I wonder why I found them so strange. There are so many around, now, since the last war. The Germans have their own newspaper, the *Montrealer Nachrichten*. In those days, a foreigner was either a workman or a refugee. Now, of course, it is quite different. My husband has German and Belgian and Norwegian colleagues—all thoroughly decent, with charming wives. Our children have been taught One World (although not *too* much). They have learned that a tailor in Oslo is the same as a tailor in Montreal, and I suppose believe it. I know that an engineer from Oslo is just the same as an engineer from Montreal. He gets just as drunk. His children are as spoiled. His wife disappears from the party to have a good cry in the bathroom, and some other woman has to fetch her and bring her back, murmuring, "He didn't mean it"—just like one of us. If I were to meet one of Isobel's friends now I might not find him so odd. But then! She knew Greeks, Italians, refugees, Jews; people from the north end of the city who could not pronounce "*th*" and never would. She knew French-Canadians—not foreign, but young, sullen and blasphemous; my generation, but a class unknown to me.

In Isobel's apartment, with honey in my hand, my excuse for being there, I encountered her friends. I remember the faces full of mobility and impatience, the bad accents, the false promises, the talk of getting away. It was never clear where anyone was going, but to hear them go on there wouldn't be anyone left here the minute the barrier of war was up. Those faces, those ambitions, my mother would have dismissed at once. Such people were unplaceable, and that was that.

To Isobel's friends I was wonderfully placeable. I see myself arriving and I see myself in their eyes. They imagine the world of bland blond faces I have come from; they invent my evenings of movies and innocent dinners with the girls from my office. I see myself arriving, and finding my sister up, smoking. One of her friends sprawls on the unmade bed. He is a dark boy of twenty. Why isn't he in uniform, I think, enjoying my mother's certain reaction. It may have happened dozens of times; it may have happened once. There are years between then and now. I have four children, and Isobel vanished to Venezuela in 1948. Some people think she died in a sailing accident (her companion was drowned that time) and others think she died of a kidney disease, and some confuse us, thinking that Jean made a bad marriage, or Jean is dead. They have forgotten who was good and who was bad. This is a small memory, of no importance: one sister visits another. Words are omitted, and the wrong things said—wounding, hopeless, inevitable.

Say that it happened once, my arrival on a winter day with the jar of honey and the magazine. I leave my coat to shed its snow on the radiator in the hall. Isobel's apartments are all the same: hall, arch, living room, cube of kitchen, smell of paint, plaster falling like snow. I step out of my snow boots and pad into the living room in stocking feet. Isobel throws me her scuffed moccasins which are dirty and too big for me. She wears knitted after-ski socks on her feet and looks ridiculous, with the printed wrapper on her back. My eyes water, my nose runs. This is a bad climate for women. There is the friend, young, unknown, sure of himself, shedding ashes on the floor.

"That your sister?" he says, or, "I didn't know you had a sister." Isobel might have spared me that.

Isobel's sister, Jean Price, sits down, crosses her ankles, clasps her hands, smiles. She is not rude, and says, How do you do? The stranger takes her in. She is shorter than Isobel, has small feet, is neater. Her hair is a sensible length (Isobel's straggles over the wrapper) and she is well polished, as if the surface of body, hair, skin, eyes, nails, were of a single substance, a thin shell. There is a faint web of lines at the outer corner of each eye, but no one but Jean has seen them. Isobel makes coffee, and pours me a cup. She stands, feet apart, and gives me the cup without a saucer. She does this with a grand air, as if bestowing a treasure. Suzanne Moreau has said that Isobel really thinks she is giving something splendid when she hands one a cup of coffee or a light for a cigarette. Suzanne has said that Isobel is lavish; she has painted a portrait of my sister curiously decorated, trailing feathers and loops of colored stones. The face in the picture is ugly and sharp. Isobel in the picture reminds me of a bird; Suzanne has called it "Personnage aux Plumes."

"Well, I'm sure it's very interesting," I said when it was shown me.

No one has ever painted me as a personage with plumes.

Isobel's sister, unlavish, is decent in an old-rose cashmere sweater and matching cardigan knitted by an aunt in Scotland. She wears a brown tweed skirt, pearls (husband's family's wedding present) and husband's fraternity pin.

"So you're Isobel's *sister*?" Mocking little face.

"I'm afraid I am. She certainly keeps her family in the dark." Flat, the flat Allenton laugh. Isobel gives me a look. The friend, suddenly impatient, wants me to go so that he can get on with his conversation. When I am there Isobel will not speak. Into this social vacuum (I shall not go) I make conversation. I speak of the season; of my job. They've never had a girl in that job before. It used to be reserved for graduate engineers. My husband was in that department, but after the war I don't think he'll go back. It will seem tame after everything he's been through. What do I do? Well, I take industrial maps of all these cities and . . . it's painstaking work. If I keep on, I shall have to get glasses. The fluorescent lighting is bad. Some people say it makes you depressed. A man I know lost his sight. A man I heard about tried to kill himself with iodine. Some people have been in the same department thirty years and they say they've definitely been more depressed since the fluorescent lighting was put in. They can't change it now. With a war on, where would they get anything else?

"God, you sound like Mother," my sister says.

The young man seems to become larger at this. He relaxes, smiles, scatters more ashes on the floor. He asks me questions now: what do I feel about the Russians? Not what do I think, mark you: he takes it for granted that I am all instinct and prejudice. He fancies I am an earnest conservative and hopes I am a Protestant bigot. He has heard about them, but thinks they will soon be extinct. Isobel, silent, making faces when she swallows coffee because it hurts her throat, is no help to me. Panic. I fall back on my mother, on her innocent assumption that the other person is waiting for her to set the tone. Something new enters my manner. I sit up. I examine him, kindly. The stranger feels it. My manner fills the room: whatever it is, it will daunt him all his life. His father is a tailor on Tupper Street. He never got beyond public school. He has a talent for poetry, but who has not? His father is a chauffeur in Vancouver, but no one in Montreal must know. He was in a reforma- tory from the age of fourteen. His sister has an illegitimate child. Vicis- situdes, the troubles we call handicaps, rise like waves. He is a German refugee and his father was a professor of philosophy but he is nothing under a kind Canadian stare. He will never make it; if he marries, his children will never fit in.

Do you see how difficult it was? And here was I, anxious to be friendly, quite without pride. No wonder my sister despised me. In the end we were all three apart, for inevitably Isobel became impatient with the cringing stranger too. But the greatest distance was between us, the sisters. In the end I said something petty or aggrieved, and put on my coat and boots and went back to my office. All afternoon I would think, she didn't even thank me. I would tell my mother about it next time I spent a weekend in Allenton. I would tell the whole story, end- ing with, "She didn't even say thanks."

"Isa is selfish," my mother would say, with the complacency that meant Isobel could afford to be. "Looks aren't everything," she might add. That made it worse. Isobel lives in Venezuela now, in a climate I can only imagine. I think of her in winter and darkness, in the black January of Montreal. When I dream of her she stands bareheaded, her coat flying open. She wears her fur-topped Russian boots, and holds a handbag slung over one shoulder by a buckled strap. The face is evasive, turned away. She has nothing to say. She will not speak to me out of her death, or out of my dreams, where, in theory, I ought to have things as I want them. She walked toward me out of the dark once: I was about to say, "She looked like that the first time I saw her"—I don't know why, for we had been seeing each other all our lives. The city was silent and abandoned; nothing moved. Because of the gasoline rationing there were few cars at night, and after a fall of snow the streets were white and untouched as country roads. I was plodding westward along Sherbrooke Street after a dinner with my husband's sister. My head was down, against the wind. The wind dropped, and I looked up and saw Isobel and Alec Campbell. They emerged out of the dark and took form as a couple. Isobel was tall as he. She listened to something he was telling her. They leaned inward as they walked, as if both had received an injury and were helping each other stand up. Isobel's face was a flower. Everything wary and closed, removed and mistrustful had disappeared. I wondered what he was telling—he was so tweedy, plaid-scarved, ordinary. He was an ordinary looking man, but that made their love affair seem all the more extraordinary, as if there were something I should see, clear as morning. Alec was secretive, like Isobel. They had that in common: I imagined they told each other that they were special, like no lovers who had ever existed. Whenever I tried to imagine the conversation of lovers it was like that. I was twenty-seven and married but fanciful as a little girl. I had an idea about love, and I thought my sister knew the truth. Until the time of my own marriage I had sworn I would settle for nothing less than a certain kind of love. However, I had become convinced, after listening to my mother and to others as well, that a union of that sort was too fantastic to exist; nor was it desirable. The reason for its undesirability was never plain. It was one of the definite statements of rejection young persons must learn to make; "Perfect love cannot last" is as good a beginning as any.

When Isobel saw me her face closed. She probably knew that I was coming from my ritual meal with my sister-in-law and that, if nothing else, would have annoyed her. She may even have believed I was out in the snowy street at half-past eleven at night purposely to irritate her. Alec, who was simpler, looked uneasy. He was a teacher, married, a father, and penniless. "She sure can pick men," our brother Frank had said, when I told him about Alec. Neither of us had liked her husband, Davy Sullivan, either. Alec may have known that I saw his wife twice a week at our work committee. Only two nights before, Bitsy had set my arm after an imaginary air raid, and said that if I accidentally swallowed poison, having lost my reason under the bombs, she would prescribe flour and water to make me vomit. Upon which she received a further badge or certificate of some sort. I had done my share too. I had treated Bitsy for an imaginary epileptic seizure. I had stuck a pencil across her tongue so that she wouldn't swallow the tongue and choke. She had bitten the pencil in a spasm of giggles. I had the pencil now, in my purse, with tiny indentations in the yellow paint.

Isobel's lips were chapped. She shook back her light ribbons of hair, and revealed her cold and slightly swollen pink ears. She had never prized her beauty. Our mother, who had dreamed of having a pretty daughter she could dress, had been given a pretty daughter who positively did not wish to be dressed.

"Come and have a drink with us," said Alec, who was kind. Our breath hung between us in white clouds and there was something marble and monumental about the group we formed in our winter clothes on the white street. Alec tried gently to pull away from my sister's arm, but she tightened her hold, and he smiled. All of that was secret and I'm sure they thought I didn't see. "I'll see that you get home," he said, as if that were the reason for my hesitating, keeping them still on the frozen street. Isobel gave no sign. The last faint trace of her smile was dying. I knew that I must not follow them to a bar. I could pry into my sister's life, but not when he was there. He would sense it. Besides, they were such a solid being that I would be invisible beside them. They were the lighted window; I was the watcher on the street.

In an excess of chattiness I said that I was walking home, all the way. We were stamping and shuffling like horses. I knocked one hard solid snow boot against the other. "I don't seem to be sleeping well," I said seriously. "I find that walking at night sort of helps. I'm against taking pills, aren't you?"

Alec gave me the shadow of a look of interest—all the interest he could spare from my sister, from the pressure of her arm, from her presence on the dark street—and said, "Try not to think you can't sleep. The more you're afraid the harder it is to sleep."

Isobel glanced at me too, almost with curiosity. No, it was pity. All at once I felt as if the absence of love in my life, my solitude, my chastity, were visible and ugly as a disease. I felt dreary and defiled before these sinners. They were right and I was wrong. The figure I represented, historically permitted, morally correct—the wife of the soldier, untouched, waiting his return—I would have thrown away in a minute for a fragment of their mystery. The cleanliness of my clothing, my washed hair, my washed, deodorized, unwanted person, even the coldness of the night, with its white suggestion of purity, mocked my condition. I saw no end to it, and I knew I could not stay near Alec and my sister. I walked on, brusquely, smiling back at them, saying something like, "See you soon" (untrue), or "Have a good time"—as if they needed my wishes.

What I had told Alec was absurd. It would not have occurred to me to walk every night. The city at night was too cold, too silent. The light lay under street lamps in pools of blue. I was afraid of purse-snatchers. When I couldn't sleep I took a sleeping pill. That night, however, I did walk home, all the way, and it was late before the anguish awakened in me by the sight of them died down. I thought that my sister ought to have helped me, but even now I don't see what she could have done.

4

I am afraid I have given two misleading impressions: one that I was jealous of my sister, the other that I married without love. At twenty-four I was ready to love anyone. I had never left home. I had not been sent to boarding school, like Isobel and Frank, and when I was ready for college, and in robust health, my mother decided I was delicate and would never stand the strain.

It was Isobel who brought Tom Price to the family. She invited him for a weekend at the lake. I remember the car stopping and Isobel jumping out and running along the drive as if escaping. Her friend, the stranger, seemed deliberate and slow. He rolled up the windows because it was a gray afternoon and put the car keys in his pocket. If I were to see him now, for the first time—as he was then, as I am now—I would think, Young army captain, loves his uniform, loves the war. Then, I thought, He looks too old for his rank. He was thirty-three.

My mother instantly saw in Tom a man who would do. He would do for either daughter. He had the cautious humor, the stern but reassuring face she admired in men. All weekend Isobel bothered us about a cat—a deaf, mangy cat named Julie my mother had had destroyed. That is, my mother had given the cat to the grocer in the village down at the end of the lake and asked him to find Julie a good home. A day later M. Robineau, the grocer, said Julie had disappeared. My mother translated this to mean "ran away."

"She ran away because you brought her down here," said Isobel. "Cats always run away from strange houses. She's trying to get back to Allenton. She's walking all those miles. She's so old . . . she doesn't know where we are."

I have said that we are not a family of weepers. The dryness of Isobel's face is before me now. I think of her that Saturday and Sunday calling "Julie, Julie," bumping along the shore in a boat, calling into strange cottages. Children mocked her: "Julie, Julie," came to us in a chorus of young voices as we sat inside the cottage late Sunday afternoon. Light rain spattered on the window netting. Isobel closed the screen door behind her and said, "Julie's drowned. The Robineau kids took her out in their boat and threw her in the lake. They hit her with an oar but she was still alive when they left her there."

"Julie ran away," said my mother, knitting.

There might have been a kinder way of putting old Julie to sleep, but my mother could hardly be blamed because French-Canadian villagers are cruel to animals. She had handed Julie in a basket to M. Robineau and said, "Find it a good home." For my mother the matter ended there. Isobel was always collecting animals, and Julie was the worst of the lot: in spite of her age she still inundated us with litters.

Isobel sat down and pretended to read. She picked up the first book she saw and opened it anywhere. In an atmosphere of extinguished quarrels Tom, her guest, began to pay attention to me. He looked at me with Isobel there, in the same room. Isobel was presumptuous. She judged us, the adults. She was eighteen but she thought she was fifty. My mother glanced at me and then at Tom. She was knitting for Frank, who was overseas. Tom would do for either daughter and he was likely to choose me. The weight of her personality, her moral strength, her contempt for men and her knowledge of their weaknesses, were now on my side. My mother backed the winner. Tom answered her gentle questions: he was a civil engineer; he had one married sister; both parents were still living; he worked in the industrial research office of a railway; he was going overseas, he supposed, any day now. Once, when her scrutiny of him ceased, when he thought he was not being watched, he sighed and relaxed and rubbed the back of his neck.

"Isobel is a rude child, I'm afraid," said my mother placidly, testing his interest, as though Isobel were out of earshot.

"I guess she feels badly about her cat," he said. If Isa had looked up at him then he would never have married me. She turned a page, indicating that she had heard but wanted no part of us. My mother and I were cold and still. I felt our unity. She and I were grown women. We knew what we were doing. Isobel was a silly girl.

She was a silly girl, there, with her legs bent under her, curled in an armchair, pretending to read. She was older than I was in one kind of experience—she had already had a lover. I knew, because Frank had found out and there had been an unholy row between them, which I overheard. Frank considered himself guardian of his sisters' virtue, but as I listened—they were in Frank's room, I on the stairs—I was astonished to realize that his principal objection was only Isobel's choice.

"Are you going to marry him?" said Frank.

"Of course I'm not," said Isobel. "I'm seventeen, for God's sake. I don't want to marry anybody and even if I did it wouldn't be him. I wouldn't marry someone just because of *that*."

"Don't get yourself caught," said Frank. "Don't tell Jean."

"Jean!"

I was poised, a little below Frank's door, hand on the bannisters. "Don't tell Jean": that was unkind of them, but no matter. "Are you going to marry him?" should surely have been, "Do you think he'll want to marry you now?" Isobel ought to be beaten. If she were my sister I'd take a strap to her: I mean—correcting the thought—if I were her brother.

That had been nearly a year ago. Now Frank was in England, Isobel was eighteen, and Tom (was he the lover?) was taking notice of me. He had never been her lover: I learned that later. He had wanted to marry her, though. My mother told me, after Tom and I were married, after he was overseas. He had proposed to Isobel that weekend, on the way down to the lake, and Isobel had refused him. Isobel said "No," and darted out of the car in search of her cat. She told Tom she never wanted to marry. She was not going to marry him, or Davy Sullivan. She did not want children, because mothers were abominable and she did not intend to be one. Those were her ideas at eighteen. It must have been a shock to poor Tom. He did not expect girls to have ideas about anything.

The night he asked me to marry him, a few weeks after this, I went to my mother's room and knelt by her bed and said, "Tom's smashed up his brother-in-law's car. We aren't hurt, so don't worry. We want to get married right away because he's going overseas." She sat up in bed, two pillows behind her. She closed the book she had been reading but held her finger between the pages. My marriage was a temporary interruption; she would go on reading for years after I left. She seemed amused. In the pupil of her eye I thought I saw a door closing, far down a tiny corridor.

She's thrown Tom and me together, I thought. She's wanted this.

It was months before I understood that pinpoint amusement—before she told me he had proposed to Isobel first. Isobel had refused him because he was too old, too old, repeated my mother (he still thinks he married too young), and because she was passionately in love with Davy Sullivan and intended to marry no one but him.

Both versions of what Isobel had to say came from my mother. Perhaps Tom told her one story and Isobel another; perhaps she made the whole thing up. I ought to put the two accounts before Tom and let him take his pick. When he was overseas, at the beginning of our marriage, I imagined all the questions I would ask when he came back; but then the personal nature of marriage made it too difficult. I could pour out my life to a stranger—at least I did, once—but with Tom I was shy. There are questions I could ask, even now, if I thought I was safe. It was a long time ago, his having wanted Isobel, but the wrong question might still pull down the house. You can never be certain of that house, even if it has been standing twenty years.

Did he ask me to marry him so that he could be near her? Of course he would say no. The question is childish. Did he think he would wake up one day and find my sister instead of me in his bed? Did he believe I could lose five years, grow four inches, speak with a different voice? Did he think I would become bored with Jean and decide to be Isobel? No, no and no, he would say. It is better not to ask, even now; for what if he said no, but thought to himself yes, yes. The house could still come down. When we thought she was dying we talked out of character, and sounded deranged. We admitted we loved her—we who dread the word. We would rather say we adore: it is so exaggerated it can't be true. Adore equals like, but love is compromising, eternal. When my sister lay dying Tom said, "She always smelled of gardenias." Isobel never wore perfume. I don't know what he meant; it was an extraordinary thing for Tom to have said.

He proposed to me after an automobile accident. He was spending a forty-eight hour leave with us, again at the lake—no longer Isobel's guest, but a family friend—and on our way back from a party he ran his brother-in-law's car into the wall of a garage. The wall came out of the dark. I thought, That's what it's like to be killed. Tom says I seemed to be sleeping and then I opened my eyes and said calmly, "All we can do is leave the car here and walk home." The tension between us during the walk made it clear something would happen. It was the first shared experience: the accident. I know of marriages that keep going on less than that. We stumbled in the dark, holding on to each other. I was closer to him than I had ever been to my father or brother, and I was not afraid of him. I was never afraid of Tom. We swam in the lake and made love on the dock. I knew what I was doing, I was not afraid of him, or of the shock part of the accident. I knew he would marry me. I decided to love him with a determination I had never shown about anything else. He asked me to marry him after we were dressed; not as an afterthought, but perhaps part of the accident too. He said he wanted to get married as quickly as possible because he was going overseas. I crept to my mother's room and knelt by her bed. In the morning Tom and I were not clandestine lovers, like Davy and Isobel, but an engaged couple with everyone's blessing. We did not make love again until after we were married. There wasn't time, we were seldom alone, and I avoided it because of the pain. Days afterward I was seized by pain that doubled me in two. I told him that. I was not afraid to tell him about the pain, or about the stains on the dock I had to scrape away with a knife. I could tell him that, even at the beginning. He always listened to me, but there was this—he never said that he loved me, and I was too shy to ask if he did.

At my wedding in Allenton Isobel was center of things. Her escapade with Davy Sullivan had been discovered and they were to be married, and soon. She had told Frank she would never marry "because of *that*" and yet she did. Her wedding took place two days before her nineteenth birthday, but some people said she was seventeen, or even sixteen. At her wedding any number of uninvited guests crowded in. No one approved of Davy, but everyone wanted to see what he was like.

Tom went overseas almost at once, and I moved to Montreal. First I stayed with my sister-in-law, who was still distressed about the smashed car. "You young people drink so much nowadays," she said, as if I were Isobel. Then, my first act of independence, I rented a room in a boarding house and went there, and then I shared an apartment on Queen Mary Road with a girl who worked in my building. I had a job, now, in Tom's old office. I met Alma Summer there. She could never have been mistaken for one of my mother's daughters, but my mother liked her well enough. It was Alma who found the apartment, and, as I had never lived in an apartment, except for the few weeks with my sister-in-law, I thought it seemed a bohemian, almost glamorous thing to do. Alma told me that if it weren't for the war, and the scarcity of places to live, she would never have signed the lease. She read the names on the mailboxes and declared we must surely be the only Protestants. "We're a little island here, Jeannie," she said. "Look at them— Gordeaux, Magione, Brondfield, Leroux, Godl, Dupay, Eschmann, Skiba, Thibeouf, di Gorbio . . ."

"Nonsense," I said. "There's a White, and a Jones."

"I don't trust them," said Alma.

From our kitchen we heard the services bellowed over a loudspeaker from St. Joseph's Oratory, and we saw the pilgrims going up the steps of the shrine on their knees. Armies of pilgrims with uniformed brass bands came from outside the city and they all climbed on their knees. "If they're so crazy about uniforms," Alma said, "why don't they join up? They could get into real uniforms and do something. There's a war on." I said nothing; I had been brought up not to say what I thought. Alma, who was from a small Ontario town, believed that Catholics sent a quarter of their incomes directly to the Pope. "It's a shame," she said, "when you think of how poor they are." She watched them from the kitchen window. The windowsill, with its soot and grit and ration books and milk tickets and parsley in a tumbler of water, was her protection against the Oratory and all the horrors it contained: pilgrims' crutches, and one hideous relic—a man's heart in a bottle. I'm sure she would have set a machine gun on the window sill if she could—not in attack: in defense. She was a plump girl with gentle eyes. She could not pronounce the letter "*r*" and had been encouraged to use a baby lisp by her closest friend, Mr. Callwood. I never saw a photograph of him, never heard his voice on the telephone, and never learned his Christian name. "Mr. Callwood says . . ." Alma would begin, and turn pink with love and distress. She slept in our living room, where a revolving electric log in the grate made her feel cozy. Most of our furniture was Alma's, and so were the rules by which we lived. She had always lived with women, and it was she who explained about taking turns with the cleaning, the shopping, and carrying the garbage out.

Our rooms were separated by a curtain on a rod, and it comes to me now that she had taken the door off its hinges because it was unfriendly and could be shut. I remember the gradual slackening, the hysterical untidiness that soon prevailed. I, who at Allenton would not have emerged from my room with a pin in my hair, now faced Alma at breakfast with cream still on my face and my head a helmet of snails. Our conversation turned on the thoughts of idle or unloved women: we were spellbound by the condition of our skin, the fragility of our fingernails, our cramps, our aches, our migraine headaches, our dreams, our pre-and post-menstrual depressions; we brewed hot water bottles and fed each other aspirin. We had nothing in common except that we were women, and we had to make that do.

From this Sargasso of scarves, stockings, lipsticks, damp towels, pins, uncapped toothpaste tubes, we emerged every morning side by side, clean, smooth, impeccable as eggs. Side by side we descended the stairs, emerged on the street, and waited for our streetcar. We traveled to work, still talking about skin, nails, pains and dreams. Arriving at our building we went at once to the third-floor washroom to powder the wings of our noses and comb our hair. Our energies were spent making certain that our teeth gleamed, our eyes shone, and that we did not under any circumstances smell of sweat. We were not beauties, mind you: all that effort was required just to keep us moderately decent. In summer our short cotton dresses were rigid with starch. Our skirts were lampshades. Our damp hands were encased in spotless gloves. Home again, we became like our rooms. We assumed the shapelessness, the deliberate sloppiness of rooms shared by women whose hopes are somewhere else. The feeling here was of waiting, as the feeling in Allenton, years later, was of death.

Alma was waiting for Mr. Callwood's wife to die of diabetes. Sometimes when Mrs. Callwood was in hospital, undergoing treatment, or visiting her old mother in Nova Scotia, Alma abandoned Queen Mary Road and lived in Mrs. Callwood's house. She would return full of sniffy criticism of Mrs. Callwood's housekeeping. Her plants were puny and untended, her bedsheets yellow, her preserves more ersatz than they need be even in wartime. "Don't the neighbors notice you?" I asked her once. Alma thought that a poor question. We could discuss Mrs. Callwood's bedsheets but we had to pretend Alma had never been in Mrs. Callwood's bed. I remember about Alma two things more: she had twenty curved imitation tortoise-shell combs, each with a bow ribbon of different color attached. Once a month she washed and ironed and retied all the ribbons and then wore a new comb every day, over a small, straying chignon. Once she remarked in a helpless, frightened way, "Believe me, Jean, you never know what goes on any place once the door's closed."

Alma tried to kill herself in 1952. I think she went to live with a niece in Windsor—we lost track. If I had known more about depression I would have guessed she might try to do something foolish. Often when I came in at night after a movie or from my war-work meeting I would find the living room dark and Alma fast asleep. She lay on her divan, fully dressed, under her gray squirrel coat. I would take off my boots and pad past the couch where she breathed like someone with a heavy cold. She would speak with great clarity and unhappiness phrases like "my red cable-stitch sweater" and "got off at the wrong stop." The room would be cold and stale. She had forgotten to disconnect the revolving log that sent bubbles of orange light over the ceiling and walls, over sorrowing unconscious Alma, over Churchill disguised as a bulldog sitting on the Union Jack. I would push aside the mulberry curtain and switch on my bedside lamp. The bar of light falling on her face made Alma turn to the wall, and I could extinguish the bubbling log. Hours later I might hear her groan, rise, undress, and crawl back to bed. We never talked about it. I know that when I was away, weekends, she took a pill that gave her five hours' sleep. If she woke up and discovered it was still Sunday she wandered drowsily into the bathroom and swallowed another five hours' oblivion. She revealed this to me in a casual remark, but we did not go on with it. Our greatest intimacy was probably the sight of each other's underwear drying in the bathroom. With mutual prudery we never asked favors, and never had debts.

I had been living with Alma three years when her cousin, a girl in the Air Force, passing through on her way to Halifax and overseas, asked if she could spend the night with us. Alma went to endless trouble, combining our ration books to buy a little roast of veal, which she rolled up with bread and onion stuffing to make it seem more. She bribed the grocer for beer, which was scarce, and laid dinner on a card table in front of the fireplace. There was a wrapped present before her cousin's plate—an Elizabeth Arden traveling kit, I think it was: something Alma thought her cousin would never find in England. We worked all day that Sunday making the apartment neat, putting stray objects behind cushions and just generally out of sight. Alma talked about her cousin in an odd way, as if she were expecting a man. When Mona Summer walked in that evening, so emphatically uniformed that the uniform might have been ambling by itself, I wondered if Alma had connected "uniform" and "Air Force" and "overseas" to create a phantom airman and not her cousin at all. She hesitated before kissing Mona. Mona was only a girl. Why had we cleaned the apartment, bribed the grocer, stuffed a roast?

Mona stalked about and flung herself into chairs like an adolescent boy. She was a woolly-headed girl of nineteen with enormous teeth.

She drank like a man and had a man's way of holding a cigarette and glass. The uniform was cruel: the skirt seemed a sack, and the tunic a bolster stuffed with straw. She had the feminine military face: round cheeks, snub nose, large mouth and piggy, impudent eyes. I remember her grubby hands and her bulging calves. She could have been the comic Air Force girl-chum in a brave English film. Alma now gave her cousin the sober reverence due to a hero. If Mona was not a pilot, we would continue to treat her like one. She was a stenographer, and going overseas to do the same job Alma performed here, in Montreal. All the same I could see that Alma felt inferior, as if her own life were without direction. She told Mona that I was the wife of an officer and the sister of an airman and that my sister's husband had been wounded in Italy. This was said with an air of offering me. Mona gave me a hard and impertinent stare.

The log revolved. We ate the veal and drank the beer. Mona spoke of her commanding officer—her ma'am. Ma'am had a code of honor; she had ideals. She could tell whether you were lying by looking in your eyes. "Our Ma'am is a real Christian, not like some," said Mona.

After dinner, when Alma and I were clearing away the plates, we decided in rapid whispers that Mona would sleep with me. Alma's couch was even narrower than my small bed. In cheerful proximity Mona and I undressed and hung our skirts on hangers. The hostess, I offered cream, Kleenex, and bobby pins. We put up our hair. We washed stockings, and brushed our teeth. I opened the window, letting in the noise of streetcars and a tide of black winter air. We got into bed and lay like mummies, side by side. Her rayon underwear, all strings and straps, had been dropped on the carpet. She turned in bed and yawned and stuck her little flannelled rump against my hip.

"Don't you want to sleep spoons?" she said. "The bed's so small."

"No, I don't."

"Well, don't mind me if I'm all over, then," said Mona, not in the least offended. "Ma'am says I'm just awful." After a silence she said in the dark, "I wish she was here to say goodnight." She gave another carefree boyish yawn. In the next room poor Alma, who had taken a pill, sank and murmured into sleep under her gray squirrel coat. "Have you got a boy friend?" Mona said.

"Mona, go to sleep," I said.

"I can't sleep," said Mona. "The bed's too small." She turned her head slightly and whispered, "You can't sleep, either. Do you want to play?"

"Go to sleep," was all I said.

When I awoke in the morning merry Mona was clambering over me on her way to breakfast. It was a quarter past seven on a winter day and the day was dark. I decided not to get up. I would stay here, at home, in my own bed, to which I had an unqualified right. The railway could flourish and the war be won without my aid. I lay with my hands behind my head and I remember this: I stared at the dark and hated Isobel. I hated Tom because he had gone away and left me with the Almas and Monas, but what Isobel had to do with that morning is not clear. I suppose I thought she was having a better time.

5

My father, who has become too deaf to listen to reason, bores us with news of the weather. We have lost the sense of seasons; our climate has been degenerating since the first nuclear explosion in Nevada a generation ago. He remembers that radioactive clouds traveled from Nevada to upstate New York and that all the exposed negatives in the Kodak laboratories in Rochester were damaged. He says he saw a news item about it in an early edition of a Montreal paper, but that in the later editions it had been left out. Did we read it then? Do we think about it now? He has also noticed that salt is less salty than it used to be and that sugar has lost its sweetness. When Tom and I lunch with my old parents my father begs us to taste the salt and sugar and say we agree. Tom, who is rational, argues. I cannot be made to remember. My father is old and talkative. My mother is quiet. Her brown-spotted hands tighten and flex, and I can see she is full of silent answers.

Salt, sugar, and the seasons: our summer is cold smoke in air-conditioned rooms, our autumn a summer misplaced. Autumn was spring, a false promise, in the old days. The first metallic morning reminded us that everything could change, and with this false beautiful expectation we were tricked into winter. By Christmas I knew the promise had been a lie, and in January, when the heart of the city was slow as the heart in sleep, I knew I would not survive. Every spring I was alive and had survived. One February day in 1945 I was still living and had nearly emerged from the winter alive. The days drew out by two minutes every twenty-four hours. Mr. Prescott, the Chief Engineer of the Industrial Development section of the railway office where Tom had worked, and where I now performed a superfluous but patriotic task, said that this was so. At any moment I might become Tom's widow. The ambition of eight chattering stenographers at the far end of the room was to become like me: each of them wanted to marry a brave boy, live for a few days and nights with him—every day and night the last—and then write letters to him for ever and ever. A translucid comb of icicles hung at the window next to my desk. Looking into the comb of the wavy gray winter sky and the wavy brown office building next to ours, Mr. Prescott said, "We're gaining two minutes a day now. It's nearly spring." The day I had news that my brother had died Mr. Prescott said, "Look at that sky, Mrs. Price," and through the now dazzling icicles I saw blue, plain blue, a sky like a plate.

In our overheated office thirty people idled, cast up by the war. There were middle-aged men, veterans of that earlier war they never stopped describing, and a veteran of the present war, Wing-Commander Meadmore, who wore the Air Force uniform and a shabby greatcoat he was no longer entitled to, but no one thought less of him for that. We were accustomed to Majors and Colonels from the other, boring war. I remember their bristling mustaches and unbrushed suits. They stank of beer and strong tea. Elderly Major Currie kissed my mouth at an office party and called me "little girl." It was like being held one second too long by an old family friend. Children know when a kiss must end, but I was twenty-eight and had better manners and fewer defenses than a child. Wing-Commander Meadmore, our recent veteran, sharing my lunch of hardboiled egg sandwiches one day, said, "I felt funny just then."

"What do you mean?"

We sat facing each other at an empty drawing table. The lights were thriftily dimmed on this dark winter noon. Wing-Commander Meadmore's skin became lumpy and porous and his smell unclean. He turned away, raised an arm slowly as if to bless me, and uttered a cry. I heard Julie drowning in the lake, hit by an oar. Having nursed Bitsy Campbell in a make-believe fit, I was able to prevent Wing-Commander Meadmore from swallowing his tongue. Afterwards he said, "I fainted." An invocation was required, but instead of an exorcist we had Jean Price, possessor of a First Aid certificate. I treated him so carefully and with such tact that anything he, or his possessed soul, might have revealed to me was stilled. I was not consciously avoiding the Devil: I would have been just as tactful with God. We permitted the existence of God without discussing Him, and He existed without the Devil. I put a pencil over Wing-Commander Meadmore's tongue, undid his tie and collar, and slipped my rolled cardigan beneath his head. The stenographers and the office boys eating sandwich lunches said he put them off their food. He smelled as if he were rotting. Presently two of the men helped him to the infirmary—"Come on, kid, you're fine"— where he slept and wakened to say, "I fainted." We ventilated the office and opened the windows to the wind and soot and graywool sky. I washed my hands to rid them of the corruption they had touched, and rubbed them with Hind's Honey and Almond lotion.

"Do you think he knows?" said Mr. Prescott.

"No," I said, without wondering if it were true. "It's better that way."

"Poor chap had a knock on the head," said Mr. Prescott.

"In my personal opinion," said young Moray Mackenzie, called up and leaving in a fortnight, "the company shouldn't be forced to take back just any vet, just because he is a vet. If I come back and I'm not fit for a good day's work I won't expect to be kept on out of charity."

"Hear, hear," said Mr. Prescott.

Moray Mackenzie only a month ago would have been squashed by any of us if he had introduced an opinion about anything. Now, leaving us, he was the office hero. He lounged, smoking, knocking ash on the floor. Standing before me he said, "I'm middle class and proud of it"—surely not in argument. I would have never said anything that could provoke an unpleasant answer. We must have been in deep accord.

The third-floor washroom, where, under running water, I cleansed my hands of Wing-Commander Meadmore, overlooked the harbor. Moray Mackenzie has passed on a story that German spies spent their time there, watching the movements of ships. He was reprimanded for spreading rumors, but Alma heard about it and was alarmed. She longed to catch Peter Lorre or Eric von Stroheim peering out of the window of the Ladies', but never did. The fact that the harbor was closed in winter failed to console Alma. She would have preferred a harbor open the year round, and spies continually at work. If the spy had been with me now he would have seen a narrow street and gritty snow and a dark Greek restaurant. Even when the street was busy, rattling with streetcars, it had the empty look of a place where nobody lives. At night migrations of rats took place. Our toothless night watchman, who wore his decorations from the Boer War, said it was a sight you could never forget: The rats crossed the street from cellar to cellar. It occurred to me that South African and Indian and Australian railways were run from buildings like this and that they had the same night watchmen and invisible spies and the same armies of rats. That was the trace of Empire: the dark brown buildings, the old men with their medals. This street seemed to me to belong to an extremely ancient period of history. I had never seen anything older and it did not enter my head that a single stone or pediment or Victorian gargoyle could ever vanish or be replaced.

"The girls are up in Montreal with war jobs," my mother liked to say. Every morning I was given a supply of industrial maps of the cities of Canada served by the railway, and I painted the sewers and waterworks yellow and mauve. I had a box of water colors for my exclusive use, and four fine brushes in a jam jar. I had clean cloths, a cold cream pot for fresh water, stacks of blotting paper, and a pad on which to rest my hand so that it would not soil the map. An envious stenographer was ordered to see that my supplies never ran short. Before the war, during the depression, a degree in civil engineering had been required for this post. Now, with a shortage of qualified men, the railway was happy to have me. My qualifications for this or any job were that I had taken lessons in geography and ancient history from an old friend of my mother's and had also been taught to play the violin.

I painted mauve and yellow pipelines all day, and scarcely ever let the brush slip out of the guide drawn for me. I sat, perched high on a draftsman's stool, my hair falling in smooth plaques as I bent my head. In a heap at the upper lefthand corner of my desk were my watch, my charm bracelet, my engagement ring, and Tom's fraternity pin. The dressing and doffing ritual took place in the morning, before and after lunch, and at half-past five. No one thought it odd of me, for nearly every person there depended upon some finicky personal ceremony before the day's work could begin. One sharpened pencils, another watered the sweet-potato plant that grew out of a peanut-butter jar on a windowsill. Mr. Prescott cut up the morning paper and filled little envelopes with mysterious clippings. The older men were fretful about possessions no one must touch: slide rules, calendars, graph paper, and in one inexplicable case, a colored photograph of the Dionne quintuplets as infants. I would swear today, and would have certainly sworn then, that everyone in the room was harmless and sane. The office was over-heated, the lighting system hard on the nerves, and we were cast up by the war. Safe and high and dry was Wing-Commander Meadmore, the possessed, who spent his working time tracing the cabooses that American railroads were forever pinching from Canada and then abandoning on sidings in the Middle West. The wartime shortage of cabooses obliged him to search for each like a missing friend, by number, through grimy, fifth-carbon leading-sheets. Aloud he muttered numbers, and sometimes the names of towns: Stony River, Chicoutimi.

When Frank was killed, the days were drawing out by two minutes in twenty-four hours, and the sky was blue as a plate. The telephone on Mr. Prescott's desk rang for me. It was my mother, in Allenton. She asked about my health and gave me news of hers before mentioning that Frank was dead.

"But he's just got there," I said, for it was barely five weeks since Isobel and I had seen him before he left for Halifax and "there." Frank was intended to survive this war, and someone like Davy Sullivan to be killed; but a mistake was made, for Frank was never seen again and it was Davy who came back. My brother had been overseas, and repatriated to Canada after typhoid fever. After a long leave he volunteered to return. He wanted to marry an English girl.

"Can you leave your job?" I heard, shrill and faint. Even now my mother maintained the legend of Isobel and me in natty uniforms with red crosses on our berets. "I think your father would like it if you girls could come down for a couple of days." Frank had been our father's child. It was our mother who wanted the daughters now.

"Is he killed or missing?" This was the crisis, and this was the manner bred since the cradle. All our training was directed towards the emergency, towards how to behave when the moment came. It was for this conversation that I had learned to go blank in the presence of worry and pain, and had been taught it was foolish to weep.

"Killed," said the insect voice, with a hint of melancholy triumph, as if to say it could not have been otherwise. She knew, but did not tell me then, that Frank died in a foolish accident. A coping stone fell on his head. He was on leave in Brighton, with his bride. It might just as easily have been someone else.

"I'll get Isa. We'll come down on the six o'clock."

"It's a slow train. I'll keep dinner for you," my mother said.

The stenographers had stopped rattling the wrappers of their candy bars. I saw on Major Currie a look of soft indecent concern. Every day he read the Killed-Wounded-Missing columns in the *Montreal Star* aloud, tracing the names with his finger. "There's a Duncan," he said once. "Would that be your brother, Mrs. Price?" I learned over the telephone and spoke to Mr. Prescott, who had opened a drawer and pretended to rearrange its contents the instant I said "killed."

"It's about my brother," I said softly. "He's been killed, but I don't know anything more. I think my sister and I should go home."

"Oh, yes." He looked up, unwillingly, with kind, worried eyes. "Take all the time your people need." Adopting my tone, he lowered his voice, as though we were discussing something shameful, a scandal, something no decent family would want known. After I had gone he might stroll across to one of the engineers—perhaps Wing-Commander Meadmore—and say, "It was her brother." The answer would be that it was too bad, but what could you expect in times like these. From "I felt funny just then" to "I fainted" was the truth about times like these, but Wing-Commander Meadmore had never seen himself, and could not know that he died before our eyes, and smelled of his death. I often heard him say, "It's the chance he took," when evil Major Currie came upon a Killed-Wounded-Missing name one of us knew. When Mr. Prescott's son had been killed in the invasion of Europe, the summer before, Mr. Prescott stayed away from the office ten days, giving as an apologetic excuse, "My wife is taking it hard." When he returned he said to me mildly, "I suppose you know about the boy." Months afterwards, he told me with the same gentle discretion that he had established contact with his son through a medium in Rosemount. The lad told the medium he was happy on the other side. "I'm glad, for the wife's sake," Mr. Prescott said.

"What did he expect?" Wing-Commander Meadmore asked me. "What did he go over there for?" Wing-Commander Meadmore, he of the upraised arm and dying animal cry, had expected it. We all expected it, of course. Mr. Prescott developed a tic after his son was killed, an almost imperceptible flutter of the lid of an eye.

I had to fetch Isobel. That was now the most important thing. I would arrive at her office unannounced and bring her the news.

She worked in the maid's room of a large and dirty flat that had been let, furnished, to Czechoslovakian refugees. Madame Adele Tessignier, Isobel's employer, lived in the room and used it as an office, giving her tenants the housing shortage as reason. The refugees must have thought that was the way things were done in Canada, for they never complained.

The building was full of grime and mirrors, and the elevators moved on frayed ropes: but the block had been fashionable thirty years earlier, and the flats were still sought after and highly priced. I saw stiff elderly couples and had glimpses of firescreens. "Rooms full of candy dishes," Isobel had said once, describing as best she could.

I did not think about Frank. I walked, in my snow boots, under a cloudless sky, and thought about Isobel, and Madame Tessignier, and our friend Suzanne Moreau, who was giving a party that night; and when I arrived at the dark and sooty place where my sister worked, I thought, she'll wonder what I'm doing here like this, in the middle of the day.

The maid's room, the office, had its own entrance. From the dark hallway I heard my sister's voice, rapid and light, saying obviously into a telephone, "Is there a garage? Are you leaving the linen and dishes?"

I was astonished years later when Davy Sullivan said, "Madame Tessignier is a crook. In any town but Montreal she'd have been in jail years ago. Isobel's a crook too. She loved the job. She was made for it." I protested, reminding Davy of Isobel's poverty, of the corners she could get into where a dollar-fifty made all the difference. He said that Isobel wasn't interested in money, but in being near someone who was dishonest; it excited her; it excited her to lend her charming face and pretty voice to the business of duping refugees and families who would pay anything for a roof. Davy always went too far. There was a wartime shortage of apartments just as there was of cabooses, and if Isobel hadn't taken that job someone else would. It couldn't have been much fun for her, moving from place to place with Barney, losing half her husband's letters because her address changed so often. I told Davy so, but it was impossible to make him ashamed.

I knocked on the door, and Madame Tessignier, whose bed was behind it, and who spent her time on that bed, let me in. Her fat arm, covered with blue satin—she lived in dressing gowns—barred the way for a moment, and then she recognized me and said, "Eesa, it's your little *sœur*." In the new role of little *sœur* I stepped inside, falsely smiling, and Madame Tessignier said, "You have brought in the cold of the street." She lay down on the bed, and drew an eiderdown from the feet up to her chin. On the shelves surrounding her bed were files, magazines, lists of inventories of furnished apartments, and a photograph of Jean-Claude, a sullen adolescent son. Isobel knew little about Monsieur Tessignier, except that his wife had him followed by detectives for the dismal pleasure she took in reading their reports. She had no intention of granting him the divorce he had urgently been demanding for years, and the detectives were the only financial extravagance she allowed herself. Isobel made a sign to me, a vague wave of the hand, and went on with her inquiry.

"The war is nearly over," said Madame Tessignier, "and the Jews are taking everything."

She seemed deeply unhappy, so small, fat, and round, her hair dyed blue, her face pink, pressed into shape like soft wax.

"Sit on the bed, dear Jean," she said. "I would offer you a chair, but I cannot afford to buy one, and besides the office is so crowded I wouldn't know where to put it. Don't sit too close to me. There, at the foot of the bed. Let us not interrupt sweetest Isobel, who has discovered a completely furnished house. The owners have been called to Ottawa. The house will make many people happy. We can easily get three couples into it. Sweetest Isobel will get them to leave everything behind. That child is an angel."

I sat as far from her as I could, remembering her fear of microbes and germs from the street. Madame Tessignier's clothes were in cases under the bed. One of the filing cabinets was full of hoarded food. On Isobel's desk were a buttery knife and some greasy papers, the remains of a private feast. Sometimes Madame Tessignier was obliged to live in one of the apartments she intended to sublet—during the holidays, for instance, when Jean-Claude had to be decently housed. The prospect terrified her; every day was torment when she thought of the money lost. She was as incompetent as my sister at assembling even the rudiments of living—say, a bed, a table, a chest of drawers—and she always scuttled back to the office and maid's room with relief. Once I remember her in a large new building, living in five rooms with nothing but a bed and a grand piano. She complained that she had to take all her meals standing up, because she used the piano as a table, and that she could not understand why people lived in apartments when an office was so obviously the best place to be.

Isobel put down the telephone. I said, so casually that I knew Isobel would forever despise me, "Mother's just called. Frank's been killed. She'd like us to come down tonight. There's that slow train around six. We might as well get it."

From Isobel's slight frown she might have been thinking about nothing except the train. Madame Tessignier gave a puppy cry. Her mouth widened, her eyes stared, and she put her fat hands to her ears, as if to prevent their receiving further horrors. Instead of applauding the performance Isobel gave her employer a look of great irritation and said, "I'm going to wash." She slammed into the maid's bathroom—where Madame Tessignier kept more food, and a number of coats and dresses on the shower rail—and only then did Madame Tessignier remove her hands. Her first words for Frank were, "Oh my poor Jean-Claude. I am a mother, dear Jean." Jean-Claude was young, and safe in boarding school. Once when Isobel visited the school, he led her into the chapel and kissed her and tried to put his hand inside her sweater. He begged her never to tell—not about the kiss, but about her being in the chapel. It had never been defiled by a woman's presence before.

Isobel returned. She took her coat and scarf from the top of a filing cabinet, where they were rolled in a ball, and sat down to pull on her snow boots. She suddenly pressed her head on the metal surface of the filing cabinet. "I feel sick, I feel so sick," she said softly.

"She loved her brother," said Madame Tessignier, as if I were a stranger.

Frank and Isobel had never got on. Isobel was younger than he, but tougher, a bully. They had often been torn apart in grim and frightening physical quarrels when they were small. When Isobel was only seven she stuffed his mouth full of dirt and grass, and, later, Frank was punished by our father for not defending himself. They had in common one memory: they had both been delicate in health as children, subject to pneumonia and bronchial complaints. Consequently, they spent two winters with a relation of our father who had a small hotel in the Laurentian mountains. This relation, a woman my mother considered friendly but common, promised to be a second mother to them. However, it became increasingly evident from the children's behavior that they were running wild, and that our father's relation had no notion of what a mother ought to be. Our mother also felt that Isobel's character was suffering because she dominated Frank (no one thought of what it was causing Frank) and they were eventually decreed cured, no longer TB types, and dispatched to separate boarding schools in Ontario. They had in common a memory of winter and sun; of choosing whatever they wanted to eat in the hotel dining room—I believe this shocked our mother more than anything else. They could speak French, of a sort, and had experienced a rhythm of life foreign to me. Only occasionally some word, or gesture, would bring them together within this memory, and they would glance at each other, in accord. My mother never encouraged this; but still the memory must have persisted for Isobel, and the person who could share it had gone. So I thought that if Isobel was now feeling sick, it was because in losing Frank she lost two winters of childhood.

Madame Tessignier lay back on her dirty pillows and spoke as if describing monuments to war, motherhood, and the future of nations. She squeezed out a tear—the first I saw shed for Frank. There was a silence. Isobel wound her scarf around her collar, picked up her gloves, and said, "There."

"You know, little Jean," said Madame Tessignier, "business is terrible. There isn't much time. The war will be over soon, everyone says so, and the Jews are taking everything."

I responded. Business was bad? Did she think the war nearly over?

"As a matter of fact," my sister said, "business is good. And the Jews are taking what you've left." She swept oddments off her desk into her open handbag. "Collusion pays."

"I say nothing, because you are suffering," said Madame Tessignier, closing her eyes. "I say only this: the war will soon be over, and we will look back on these years as the happiest of our lives."

"Well, goodbye," said Isobel. She stood with her feet apart, like a child. "I'll be back soon."

Madame Tessignier began to weep, seriously this time. "How can I manage without you?" she said.

"It doesn't matter, does it, if business is over and the Jews have taken everything?" said Isobel.

"Sweetest Jean," said Madame Tessignier to me. "Tell your mother that another mother sends her heart. Her *heart*."

"Thank you," I said, and I did feel guilty about leaving the poor weeping woman alone.

Isobel, without looking at me, began to speak with an intensely pronounced, "Listen!" as if she could not be certain of my attention. "Listen, don't you feel sorry for *her*. You ought to see some of the places she rents to Jews—to refugees, I mean. If there's an ironing board and an egg-beater she says it's a furnished apartment. You should see the key money they pay. She finds out what they've got in the bank. I don't know how. She knows everybody. And then she says the price of the lease, just the lease, not counting the rent, will be just that—whatever she knows they've got. They're used to paying for leases in Europe and they think it's done that way here too. They don't think it's legal, but they're not used to anything being legal. Well, she's got a big rival now.

He's a refugee and a lot of the refugees go to him because they think he's safer than a Canadian. Don't worry about *her*. He's smart, but she knows everybody. She'll win. I've met him. He's a snake, but she's a fat little squirrel with sharp little teeth and she'll..."

She stopped abruptly. The building was full of squeaks and the hum and wheezing of ancient elevators. The elevator bell, after I had pressed it, left a coating of grease on my finger. A hunchback in uniform let us in. We pretended not to see him. The other passenger was a servant wearing a windbreaker over her cotton dress. "Listen," said Isobel again, "we're supposed to go to Suzanne's tonight. At least I am, and I guess she invited you too. It's her birthday. Twenty-three."

"No, twenty-four," I said.

"We're the same age," said Isobel. "I talked to her this morning."

"All I can say is, she was twenty when I met her four years ago, but have it your own way." I sounded like our mother: flat and calm and certain I was right.

It was part of the quality of that day that we should discuss Suzanne Moreau all the way out and into the street, and through a series of short-cut alleys to the street where Isobel lived. We walked on cinders and garbage and snow that looked winters old. From the basement kitchen of a restaurant rose a smell that made me cover my face with my gloved hands. We kept on about Suzanne Moreau, saying we must call her, yes, that one of us must ring and explain why we could not be at her party that night; and yet the "why" was left out of our talk. My sister was still pale and the skin around her eyes seemed bruised. She talked as if she were trying to use her breath, be rid of it, as people do when they fear that an intake of cold air will make them sick. She let me into her flat and kicked off her boots, and dropped her coat on the floor. She had lived here three months without being obliged by Madame Tessignier to move on. I had never known her to stay as long as that anywhere. In these rooms we had last seen Frank: he had spent his last days of leave in Montreal with Isobel.

I picked up her coat and placed her boots neatly in the hall closet.

"I suppose business *is* bad, or Madame Tessignier would have rented this place by now," I said.

"No, it's blackmail, just blackmail. I don't care where I live, but I like scaring her. It's a game. I know so much about her, you see. Her sister has a call house. Suzanne—it's a coincidence—is on the call house party line. She doesn't know it's Madame Tessignier's sister, but I know. I don't care, I don't care about other people's business." She meant that I did, I suppose. She laughed, telling me this. The telephone was on the floor and she knelt down to it, dialing Suzanne's number. We smiled at each other. I had forgotten why we had left our offices—our war jobs—in the middle of the day. I was in Isobel's flat without a false excuse, and could observe the bed, the books, the traces of her life.

"Doesn't answer." She padded around the room in stocking feet, pulling out drawers, opening cupboards. Searching for something—a suitcase?—she pulled our wet snowboots out of the hall closet and dropped them on the polished floor. Her boots were huge, fur-lined; mine were small, the black velvet white where snow had stained it. They lay, ugly, in spreading pools of melted snow. I found myself worrying about the effect on the polished floor, but knew that if I said so Isobel would call me the worst appellation in her vocabulary, an Allenton Mum.

She slept more or less on the floor, on a thin mattress and springs Madame Tessignier had lent her. With half-understood prudishness I sat down on the floor with my back to this bed; it had something to do with Isobel and Alec, and it was something I didn't want to consider too specifically lest my thoughts show on my face. I took the telephone now and called Suzanne. The telephone rang and rang. Isobel had found a paper shopping bag with the name of a grocery store printed upon it. Into this she crammed a toothbrush wrapped in a bit of Kleenex, and wildly folded pajamas. Looking round, distracted, evidently wondering if more objects were required for an absence of four days, she rolled up a sweater and a blouse and thrust those into the bag too. Satisfied, she picked up Barney, who, aware of disaster, had been sitting on the windowsill. He had been moved about so often he had lost his instinct of fear, but not of apprehension. When Isobel picked him up, now, to bear him away to the janitor, he let himself go limp, resigned.

"A fatalist. A Slav, this cat," said Isobel.

The telephone rang in Suzanne's empty rooms. I imagined her kitchen table covered with empty bottles and piles of magazines, and the record albums left behind by her friends. I imagined her towering and surrounded by a multitude of tiny refugees, pin-sized, with anxious pin-sized faces. I saw the paintings on the wall and the frames stacked on chairs. Her bedroom was the size of a cupboard and nearly filled with an unmade bed. It must be curious, empty, except for the emphatic telephone now. "Of course Suzanne's studio is unspeakably filthy," I felt obliged to explain to my invisible mother. The ringing filled the kitchen and the bathroom, where sheets soaked in a rimmed tub. I had never seen her bathtub when it was not being used as a laundry. I could not imagine Suzanne in a perfumed bath; the smell of her bathroom was of Javelle water.

I heard Isobel in the kitchen now collecting Barney's sandbox and drinking bowl. I let the telephone ring three times more and hung up. If Suzanne was home, and not answering, she must have been cursing richly in two languages by this time. It was just as well that I hadn't reached her: I would have stumbled in my explanation about Frank. Suzanne looked at the war as an English-Canadian affair and the death of our brother would be our doing—our collective error, our guilt. Yet she was married to an army private who was in Europe, too. He was a prisoner of war. She was called by her maiden name, Moreau, and scarcely anyone realized she had ever been married. I had never seen his photograph. He had been taken prisoner at Dieppe, in 1942, and vanished from her life. I think she forgot him because she could not imagine where he was. She had never been out of the Province of Quebec, and her mind's eye could not reach the real place we had seen as a make-believe country in films. She could not see the barracks of a prison camp because she had already seen them, gray and white, with film stars suffering and escaping and looking like no one she knew. Surely there was a true landscape—gray, flat, spotted with gray trees and gray wooden houses, where foreign people with gray faces walked in the rain? We all received letters that were real enough, but the letters told us that everything we saw and read was a lie. Davy, Isobel's husband, saw a documentary film about Italy and even though it was a truthful film, and he saw himself, a glimpse of himself, he wrote that it was a lie. "I went out and puked," said Davy's letter—the only letter of his my sister ever showed me. It was Suzanne's husband's bad luck to have disappeared into a sham landscape. The men we knew dissolved in a foreign rain. I think she did not expect ever to see him again.

"Suzanne doesn't answer," I said, when Isobel returned.

"Never mind. We'll call from home tonight."

"I've got to go and pack now," I said.

"You don't need anything," said Isobel. "You can buy a toothbrush. We'll miss the train."

Now that was unreasonable, for it was only a little after four o'clock. Isobel simply could not be bothered coming with me to Alma's apartment. She was irritated by its red maple furniture and the picture of Bulldog Churchill. She knew it was Alma's taste, but blamed me. I hadn't Isobel's advantages, I now thought meanly. I couldn't afford to live alone, and had no one to blackmail into letting me have a free apartment.

"Don't come, we can meet at the station," I said.

She was so self-centered, so unconcerned, with her love and her cat and her good looks and her shopping bag. All she wanted was to get me out of the way so that she could call Alec and tell him she was leaving; and that was enough to silence and humble me, it seemed so important. Isobel followed me to the door as if I had said nothing.

"We'll take a taxi to your place," she said. "I'll pay." I interpreted this as an insult, knowing she considered me avaricious. I was saving money against my husband's return. We had already discussed this. Why need I always defend myself, when I was in the right?

Two hours had now passed since our mother had called me. My sister and I ground up Côte des Neiges Road in an overheated taxi. One of the chains around the tires had broken and made an irregular beating sound. Even that was enough to distract me.

It seemed wrong when I thought of it later. I scarcely mourned my brother; it seems to me now that I ought to pay for my indifference. But that series of incidents, feeling nagged by the need to cancel a party, or being offended when there was no cause for it, or thinking about the beating of a broken chain on the road, continued to drag on and away from the reason for my being out and alone with my sister on a working day. I withdrew from my brother's death into a living country of wrangles and arrangements and sharing taxis; of packing and snatching

Alma's stockings from the towel rack instead of my own; of leaving
Alma a note; of buying magazines and cigarettes and tickets for a train:
all of it took Frank's share of my time. Although I speak now of his
death, his death did not occur. What happened was that he was never
seen again. He disappeared, like Suzanne's husband, in an unfamiliar
landscape, under cinema rain, and we never saw him again.

At the station Isobel bought chewing gum because she thought she
might be trainsick. Then it was dark, and the blackened windows of
the train gave her boned face back like a dramatic photograph. "I feel
sick, I really do," she said, leaning back and closing her eyes. I bought
candy from the vender—Commando Crunch, which was all he had
left—but Isobel asked me not to unwrap it in her presence. She said
the smell of ersatz chocolate would finish her. We discussed why this
should be so. These diversions occupied us. I ate my patriotic candy,
and proved to Isobel that she was not really sick. When we reached
Allenton we found our mother bound with trifles and worries, the
crumbs of life, and there we were, an ordinary family, wondering only
how it was that we were together at such an odd time of the week, and
at such an unlikely time of the year. We spoke of the train journey, and
arranged where we were to sleep. Our parents now slept apart, and my
mother occupied what was still called the girls' room. Isobel was put
in a spare room full of jam jars and apples on shelves. "You'll sleep well
there," my mother said. "Apples give you pleasant dreams." I was to
have Frank's bed. I unpacked in his room as if it were the most natural
place to be. We were so busy with the details involved by our simply
being here, at home, together, that it was some time before we spoke
about him at all.

6

"Poor Frank," our mother said. That was the principal change when
we did speak about him: the new little word "poor." Our mother walked
about the glassed-in sun porch, where she had lighted a kerosene stove
not so much for our comfort as to assure the survival of her plants. She
seemed to be walking with a reason for walking, not simply drifting

or nervously pacing. She walked up and down, past the wicker sofa and the wicker table, and pulled dead bits off the geraniums, and she sighed, and said, "Poor Frank." It was half-past six o'clock, too dark for reading. The pattern of the pierced stove, like a hoop of bright embroidery, became distinct on the ceiling. Isobel read, her face nearly pressed to the book. She was reading *Anne of Green Gables*, which had belonged to both of us, but had her name on the flyleaf. Our mother said, "You're a silly girl, you'll ruin your eyes," and, stopping by the door, where the light was, suddenly revealed the porch in its winter shabbiness and our father in his wretchedness. He sat, physically shrunken, at the far end, where a draft seeped through the ill-fitted double windows. The panes went black and reflected us: Isobel reading, our mother erect by the door, our father mourning and small. We were in a lighted cage. We could be seen from the street. Anyone going by in the snow would think, The Duncans have lost their boy, the girls are down from Montreal.

"There's a kind of inner serenity about you," dear Alma Summer had once said to me. Was there, now? I smiled at myself in the black glass.

"Would you girls eat floating island for dessert tonight?" our mother said. "Because if you'd like it, I'll make it right now." We considered it. I could not help considering it. Floating island? Isobel looked up from her reading and lowered the book to her lap. It was so important. "Isa," our mother went on, "I want you to give me all your sweaters tomorrow, everything you've brought. I don't know what you've been washing that sweater with, but it wasn't Lux."

Across the snowy lawn we saw into our neighbors' lighted living room. The neighbors were careful not to look at us, but they must have said, "The Duncans have lost their boy."

The ghost in the Allenton house cannot be Frank's. If Frank had left part of himself there I would have felt him then, that night. He left no trace; nothing of him came back.

We had sat here, Isobel and I side by side, at Christmastime. There were evergreen wreaths with electric candles in three of the windows, and a Christmas tree in the bay window of the room behind us; and we had looked straight over the lawn to our neighbor's tree. Frank was here, on embarkation leave. Light haired, stiff shouldered, sharp nosed, he sat in the middle of the porch on a wicker chair and was polite to aunts. The aunts, our mother's sisters, talked about their own sons, who had done well in the war and were higher ranking than Frank. Everyone they knew had done well in this war; they knew a milkman who was a major. Isobel smoked one cigarette after the other because she knew it would annoy our father's mother, our least-liked relation. Our father was being dreary over Ypres. Whenever anyone spoke to Frank, our father butted in with a reminder of the war he had been in, and boasted about the lice, the rats, and the dirty water, and rolled his eyes at the mention of "France." "*Auprès de ma blonde*," our staid father intoned, and my mother's glance met mine; her look told me that he'd had too much to drink, but that this was a permissible occasion and she was not going to do anything about it.

Our mother was behaving strangely too. She seemed to have mixed, tumultuous feelings about Frank now that it appeared he might be killed after all. She had always said she knew nothing about the training of boys; they were boisterous, hard to understand, and inevitably faithless. She would have wanted an ideal daughter, as pretty as Isobel and tractable as Jean. In a way she had nothing, and was about to lose the boy. Her odd behavior that day took the form of brusque assaults of tenderness that sent Frank pale with dismay. We said little about his leaving then, just as now, six weeks later, we said next to nothing about his death. At Christmas we spoke of the dinner we had eaten, and the snow weighing the branches of the trees, and of the coal shortage. We spoke of Frank's journey as if he were going to a football game in another town. Isobel was restless on the creaking wicker sofa; she crossed her long legs and blew cigarette smoke so that our least-liked grandmother could go through an exaggerated pantomime of having to beat it away. Isobel looked severely from face to face. "Being direct" was her preferred expression then—I think she had it from Suzanne— and I suppose she wanted everyone to make a statement, as in one of those plays where every character suddenly says what he thinks in the most disconcerting manner imaginable. If Frank had never given us great cause for pride, he had never until recently given us cause for alarm: I expect she wanted statements made about that. Our mother should have said, "I have never loved you enough," and our father, "I love you but I am envious." Frank, stiff, silent Frank, ought to have said—if one were to complete the deranged dialogue—"I don't want to go back. I've had enough. But appearances are in favor of my going. I secure my parents' position. I assure myself of their esteem. Besides, I am bored here and have nothing to do, and I have a girl in England who must be married."

Our upright brother had left behind a girl whose daughter had since been born. We spoke of Enid decently as his fiancée. News of her misfortune had passed through the family from hand to hand, like a forfeit. The event ought to have satisfied our father once and for all about Frank's possible girlishness, but he seemed taken aback and never mentioned it. Enid was already writing our mother her first stoic letters about hardship and destruction, mentioning her own troubles in such a delicate way that she seemed to avoid and take them for granted all at once. Our mother, far from innocent, almost never taken in, said that Enid was plucky, and that those English girls couldn't be having much fun, what with all the rationing and the danger. "They've got our men," I said once, suddenly, not knowing I had an opinion about it until the words were out. My mother answered in a low, intense, and anxious voice, as close to passion as I had ever seen her. England was a permitted emotional channel; one could be as worked up as one liked over the white cliffs of Dover. Enid was of the same race as Churchill and the King and Queen. She was excused.

Dutiful Frank stayed in Allenton twelve days of his leave. On the thirteenth and next to last day he was sent up to Montreal like a bundle of laundry, our mother having announced that what he wanted now was the company of his sisters. She had no qualms about deciding what other people wanted, and the odd thing was that they usually ended up wanting what she had decided. Frank arrived in Montreal announcing that he wanted to see his sisters. He had seen us ten days before, at Christmas, and we had said goodbye then. Isobel and I had a scrambled discussion by telephone about where he was to stay. Unexpectedly Isobel said she would have him. They quarreled so much when they were together that I often forgot they were really close friends. Isobel's apartment was small, but she could put a camp cot in the hall, which she would borrow from some other Tessignier hovel.

I met Frank at the station on Saturday afternoon. He was leaving Monday. He kissed me solemnly and gave me news of our parents. I explained about his staying with Isobel; he was instantly suspicious.

"What's her place like?"

"All right, but bare. It's not hers. It's one of Madame Tessignier's so-called furnished apartments. Isa lives around in these places till they're rented. She moves every few weeks. She doesn't pay any rent or gas or light. Don't tell Mother."

"That's darned nice, about the gas and light," said Frank.

I told him that the apartment was over a garage, and sometimes the noise from the garage drove everybody but Isobel mad. It was sunny (I was answering Frank's questions) and Isobel could see cheerful happenings on the street: drunks beating their girls, and American tourists looking for butter and meat. I had realized that morning that Frank was the head of the family, for even Isobel had been in panic about what he might think of her way of life. She had borrowed a red counterpane from Suzanne, a remnant of Suzanne's homespun old Quebec period, and begun painting the kitchen cupboards. I had collected for her a pillow, a blanket, a lamp, and a blue glass bowl that had been one of my wedding presents. Isobel was grateful for everything. We were both of us nervous as birds.

She was warm and cheerful when I returned with Frank, and threw her arms around him. "I've got a huge bottle of rye," she said to him. "All for you, only you have to drink it here."

The camp cot lay in pieces on the hall floor, with my folded blanket. "I hope to God you know how to put that thing up," she said, "because I don't." The room smelled of fresh paint, of the apples she had put in my blue glass bowl, and of Isa's own blond fragrance. I remember now why Tom said she smelled of gardenias. There were four long yellow tulips in a milk bottle on the windowsill; they threw their shadows on the bare floor, in a rectangle of pure winter sun.

"It looks almost furnished," I said. "There's even a chair."

"A friend of mine made it," said Isobel proudly. It was canvas chair shaped like a hammock on tiny wire legs. Frank sat down on its edge and was immediately toppled back into it. I got him a chair from the kitchen, a sensible wooden upright chair, and he sat down on that. He looked at Barney, curled on the bed, and offered the information that our mother disliked cats.

"Has she ever liked anything, except this damned war?" said Isobel, pouring rye into three tumblers lined up on the windowsill.

"Now, Isa," said Frank, comfortably, in a male head-of-family role. When the three of us were alone he took on this air. He thought his sisters' destinies depended on his strength of character and his judgment. If he could, he would have put us under glass bells, protected from dust and the elements, until he could decide what was to be done. He did not consider us married. Our husbands had never been there, except as pictures. Frank was too mild to believe that women should be driven, but there was no doubt he was convinced they ought to be led. "Why don't you get Mum to send you some furniture?" he said, looking around the room. This was his way of commenting on the canvas chair.

"The apartment isn't hers," I said. "I told you."

"I guess you can't buy much stuff now," he said.

"There's a war on," I said primly, sitting on the bed, trying to stroke Barney.

"All the same, you'd think they would . . ." Either Frank often forgot to finish his sentences, or I forgot to listen to the end. He sniffed the fresh paint and said, "Is it safe to sleep here?" Then he said, "This is a new place, isn't it? I mean, it's remodeled. It's funny, this Mrs. Tessignier getting permission to remodel a building in wartime. A whole apartment house."

"She just has this one apartment," I said.

"The Carters at home couldn't even get permission to build a garage. Who owns this place, anyway?"

"Madame Tessignier," I said.

"She rents it. Who does she rent it from?"

"A man called Farrow," Isobel said, adding ice and water to our drinks.

She turned to the telephone a split second before it rang. She picked it up from the floor and put it on the windowsill; she leaned on the sill, partly screened from me by her long hair, her eyes absently looked away, out the window, into the sunny, frozen day. All the roads that separated her from Frank, from me, led her to Alec; I was sure it was he. Her voice, after the first words, dropped, became gentle and trusting. I sat on the red counterpane, warmed by the sight of the oblong of sun on the floor, and told myself I was warmed by the sudden presence of love. To my horror and shame, tears came to my eyes, but then Barney jumped on my lap, and I stroked him and bent my head while Isobel talked. Frank picked up a book, discovered it was verse, and put it down. Isobel was removed from us to a warmer world, to a climate I could sense but not capture, like a secret, muddled idea I had of Greece, or the south, or being warm. What she said was ordinary enough. She said:

"Frank's here. He's on his way overseas. He's sleeping here for the weekend. No, I think he likes the idea. Jean's here. We're going to take him to Suzanne's. Oh, one of her parties. It'll be either for a refugee or a pansy, they're the only people she knows these days. You know, it happened again. I knew the phone was going to ring. Oh, about half a second before. ESP. No, don't laugh. It *is* ESP. I'll tell you when I see you. Soon. Soon, soon. What? Are you alone? Well, I thought so. That remark. Yes, soon. Goodbye. Soon. Goodbye."

When she turned back to us we had had time to adjust our faces and perhaps our thoughts. Frank had picked up the book again and opened it, and I was able to look with no question in my eyes.

"Which Farrow is that?" said Frank.

"Farrow?" said Isobel.

"Who owns this place," said Frank patiently. "Farrow, did you say, or Farrell?"

"The Farrows of Upper Galicia," said Isa, still smiling, still in the voice she had used with Alec, as if the break could not be made all at once. "Of Upper Galicia. A special branch."

"I thought so," my brother said, with great satisfaction. He put the book down. "That's exactly what I thought. The names they take! I don't know why the real Farrows don't sue."

He was driving Isa away. She looked absent, indifferent, now, as she did at Allenton, retreating from the family, "behaving." She handed Frank his glass rather abruptly, and gave me mine with a gesture less brusque.

"Farrow," said Frank, as if determined to drive her still farther off. If it had been in my power to make a decision of that sort, I might have hit him with the blue glass wedding present.

"Don't bother about it," I said, stroking the cat, slowly. "The real money behind this place is all Scot. Farrow's only a small partner, a midget. The money is a man called MacKenzie Hamilton."

"I don't believe it," said Frank. Nevertheless he was silent for half a minute. It was difficult for him to find fault with the integrity of a Scot. Our father believed that Scottish blood was the best in the country, responsible for our national character traits of prudence, level-headedness, and self-denial. If anyone doubted it, our father said, the doubter had only to look at the rest of Canada: the French-Canadians (political corruption, pusillanimity, hysteria); the Italians (hair oil, used to bootleg in the 'twenties, used to pass right through Allenton); Russians and Ukrainians (regicide, Communism, pyromania, the distressing cult of nakedness on the West Coast); Jews (get in everywhere, the women don't wear corsets); Swedes, Finns (awful people for a bottle, never save a cent); Poles, hunkies, the whole Danubian fringe (they start all the wars). The Irish were Catholics, and the Germans had been beyond the pale since 1914. The only immigrant group he approved of were the Dutch. A census had revealed that although there were a quarter-million of them in the country, they were keeping quietly to themselves on celery farms in Western Ontario, saving money, not setting fire to anything, well-corseted, and out of politics. Their virtue, in fact, was that until the census one needn't have known they existed.

Frank continued to eye me suspiciously. Isobel was completely absent, sitting in the canvas chair. I said, "Farrow's hard working. He's only been in Canada three years, but he's got all his kids in good schools." (Frank would love that.) "But this MacKenzie Hamilton, now, he's only been here seven months, and he owns most of Peel Street."

There was a long silence. Frank mulled this over; he looked at the white wall and moved his lips. Like our father, Frank respected people who had made money, providing they were not Italian, Irish, Ukrainian and so forth, in which case the rise in wealth was put down to political chicanery and the complete absence of any sort of moral sense. Frank could not criticize the Galician Farrow without involving MacKenzie Hamilton as well. I had invented MacKenzie Hamilton, which poor Frank suspected.

"This Farrow," said Frank, finally. "Why'd he come to Canada?" I could see straight into the thicket of Frank's thinking to the tiny, sunlit clearing he had now discovered. The Scot had come to Canada willingly, because it was a country with a great future: MacKenzie Hamilton stood with his head tilted back and his hands outspread, on a background of pigmy pines. Galician Farrow had come here because he had nowhere else to go. Why wasn't he in uniform, fighting for Galicia?

Isobel suddenly woke up. She said, "Frank, for God's sake cut it out. I get enough of that from Madame Tessignier. If you start about the refugees I'll tell you about my unhappy childhood, and it'll bore you as much as you're boring us now."

"I haven't anything against anybody," said Frank.

"Don't be Christly," said Isa.

"There'll be refugees at the party tonight," I said. "Suzanne has discovered Europe."

"I'm sorry I bored you," said Frank earnestly. "We had exactly the same childhoods, so I don't see how yours could have been unhappy."

He wore his uniform as if he had never worn anything else. With his sandy hair, thin face, blue eyes, he looked as if he had been born to be photographed, in uniform, for the *Montreal Star*. We emptied the bottle, slowly, and the oblong of sun moved over the low red bed, over Barney, over me, and the room grew pale with the winter afternoon, then dark, and Isobel lit the lamp I had brought her that morning. In the new light we seemed softened by the experience of the day. The ashtrays were heaped. Instead of emptying them Isobel brought plates from the kitchen. We played Isobel's Charles Trenet records on a record player I'd never seen before. I guessed that it was a Christmas present from Alec. We played Noel Coward songs for Frank, who was drunk and solemn. He grew protective; assertive; we were his sisters. He observed that I was too pale and Isobel thin. He wondered if it was safe to sleep here, with the smell of paint, but this time his concern was for Isobel and not himself. He said the word "sister" as if it were a figure he had to explain. He looked pleading. All he demanded of us was that we be exactly like the sister he was describing. It was all he demanded of any human being: to be nothing more than a word suggested—sister or mother or husband or friend. A concern for some new, personal idea (brother-in-law) now made him look around the room and ask about Davy's picture. Isobel had put her husband's picture away. It was an enlarged snapshot of a funny clownish boy. She had put it away because it had been taken when he was eighteen and she found that she was writing year after year to a grinning boy instead of to a man of twenty-four. She could not understand the letters she received, and so she supposed he was writing to a much younger girl too. I would never have dared ask the question about Davy's picture. Isobel told Frank why she had put it away as if Frank were her conscience.

"Yes, I know what you mean," said Frank. "But just the same I'd leave it out somewhere. This way, it looks as if you didn't care."

Presently—I must have gone to sleep on the bed—I heard Frank say, "I don't know why, but I never liked a book like I liked *Butterfield 8*."

"You can't say 'like a book like I liked,'" said my sister. The pupils of her eyes were huge. "I don't know what you are supposed to say but I know it isn't 'like a book like I liked.'"

Frank said, "Yes, and you know something else? A book like that, I wouldn't give it to my mother to read."

"Neither would I," said Isobel. "If I had a mother I wouldn't let her read anything. Look at Jean, sound asleep with her eyes open."

"Ears too," said Frank, but I must have dreamed that Frank said this, for it was superimposed with the words, "The bottle's killed." My memory after that is our being all three in a restaurant, eating fried chicken, on the way to Suzanne's party. It was January 1945. We sat in a booth in a restaurant. Snow fell heavily on the street outside. I have forgotten if any important historical events were then taking place.

My concern was the party, and whether Frank would like Suzanne. I think that was how it was. I am the only person who can tell the truth about anything now, because I am, in a sense, the survivor. Suzanne is still alive, but I never see her. She must be in her forties. I imagine her thin and hard with hard dyed hair. She was twenty-three then. I was proud of her because Isobel liked her, and because I had met her first. We had lived in the same boarding house when I came up to Montreal, the summer I was married. I had never in my life lived in a city during a heat wave. In this worn and dusty house I heard gusts of words and music, the creaks and slams and the dropped hangers and vague exclamations that seemed to me all of life. Sitting by the window one breathless July night I recognized for the first time the feeling of a city. Suzanne had never known anything else. She was so fierce, white-skinned, black-haired, that if she had not spoken to me first I would never have had enough courage to say hello. She was just out of Beaux-Arts and living on her husband's service allowance and a part-time job as a waitress. She crashed through life, like the farmers in the north of Quebec who, settling on new land, cut every tree in sight just because nothing must stand. Suzanne crashed on, dragging with her a younger sister, Huguette, who was sweet-faced and barely literate, cutting down everything she saw standing. The two girls were out of a slum in the east end of a city I could barely imagine.

I remember Suzanne's telling me straight away that she had a lover. He was a professor who had lost his post at the Beaux-Arts owing to some intrigue I was unable to follow. He had a second mistress, who satisfied certain needs for the professor Suzanne could but partially gratify. She did not say what they were and I had no idea even approaching the sexual reality she was talking about. Suzanne had a simple view of life and love then; she thought a man of genius had a right to as many women as he appeared to need. Her feelings toward him were almost maternal. I once accompanied her on a Sunday morning. The professor having been on a bender of three or four days with the second mistress, Suzanne began to fret in case he hadn't found time to eat during these busy hours, and we traveled miles by streetcar in order to leave a loving message and a bit of raw steak in his apartment mailbox. Years later I was disappointed to meet the professor at one of her parties. He sat in a corner, wan and moth-eaten, gray-haired, dressed with a Sunday air like a local farmer in town for the weekend. That, indeed, was his origin, and a long prewar residence in Paris had done nothing to modify his looks. Suzanne, furious with me for saying so, remarked that I was a hopeless provincial and would never be anything else, since I lacked imagination and could rely on nothing but the evidence of my experience. I begged her forgiveness and admitted she was right. I had never been to Paris and could only imagine how people there might differ from farmers.

Suzanne met Isobel through me (oh, the pride of that introduction!) and it was Isobel who found Suzanne her studio on Oxenden Street—two north-facing rooms so dank and ratridden that even Madame Tessignier could not disguise them as nests for refugees or servicemen. Slowly, Isobel and Suzanne became friends. A pattern of friends and encounters took form, and after a time I saw Isobel only at Suzanne's parties.

"Isa won't get in any trouble there," I remember saying to my mother. "Suzanne only knows pansies." In relation to my mother, something always compelled me to be disloyal to my friends. Suzanne's friends, now, were young refugees. They seemed to me alike, and examined me in the same tense-mouthed manner. I was considered the symbol of English Canada. I told my mother so, and we laughed. Then I was ill with remorse, for Suzanne had been abrupt but generous with me always. I remember her thrusting into my hands a drawing of hers I had liked, or a pair of nylon stockings some man, perhaps one of her sister's racketeer boy friends, had given her. I remember walking away from her studio down a curved, foggy street, while flower-shaped lamps came out of the fog, and the cobbles of the street shone as if they had risen from the sea; I held the little parcel of whatever it was she had given me—stockings, or a rolled-up sketch—and I remember thinking, Now, this is the happiest moment of my life, I shall never be happier than now.

I hoped that in the presence of Frank Suzanne would not be too openly ironic about the war. Her new cult of refugees had taught her to say "anti-fascist," but she could not get over her idea of war as a social event for the English. I needn't have worried. Frank was given the same wary care as visiting parents in boarding school. One of Suzanne's new friends offered him a cigarette with trembling hands. In that atmosphere, where everyone represented something other than himself, Frank in his uniform was simply heroic. The uniform represented the fight for democracy and the betterment of mankind, and his physical coloring gave him the Anglo-Saxon appearance required for decent fighting. He was off to rescue any number of less fortunate people, many of them darker than himself. His conventional manners stood for order, and his unloquaciousness was the modesty of the doomed. Family instinct compelled me to stay by his side until Suzanne suddenly emerged and said, "Can't I talk to this boy?" She took his arm and guided him around the studio, making people move when they were in his way. "Did you paint all this?" I heard Frank say. Suzanne scarcely ever showed anyone her paintings in this way, but perhaps she had never known anyone like Frank. She looked at him from time to time as they circled the room, saying little. She was not mocking, as she often had been with me, but almost supplicating. Was Frank the person she wanted to reach? I was certain he would say "What are they supposed to be?" of her pictures, but to my astonishment he thought that everything looked like something. It was the first abstract art he had seen, except in magazines, and that was what he thought: everything looked like something. He saw a beach scene with children playing, Japanese women crossing a bridge, a plane smashed on a mountain, a table and window and somebody's frightening head at the window. He saw a fish in a bowl with flowers behind the bowl.

"Good," said fierce Suzanne, showing her white teeth when she laughed. She was a black and white girl: white teeth, white skin, black hair, a black scowl. She was dirty: I mean by that physically dirty. She slipped her arm around Frank, an incredible mark of her favor; but he moved slightly when she touched him, and I wondered for the first time what Enid was like.

My sister lay on the double bed in the next room, her head on her hand, her straight hair covering the hand, and stared at a boy from Halifax who was reciting, from memory, the opening sentences of his novel. The party was being given for him. "I thought he was a genius," said Suzanne. "My mistake." The new boy, the mistake, looked miserable. He sat beside Isobel, and droned on: "He walked through the hall. A rose fell. Roses, he thought. Blood." He would not have Isobel to himself for long. In a few minutes she would be surrounded by the men to whom she was nearly a legend: the young mistress of a middle-aged man to whom she was completely faithful. She looked as if love absorbed her so completely that she hadn't time for the ordinary cares of life. I observed her cracked, scuffed moccasins, and the blouse slipping out of the band of the skirt. She looked at the novelist with great kindness.

"I want to ask you a question," said an unknown man. "Why'n't you ever get tight? Why'n't you let yourself go?" Earnest, red-eyed, watery-kind—I have no idea who he was. I said crossly, "Well, I am tight, if you want to know," but he thought I was making fun of him.

Suzanne showed Frank a poem written by the boy from Halifax. The boy was still clinging to Isobel, as if he knew by now that Suzanne considered him a mistake. Suzanne read aloud: "And wash my sweating face."

"Lousy, eh?" she said, but Frank thought it was good. He said she had never been in the service and knew nothing about sweat.

"I've been poor, I've lived where there wasn't any water," said Suzanne, who was proud of this.

Frank was entranced, polite, and receptive. I had never known him. I heard Suzanne telling him about her party line, which was connected with a call house on Pine Avenue. She had once heard a distinguished lawyer say to a distinguished colleague, "Come right away, she's got high school girls." Frank smiled, a grave, friendly smile I had never seen, as if he might have been either of those two men. It was a pity I could not see him for the first time, now, without knowing he resembled our father, or had been bullied, and had left in England an illegitimate child.

Some of Suzanne's refugees had formed a circle, sitting on the floor, with their beer glasses inside the magic ring. They sang softly, "Freiheit." There was a girl with them, a little blond girl who had fallen in love with one of them. Her hand was in his and she swayed, her eyes closed, and sang "Freiheit." I knew in an instant that Frank wouldn't like this. The refugees could sing anything they chose, but not the Canadian girl. He looked at the girl and his mouth closed as if on a secret. Suzanne noticed nothing. She and Frank sat side by side on a table and I stood before them. She went on telling him about the party line. It would seem curious to him, subversive even, to sing freedom during a war. The very idea was anti-duty. One could be anti-duty or anti-government or even antiwar if one were a crackpot, but one had better not be anti-circumstance. It was against the circumstance to sing of freedom now. "*Freiheit*" said the little blond girl emphatically, eyes shut, swaying.

We were nearly the last to leave. We walked in snow, our arms linked, and in the curtain of snow Frank said, "Good party. That Suzanne, she's got a sense of humor." He shook his head at the memory of her, smiling and secretive. Snow lay thicker and thicker on our shoulders and our hair and the stuff of our coats. Frank suddenly said, "Did you see the girl singing?"

"Which one?" said Isobel.

"On the floor, singing in German. A little blonde."

"I was in the other room," my sister said.

"I saw her," I said.

"Well, she looks like Enid," said Frank. "That's what she looks like, the same hair and all. Enid can sing too."

"I'll ask Suzanne who she is," said Isobel.

His answer was, "You know what I said before? About Davy's picture? I'd leave it out if I were you. This way, it looks bad. Whatever your personal feelings are you shouldn't make it look as if you don't care."

They put me into a taxi then, and Frank instructed the driver to drive with care; he was taking over my destiny again. He and Isobel walked on in the snow. I slept through the next day, Sunday, and when I rang Isobel's number in the evening there was no reply. They had gone to a movie. On Monday he went to the station alone. We did not say goodbye, and I never saw him again.

In February, from the train that was taking Isobel and me to Allenton, we saw another lighted train pass with such speed that we might have been standing still. The drawn-out sweeping whistle rushed by the windows. It was the Boston train, which had seemed to me on winter nights before I married the sound of hope and escape. Afterwards it was the sound of nostalgia, as if there were a journey I had once made and now remembered. "Oh, you know, he isn't better off!" Isobel cried as if I had said it were possible. She said it to our reflections in the train window. It was all I ever heard her say about Frank.

7

Our period of family mourning continued for three days. One night I saw, or thought I saw, or may have dreamed, that my father sat on the stairs weeping. Our mother stood a few steps below him so that their faces were nearly level. She was in a flannel dressing gown, a plait of gray hair undone and over one shoulder. Patient, waiting, she held a glass of water to his lips as if control could be taken like a pill. Everything in that scene, which I must have dreamed, spoke of the terror of pity. "The girls are home," she said, for fear that we wake and see him and join him in grieving aloud.

On the last night Isobel came into Frank's room. I was sitting up in Frank's bed writing to my husband. Tom was in Holland. I wrote to a legendary husband, in a place I assumed must exist. Both of us wrote frequently, as if we wanted to say, "I am doing my best, I am not to blame." I had curled the ends of my hair and tied round the curls a coral chiffon scarf I had found in my overnight case. It must have been a scarf belonging to Alma, snatched from the towel rack together with Alma's stockings. Isobel peered round the door; I think she smiled. "Can I come in for a minute? Wait, I'll shut the window." She crossed the room and disappeared behind the drawn curtains. "There's snow all over the floor," she said, emerging. "How do you stand it, sitting there in the cold?" Her voice was light and full of life. I never could match the breathless child's voice with someone who seemed to me so closed and careful. That day my mother and I had listened to a radio interview with a returned soldier. "What are your first impressions of good old Montreal?" asked the bright announcer. "The girls have these awful voices," said the new repatriate. "Thank *you*," my mother said, turning him off.

Isobel sat down, shivering, at the foot of the bed. Her hair was streaky and dark at the roots, as if it had been dyed. Our mother had mentioned it that evening: "Isa, when did you last give your head a good wash?"

"The other day," my sister said, indifferently. "It's all going dark. I must be getting a cold or something."

"Fine hair is a curse," our mother said, with the pride one owed a divine affliction.

Isobel propped her elbow on the iron bedstead and dropped her head on her hand. It was a romantic pose—knees bent, one hand palm upward on her lap. She resembled the tired figures named "Hope" and "Waiting" on colored postcards of the First World War. She moved, sighed, smiled at me, and for a moment I saw why Suzanne had called Isobel lavish. *Personnage aux Plumes*. A golden bird. How foolish all of that was, when I think of it soberly! She was a tall, slouching, untidy girl in a faded dressing gown. There was no limit to my delusions then. They were fed in solitude, on the wildness of people like Suzanne. I had no reason then to live in reality, as I have now. Looking back and down from reality, I can correct the story about plumes: Isobel was considered attractive, though not a perfect beauty, and she was not lavish, and not golden, and not a bird. Those are fancies.

"What do you do when you can't sleep?" Isobel said. I had asked Alec about sleeping once, on Sherbrooke Street.

I said, "Alma gives me a pill."

"Where does she get them?"

"From the nurse at the office infirmary. That nurse is insane," I said. "She gives out phenobarb and codeine like candy. Some of the old girls in the company live on it."

"Listen," Isobel said. "I'm pregnant. That's why I feel sick all the time. I think being sick is only being frightened. I'm two months. I knew it when Frank was here. I wasn't certain but I knew."

"Don't tell Mother."

"Mother! Why do you think I'm telling you?"

She hadn't shut the window properly. I felt a draft of thin snowy air.

From that moment I stopped being the stranger on the dark street and I moved into the bright rooms of my sister's life. The doors were opened to me; everything had been leading to my entrance, my participation. Frank's old room, with his faded collection of butterflies and his maps and his schoolbooks in a glassfront case, disappeared with his memory. If Isobel needed me, then I had overcome the common inheritance, the family walls. I was up and closing the window against the draft before she had finished speaking. On my way back to bed I pulled a corner of the blanket over her bare feet. She seemed to have the lassitude of pregnancy, the droop of wrist, the relaxed fingers. She did not notice that I had covered her feet. The dressing gown she wore had belonged to both of us years before. It was inches short for her long arms. She said, "When we were kids we couldn't get away with a midnight talk, could we? We'd hear 'Jean-an-Isa. Isa-an-Jean. Quiet. It's late.' You know, for years I thought Mother could read our minds and see through walls."

"I still think it."

"I hate nicknames," Isobel said. "Isa. Isn't that ugly? Jean, now, that's plain."

"Mother thought I'd be plain."

"Mother didn't think anything. She named you after Granny Stewart, only Granny Stewart left it all to charity. Plain names are better, and there mustn't be nicknames. I say Alec, not Al. I'm the only person who does. I think his wife says Al, when she doesn't say 'My husband, Mr. Campbell.' Al sounds like somebody's no-good brother drinking beer in a tavern."

Our wishes are granted when we are least ready. How often had I prowled around her house, waiting for a word, a half-open door, a sleeping sentry, so that I could see what it was to be Isobel, to have Alec, to be loved? The door opened, but I was unprepared.

It wasn't easy, this business with Alec, said Isobel calmly. He had the wife to support, and the children. When Isobel and Alec married—as of course they would—Isobel would have to keep on working. She knew she would work all her life for Bitsy and Bitsy's children. She didn't mind. There was Davy. She didn't want me to think she didn't care about Davy. She knew I disliked him, but did I know him, really? Wasn't I a bit prejudiced? What had he ever said to me that was impolite? She wrote Davy all the time, but she was writing to a kid. With Alec it wasn't the same thing. Alec was older. When she measured

Davy against Alec she saw that Davy wasn't growing. He hadn't moved. Of course it wasn't his fault. The army was adolescent. Alec said so. Did I know, Davy still had that business about Thomas Wolfe? Yes, still, and he went on about Wolfe in nearly every letter. Wasn't he ever going to read anything else? Davy was still where they had been a long time ago. How many years? She had loved Davy, but Davy couldn't help her now. He needed help himself. He was a little peculiar, a little too young; and she was a little crazy too, so it would never do, she and Davy together. Alec had said so. Had I never noticed she was a little crazy? Well, she was. She knew it. Sometimes she had to stop while she was doing something ordinary, some commonplace thing like brushing her hair or looking for a postage stamp, and she had to say, "Is this the right thing to be doing? Am I right?" and she would be full of fear in case she had been about to do the wrong thing. Every step she took might be a step in a trap. Am I right? she had to keep saying. Is this all right? Am I doing what I ought to be doing? Alec knew. He kept her sane. He was the rock. As long as he was there she could behave like other people. She might have spent her life being a little weak, a little frightened, if it hadn't been for him. It was the only kind of love, Isobel said calmly. Alec had told her so. He had said it was the best thing in the world for her, this secret. You need to have someone between you and the rest, she said; someone between you and the others, blotting out the light.

She may not have said "blotting out the light," and I may distort the remembered scene if I say she put up her hand, flat, to indicate the kind of shutting out.

This had been spoken in the most simple tone. There was no intensity, and no drama in her voice. Nevertheless I had the feeling that I had been listening to something completely astonishing and greatly intimate. I understood as I had just before the automobile crash with Tom the inevitability of dying: I experienced again the pool of saliva under the tongue and the swollen lips. The words I had thought then came back now: That is what it is like. I understood she had told me something I wanted to know. I would have gone once more to the window, for the sake of something to do, but there was no real reason for moving. I sat straight, knees bent, and clasped my knees with hands

as thick as pieces of wood. What had troubled me? The words, Someone between you and the rest? The wall suddenly there, immovable, in
the headlights of the car?

Presently I thought she had said everything and I allowed my hands
to come apart. The movement brought Isobel to life. "I'm afraid of
Alec's children," she said. "They frighten me. I saw them once in his
car. He was driving and he saw me, but he didn't know me. He saw me
but he didn't *know*. When he's not with them he doesn't know anyone
but me." More silence. She sighed, smiled, played with the edge of the
blanket I had turned over her feet. I had a vain reaction. I began to
undo the coral chiffon scarf, which I knew was making me very homely,
and take the pins out of my hair. Isobel would come and live with me.
Alma would have to go. She would pack her ribboned combs and her
red maple furniture and go.

"You know why I've told you, don't you?" Isobel said. "I don't need
just an address. I don't need just good advice."

"You don't need any address except mine. You don't have to go
anywhere except with me."

"I don't need an address," Isobel said again. "I can get that from
Suzanne. I don't need advice about drinking gin or taking boiling-hot
baths. I need somebody's whole attention."

"Who else is there?" I said, creating a fantasy that we were sisters,
therefore confidants, therefore friends.

She gave me an exasperated and deliberately wounding glance.
"There's Suzanne," she said. "She's sensible, she minds her own business,
she doesn't preach. But that works both ways. She minds her own
business when you're in trouble too. Madame Tessignier can pray for
me. But I want somebody's whole attention. I don't want to be alone."

"What about him?" I said bravely.

"There's nothing he can do, is there? I'm not going to tell him until
it's over." She spoke in the obstinate way our mother detested. She was
afraid. I thought again, Someone between you and the rest. There was
a flaw in the story, just as some people said there was a flaw in her face.
Isobel was watching me now. We were sisters, rather alike, in our
brother's room, having a midnight talk. Isobel watched me, with the
expression one of Suzanne's refugees wore when he was trying to explain

in faulty English how things had been at home. Someone who has lost his language wears that look, that despair. Fear, despair: despair is too loud for the quiet night. Remove the word, leave Isobel with cheek on hand, eyes gone yellow in the light of the lamp.

It was plain and simple: She was in trouble and needed me. Pretend I had never circled her life, been the stranger on the street, afraid to meet the eyes of another stranger looking out. "Afraid" is too loud, too. There remains Isobel, then, cheek on hand, a little tired. I remain bolt upright in bed, hugging my knees. Forget despair, fear. We were very ordinary. Leave us there, with the lamp like a ship and the anchors round the shade, and the map on the wall with the Empire in pink, and my sister and I at opposite ends of the bed, with our childhoods between us going on to the horizon without a break. It was so plain and simple; and I thought that unless we could meet across that landscape we might as well die, it was useless to stay alive. She was the most beautiful girl I had ever known, even now, with her hair dark at the roots, her eyes yellow and circled; she was still the most elusive, the most loved. I moved forward, kneeling, in the most clumsy movement possible. It was dragging oneself through water against the swiftest current, in the fastest river in the world; I knelt on the bed near my sister and took her thin relaxed hand in mine. We met in a corner of the landscape and she glanced at me, then slid her hand out of mine and said, "Oh, don't."

I said, "I only meant I would give you what you said, you know, my whole attention."

"I know that," said Isobel. She tried to smile and I tried to return the smile, but I had attempted something beyond our capacities. I drew back and got under the blankets again. Isobel groped with her feet for her slippers. "I didn't bring them," she said to herself. She bowed her head. "I know you'll help me," she said. "That's why I told you. Everything is easy for you. You've got all the wheels turning."

She stood up, shivering as her feet touched the cold floor. She closed the door behind her and I sat still. Her movements cried her defeat. She wanted my attention, and would pay for it. She would tell me about Davy and Alec and life and love. She would tell me everything I wanted to know. She would never shut the door again and leave me on the street. Neither Suzanne nor Alec could give her what she could have from me: the whole attention. She needed it, and she would pay.

I left the scarf and pins on Frank's night table. It no longer mattered whether my hair was straight or curled. I saw the curtains tremble in the draft and went to the window. There is no condition of snow I have not observed, from the first fall to the mild deceptive stillness at night, close to the end of winter, when a dark breath, indrawn and held, warns that death is returning after all. I opened the window to this held breath and knew that winter was still here and might never come to an end.

I continued my letter to Tom. I wrote: "Mother is taking it well, as you might expect from her, but Dad feels it. Isa . . ." It wouldn't hurt to tell him about her. Why not describe the visit to my room and say that she needed me? It would be something to write into the void. Reading my letter in Holland (what was Holland?) he might remember something about me he had forgotten. His memory is for dates, not for feelings; even today he will insist that we last saw Isobel in 1958 and not 1955, as I tell it. He might realize he had not known me well, and he might write, "I was interested in your letter because . . ." It wouldn't hurt. Had he not loved her before proposing to me? Had she not refused him in the car that June day when she was eighteen and in love with Davy Sullivan? Why not tell him that Isobel and I could not look at each other? I wrote: "I don't think I've ever told you, but poor Isa is having a bad time. She's been having an affair with a married man and now she thinks she's pregnant. Don't mention it to anyone." That was how it was. If I sent the letter, the strangeness would be in having written, "Poor Isa," but it would be Isobel delivered, Isobel destroyed. The story could wait. It would always be there to tell. I might never tell it, but there is something in waiting for the final word. One day Isobel might be "poor Isa" in Tom's eyes. He would see and judge for himself.

He would see and judge providing he was not killed; providing the winter ended and we had survived. Madame Tessignier hoped it would never end—the night, the winter, the war. I suspected, then, sitting in Frank's unhaunted room, that all of us, save my brother, were obliged to survive. We had slipped into our winter as trustingly as every night we fell asleep. We woke from dreams of love remembered, a house re-covered and lost, a climate imagined, a journey never made; we woke dreaming our mothers had died in childbirth and heard ourselves saying, "Then there is no one left but me!" We would waken thinking the earth must stop, now, so that we could be shed from it like snow. I knew, that night, we would not be shed, but would remain, because that was the way it was. We would survive, and waking—because there was no help for it—forget our dreams and return to life.

THE FLOWERS OF SPRING

BECAUSE it was a spring day, and because she liked to arrive at the hospital with her arms laden, Estelle brought her husband a bunch of daffodils. They lay now, still untouched, on the foot of his bed.

Malcolm was up. That is, he was in a wheelchair. He had not mentioned the flowers, and had in fact barely spoken at all. After the first perfunctory greeting he had turned to the magazines Estelle had piled on his lap and was greedily absorbed in the new pages.

This is what he lives for from week to week, she thought. It isn't seeing me, regardless of what the doctor says.

They had given Malcolm another of those hospital haircuts, all in tufts with a band of scalp showing at the neck and ears. His face was as white as the pages he turned, and his hands were thin. Surely it was warm enough to begin putting the men in the sun, like plums to be ripened. It was a childish picture, but she amused herself with it for a while. There was nothing to do in any case but wait until Malcolm had read every title and seen every picture.

It was easy for Estelle to sit quietly. She was not a fidget by nature and silence pleased her, provided she had something to think about. She did not care to think about Malcolm, it was true, but watching him lightened her conscience. She felt that she was evaluating his progress (there was none) and checking on the hospital care. It seemed abominable to her, but Malcolm seldom complained.

She watched him now as with the grave care of a child he examined the photograph of a long-legged girl who had been named queen of something. The girl wore a white bathing suit and crown of flowers and she stood looking over her shoulder as if in surprise. Malcolm's eyes went from her round bottom to the blue buttons of her eyes. Then he read once more the words printed underneath.

The army made him very thorough, Estelle thought without humor. Actually, she was certain the girl meant nothing. Three years in a ward had given Malcolm the curious unsexual look you see on faces of invalids or on men in homes for the aged. His face had lost form, the features were blurred. The only sharpness was in the line from that terrible haircut. Finally he closed the last cover and looked up:

"And?"

Jolted, she began rapidly: "Why, as I told you, or wrote you perhaps, I went and looked at one of those garden development things. But I think you have to have a child to be accepted. And I think you would hate it. The place is awash with garbage cans and frightfully gerry-built."

"I'd like to get out of here."

But he said it without rancor. It was something they both knew. Estelle pushed her fists under the collar of her coat until she felt the tweed on her face. Reassured, she went on:

"In any case, I should think the veteran people would do something."

"Why don't you see them?"

"I have," she cried, "a thousand times." This was not quite true. More accurately, she had been approached on the case of Riley, Malcolm A., whose morale would be considerably improved outside a hospital. Did she consider herself married, they had asked? All they asked, for Patient Riley, was an answer.

"But they don't know how difficult it is," she went on.

"I'm sure," said Malcolm with indifference. It was a subject he was glad to drop. He smiled politely, as if she were a guest to be entertained.

"We have a magazine now," he said after a silence.

"Oh?"

He turned his chair neatly (Estelle closed her eyes) and from the drawer of his night-table produced a small magazine. Estelle took it, turning the pages with embarrassment. It was one of her conceits never to be ill, and the sickness of others filled her with disgust.

You would think they were proud of it, she thought, looking at picture after picture of paralyzed men driving automobiles and cheering at baseball games. It was the wives who interested her most and she searched their faces for despair and discontent. If the feelings existed they photographed badly.

It's unnatural, Estelle decided. She felt sorry for Malcolm. He had chosen poorly. She had been a charming bride (she believed) but a delinquent wife. Even now, after four years, she could not bring herself to discuss Malcolm's illness even though his doctor had urged her to do so. The same doctor must have been speaking to Malcolm for he began shifting about and frowning as if he had a speech to deliver.

First he took the magazines from his lap and, with the meticulousness he had developed, laid them next to the daffodils, straightening them like a pair of shoes. Then he wheeled his chair toward her, leaning forward as if they were conspirators. He clasped his hands, another wheelchair mannerism he had acquired.

"What do you do with yourself all day?" he asked. It was like a line in a badly rehearsed play. But it was a good sign, a healthy sign, and an imaginary doctor stood behind Estelle prodding her backbone. "Go on," said the doctor's voice. "Help him out."

"You know," she exclaimed. "I work, I still work. I read, sometimes I go out."

"And you hunt for an apartment," he finished. After a moment he went on:

"Who are your friends? Do you ever see any of the people we knew?"

"We didn't know many together."

"I know," he said, "but there were some. And you shouldn't be too much alone."

Now she was certain it was the doctor's helping hand.

"I see the Aylmers," she said, "and I used to see Harvey—you liked him, didn't you—but he married and I didn't like his wife."

Malcolm nodded as if to say he had heard of it.

"All the people we knew have moved away," she said, "or they have changed jobs or married."

"How about Bill Hedges?" Malcolm asked abruptly. "He was a friend of mine, oh, long before I knew you. He came up here, it must have been more than a year ago. I asked him to look you up. Did he ever do that?"

"We had dinner," she said. "I think I mentioned it."

"How did you like him?"

"All right."

"He's a hell of a nice guy."

"Mmm."

"Too bad he doesn't live here now. He might take you out once in a while."

"I suppose so."

"But he said he might be coming back," Malcolm pursued. "Do you know if he did?"

She shook her head vaguely and looked down at her hands. The ten red beetles of her nails marched in formation across her lap. Malcolm looked at them too and laughed. "Women!" he said and the tone of it shocked her more profoundly than anything he had said since his illness. There was a trace of senility in his voice (she could think of no other word for it) and she looked around the ward to see if anyone else had noticed. But the visitors sat in their decent little groups and Estelle burst out:

"Oranges and checkerboards! Is that all you see on visiting days?"

"Why no," he said pleasantly. "Some people bring spring flowers but it isn't considered a good idea. It makes work for the nurses, there's no place to keep them, and I forget to change the water. That's why I think you should take the daffodils away when you leave. It was nice of you to bring them but you probably have more space for them."

He laid the flowers gently on her lap across her hands. The paper around them was soaked through but the daffodils were firm and brilliant.

"Of course," said Estelle. "But what is a suitable gift for you? A game of chess?"

She clutched the flowers, appalled at herself. But Malcolm had no guile.

"Take them home, the flowers I mean, and put them in water," he said.

Gratefully, as if a signal bell had sounded, she began to assemble her scattered belongings: gloves, hat, cigarettes (should she leave them for Malcolm?), purse, coat to be buttoned, hair quickly combed, and all the while the daffodils rolling off her lap, and juggled from hand to hand.

"What is the matter with me?" she cried at last, for a bracelet which had been straining at its catch now sprang open and became hopelessly caught in the sleeve of her coat.

"Don't bother," she added hastily, "you can't fix it and I seem to be together at any rate."

Standing, she bent to kiss his cheek, which was as dry as cotton. He smells of wards, bedsheets and flannel dressing-gowns, she thought, and they tell me that unless I do something quickly I will burn in Hell forever.

"Goodbye," she said, "and if you need anything let me know."

Accustomed to platitudes, she heard her own words with surprise.

"Poor Malcolm," she said. "I am sorry. I get more foolish every year."

"You're not supposed to call attention to your lapses," he reminded her. "And you're not supposed to say 'poor Malcolm.' It's considered bad therapy. Didn't the doctor ever tell you?"

He was, for the first time in months, quite at ease. Help him out, the doctor whispered again, but she scarcely heard him. When it had first become clear that Malcolm would never walk or be well he had stopped dealing with her as a person. His manner made it plain that she was part of his existence but not the best part. Aggrieved, she thought: He wanted to be a shadow in a wheelchair and that is what he became. If he wanted anything else he should have begun a long time ago.

She stood, clutching her flowers, and saw that Malcolm was watching with a full appraising gaze.

"You're better looking," he said.

"Better looking?"

"Than when I met you. You seem taller. Could you have grown?"

"I could scarcely have grown," Estelle said. "I was twenty-five when we were married."

"I've forgotten how old I am," said Malcolm.

"And I am now thirty-two," she finished with determination.

Malcolm leaned forward over his clasped hands, looking up at her face. Their eyes met and he said:

"But you're better looking. Do you think that's a great deal?"

Was it the doctor again? But she was done with looking for motives and openly glanced at her watch.

"If we are going to talk again I had better sit down," she said.

Malcolm shook his head. "No, go on, walk to the door," he said. "I've forgotten how you walk."

He had time to see her furious astonished face for a moment before she turned and raced for the door. Halfway across the room she stopped. The entire room must be watching her disgraceful leave-taking with the eyes of her husband fixed on her back. At the door she turned; she had to see what was happening. No one was looking at her and Malcolm was opening a book.

Outside, she fled like a truant down the corridor, thinking: Disgusting, those idiot doctors. Rage at Malcolm's own doctor welled up for she was certain that inept and fumbling little man had persuaded Malcolm to (she could hear him now) make a fresh start, talk it out, put things on a sound basis. At least, she thought wildly, before today we knew where we were at.

Dr. Zatz, and was ever a name more fittingly wed to its bearer, was short and gave the impression of being close to tears. For three years and more he had been hovering over Malcolm and, when he could, around Estelle, assuring them that many couples in their unfortunate situation were quite happy. He was everything Estelle distrusted. He perspired, he was profuse, he was emotional. His wife, it had given Estelle joy to learn, was called Nadra. But she had never hated him more than at this moment, for he was waiting for her at the elevator.

"Mrs. Riley!" he exclaimed. "How are you. And your flowers," he added irrelevantly.

"I am very well." Dr. Zatz produced from Estelle the faintest trace of an English accent. "But I'm afraid Malcolm isn't. Someone in the hospital has been upsetting him."

"Oh?" The little doctor looked at his shoes. Unlike his colleagues, he persisted in liking Mrs. Riley. She was not impossible, he maintained. She would come round. And though rudeness quivered on his tongue he merely answered agreeably:

"I can't think who would do that. Malcolm is very popular here. As for his being unwell, he's as well as he'll ever be."

It was for remarks like this that Estelle detested the doctor.

"Which means," the little man went on, "that he is not better off here than he would be anywhere else, if you follow."

Estelle, trying to think of something at once crushing and placating, was saved by a mite of a woman, smaller even than Dr. Zatz, who arrived gasping that she had been searching for him everywhere. They whispered excitedly and Estelle rang for the elevator, turning away to show that as far as she was concerned the interview was at an end. Gratefully she saw a square of light slide down and the door of the elevator opened.

"Mrs. Riley," the doctor called, "just a moment. Mrs. Tyson from the staff wants to meet you."

Her back to the silent crowd in the elevator, Estelle murmured:

"No time now. Next week, delighted," and she raised her gloved hand as the door closed. There was no need to tell her who Mrs. Tyson was. The knit suit and frumpy pearls, the graying hair and anxious face spelled to Estelle Social Service. They must be desperate, really desperate, she thought, trying to maneuver her watch into position around the daffodils.

The hospital was so dark that she was surprised to see the sun outside. Her sense of release was so great that she wanted to run but instead picked her way soberly through the puddles left by an early rain. She paused at the corner and looked down the street. There might be a taxicab nearby, but she liked to wait out of sight of the hospital, which seemed to loom at her back like a forest. Leaving, it was her habit to glance apprehensively behind. I'll look back only once, she thought, giving in comfortably, and turned to see a familiar automobile at the curb.

"Bill," she cried, as the driver leaned over to open the door. "This is the best thing that's happened all day."

"I was here before," he said, "but the cop made me move. So I went away to pick up some things and came back. Get in."

On the back seat were a pile of newspapers, a pastry box, and a bottle of milk. It pleased him to be domestic. And no wonder, she thought spitefully, when he has only to play at it and can change to another game whenever he likes.

She was well out of sorts, which was unusual. It was the doctor, Estelle decided, and she hoped Bill would notice nothing. He made no comment on the daffodils, which she had placed between them. But then she was accustomed to the gigantic indifference his friends mistook for tact.

"How did it go?" he asked, prepared to have the subject dismissed.

"Terribly," she said unexpectedly. Just as she and Malcolm had never discussed themselves, so she and Bill never talked about Malcolm. She thought: I'm behaving like Malcolm. But she went on perversely: "He's fed up, and the hospital is fed up, and he talked about you."

"Well?"

"He said I was pretty and he asked if I ever saw you."

"And you said yes."

"I wish you would listen," she said. "I think he's fond of me and it made him unkind. And you know me, I blow hot and cold about everything."

He looked at her briefly and laid a hand on her knee. Her distress was normal but the solution was not his to suggest. It was Estelle's problem. He had trained himself to veer from it with the dexterity of a goldfish.

"You're no help," she said, and although he was silent, the phrase "What do you expect?" formed between them as tangibly as the daffodils. They drove on in comfortless quiet and Bill put his hand back on the wheel. She saw that he was frowning. Even his moods had a freedom denied Malcolm. Bill could act, and it was difficult to believe that Malcolm had ever been like him. She pulled away with horror from thoughts of Malcolm. After all, what was there to do with Bill but marvel at a selfishness so pure her own irresolution seemed muddy beside it?

"You put the car away," she said as they drew up to the curb. "I'll take the parcels up and we'll have time for several drinks before dinner."

"Fine." He was pleasant again. His temper was even; he was like Estelle, counting on others to keep the air clear. But today Estelle's teeth came together as if she had eaten something bitter.

It would take very little, she thought, to make me behave foolishly; lose my temper; insult someone.

She became angry, for example, at the door of the apartment building. She had put the milk, the pastry box, and the flowers on the floor while she searched for the doorkey. Then as she was picking them all up the door slammed and she had to start over. That happened twice. At the end she was sobbing, though without tears, and solved it finally by ringing the bell of an apartment on the top floor and scurrying in at the answering buzz. She looked quickly into the mailbox marked WM. HEDGES and ran upstairs before the top-floor tenant could call out.

Entering Bill's apartment alone always gave her the feeling of meeting a hostile woman, for any imprint she made on the rooms left with her each morning. Like water closing over a stone the air took back its own shape. The furniture told her she was on sufferance far more plainly than Bill's silence ever had.

What was there belonging to her, when you thought of it? A few books, and they could be packed. Clothes in the closets; perfume which sometimes hung in the air; stockings drying; but nothing with a permanent place. There was nothing to account for her presence except an extra laundry bill.

She put her coat in the hall closet, making a point of disarranging Bill's things. Then she took her bundles to the kitchen, kicking off her shoes as she went.

The drinks: it would cheer him immensely to have a drink waiting. Since she had no place here, she might as well have a function, and that of an efficient mistress was as worthwhile as any. The door opened as she was stirring martinis in Bill's glass mixer. She heard him pick up the papers she had left in the hall and start for the living room.

"You left your shoes here," he called reprovingly. Estelle gave the kitchen door a push.

"I can't hear you," she said under her breath. She put the mixer on the tray with glasses and was on her way out when she caught sight of the daffodils. At least they are mine, she thought, particularly in view of the fact that Malcolm didn't want them.

She set the tray beside the sink and began to search through the cupboards for something to put them in. There was nothing, nothing at all except a cocktail shaker that was too small and an ice bucket that was too large. There was a silver water pitcher, she remembered, but Bill had filled it with tulips in the living room. In the kitchen, she discovered with astonishment, there was not so much as an empty milk bottle.

There was the martini mixer, but it was full of Bill's drinks. She could put them in the little shaker and put the flowers in the mixer but Bill would disapprove; he liked things thus and so. She sat on the kitchen stool with her hand against the refrigerator and began to cry. It was the first time she had cried for years, which made it all the more difficult to explain to Bill, when he came to see what was wrong, that she was weeping because there was no place anywhere for the daffodils.

SATURDAY

I

AFTER the girl across the aisle had glanced at Gérard a few times (though he was not talking to her, not even trying to), she went down to sit at the front of the bus, near the driver. She left behind a bunch of dark, wet, purple lilac wrapped in wet newspaper. When Gérard followed to tell her, she did not even turn her head. Feeling foolish, he suddenly got down anywhere, in a part of Montreal he had never seen before, and in no time at all he was lost. He stood on the curb of a gloomy little street recently swept by a spring tempest of snow. A few people, bundled as Russians, scuffled by. A winter haze like a winter evening sifted down through a lattice of iron and steel. The sudden lowering of day, he saw, was caused by an overhead railway. This railway was smart and new, as if it had been unpacked out of sawdust quite recently and snapped into place.

What was it for? "Of all the unnecessary…" Gérard muttered, just as his father might. Talking aloud to oneself was a family habit. You could grumble away for minutes at home without anyone's taking the least notice. "Yes, they have to spend our money somehow," he went on, just as if he were old enough to vote and pay taxes. Luckily no one heard him. Everyone's attention had been fixed by a funeral procession of limousines grinding along in inches of slush. The Russian bundles crossed themselves, but Gérard kept his hands in his pockets. "Clogging up the streets," he offered, as an opinion about dying and being taken somewhere for burial. At that moment the last cars broke away, climbed the curb, and continued along the sidewalk. Gérard pressed back to the wall behind him, as he saw the others doing. No one appeared astonished, and he supposed that down here, in the East End, where there was a funeral a minute, this was the custom. "Otherwise you'd never have any normal traffic," he said. "Only all these hearses."

He thought, all at once, Why is everybody looking at me?

He was smiling. That was why. He could not help smiling. It was like a cinématèque comedy—the black cars in the whitish fog, the solemn bystanders wiping their noses on their gloves and crossing themselves, and everyone in winter cocoon clothes, with a white bubble of breath. But it was not black and gray, like an old film: it was the color of winter and cities, brown and brick and sand. What was more, the friends and relations of the dead were now descending from their stopped cars, and he feared that his smile might have offended them, or made him seem gross and unfeeling; and so, in a propitiatory gesture he at once regretted, he touched his forehead, his chest, and a point on each shoulder.

He had never done this for himself. Until now, he had never craved approval. From the look of the mourners, they were all Protestants anyway. He wanted to tell them he had crossed himself by mistake; that he was an atheist, from a singular and perhaps a unique family of anti-clerics. But the mourners were too grieved to pay attention. Even the men were sobbing. They held their hands against their mouths, they blinked and choked, they all but doubled over with pain—they were laughing at something. Perhaps at Gérard? Well, they were terrible people. He had always known. He was relieved to see one well-behaved person among them. She had been carried from her car and placed, with gentle care, in a collapsible aluminum wheelchair. Loving friends attended her, one to hold her purse, another to tie her scarf, a third to tuck a fur robe around her knees. Gérard had often been ill, and he recognized on her face the look of someone who knows about separateness and nightmares and all the vile tricks that the body can play. Her hair was careless, soft, and long, but the face seemed thirty, which was, to him, rather old. She turned her dark head and he heard her say gravely, "Not since the liberation of Elizabeth Barrett..."

The coffin lay in the road. It had been let down from a truck, parked there as if workmen were about to jump out and begin shoveling snow or mending the pavement. The dead man must have left eccentric instructions, Gérard thought, for his coffin was nothing more than pieces of brown carton stapled together in a rough shape. The staples were slipping out: that was how carelessly and above all how cheaply the thing had been done. Gérard had a glimpse of a dark suit and a watch chain before he looked away. The hands, he saw, rested upon a long white envelope. He was to be buried with a packet of securities, as all Protestants probably were. The crippled woman touched Gérard on the arm and said, "Just reach over and get it, will you?"—that way, casually, used to service. No one stopped Gérard or asked him what he thought he was doing. As he slipped the envelope away he knew that this impertinence, this violation, would turn the dead man into a fury where he was concerned. By his desire to be agreeable, Gérard had deliberately and foolishly given himself some bad nights.

Jazz from an all-night program invaded the house until Gérard's mother, discovering its source in the kitchen, turned the radio off. She supposed Gérard had walked in his sleep. What else could she think when she found him kneeling, in the dark, with his head against the refrigerator door? Beside him was a smashed plate and the leftover ham that had been on it, and an overturned stool. She knelt too, and drew his head on her shoulder. His father stood in the doorway. The long underwear he wore at all times and in every season showed at his wrists and ankles, where the pajamas stopped. Without his teeth and without his glasses he seemed younger and clearer about the eyes, but frighteningly helpless and almost female. His head and his hands were splashed with large, soft-looking freckles.

"He looks so peaceful," the old man said. "This is how he always looks when we aren't around."

She did not answer, for once, "Oh, nobody cares," but her expression cried for her, "What useless, pointless remark will you think of next?" She clasped her son and tried to rock him. As Gérard resisted, she held still. Of all her children, he was the one with whom she blundered most. His uneven health, his moods, his temper, his choked breathing were signs of starvation, she had been told, but not of the body. The mother was to blame. How to blame? How? Why not the father? They hadn't said. Her daughters were married; Léopold was still small; in between came this strange boy. One of Queen Victoria's children had been flogged for having asthma. Why should she think of this now? She had never punished her children. The very word had been banned.

Gérard heard his father open the refrigerator and then heard him pouring beer in a glass.

"He's been out with his girl," his father said. "She's no Cleopatra, but it's better than having him queer."

All Gérard felt then was how her grip slackened. She said softly, "Get rid of that girl. Just until you've passed your exams. Look at what she's doing to you. One day you'll meet her in the street and you'll wonder why you fought with your mother over her. Get rid of her and I'll believe everything you ever say. You've never walked in your sleep. You came in late. You were hungry..."

"What about the funeral?" the old man said. "Whose funeral?"

"Leave him," said his mother. "He's been dreaming."

Gérard, no longer refusing, let his mother rock him. If it had been a dream, then why in English? Dreaming in English made him feel powerless, as if his mind were dying, ill-fed from the soil. They spoke English at home, but he, Gérard, tried to dream in French. He read French; he went to French movies; he tried to speak it with his little brother; and yet his mind made fun of him and sent up to the surface "Elizabeth Barrett." The family had not deserted French for social betterment, or for business reasons, but on the matter of belief that set them apart. His mother wanted English to be freedom, at least from the Church. There were no public secular schools, but that was only part of it. Church and language were inextricably enmeshed, and you had to leave the language if you wanted your children brought up some other way. That was how it was. It was as simple, and as complex, as that. But (still pressed to his mother) he thought that here in the house there had never been freedom, only tension and conversation (oh, such a lot of conversation!) and a few corrupted qualities disguised as "speaking your mind," "taking a stand," and "drawing the line somewhere." Caressed by his mother, he seemed privileged. Being privileged, he weakened, and that meant even his rage was fouled. He had so much to hate that he seemed to carry in his brain a miniature Gérard, sneering and dark.

"If you would just do something about your children instead of all the time thinking about yourself," he heard his mother say. "Oh, anything. Do anything. Who cares what you do now? Nobody cares."

There had been a shortage of bedrooms until Gérard's five sisters married. His mother kept for her private use a sitting room with periwinkle paper on the walls. It could have done as a bedroom for the two boys, but her need for this extra space was never questioned. She had talks with her daughters there, and she kept the household accounts. Believing it her duty, she read her children's personal letters and their diaries as long as they lived under her roof. She carried the letters to the bright room and sat, leaning her head on her hand, reading. If someone came in she never tried to hide what she read, or slip it under a book, but let her hand fall, indifferently. In this room Gérard had lived the most hideous adventure of his life. Sometimes he thought it was a dream and he willed it to be a dream, even if it meant reversing sleeping and waking forever and accepting as friends and neighbors the strangers he saw in his sleep. He would remember it sometimes and say, "I must have dreamed it." His collection of pornography was heaped in plain sight on his mother's desk. There were the pictures, the books carefully dissimulated under fake covers, and the postcards from France and India turned face down. His mother sat with these at her elbow, and, of course, he could see them, and she said, "Gérard, I won't always be here. I'm not immortal. Your father is thirty years older than I am but he didn't have to bear his own children and he's as sound as this house. He might very well outlive me. I want you to see that he is always looked after and that he always uses saccharine to sweeten his tea. There is a little box I slip in his pajama pocket and another in the kitchen. Promise me. Now, the sweater you had on yesterday. I want to throw it out. It's past mending. I don't want you to sulk for a week, and that's why I'm asking you first." He wanted to say, "Those things aren't mine, I've got to give them back." He saw through her eyes and all at once understood that the cards from India were the worst of all, for they were all about people scarcely older than Léopold, and the reason they looked so funny was that they were starving to death. All Gérard had seen until now was what they were doing, not who they were, or could be. Meanwhile the room rocked around him, and his mother stood up to show that was all she had to say.

She did not sleep in the pretty room, but in a Spartan cell where there were closets full of linen and soap, and a shelf of preserves behind a curtain, and two painters' stepladders, and two large speckled mirrors in gilt frames. One wall was covered with photographs of a country house the children had never seen, and of her old convent school. The maid, when there was one, went freely in without knocking if she needed a jar of fruit or clean bedsheets. Even when her daughters married and liberated their rooms one by one, she stayed where she was. The bed was hard and narrow and the old man could not comfortably spend the night. For years Gérard had slept in a basement room that contained a Ping-Pong table, and from which he could hear, at odd hours, the furnace coming to life with a growl. A lighted tank of tropical fish separated two divans, one of which was used now by his father, now by his little brother. He had never understood why his father would suddenly appear in the middle of the night, and why the little brother, aged three and four and five, was led, stumbling and protesting, to finish the night in his mother's bed. Gérard was used to someone's presence at night, the warm light of the tank had comforted him. Now that he had a room of his own and slept alone in it, he discovered he was afraid of the dark.

His mother sat by his bed, holding his hand, until he pretended to be asleep. His door was open and a ray from the passage bent over the bed and along the wall. "I'm sure I must be pale," she said, though her cheeks and brow were rosy. She believed her children had taken her blood to make their own and that hers was diminished. Having had seven babies, she could not have left much over a pint. Bitterly anticlerical, she sometimes hinted that nuns had the best of it after all. Gérard had been wrong to wake her; he had no business walking in his sleep. Tomorrow was what she called "a hell day." It was Léopold's ninth birthday, she was without help, and twenty-two people were going to sit down to lunch. Directly after the meal, she was to take all the uneaten cake to an aged religious who had once been a teacher of hers and was now ending her life bedridden in a convent for the old. The home was seventy miles north of the city, but might have been seven hundred. One son-in-law had undertaken to drive her. Instead of coming back with him, she proposed to spend the night. This meant that another son-in-law would have to fetch her the next day. The interlocked planning this required surpassed tunnelling under the Alps. "Hell day," she said, but she said it so often that Gérard supposed most days were some kind of hell.

The first thing he did when he wakened was light a cigarette, the second turn on his radio. He felt oddly drunk, as if he might miss his footing stumbling down to breakfast. She was already prepared for the last errand of the day. She wore a tweed suit and her overnight case stood in the hall. She moved back and forth between the kitchen and the dining room. His father, still in underwear and pajamas, sat breakfasting at the counter in the kitchen. She paused and watched him stir too much sugar into his coffee, but did not, this time, remark on it. The old man, excited, tapped his spoon on his saucer.

"It was a movie," he said. "Your dream. I saw it, I think, in a movie about an old man. You've dreamed an old man's dream. I've looked through the paper," he said, pushing it toward his son. "There's nothing about that funeral. It couldn't have been a funeral. Anyway, not anyone important."

"Leave him," said the mother, patiently. "He dreamed it. There is something you can do today. Take over the dog. *Completely*. Léopold has him now." Gérard knew it was his father thus addressed. He held his cup in both hands. "As for you, Gérard, I want a word with you."

"Another thing I thought," continued the old man. "Maybe they were making a movie around there and you got mixed up with the crowd. What you took for a railway was some kind of scaffolding, cameras. Eh?"

"Gérard, I want you to..." She turned to her husband: "Back me up! He's your son, too! Gérard, I want you to tell that girl you're too young to be tied to one person." Her face was blazing, her eyes brilliant and clear. "What will you do when she starts a baby? Marry her? I want you to tell that girl there's no money to inherit in this family, and that after Léopold's education is finished there won't be a cent for anybody. Not even us."

"She's not really a dancer," said the old man, forestalling the next bit. "She gives dancing *lessons*. It's not the same thing."

"I don't care what she gives. What about your son?"

Gérard was about to say, "I did tell her," but he remembered, "I never got there. I only started out."

He stopped hearing them. He had set his cup down as his mother spoke his name, and pushed it to the back of the counter. As his father handed him the paper, he remembered, he had taken it with his left hand, and opened it wide instead of carefully folding it, as he usually did. This was so important that he did not hear what was said after a minute or two. He had always given importance to his gestures, noticing whether he put his watch or his glasses to the left or the right of a bedlamp. He always left his coffee cup about four inches from the edge of the counter. When he studied, he piled his books on the right, and whatever text he was immediately using was at his left hand. His radio had to be dead center. He saw, and had been noticing for some time, that his mind was not keeping quiet order for him anymore and that his gestures were not automatic. He felt that if he did not pay close attention to everything now, something literally fantastic could happen. Gestures had kept things controlled, as they ought to be. Whatever could happen now was in the domain of magic.

2

The conviction that she was married against her will never leaves her. If she had been born royal it could not have been worse. She has led the life of a crown princess, sapped by boredom and pregnancies. She told each of her five daughters as they grew up that they were conceived in horror; that she could have left them in their hospital cots and not looked back, so sickened was she by their limp spines and the autumn smell of their hair, by their froglike movements and their animal wails.

She liked them when they could reason, and talk, and answer back—when they became what she calls "people."

She makes the girls laugh. She is French-Canadian, whether she likes it or not. They see at the heart of her a sacrificial mother; her education has removed her in degree only from the ignorant, tiresome, moralizing mother, given to mysterious female surgery, subjugated by miracles, a source of infinite love. They have heard her saying, "Why did I get married? Why did I have all these large dull children?" They have heard, "If any of my children had been brilliant or unusual, it would have justified my decision. Yes, they might have been narrow and warped in French, but oh how commonplace they became in English!" "We are considered traitors and renegades," she says. "And I can't point to even one of my children and say, 'Yes but it was worth it—look at Pauline—or Lucia—or Gérard.'" The girls ought to be wounded at this, but in fact they are impermeable. They laugh and call it "Mother putting on an act." Her passionate ambition for them is her own affair. They have chosen exactly the life she tried to renounce for them: they married young, they are frequently pregnant, and sometimes bored.

This Saturday she has reunited them, the entire family and one guest, for Léopold's ninth birthday. There are fourteen adults at the dining-room table and eight at the children's, which is in the living room, through the arch. Léopold, so small he seems two years younger than nine, so clever and quick that other children are slightly afraid of him, keeps an eye on his presents. He has inherited his brother's electric train. It is altogether old-fashioned; Gérard has had it nine years. Still, Léopold will not let anyone near it. It is his now, and there-fore charmed. If any of these other children, these round-eyed brats with English names, lays a hand on the train, he disconnects it; if the outrage is repeated, he goes in the kitchen and stands on a stool and turns off the electricity for the whole house. No one reprimands him. He is not like other children. He is more intelligent, for one thing, and so much uglier. Unlike Gérard, who speaks French as if through a muslin curtain, or as if translating from another language, who wears himself out struggling for one complete dream, Léopold can, if he likes, say anything in a French more limpid and accurate than anything they are used to hearing. He goes to a private, secular school, the only French one in the province; he has had a summer in Montreux. Either his parents have more money than when the others were small, or they have chosen to invest in their last chance. French is Léopold's private language; he keeps it as he does his toys, to himself, polished, personal, a lump of crystalline rock he takes out, examines, looks through, and conceals for another day.

Léopold's five sisters think his intelligence is a disease, and one they hope their own children will not contract. Their mother is *bright*, their father is *thoughtful* (*deep* is another explanation for him), but Léopold's intelligence will always show him the limit of a situation and the last point of possibility where people are concerned; and so, of course, he is bound to be unhappy forever. How will he be able to love? To his elder brother, he seems like a small illegitimate creature raised in secret, in the wrong house. One day Léopold will show them extraordinary credentials. But this is a fancy, for Léopold is where he belongs, in the right family; he has simply been planted—little stunted, ugly thing— in the wrong generation. The children at his table are his nieces and nephews, and the old gentleman at the head of the adult table, the old man bowed over a dish of sieved, cooked fruit, is his father. Léopold is evidence of an old man's foolishness. His existence is an embarrassment. The girls wish he had never been born, and so they are especially kind, and they load him with presents. Even Gérard, who would have found the family quite complete, quite satisfactory, without any Léopold, ever, has given the train (which he was keeping for his own future children) and his camera.

When Léopold is given something, he walks round it and decides what the gift is worth in terms of the giver. If it seems cheap, he mutters without raising his eyes. If it seems important, he flashes a brief, shrewd look that any adult, but no child, mistakes for a glance of complicity. The camera, though second-hand, has been well received. It is round his neck; he puts down his fork and holds the camera and makes all the children uneasy by staring at each in turn and deciding none of them worth an inch of film.

"Poor little lad," says his mother, who flings out whatever she feels, no matter who is in the way. "He has never had a father—only a grandfather."

The old man may not have heard. He is playing his private game of trying to tell his five English-Canadian sons-in-law apart. The two Bobs, the Don, the Ian, and the Ken are interchangeable, like postage stamps of the Queen's profile. Two are Anglicans, two United Church, and the most lackluster is a Lutheran, but which is he? The old man lifts his head and smiles a great slow smile. His smile acquits his daughters; he forgives them for having ever thought him a shameless old person; but the five sons-in-law are made uneasy. They wonder if they are meant to smile back, or something *weird* like that. Well, they may not have much in common with each other, but here they are five together, not isolated, not alone. Their children, with round little noses, and round little blue eyes, are at the next table, and two or three babies are sleeping in portable cots upstairs.

It is a windy spring day, with a high clean sky, and black branches hitting on the windows. The family's guest that day is Father Zinkin, who is dressed just like anyone, without even a clerical collar to make him seem holy. This, to the five men, is another reason for discomposure; for they might be respectful of a robe, but *what* is this man, with his polo-necked sweater and his nose in the wine and his rough little jokes? Is he really the Lord's eunuch? I mean, they silently ask each other, would you trust him? You know what I mean ... Father Zinkin has just come back from Rome. He says that the trees are in leaf, and he got his pale jaundiced sunburn sitting at a sidewalk café. This is Montreal, it is still cold, and the daughters' five fur coats are piled upstairs on their mother's bed. They accept the news about Rome without grace. If he thinks it is so sunny in Rome, why didn't he stay there? Who asked him to come back? That is how every person at that table feels about news from abroad, and it is the only sentiment that can ever unite them. When you say it is sunny elsewhere, you are suggesting it is never sunny here. When you describe the trees of Rome, what you are *really* saying is there are no trees in Montreal.

Why is he at the table, then, since he brings them nothing but unwelcome news? The passionately anti-clerical family cannot keep away from priests. They will make an excuse: they will say they admire his mind, or his gifts with language—he speaks seven. He eats and drinks just like anyone, he has traveled, and been psychoanalyzed, and is not frightened by women. At least, he does not seem to be. Look at the way he pours wine for Lucia, and then for Pauline, and how his tone is just right, not a scrap superior. And then, he is not Canadian. He does not remind them of anything. None of the children, from Lucia, who is twenty-nine, to Léopold, nine today, has been baptized. Father Zinkin sits down and eats with them as if they were. Until the girls grew up and married they never went to church. Now that they are Protestants they go because their husbands want to; so, their mother thinks, this is what all the fighting and the courage came to, finally; all the struggling and being condemned and cut off from one's own kind: the five girls simply joined another kind, just as stupid.

No, thinks the old father at the head of the table: more stupid. At any rate, less interesting. Less interesting because too abstract. You would have to be a genius to be a true Protestant, and those he has met ... At night, when he is trying to get to sleep, he thinks of his sons-in-law. He remembers their names without trouble: the two Bobs, the Don, the Ian, and the last one—Keith, or Ken? Ken. Monique married Ken. Alone, in the dark, he tries to match names and faces. Are both Bobs thin? Pink in the face? Yes, and around the neck. They lose their hair young—something to do with English hairbrushes, he invents. The old man droops now, for the sight of his sons-in-law can send him off to sleep. His five daughters—he knows their names, and he knows his own sons. His grandchildren seem to belong to a new national type, with round heads, and quite large front teeth. You would think some Swede or other had been around Montreal on a bicycle so as to create this new national type. Sharon, and Marilyn and Cary and Gary and Gail. Cary and *Gary.*

"Nobody cares," his wife says, very sharply.

He has been mumbling, talking to himself, saying the names of children aloud. She minds because of Father Zinkin. When she and her husband are alone, and he talks too much, repeats the same thing over and over, she squeezes her eyes until only a pinpoint of amber glows between the lids, and she squeezes out through a tight throat, "All right, all *right,*" and even, "Shut UP" in a rising crescendo of three. Not even her children know she says "Shut up" to the old man; "nobody cares" is just a family phrase. When it is used on Don Carlos, the basset, now under the children's table, it makes him look as if he might cry real tears.

She speaks lightly, quickly now, in English. She sits, very straight, powdered and pretty, and says, in a musical English all her own, not the speech of the city at all, "They say Jews look after their own people, but it's not true. I was told about some people who had a very old sick father. They had to tie him to a chair sometimes, because he would go downtown and steal things or start to cry in the street. As they couldn't afford a home for him, and he wouldn't have gone anyway, they decided to leave him. They moved half the furniture away and the old man sat crying on a chair and saw his family go. He sat weeping, not protesting, and his children slouched out without saying goodbye. Yes, he sat weeping, a respectable old man. Now, this man's wife gave Russian lessons to earn her living, and one day, when she was giving a lesson to a woman I know, she said, 'Come to the window.' My friend looked out and saw an old-fashioned Jew going by. The woman said, 'That was my husband.' She seemed pleased with herself, as though she had done what was right for her children."

"Was he dead?" asks Gérard. He is always waiting for some simple, casual confirmation about the existence of ghosts.

"No, of course not. He was just an old man, and someone had taken him in. Some Russian. So," she concedes, "he was looked after." But, as she likes her stories cruel, so that her children will know more about life than she once did, unhappy endings are her habit. She feels obliged to add, "Someone took him in, but probably gave him a miserable time. He must be dead now. This was long ago, during the last war, when people were learning Russian. It was the thing to do then."

Her children are worried by this story, but perhaps the father has not heard it. He is still eating his fruit, taking a mouthful and then forgetting to swallow. Suddenly something he has been thinking silently must have excited him, for he taps his spoon on the edge of the glass dish.

"As you get old you lose everything," he says. "You lose your God, if you ever had one. When you know they want you to die, you want to live. You want to be loved. Even that."

His children are so embarrassed, so humiliated, they feel as if ashes and sand were being ground in their skins. The sons-in-law are revolted. They look at their plates. Honestly, they can never come to this house without something being said about religion or something personal.

"You lose your parents," the old man continues. "You have to outlive them. Everything is loss." Before they can say "nobody cares" he is off once more: "No need for priests," he mutters. "If there is no sin, then no need for redemption. Dead words. Tell me, Father whoever you are," (he asks the glass dish of fruit) "will you explain why these words should be used?" Muttering—he has been muttering all his life.

"Oh, shut *up*," they are thinking. A chorus of silent English: "Shut *up*!" If only the old man could hear the words, he would see a great black wall; he would hear a sigh, a rattle, like the black trees outside the windows, hitting the panes.

The old man shakes his head over his plate: No, no, he never wanted to marry. He wanted to become a priest. Either God is, or He is not. If He is, I shall live for Him. If He is not, I shall fight His ghost. At forty-nine he was married off by a Jesuit, who was an old school friend. He and the shy, soft, orphaned girl who had been placed in a convent at six, and had left it, now, at eighteen, exchanged letters about comparative religion. She seemed intelligent—he has forgotten now what he imagined their life could ever be like. Presently what they had in common was her physical horror of him and his knowledge of it, and then they had in common all their children.

3

When the old man had finished his long thoughts, everyone except Gérard and Father Zinkin had disappeared. The small children were made to kiss him—moist reluctant mouths on his cheek—"before Granpa takes his nap." Léopold, who never touched anyone, looked at him briefly through his new camera and said softly to him, and only to him, "*Il n'y a pas assez de lumière.*" Their dark identical eyes reflected each other. Then everyone vanished, the women to rattle plates in the kitchen, Léopold to his room, the five fathers to play some game with the children at the back of the house. He sat in his leather armchair, sometimes he slept, and he heard Gérard protesting, "I know the difference between seeing and dreaming."

"Well, it was a waking dream," said the priest. "There is no snow on the streets, but you say there had been a storm."

The old man looked. The white light in the room surely was the reflection of a snowy day? The room seemed filled with white furniture, white flowers. The priest, because he was dressed like Gérard, tried to sound like a young man and an old friend. Only when the priest turned his head, seeking an ashtray, did the old man see what Father Zinkin knew. His interest in Gérard was intellectual. His mind was occupied with its own power. The old man imagined him, narrow, suspicious, in a small parish, lording it over a flock of old maids. They were thin, their eyebrows met over their noses.

Gérard said, "All right, what if I was analyzed? What difference would it make?"

"You would be yourself. You would be yourself without *effort*."

The old man had been waiting for him to say, "it would break the mirror"; for what is the good of being yourself, if you are Gérard?

"What I mean is, you can't understand about this girl. So there's no use talking about her."

"I know about girls," said the other. "I went out. I even danced."

It struck the old man how often he had been told by priests they knew about life because they had, once, danced with girls. He was willing to let them keep that as a memory of life, but what about Gérard, as entangled with a woman as a man of thirty? But then Gérard lost interest and said, "I'd want to be analyzed in French," so it didn't matter.

"It wouldn't work. Your French isn't spontaneous enough. Now, begin again. You were on the street, it was daylight, then you were in the kitchen in the dark."

How the old man despised this self-indulgence! He felt it was not his business to put a stop to it. His wife stopped it simply by coming in and beginning to talk about herself. When she talked about her children she seemed to be talking about herself, and when the priest said, to console some complaint she was making, "The little one will be brilliant," meaning Léopold, he seemed to be prophesying a future in which she would shine. Outside, the others were breaking up into groups, carrying cots, ushering children into cars. It would take a good ten minutes, and so she sat perched on the arm of a sofa with her hat on her head and her coat on her arm, and said, "Léopold will be brilliant, but I never wanted him. I'd had six children, five close together. French Canadians of our background, for I daren't say class, it sounds so ... Well, we, people like ourselves, do *not* usually have these monstrous families, regardless of what you may have been told, Father. My mother had no one but me, and when she tried having a second child, it killed her. When I knew I was having Léopold I took ergot. I lay here, on this very sofa, in the middle of the afternoon. Nothing happened, and nothing showed. He was born without even a strawberry mark to condemn me."

She likes to shock, the old man remembered. How much you can take is measure of your intelligence. So she thinks. Oddly enough, she can be shocked.

She stopped speaking and sighed and smoothed the collar of her coat. When she thought, "My son Gérard is sleeping with a common girl," it shocked her. She thought, now, seeing him slouch past the doorway, scarcely able to wait for the house to empty so that he could go off and find that girl and spend a disgusting Saturday night with her, "Gérard knows. He looks at his father, and me, and now he knows. Before, he only thought he knew. He knows now why the old man follows me up the stairs."

She said very lightly, "My son has sex on the brain. It's all he thinks about now. I suppose all boys are the same. You must have been that way once, Father." Really, that was farther than she had ever gone. The priest looked like a statue resembling the person he had been a moment before.

Once she had departed the house seemed to relax, like an animal that feels safe and can sleep. The old man was to walk the dog and do something about his children. Those had been his instructions for the day. Oh, yes, and he was to stop thinking about himself.

He put on his hat and coat and walked down the street with Don Carlos. Don Carlos dug the wet spring lawns with tortoiseshell nails.

Let off the leash, he at once rolled in something horrible. The old man wanted to scold, but the wind made all conversation between himself and the dog impossible. The wind suddenly dropped; it was to the old man like a sudden absence of fear. He could dream as well as Gérard. He invented: he and Don Carlos went through the gap of a fence and were in a large sloping pasture. He trod on wildflowers. From the spongy spring soil grew crab apple trees and choke cherries, and a hedge of something he no longer remembered that was sweet and white. Presently they—he and the dog—looked down on a village and the two silvery spires of a church. He saw the date over the door: 1885. The hills on the other side of the water were green and black with shadows. He had never seen such a blue and green day. But he was still here, on the street, and had not forgotten it for a second. Imagination was as good as sleepwalking any day.

Léopold stood on the porch, watching him through his camera. He seemed to be walking straight into Léopold's camera, magically reduced in size.

"Why, Léo," he said. "You're not supposed to be here," not caring to show how happy it made him that Léopold was here. They were bound so soon to lose each other—why start?

"Wouldn't."

"Wouldn't what?"

"Wouldn't go to Pauline's. She's coming back to get us for supper."

"I don't want anything more to eat today."

"Neither do I. And I'm not going."

Who would dare argue with Léopold? He put his camera down. One day he would have the assurance of a real street, a real father, a real afternoon.

"Well, well," his father said. "So they're all gone." He felt shy. He would never have enough of Léo—he would never know what became of him. He edged past and held the door open for the dog.

"All gone. *Il n'y a que moi.*" Léopold, who never touched anyone, pressed his lips to his father's hand.

UP NORTH

WHEN THEY woke up in the train, their bed was black with soot and there was soot in his Mum's blondie hair. They were miles north of Montreal, which had, already, sunk beneath his remembrance. "D'you know what I sor in the night?" said Dennis. He had to keep his back turned while she dressed. They were both in the same berth, to save money. He was small, and didn't take up much room, but when he woke up in that sooty autumn dawn, he found he was squashed flat against the side of the train. His Mum was afraid of falling out and into the aisle; they had a lower berth, but she didn't trust the strength of the curtain. Now she was dressing, and sobbing; really sobbing. For this was worse than anything she had ever been through, she told him. She had been right through the worst of the air raids, yet this was the worst, this waking in the cold, this dark, dirty dawn, everything dirty she touched, her clothes—oh, her clothes!—and now having to dress as she lay flat on her back. She daren't sit up. She might knock her head.

"You know what I sor?" said the child patiently. "Well, the train must of stopped, see, and some little men with bundles on their backs got on. Other men was holding lanterns. They were all little. They were all talking French."

"Shut up," said Mum. "Do you hear me?"

"Sor them," said the boy.

"You and your bloody elves."

"They was people."

"Little men with bundles," said Mum, trying to dress again. "You start your fairy tales with your Dad and I don't know what *he'll* give you."

It was this mythical, towering, half-remembered figure they were now traveling to join up north.

Roy McLaughlin, traveling on the same train, saw the pair, presently, out of his small red-lidded eyes. Den and his Mum were dressed and as clean as they could make themselves, and sitting at the end of the car. McLaughlin was the last person to get up, and he climbed down from his solitary green-curtained cubicle conspicuous and alone. He had to pad the length of the car in a trench coat and city shoes—he had never owned slippers, bathrobe, or pajamas—past the passengers, who were drawn with fatigue, pale under the lights. They were men, mostly; some soldiers. The Second World War had been finished, in Europe, a year and five months. It was a dirty, rickety train going up to Abitibi. McLaughlin was returning to a construction camp after three weeks in Montreal. He saw the girl, riding with her back to the engine, doing her nails, and his faculties absently registered "Limey bride" as he went by. The kid, looking out the window, turned and stared. McLaughlin thought "Pest," but only because children and other men's wives made him nervous and sour when they were brought around camp on a job.

After McLaughlin had dressed and had swallowed a drink in the washroom—for he was sick and trembling after his holiday—he came and sat down opposite the blond girl. He did not bother to explain that he had to sit somewhere while his berth was being dismantled. His arms were covered with coarse red hair; he had rolled up the sleeves of his khaki shirt. He spread his pale, heavy hands on his knees. The child stood between them, fingertips on the sooty window sill, looking out at the breaking day. Once, the train stopped for a long time; the engine was being changed, McLaughlin said. They had been rolling north but were now turning west. At six o'clock, in about an hour, Dennis and his mother would have to get down, and onto another train, and go north once more. Dennis could not see any station where they were now. There was a swamp with bristling black rushes, red as ink. It was the autumn sunrise; cold, red. It was so strange to him, so singular, that he could not have said an hour later which feature of the scene was in the foreground or to the left or right. Two women wearing army battle jackets over their dresses, with their hair piled up in front, like his mother's, called and giggled to someone they had put on the train. They were fat and dark—grinny. His mother looked at them with detestation, recognizing what they were; for she hated whores. She had always acted on the desire of the moment, without thought of gain, and she had taken the consequences (Dennis) without complaint. Dennis saw that she was hating the women, and so he looked elsewhere. On a wooden fence sat four or five men in open shirts and patched trousers. They had dull, dark hair, and let their mouths sag as though they were too tired or too sleepy to keep them closed. Something about them was displeasing to the child, and he thought that this was an ugly place with ugly people. It was also a dirty place; every time Dennis put his hands on the window sill they came off black.

"Come down any time to see a train go by," said McLaughlin, meaning those men. "Get up in the *night* to see a train."

The train moved. It was still dark enough outside for Dennis to see his face in the window and for the light from the windows to fall in pale squares on the upturned vanishing faces and on the little trees. Dennis heard his mother's new friend say, "Well, there's different possibilities." They passed into an unchanging landscape of swamp and bracken and stunted trees. Then the lights inside the train were put out and he saw that the sky was blue and bright. His mother and McLaughlin, seen in the window, had been remote and bodiless; through their transparent profiles he had seen the yellowed trees going by. Now he could not see their faces at all.

"He's been back in Canada since the end of the war. He was wounded. Den hardly knows him," he heard his mother say. "I couldn't come. I had to wait my turn. We were over a thousand war brides on that ship. He was with Aluminium when he first came back." She pronounced the five vowels in the word.

"You'll be all right there," said McLaughlin. "It's a big place. Schools. All company."

"Pardon me?"

"I mean it all belongs to Aluminum. Only if that's where you're going you happen to be on the wrong train."

"He isn't there now. He hates towns. He seems to move about a great deal. He drives a bulldozer, you see."

"Owns it?" said McLaughlin.

"Why, I shouldn't *think* so. Drives for another man, I think he said."

The boy's father fell into the vast pool of casual labor, drifters; there was a social hierarchy in the north, just as in Heaven. McLaughlin was an engineer. He took another look at the boy: black hair, blue eyes. The hair was coarse, straight, rather dull; Indian hair. The mother was a blonde; touched up a bit, but still blond.

"What name?" said McLaughlin on the upward note of someone who has asked the same question twice.

"Cameron. Donald Cameron."

That meant nothing, still; McLaughlin had worked in a place on James Bay where the Indians were named MacDonald and Ogilvie and had an unconquered genetic strain of blue eyes.

"D'you know about any ghosts?" said the boy, turning to McLaughlin. McLaughlin's eyes were paler than his own, which were a deep slate blue, like the eyes of a newly born child. McLaughlin saw the way he held his footing on the rocking train, putting out a few fingers to the window sill only for the form of the thing. He looked all at once ridiculous and dishonored in his cheap English clothes—the little jacket, the Tweedledum cap on his head. He outdistanced his clothes; he was better than they were. But he was rushing on this train into an existence where his clothes would be too good for him.

"D'you know about any ghosts?" said the boy again.

"Oh, sure," said McLaughlin, and shivered, for he still felt sick, even though he was sharing a bottle with the Limey bride. He said, "Indians see them," which was as close as he could come to being crafty. But there was no reaction out of the mother; she was not English for nothing.

"You seen any?"

"*I'm* not an Indian," McLaughlin started to say; instead he said, "Well, yes. I saw the ghost, or something like the ghost, of a dog I had."

They looked at each other, and the boy's mother said, "Stop that, you two. Stop that this minute."

"I'll tell you a strange thing about Dennis," said his mother. "It's this. There's times he gives me the creeps."

Dennis was lying on the seat beside her with his head on her lap.

She said, "If I don't like it I can clear out. I was a waitress. There's always work."

"Or find another man," McLaughlin said. "Only it won't be me, girlie. I'll be far away."

"Den says that when the train stopped he saw a lot of elves," she said, complaining.

"Not elves—men," said Dennis. "Some of them had mattresses rolled up on their backs. They were little and bent over. They were talking French. They were going up north."

McLaughlin coughed and said, "He means settlers. They were sent up on this same train during the depression. But that's nine, ten years ago. It was supposed to clear the unemployed out of the towns, get them off relief. But there wasn't anything up here then. The winters were terrible. A lot of them died."

"He couldn't know that," said Mum edgily. "For that matter, how can he tell what is French? He's never heard any."

"No, he couldn't know. It was around ten years ago, when times were bad."

"Are they good now?"

"Jeez, after a *war*?" He shoved his hand in the pocket of his shirt, where he kept a roll, and he let her see the edge of it.

She made no comment, but put her hand on Den's head and said to him, "You didn't see anyone. Now shut up."

"Sor 'em," the boy said in a voice as low as he could descend without falling into a whisper.

"You'll see what your Dad'll give you when you tell lies." But she was halfhearted about the threat and did not quite believe in it. She had been attracted to the scenery, whose persistent sameness she could no longer ignore. "It's not proper country," she said. "It's bare."

"Not enough for me," said McLaughlin. "Too many people. I keep on moving north."

"I want to see some Indians," said Dennis, sitting up.

"There aren't any," his mother said. "Only in films."

"I don't like Canada." He held her arm. "Let's go home now."

"It's the train whistle. It's so sad. It gets him down."

The train slowed, jerked, flung them against each other, and came to a stop. It was quite day now; their faces were plain and clear, as if drawn without shading on white paper. McLaughlin felt responsible for them, even compassionate; the change in him made the boy afraid.

"We're getting down, Den," said his Mum, with great, wide eyes. "We take another train. See? It'll be grand. Do you hear what Mum's telling you?"

He was determined not to leave the train, and clung to the window sill, which was too smooth and narrow to provide a grip; McLaughlin had no difficulty getting him away. "I'll give you a present," he said hurriedly. But he slapped all his pockets and found nothing to give. He did not think of the money, and his watch had been stolen in Montreal. The woman and the boy struggled out with their baggage, and McLaughlin, who had descended first so as to help them down, reached up and swung the boy in his arms.

"The Indians!" the boy cried, clinging to the train, to air; to anything. His face was momentarily muffled by McLaughlin's shirt. His cap fell to the ground. He screamed, "Where's Mum? I never saw *any*thing!"

"You saw Indians," said McLaughlin. "On the rail fence, at that long stop. Look, don't worry your mother. Don't keep telling her what you haven't seen. You'll be seeing plenty of everything now."

MY HEART IS BROKEN

"WHEN that Jean Harlow died," Mrs. Thompson said to Jeannie, "I was on the 83 streetcar with a big, heavy paper parcel in my arms. I hadn't been married for very long, and when I used to visit my mother she'd give me a lot of canned stuff and preserves. I was standing up in the streetcar because nobody'd given me a seat. All the men were unemployed in those days, and they just sat down wherever they happened to be. You wouldn't remember what Montreal was like then. *You* weren't even on earth. To resume what I was saying to you, one of these men sitting down had an American paper—the *Daily News*, I guess it was— and I was sort of leaning over him, and I saw in big print JEAN HAR-LOW DEAD. You can believe me or not, just as you want to, but that was the most terrible shock I ever had in my life. I never got over it."

Jeannie had nothing to say to that. She lay flat on her back across the bed, with her head toward Mrs. Thompson and her heels just touching the crate that did as a bedside table. Balanced on her flat stomach was an open bottle of coral-pink Cutex nail polish. She held her hands up over her head and with some difficulty applied the brush to the nails of her right hand. Her legs were brown and thin. She wore nothing but shorts and one of her husband's shirts. Her feet were bare.

Mrs. Thompson was the wife of the paymaster in a road-construction camp in northern Quebec. Jeannie's husband was an engineer working on the same project. The road was being pushed through country where nothing had existed until now except rocks and lakes and muskeg. The camp was established between a wild lake and the line of raw dirt that was the road. There were no towns between the camp and the railway spur, sixty miles distant.

Mrs. Thompson, a good deal older than Jeannie, had become her best friend. She was a nice, plain, fat, consoling sort of person, with varicosed legs, shoes unlaced and slit for comfort, blue flannel dressing gown worn at all hours, pudding-bowl haircut, and coarse gray hair. She might have been Jeannie's own mother, or her Auntie Pearl. She rocked her fat self in the rocking chair and went on with what she had to say: "What I was starting off to tell you is you remind me of her, of Jean Harlow. You've got the same teeny mouth, Jeannie, and I think your hair was a whole lot prettier before you started fooling around with it. That peroxide's no good. It splits the ends. I know you're going to tell me it isn't peroxide but something more modern, but the result is the same."

Vern's shirt was spotted with coral-pink that had dropped off the brush. Vern wouldn't mind; at least, he wouldn't say that he minded. If he hadn't objected to anything Jeannie did until now, he wouldn't start off by complaining about a shirt. The campsite outside the un-curtained window was silent and dark. The waning moon would not appear until dawn. A passage of thought made Mrs. Thompson say, "Winter soon."

Jeannie moved sharply and caught the bottle of polish before it spilled. Mrs. Thompson was crazy; it wasn't even September.

"Pretty soon," Mrs. Thompson admitted. "Pretty soon. That's a long season up here, but I'm one person doesn't complain. I've been up here or around here every winter of my married life, except for that one winter Pops was occupying Germany."

"I've been up here seventy-two days," said Jeannie, in her soft voice. "Tomorrow makes seventy-three."

"Is that right?" said Mrs. Thompson, jerking the rocker forward, suddenly snappish. "Is that a fact? Well, who asked you to come up here? Who asked you to come and start counting days like you was in some kind of jail? When you got married to Vern, you must of known where he'd be taking you. He told you, didn't he, that he liked road jobs, construction jobs, and that? Did he tell you, or didn't he?"

"Oh, he told me," said Jeannie.

"You know what, Jeannie?" said Mrs. Thompson. "If you'd of just listened to me, none of this would have happened. I told you that first day, the day you arrived here in your high-heeled shoes, I said, 'I know this cabin doesn't look much, but all the married men have the same sort of place.' You remember I said that? I said, 'You just get some curtains up and some carpets down and it'll be home.' I took you over and showed you my place, and you said you'd never seen anything so lovely."

"I meant it," said Jeannie. "Your cabin is just lovely. I don't know why, but I never managed to make this place look like yours."

Mrs. Thompson said, "That's plain enough." She looked at the cold grease spattered behind the stove, and the rag of towel over by the sink. "It's partly the experience," she said kindly. She and her husband knew exactly what to take with them when they went on a job, they had been doing it for so many years. They brought boxes for artificial flowers, a brass door knocker, a portable bar decorated with sea shells, a cardboard fireplace that looked real, and an electric fire that sent waves of light rippling over the ceiling and walls. A concealed gramophone played the records they loved and cherished—the good old tunes. They had comic records that dated back to the year I, and sad soprano records about shipwrecks and broken promises and babies' graves. The first time Jeannie heard one of the funny records, she was scared to death. She was paying a formal call, sitting straight in her chair, with her skirt pulled around her knees. Vern and Pops Thompson were talking about the Army.

"I wish to God I was back," said old Pops.

"Don't I?" said Vern. He was fifteen years older than Jeannie and had been through a lot.

At first there were only scratching and whispering noises, and then a mosquito orchestra started to play, and a dwarf's voice came into the room. "Little Johnnie Green, little Sallie Brown," squealed the dwarf, higher and faster than any human ever could. "Spooning in the park with the grass all around."

"Where is he?" Jeannie cried, while the Thompsons screamed with laughter and Vern smiled. The dwarf sang on: "And each little bird in the treetop high/Sang 'Oh you kid!' and winked his eye."

It was a record that had belonged to Pops Thompson's mother. He had been laughing at it all his life. The Thompsons loved living up north and didn't miss cities or company. Their cabin smelled of cocoa and toast. Over their beds were oval photographs of each other as children, and they had some Teddy bears and about a dozen dolls.

Jeannie capped the bottle of polish, taking care not to press it against her wet nails. She sat up with a single movement and set the bottle down on the bedside crate. Then she turned to face Mrs. Thompson. She sat cross-legged, with her hands outspread before her. Her face was serene.

"Not an ounce of fat on you," said Mrs. Thompson. "You know something? I'm sorry you're going. I really am. Tomorrow you'll be gone. You know that, don't you? You've been counting days, but you won't have to anymore. I guess Vern'll take you back to Montreal. What do you think?"

Jeannie dropped her gaze, and began smoothing wrinkles on the bedspread. She muttered something Mrs. Thompson could not understand.

"Tomorrow you'll be gone," Mrs. Thompson continued. "I know it for a fact. Vern is at this moment getting his pay, and borrowing a jeep from Mr. Sherman, and a Polack driver to take you to the train. He sure is loyal to *you*. You know what I heard Mr. Sherman say? He said to Vern, 'If you want to send her off, Vern, you can always stay,' and Vern said, 'I can't very well do that, Mr. Sherman.' And Mr. Sherman said, 'This is the second time you've had to leave a job on account of her, isn't it?,' and then Mr. Sherman said, 'In my opinion, no man by his own self can rape a girl, so there were either two men or else she's invented the whole story.' Then he said, 'Vern, you're either a saint or a damn fool.' That was all I heard. I came straight over here, Jeannie, because I thought you might be needing me." Mrs. Thompson waited to hear she was needed. She stopped rocking and sat with her feet flat and wide apart. She struck her knees with her open palms and cried, "I *told* you to keep away from the men. I told you it would make trouble, all that being cute and dancing around. I said to you, I remember saying it, I said nothing makes trouble faster in a place like this than a grown woman behaving like a little girl. Don't you remember?"

"I only went out for a walk," said Jeannie. "Nobody'll believe me, but that's all. I went down the road for a walk."

"In high heels?" said Mrs. Thompson. "With a purse on your arm, and a hat on your head? You don't go taking a walk in the bush that way. There's no place to walk *to*. Where'd you think you were going? I could smell Evening in Paris a quarter mile away."

"There's no place to go," said Jeannie, "but what else is there to do? I just felt like dressing up and going out."

"You could have cleaned up your home a bit," said Mrs. Thompson. "There was always that to do. Just look at that sink. That basket of ironing's been under the bed since July. I know it gets boring around here, but you had the best of it. You had the summer. In winter it gets dark around three o'clock. Then the wives have a right to go crazy. I knew one used to sleep the clock around. When her Nembutal ran out, she took about a hundred aspirin. I knew another learned to distill her own liquor, just to kill time. Sometimes the men get so's they don't like the life, and that's death for the wives. But here you had a nice summer, and Vern liked the life."

"He likes it better than anything," said Jeannie. "He liked the Army, but this was his favorite life after that."

"There," said Mrs. Thompson. "You had every reason to be happy. What'd you do if he sent you off alone, now, like Mr. Sherman advised? You'd be alone and you'd have to work. Women don't know when they're well off. Here you've got a good, sensible husband working for you and you don't appreciate it. You have to go and do a terrible thing."

"I only went for a walk," said Jeannie. "That's all I did."

"It's possible," said Mrs. Thompson, "but it's a terrible thing. It's about the worst thing that's ever happened around here. I don't know why you let it happen. A women can always defend what's precious, even if she's attacked. I hope you remembered to think about bacteria."

"What d'you mean?"

"I mean Javelle, or something."

Jeannie looked uncomprehending and then shook her head.

"I wonder what it must be like," said Mrs. Thompson after a time, looking at the dark window. "I mean, think of Berlin and them Russians and all. Think of some disgusting fellow you don't know. Never said hello to, even. Some girls ask for it, though. You can't always blame the man. The man loses his job, his wife if he's got one, everything, all because of a silly girl."

Jeannie frowned, absently. She pressed her nails together, testing the polish. She licked her lips and said, "I was more beaten up, Mrs. Thompson. It wasn't exactly what you think. It was only afterwards I thought to myself, Why, I was raped and everything."

Mrs. Thompson gasped, hearing the word from Jeannie. She said, "Have you got any marks?"

"On my arms. That's why I'm wearing this shirt. The first thing I did was change my clothes."

Mrs. Thompson thought this over, and went on to another thing: "Do you ever think about your mother?"

"Sure."

"Do you pray? If this goes on at nineteen—"

"I'm twenty."

"—what'll you be by the time you're thirty? You've already got a terrible, terrible memory to haunt you all your life."

"I already can't remember it," said Jeannie. "Afterwards I started walking back to camp, but I was walking the wrong way. I met Mr. Sherman. The back of his car was full of coffee, flour, all that. I guess he'd been picking up supplies. He said, 'Well, get in.' He didn't ask any questions at first. I couldn't talk anyway."

"Shock," said Mrs. Thompson wisely.

"You know, I'd have to see it happening to know what happened. All I remember is that first we were only talking..."

"You and Mr. Sherman?"

"No, no, before. When I was taking my walk."

"Don't say who it was," said Mrs. Thompson. "We don't any of us need to know."

"We were just talking, and he got sore all of a sudden and grabbed my arm."

"Don't say the name!" Mrs. Thompson cried.

"Like when I was little, there was this Lana Turner movie. She had two twins. She was just there and then a nurse brought her in the two twins. I hadn't been married or anything, and I didn't know anything, and I used to think if I just kept on seeing the movie I'd know how she got the two twins, you know, and I went, oh, I must have seen it six times, the movie, but in the end I never knew any more. They just brought her the two twins."

Mrs. Thompson sat quite still, trying to make sense of this. "Taking advantage of a woman is a criminal offense," she observed. "I heard Mr. Sherman say another thing, Jeannie. He said, 'If your wife wants to press a charge and talk to some lawyer, let me tell you,' he said, 'you'll never work again anywhere,' he said. Vern said, 'I know that, Mr. Sherman.' And Mr. Sherman said, 'Let me tell you, if any reporters or any investigators start coming around here, they'll get their ... they'll never ...' Oh, he was mad. And Vern said, 'I came over to tell you I was quitting, Mr. Sherman.'" Mrs. Thompson had been acting this with spirit, using a quiet voice when she spoke for Vern and a blustering tone for Mr. Sherman. In her own voice, she said, "If you're wondering how I came to hear all this, I was strolling by Mr. Sherman's office window—his bungalow, that is. I had Maureen out in her pram." Maureen was the Thompsons' youngest doll.

Jeannie might not have been listening. She started to tell something else: "You know, where we were before, on Vern's last job, we weren't in a camp. He was away a lot, and he left me in Amos, in a hotel. I liked it. Amos isn't all that big, but it's better than here. There was this German in the hotel. He was selling cars. He'd drive me around if I wanted to go to a movie or anything. Vern didn't like him, so we left. It wasn't anybody's fault."

"So he's given up two jobs," said Mrs. Thompson. "One because he couldn't leave you alone, and now this one. Two jobs, and you haven't been married five months. Why should another man be thrown out of work? We don't need to know a thing. I'll be sorry if it was Jimmy Quinn," she went on, slowly. "I like that boy. Don't say the name, dear. There's Evans. Susini. Palmer. But it might have been anybody, because you had them all on the boil. So it might have been Jimmy Quinn—let's say—and it could have been anyone else, too. Well, now let's hope they can get their minds back on the job."

"I thought they all liked me," said Jeannie sadly. "I get along with people. Vern never fights with me."

"Vern never fights with anyone. But he ought to have thrashed *you*."

"If he . . . you know. I won't say the name. If he'd liked me, I wouldn't have minded. If he'd been friendly. I really mean that. I wouldn't have gone wandering up the road, making all this fuss."

"Jeannie," said Mrs. Thompson, "you don't even know what you're saying."

"He could at least have liked me," said Jeannie. "He wasn't even friendly. It's the first time in my life somebody hasn't liked me. My heart is broken, Mrs. Thompson. My heart is just broken."

She has to cry, Mrs. Thompson thought. She has to have it out. She rocked slowly, tapping her foot, trying to remember how she'd felt about things when she was twenty, wondering if her heart had ever been broken, too.

ORPHANS' PROGRESS

WHEN THE Collier girls were six and ten they were taken away from their mother, whom they loved without knowing what the word implied, or even that it existed, and sent to their father's mother. Their grandmother was scrupulous about food, particularly for these underfed children, and made them drink goat's milk. Two goats bought specially to supply the orphans were taken by station wagon to a buck fifty miles away, the girls accompanying them for reasons of enlightenment. A man in a filling station was frightened by the goats, because of their oblong eyes. The girls were not reflected in the goats' eyes, as they were in each other's. What they remembered afterwards of their grandmother was goat's milk, goat eyes, and the frightened man.

They went to school in Ontario now, with children who did not have the same accent as children in Montreal. When their new friends liked something they said it was smart. A basketball game was smart, so was a movie: it did not mean elegant, it just meant all right. Ice cream made out of goat's milk was not smart: it tasted of hair.

Their grandmother died when the girls were seven and eleven and beginning to speak in the Ontario way. Their mother had been French-Canadian—they were now told—but had spoken French and English to them. They had called her Mummy, a habit started when their father was still alive, for he had not learned French. They understood, from their grandmother, and their grandmother's maid, and the social worker who came to see their grandmother but had little to say to them, that French was an inferior kind of speech. At first, when they were taken away from their mother, Cathie, the elder girl, would wake up at night holding her head, her elbows on her knees, saying in French, "My head hurts," but a few minutes later, the grandmother having applied cold wrung-out towels, she would say in English, "It's better."

Mildred had pushed out two front teeth by sucking her thumb. She had been doing that forever, even before they were taken away from their mother. Ontario could not be blamed. Nevertheless, their grandmother told the social worker about it, who wrote it down.

They did not know, and never once asked, why they had been taken away. When the new social worker said to Cathie, "Were you disturbed because your mother was unhappy?" Cathie said, "She wasn't." When the girls were living with their mother, they knew that sometimes she listened and sometimes could not hear; nevertheless, she was there. They slept in the same bed, all three. Even when she sat on the side of the bed with her head hanging and her undone jagged-cut hair hiding her eyes, mumbling complaints that were not their concern, the children were close to her and did not know they were living under what would be called later "unsheltered conditions." They never knew, until told, that they were uneducated and dirty and in danger. Now they learned that their mother never washed her own neck and that she dressed in layers of woolen stuff, covered with grease, and wore men's shoes because some man had left them behind and she liked the shape or the comfort of them. They did not know, until they were told, that they had never been properly fed.

"We ate chicken," said Cathie Collier, the elder girl.

"They say she served it up half raw," said their grandmother's maid. "Survet" said the maid for "served," and that was not the way their mother had spoken. "The sheets was so dirty, the dirt was like clay. All of yez slept in the one bed," said the maid.

"Yes, we slept together." The apartment—a loft, they were told, over a garage; not an apartment at all—must still exist, it must be somewhere, with the piano that Mildred, the little one, had banged on with her palms flat. What about the two cats who were always fighting or playing, depending on their disposition? There were pictures on the wall, their mother's and the children's own drawings.

"When one of the pictures was moved there was a square mass of bugs," said the grandmother's maid. "The same shape as the pitcher."

"To the day I die," said the social worker from Montreal to her colleague in Ontario, "I won't forget the screams of Mildred when she was dragged out of that pigsty." This was said in the grandmother's parlor, where the three women—the two social workers, and the grandmother—sat with their feet freezing on the linoleum floor. The maid heard, and told. She had been in and out, serving coffee, coconut biscuits, and damson preserves in custard made of goat's milk. The room was heated once or twice a year: even the maid said her feet were cold. But "To the day I die" was a phrase worth hearing. She liked the sound of that, and said it to the children. The maid was from a place called Waterloo, where, to hear her tell it, no one behaved strangely and all the rooms were warm.

Thumb-sucker Mildred did not remember having screamed, or anything at all except the trip from Montreal by train. "Boy, is your grandmother ever a rich old lady!" said the maid from Waterloo. "If she wasn't, where'd you be? In an orphung asylum. She's a Christian, I can tell you." But another day, when she was angry with the grandmother over something, she said, "She's a damned old sow. It's in the mattress and she's lying on it. You can hear the bills crackle when you turn the mattress Saturdays. I hope they find it when she dies, is all I can say."

The girls saw their grandmother dead, in the bed, on that mattress. The person crying hardest in the room was the maid. She had suddenly dyed her hair dark red, and the girls did not know her, because of her tears, and her new clothes, and because of the way she fondled and kissed them. "We'll never see each other again," said the maid.

Now that their grandmother had died, the girls went to live with their mother's brother and his wife and their many children. It was a suburb of Montreal called Ahuntsic. They did not see anything that reminded them of Montreal, and did not recall their mother. There was a parlor here full of cut glass, which was daily rubbed and polished, and two television sets, one for the use of the children. The girls slept on a pull-out divan and wrangled about bedclothes. Cathie wanted them pushed down between them in a sort of trough, because she felt a draft, but Mildred complained that the blankets thus arranged were tugged away from her side. She was not properly covered and afraid of falling on the floor. One of their relations (they had any number here on their mother's side) made them a present of a box of chocolate almonds, but the cousins they lived with bought exactly the same box, so as to tease them. When Cathie and Mildred rushed to see if their own box was still where they had hidden it, they were bitterly mocked. Their Ontario grandmother's will was not probated and every scrap of food they put in their mouths was taken from the mouths of cousins: so they were told. Their cousins made them afraid of ghosts. They put out the lights and said, "Look out, she is coming to get you, all in black," and when Mildred began to whimper, Cathie said, "Our mother wouldn't try to frighten us." She had not spoken of her until now. One of the cousins said, "I'm talking about your old grandmother. Your mother isn't dead." They were shown their father's grave, and made to kneel and pray. Their lives were in the dark now, in the dark of ghosts, whose transparent shadows stood round their bed; soon they lived in the black of nuns. Language was black, until they forgot their English. Until they spoke French, nothing but French, the family pretended not to understand them, and stared as if they were peering in the dark. They very soon forgot their English.

They could not stay here with these cousins forever, for the flat was too small. When they were eight and twelve, their grandmother's will was probated and they were sent to school. For the first time in their lives, now, the girls did not sleep in the same bed. Mildred slept in a dormitory with the little girls, where a green light burned overhead, and a nun rustled and prayed or read beside a green lamp all night long. Mildred was bathed once every fortnight, wearing a rubber apron so that she would not see her own body. Like the other little girls, she dressed, in the morning, sitting on the floor, so that they would not see one another. Her thumb, sucked white, was taped to the palm of her hand. She caught glimpses of Cathie sometimes during recreation periods, but Cathie was one of the big girls, and important. She did not play, as the little ones still did, but walked up and down with the supervisor, walking backwards as the nun walked forward.

One day, looking out of a dormitory window, Mildred saw a rooftop and an open skylight. She said to a girl standing nearby, "That's our house." "What house?" "Where Mummy lives." She said that sentence, three words, in English. She had not thought or spoken "Mummy" since she was six and a half. It turned out that she was lying about the house. Lying was serious; she was made to promenade through the classrooms carrying a large pair of shears and the sign I AM A LIAR. She did not know the significance of the shears, nor, it seemed, did the nun who organized the punishment. It had always been associated with lying, and (the nun suddenly remembered) had to do with cutting out the liar's tongue. The tattling girl, who had told about "Where Mummy lives," was punished too, and made to carry a wastebasket from room to room with I AM A BASKET-CARRIER hung round her neck. This meant a tale-bearer. Everyone was in the wrong.

Cathie was not obliged to wear a rubber apron in her bath, but a muslin shift. She learned the big girls' trick, which was to take it off and dip it in water, and then bathe properly. When Mildred came round carrying her scissors and her sign Cathie had had her twice-monthly bath and felt damp and new. She said to someone, "That's my sister," but "sister" was a dark scowling little thing. "Sister" got into still more trouble: a nun, a stray from Belgium, perhaps as one refugee to another, said to Mildred, swiftly drawing her into a broom-cupboard, "Call me Maman." "Maman" said the child, to whom "Mummy" had meaning until the day of the scissors. Who was there to hear what was said in the broom-cupboard? What basket-carrier repeated that? It was forbidden for nuns to have favorites, forbidden to have pet names for nuns, and the Belgian stray was sent to the damp wet room behind the chapel and given flower-arranging to attend to. There Mildred found her, by chance, and the nun said, "Get away, haven't you made enough trouble for me?"

Cathie was told to pray for Mildred, the trouble-maker, but forgot. The omission weighed on her. She prayed for her mother, grandmother, father, herself (with a glimpse in the prayer of her own future coffin, white) and the uncles and aunts and cousins she knew and those she had never met. Her worry about forgetting Mildred in her prayers caused her to invent a formula: "Everyone I have ever known who is dead or alive, anyone I know now who is alive but might die, and anyone I shall ever know in the future." She prayed for her best friend, who wanted like Cathie to become a teacher, and for a nun with a mustache who was jolly, and for her confessor, who liked to hear her playing the Radetzky March on the piano. Her hair grew lighter and was brushed and combed by her best friend.

Mildred was suddenly taken out of school and adopted. Their mother's sister, one of the aunts they had seldom seen, had lost a daughter by drowning. She said she would treat Mildred as she did her own small son, and Mildred, who wished to leave the convent school, but did not know if she cared to go and live in a place called Chicoutimi, did not decide. She made them decide, and made them take her away. When the girls were fifteen and nineteen, and Mildred was called Desaulniers and not Collier, the sisters were made to meet. Cathie had left school and was studying nursing, but she came back to the convent when she had time off, not because she did not have anywhere else to go, but because she did not want to go to any other place. The nuns had said of Cathie, laughing, "She doesn't want to leave—we shall have to push her out." When Cathie's sister, Mildred Desaulniers, came to call on her, the girls did not know what to say. Mildred wore a round straw hat with a clump of plastic cherries hanging over the brim; her adoptive brother, in long trousers and bow tie, did not get out of the car. He was seven, and had slick wet-looking hair, as if he had been swimming. "Kiss your sister," said Mildred's mother, to Cathie, admonishingly. Cathie did as she was told, and Mildred immediately got back in the car with her brother and snatched a comic book out of his hands. "Look, Mildred," said her father, and let the car slow down on a particular street. The parents craned at a garage, and at dirty-legged children with torn sneakers on their feet. Mildred glanced up and then back at her book. She had no reason to believe she had seen it before, or would ever again.

WITH A CAPITAL T

For Madeleine and Jean-Paul Lemieux

IN WARTIME, in Montreal, I applied to work on a newspaper. Its name was *The Lantern*, and its motto, "My light shall shine," carried a Wesleyan ring of veracity and plain dealing. I chose it because I thought it was a place where I would be given a lot of different things to do. I said to the man who consented to see me, "But not the women's pages. Nothing like that." I was eighteen. He heard me out and suggested I come back at twenty-one, which was a soft way of getting rid of me. In the meantime I was to acquire experience; he did not say of what kind. On the stroke of twenty-one I returned and told my story to a different person. I was immediately accepted; I had expected to be. I still believed, then, that most people meant what they said. I supposed that the man I had seen that first time had left a memorandum in the files: "To whom it may concern—Three years from this date, Miss Linnet Muir will join the editorial staff." But after I'd been working for a short time I heard one of the editors say, "If it hadn't been for the god-damned war we would never have hired even one of the god-damned women," and so I knew.

In the meantime I had acquired experience by getting married. I was no longer a Miss Muir, but a Mrs. Blanchard. My husband was overseas. I had longed for emancipation and independence, but I was learning that women's autonomy is like a small inheritance paid out a penny at a time. In a journal I kept I scrupulously noted everything that came into my head about this, and about God, and about politics. I took it for granted that our victory over Fascism would be followed by a sunburst of revolution—I thought that was what the war was about. I wondered if going to work for the capitalist press was entirely moral. "Whatever happens," I wrote, "it will be the Truth, nothing half-hearted, the Truth with a Capital T."

The first thing I had to do was write what goes under the pictures. There is no trick to it. You just repeat what the picture has told you like this:

"Boy eats bun as bear looks on."

The reason why anything has to go under the picture at all is that a reader might wonder, "Is that a bear looking on?" It looks like a bear, but that is not enough reason for saying so. Pasted across the back of the photo you have been given is a strip of paper on which you can read: "Saskatoon, Sask. 23 Nov. Boy eats bun as bear looks on." Whoever composed this knows two things more than you do—a place and a time.

You have a space to fill in which the words must come out even. The space may be tight; in that case, you can remove "as" and substitute a comma, though that makes the kind of terse statement to which your reader is apt to reply, "So what?" Most of the time, the Truth with a Capital T is a matter of elongation: "Blond boy eats small bun as large bear looks on."

"Blond boy eats buttered bun . . ." is livelier, but unscrupulous. You have been given no information about the butter. "Boy eats bun as hungry bear looks on," has the beginnings of a plot, but it may inspire your reader to protest: "That boy must be a mean sort of kid if he won't share his food with a starving creature." Child-lovers, though less prone to fits of anguish than animal-lovers, may be distressed by the word "hungry" for a different reason, believing "boy" subject to attack from "bear." You must not lose your head and type, "Blond bear eats large boy as hungry bun looks on," because your reader may notice, and write a letter saying, "Some of you guys around there think you're pretty smart, don't you?" while another will try to enrich your caption with, "Re your bun write-up, my wife has taken better pictures than that in the very area you mention."

At the back of your mind, because your mentors have placed it there, is an obstruction called "the policy factor." Your paper supports a political party. You try to discover what this party has had to say about buns and bears, how it intends to approach them in the future. Your editor, at golf with a member of parliament, will not want to have his game upset by: "It's not that I want to interfere but some of that bun stuff seems pretty negative to me." The young and vulnerable reporter would just as soon not pick up the phone to be told, "I'm ashamed of your defeatist attitude. Why, I knew your father! He must be spinning in his grave!" or, more effectively, "I'm telling you this for your own good—I think you're subversive without knowing it."

Negative, defeatist, and subversive are three of the things you have been cautioned not to be. The others are seditious, obscene, obscure, ironic, intellectual, and impulsive.

You gather up the photo and three pages of failed captions, and knock at the frosted glass of a senior door. You sit down and are given a view of boot soles. You say that the whole matter comes down to an ethical question concerning information and redundancy; unless "reader" is blotto, can't he see for himself that this is about a boy, a bun, and a bear?

Your senior person is in shirtsleeves, hands clasped behind his neck. He thinks this over, staring at the ceiling; swings his feet to the floor; reads your variations on the bear-and-bun theme; turns the photo upside-down. He tells you patiently, that it is not the business of "reader" to draw conclusions. Our subscribers are not dreamers or smart alecks; when they see a situation in a picture, they want that situation confirmed. He reminds you about negativism and obscuration; advises you to go sit in the library and acquire a sense of values by reading the back issues of *Life*.

The back numbers of *Life* are tatty and incomplete, owing to staff habits of tearing out whatever they wish to examine at leisure. A few captions, still intact, allow you to admire a contribution to pictorial journalism, the word "note":

"American flag flies over new post office. Note stars on flag."

"GI waves happily from captured Italian tank. Note helmet on head."

So, "Boy eats bun as bear looks on. Note fur on bear." All that can happen now will be a letter asking, "Are you sure it was a bun?"

From behind frosted-glass doors, as from a leaking intellectual bath, flow instructions about style, spelling, caution, libel, brevity, and something called "the ground rules." A few of these rules have been established for the convenience of the wives of senior persons and reflect their tastes and interests, their inhibitions and fears, their desire to see close friends' pictures when they open to the social page, their fragile attention span. Other rules demand that we pretend to be independent of British foreign policy and American commerce—otherwise our readers, discouraged, will give up caring who wins the war. (Soon after victory British foreign policy will cease to exist; as for American commerce, the first grumbling will be heard when a factory in Buffalo is suspected of having flooded the country with defective twelve-inch pie tins.) Ground rules maintain that you must not be flippant about the Crown—an umbrella term covering a number of high-class subjects, from the Royal Family to the nation's judicial system—or about our war effort or, indeed, our reasons for making any effort about anything. Religions, in particular those observed by decent Christians, are not up for debate. We may, however, describe and denounce marginal sects whose puritanical learnings are even more dizzily slanted than our own. The Jehovah's Witnesses, banned as seditious, continue to issue inflammatory pamphlets about Jesus; patriotic outrage abounds over this. The children of Witnesses are beaten up in public schools for refusing to draw Easter bunnies. An education officer, interviewed, declares that the children's obstinate observance of the Second Commandment is helping Hitler. Everyone knows that the Easter bunny, along with God and Santa Claus, is on our side.

To argue a case for the children is defeatist; to advance reasons against their persecution is obscure. Besides, your version of the bunny conflict may be unreliable. Behind frosted-glass doors lurk male fears of female mischief. Women, having no inborn sense of history, are known to invent absurd stories. Celebrated newspaper hoaxes (perpetrated by men, as it happens) are described to you, examples of irresponsible writing that have brought down trusting editors. A few of these stories have been swimming, like old sea turtles, for years now, crawling ashore wherever British possessions are still tinted red on the map. "As the niece of the Governor-General rose from a deep curtsey, the Prince, with the boyish smile that has made him the darling of five continents, picked up a bronze bust of his grandmother and battered Lady Adeline to death" is one version of a perennial favorite.

Privately, you think you could do better. You will never get the chance. The umpires of ground rules are nervous and watchful behind those doors. Wartime security hangs heavy. So does the fear that the end of hostilities will see them turfed out to make way for war correspondents wearing nonchalant mustaches, battered caps, carelessly-knotted white scarves, raincoats with shoulder tabs, punctuating their accounts of Hunnish atrocities perceived at Claridges and the Savoy with "Roger!" and "Jolly-oh!" and "Over to you!"

Awaiting this dreadful invasion the umpires sit, in shirtsleeves and braces, scribbling initials with thick blue pencils. "NDG" stands for "No Damned Good." (Clairvoyant, you will begin to write "NBF" in your journal meaning "No Bloody Future.") As a creeping, climbing wash of conflicting and contradictory instructions threatens to smother you, you discover the possibilities of the quiet, or lesser, hoax. Obeying every warning and precept, you will write, turn in, and get away with, "Dressed in shoes, stockings and hat appropriate to the season, Mrs. Horatio Bantam, the former Felicity Duckpond, grasped the bottle of champagne in her white-gloved hand and sent it swinging against the end of HMCS *Make-weight* that was nearest the official party, after which, swaying slightly, she slid down the ways and headed for open waters."

As soon as I realized that I was paid about half the salary men were earning, I decided to do half the work. I had spent much of my adolescence as a resourceful truant, evolving the good escape dodges that would serve one way and another all my life. At *The Lantern* I used reliable school methods. I would knock on a glass door—a door that had nothing to do with me.

"Well, Blanchard, what do you want?"

"Oh, Mr. Watchmaster—it's just to tell you I'm going out to look something up."

"What for?"

"An assignment."

"Don't tell *me*. Tell Amstutz."

"He's organizing fire-drill in case of air-raids."

"Tell Cranach. He can tell Amstutz."

"Mr. Cranach has gone to stop the art department from striking."

"*Striking*? Don't those buggers know there's a war on? I'd like to see Accounting try that. What do they want now?"

"Conditions. They're asking for conditions. Is it all right if I go now, Mr. Watchmaster?"

"You know what we need around here, don't you? One German regiment. Regiment? What am I saying? *Platoon*. That'd take the mickey out of 'em. Teach them something about hard work. Loving your country. Your duty. Give me one trained German sergeant. I'd lead him in. 'O.K.—you've been asking for this!' Ratatatat. You wouldn't hear any more guff about conditions. What's your assignment?"

"The Old Presbyterians. They've decided they're against killing people because of something God said to Moses."

"Seditious bastards. Put 'em in work camps, the whole damned lot. All right, Blanchard, carry on."

I would go home, wash my hair, listen to Billie Holiday records.

"Say, Blanchard, where the hell were you yesterday? Seventy-nine people were poisoned by ham sandwiches at a wedding party on Durocher Street. The sidewalk was like a morgue."

"Actually, I just happened to be in Mr. Watchmaster's office. But only for a minute."

"Watchmaster's got no right to ask you to do anything. One of these days I'm going to close in on him. I can't right now—there's a war on. The only good men we ever had in this country were killed in the last one. Look, next time Watchmaster gets you to run his errands, refer it to Cranach. Got that? All right, Blanchard, on your way."

No good dodge works forever.

"Oh, Mr. Watchmaster, I just wanted to tell you I'm going out for an hour or two. I have to look something up. Mr. Cranach's got his door locked, and Mr. Amstutz had to go home to see why his wife was crying."

"Christ, what an outfit. What do you have to look up?"

"What Mussolini did to the Red Cross dogs. It's for the 'Whither Italy?' supplement."

"You don't need to leave the building for that. You can get all you want by phone. You highbrows don't even know what a phone is. Drop around Advertising some time and I'll show you down-to-earth people using phones as working instruments. All you have to do is call the Red Cross, a veterinarian, an Italian priest, maybe an Italian restaurant, and a kennel. They'll tell you all you need to know. Remember what Churchill said about Mussolini, eh? That he was a fine Christian gentleman. If you want my opinion, whatever those dogs got they deserved."

Interviews were useful: you could get out and ride around in taxis and waste hours in hotel lobbies reading the new American magazines, which were increasingly difficult to find.

"I'm just checking something for *The Lantern*—do you mind?"

"Just so long as you don't mar the merchandise. I've only got five *Time*, three *Look*, four *Photoplay* and two *Ladies' Home*. Don't wander away with the *Esquire*. There's a war on."

Once I was sent to interview my own godmother. Nobody knew I knew her, and I didn't say. She was president of a committee that sent bundles to prisoners-of-war. The committee was launching an appeal for funds; that was the reason for the interview. I took down her name as if I had never heard it before: Miss Edna May Henderson. My parents had called her "Georgie," though I don't know why.

I had not seen my godmother since I was eight. My father had died, and I had been dragged away to be brought up in different cities. At eighteen, I had summoned her to a telephone: "It's Linnet," I said. "I'm here, in Montreal. I've come back to stay."

"Linnet," she said. "Good gracious me." Her chain-smoker's voice made me homesick, though it could not have been for a place—I was in it. Her voice, and her particular Montreal accent, were like the unexpected signatures that underwrite the past: If this much is true, you will tell yourself, then so is all the rest I have remembered.

She was too busy with her personal war drive to see me then, though she did ask for my phone number. She did not inquire where I had been since my father's death, or if I had anything here to come back to. It is true that she and my mother had quarreled years before; still, it was Georgie who had once renounced in my name "the devil and all his works, the vain pomp and glory of the world, with all covetous desires of the same, and carnal desires of the flesh." She might have been curious to see the result of her bizarre undertaking, but a native canny Anglo-Montreal prudence held her still.

I was calling from a drugstore; I lived in one room of a cold-water flat in the East End. I said, "I'm completely on my own, and entirely self-supporting." That was so Georgie would understand I was not looking for help; at all events, for nothing material.

I realize now how irregular, how fishy even, this must have sounded. Everybody has a phone, she was probably thinking. What is the girl trying to hide?

"Nothing" would have been the answer. There seemed no way to connect. She asked me to call her again in about a month's time, but of course I never did.

My godmother spent most of her life in a block of granite designed to look like a fortress. Within the fortress were sprawling apartments, drawn to an Edwardian pattern of high ceilings, dark corridors, and enormous kitchens full of pipes. Churches and schools, banks and prisons, dwellings and railway stations were part of an imperial contravallation that wound round the globe, designed to impress on the minds of indigenous populations that the builders had come to stay. In Georgie's redoubt, the doorman was shabby and lame; he limped beside me along a gloomy passage as far as the elevator, where only one of the sconce lights fixed to the paneling still worked. I had expected someone else to answer my ring, but it was Georgie who let me in, took my coat, and indicated with a brusque gesture, as if I did not know any English, the mat where I was to leave my wet snowboots. It had not occurred to me to bring shoes. Padding into her drawing room on stockinged feet, I saw the flash photograph her memory would file as further evidence of Muir incompetence; for I believe to this day that she recognized me at once. I was the final product, the last living specimen of a strain of people whose imprudence, lack of foresight, and refusal to take anything seriously had left one generation after another unprepared and stranded, obliged to build life from the ground up, fashioning new materials every time.

My godmother was tall, though not so tall as I remembered. Her face was wide and flat. Her eyes were small, deep-set, slightly tilted, as if two invisible thumbs were pulling at her temples. Her skin was as coarse and lined as a farm woman's; indifference to personal appearance of that kind used to be a matter of pride.

Her drawing room was white, and dingy and worn-looking. Curtains and armchairs needed attention, but that may have been on account of the war: it had been a good four years since anyone had bothered to paint or paper or have slipcovers made. The lamps were blue-and-white, and on this winter day already lighted. The room smelled of the metallic central heating of old apartment buildings, and of my godmother's Virginia cigarettes. We sat on worn white sofas, facing each other, with a table in between.

My godmother gave me Scotch in a heavy tumbler and pushed a dish of peanuts towards me, remarking in that harsh evocative voice, "Peanuts are harder to find than Scotch now." Actually, Scotch was off the map for most people; it was a civilian casualty, expensive and rare.

We were alone except for a Yorkshire terrier, who lay on a chair in the senile sleep that is part of dying.

"I would like it if Minnie could hang on until the end of the war," Georgie said. "I'm sure she'd like the victory parades and the bands. But she's thirteen, so I don't know."

That was the way she and my parents and their friends had talked to each other. The duller, the more earnest, the more literal generation I stood for seemed to crowd the worn white room, and to darken it further.

I thought I had better tell her straightaway who I was, though I imagined she knew. I did not intend to be friendly beyond that, unless she smiled. And even there, the quality of the smile would matter. Some smiles are instruments of repression.

Telling my new name, explaining that I had married, that I was now working for a newspaper, gave an accounting only up to a point. A deserted continent stretched between us, cracked and fissured with bottomless pits over which Georgie stepped easily. How do you deal with life? her particular Canadian catechism asked. By ignoring its claims on feeling. Any curiosity she may have felt about such mysteries as coincidence and continuity (my father was said to have been the love of her life; I was said to resemble him) had been abandoned, like a game that was once the rage. She may have been unlucky with games, which would explain the committee work; it may be dull, but you can be fairly sure of the outcome. I often came across women like her, then, who had no sons or lovers or husbands to worry about, and who adopted the principle of the absent, endangered male. A difference between us was that, to me, the absence and danger had to be taken for granted; another was that what I thought of as men, Georgie referred to as "boys." The rest was beyond my reach. Being a poor judge of probabilities, she had expected my father to divorce. I was another woman's child, foolish and vulnerable because I had lost my dignity along with my boots; paid to take down her words in a notebook; working not for a lark but for a living, which was unforgivable even then within the shabby fortress. I might have said, "I am innocent," but she already knew that.

My godmother was dressed in a jaunty blue jacket with a double row of brass buttons, and a pleated skirt. I supposed this must be the costume she and her committee wore when they were packing soap and cigarettes and second-hand cheery novels for their boys over there in the coop. She told me the names of the committee women, and said, "Are you getting everything down all right?" People ask that who are not used to being interviewed. "They told me there'd be a picture," she complained. That explained the uniform.

"I'm sorry. He should be here now."

"Do you want me to spell those names for you?"

"No. I'm sure I have them."

"You're not writing much."

"I don't need to," I said. "Not as a rule."

"You must have quite a memory."

She seemed to be trying to recall where my knack of remembering came from, if it was inherited, wondering whether memory is of any use to anyone except to store up reasons for discord.

We gave up waiting for the photographer. I stood stork-like in the passage, pulling on a boot. Georgie leaned on the wall, and I saw that she was slightly tight.

"I have four godchildren," she said. "People chose me because I was an old maid, and they thought I had money to leave. Well, I haven't. There'll be nothing for the boys. All my godchildren were boys. I never liked girls."

She had probably been drinking for much of the day, on and off; and of course there was all the excitement of being interviewed, and the shock of seeing me: still, it was a poor thing to say. Supposing, just supposing, that Georgie had been all I had left? My parents had been perfectly indifferent to money—almost pathologically so, I sometimes thought. The careless debts they had left strewn behind and that I kept picking up and trying to settle were not owed in currency.

Why didn't I come straight out with that? Because you can't—not in that world. No one can have the last retort, not even when there is truth to it. Hints and reminders flutter to the ground in overheated winter rooms, lie stunned for a season, are reborn as everlasting grudges.

"Goodbye, Linnet," she said.

"Goodbye."

"Do you still *not* have a telephone?" No answer. "When will it come out?" She meant the interview.

"On Saturday."

"I'll be looking for it." On her face was a look I took to mean anxiety over the picture, and that I now see to have been mortal terror. I never met her again, not even by accident. The true account I wrote of her committee and its need for public generosity put us at a final remove from each other.

I did not forget her, but I forgot about her. Her life seemed silent and slow and choked with wrack, while mine moved all in a rush, dislodging every obstacle it encountered. Then mine slowed too; stopped flooding its banks. The noise of it abated and I could hear the past. She had died by then—thick-skinned, chain-smoking survivor of the regiment holding the fort.

I saw us in the decaying winter room, saw the lamps blazing coldly on the dark window panes; I heard our voices: "Peanuts are harder to find than Scotch now." "Do you send parcels to Asia, or just to Germany?"

What a dull girl she is, Georgie must have thought; for I see, now, that I was seamless, and as smooth as brass; that I gave her no opening.

When she died, the godsons mentioned in her will swarmed around for a while, but after a certain amount of scuffling with trustees they gave up all claim, which was more dignified for them than standing forlorn and hungry-looking before a cupboard containing nothing. Nobody spoke up for the one legacy the trustees would have relinquished: a dog named Minnie, who was by then the equivalent of one hundred and nineteen years old in human time, and who persisted so unreasonably in her right to outlive the rest of us that she had to be put down without mercy.

THE OLD PLACE

THE HOUSE they had abandoned was eighteen miles from Pough-keepsie, in a valley almost deserted because of a bad road. Traffic had been diverted to the new highway in 1938; scarcely anything passed now, except the mailman's old Pontiac, halting with catalogues at boxes called Trapp, Arnheim, Clinton, Knickerbocker, and Van Loo, and the milk truck from Mr. Trapp's farm. The farmhouses, bleak and run-down, swarming with dirty blond children, were close to the road, with neither wall nor fence to hide their sagging porches and lines of wash. Except for the Arnheim place, which belonged to city people, and combined the traditionally pretty components of white walls, green roof, authentic stoop, and Virginia creeper, and the Trapps', which maintained a modicum of order and prosperity, showing the intense hard labor and avariciousness of the Trapp family, the valley, the road, gave an impression of failure and fatigue. Failure had run along the road as if it were the bed of a river, confined to a doomed stretch of valley and a shiftless few. Not three miles distant began the proper Dutchess County landscape, the calendar-art farms, the fat silos, the sleek, black Aberdeen Angus picturesquely dotting the hills.

The Arnheim place was in a hollow, but the fields around it sloped off at such a shallow angle that the windows were never cut off from sun. The walls of Dennis's room, covered with an old, glazed, misty-colored paper, drank in the sun like a yellow pool. His window looked west, over his mother's plum trees to Mr. Trapp's pasture, his Holsteins, and his three black walnut trees. Dennis's mother told him that those trees were beautiful, and very old. She said that his father's ancestors had loved them too; otherwise they would never have left them stand-ing in the middle of a valuable field. The Arnheims had owned most of the land in that area about two hundred years before. "Just think, Dennis, love," his mother would say. "Every morning of your life you can wake up and see those trees, just as your great-grandfather and great-great-grandfather did."

When Mr. Trapp decided to cut the trees down because he wanted to put corn in that field and the roots were in the way, Dennis stationed himself at his bedroom window, the better to watch. What he saw was his mother, running along the deserted road, crying, begging Mr. Trapp not to cut them down. She really behaved badly, making such a fool of herself that word of the scene drifted up the valley and into town. People said that Mrs. Arnheim was not only lame, but demented. It came back to Dennis, that story; it kept coming back for years. She did limp slightly, particularly when she was tired; a bone had been badly set after a skiing accident. Dennis could see her from his window, in a flowered cotton dress, arms bare and brown, hair bleached from swimming and sun. He could see how Mr. Trapp and Mr. Trapp's sons exchanged sly smiles as they got on with their business. She did look demented at that moment, and she limped more than she usually did, as if the futility of fighting against destruction, against people bound by their natures to destroy, had taken all her control. She limped back into the house, weeping, wiping her eyes.

That was one of Dennis's first complete memories. He remembered the whole scene, the words cried out on the quiet field, the quality of the day, the pattern of his mother's dress. It must have been around 1942, when he was six. It was late summer, and his father was overseas. His father could not have been long gone; there was still the feeling of him about the house. Dennis was bitterly ashamed of his mother that day, and the shame returned with the memory, even years after. When she tried to involve him in her public breakdown, tried to force him to feel badly too, he almost yelled in her face that he didn't care about the trees, he *wanted* Mr. Trapp to cut them down. It would have surprised her very much if he had yelled anything at all; he was a small boy, soft-eyed, big-eared, very like one of the field mice that crept into the house when they were asleep and hid grain in their shoes.

It had been sunny that day. He remembered later how sun would lie in their valley like water, like something dense and consistent. His recollections of childhood were all sunny, soaked in sun, the color of honey. When he thought of the house after the death of his mother, he saw her in the garden, in sun, difficult to distinguish, as if she were in a snapshot taken when the light was too intense.

He thought of his mother months after her death, after the shock and strangeness had passed away. He had abandoned college by then, and was working as a junior draftsman in an electrical equipment plant in Maine. He had been there four months when his stepfather wrote, asking if he wanted to sell the old house. The stepfather, Dr. Meyer, had nothing to do with the place; it had passed directly to Dennis after his own father's death. But Meyer was lonely, and perpetually worried by unfinished business. He told Dennis that he would try to find a buyer, and make a proper catalogue of the furniture and books. It would give him, Meyer, something to do.

Dennis hadn't lived in the house for years. When he was ten, a stupid divorce wrangle, the refusal of either parent to give in on a question of property, had driven them all away. His father went back to New York; his mother took an apartment in the nearest small town, where Dennis went to school. Five years after that, Dennis's father was killed in Korea. The house came to him. He and his mother could have returned, but didn't. Mrs. Arnheim was established in the town; she said that it was better for Dennis, less isolated, nearer school. She was a hero's widow now, for the divorce had never gone through. Dennis didn't know, and never discovered, which of his parents had opposed it. There were only half-recollected words, a feeling of anger in a room, voices quarreling in the night, ceasing abruptly when he called out. He remembered a maid running out into the garden with him because his parents were fighting inside; really fighting, hitting. They had run out of accusations, and one of them (he would never know which) had been goaded into something nearly murderous.

He didn't know what to tell his stepfather about the house. He felt as though it should be let stand as it was, the tiles gradually slipping off the roof, the mice nesting in the furniture piled in the garage. He and his mother had almost preferred it as a ruin. They had visited it throughout his adolescence, three or four times a year, most often in summer or spring. His mother would slip the rusted chain off the gate and Dennis would follow along the weed-grown gravel drive. There was a ritual to their visits, the solemn, inevitable progression of a myth. His mother would say, "Look at those peacock tulips, Dennis. Wouldn't you think they'd freeze? The roots must be striking deeper every year." The asparagus bed was a forest; the raspberry canes a hopeless tangle of burdock and wild morning glory. His mother would say, "Dennis, love, to save the raspberries from frost one time we ran out with the bedsheets and flung them over." They would walk in and out of half-empty rooms, pointing out the growing patches of damp, like maps, on the ceilings. Along the paths of the ruined garden, they saw the indestructible flowers, the weed-choked but still living April corners. "*Look* at those daffodils! I declare, Dennis, they seem to like it." They relived a portion of life, the sunny years of solitude and war.

These visits never saddened them. Rather, they feared that a stranger might one day buy the house and eliminate years of their existence by the simple act of tidying up. It was a ruin, but their own. Instead of a contented: "Do you remember, Dennis, how happy we were?" might emerge the belief that they had never been happy here at all. Dennis never questioned his mother's assertion of their common happy past. It was now almost the only thing that bound them together. He was a disappointment to her in many ways, less subtle and intelligent than she might have wished, scarcely interested in books, indifferent to nature, incapable of demonstration, which, to her, meant a character devoid of love. Generously, she blamed her own deficiencies. She had not known how to bring out the best in her son. She blamed his schooling, too, and most particularly his modern, well-built high school, with its hearty, neurotic teachers, its implicit contempt for scholarship and the visionary mind. Dennis was, or seemed to his mother, slow, secretive, and tiresomely single-minded. He read nothing but *Life* and comic books until he was fifteen, when he suddenly developed a taste for Conrad. He then read everything he could find in the school library, and everything his mother ordered from New York, and then, just as abruptly, went back to pictures and unicellular thought. He was often silent, and gave the impression, sitting alone, staring at the carpet, of a player brooding at chess. Mrs. Arnheim was skeptical of silence. She did not believe that still water ran deep; not in her husband's son.

Dennis's silence was probably owing to the amount of energy he spent trying to resolve the contradictions of life. His mother was right, to some extent, about his schooling: he lacked vocabulary and had never been offered even the most rudimentary image of systematic thought. He loved the old house, but he didn't want to live there. He loved the idea that there had been Arnheims before there had been Trapps, but he was stonily uninterested in the four family portraits now stacked in the garage, the black-eyed, blankly staring German merchants and their rosy-faced wives. It was all too far away, and of no assistance. He remembered sun and his room and the sound of Mr. Trapp's mowing machine; those years were the base of his life, the good beginning. Where did that other memory fit, then, of his father's saying something, and the maid running with Dennis into the garden, pretending it was for fun?

When he was seventeen, his mother married again. She had been "engaged" for more than a year, but wanted Dennis to finish high school before she changed his life with such a drastic step. She might have spared herself the delay, for he failed in two of his Regents' examinations, and the average of the others was sixty-four. It meant that he could not follow his father to Amherst, nor, for that matter, be admitted to any reputable college at all. His mother did not reproach him; she set to work pulling strings. In the middle of July she sent for him (he was at his first good summer job, at the plant in Maine) and he came home at great bother and expense to be told that she had secured his admission to a small but decent college near Buffalo, and that she would like to marry Dr. Meyer, if Dennis didn't feel it would shatter his sense of security. Dennis thanked her tepidly for the news about the college; about Meyer, he told her, in effect, that her life was her own.

Rudolf Meyer was an immigrant doctor who had set up practice in Poughkeepsie after the war. Mrs. Arnheim had gone to see him about her foot, which had begun to trouble her again. He was helpful, and he interested her, and they rapidly became friends. Meyer liked to talk, and Dennis's mother asked nothing better than to listen. Talk about himself tumbled like a waterfall, but even the enormous number of facts he threw out left him mysterious, difficult to place. He said he was Russian, but he also said he was Viennese. He had lived for many years in Geneva, among a turbulent crowd of émigré Russians. He spoke excellent German. He said that his mother was Hungarian and that his first wife had been the most beautiful woman in Central Europe. He had been attached to the finest hospitals of Vienna, Geneva, and Zurich, and he had this information printed on his professional writing paper. His past life floated over their heads, tantalizing and brilliant, like a cluster of escaped balloons. Some facts were incontestable: he was a doctor, with a degree from Vienna. He had a daughter by his first marriage, who was a social worker in Geneva. He had been in a concentration camp: his number was tattooed just above his right wrist. However, and this was typical, he said he had been in no fewer than six: Auschwitz, Ravensbruck, Belsen, Dachau, Mauthausen, and Buchenwald. He was huge and tall and well-muscled, and said he had been fencing champion of Vienna and amateur boxing champion of Austria. Gray curly hair stood straight up all over his head like a tangled wire wreath. He wore double-focus spectacles, which fit badly, so that he had to throw back his head to get a good view through the lower half-circle. This pose made him appear haughty. Indeed, Dennis's first view of his future stepfather had been all chin. He loved food and drink, and made futile scenes in the chintzy, innocent, Colonial eating places north of Poughkeepsie. The scenes were over the texture of omelets or the temperature of wine. When he was angry he roared, and his face became, literally, the color of wine. Dennis was ashamed of these tantrums (he had no other emotional resource) but his mother would listen with a quiet, gentle smile. After all, the scenes were created on her behalf: "Do you expect my wife, a woman of taste and culture, to eat this filth?" Meyer would demand. Fortunately, his accent was such that very few people could understand what was troubling him. The waitress, helpful, might bring more ice water, or remove the restaurant cat. "I am sorry, my dear, to have brought you to such a place," he would say to Dennis's mother, his high Beaujolais flush receding as he calmed down. On the other hand, he could be just as irascible with his wife. Dennis, home from college for Thanksgiving, saw his stepfather get up from the table, put on his coat, and storm out of the house because he believed he had not been offered cranberry sauce. His mother's reaction was almost as unsettling. She smiled and said, "The poor boy, now he'll go to a diner and make himself sick with greasy bacon and eggs." She took her fifty-five-year-old child's dinner and kept it warm for him in the oven.

Dennis had never had an intimate or even a personal discussion with his mother in his life, but even a mind as guarded as his questioned the idea of these two unlikely people living together. His mother explained it by saying that she had once been happily married and felt no qualms about risking it again. This was the story she offered outsiders, and she forgot herself sufficiently to offer it to her son. Her second explanation was that Meyer needed her, and that she liked to be needed now that Dennis was growing up. That was probably true. She could cry over him as she had once cried over trees. He told her about war and vileness and indignity; about the base and grasping conduct he had witnessed in other human beings under stress. She would listen, deeply affected, curled on a couch like a little girl. She was still pretty; even Dennis, who never really *saw* her, was conscious of her effect on other people. Her face was expressive and tender. The rooms she furnished reflected her personal aura of clarity, order, and comfort. He thought, without rancor, that tempestuous Dr. Meyer was fortunate in his new wife.

He had tried for a time to feel that his mother's marriage was a betrayal of his father, but was unable to work the idea into anything real. His mother had been scrupulous in her attitude toward the absent parent. For the sake of Dennis's sense of security, she constructed the image of an admirable parent, temporarily absent, deeply interested in his son. Dennis had played the game along with her. After his father's death, he put up a special shelf in his room on which he kept his father's picture, his decorations, and the newspaper clippings concerning his death. It was a cult of images, not of feelings; for the truth was that the happiest time of his life had been when he was living alone with his mother in the old place, with his father at war.

Dennis's mother and stepfather moved to Poughkeepsie, where the doctor had bought a house. A room was set aside for Dennis. It contained a few of his things, but he slept in it only at Christmas and Easter. Without joy, he had embarked on his four-year internment in the small college near Buffalo that had admitted him in spite of his low credits. Most of the students were on Dennis's academic level. The staff was sour and underpaid. There was a creative writing course and a resident poet. Dennis felt as if he had been thrust into limbo and that his real life could not begin until he had shaken the dust of this place. Twice he left and took a factory job, driven by the desperate conviction that he was wasting time and living in a manner he could classify only as untrue. On both occasions his mother persuaded him to go back. She told him that there was no hope for anyone without a degree from some or other college; that without one he would spend his future sharpening knives or stringing tennis rackets.

She knew better, of course; but she had resigned herself to the idea that her son was not a scholar, and she was trying to project an image of life from his, the commercial, point of view. She imagined him, vaguely, in some sort of business. Knowing nothing whatever about the conduct of business, she wanted to equip him as best she could. She managed to keep him in college three years.

From time to time, since his marriage, Meyer had spoken of going to Europe, and finally, the summer before Dennis's senior year, he arranged his affairs so that he could be away six months. Generously, he invited Dennis, who was to travel with them during the summer, returning home alone in September. Dennis accepted without enthusiasm. He would rather have taken a job. The aim of Meyer's visit abroad seemed to him so entirely fantastic that he could not imagine himself involved. Dr. Meyer had conceived the extraordinary notion of revisiting the concentration camps in which he had been interned and showing them to his wife. He also wanted to look at the other camps, those he hadn't seen, but about which he knew everything: the caloric value of the meals, the names of the officers in charge, the nature of the forced labor, the number of deaths. He had become an expert on the camps, and could speak for hours on their relative amenities (Dachau had been better than Auschwitz) and their genocidal efficiency. His wife would listen to these expositions, neither bored nor repelled.

Sometimes Dennis thought he heard a curious echo of his mother in Meyer's words. "Birkenau was the extermination camp for Auschwitz. It was about two miles away," he would drone. "Trains came from every part of Europe. There were trains every day. It had its own railway station. Jews from Warsaw were sent to Treblinka. From Dachau one was sent to Schloss Hartheim for gassing. Frenchwomen went to Ravensbruck. There were many intellectuals." The echo Dennis heard, or thought he heard, was of, "Isn't it funny how the tulips survive? Isn't it funny how the Iceland poppies keep coming up and up? Dennis! Remember it all?"

Another object of the trip to Europe was to meet Charlotte, Meyer's daughter. Dennis's mother dwelt on this. She and Charlotte had exchanged letters through the years, and Charlotte's letters had established a few details of her father's past. He was a Russian Jew. His first wife had been Viennese. Charlotte herself had been deported from Vienna and would never live there again. In one curious letter, she passionately stated that her personal culture, her way of thinking, was Swiss and French.

They sailed at the end of June with half-empty suitcases, which, like Mrs. Meyer's eager and receptive imagination, they planned to bring home filled. As they neared the old continent, and particularly after they had arrived, some sureness in Meyer reasserted itself. He made scenes, but people seemed to understand him, and scuttled about. He received glances, but he was obeyed. He showed his American passport whenever he could, and said to everyone that he was an American citizen. He was competent in Europe; he knew how to travel, and how to be served. He knew where to eat decently in London and where to buy china plates. He spoke French in Paris, and made himself understood in Rome. Dennis's mother was proud and delighted. She smiled at everyone in Europe, and found everything better than at home. As for Dennis, the whole experience was so out of the ordinary, so removed from anything he would have chosen for himself, that it made no impression at all. He helped his mother carry parcels, and escaped to American movies whenever he could. Meyer seemed in no hurry to get to Geneva. He seemed to want to guide his wife through every other country first, leaving a passage of time clear for the visit to his daughter and the pilgrimage to the camps. In Geneva, he said, they would hire a car and drive at leisure through Germany to the north.

In August, battered by travel, they arrived in Geneva. Charlotte did not meet them at the station, nor did she call their hotel. Instead, she sent around a formal note inviting them to tea. Dennis's mother said, "I could say it's just formal and European, only, you know, Dennis, I'm not that stupid. I think they just don't get along. Maybe he gets on her nerves, or maybe it's the other way around."

Charlotte lived in a small furnished apartment on a street that could have been in Boston. Her windows looked out on a court, and, although they arrived at three o'clock, all the lights were turned on inside. Charlotte's hair was reddish and thick. She wore a gray tailored suit, old-fashioned in cut, and rather ill-fitting. She was twenty-seven, but looked, to Dennis, thirty-five. He knew about Russians in Geneva from *Under Western Eyes*. He had these odd pockets of information from the only territory his mind had explored. He expected circumstances, when they coincided, to fit. He was disappointed. Charlotte did not look Russian at all.

She took their coats, polite. It was August, but as dismal as November. Walking through the streets, they had felt as if winter might come down on their heads; as if, changing countries, they had inadvertently moved into the wrong time of the year. Charlotte stood rigid in her father's embrace, and then stood apart, patient, while he broke down. "My little girl," he said hoarsely. "My little girl."

"We shall have tea at once," Charlotte said, showing them where they might sit.

She seemed to want to move quickly into the ritual of tea so that they would stop standing around making pointless or emotional remarks. She discovered she had forgotten lemons, and Dennis was dispatched to get some. She pressed money into his hand, almost gasping with impatience when he tried to refuse it. He had the feeling that everyone was doing the wrong thing. It was the first time he had been sent on a normal errand during this tour: the few moments inside the Geneva grocery had a quality of reality that had been missing until now and that never returned again. When he got back to the flat, the three were sitting around a huge tea-table, quite far apart. In the center of the table was a dying azalea in a pot, surrounded by spoons, china, and platters of little cakes. There was enough food for at least ten persons. A light turned on directly over the table gave the scene an old-fashioned air, like a postcard photo of some extinct royal family posed for a studio portrait.

"You came out of camp first," Dennis's mother was saying, in her soft, pretty voice. There was a little line between her eyebrows, and her son recognized the nervous supplication, the unnecessary assumption of guilt that was, to him, the most perplexing side of her nature. She seemed to be genuinely sorry that she had never been exiled, slandered, deported, crowded into a verminous hut, or deprived of food.

Well, Dennis suddenly thought with energy, *he* didn't mind. He had no desire to suffer, no, none at all. It was just like Mr. Trapp's trees. If they ever mentioned the trees again he would tell her that Mr. Trapp was right. If the roots interfered with the corn, and if he thought the corn more important than the trees, then he was right to cut them down.

"Oh, Dennis," said his mother, suddenly bringing him into the scene. "And we sat there in our lovely garden, not doing a thing for anybody."

Charlotte answered for him. "He was only a little boy," she said. "What could he have done? In any case, it had nothing to do with him."

That settled that, and Dennis looked at her, but Charlotte was not interested in him. She was far more elegant than her father, in spite of the shabby suit; and, of course, more controlled. Her English was careful, her sense of social behavior acute. She tried to ask about their reactions to Paris, but they were enmeshed in the past. The telephone called her, and there, speaking in French, out of the room, she sounded gay and urgent, as if she had suddenly achieved her full personality. Picking up the telephone she said "Oui, ici Mademoiselle May-air," which sounded so different from plain American Meyer that Dennis wondered how she and her father found anything to say to each other at all.

When she came back from the telephone, having told someone not to come until six o'clock, they were still on the subject of camps. "I suppose you came out and then looked everywhere for your father?" Dennis's mother said to her.

"Well, those were funny times," said Charlotte, with a slow smile, as if still thinking of the person at the telephone.

"I looked for her," said Meyer, heavily. "I had typhoid. I crawled out to the road from the camp hospital every day, and lay there, in the ditch, in the dirt, watching the refugees going along the road, asking everybody for news of my Lotte."

"I wasn't walking," said Charlotte, looking at her fingers, smiling. "I had American transport all the way, yes, all the way to Vienna."

"And you had typhoid!" said Dennis's mother, as if hearing this story for the first time.

"I was cured," said Meyer, peering under his glasses. "But I was weak."

"Typhus," murmured Charlotte, still smiling. "Not typhoid, typhus."

"She was only a little girl," said Meyer. His head suddenly fell forward. "A little girl who had been through too much and had no heart left. She asked for no one. No one. They told me when I got back. The truth is she has no natural feelings."

"She was afraid of what she might find," said Dennis's mother, with, again, the look of anxious supplication.

"Well, you see," said Charlotte, changing only the inflection of the sentence, "those were funny times." She remembered that they had come to tea and jumped up from her chair, offering cakes as if she were a servant, holding out the loaded plates, taking nothing herself. Dennis's mother said, "Oh, *thank* you," but Meyer could not rise above the surface of his gloom. He seemed to be accusing them all, his stepson, his daughter, his wife. "Perhaps you prefer iced tea," said Charlotte to Dennis's mother. The party was obviously a failure, although what measure of success any of them could have expected had been doomed at the outset by Meyer's tears. Charlotte, reacting mechanically to a social situation, clung to the idea of food and drink. Ice in the tea would make the difference. It was a suggestion that the bitter weather outside made absurd; indeed, the tea-table was hedged by an electric radiator and a gas fire. "No, no," said Charlotte, covering the protests. "Americans like iced drinks. I had forgotten."

"Dennis will help," said his mother, clearly defeated by the prospect of starting tea all over again.

Dennis went into the kitchen. The ice tray in the tiny refrigerator was stuck fast. Charlotte, coming in behind him, banged the tray with a huge pair of kitchen shears. She said in a low, matter-of-fact voice, "You seem a nice boy. Could you get them out of here soon?" He knew that he should be angry, that he should say, "That happens to be my mother," but he merely nodded, holding the ice tray under a stream of water, and said, "Soon as I can." It seemed to him that Charlotte was behaving the only way she could.

Ice failed to revive the party, and Dennis had no trouble getting them away. His mother was shocked, and said so. She thought Charlotte a monster. "Natural feelings" was an archaic term, she said, but it expressed something civilized in human relations. Her husband was right. Charlotte had no natural feelings at all. She fussed about it for a day or two, and then forgot Charlotte, for she and her husband were beginning their pilgrimage to Germany and Dennis sailing for home alone. He was returning to America with the same half-hearted despair he had felt coming away; a mirror image of himself in limbo. Of his summer in Europe, he retained two sharp memories: shopping for lemons in Geneva, and the voice of Charlotte saying "Mademoiselle May-air." That wasn't much to tell the resident poet. They had told him at the plant in Maine that there would be a job for him whenever he was ready for it. There suddenly seemed to him only one form of living possible, and he wondered why he had put it off until now. Instead of returning to college, he went straight to Maine. College seemed to him, more than ever, an unnecessary prolonging of childhood, a retreat from life. When he took a furnished room and unpacked his clothes in the plant town, he felt as if he had freed himself from something gritty and shadowed, an undefined menace that could have hampered him for life. He was twenty that autumn, and had already wasted time.

His mother wrote him regularly, telling him, with a determined absence of reproach, that his life, his choice for the future, was his own. She said nothing about stringing rackets or grinding knives, but she asked what it was all leading to, and blamed herself. His schools had never brought out the best in him, and he had missed a father's guiding hand. She described the German autumn landscape and begged him for news. Dennis found it hard to know what to write, except that he had a job as junior draftsman, was going to night classes at the plant, and had a room with a family of Germans who had been over three years and already owned a house. The first week in November, his mother's usual letter failed to come, and ten days later came a long and partially incoherent letter from Meyer. He said that they had been in an automobile crash outside Munich. He was still in hospital; Dennis's mother had been killed at once. He had not cabled because he had been in a coma, and after he recovered consciousness it seemed too late for a wire. He had felt that it would be less of a shock for Dennis if he wrote. He said that it had been his fault, that he should never have taken his wife out of her environment and into a strange country with strange signs along the roads. He begged Dennis to forgive him. He said that he was old and wanted to die.

The only letter it seemed possible for Dennis to write was one telling Meyer not to blame himself.

Meyer returned from Europe after a month. He went to a nursing home, where Dennis visited him. He did seem much older, and he wept almost unceasingly, as if it were nearly a natural reflex with him now, like breathing. He had engaged a lawyer, he said, and he wanted Dennis to know that he was scrupulously collecting everything of value belonging to his wife, all the little knick-knacks and trinkets, and would remit these to her son. The lawyer would see to it.

"You shouldn't worry about things like that," Dennis said, embarrassed.

Meyer then showed him a letter from Charlotte. "I have no daughter," he said. "Read it. Cold, cold." Dennis read very little French, but it was evident that Meyer's emotional demands for sympathy and love froze his daughter. She was sorry, more sorry than he might believe, about his wife's death, she wrote; at the same time, she could not replace his wife. She couldn't fill the role he needed, because it was a lifetime job, and she had her own life to consider. She was sorry about that, too.

His mother's death was still unreal. He found himself thinking, objectively, quite outside the situation, that Charlotte was hard, but truthful, and that Meyer was going to find life difficult without his tender and all-feeling wife.

He went back to his job, and Meyer, soon afterward, returned to Poughkeepsie. He was partly bedridden, and spent much of his time going over old papers, documents that proved he had been fencing champion of Vienna and had once been married to the most beautiful woman of Central Europe. Some of these papers, pinned into cardboard covers, he sent Dennis, with the lettered command in red ink: "Valuable. Please Return." He wrote to Dennis about the house, receiving a reply that was neither yes nor no. In the spring, he thought of Dennis and wrote again.

"Soon I expect to die," this letter said. "I have little money to leave and I must think of my poor Charlotte. Your mother's long medical history of which you can inform yourself at competent authorities (for all the papers are there and the truth is she had tuberculosis of the bones) has used all my resources. Also, her funeral and burial in Munich, involving two separate payments. After her death a bill came to me for a dressing table skirt, glazed chintz, six-sixty a yard. Imagine my feelings, thinking of her sewing this.

"I do not intend to leave you with nothing. In my home will be found a General Electric refrigerator, a deep-freeze full to the lid, a pair of valuable opera glasses of a kind they don't make anymore, a library of medical books, some in Russian, some in German, and other tangible goods. By tangible goods I mean goods that can be converted to cash. After my death these objects will be yours. Take them and sell them. The proceeds will enable you to live for several years in great comfort."

In response to this letter, Dennis went to see his stepfather. It was Easter weekend. Friends from the plant drove him to Albany, and he took a train from there. He found his stepfather in the small semi-modern house he had bought after his marriage, nearly four years before. Everything in the house had been chosen by his mother. For the first time since her death he was acutely conscious of her physical absence: the mirrors, the white-shaded lamps, the patterns of ivy and yellow-hearted flowers, recalled to him the atmosphere in which he had grown up, the house, the valley, the clarity, the sun.

Meyer was in his room, in bed. He wore a dressing gown held together with a cameo pin. His hair was quite white. He pulled Dennis toward him and kissed him on both cheeks. Released, Dennis sat down at the foot of the bed, clearing away a small tangle of socks, papers, and woolen scarves. It was a warm, clear evening, but Meyer was wrapped in wool like a cocoon. He said nothing about expecting to die, but spoke of his illness, his loneliness, and of his wife. After a time Dennis realized he was speaking of Charlotte's mother. Suddenly, switching to the present, he said, "You know, she saw three of them. We couldn't get to every one. But she did see three. The camps. You know." Dennis said nothing. An accusation arose in his mind, but then, Meyer had already accused himself. "Dachau," said Meyer, frowning. "Do you know, they are tearing some of them down?"

"Just as well," said Dennis.

Meyer wore the same perplexed look as Dennis's mother when she spoke of the old place, saying, "Dennis, love, remember how we saved the raspberries from frost? Remember the Iceland poppies? Remember how happy we were?"

"It's just that they could be used for something, the buildings," Meyer said. He sounded helpless. "They were sturdy enough."

"I guess no one would want to live in them," Dennis said.

At that moment he did not understand that his mother was dead. She might have been in Europe all winter, and at the moment be in another part of the house. The closet was full of her dresses and her sachets of dried carnations were tied to the hangers. At any instant she might come in and say, "Oh, Dennis, it was really awful over there, I kept thinking of those poor people!"

"I took pictures," Meyer said. He pulled open the drawer of the table by his bed and found envelopes stuffed with photographs. Dennis took them and saw what Meyer had done. He had photographed the empty barracks, the disused railway sidings, the graveled paths, the fences enclosing silence and space. "Before they tear it all down," Meyer said. "You *know*." He leaned over, pointing. "In this place I was tattooed. Here there were many Greeks."

Dennis looked at them with great care, at the sunny autumn lawns. The feeling of silence in the photographs conveyed itself into the room; he felt as if he were holding squares of silence in his hands. He returned the pictures and Meyer put them away.

"Are you going to visit your old house?" Meyer said. "You could take my car."

"I don't know," said Dennis, distracted. The cold sun of another country filled the room. Meyer should never have taken his mother away. "My mother liked it," he said. "She liked it in spring. She liked to see how the bulbs kept coming up through the weeds. Sometimes she'd find something, one of my toys. She liked that."

"If you would like to go tomorrow..." Meyer said.

"I guess I won't," Dennis said. "I really came down to see you. To-morrow I'll have to go back to Albany. I'm picking up these friends. They're driving me back. Maybe we should sell the place. I don't know. You said you could do it. You said you wanted to. Do what you like. Anything you do is all right."

"It will keep me alive," said Meyer jokingly. "An inventory must be made. I shall catalogue every thing in every box." Forcing himself to take an interest in this slack-faced indifferent boy, he said, "Do you like this job? You have a comfortable room?"

"I live with these Germans," Dennis said. It was all he could say.

He lived with a prospering family of Germans who had come out after the war. On Friday nights he went shopping with them in their car. He wore the uniform of his job and position in the plant—a pat-terned sports shirt and unpressed trousers. He lived easily with these people; he admired their energy and was excited by their vulgarity. They never talked of the past. The population of the town was restless, moving. It was a town that had grown since the war. There were Ger-mans, French-Canadians, and Finns. He thought, vaguely, that Amer-ica must have been like this fifty or sixty years ago. When people moved up in the plant they left their old associations behind without nostal-gia. They were the hardest-working and the most restless people he had ever known. The coarseness, the looseness of the relationships, was almost a reassurance; when he left, as he certainly would one day, he would never have to go back. There was nothing to go back to there.

THE PRODIGAL PARENT

WE SAT on the screened porch of Rhoda's new house, which was close to the beach on the ocean side of Vancouver Island. I had come here in a straight line, from the East, and now that I could not go any farther without running my car into the sea, any consideration of wreckage and loss, or elegance of behavior, or debts owed (not of money, of my person) came to a halt. A conqueror in a worn blazer and a regimental tie, I sat facing my daughter, listening to her voice—now describing, now complaining—as if I had all the time in the world. Her glance drifted round the porch, which still contained packing cases. She could not do, or take in, a great deal at once. I have light eyes, like Rhoda's, but mine have been used for summing up.

Rhoda had bought this house and the cabins round it and a strip of maimed landscape with her divorce settlement. She hoped to make something out of the cabins, renting them weekends to respectable people who wanted a quiet place to drink. DUNE VISTA said a sign, waiting for someone to nail it to a tree. I wondered how I would fit in here—what she expected me to do. She still hadn't said. After the first formal Martinis she had made to mark my arrival, she began drinking rye, which she preferred. It was sweeter, less biting than the whiskey I remembered in my youth, and I wondered if my palate or its composition had changed. I started to say so, and my daughter said, "Oh, God, your accent again! You know what I thought you said now? 'Oxbow was a Cheswick charmer.'"

"No, no. Nothing like that."

"Try not sounding so British," she said.

"I don't, you know."

"Well, you don't sound Canadian."

The day ended suddenly, as if there had been a partial eclipse. In the new light I could see my daughter's face and hands.

"I guess I'm different from all my female relatives," she said. She had been comparing herself with her mother, and with half sisters she hardly knew. "I don't despise men, like Joanne does. There's always somebody. There's one now, in fact. I'll tell you about him. I'll tell you the whole thing, and you say what you think. It's a real mess. He's Irish, he's married, and he's got no money. Four children. He doesn't sleep with his wife."

"Surely there's an age limit for this?" I said. "By my count, you must be twenty-eight or -nine now."

"Don't I know it." She looked into the dark trees, darkened still more by the screens, and said without rancor, "It's not my fault. I wouldn't keep on falling for lushes and phonies if you hadn't been that way."

I put my glass down on the packing case she had pushed before me, and said, "I am not, I never was, and I never could be an alcoholic."

Rhoda seemed genuinely shocked. "I never said *that*. I never heard you had to be put in a hospital or anything, like my stepdaddy. But you used to stand me on a table when you had parties, Mother told me, and I used to dance to 'Piccolo Pete.' What happened to that record, I wonder? One of your wives most likely got it in lieu of alimony. But may God strike us both dead here and now if I ever said you were alcoholic." It must have been to her a harsh, clinical word, associated with straitjackets. "I'd like you to meet him," she said. "But I never know when he'll turn up. He's Harry Pay. The writer," she said, rather primly. "Somebody said he was a new-type Renaissance Man—I mean, he doesn't just sit around, he's a judo expert. He could throw *you* down in a second."

"Is he Japanese?"

"God, no. What makes you say that? I already told you what he is. He's white. Quite white, *entirely* white I mean."

"Well—I could hardly have guessed."

"You shouldn't have to guess," she said. "The name should be enough. He's famous. Round here, anyway."

"I'm sorry," I said. "I've been away so many years. Would you write the name down for me? So I can see how it's spelled?"

"I'll do better than that." It touched me to see the large girl she was suddenly moving so lightly. I heard her slamming doors in the living room behind me. She had been clumsy as a child, in every gesture like a wild creature caught. She came back to me with a dun folder out of which spilled loose pages, yellow and smudged. She thrust it at me and, as I groped for my spectacles, turned on an overhead light. "You read this," she said, "and I'll go make us some sandwiches, while I still can. Otherwise we'll break into another bottle and never eat anything. This is something he never shows *anyone*."

"It is my own life exactly," I said when she returned with the sandwiches, which she set awkwardly down. "At least, so far as school in England is concerned. Cold beds, cold food, cold lavatories. Odd that anyone still finds it interesting. There must be twenty written like it every year. The revolting school, the homosexual master, then a girl—saved!"

"Homo *what*?" said Rhoda, clawing the pages. "It's possible. He has a dirty mind, actually."

"Really? Has he ever asked you to do anything unpleasant, such as type his manuscripts?"

"Certainly not. He's got a perfectly good wife for that."

When I laughed, she looked indignant. She had given a serious answer to what she thought was a serious question. Our conversations were always like this—collisions.

"Well?" she said.

"Get rid of him."

She looked at me and sank down on the arm of my chair. I felt her breath on my face, light as a child's. She said, "I was waiting for something. I was waiting all day for you to say something personal, but I didn't think it would be that. Get rid of him? He's all I've got."

"All the more reason. You can do better."

"Who, for instance?" she said. "You? You're no use to me."

She had sent for me. I had come to Rhoda from her half sister Joanne, in Montreal. Joanne had repatriated me from Europe, with an air passage to back the claim. In a new bare apartment, she played severe sad music that was like herself. We ate at a scrubbed table the sort of food that can be picked up in the hand. She was the richest of my children, through her mother, but I recognized in her guarded, slanting looks the sort of avarice and fear I think of as a specific of women. One look seemed meant to tell me, "You waltzed off, old boy, but look at me now," though I could not believe she had wanted me only for that. "I'll never get married" was a remark that might have given me a lead. "I won't have anyone to lie to me, or make a fool of me, or spend my money for me." She waited to see what I would say. She had just come into this money.

"Feeling as you do, you probably shouldn't marry," I said. She looked at me as Rhoda was looking now. "Don't expect too much from men," I said.

"Oh, I don't!" she cried, so eagerly I knew she always would. The cheap sweet Ontario wine she favored and the smell of paint in her new rooms and the raw meals and incessant music combined to give me a violent attack of claustrophobia. It was probably the most important conversation we had.

"We can't have any more conversation now," said Rhoda. "Not after that. It's the end. You've queered it. I should have known. Well, eat your sandwiches now that I've made them."

"Would it seem petulant if, at this point, I did not eat a tomato sandwich?" I said.

"Don't be funny. I can't understand what you're saying anyway."

"If you don't mind, my dear," I said, "I'd rather be on my way."

"What do you mean, on your way? For one thing, you're in no condition to drive. Where d'you think you're going?"

"I can't very well go that way," I said, indicating the ocean I could not see. "I can't go back as I've come."

"It was a nutty thing, to come by car," she said. "It's not even all that cheap."

"As I can't go any farther," I said, "I shall stay. Not here, but perhaps not far."

"Doing what? What *can* you do? We've never been sure."

"I can get a white cane and walk the streets of towns. I can ask people to help me over busy intersections and then beg for money."

"You're kidding."

"I'm not. I shall say—let me think—I shall say I've had a mishap, lost my wallet, pension check not due for another week, postal strike delaying it even more—"

"That won't work. They'll send you to the welfare. You should see how we hand out welfare around here."

"I'm counting on seeing it," I said.

"You can't. It would look—" She narrowed her eyes and said, "If you're trying to shame me, forget it. Someone comes and says, 'That poor old blind bum says he's your father,' I'll just answer, 'Yes, what about it?'"

"My sight *is* failing, actually."

"There's welfare for that, too."

"We're at cross-purposes," I said. "I'm not looking for money."

"Then waja come here for?"

"Because Regan sent me on to Goneril, I suppose."

"That's a lie. Don't try to make yourself big. Nothing's ever happened to you."

"Well, in my uneventful life," I began, but my mind answered for me, "No, nothing." There are substitutes for incest but none whatever for love. What I needed now was someone who knew nothing about me and would never measure me against a promise or a past. I blamed myself, not for anything I had said but for having remembered too late what Rhoda was like. She was positively savage as an infant, though her school tamed her later on. I remember sitting opposite her when she was nine—she in an unbecoming tartan coat—while she slowly and seriously ate a large plate of ice cream. She was in London on a holiday with her mother, and as I happened to be there with my new family I gave her a day.

"Every Monday we have Thinking Day," she had said, of her school. "We think about the Brownies and the Baden-Powells and sometimes Jesus and all."

"Do you, really?"

"I can't *really*," Rhoda had said. "I never met any of them."

"Are you happy, at least?" I said, to justify my belief that no one was ever needed. But the savage little girl had become an extremely careful one.

That afternoon, at a matinée performance of *Peter Pan*, I went to sleep. The slaughter of the pirates woke me, and as I turned, confident, expecting her to be rapt, I encountered a face of refusal. She tucked her lips in, folded her hands, and shrugged away when I helped her into a taxi.

"I'm sorry, I should not have slept in your company," I said. "It was impolite."

"It wasn't that," she burst out. "It was *Peter Pan*. I hated it. It wasn't what I expected. You could see the wires. Mrs. Darling didn't look right. She didn't have a lovely dress on—only an old pink thing like a nightgown. Nana wasn't a real dog, it was a lady. I couldn't understand anything they said. Peter Pan wasn't a boy, he had bosoms."

"I noticed that, too," I said. "There must be a sound traditional reason for it. Perhaps Peter is really a mother figure."

"No, he's a *boy*."

I intercepted, again, a glance of stony denial—of me? We had scarcely met.

"I couldn't understand. They all had English accents," she complained.

For some reason that irritated me. "What the hell did you expect them to have?" I said.

"When I was little," said the nine-year-old, close to tears now, "I thought they were all Canadian."

The old car Joanne had given me was down on the beach, on the hard sand, with ribbons of tire tracks behind it as a sign of life, and my luggage locked inside. It had been there a few hours and already it looked abandoned—an old heap someone had left to rust among the lava rock. The sky was lighter than it had seemed from the porch. I picked up a sand dollar, chalky and white, with the tree of life on its underside, and as I slid it in my pocket, for luck, I felt between my fingers a rush of sand. I had spoken the truth, in part; the landscape through which I had recently traveled still shuddered before my eyes and I would not go back. I heard, then saw, Rhoda running down to where I stood. Her hair, which she wore gathered up in a bun, was half down, and she breathed, running, with her lips apart. For the first time I remembered something of the way she had seemed as a child, something more than an anecdote. She clutched my arm and said, "Why did you say I should ditch him? *Why?*"

I disengaged my arm, because she was hurting me, and said, "He can only give you bad habits."

"At my age?"

"Any age. Dissimulation. Voluntary barrenness—someone else has had his children. Playing house, a Peter-and-Wendy game, a life he would never dare try at home. There's the real meaning of Peter, by the way." But she had forgotten.

She clutched me again, to steady herself, and said, "I'm old enough to know everything. I'll soon be in my thirties. That's all I care to say."

It seemed to me I had only recently begun making grave mistakes. I had until now accepted all my children, regardless of who their mothers were. The immortality I had imagined had not been in them but on the faces of women in love. I saw, on the dark beach, Rhoda's mother, the soft hysterical girl whose fatal "I am pregnant" might have enmeshed me for life.

I said, "I wish they would find a substitute for immortality."

"I'm working on it," said Rhoda, grimly, seeming herself again. She let go my arm and watched me unlock the car door. "You'd have hated it here," she said, then, pleading, "You wouldn't want to live here like some charity case—have me support you?"

"I'd be enchanted," I said.

"No, no, you'd hate it," she said. "I couldn't look after you. I haven't got time. And you'd keep thinking I should do better than *him*, and the truth is I can't. You wouldn't want to end up like some old relation, fed in the kitchen and all."

"I don't know," I said. "It would be new."

"Oh," she cried, with what seemed unnecessary despair, "what did you come for? All right," she said. "I give up. You asked for it. You can stay. I mean, I'm inviting you. You can sit around and say, 'Oxbow was a Cheswick charmer,' all day and when someone says to me, 'Where jer father get his accent?' I'll say, 'It was a whole way of life.' But remember, you're not a prisoner or anything, around here. You can go whenever you don't like the food. I mean, if you don't like it, don't come to me and say, 'I don't like the food.' You're not my prisoner," she yelled, though her face was only a few inches from mine. "You're only my father. That's all you are."

STORIES OF SOUTHERN EUROPE

BETTER TIMES

Turning the old house over to Guy and Susan Osborne, Susan's Aunt Val said, "Children, have I mentioned this before? You may hear someone prowling in the garden at night. The place is stiff with smugglers now. They come down from Italy, along the top of that cliff." She pointed in the direction of the frontier—a handsome red cliff over which falcons cried and flew. Their shadows slid impartially on the fields of Italy and France. But Guy and Susan could not see anything except the dining-room wall. Along this wall, an army of red ants bore the foundations of the house up to the roof.

One day the house would fall, the walls tunneled to paper. If it collapsed down on their heads at this moment, at lunch, Aunt Val would not have been surprised. Every crumb of wood, every floating speck of dust was disastrous. Aunt Val knew. Her hands flew out to the newly married pair in gestures of warning. Her hair was made of old doll stuffing; her hair net was down to her eyes. She was in true terror, not over the smugglers, or the ants, but lest Guy should demand the last of the macaroni-and-cheese. Guy could not know, of course, how important it was that the last of every dish be spooned onto one special, thick-rimmed china plate, and how this plate must be kept in the larder, in the dark, until the food upon it spoiled.

Hoping to distract him, glancing elsewhere, Aunt Val said, "Not only smugglers but, you know, Guy, *shiftless* young men. Young men without jobs, with nothing to do." That was tactless; Guy was also unemployed. "Italians, I mean to say," said Aunt Val hurriedly. "*They* wouldn't do a day's work if you offered solid gold." Would Guy? "I mean the sort of young men who would murder one for a pair of shoes!"

the old lady cried. Whatever else you could say about poor dear Guy, he was no murderer.

So that was the autumn prospect. But Guy kept smiling, saying "Yes" and "Quite," turning his water glass around and around, as though being murdered for his shoes were part of the season's plan. Old Val could have been just a little more lavish, he thought. Water to drink, and the mucilage cheese. The house was full of ants, and the windows, which were dirty, were smeared with rain. The most disobliging sight in nature was provided by the view—palm trees under a dark sluice of rain. Beyond a drenched hedge stood a house exactly like Aunt Val's, with spires, minarets, stained-glass windows; possibly it, too, contained a drawing room stuffed with ferns and sheeted sofas. The houses were part of a genteel settlement, built in an era of jaunty Islamic-English design, in a back pocket of the Riviera country. The district was out of fashion, crumbling, but the houses persisted; dragging their rock gardens, their humped tennis courts, they marched down the slope of a tamed minor Alp.

In the old days, Aunt Val said, except for the trees and the climate and the conversation of servants, one needn't have ever known this was France. That was how they had liked being abroad then. "Abroad" meant keeping warm, pudding at Christmas, a mutable, merchants' England everywhere you went. The people in Villa Omar and Villa Khartoum had been rich but not received; they hadn't cared. They received one another for tennis parties and fat, starchy teas. Well, it was over, Aunt Val said. Now one knew this was France. There were enormous taxes to pay. Servants were scarce . . .

The conversation might have been in England. Yet it was really France; thirty miles away was the true Riviera—white houses bristling with balconies, yachts, flags. Guy thought of that and pulled himself straighter in his chair. Pale-eyed, old war hero, nearly successful salesman—of nearly anything—he thought of the flags and the yachts, and of the present, with its gains and rewards.

Susan was looking at the ants on the wall as if she were in a dream.

She fell naturally into pretty positions, although she was not a truly pretty girl. In an ugly mood—which Guy had still to see—she might resemble a pug; when her face was not reflecting solemnity or inquisitiveness, it tended to crumple. Her ideas, her affections, were based on her having been all her life somebody's favorite godchild or niece. Watchfulness made her seem without expression. That look—empty, receptive—and her light, straight hair caused her to be compared to a medieval pageboy or a picture-book Anglo-Saxon girl, uncoarsened by Norman blood. Even Guy, who was twenty-two years older than his wife and surely centuries wiser, could mumble about porcelain cheeks and silken hair. It exasperated her; she knew about reality—her father had swindled a large sum of money once, and they had left Kenya and never gone back. She had been told only that they could never live out in Africa again, and that there had been a plot, of which her father was the victim. No one would help or trust him, or give him a job. Then both parents died; more mystery. She persistently went back to sources now, looking for specific explanations of so many puzzling affairs. She was eighteen, and she had thought that marriage was in itself an explicit sort of answer.

Guy was sure that Susan was not listening to Aunt Val. He felt as if he had been left stranded at a party with the only bore. He tried to touch her foot under the table. He deplored Susan's constant worry and thought. As he said, it put him off. It was all too deep. If only the poor little thing had been through something really big—the war.

Susan looked at the ants, but she *was* listening to Aunt Val. Sometimes out of her aunt's dotty wanderings came one sharp, disconcerting observation—just what Susan liked. Here where there were palm trees under rain and cypresses as soaked as sponges there had once been a wilderness, with wild apricot and almond trees, and the olive groves left behind by the Greeks, Aunt Val said, and you could always tell where there had been a nice English garden by two things—cypress trees and palms. Now the gardens were going back to wilderness again. The suburban mountainside belonged to falcons, peasants, smugglers and a few survivors of the old days. But it was an ordered wilderness, properly reforested, with drains, and pampas grass, and *tout confort*.

Fortunately for Guy, who would not knowingly have entered any kind of wilderness, there would be people about, agreeable people, English-speaking—English, in fact. A neighbor, Major Terry, had been in to see them before lunch. Yellow-toothed, smelling of unwashed woolen garments and cold tobacco pipes, dragged by a slavering boxer dog on a lead, Major Terry entered the drawing room, sat on a sheeted sofa, and could not take his eyes away from Guy's wife. Susan had dropped, sulking, into her chair. She wore tight Italian trousers, a black pullover, beads. The costume was a reaction from the things she had been made to wear in school, and her slight, sullen commonness was a stand in favor of reality. "Be sure to bring your little *mem-sahib*," said the Major, inviting Guy to look at anything—a chicken run, a blue hibiscus, some bound issues of *Country Life*. There hadn't been anything like Susan about for years.

"Did you hear that man?" said Susan gravely, twisting the beads, after the Major had departed. "Did you hear what he called me? '*Mem-sahib*,' he said. Why it's a dream world, Guy, a horrid Shangri-La. *Mem-sahib*! Don't they *know*?"

Guy was unwise enough to say, "They don't. That's their charm." It was unwise because he risked appearing unredeemably old to his bride. He wished again that Susan would dream more and think less. Guy admired anyone's dream, whether it was the private dream that led to Monte Carlo and a yacht or the dream of Major Terry, who said "*mem-sahib*" and inhabited empires. But Susan, unequipped for dreams, congealed life for Guy by seeing things as they were. Perhaps she was too soon out of the schoolroom. Perhaps her clear stare was not medieval, after all, but just the righteous, prying look of the form prefect. He remembered how soon after their wedding she had begun to get the drift of things, particularly of his financial affairs. She had pushed a straight lock away from her face, kept her hand there, and said maternally, "Tell me, Guy. Are you *improvident*?"

Now they were here, down at Aunt Val's, because he was improvident and could not have kept a canary with style. They were in trouble and had no money for the rent in London—although Guy kept pretending it was all frolic and spree. They were to spend the autumn caretaking for Aunt Val while she, bewildered, went to stay with terrible cousins in Wales. The plan was Susan's; for such a baby, she had a good head. It happened that because of unfair competition from the Japanese, Guy's firm had retrenched, and he was out of a job. Now he was waiting. He was waiting for a rearrangement of the planets concerned with his fate, for his close-fisted mother to increase his allowance, and for better times. He was also waiting for a letter about a post with a British firm in the Argentine. (Oil-burners—odorless oil-burners. Guy said it was just up his street. Given a chance, he would be first-rate at selling odorless oil-burners in the Argentine.)

Out of habit, he pressed a nerve in his left hip, which had been injured in an air crash during the war. This pressure caused him sharp immediate pain but relieved a feeling of weight on his left knee. It was a trick he had learned. When he stood up to walk, his limp would be less pronounced.

"There is the gin," Aunt Val said suddenly. "It is of very poor quality, and I can't think how it came into the house. You will find it under the kitchen stairs. There must be thirty bottles still."

"Thirty bottles of gin?" said Guy.

"Under the stairs. But of poor quality. I am so sorry. Everything I am leaving you is poor." She apologized for the gin, for the smugglers, even the noise of the sea. The sea was miles behind them, but the cliff was a sounding board. Often, she promised them, and was sorry about it, they would hear the beating of phantom waves.

The smugglers' passage was a kind of game. Guy liked the sound of it. First there were the border police, and the guns, and then the steep clandestine path. The path forked, Aunt Val said. One branch led the fugitives to safety, by way of a burned olive grove, remnant of an old forest fire, and a peasant's house and then her house. The other branch, which seemed to be leading to the warm lights of a town, suddenly narrowed and merged with the wall of the cliff. Often a secret traveler missed his footing in the dark and was found killed on the rocks, with a sprig of broom in his hand, grasped in the fall. But Guy said it was fair enough; there was the same sporting chance one would allow an otter, a fox or a prisoner of war.

"Oh, stop it, Aunt Val," said Susan, not quite daring to bully Guy. "There haven't been any real smugglers around here for years. There isn't anything *to* smuggle, except drugs, and that's done in a big way now, in planes, and boats. These smugglers are just wretched men from Italy looking for work in France. The Italians won't let them out and the French won't let them in, and so they come as they can. They aren't dangerous. They are just—*dispossessed.*" She loved those words: improvident, dispossessed.

Aunt Val looked at Guy. "Let us not lose our heads over these people," her small, daft eyes implored. Guy would have backed her all the way. Whatever he thought of Aunt Val's luncheon, or whatever her opinion of him as a provider for Susan, he and Aunt Val were the same kind. They bore a dozen labels that said so. Silence, camouflage, self-control, a cruel tact—these were virtues they had handled and that had tarnished in their hands. But Susan would not admit these tarnished objects as virtues. She confused her elders, set them running in moral circles, like ants whose path has been interfered with. They were too taken aback ever to say to her "How do you know?" She denounced their judgments and prodded their failings. Alas, they did not believe they had failed. "As for Major Terry," she said suddenly, as if he were the principal source of their going mentally soft and astray, "I shall have nothing to do with him. He can stare all he likes. If that drooling boxer could talk, it would have more sense."

Aunt Val began to twitter about unneighborly kindliness and borrowed gardening tools. Major Terry was kind about sharing his television. Guy merely said, "Oh, I don't know," preparing the defense of his autumn social life. An invitation to the least promising party would have sent him whistling into a clean shirt. People liked him on sight, and there were always the drinks. He could have slipped easily into life down here, or into any other. He wondered if Susan knew.

"But you must be friendly, Susan, dear," said Aunt Val, clasping the macaroni-and-cheese—saved—in her arms. "Everyone will love you. As for Guy, why, I can't count the friends he will make. Guy is so awfully nice."

Susan was about to explain that he wasn't so awfully nice, that she thought it was just the way he behaved. But she checked herself and held still. Curious, prodding, she was still not sure just how much grown people could stand being hurt.

Aunt Val went to Wales, bearing an empty bird cage she had promised the cousins years before, and two of the thirty bottles of inferior gin, so as to have refreshment during the voyage. Guy and Susan were left alone. They had not been married long, and there had been people around them in London. They went up and down stairs hand in hand, and Susan told him a little about her family—not too much. She was not certain what she ought to think. She told him what she suspected about life, and she unfolded her touchingly empty past. Guy told her about the war and, one evening, about a woman named Marigold. He had had a lot to drink, and one topic led to the next with sliding facility. Susan listened politely. She already knew. She had found a letter. Found? She systematically went through his pockets. After all, that was how schoolgirls learned to know each other well. Locked in a bathroom, she had read the letter and marveled at the ability of a man to lead two lives, or two facets of the same life, without going off his head. She read that Marigold was drowning in her marriage but that the memory of Guy kept her afloat. For some reason that Susan did not understand, Guy and Marigold had not married each other. A landscape of middle-aged resignation came into view. She observed it with a cold eye. She was not jealous. Marigold was drowning, and Guy was hers.

Aunt Val sent instructions from Wales, mostly of an economical, electricity-saving kind; the autumn rain continued to blow down from the Alps; and one day they were nearly out of funds. Susan said, "Guy, about the letter. I mean the letter about the job in the Argentine. You are expecting it, aren't you? It *is* real?"

"Oh, real as real," he said affectionately—or perhaps his tone was on the fringe of affection. It was terrible for old hero Guy, so shady, slippery and gay—it was terrible having a witness.

Luckily, there were the nights. At night he could still promise anything she wanted and make her believe in the prospect. He could give assurance of miracles. He promised that the next day would be better; the rain would stop, the letter would come. As with most cheerful men, his weak point was memory. He forgot at night what the morning had been. Mornings, far from being better, as Guy had said they would be, were the low point of their lives. Everything he touched was icy or congealed. The coffee grinder in his hands froze the blood. He held his fingers over the gas ring where he made toast. It was hours before he could bring himself to shave, because of the cold taps. Susan stayed in bed with her cooling hot-water bottles. She could make passable Turkish delight, but that wasn't called for now. Aunt Val had left them a quantity of kumquat jam, bottled—or at any rate labelled—by herself. Susan observed with uncritical interest that Guy was expert in not pushing credit too far. Occasionally he gave the grocer a rest and they lived on toast and the gin and the kumquat jam. He never minded. Susan had never seen him cast down. Her father—the Kenya absconder—became small and dark beside this sunny husband. Guy never protested against injustice—that he was forty and had been thrown out of his job, that he had a bad leg from the war and would limp all his life. But no one can exist only as a happy former hero. His real feelings were layers deep. Under his manner was a pool of gall, unadmitted, opaque. Something had gone wrong for him just after the war, either in love, or ambition, or the way the world seemed when he got up from his bed and his plaster casts. Now he would never say he missed or wanted anything. His desire for Susan was a single exception, and, as there had been no one to forbid or advise her, she had been easily won. He liked every circumstance as it came along. If liking was impossible, then he blamed the weather—something beyond one's control. It was all the weather down here. Who would have believed the south of France could be chill and wet? If the weather would change, he and Susan might enjoy strolling down to the shops; otherwise, one could make a jolly meal of jam and toast. After a time, when the nights and the prospects inevitably failed, he said that if their beds were not so damp and Susan not so entrenched in hot-water bottles, love would not be in abeyance. It had nothing to do with Susan or him; it was all in the time of year.

They waited for the letter. Every night Susan heard the smugglers in the garden. She heard whispers, footsteps, and forgot that they were only the footsteps of the dispossessed. The certainty that she was being watched by strangers froze and held every scattered alarm, every in-consequential fear that in other circumstances would have briefly brushed by. She knew that to Guy her fears were puzzling and rather dowdy. They spoiled for him the red-and-ochre cliff over which smug-glers came and falcons flew. She was afraid of strangers; it was virginal, queer. He could not understand. To him, unknown people were ghosts. He could feel neither pity nor fear where they were concerned; they did not expect it. Ghosts have no true feelings; they are mystifying, unreasonable, with no regard for privacy. The whispers in the dark, the footprints on the wet drive, the odd, abandoned clues—one shoe, or a filthy coat—were trappings of chaos. Ghosts and confusion. He was for order, and gaiety, and for dealing with living things.

For Susan's sake, he went around the garden every night with a light in his hand. Often he was bold and drunk, and if he had come face to face with a man—walked into a man and not a ghost—he would have clapped him on the shoulder, with the hearty air left over from the war, and given him a cigarette and plenty of good advice. He shone his light into the black roots of wisteria, frightening the rats, and on the palms. Sometimes there might have been a blur—a face—by the cypress wind-screen, but he was so sure the night contained no threat to him that he never called out, but turned away and limped back along the drive. Under the caked wet leaves at his feet he could hear the stirrings of small things keeping out of the rain—black beetles, spiders. "Lizards," craven Susan would have said, confusing them with scorpions, probably—some-thing that could kill with a sting. No use telling her the lizards were sleeping through the winter (rather like Guy and Susan that year) and that there were no scorpions in this part of France; none to speak of.

Susan cowered indoors, dressed for charades. She dressed as though she had simply forgotten what normal people put on their backs. One night, after seven weeks of waiting for the letter—a whole lifetime—Guy came into the house, unwinding his scarf, and called down the dark hall, "I've told you, there's nobody. Now be a good girl and give me some peace."

In the drawing room, lit like a pleasure boat, Susan knelt by the fire. She gave him a large-pupiled tipsy stare. Out of the fur fringe of an anorak hood, found in a trunk or a cupboard of Aunt Val's, her fine, straight hair sprang as if electrified. She had fastened a plaid blanket around her shoulders with a safety pin and a cameo brooch, but the brooch was open and dangling. She was down on the dove-gray rug she had stained with tea and burned with cigarettes trying to make toast on a long-handled, trembling fork. Everything he was capable of feeling about her, all the tenderness and the subdued exasperation, was called up by the sight of her now. She had been an enchanting girl, a medieval page. He had snatched her straight out of the schoolroom— quite a feat for a lame old boy. He had never wanted to marry anybody, but he could not have had her any other way. Marriage had seemed a small thing then—a sand flea. But Marigold had been right; his life was too dodgy for wives, and it was better without witnesses, alone.

Still, they were quite the picture of domestic heaven, he thought a moment later: Guy with his legs stretched toward the fire, a glass of gin in one hand and frightened Susan at his feet. Being tall, his usual view of people began with the top of the head. Susan's head—the porcelain skull, the true silk hair—had attracted him to her in the first place. He gently pushed her anorak hood away. His sentiments expanded with drink. He would have murmured some endearment, but she might turn the clear, unfocused stare in his direction and say, "The letter, Guy. Are you really expecting it? Do you think it will come?"

Without looking up at him, attending to their toast, she said, "You know, Guy, I like being married and all that, but I think I would rather go back to London, if you don't mind. I like being married and every-thing, but I think I'm too young. I mean, I think I'd rather not be married anymore." Often, alone, when Guy was asleep or looking at the television over at Major Terry's, she had wandered around the rooms and come across hibernating geckos—small house lizards—their heartbeats slowed until they were just this side of life. She turned them over, ungently, with the cruel curiosity of a child. Looking at them, she would think, Now, let me see, what am I doing? I am married to Guy Osborne and we are having a honeymoon in the south of France. Cruel, frightened, she looked up now to see what he would do.

He simply thought it was a good thing that she had decided to start a row at this moment, because he could hear someone walking in the drive and knew he would not be able to persuade her that it was the sound of a blown leaf. It was his habit to see the best in every circumstance—marriage being otherwise untenable.

He did not take her seriously. Being in the darkened winter south had led to too much brooding and talk. Every tree and stone seemed to be waiting, like them, for a minor change. But trees and stones have this advantage: they do not converse. There is talk and talk. Guy would have gone on about the war, which he had enjoyed, but Susan had got in first with her family, and her fears, and even Marigold. Poor Marigold, whom he had loved, now stuck like persistent bad luck to their marriage, their future, their uncertain life.

"Then, you see, you could just marry Marigold, and I could get a job in a coffee bar," said Susan, buttering toast.

"I couldn't and you certainly couldn't," he said. "I couldn't marry Marigold, even if I wanted to. Although the fact of the matter is, I adored her."

"You never got over her," Susan said. She had been saying this all along.

"In a way not. You see, we knew each other awfully well."

The prefect took over. "Then it would have been more honorable not to have married me. You needn't have. I wasn't *seduced*."

Guy seemed to accept this. He might have got over Marigold in time, but never the war. Tonight's drinking and arguing brought it back. His closest friends had been killed, but he thought of them as living and young. He looked, and would always look, as if he were bringing in an aircraft with all the essential parts shot away. His war record was good for jobs, although for one reason or another, not Guy's doing, they never held up; and his manner still brought down women: flower women who sobbed in bars, forgot their own names, lost their purses; soft little women, appealing as tiny animals, usually married to hopeless men. The beloved Marigold, combining essentials, was both flower and mouse. Guy's ability to recall, exclusively limited to scenes of war, made way for memories of his love. In stormier, happier times, she edged from the bar counter to the telephone and returned in tears: the husband, at home and waiting for his dinner, had been cross. But Marigold, frail thing, was not to be shoved. She dried her tears and said she would have another drink. Guy admired that.

His wife had nothing of that fierce mouselike courage. She talked about leaving him, unsettled by gin probably; but wait!

"*You* should go, actually," said Susan, now in the ugly mood he thought of as exclusively possible with women. "It is *my* aunt's house." She thought of the letters Marigold had written to him that she had read in the freezing bathroom, perched uncomfortably on the edge of the tub. "I think you should go within twenty-four hours."

He paid no attention. She would not have stayed alone a second, and it would have taken him twenty-four days to decide where to go. He slipped the bottle, the last of their hostess's gin, behind his chair. He took a drink, shuddering. "Somebody's walked on my grave," he said amiably. Obviously he never expected to have a grave, anywhere. Susan seemed to him terribly comic, telling him to clear out that way, with the plaid blanket rakishly tossed back. He could not help giving her a friendly smile.

The smile was maddening. He reacted no more than a sleeping lizard that, tormented, could not move an eye or a frozen limb. Unable to adjust his eyes to a fixed point, Guy placidly watched a transparent Susan detach herself from his wife and slip to one side. Interested, but not alarmed, his reflexes all one minute behind, he saw Susan and her double smash a clock. They could never replace that clock.

The awaited collapse came on. Susan sobbed on his lap.

"Poor little kitten!"

"You never got over Marigold. You should never have married me."

"Oh, come on. You can love different people different ways."

"I didn't think being married to you would be like this."

"Neither did I," said Guy, truthfully. "Don't cry, now. You get so worked up at night. Everything will be different in the morning."

But she shook her head—no. The weight of their marriage shifted; she rejected the promises and remembered the claims. They were sliding, as a couple, from being the gay relations from London, caretaking for a lark, to the improvident kin who must be helped; they were slipping over an invisible frontier. On one side were people with funny little debts (as Guy pretended he and Susan were) and on the other were the people who wanted such a lot but weren't able to pay for any of it.

She said helplessly, "It's just that I think I'm too young."

"Too young to be alone in London, if that's what you mean."

He remembered how she had daunted her elders, how moral she had been. Patiently he explained their present situation all over again. He had lost his job because of competition from the Danes—no, the Japanese; the Danes last time—and they had thought it would be fun to wait for better times in the South. They had given up their flat in London—remember? Susan remembered. Of course Guy was right... He was endlessly tender and kind. He must have been like that in the old days when he was prying Marigold out of bars. *Guy* was the one with the grasp on fact.

She decided to blame the house. It was far too big. One of them was always wondering what the other one was up to. If one had nothing to do and found the other occupied, the unoccupied person felt abandoned. Drawn to the warmth of the single fire, they met in the drawing room at half past five. To avoid running up a reproachable electrical bill, they kept all but the drawing room dark, giving the rest of the house over to the wind, and the scratching sounds. The area around the fireplace was cleared, the uncovered tables crowded with full ashtrays. The rest of the furniture was still hidden under sheets. On dim corner tables, jars of drooping, blackish carnations were the reminders of Susan's early efforts to make the room alive.

"All the same," she said, sniveling, drying her tears with the palms of her hands, "I know you think about Marigold. Sometimes I believe you would murder me to get rid of me, if you dared." He did not reply. He looked suddenly old and ill. It was no good; nobody was planning to murder anybody. Guy had a bad leg and hip. The cold was worse for him than for Susan, although he never mentioned it. He was waiting for news from the world; for a message. Submerged in the icy lake of his situation, he accepted this stunning shock: he was forty, he had never been able to earn a living, and in a moment of sexual insanity he had taken on a young, young wife.

As Guy had promised all along, the weather cleared in the night. A mistral blew in from the sea, sending the clouds inland to pile up against the higher Alps. It was dryly cold. Susan stood out on the terrace before the drawing room and saw that torn, stained newspapers were flapping against the hedge. Someone had been through in the night. The wind dragged at her hair. She felt everything swept back and away; her marriage was knocked down and the threadroots picked up by the wind. In the drawing room was the wreckage of the short quarrel—the smashed clock.

Evidently miracles occurred. There was a letter, and it was not from Aunt Val. She watched Guy's progress up the drive from the road, where he had been waiting for the postman to come by, as he did every day. He came up to the terrace and stood with his arm around Susan. The letter fluttered against her arm. Susan would not read it; she would take his word.

They began walking up and down the terrace arm in arm. The letter was from Guy's mother; she was sending them money, and they were to join her for the winter in Madeira. His mother was taking over from Susan's relatives; an implicit, unspoken volley was beginning. He told Susan that his mother was mean; she had always kept him on short rein, and his father before him. It was puzzling, hearing him talk about allowances as if he were a little boy. For if the house had fallen, or if Susan's hair had caught fire, he would surely have known what to do. It was just this business of earning a living, keeping jobs. They talked about Madeira, confusing it with the future in the Argentine. Susan believed. He had said the letter would come; it came. He had said the weather would change. She did not know of any more reliable prophets, or even if any existed. They agreed that everything would be different once they had made a move. They would be careful about the house they lived in—not too large, not too old; it made all the difference. Where they were going now, Guy was saying, there would be no difficulty about the climate; they would never have the weather between them again. Guy had been told it was sunny all the year around.

CROSSING FRANCE

JAMES Prescott Tynes and his friend Richard Smith cycled south from Calais, sometimes taking buses or trains for short runs, but mostly pushing along the narrow routes that ran alongside and wound in and out of the main highways of France. Even the most devious roads were dense with summer traffic and it would have been slow going for anyone in a hurry, but the boys were taking their time, going miles out of their way if they felt like it, not tied to any schedule except getting home before September. They lived on picnic food and slept in youth hostels when they found them, or under hired tents in *terrains de camping*. Prescott handled the money and the maps and decided when to take trains and where they should spend the night. He had a better head than Smithy, but Smithy was acquiescent about most things, so that part of the trip was all right. They were good friends and had been friends eight years, ever since Prescott, aged eight, had come to the prep school where Smithy's father was a master. Homesick, outraged, Prescott sobbed himself sick in the lavatories day after day, while Smithy tried to pull him together with pleas and exhortations and assurances of better things to come. They were in different schools now, and their character roles were reversed. Prescott was outgoing, good looking, dauntingly sure of himself. He wore his hair quite short, American style, and dressed in blue jeans and heavy ribbed sweaters. People in France kept telling him he resembled the late actor Chems Din, and one girl they talked to in a hostel took out a pearl-edged plastic locket she wore under her blouse and showed them a picture of James Dean looking tousled and sullen.

"Hysteria," said Prescott. But Smithy thought he seemed pleased all the same.

Smithy was quite different, red-haired, with a sharp, delicate, not quite masculine face. He attracted the sympathy and attention of older women. He detested this, and the situations it led to were dismissed by him and by Prescott as "the old-lady business." They got along well, and it was a good holiday. The only thing Smithy had to remember was not to get on Prescott's nerves. Straight at the beginning, after they had claimed their bikes and pushed them out of customs and were properly and legally on French soil, Smithy said in a sepulchral voice, "Eternal France!" The look Prescott shot him, rapid, magpie bright, was warning enough: he wasn't to make those remarks—those boneless platitudes everyone they knew called "Smithy's thoughts." Smithy had thoughts on nearly everything, and he uttered them in a slow, dismal, astonished way, as if he had just discovered the uses of English. Most people thought Smithy funny, even though he seldom tried to be. But Prescott didn't find him funny at all. He said Smithy sounded like one of the Sitwells reading aloud in a very large hall. This got on his nerves, and Smithy had to remember to keep quiet fairly often. That and the old-lady business were the only flaws. They were minor flaws, at least at the beginning.

It was a wet summer: *un été pourri*. They heard *été pourri* from Calais onward, and it was an expression that conveyed all the rotten-ness of rotting fruit. It sounded like a peach decaying on wet grass; like a melon full of wasps. The countryside in the Île de France was deep wet blotting-paper green, and the sky, between showers, a thin diluted blue. The ditches along the roads were loud with rushing water, and this sound of water running over stones followed them by day, and at night worked into Smithy's dream. They cycled down paths where chestnut and acacia branches met over their heads and they passed children looking for mushrooms under the trees. Then Smithy had to remember not to say, "This is the real France," because that would get on Prescott's nerves. When they were halfway south the rain stopped and the dark wet look of the landscape gradually lifted. The sun through the moist air stung their faces, as it does after storms. Everything was clear and light and green and blue and Smithy thought that if they had been flying they would have seen every snail glued to the stone walls, every blackberry ripening, the air was that clear. Prescott took his sweater off and cycled that way and was soon very brown; but Smithy couldn't because of having red hair and the skin that went with it. He wore a jersey with long sleeves. At one of the tourist halts where buses disgorged, he bought a straw hat with a brim. It was a feminine hat but he didn't know it. He had no idea that he looked remarkable with his pale face, and his striped jersey going endlessly down his thin waist and broomstick arms, and his girl's straw hat. By the time they came to the Mediterranean, Prescott was as brown as if he had lived there all his life, and Smithy looked as if he had never left home.

They came in sight of Nice at eleven o'clock on a dry, white day. Coming down the curving road from Grasse they saw first the red roofs, then the blue harbor and the ships. They had seen the sea from above Grasse, but it was distant, a mirage between hills, too easily confused with sky. They stopped and propped their bikes against a stone wall by the road and they both sat down on the wall. They had been on the road since dawn, but they weren't tired, only hungry, and they felt well about having crossed France without accidents or incidents or having to telegraph home. Nice wasn't their terminal, for they were going on to Italy, but it was the end of France, and there was a sense of achievement in suddenly coming on to the sea like this. Prescott took a picture, holding the camera sideways so that he could get a panoramic effect, and Smithy put alcohol on his mosquito bites. Cars went by and strangers waved at them from the bursting foreign buses and after a bit the inevitable thing happened, a middle-aged Englishwoman drew up in a sporty little Singer and asked if they were in trouble or needed a lift.

"We're only resting, thank you," said Smithy. "We've got our bikes." Prescott, who did not consider himself involved, continued taking pictures. After a few questions and a few words of praise this inquisitive woman started up the motor and drove away. She gave a jaunty backward wave and Smithy raised a limp, freckled hand.

"We are brave," said Prescott, in an exaggeratedly educated voice. "How wise we are to take this sort of adventurous holiday, which Norman Douglas would not have despised, instead of lounging about with the rest of our spoon-fed welfare-rotted generation. Things are not finished yet for Old England. The spirit of Nelson still prevails among the young. How'd you like that Norman Douglas touch?" he said, in his own voice. But Smithy, the old-lady magnet, was not reacting. He went on savagely dabbing his mosquito bites and wishing Prescott would shut up. It wasn't his fault, and it wasn't his fault either that he felt he had to answer every time and be polite.

His audience withdrawn into a stormy inner world, Prescott understood that his teasing had been taken for an attack. He rapidly turned into a different sort of old-lady imitation, one that had nothing to do with Smithy at all. This time Smithy looked up and laughed.

Prescott was paying out quantities of energy and charm keeping Smithy afloat. It seemed to him Smithy wanted a lot of props. He had charm and enough to spare, but he resented having to expend it as a kind of emotional salve.

"You ought to go on the stage," said Smithy sincerely.

"Everybody who can do an imitation thinks he can go on the stage," said Prescott. "But thanks all the same."

"I suppose your father would help you if you did want to," said Smithy, instantly envying his friend.

"He'd throw me out," said Prescott. "He wants me to be a civil servant so I can get a pension and give him a regular allowance in his old age. An international civil servant, you know, something in Geneva. He says that's the new bourgeoisie."

Smithy accepted this. Everything he knew about the Tynes family was irregular and strange. Prescott's father made documentary films of a rather lyrical nature, which Prescott professed to scorn, and his mother was a mild-hearted gently alcoholic socialist, and Smithy would have traded his own dry high-minded home life for it any day. He wondered how his friend could be so offhand about his interesting father who went all over the world making films paid for by oil companies, concrete mixers, airlines, or by Asian governments towering on the brink of Communism, who had decided to spend their American credits making narcissistic pictures about themselves. The films had no relation, ever, to oil, Asia, concrete, and so forth, and they never seemed to earn any money afterwards, but it did give Prescott's father a chance to travel and enjoy himself. Smithy's father hardly went anywhere, except to beachy villages that hadn't yet been spoiled. His mother and father would find a nice little place in Spain, say, where there were no other foreigners for the good reason that there were no decent hotels, no running water, fleas in the sand, stinging jellyfish in the surf, and it rained all the time. Then the little village would be discovered, usually by Germans and people from Liverpool, and the newcomers would take over, fleas, rain, stingers, and all, and Smithy's parents would have to find something even less attractive, in order to have it all to themselves. It was because of the discovering business that Smithy knew the more squalid fringes of Spain, Yugoslavia and Greece, but next to nothing of Italy or France. Smithy was certain his parents had never seen Nice as it was this hot morning, and that if they had been there, they would have judged it wrongly. He felt that he had overshot them, in a way, achieving something beyond their reckoning, and this was a stirring thought. It stirred his sense of opposition, his awareness of growing up, and the unfortunate platitudinous springs from which his thoughts, brimming, usually rose. He decided not to say anything about what he was feeling. It was safer that way. Changing to another subject entirely, he said, "What's the first thing you remember? In your life, I mean."

"V-E Day," Prescott said.

"I remember even before," said Smithy, "I remember a Christmas tree when I was two."

So far so good. They hadn't moved from the wall. The sun was still on them, the sea hadn't run away. Prescott broke a chocolate bar in two and gave Smithy half. Then Smithy had to say in that melancholy voice, "The deep Gregorian pool of memory."

Prescott spat out his chocolate. He exploded: "In the first place it doesn't mean anything, not one bloody thing. It only sounds as if it might mean something. You probably mean Freudian. You don't even know. You must have a mind like a meat mixer."

"I don't mean Freudian," said Smithy, "I don't go in for that much. I know what I mean."

"Well, keep it to yourself." Prescott was good-natured, but Smithy's thoughts, and the voice he used, made his hair rise, just as some people cannot bear the feel of velvet or the sound of squeaking chalk. They got on their bikes without speaking and cruised downhill. In five minutes Prescott had forgotten their last exchange, and he called to

Smithy: "We could get over to Italy today if you feel like it. There's a hostel in Ventimiglia." His parents had told Prescott not to linger on the Riviera, and he received so few instructions that he had taken this one very much to heart. He put the question to Smithy again, and again received no answer. Smithy was sulking, but Prescott, who didn't know what sulking was, and didn't always recognize it when he saw it, took this for assent.

They crawled through Nice, which was full of buses like dinosaurs, and Prescott said they could stop and bathe at Èze which his father had told him would do. Smithy answered this, but added that he was starved. Cheerful again, they bought bread and garlic sausage and made huge sandwiches of it. Then in Villefranche a terrible thing happened, the crack in the friendship that was the start of the end. They stopped in front of a souvenir shop, so that Smithy could choose postcards to send home, and an American sailor, not much older than they were, came over and spoke to them. He asked them first for a light, but neither of them smoked, then he asked them some rather old-lady questions: where they came from, and how old they were, and where they were going. Smithy replied with the same courtesy, but more unease, than he would have given an old lady. When he said they were going to Italy and across to Austria, the sailor took out his wallet and after searching through its several stuffed compartments took out a dirty little packet of Italian money and said, "You might as well take this, it's no good to me."

"I couldn't," said Smithy, bright pink under his ludicrous hat.

The sailor said, "No, go ahead, I can't use them," and shoved the money in Smithy's hand.

Smithy at once became formal and found his manner and said, "You must take my name then, and if you come to England, we can pay you back."

The sailor seemed to think that was fair enough and they exchanged names and addresses on the backs of postcards. The sailor's name was Roy Freligh, and his address was double, one in care of his ship, and one in Pennsylvania. He wished them good luck and a good trip and all the best of everything, as if he had known them for years, and it wasn't funny, but, evidently, his normal way.

The two cycled on in silence. "You shouldn't have taken the money," Prescott said at last. "It looks funny."

Smithy put on a burst of speed and instead of trailing behind, as always, pushed on ahead. He felt all wrong about the whole thing, but Prescott's remark struck him as an accusation, and he felt like getting off his bicycle and knocking Prescott down. That was perhaps the trouble, that he did nothing but ride on, first in aggressive then in defensive silence. They missed Èze, and had a look at Monte Carlo, but it was an expensive beach and they didn't stop. It was afternoon, the hottest part of the day. Traffic thickened and slowed as they neared the frontier. There was a prevalence of blue-clad white-gaitered police, of long cars from Belgium and Germany, of bad-tempered drivers, and nothing really amenable. They were on the lower road, Prescott having decided they would make better time that way. Between the stucco-fronted blocks of flats, the shuttered villas, the massive hotels with towels drying from the windows, they sometimes had glimpses of sea. They reached Menton, a mile from the frontier; hot, red-faced, speech-less, they swam off the piled-up rocks before the casino without wait-ing to find a beach. The whole venture appeared flat and hot and empty. The water was dirty and opaque, and the tourists promenading before the cafes might have been in Eastbourne.

Prescott came out of this mood first. When they were putting on their clothes, he said, "Do you know, we've been on the road thirteen hours today?"

"Feels more like thirty." In spite of his precautions Smithy had a touch of sunburn. Pulling on his shirt he said, "This feels like haircloth."

"You're a surly bastard," said Prescott amiably. "You're tired. Why don't we take a bus from here? There must be something that goes up to the frontier."

Smithy felt injured but no longer remembered why. He lagged behind Prescott and let him do everything, all the finding out about the bus, and then the arguing with the driver before he would put their bikes up on the roof. They climbed aboard and with sulky politeness he let Prescott sit near the window. He had never been so hot, so tired, so hungry, and so indifferently understood in his life. Prescott kept on pointing things out: the beach, where you couldn't put a pin between the people, and the mile or so of cars, three across, waiting to cross into Italy. The bus sailed by the stalled traffic, and Smithy supposed he ought to congratulate Prescott for having had this idea, but the thought of praising his conceited companion was intolerable. The bus let them off before a small fountain. The way to the frontier was short but uphill. They had ridden not thirty seconds when they came to a railway crossing, where a white gate was descending, and they got off their bikes and went up to the rail, and suddenly the Blue Train, almost empty, for this was the start of its run, swept nobly around the bend of the last small hill of the Alps, and rushed by with a long triumphant clatter. Even Prescott was affected; at least, he was still. Smithy thought that the train, fresh, washed, swept, really blue, began this run as if it had never done it before; came around the curve of the stony Alpille as if breaking a starting tape, parting a curtain, preparing a surprise. He realized he was giving the train a human personality and it was bad enough when he did it with animals and flowers but a train was much worse. He knew what Prescott would say. At the same time he felt compelled to repeat this idea and take the punishment of Prescott's scorn, but then the barrier went up and the cars behind them began to hoot fiercely. They pushed over the tracks and got on their bikes and changed the gears so they could climb the road to the frontier. The road was narrow, curving, steep, between walled gardens and bolted garden doors. They kept to the edge, grazing the walls. There was no pavement. A huge cypress overgrown in yellow amaranth suddenly reared up over a hedge, and Smithy found this beautiful and unexpected and wondered if the plant had become rooted in the bark of the tree. When they reached the top of the hill he mentioned it to Prescott, who was too winded to answer, and merely nodded, to indicate he had seen it, too. Smithy remembered Prescott had told him that people who worked close to the land were indifferent to the aesthetics of nature, and he was certain Prescott was thinking this now. "But I can't watch everything I say," he thought. "I can't keep on having thoughts and never speaking."

There was a cluster of cafes at the top of the hill, with terraces, and a view of a pretty harbor and a church and deeply shadowed hills; it was as if the last few feet of territory before it stopped being France should be given over to places where you could eat and drink and look at things. Smithy would have sat there straight away and eaten ice cream and looked at the harbor until it grew dark, but Prescott pointed out that would make them late, although he didn't say what it would make them late for. He also mentioned that the ice cream was better and cheaper on the Italian side. Prescott was right, of course. They pushed their bikes almost up to the customs building, and Smithy didn't say, "We are leaving France," even though he felt he owed some ritual word, simply because he had crossed the whole country, under trees and in the rain. It seemed to him wrong not to say what you were feeling. He gave Prescott a bitter look, but as Prescott was charming the customs official, a dumpy little uniformed woman, it went unnoticed. Beyond the French border station was a curving bridge, more like a shelf, really, with cliffs rising abruptly behind, and carnations growing on neat Japanese-looking terraces underneath. Then, over this bridge, were new white buildings and a sign saying ITALIA, and a green-white-red flag. Smithy was sure that the minute he set foot there, everything would change and be instantly unlike France. He expected the color of the sky and the color of the sea and the smell of the air to be transformed. They were standing before the French police inspector, holding out their blue passports, when Smithy, looking moodily to the other side, said, "The far Italian shore," more than ever in a poetry-recital tone of voice. Prescott turned to him, right before the lined-up waiting cars and all the people who understood English and the French officials, and said, "Oh my *God* Smithy shut *up*!"

Smithy knew he was going white, he felt the curious thickening of skin around his mouth. He knew it gave him a look his mother couldn't stand. Prescott thought Smithy's face had gone irregular, like someone hit during a game. His face was red and white and lumpy with pain. Prescott thought, "This is a hell of a holiday." He said, more out of curiosity than unkindness, "I'll bet you can make yourself be sick whenever you want to."

Smithy looked as if he were going to be sick there and then, and Prescott, disgusted with him, heard him say in a thick voice, "I mean to say, I can't go on not having thoughts."

"Oh, have anything you want, only get your passport fixed and let's go," he said, and pushed on without looking back.

There seemed nothing for Smithy to do but go back into France, and so he turned his bike the other way and walked off. When he looked back Prescott had already pocketed his passport and was vanishing into the file of traffic creeping along the bridge. He seemed suspended miles and miles over the carnation fields, then he was swallowed into Italy. They had broken the rule about separating. Even Prescott would have trouble with his parents over that. It was the only thing the parents, both sets, had been really firm about.

Smithy went into the first cafe he could see on the French side and sat down where there was a good view toward the sea. He had only a few francs in his pocket, and he knew that Prescott would have to come back, because he was carrying all the maps and the money and couldn't leave Smithy like this. He knew Prescott would realize it before long and come back. He stared straight at the harbor, trying to think of something appropriate to this view. It seemed to him that he was so often hurt and made to seem in the wrong, and he was always walking off because he couldn't think of what else to do, and people were always having to come after him. The worst of it all was that now he was alone he wasn't having thoughts. He wasn't thinking of anything at all. Lights went on like drops of water around the edge of the bay. The cypresses looked theatrical, cut out of cardboard and propped in place. Surely there was a thought in his head suitable for this? The row had been all over nothing. There was nothing in his head at all. It was too late, too late to start back on the fringe of the day and live it all over differently. It was too late to change Prescott's feelings, and he supposed that it was too late to change his own character and that it was going to be like this all his life.

Prescott was back in ten minutes. He must have realized about the money before he'd gone anywhere. He sat down at Smithy's table and asked for a pêche Melba without saying anything about its being better on the Italian side.

"There's an officer with a beard over there," Prescott said. "He looks like James Robertson Justice. There's an Aston Martin with its guts out. You should hear the driver. I saw a place where I think we can eat." You could tell he had taken an attitude. He was making the best of it, because they weren't to separate, and it was either get on together or go home, and Prescott wanted to go on through North Italy and up into Austria. He was going to be good about Smithy and let him talk all he wanted: but he would never do a holiday with him again. All that was implicit. Smithy knew the rest of the trip would be all right, but not the same; and although he would have given anything to change things, it would never be the same again as before they had the row, when they were still coming across France.

THE MOABITESS

ELDERLY Miss Horeham, though timid and poor, did not shrink from a row on that account, particularly when she imagined that something was expected of her. It was she, in the end, who cornered Mme. Arnaud in the passage and complained about the noise the Oxleys made. The others marveled at her nerve, for she was known to be someone who wouldn't say boo to a goose. But then, Miss Horeham had the room next to the Oxleys, with only the thin wall between, and she had probably had enough.

"It's a disgrace, you know," Miss Horeham whispered, blinking, drawing rapid little breaths between words; she really was excruciatingly timid, and this business of going outside herself took all her strength.

Mme. Arnaud said she did not understand. She did not understand what Miss Horeham meant by disgrace.

Well, it was the way the Oxleys quarreled in the night, said Miss Horeham, apologizing with her eyes for having to bring up that sort of thing. It was the things they said—particularly Mr. Oxley. You could hear them all over the floor. Mr. Wynn had heard them. Mme. Brunhof had heard. Those people from Liverpool had probably heard, too.

It was all so clear to Miss Horeham, this picture of the *pension* tenants roused and trembling in their rooms. But Mme. Arnaud still screwed up her eyes and frowned. She folded her hands on her filthy apron. She said, "*Et alors?*"

Mrs. Oxley, Miss Horeham whispered, bending close, Mrs. Oxley might find life hard, but she was a married woman. If she didn't want to be a married woman, if she didn't care about . . . that side of life . . . why did she marry? There were plenty of women who didn't care about life . . . about that side of life . . . and they simply never married.

All this was more than she had intended to say, and she would never have brought it all out so courageously, especially that last bit about marriage, if she hadn't had the wine at lunch. Departing guests, the nice Lawrences from Wimbledon, had left her the remains of their wine—half a liter of red. So now there was a grape-colored flush on Miss Horeham's cheeks, and she was saying everything that came into her head.

"If you don't like your room, I can move you back to the attic," said Mme. Arnaud. The passage was dark and smelled of the cauliflower they had been given for lunch, and all at once Mme. Arnaud, with her dirty apron, and the black mustache on her upper lip, seemed the dark wielder of power Miss Horeham had known as a child, after her mother died and delivered her into servants' hands.

"I meant change their room, not mine," she said faintly.

Mme. Arnaud pushed by her and went into the kitchen. She had other things to do, such as disguise the remains of the cauliflower so that it could be served up again that night. It was November, out-of-season on the Riviera; she had few enough people as it was, without offending the Oxleys for the sake of mad Miss Horeham.

"We are at their mercy," Miss Horeham said, stepping into the lounge. The encounter had stimulated her and widened the world, usually limited to her room and her own face in the glass. "We are at the mercy of hotel-keepers. And with all the decent places closed until Christmas, we are obliged to stay here and suffer the inconveniences."

Nobody replied. There was no assenting ripple from among the stuffed chairs and potted ferns. Mr. Wynn didn't so much as lower the *Daily Telegraph*. For one thing, Mrs. Oxley was in the room—the very person complained about; it couldn't have been more tactless. And then they had known that Mme. Arnaud would never take Miss Horeham's word. Everyone knew that she paid next to nothing, and that every summer, in the good season, she was moved to a small kiln of a room under the roof. The poor thing had lived abroad too long to be eligible for a pension at home; it was really a shame. Mr. Wynn had tried to do something about it, but even the welfare state had its rules.

Miss Horeham walked once about the lounge, as if seeing the travel posters on its walls for the first time, then sat down in her usual place, on a stone-hard upholstered sofa adrift in the room, away from lamps and footstools and magazines. This did not trouble her in the least, for she came to the lounge only to see the others, and the position of the sofa was such that the rest could escape her gaze only by swiveling around with their backs to her, and no one ever had the courage to do this. They were down from their afternoon naps now. There was Mr. Wynn with the *Telegraph*, and little Mrs. Oxley reading *Vogue*, and Mme. Brunhof writing a letter. The people from Liverpool—father and mother and nearly grown sons—stood at separate windows, looking with mute despair at the rain, which came off the Alps in gusts, like gray veils, to merge with the gray fog on the sea. Buses, wet and cold as toads, crawled along the sea road. The last of the zinnias in the garden were being battered into the ground.

"It usen't to rain like this before the war," said Miss Horeham, fixing her eyes on Mr. Wynn's paper, but without seeing it. She had a small, particular field of vision, as if her eye were eternally pressed to a knothole. Everything else was quite blurred. "It never rained at the villa in the old days," she said in a droning voice. "When father died, I gave it up. The villa was called La Bella. That was for me." She stuttered so at the memory that the others thought she would choke.

Mr. Wynn rustled the *Daily Telegraph*. He knew all about La Bella by now. "Do read us something," said little Mrs. Oxley, putting down her *Vogue*. "Some interesting bit."

He read where his eyes rested, if only to put a halt to that droning voice. "The Queen wore mauve, while the Queen Mother . . . trimmed with fox . . . Rain failed to dampen the spirits of a large crowd . . ."

Temporarily stilled, Miss Horeham contemplated them all with grave good will. She had fought their battle with Mme. Arnaud, as she used to battle for her father in the old days, in the war. She had been straight as an arrow—not a gray hair until she was forty-three. The curls around her face were yellow-gray now, her eyes were sunken, and the skin around them was dark. She wore long-sleeved dresses in gray, violet, or brown. Most of her dresses had been given her, and although many of the castoff things that came her way were gay and bright, she felt she oughtn't wear anything cheerful. She felt as if "Charity" should be written on her in letters four feet high, so that wherever her father was, in whatever dark passage of the dead, he might see the word and doubly perish with shame. If there was another annihilation after death, then let it come to Mr. Percy Horeham, who had irresponsibly departed from life in 1946 and left his maiden daughter not a penny, not a franc, nothing but debts. She had nursed him through the war, through the Occupation, under the very noses of Italians and Germans—all those strangers! She had walked seven miles to buy him an egg! And still she had had no allowance but had had to beg for everything from the locked box under the bed, so that all her life she had no idea of money, of what things ought to cost. She did not doubt that the dead knew what went on among the living. Let him see now what had become of the remnants of his house—a solitary daughter in castoff dresses in the lounge of a third-class *pension*. Let him see! Let him perish!

Thinking this, she smiled, and Mrs. Oxley thought, She's not a bad old thing. It must be awful to be alone ... Mrs. Oxley had not only a husband to quarrel with but also a son of four. "Do you like being read things?" she said to Miss Horeham, when Mr. Wynn had stopped about the party in the rain.

"At the villa we never read—only the Bible," said Miss Horeham, which was true. There wasn't another book at La Bella, aside from her prizes from school, put away in a box. But there was the Bible, and the two of them had known it by heart.

Miss Horeham moved her lips to say again, "We are at their mercy," but she had lost the thread, and only liked the Biblical sound it made. She went on smiling. She was thinking of the Bible and the old days, and of what a nice time of year this was; in spite of what she had said about its being off season, it was really the period she liked best. When the rain stopped, the sun came out, unnaturally large and bright, like a flower forced into bloom. But it was never high in the sky, and the shadows of people walking in the *pension* gardens stretched like the long shadows of a summer evening; noon was a brilliant evening. In Miss Horeham's vision of life this was the climate in which everything took place. On November nights, the world closed comfortably in. They were the same people in the same lounge, but at night they were held by the dark corners of the room, drawn together in the dim pools of light from the low-watt lamps beside their chairs: Mr. Wynn, pensioned from the Admiralty, and Mme. Brunhof, who lived here between in-vitations to the houses of rich old friends, and little Mrs. Oxley with her son. Mr. Oxley, that disturbing influence at night, disturbed Miss Horeham even more by not staying quietly in the lounge after dinner. He and the Liverpool lot, who had imagined the Riviera as being very different, would make off straight after their meal, down the road to the Bar du Midi. They never came back until just before twelve, when the *pension* door was locked. What fun was there in the bar? There was nothing to see from there but the sea and the odd, starry light of a fishing boat, or the moon rising over an Alp. "When you've seen it once, you've seen it forever," Mr. Wynn always said. And as for the bar itself, there was no one English there; you couldn't even talk.

Mrs. Oxley sat in a large armchair with little Tom on her lap. He was afraid to stay alone upstairs, and she had to wait until he was sound asleep and then carry him up. Sometimes kind Mr. Wynn carried him for her. She was twenty-six and plump, with skin like an apricot. Her eyes, her fat little hands, her full lips suggested she was the last person in the world to deny that side of life, but even without Miss Horeham to inform them the others would have understood that things were not well with the Oxleys. "Don't wake me up when you come in," she would tell her husband as he started out for "just a turn down the road." A quick resentful look would pass between them. He was a fair man with light-blue eyes, and he colored easily. Pink with anger, he would stride off, wearing flannels and a blazer with the crest of an obscure school. The Oxleys lived in South Africa because of his job, and were in Europe for a leave of three months.

"When Tom was born, I nearly died," Mrs. Oxley once said, after her husband had gone. The others took this to mean she knew they heard the night quarrels and wanted to give a decent explanation.

Miss Horeham nodded her yellow-gray curls, as if she knew all about that. "They are dreadful," she murmured vaguely, but whether she meant men or births or quarrels she was not quite sure. Her eyes turned to Mr. Wynn—to his fine white hands, his cropped gray hair, his color-less lips. She watched the delicate way he inserted a cigarette in an amber holder. She admired the white of his cuffs. Even his newspapers seemed cleaner and crisper than other people's. She remembered a dream of a union that had nothing to do with quarrels at night or damp bath towels on the floor or someone using your comb. It was an ancient girlhood dream, small and removed now, and she had to dig under the leaves of her memory to find it—an early dream of living with someone rather like Mr. Wynn and sharing with him a cold immaculate bed. But the dream retreated. It was small and bright and slipped under the leaves again. She knew about living in the same house with men; she had nursed her ailing father for years and years.

Mr. Wynn loved children. "Isn't it time for me to carry little Tom upstairs?" he would ask. And Mrs. Oxley, who would not have surrendered him to anyone else, would let Mr. Wynn take Tom from her arms. "It's a wonderful age," he would say, looking down on the flushed, sleeping child.

"I wish he needn't grow up. I never want him to change."

"No, he mustn't."

They would go up the stairs together, quietly, so as not to wake Tom, and after a few minutes Mr. Wynn would descend alone and pick up his paper again. Sometimes it was Mme. Brunhof who got up to go first, leaning on her cane. She was an Englishwoman, in spite of her name.

"Who is she?" Mrs. Oxley had asked.

A direct question of this sort plunged Miss Horeham into uncertainty. She struggled to emerge. "Mme. Brunhof—well, you see, she is English. Oh, very English indeed." It was so difficult to find the right words, the most delicate explanation. "Mme. Brunhof was closely associated for many years—years ago, of course—with an *important person*. We believe it to have been—oh, someone very grand." Her love of established order rose and checked the disloyal suspicion. She could not bring it out.

Mr. Wynn gave an irritated cough and told the royal name.

"Goodness," said Mrs. Oxley, but without real interest. It was all so long ago. She stretched one of Tom's brown curls. It sprang back.

"He married her off to this Brunhof, after he was fed up with her," said Mr. Wynn, who could be surprisingly coarse. "An Austrian count."

"An Alsatian baron," said Miss Horeham, making a fluttering motion with her hands at being obliged to contradict.

"She must have been good-looking," Mrs. Oxley said.

"You can see the traces still. She must be seventy-five."

"Eighty," gasped Miss Horeham.

"You're all I care about in the whole world," Mrs. Oxley whispered.

Miss Horeham suddenly blinked and peered sharply out of the small universe in which she lived. Did she mean Tom, or Mr. Wynn? She meant Tom, of course, for she was rocking him gently in her chair.

Night after night, November went on like this, and it was the best season, even though there were fewer people to give Miss Horeham old dresses and half bottles of wine. The world drew into itself, became smaller and smaller, was limited to her room, her table in the dining room, her own eyes in the mirror, her own hand curved around a glass. Dreams as thick as walls rose about her bed and sheltered her sleep— unless the Oxleys quarreled. Then she would lie awake in the dark, her heart ticking rapidly and dryly, like her father's old watch.

What made this peaceful order stop? Why did it stop? What made Mr. Oxley quarrel with kind Mr. Wynn? Miss Horeham had never heard anything like it. There was Mrs. Oxley out in the hall or on the staircase—probably in her nightdress, for it was very late—wailing "Oh, it's a mistake! He came to see Tom!" and Mr. Oxley yelling until they heard him in the basement. Mme. Arnaud came out and shouted louder than anyone else. From Mr. Wynn there was no sound. Oh, it was terrible; the harsh night broken with shouts, like being taken on a night journey when one was a child: the flashing lights, the strange voices, the names of unknown stations swimming by. Miss Horeham lay flat on her back and recited at random from Proverbs: "A virtuous woman is a crown to her husband: but she that maketh ashamed is as rottenness to his bones." It was the first thing that came into her head. What came next? "He that tilleth ..." No, that came later. "The thoughts of the righteous are right." She repeated this until the noise had stopped, and then she fell back into sleep.

In the morning she was sure she must have dreamed it, but at breakfast Mr. Wynn was not at his place, and at the Oxleys' table there were only Mr. Oxley, looking mulish, and little Tom, perfectly calm

but hugging a girl's doll. Mme. Brunhof did not say good morning to
Mr. Oxley. Mme. Arnaud was siding with Mr. Wynn. She said that
Mr. Oxley had been drunk, and that she would not have South Africans
again. Miss Horeham tried not to see anything; she tried to pretend
nothing had happened at all. But then in the garden she had to run
into the Oxleys, and see Mrs. Oxley sitting bolt upright on a wrought-
iron chair, and Mr. Oxley standing with Tom.

"Don't take him away from me today!" said Mrs. Oxley. "I ask as a
special favor. Don't take him today. He's never been away from me for
a minute."

"He's going to be five," said Mr. Oxley. "He can go with his own
father to the beach."

"Where's my dolly?" said Tom.

"You're too big," his father said. "Forget it."

"He's not yet five!" cried Mrs. Oxley in a kind of wail.

"He's not to have it," said Mr. Oxley, suddenly very red, for he saw
Miss Horeham, hands clasped to her heart, all in gray-brown today,
like a little thrush.

"You're taking it out on him," said Mrs. Oxley. She had not yet seen
their witness.

Mr. Wynn was not down to lunch, or to dinner. Miss Horeham
kept glancing at his table. It was upsetting, like a day with no post. The
Oxleys were all together, eating in silence. That evening, father and son
were both red in the face, because they had been sitting on the beach.

Tom had brought a colored stone from the beach. He held it in one
hand and ate with the other. Suddenly, as if he had been good too long,
he flung the stone across the room, and it hit Miss Horeham on the
arm and fell on the carpet. She bent down and picked it up. "Naughty
boy," said both parents, but without much heart behind it. They seemed
both of them worn out with this day.

"What a charming present," Miss Horeham said. "Everyone gives
me things."

The Oxleys went up to their room after dinner. Then Mme. Brunhof went, and the Liverpool people, and then, since there was nothing
to stay up for, Miss Horeham left her sofa and sadly climbed the stairs.
There was a light under the Oxleys' door and a light under Mr. Wynn's,

but there was no sound. From her own room, Miss Horeham could hear the Oxleys, talking in low voices of ordinary things. They talked about the end of their leave in Europe, and of the things they had bought and now regretted—a white nylon pullover that had gone yellow in the wash, a bathrobe of toweling, four butter plates shaped like vine leaves, with butter knives to match.

"Give it all to the old trout," said Mr. Oxley.

Miss Horeham meekly bowed her head, although there was no one to see. Beggars couldn't be choosers, she knew. But the gifts came into the small, clear field of light, moved across it, and vanished into the blur.

An hour later, the house was so quiet you could hear the maids leave the kitchen and crunch down the gravel path in the garden on their way home. It was quieter than it had been since the arrival of the Oxleys, yet Miss Horeham could not settle down to sleep. There were woolly knitted bootees on her feet, and she wore a warm nightdress, and she had no aches or pains, and had not forgotten to pray. She tried to send herself off with Proverbs, but could not. At last she rose and turned on the light and drew on a dressing gown. Tom's stone was on the table by her bed. I had better put it away, she thought. It was a present, and besides it might be rare. She removed two cushions from what appeared to be a window seat, and revealed a small trunk. The key to the trunk hung around her neck on a string. Kneeling, she opened the trunk and began to take out her treasures—all the secret things she could have sold for pounds and pounds and pounds. Oh, how they would die if they knew—all those people who left her wine and dresses and gave her stones! How they would simply die! But none of them knew—not the sleeping Oxleys, or Mme. Brunhof, nor Mr. Wynn. Perhaps he was awake and brooding over last night's misunderstanding; a scene of that sort must have been dreadful for a man like Mr. Wynn. But he was already removed to the blurry world beyond her field of vision, and the little beam she had thrown in his direction flickered out.

She removed the first tray. There was her father's old collection of butterflies in a glass box; they must be worth something. At any rate, they were very gay. There was the scarf from Sicily, and the broken amber beads in a little cardboard box, and the box of Christmas soap, so precious it had never been used. There were the smoked mother-of-pearl buttons from her grandfather's waistcoat, and nineteen prewar stamps from India and Ceylon. She began to empty the trays still more rapidly. Three gold sovereigns in a leather bag. An orange stuck with cloves and tied with velvet ribbons; you never saw those now. The head of the "Madonna of the Chair," painted on ivory. A pewter plate with a date scratched on its back. Her prize books from school, with her name inside. A locket of garnets on a silver chain. A Spanish shawl, heavy embroidery on pink silk. A box from Italy inlaid with little colored stones and PERUGIA spelled in green. A bundle of clippings about the 1937 Coronation. Her father's letters to her, when she was still in school: "Dearest Girl..."

She stroked the striped Sicilian scarf and lifted it out of its tray and put it over her head. Mme. Arnaud grumbled at that locked trunk, when it had to be moved to and from the attic room. But she never dreamed of what it contained—not for one moment.

Miss Horeham sat down at the dressing table and solemnly regarded herself in the glass. Sometimes with that scarf on she looked like Ruth the Moabitess, and sometimes Bath-shebah, and sometimes even Rebekah, for Rebekah on seeing Isaac had put up her veil. But it was as Ruth that she fancied herself, a Moabitish woman with hoops in her ears and a red-green-black striped veil. "Dearest Girl," he had written when she was young; and how they had acted out the glorious stories— Samson and his traitress, and Boaz and Ruth. Well, it had all been harmless and a secret, and gave them the feeling that something rich was being lived at La Bella, something nobody knew. They had never read anything other than the Bible together. Not even the *Daily Mail*. And then his illness, and the slobbering, and having to shave him, for he wouldn't have anyone else, and even that wasn't the worst. In the end he hadn't known her, but then he opened his dying eyes and called her Ruth. He looked old and evil and cunning, going into his death. But he still knew her as Ruth, with hoops in her ears and the green-red-black striped veil.

It was only a Sicilian scarf, of course, bought on such an innocent holiday years ago. Staring in the mirror, she did not see her dressing gown or the yellow-gray curls. She saw her own eyes, until she was dazzled by the very sight of them. Everything else fell away. Her eyes were the center of the house, of the world. And there in the next room lay the Oxleys, and never guessed what Miss Horeham was really like. Mme. Brunhof never guessed, or Mr. Wynn. Nobody guessed at all. She smiled at herself, for of everyone in the house only Miss Horeham had favor in the sight of the Lord.

Oh, how they would all die if they knew! Oh, how they would all of them die!

ABOUT GENEVA

GRANNY was waiting at the door of the apartment. She looked small, lonely, and patient, and at the sight of her the children and their mother felt instantly guilty. Instead of driving straight home from the airport, they had stopped outside Nice for ice cream. They might have known how much those extra twenty minutes would mean to Granny. Colin, too young to know what he felt, or why, began instinctively to misbehave, dragging his feet, scratching the waxed parquet. Ursula bit her nails, taking refuge in a dream, while the children's mother, Granny's only daughter, felt compelled to cry in a high, cheery voice, "Well, Granny, here they are, safe and sound!"

"Darlings," said Granny, very low. "Home again." She stretched out her arms to Ursula, but then, seeing the taxi driver, who had carried the children's bags up the stairs, she drew back. After he had gone she repeated the gesture, turning this time to Colin, as if Ursula's cue had been irrevocably missed. Colin was wearing a beret. "Wherever did that come from?" Granny said. She pulled it off and stood still, stricken. "My darling little boy," she said, at last. "What have they done to you? They have cut your hair. Your lovely golden hair. I cannot believe it. I don't want to believe it."

"It was high time," the children's mother said. She stood in the outer corridor, waiting for Granny's welcome to subside. "It was high time someone cut Colin's hair. The curls made such a baby of him. We should have seen that. Two women can't really bring up a boy."

Granny didn't look at all as if she agreed. "Who cut your hair?" she said, holding Colin.

"Barber," he said, struggling away.

"Less said the better," said Colin's mother. She came in at last, drew off her gloves, looked around, as if she, and not the children, had been away.

"He's not my child, of course," said Granny, releasing Colin. "If he were, I can just imagine the letter I should write. Of all the impudence! When you send a child off for a visit you expect at the very least to have him returned exactly as he left. And you," she said, extending to Ursula a plump, liver-spotted hand, "what changes am I to expect in you?"

"Oh, Granny, for Heaven's sake, it was only two weeks." She permitted her grandmother to kiss her, then went straight to the sitting room and hurled herself into a chair. The room was hung with dark engravings of cathedrals. There were flowers, red carnations, on the rickety painted tables, poked into stiff arrangements by a maid. It was the standard seasonal Nice *meublé*. Granny spent every winter in rented flats more or less like this one, and her daughter, since her divorce, shared them with her.

Granny followed Ursula into the room and sat down, erect, on an uncomfortable chair, while her daughter, trailing behind, finally chose a footstool near the empty fireplace. She gave Granny a gentle, neutral look. Before starting out for the airport, earlier, she had repeated her warning: There were to be no direct questions, no remarks. It was all to appear as natural and normal as possible. What, indeed, could be more natural for the children than a visit with their father?

"What, indeed," said Granny in a voice rich with meaning.

It was only fair, said the children's mother. A belief in fair play was so embedded in her nature that she could say the words without coloring deeply. Besides, it was the first time he had asked.

"And won't be the last," Granny said. "But, of course, it is up to you."

Ursula lay rather than sat in her chair. Her face was narrow and freckled: She resembled her mother who, at thirty-four, had settled into a permanent, anxious-looking, semi-youthfulness. Colin, blond and fat, rolled on the floor. He pulled his mouth out at the corners, then pulled down his eyes to show the hideous red underlids. He looked at his grandmother and growled like a lion.

"Colin has come back sillier than ever," Granny said. He lay prone, noisily snuffing the carpet. The others ignored him.

"Did you go boating, Ursula?" said Granny, not counting this as a direct question. "When I visited Geneva, as a girl, we went boating on the lake." She went on about white water birds, a parasol, a boat heaped with colored cushions.

"Oh, Granny, no," said Ursula. "There weren't even any big boats, let alone little ones. It was cold."

"I hope the house, at least, was warm."

But evidently Ursula had failed to notice the temperature of her father's house. She slumped on her spine (a habit Granny had just nicely caused her to get over before the departure for Geneva) and then said, unexpectedly, "She's not a good manager."

Granny and her daughter exchanged a look, eyebrows up.

"Oh?" said Ursula's mother, pink. She forgot about the direct questions and said, "Why?"

"It's not terribly polite to speak that way of one's hostess," said Granny, unable to resist the reproof but threatening Ursula's revelation at the source. Her daughter looked at her, murderous.

"Well," said Ursula, slowly, "once the laundry didn't come back. It was her fault, he said. Our sheets had to be changed, he said. So she said Oh, all right. She took the sheets off Colin's bed and put them on my bed, and took the sheets off my bed and put them on Colin's. To make the change, she said."

"Dear God," said Granny.

"Colin's sheets were a mess. He had his supper in bed sometimes. They were just a mess."

"Not true," said Colin.

"Another time . . . ," said Ursula, and stopped, as if Granny had been right, after all, about criticizing one's hostess.

"Gave us chocolate," came from Colin, his face muffled in carpet.

"Not every day, I trust," Granny said.

"For the plane."

"It might very well have made you both airsick," said Granny.

"Well," said Ursula, "it didn't." Her eyes went often to the luggage in the hall. She squirmed upright, stood up, and sat down again. She rubbed her nose with the back of her hand.

"Ursula, do you want a handkerchief?" said Granny.

"No," said Ursula. "Only it so happens I'm writing a play. It's in the suitcase."

Granny and the children's mother looked at each other again. "I *am* pleased," Granny said, and her daughter nodded, agreeing, for, if impertinence and slumping on one's spine were unfortunate inherited tendencies, this was something else. It was only fair that Ursula's father should have bequeathed her *something* to compensate for the rest. "What is it about?" said Granny.

Ursula looked at her feet. After a short silence she said, "Russia. That's all I want to tell. It was her idea. She lived there once."

Quietly, controlled, the children's mother took a cigarette from the box on the table. Granny looked brave.

"Would you tell us the title, at least?" said Granny.

"No," said Ursula. But then, as if the desire to share the splendid thing she had created were too strong, she said, "I'll tell you one line, because they said it was the best thing they'd ever heard anywhere." She took a breath. Her audience was gratifyingly attentive, straining, nearly, with attention and control. "It goes like this," Ursula said. "'The Grand Duke enters and sees Tatiana all in gold.'"

"Well?" said Granny.

"Well, what?" said Ursula. "That's it. That's the line." She looked at her mother and grandmother and said, "*They* liked it. They want me to send it to them, and everything else, too. She even told me the name Tatiana."

"It's lovely, dear," said Ursula's mother. She put the cigarette back in the box. "It sounds like a lovely play. Just when did she live in Russia?"

"I don't know. Ages ago. She's pretty old."

"Perhaps one day we shall see the play after all," said Granny. "Particularly if it is to be sent all over the Continent."

"You mean they might act in it?" said Ursula. Thinking of this, she felt sorry for herself. Ever since she had started "The Grand Duke" she could not think of her own person without being sorry. For no reason at all, now, her eyes filled with tears of self-pity. Drooping, she looked out at the darkening street, to the leafless trees and the stone facade of a public library.

But the children's mother, as if Granny's remark had for her an entirely different meaning, not nearly so generous, said, "I shall give you the writing desk from my bedroom, Ursula. It has a key."

"Where will you keep your things?" said Granny, protesting. She could not very well say that the desk was her own, not to be moved. Like everything else—the dark cathedrals, the shaky painted tables— it had come with the flat.

"I don't need a key," said the children's mother, lacing her fingers tightly around her knees. "I'm not writing a play, or anything else I want kept secret. Not anymore."

"They used to take Colin for walks," said Ursula, yawning, only vaguely taking in the importance of the desk. "That was when I started to write this thing. Once they stayed out the whole afternoon. They never said where they'd been."

"I wonder," said her mother, thoughtful. She started to say something to Ursula, something not quite a question, but the child was too pre- occupied with herself. Everything about the trip, in the end, would crystallize around Tatiana and the Grand Duke. Already, Ursula was Tatiana. The children's mother looked at Ursula's long bare legs, her heavy shoes, her pleated skirt, and she thought, I must do something about her clothes, something to make her pretty.

"Colin, dear," said Granny in her special inner-meaning voice, "do you remember your walks?"

"No."

"I wonder why they wanted to take him alone," said Colin's mother. "It seems odd, all the same."

"Under seven," said Granny, cryptic. "Couldn't influence girl. Too old. Boy different. Give me first seven years, you can have rest."

"But it wasn't seven years. He hasn't been alive that long. It was only two weeks."

"Two very impressionable weeks," Granny said.

"I understand everything you're saying," Ursula said, "even when you talk that way. They spoke French when they didn't want us to hear, but we understood that, too."

"I fed the swans," Colin suddenly shouted.

There, he had told about Geneva. He sat up and kicked his heels on the carpet as if the noise would drown out the consequence of what he had revealed. As he said it, the image became static; a gray sky, a gray lake, and a swan wonderfully turning upside down with the black rubber feet showing above the water. His father was not in the picture at all; neither was *she*. But Geneva was fixed for the rest of his life: gray, lake, swan.

Having delivered his secret he had nothing more to tell. He began to invent. "I was sick on the plane," he said, but Ursula at once said that this was a lie, and he lay down again, humiliated. At last, feeling sleepy, he began to cry.

"He never once cried in Geneva," Ursula said. But by the one simple act of creating Tatiana and the Grand Duke, she had removed herself from the ranks of reliable witnesses.

"How would you know?" said Granny bitterly. "You weren't always with him. If you had paid more attention, if you had taken care of your little brother, he wouldn't have come back to us with his hair cut."

"Never mind," said the children's mother. Rising, she helped Colin to his feet and led him away to bed.

She stood behind him as he cleaned his teeth. He looked male and self-assured with his newly cropped head, and she thought of her husband, and how odd it was that only a few hours before Colin had been with him. She touched the tender back of his neck. "Don't," he said. Frowning, concentrating, he hung up his toothbrush. "I told about Geneva."

"Yes, you did." He had fed swans. She saw sunshine, a blue lake, and the boats Granny had described, heaped with colored cushions. She saw her husband and someone else (probably in white, she thought, ridiculously bouffant, the origin of Tatiana) and Colin with his curls shorn, revealing ears surprisingly large. There was nothing to be had from Ursula—not, at least, until the Grand Duke had died down. But Colin seemed to carry the story of the visit with him, and she felt the faintest stirrings of envy, the resentfulness of the spectator, the loved one left behind.

"Were you really sick on the plane?" she said.

"Yes," said Colin.

"Were they lovely, the swans?"

But the question bore no relation to anything he had seen. He said nothing. He played with toothpaste, dawdling.

"Isn't that child in bed yet?" called Granny. "Does he want his supper?"

"No," said Colin.

"No," said his mother. "He was sick on the plane."

"I thought so," Granny said. "That, at least, is a fact."

They heard the voice of Ursula, protesting.

But how can they be trusted, the children's mother thought. Which of them can one believe? "Perhaps," she said to Colin, "one day, you can tell me more about Geneva?"

"Yes," he said, perplexed.

But, really, she doubted it; nothing had come back from the trip but her own feelings of longing and envy, the longing and envy she felt at night, seeing, at a crossroad or over a bridge, the lighted windows of a train sweep by. Her children had nothing to tell her. Perhaps, as she had said, one day Colin would say something, produce the image of Geneva, tell her about the lake, the boats, the swans, and why her husband had left her. Perhaps he could tell her, but, really, she doubted it. And, already, so did he.

THE ACCIDENT

I WAS TIRED and did not always understand what they were asking me. I borrowed a pencil and wrote:

PETER HIGGINS

CALGARY 1935—ITALY 1956

But there was room for more on the stone, and the English clergyman in this Italian town who was doing all he could for me said, "Is there nothing else, child?" Hadn't Pete been my husband, somebody's son? That was what he was asking. It seemed enough. Pete had renounced us, left us behind. His life-span might matter, if anyone cared, but I must have sensed even then that no one would ever ask me what he had been like. His father once asked me to write down what I remembered. He wanted to compose a memorial booklet and distribute it at Christmas, but then his wife died, too, and he became prudent about recollections. Even if I had wanted to, I couldn't have told much—just one or two things about the way Pete died. His mother had some information about him, and I had some, but never enough to describe a life. She had the complete knowledge that puts parents at a loss, finally: she knew all about him except his opinion of her and how he was with me. They were never equals. She was a grown person with part of a life lived and the habit of secrets before he was conscious of her. She said, later, that she and Pete had been friends. How can you be someone's friend if you have had twenty years' authority over him and he has never had one second's authority over you?

He didn't look like his mother. He looked like me. In Italy, on our wedding trip, we were often taken for brother and sister. Our height,

278

our glasses, our soft myopic stares, our assurance, our sloppy comfortable clothes made us seem to the Italians related and somehow unplaceable. Only a North American could have guessed what our families were, what our education amounted to, and where we had got the money to spend on traveling. Most of the time we were just pie-faces, like the tourists in ads—though we were not as clean as those couples, and not quite as grown-up. We didn't seem to be married: the honeymoon in hotels, in strange beds, the meals we shared in cheap, bright little restaurants, prolonged the clandestine quality of love before. It was still a game, but now we had infinite time. I became bold, and I dismissed the universe: "It was a rotten little experiment," I said, "and we were given up long ago." I had been brought up by a forcible, pessimistic, widowed mother, and to be able to say aloud "we were given up" shows how far I had come. Pete's assurance was natural, but mine was fragile, and recent, and had grown out of love. Traveling from another direction, he was much more interested in his parents than in God. There was a glorious treason in all our conversations now. Pete wondered about his parents, but I felt safer belittling Creation. My mother had let me know about the strength of the righteous; I still thought the skies would fall if I said too much.

What struck me about these secret exchanges was how we judged our parents from a distance now, as if they were people we had known on a visit. The idea that he and I could be natural siblings crossed my mind. What if I, or Pete, or both, had been adopted? We had been raised in different parts of Canada, but we were only children, and neither of us resembled our supposed parents. Watching him, trapping him almost in mannerisms I could claim, I saw my habit of sprawling, of spreading maps and newspapers on the ground. He had a vast appetite for bread and pastries and sweet desserts. He was easily drunk and easily sick. Yes, we were alike. We talked in hotel rooms, while we drank the drink of the place, the *grappa* or wine or whatever we were given, prone across the bed, the bottle and glasses and the ashtray on the floor. We agreed to live openly, without secrets, though neither of us knew what a secret was. I admired him as I could never have admired myself. I remembered how my mother, the keeper of the castle until now, had said that one day—one treeless, sunless day—real life would overtake me, and then I would realize how spoiled and silly I had always been.

The longest time he and I spent together in one place was three days, in a village up behind the Ligurian coast. I thought that the only success of my life, my sole achievement, would be this marriage. In a dream he came to me with the plans for a house. I saw the white lines on the blue paper, and he showed me the sunny Italian-style loggia that would be built. "It is not quite what we want," he said, "but better than anything we have now." "But we can't afford it, we haven't got the capital," I cried, and I panicked, and woke: woke safe, in a room of which the details were dawn, window, sky, first birds of morning, and Pete still sleeping, still in the dark.

The last Italian town of our journey was nothing—just a black beach with sand like soot, and houses shut and dormant because it was the middle of the afternoon. We had come here from our village only to change trains. We were on our way to Nice, then Paris, then home. We left our luggage at the station, with a porter looking after it, and we drifted through empty, baking streets, using up the rest of a roll of film. By now we must have had hundreds of pictures of each other in market squares, next to oleanders, cut in two by broomstick shade, or backed up, squinting, against scaly noonday shutters. Pete now chose to photograph a hotel with a cat on the step, a policeman, and a souvenir stand, as if he had never seen such things in Canada—as if they were monuments. I never once heard him say anything was ugly or dull; for if it was, what were we doing with it? We were often stared at, for we were out of our own background and did not fit into the new. That day, I was eyed more than he was. I was watched by men talking in dark doorways, leaning against the façades of inhospitable shops. I was traveling in shorts and a shirt and rope-soled shoes. I know now that this costume was resented, but I don't know why. There was nothing indecent about my clothes. They were very like Pete's.

He may not have noticed the men. He was always on the lookout for something to photograph, or something to do, and sometimes he missed people's faces. On the steep street that led back to the railway station, he took a careful picture of a bakery, and he bought crescent-shaped bread with a soft, pale crust, and ate it there, on the street. He wasn't hungry; it was a question of using time. Now the closed shutters broke out in the afternoon, and girls appeared—girls with thick hair, smelling of jasmine and honeysuckle. They strolled hand in hand, in light stockings and clean white shoes. Their dresses—blue, lemon, the palest peach—bloomed over rustling petticoats. At home I'd have called them cheap, and made a face at their cheap perfume, but here, in their own place, they were enravishing, and I thought Pete would look at them and at me and compare; but all he remarked was "How do they stand those clothes on a day like this?" So real life, the gray noon with no limits, had not yet begun. I distrusted real life, for I knew nothing about it. It was the middle-aged world without feeling, where no one was loved.

Bored with his bread, he tossed it away and laid his hands on a white Lambretta propped against the curb. He pulled it upright, examining it. He committed two crimes in a second: wasted bread and touched an adored mechanical object belonging to someone else. I knew these were crimes later, when it was no use knowing, no good to either of us. The steering of the Lambretta was locked. He saw a bicycle then, belonging, he thought, to an old man who was sitting in a kitchen chair out on the pavement. "This all right with you?" Pete pointed to the bike, then himself, then down the hill. With a swoop of his hand he tried to show he would come straight back. His pantomime also meant that there was still time before we had to be on the train, that up at the station there was nothing to do, that eating bread, taking pictures of shops, riding a bike downhill and walking it back were all doing, using up your life; yes, it was a matter of living.

The idling old man Pete had spoken to bared his gums. Pete must have taken this for a smile. Later, the old man, who was not the owner of the bike or of anything except the fat sick dog at his feet, said he had cried "Thief!" but I never heard him. Pete tossed me his camera and I saw him glide, then rush away, past the girls who smelled of jasmine, past the bakery, down to the corner, where a policeman in white, under a parasol, spread out one arm and flexed the other and blew hard on a whistle. Pete was standing, as if he were trying to coast to a stop. I saw things meaningless now—for instance that the sun was sifted through leaves. There were trees we hadn't noticed. Under the leaves he seemed under water. A black car, a submarine with Belgian plates, parked at an angle, stirred to life. I saw sunlight deflected from six points on the paint. My view became discomposed, as if the sea were suddenly black and opaque and had splashed up over the policeman and the road, and I screamed, "He's going to open the door!" Everyone said later that I was mistaken, for why would the Belgian have started the motor, pulled out, and *then* flung open the door? He had stopped near a change office; perhaps he had forgotten his sunglasses, or a receipt. He started, stopped abruptly, hurled back the door. I saw that, and then I saw him driving away. No one had taken his number.

Strangers made Pete kneel and then stand, and they dusted the bicycle. They forced him to walk—where? Nobody wanted him. Into a pharmacy, finally. In a parrot's voice he said to the policeman, "Don't touch my elbow." The pharmacist said, "He can't stay here," for Pete was vomiting, but weakly—a weak coughing, like an infant's. I was in a crowd of about twenty people, a spectator with two cameras round my neck. In kind somebody's living room, Pete was placed on a couch with a cushion under his head and another under his dangling arm. The toothless old man turned up now, panting, with his waddling dog, and cried that we had a common thief there before us, and everyone listened and marveled until the old man spat on the carpet and was turned out.

When I timidly touched Pete, trying to wipe his face with a crumpled Kleenex (all I had), he thought I was one of the strangers. His mouth was a purple color, as if he had been in icy water. His eyes looked at me, but he was not looking out.

"Ambulance," said a doctor who had been fetched by the policeman. He spoke loudly and slowly, dealing with idiots.

"Yes," I heard, in English. "We must have an ambulance."

Everyone now inspected me. I was, plainly, responsible for something. For walking around the streets in shorts? Wasting bread? Conscious of my sweaty hair, my bare legs, my lack of Italian—my nakedness—I began explaining the true error of the day: "The train has gone, and all our things are on it. Our luggage. We've been staying up in that village—oh, what's the name of it, now? Where they make the white wine. I can't remember, no, I can't remember where we've been. I could find it, I could take you there; I've just forgotten what it's called. We were down here waiting for the train. To Nice. We had lots of time. The porter took our things and said he'd put them on the train for us. He said the train would wait here, at the border, that it waited a long time. He was supposed to meet us at the place where you show your ticket. I guess for an extra tip. The train must have gone now. My purse is in the duffelbag up at the the . . . I'll look in my husband's wallet. Of course that is my husband! Our passports must be on the train, too. Our traveler's checks are in our luggage, his and mine. We were just walking round taking pictures instead of sitting up there in the station. Anyway, there was no place to sit—only the bar, and it was smelly and dark."

No one believed a word of this, of course. Would you give your clothes, your passport, your traveler's checks to a porter? A man you had never seen in your life before? A bandit disguised as a porter, with a stolen cap on his head?

"You could not have taken that train without showing your passport," a careful foreign voice objected.

"What are you two, anyway?" said the man from the change office. His was a tough, old-fashioned movie-American accent. He was puffy-eyed and small, but he seemed superior to us, for he wore an impeccable shirt. Pete, on the sofa, looked as if he had been poisoned, or stepped on. "What are you?" the man from the change office said again. "Students? Americans? No? What, then? Swedes?"

I saw what the doctor had been trying to screen from me: a statue's marble eye.

The tourist who spoke the careful foreign English said, "Be careful of the pillows."

"What? What?" screamed the put-upon person who owned them.

"Blood is coming out of his ears," said the tourist, halting between words. "That is a bad sign." He seemed to search his memory for a better English word. "An *unfortunate* sign," he said, and put his hand over his mouth.

Pete's father and mother flew from Calgary when they had my cable.

They made flawless arrangements by telephone, and knew exactly what to bring. They had a sunny room looking onto rusty palms and a strip of beach about a mile from where the accident had been. I sat against one of the windows and told them what I thought I remembered. I looked at the white walls, the white satin bedspreads, at Mrs. Higgins' spotless dressing case, and finally down at my hands.

His parents had not understood, until now, that ten days had gone by since Pete's death.

"What have you been doing, dear, all alone?" said Mrs. Higgins, gently.

"Just waiting, after I cabled you." They seemed to be expecting more. "I've been to the movies," I said.

From this room we could hear the shrieks of children playing on the sand.

"Are they orphans?" asked Mrs. Higgins, for they were little girls, dressed alike, with soft pink sun hats covering their heads.

"It seems to be a kind of summer camp," I said. "I was wondering about them, too."

"It would make an attractive picture," said Pete's mother, after a pause. "The blue sea, and the nuns, and all those bright hats. It would look nice in a dining room."

They were too sick to reproach me. My excuse for not having told them sooner was that I hadn't been thinking, and they didn't ask me for it. I could only repeat what seemed important now. "I don't want to go back home just yet" was an example. I was already in the future, which must have hurt them. "I have a girl friend in the Embassy in Paris. I can stay with her." I scarcely moved my lips. They had to strain to hear. I held still, looking down at my fingers. I was very brown, sun streaks in my hair, more graceful than at my wedding, where I knew they had found me maladroit—a great lump of a Camp Fire Girl. That was how I had seen myself in my father-in-law's eyes. Extremes of shock had brought me near some ideal they had of prettiness. I appeared now much more the kind of girl they'd have wanted as Pete's wife.

So they had come for nothing. They were not to see him, or bury him, or fetch home his bride. All I had to show them was a still unlabeled grave.

When I dared look at them, I saw their way of being was not Pete's. Neither had his soft selective stare. Mr. Higgins' eyes were a fanatic blue. He was thin and sunburned and unused to nonsense. Summer and winter he traveled with his wife in climates that were bad for her skin. She had the fair, papery coloring that requires constant vigilance. All this I knew because of Pete.

They saw his grave at the best time of day, in the late afternoon, with the light at a slant. The cemetery was in a valley between two plaster towns. A flash of the sea was visible, a corner of ultramarine. They saw a stone wall covered with roses, pink and white and near-white, open, without secrets. The hiss of traffic on the road came to us, softer than rain; then true rain came down, and we ran to our waiting taxi through a summer storm. Later they saw the station where Pete had left our luggage but never come back. Like Pete—as Pete had intended to—they were traveling to Nice. Under a glass shelter before the station I paused and said, "That was where it happed, down there." I pointed with my white glove. I was not as elegant as Mrs. Higgins, but I was not a source of embarrassment. I wore gloves, stockings, shoes.

The steep street under rain was black as oil. Everything was reflected upside down. The neon signs of the change office and the pharmacy swam deeply in the pavement.

"I'd like to thank the people who were so kind," said Mrs. Higgins. "Is there time? Shirley, I suppose you got their names?"

"Nobody was kind," I said.

"Shirley! We've met the doctor, and the minister, but you said there was a policeman, and a Dutch gentleman, and a lady—you were in this lady's living room."

"They were all there, but no one was kind."

"The bike's paid for?" asked Mr. Higgins suddenly.

"Yes, I paid. And I paid for having the sofa cushions cleaned."

What sofa cushions? What was I talking about? They seemed petrified, under the glass shelter, out of the rain. They could not take their eyes away from the place I had said was *there*. They never blamed me, never by a word or a hidden meaning. I had explained, more than once, how the porter that day had not put our bags on the train after all but had stood waiting at the customs barrier, wondering what had become of us. I told them how I had found everything intact—passports and checks and maps and sweaters and shoes...They could not grasp the importance of it. They knew that Pete had chosen me, and gone away with me, and they never saw him again. An unreliable guide had taken them to a foreign graveyard and told them, without evidence, that now he was there.

"I still don't see how anyone could have thought Pete was stealing," said his mother. "What would Pete have wanted with someone's old bike?"

They were flying home from Nice. They loathed Italy now, and they had a special aversion to the sunny room where I had described Pete's death. We three sat in the restaurant at the airport, and they spoke quietly, considerately, because the people at the table next to ours were listening to a football match on a portable radio.

I closed my hand into a fist and let it rest on the table. I imagined myself at home, saying to my mother, "All right, real life has begun. What's your next prophecy?"

I was not flying with them. I was seeing them off. Mrs. Higgins sat poised and prepared in her linen coat, with her large handbag, and her cosmetics and airsickness tablets in her dressing case, and her diamond maple leaf so she wouldn't be mistaken for an American, and her passport ready to be shown to anyone. Pale gloves lay folded over the clasp of the dressing case. "You'll want to go to your own people, I know," she said. "But you have a home with us. You mustn't forget it." She paused. I said nothing, and so she continued, "What are you going to do, dear? I mean, after you have visited your friend. You mustn't be lonely."

I muttered whatever seemed sensible. "I'll have to get a job. I've never had one and I don't know anything much. I can't even type—not properly." Again they gave me this queer impression of expecting something more. What did they want? "Pete said it was no good learning anything if you couldn't type. He said it was the only useful thing he could do."

In the eyes of his parents was the same wound. I had told them something about him they hadn't known.

"Well, I understand," said his mother, presently. "At least, I think I do."

They imagine I want to be near the grave, I supposed. They think that's why I'm staying on the same side of the world. Pete and I had been waiting for a train; now I had taken it without him. I was waiting again. Even if I were to visit the cemetery every day, he would never speak. His last words had not been for me but to a policeman. He would have said something to me, surely, if everyone hadn't been in such a hurry to get him out of the way. His mind was quenched, and his body out of sight. "You don't love with your soul," I had cried to the old clergyman at the funeral—an offensive remark, judging from the look on his face as he turned it aside. Now I was careful. The destination of a soul was of no interest. The death of a voice—now, that was real. The Dutchman suddenly covering his mouth was horror, and a broken elbow was true pain. But I was careful; I kept this to myself.

"You're our daughter now," Pete's father said. "I don't think I want you to have to worry about a job. Not yet." Mr. Higgins happened to know my family's exact status. My father had not left us well off, and my mother had given everything she owned to a sect that did not believe in blood transfusions. She expected the end of the world, and would not eat an egg unless she had first met the hen. That was Mr. Higgins' view. "Shirley must work if that's what she wants to do," Mrs. Higgins said softly.

"I do want to!" I imagined myself, that day, in a river of people pouring into subways.

"I'm fixing something up for you, just the same," said Mr. Higgins hurriedly, as if he would not be interrupted by women.

Mrs. Higgins allowed her pale forehead to wrinkle, under her beige veil. Was it not better to struggle and to work, she asked. Wasn't that real life? Would it not keep Shirley busy, take her mind off her loss, her disappointment, her tragedy, if you like (though "tragedy" was not an acceptable way of looking at fate), if she had to think about her daily bread?

"The allowance I'm going to make her won't stop her from working," he said. "I was going to set something up for the kids anyway."

She seemed to approve; she had questioned him only out of some prudent system of ethics.

He said to me, "I always have to remember I could go any minute, just like that. I've got a heart." He tapped it—tapped his light suit. "Meantime you better start with this." He gave me the envelope that had been close to his heart until now. He seemed diffident, made ashamed by money, and by death, but it was he and not his wife who had asked if there was a hope that Pete had left a child. No, I had told him. I had wondered, too, but now I was sure. "Then Shirley is all we've got left," he had said to his wife, and I thought they seemed bankrupt, having nothing but me.

"If that's a check on a bank at home, it might take too long to clear," said his wife. "After all Shirley's been through, she needs a fair-sized sum right away."

"She's had that, Betty," said Mr. Higgins, smiling.

I had lived this: three round a table, the smiling parents. Pete had said, "They smile, they go on talking. You wonder what goes on."

"How you manage everything you do without a secretary with you all the time I just don't know," said his wife, all at once admiring him.

"You've been saying that for twenty-two years," he said.

"Twenty-three, now."

With this the conversation came to an end and they sat staring, puzzled, not overcome by life but suddenly lost to it, out of touch. The photograph Pete carried of his mother, that was in his wallet when he died, had been taken before her marriage, with a felt hat all to one side, and an organdie collar, and Ginger Rogers hair. It was easier to imagine Mr. Higgins young—a young Gary Cooper. My father-in-law's blue gaze rested on me now. Never in a million years would he have picked me as a daughter-in-law. I knew that; I understood. Pete was part of him, and Pete, with all the girls he had to choose from, had chosen me. When Mr. Higgins met my mother at the wedding, he thanked God, and was overheard being thankful, that the wedding was not in Calgary. Remembering my mother that day, with her glasses on her nose and a strange borrowed hat on her head, and recalling Mr. Higgins' face, I thought of words that would keep me from laughing. I found, at random, "threesome," "smother," "gambling," "habeas corpus," "sibling."...

"How is your mother, Shirley?" said Mrs. Higgins.

"I had a letter... She's working with a pendulum now."

"A pendulum?"

"Yes. A weight on a string, sort of. It makes a diagnosis—whether you've got something wrong with your stomach, if it's an ulcer, or what. She can use it to tell when you're pregnant and if the baby will be a girl or a boy. It depends whether it swings north-south or east-west."

"Can the pendulum tell who the father is?" said Mr. Higgins.

"They are useful for people who are afraid of doctors," said Mrs. Higgins, and she fingered her neat gloves, and smiled to herself. "Someone who won't hear the truth from a doctor will listen to any story from a woman with a pendulum or a piece of crystal."

"Or a stone that changes color," I said. "My mother had one of those. When our spaniel had mastoids it turned violet."

She glanced at me then, and caught in her breath, but her husband, by a certain amount of angry fidgeting, made us change the subject. That was the one moment she and I were close to each other—something to do with quirky female humor.

Mr. Higgins did not die of a heart attack, as he had confidently expected, but a few months after this Mrs. Higgins said to her maid in the kitchen, "I've got a terrible pain in my head. I'd better lie down." Pete's father wrote, "She knew what the matter was, but she never said. Typical." I inherited a legacy and some jewelry from her, and wondered why. I had been careless about writing. I could not write the kind of letters she seemed to want. How could I write to someone I hardly knew about someone else who did not exist? Mr. Higgins married the widow of one of his closest friends—a woman six years older than he. They traveled to Europe for their wedding trip. I had a temporary job as an interpreter in a department store. When my father-in-law saw me in a neat suit, with his name, HIGGINS, fastened to my jacket, he seemed to approve. He was the only person then who did not say that I was wasting my life and my youth and ought to go home. The new Mrs.

Higgins asked to be taken to an English-speaking hairdresser, and there, under the roaring dryer, she yelled that Mr. Higgins may not have been Pete's father. Perhaps he had been, perhaps he hadn't, but one thing he was, and that was a saint. She came out from under the helmet and said in a normal voice, "Martin doesn't know I dye my hair." I wondered if he had always wanted this short, fox-colored woman. The new marriage might for years have been in the maquis of his mind, and of Mrs. Higgins' life. She may have known it as she sat in the airport that day, smiling to herself, touching her unstained gloves. Mr. Higgins had drawn up a new way of life, like a clean will with everyone he loved cut out. I was trying to draw up a will, too, but I was patient, waiting, waiting for someone to tell me what to write. He spoke of Pete conventionally, in a sentimental way that forbade any feeling. Talking that way was easier for both of us. We were both responsible for something—for surviving, perhaps. Once he turned to me and said defiantly, "Well, she and Pete are together now, aren't they? And didn't they leave us here?"

JEUX D'ÉTÉ

LATE IN the afternoon, when their work was done, the young men of the town sailed their boats along the coast, out past the big hotels where foreigners stayed. They drifted in a wide, restless half circle around the private beaches belonging to the hotels. They liked to look at the foreign people and at the girls. The foreigners carried portable radios and smoked expensive cigarettes and their voices—French, German, and English—floated over the calm Adriatic bays and rocky shore. The hotels, up on a low cliff behind the beaches, were square and imposing, built before the war and the People's Revolution. Now the hotels were said to belong to the people, and it was perhaps because of this ownership that the people hung about at a distance, staring in. There were Yugoslavs as well as strangers in the hotels—well-to-do civil engineers, and meritorious members of the police—but the young men were not interested in any of them. One would have said, indeed, that they failed to see them.

The chief magnet those last, hot days of July was a trio of girls on the beach of the Hotel Marina. All day, every day, the girls lay, stretched like offerings, on the warm rocks, under a sun that bleached their hair and turned their faces brown. They had neat hair and straight teeth, and they wore frilly skirted bathing suits that covered the tops of their rather fat legs.

"American women are said to have the finest legs in the world," one of the dining-room waiters remarked, as if he had been deceived. He hung over the railing of the dining terrace, watching the three motionless girls. From the pocket of his white jacket he fished out two butts he had saved from the breakfast ashtrays. He offered one to his companion, another waiter, who lit both, flipping the match down among the bathers.

"They aren't women," his companion said. "They are little girls."

"They think they are women."

Nancy and Patty and Linda were conscious of being observed. Even without opening their eyes, they could tell when men were looking. They always smiled at the waiters—the right sort of smile, friendly but distant—and they swam cautiously, tentatively, around the anchored boats and the blond young men from town. Nancy and Patty were sisters; Linda was a friend. The three were being clucked through Europe by a Miss Baxter, a professional chaperone, who, though careful, had decided that no harm could come to them on the beach, and had gone off to town today on the pretext of visiting churches. The girls had been looking at things in Italy and were shortly to be looking at things in Greece. They had looked at everything in Paris, in Nice, in Florence, in Rome and in Venice, all in less than four weeks. It had been cold in Paris and hot in Rome and smelly in Venice, and this beach, halfway down the Dalmatian coast, was the best part of the trip. They were good-tempered girls. They made no demands on the strange things they saw, or the strange people they met, and they had left a bland, favorable impression with the travel agents and consular officials with whom they had come in contact. To the undiscerning, they were alike as triplets. Miss Baxter could tell them apart, though. So could the boys in the boats.

Nancy and Patty lay with their eyes shut, silent, as if speech might interfere with the business of getting brown. The advantages of having spent the summer abroad were easily outweighed by the fear that in the autumn they would be paler than their friends. Secretly, they wished they had stayed home and gone up to the lake; but it was a wish neither of them expressed, not even to each other. Someone had told them that there were no beaches in Greece—none, at least, where they would be staying. They were determined to grasp all the benefits possible from these few days of sun. Only Linda seemed unable to settle down. She looked at the sea and then up at the waiters. Suddenly she got up, with no explanation, and climbed the concrete steps that led up to the hotel. Her departure had the effect of a signal. The sisters behaved as if an inhibiting force had been removed. Patty rolled over, sighing. Nancy knelt, blinking. She looked at the shallow side of the rocks, and at the part where it was safe to dive.

"Going in?" said Patty.

Nancy shook herself like a little dog, cold at the thought of the water she would strike. She climbed to the top of the piled-up rocks, gathered courage and suddenly dived.

The boat nearest the beach was painted blue. One of the boys on board smoked a cigarette, the other sat with his feet over the side, moving them in the colorless water. He watched the girl who was swimming out to them. Both boys were fair, and nearly black with sun. Nancy caught a rope and, with the other hand, pushed back her dripping hair.

"I like your boat," she said.

"Come on, then," said the boy with the cigarette. He bent over and held out his hand.

"Uh-uh." She shook her head vigorously. Her eyelashes were stuck together in points with water. The boy with the cigarette lay prone. He edged closer to the side. He looked at her and then, suddenly giving up, lowered his head on his crossed arms.

"Come with us," said his friend, slowly, with great concentration. He had to fish each word from a sea teeming with English expressions.

"Oh, for goodness' sake," said the girl. "Can't a person even talk about your boat without starting something?"

The boy smoking had not understood. He said to his friend, "Ask her to come for a sail. Tell her we'll go around the island."

His friend shook his head impatiently, and the girl let go of the rope. She pushed herself out with a long backstroke and then turned over and swam to shore. They watched her pick her way out on the shallow side of the pier, over rocks perilous with sea urchins.

The boy smoking threw his cigarette into the calm water. He said, "Why does she always come out, then? They're crazy, I think."

"The other girl would come," said his friend. He looked at the dry rocks above the shore, where Linda, back from the hotel, was settling down on a towel. "That's the one," he said, with an assurance that would not have surprised the sisters. Men had followed the girls in Italy, but only Linda's door had been nearly broken down. She was not prettier, or fairer, or better dressed. But she was the one Miss Baxter watched, and, with a resigned concession to the workings of nature, so did Nancy and Patty.

It took Linda, as always, about three minutes to arrange herself on a beach towel. "I've had a letter," she said, at last. "Remember that reporter we met in Florence, the one that was taking pictures for that Italian magazine?"

The sisters exchanged a look. The reporter, like every other man encountered on the trip, had shown an undisguised preference for Linda. "He wants to know if we're coming back through Italy," she went on. "They're trying out a new kind of submarine in Genoa or someplace. He wants me to go down in it, in the submarine. He says he'll take my picture. As he says, how can you make a submarine interesting all by itself? He says the story needs me. He says they'll put me on the cover."

"On what cover?" said Nancy. She longed to ask how he had known where to write, but felt it an unnecessary diversion.

"Oh, of some magazine."

The sisters were silent. They were by no means plain, and it seemed unfair that Linda should have everything. One of us would have had a chance if Linda hadn't been along, Nancy thought.

"I've cabled home," Linda said. "That's why I went up to the hotel just now. I thought I'd better do it and get it over with. I've asked my parents if it's all right. Baxie wasn't around, so I sent the cable myself."

"Why a cable?" said Patty. "Couldn't you have just written?"

"He wants an answer right away. Anyway, it's better to have your parents' consent; it's only polite. You sort of have to have it," said Linda, calmly, as if she were frequently involved in these emergencies. "I cabled, 'Offered chance to go down in new-type submarine for magazine cover please cable immediate permission.' Soon as I get the answer, I'll tell him yes."

"Well, I suppose your parents would hardly refuse," said Patty. "I mean, it's a once-in-a-lifetime chance."

"They might," said Linda, frowning. "They don't know it's a responsible sort of submarine, with officers and everything. They don't know there're going to be reporters and people around, and they don't know it isn't going to cost them any more money. I couldn't get all that in."

"You could have got in 'expenses paid,'" said Nancy. "Anyway, they probably wouldn't mind if they did have to pay something, for a thing like that."

"I wouldn't ask them for more money," said Linda, virtuously.

At this point, a display of virtue was insupportable.

"*Naturally* you wouldn't ask for any more," said Nancy. "*Naturally*. It happens to be free." She added, "You didn't even tell them which navy it was."

"I forgot."

After a silence, Patty said, "I'll bet your parents won't want you to be on the cover. Ours certainly wouldn't."

"No," said Nancy, "and what's more I wouldn't like it. Not for myself."

"Neither would I," her sister said.

"Well, it wouldn't be either of you, anyway," said Linda, "so it doesn't matter." She lay flat on her back, looking dreamily—but with slightly narrowed eyes, as if there were calculation in the dream—up to the fringe of pine that hung over the edge of the cliff. There was so much truth in her remark that the others were not offended. Linda's success was inevitable, she would be famous first, married first, everything first. Unable to compete, they tacitly decided to share the excitement of her career.

"Wait till Baxie hears it," Patty said. "She'll be thrilled. It's a lot more exciting than her old churches."

"Poor Baxie," Linda said, closing her eyes, giving herself up to the deliciousness of sun and of being pretty and desired. "Churches are Baxie's kind of fun, I guess."

As it happened, Miss Baxter was spending the afternoon in a café. The café was on a square facing what seemed to be a very old church. Conscientiously, she noted every feature of the church and of the square, so that she could tell the girls about it later on. The girls were not allowed to sit in cafés. They had promised their parents before sailing.

Cozy with guilt, Miss Baxter wondered if she was being fair in enjoy-ing something her charges were not permitted. Returning to her exer-cise in observation, she recorded swallows, two sailors in uniform, a Gothic fountain, the absence of motorcars, and the fact that every window shutter on the square was painted the same shade of green. She was in a mood to find everything lovely; the glass she drank from seemed enchanting, and a poster announcing a summer festival with the words SUMMER GAMES—JEUX D'ÉTÉ struck her as being something of great significance and charm.

Her companion, a shabby gentleman from a tourist office, ordered slivovitz for them both. He was fat and amiable and anxious to improve his English. He carried a dictionary and looked everything up before he spoke. Miss Baxter gravely assisted him. To her charges, she appeared plain and effaced. However, the man from the tourist office was not the first to have asked for help with the English language. Miss Baxter's blue eyes held a kind of watery sympathy. She wore soft pastel suits with felt flowers pinned to the lapel, and blouses with pleated jabots. Part of the year, she taught history in a girls' boarding school. Summers, she hired herself out as a governess, chaperone, companion—anything that promised a season of travel or country living. This summer was particularly wonderful, for the girls' parents had let her choose the travel plan and given them all a large allowance. She was almost excru-ciatingly grateful. Three times a week she sent the parents a dull, detailed account of the places they had visited and the things they had seen. "We particularly enjoyed seeing the lovely Gold Staircase of Venice," she had written. "Linda was intrigued by the amusing round hats worn by the Italian gentlemen of the Renaissance. In the morning we hired a gondola. The girls were amused at the bargaining required in hiring this conveyance. Nancy remarked . . ." Three times a week she put this sort of thing in the post, closing each letter with her fulsome thanks. She wanted to thank the parents, but she also wanted to let them know that they were getting their money's worth. When she was with the girls, she talked incessantly. She felt that she was not doing her duty or earning her keep if she kept a single impression to herself. Sometimes, talking on and on, she obliterated the scene she was so anxious they should take away with them. She had been deeply moved in Venice by a small thing, the reflection of water from the canal outside shining on the ceiling of the room. She had pointed it out to the girls, one of whom had said indulgently, "Honestly, Baxie!" Yet she remembered it now, and she remembered Florence because for breakfast she had been given a fresh fig that was cold as water and tasted of cream. She also remembered how the bootboy in Florence had pointed to her bed, then her, then himself, then clasped his hands and put his head against them.

"Did you care for Italy?" said her companion politely. He waved a fly away from his drink.

Miss Baxter considered her answer with care. The Croats and the Italians, she knew, were traditional enemies. "It is difficult to travel in a Latin country with a party of girls," she said. Her drink smelled of warm fruit. She drank the last of it and felt patches of heat covering her cheeks.

He smiled sympathetically and said, "It will be different here."

"I know." Tears started to her eyes. How kind he was, how kind they all were, how kind the Florentine bootboy had been, how lovely the swallows were, swooping across the square!

"We are not like the Italians," he said. The waiter took away their small glasses and set fresh drinks before them.

"Thank goodness for that," Miss Baxter murmured, not really listening.

"Our boys are good boys," the man said. What he next had to say he assembled from his dictionary. Miss Baxter sipped her new drink, smiling at everyone. He had found the words: "I should say that, with our people, what matters is only the pure animal pleasure of making love." Uttered in bald English, it sounded quite wrong. Hastily, he ruffled his dictionary again.

"I'm sure," said Miss Baxter, still dreamy. The word "pure" had taken hold and she derived a sleepy pleasure from the idea of her girls purely in love. She had been so often in love herself, and fell so easily into romantic difficulties! The man from the tourist bureau seemed in no hurry to get back to work. Miss Baxter was perfectly content to sit on beside him. Conversation became at once halting and discursive: she remembered that they represented countries politically apart. Although not in the least politically minded, it seemed to her natural that the subject might arise, and destroy this new relationship—warm, sleepy, pleasantly sensuous. It was possible that he, too, felt this constraint. Their talk became slower. An awareness of what they were really about, and of what this was bound to lead to, surrounded them like—Miss Baxter thought—a warm little cloud. All the same, it made it difficult to get on with the normal interchange of polite speech, particularly between strangers who barely spoke the same tongue. It was almost seven o'clock before the lengthening shadows of buildings on the square reminded her of how long she had been away. Yawning, her companion paid for their drinks. For the moment, they were glad to part.

The man from the tourist office admired her frilled blouse. "Our women are like men," he said, holding her hand. "It is your femininity we find appealing." The "you" was collective—Miss Baxter was too modest to accept the entire tribute for herself—yet something like intimacy established itself, as if they had been though danger together, and Miss Baxter, brushing something invisible from her cheek, agreed that femininity was important. They made an appointment to meet on Sunday.

"It is our last day," she said, already savoring Sunday, and feeling warmly sad at the parting to follow.

Panic came during the walk back to the hotel. The road from town was long and hot, and the flaming oleanders cast a thin lacy shade. How could she have left her girls alone, on the beach, for an entire afternoon? I cannot be trusted, she thought. It was a thought she wore with comfort. It became her, like the curly lines of her clothes and the almost liquid anxiety in her eyes. She thought about Sunday, and the man from the tourist office. He was fat and affable. He was a *kind* man, she thought, halting in a patch of shade. But her charges, her girls! They might have drowned, or had indigestion, or disappeared in a sailboat with the blond young men from town. The pure animal pleasure of making love, the man had said. Perhaps he had been trying to warn her. The trouble had been his voice, so very reassuring, it had prevented her from taking in the import of his words. By the time she reached the hotel, anxiety was like a rope around her throat, and her voice, when she asked the desk clerk if he had seen her girls, was hoarse and uncontrolled.

"Your girls are here," said Linda, behind her. They had dressed for the evening in fresh, cool blouses and skirts. Their hair, streaked with sun and salt, was brushed, their lips rouged and expectant. Their expectancy terrified Miss Baxter; they seemed to her terribly in danger. I left them alone for most of a day in a country where anything might happen, she said to herself, but even as she produced the thought, she knew that the danger she had left them exposed to was not political. The truth was that she herself had always been expectant, still was (What about Sunday? What about the man from the tourist bureau?), and her life was strewn with errors and moves of unsurpassable stupidity.

"Oh, Baxie!" Nancy cried, falsely enthusiastic. "Guess what! Linda's been asked to go down in a submarine, and she's cabled home for permission."

Even if I were perfectly sober and could consider this rationally, Miss Baxter thought, I could not consider myself a greater failure than at this moment.

"I wish you had discussed it with me first," she said. "It was up to me to send the cable. What will Linda's parents think of me? After all they've spent."

"It's not going to cost them anything," Linda said sulkily.

"I mean, after all they've spent for me," said Miss Baxter. "Oh, I cannot bear it. No, no, don't tell me who has invited Linda to go down in a submarine. One of those boys in the sailboats…"

They denied it together, indignant. Linda said, "Honestly, Baxie, when you get like that, a person doesn't know what to do with you. It's not your fault. You couldn't help it if he asked me."

"Who?"

"This reporter," Nancy said. "You know, the one we met in Florence. The one that told us to be careful in Italy not to talk to married men."

"Yes, but then we met this other man, remember?" said her sister. "That sort of nice married man with the mustache, on the train, the one that told us never to talk to *single* men?"

Miss Baxter was not to be diverted. "I said nothing in any of my letters home about a reporter. What on earth are your parents going to think now? If only you girls would try to understand my position, my... my position," she said.

"Oh, Bax," said Linda, affectionately. She put her arm about Miss Baxter's shoulders and said, "What's your position, Baxie?"

The elating effect of the slivovitz had worn off just enough to give her a headache. But she still retained an alcoholic feeling of clarity. "My position is that I owe your parents a great deal in return for this trip. Your position is that you are spoiled, silly and rich."

She spoke so quietly that it was a moment or so before any of the girls realized a scene had been created. They looked at one another. They considered her reference to money indelicate in the extreme, but none of them could say so. They had been brought up to deprecate extravagance and to say that they couldn't afford things. Also, they felt that Baxie had no right to divert attention from Linda to herself. This was Linda's moment; even Baxie, unworldly though she was, ought to realize it.

In silence they filed out to the dining terrace for dinner. In silence they attempted to sulk; but they kept forgetting they were annoyed and even found themselves commenting on Miss Baxter's description of a church.

"How long will we be in Greece?" Linda said.

"A week."

"A whole week!" It was impossible to tell whether her exclamation meant joy or dismay.

"A whole week for all of Greece," Miss Baxter said. "Then back to Paris and home. We shall have had the best of it by then. August is so hot. We've had the best part of the summer. There's only tomorrow here and then Sunday, our last day."

"Our last day," Nancy said, working herself up to a feeling of nostalgia.

"I'll have my answer by then," Linda said, looking dreamily out to the warm summer sea. "I'll have my cable and I can tell him yes, and then we'll have Greece and then there's my submarine. Oh, Baxie!"

"I know," Miss Baxter said. "Only don't count on it, Linda dear."

But this was so preposterous that none of them bothered to reply.

IN ITALY

"THE JOKE of it is," Henry kept saying, "the joke is that there's nothing to leave, nothing at all. No money. Not in any direction. I used up
most of the capital years ago. What's left will nicely do my lifetime."

Beaming, expectant, he waited for his wife to share the joke. Stella
didn't think it as funny as all that. It was a fine thing to be told, at this
stage, that there was no money, that your innocent little child sleeping
upstairs had nothing to look forward to but a lifetime of work. She
had just been bathing the innocent child. Usually, her evening task
consisted only of kissing it good night, for the Mannings were fortunate
in their Italian servants, who were efficient, loyal, and cheap.

"They don't let Stella lift a finger," Henry always told visitors. "Where
can you get that kind of loyalty nowadays, and at such little cost? Not
in England, I can tell you."

There had been two babies in the bath. The boy was Stella's; in the
midst of less cheerful thoughts, it was still a matter of comfort that she
had produced the only boy in the Manning family, the heir. The other
baby, a girl, was, Stella supposed, her grandchild. That is, she was
Henry's grandchild. It was too much, really, to be expected to consider
oneself a grandmother at twenty-six. Stella pulled down her cardigan
sleeves, brushing at the wet spots where the babies had splashed. In the
presence of Henry's grown daughter, she had been grave and devoted,
had knelt on the cold bathroom floor, as if no one, not even the most
cheap and loyal of Italian servants, could take a mother's place.

Peggy, the daughter, had lounged in the doorway, not offering to
help. She looked amused. "Doesn't Max Beerbohm live near here?" she
said. "I expect everyone asks that."

"We know no one of that name," said Stella, soberly. "Henry says he came to Italy to meet Italians."

"I see," said Peggy. She shifted from one bony leg to the other, started to say something, changed her mind. She turned the talk to Henry. "How like the poor old boy to think he can go native," she said. "Actually, he chose this part of the coast because it was full of English. They must be doddering, most of them. It must be ghastly for you, at your age."

All Stella retained from this was the feeling that Henry had been criticized. She no more liked having him referred to as "the old boy" than she enjoyed Peggy's repeated references to Stella's youth. She was only ten months younger than her stepdaughter, but Peggy made it sound years. Of course, Peggy looked older, always would. She said of herself, as if the idea pleased her, that she had been born old. The features that were attractive in Henry had been dismayingly caricatured in his child. Peggy was too tall, too thin, her teeth were too large and white. Slumped in the doorway, she looked like a cynical horse.

There were so many things one could retort to Peggy, replies at once cutting and polite; the trouble was, Stella never thought of them in time. Now, embroiled in an unaccustomed labor (dressing her son for the night), she could not give her mind to anything else. She held the baby on her lap, struggling with him and with garments that seemed to have no openings or fastenings.

"Why don't you put it down on something, the infant, I mean," said Peggy. "You'll never manage that way. He's too lively and fat. And mine should be out of the bath. She'll catch pneumonia in this room." She beckoned to Stella's nurse, who, hovering in the passage, had been waiting to pounce.

"My little boy doesn't feel the cold," said Stella, unable to make this sound convincing. She dreaded her own baths here. The bathroom had been converted from something—a ballroom, she often thought. A chandelier in the form of glass roses dropped from the ceiling. The upper half of the walls was brown, except where paint had flaked away to reveal an undercoat of muddy blue. The bathroom grieved Stella more than any other part of the house. She knew that a proper bathroom should be small, steamy, draftless, and pale green, but try to convince

Henry! The villa was only a rental, and even if they lived in it the rest of their lives, nothing would induce him to put a penny into repairs.

"Be sure that the nursery is warm," said Stella, surrendering the baby to its nurse with exaggerated care, as if it were an egg. "Mrs. Burleigh is worried about the cold."

But it was hopeless. No room could be kept warm. The rest of the house was of a piece with the bathroom, in style and in temperature. The ceilings were blistered and stained with damp; the furnishings ran to beaded lampshades and oil paintings of Calabrian maidens holding baskets of fruit. The marble staircase—a showpiece, Henry said—was a funnel of icy air. There was no heating, other than a fireplace in the dining room and a tiny open stove in the library. Over this stove, much of the year, Stella sat, crouched, reading *Lady* and *Woman's Own*, which her mother sent regularly from England.

Henry never seemed to notice the cold. He spent the mornings in bed writing letters, slept after lunch until five, drank until dinner, and then played bridge with the tattered remnants of the English colony, relics of the golden period called "before the war." "Why don't you do something—knit, for instance," he would tell Stella. "Sitting still slows the blood. That's why you're always shivering and complaining."

"Knitting isn't exercise," she would say, but after delivering an order or an opinion Henry always stopped paying attention.

Stella might have found some reason to move around if Henry hadn't had such definite ideas about getting value for money. She would have enjoyed housework, might even have done a little cooking, but they had inherited a family of servants along with the house. Their wages seemed so low, by English standards, that Henry felt offended and out-of-pocket if his wife so much as emptied an ashtray. Patient, he repeated that this was Italy. Italy explained their whole way of life: it explained the absence of heating and of something to do. It explained the wisteria trellis outside, placed so that no sun could enter the ground-floor rooms. During the summer, when the sudden heat rendered the trellis useful, it was Henry's custom to sublet the house, complete with staff, and move his family to a small flat in London. The flat was borrowed. Henry always managed that.

Although she spent much of the year abroad pining for England

and reading English recipes, Stella was a country girl, alarmed and depressed by London. Her summers were nearly as lonely as her long Italian winters, for Henry, having settled her in London with a kindly injunction to go and look at shops, spent his holiday running around England visiting old cronies. He and Stella always returned to Italy after a stay of exactly three months less one day, so that Henry would not be subject to income tax.

"I've organized life for a delightful old age," Henry often said, with a gesture that included his young wife.

At times, a disconcerting thought crept into Stella's waking dreams: Henry was thirty years older than she, and might, presumably, die thirty years sooner. She would be free then, but perhaps too old to enjoy it. He might die a little earlier. He took frightfully good care of himself, with all that rest and those mornings in bed; but then he drank a lot. Did drink prolong or diminish life? Doctors were against it, but Stella knew of several old parties, particularly down here, who flourished on a bottle of brandy a day. A compound of middle-class virtues, she was thoroughly ashamed of this thought. Questioned about her life abroad, she was enthusiastic, praising servants she could neither understand nor direct, food that made her bilious, and a race of people ("so charming and childlike") who seemed to her dangerous and dishonest. Many people in England envied her; it was agreeable to be envied, even for a form of life that didn't exist. Peggy, she knew, envied her more than anyone in the world.

"It's wasted," Peggy had said at Stella's wedding, and Stella had overheard her. "That poor little thing in Italy? She'll be bored and lonely and miserable. It's like giving a fragile and costly toy to a child who would rather have a hammer and bricks." Stella had been too rushed and excited that day to pay much attention, but she had recorded for future scrutiny that Peggy was a mean, jealous girl.

"We adore Italy," said Stella now, playing her sad, tattered card. What were some of the arguments Henry used? "Servants are so loyal," she said. "Where can you get that loyalty nowadays?"

"I don't know what you mean by loyalty now," said Peggy. "You are much too young to remember loyalty then."

Stella looked depressed. No one ever answered Henry that way. She began, "I only meant—" But if you had to make excuses, where was the triumph?

"I know what you meant," said Peggy, softer. "Only don't catch that awful servant thing from Henry. He's gone sour and grasping, I think. He used to be quite different, when he still believed the world was made for people of his sort. But don't you get that way. There's no reason for it, and you're much too young. It will make you unfit for life anywhere but here, a foreigner in a foreign country with just a shade more money than the natives."

Peggy spoke with a downward drop at the end of each sentence, as if there could be no possible challenge. She was so sure of herself, and yet so plain. That was class, Stella thought, unhappy. She remembered something else she had heard Peggy say: "She's a nice little creature, but so bloody genteel." In Stella's milieu, one did not say "bloody," and one spoke of one's parents with respect. Stella had thought: They're worse than we are. It was the first acknowledgment she had made to the difference between Henry and herself (other than a secret surprise that he had chosen her) and it was also her first criticism. Since then, she had acknowledged it more and more, and, each time, felt a little stronger. She permitted Henry to correct some of the expressions she used—"Christ, Stella," was his usual educative remark—but, inwardly, she had developed a comforting phrase. We may be common, she would think, but we're really much nicer. She felt, in a confused way, that she was morally right where Henry was wrong in any number of instances, and that her being right was solidly based on being, as Peggy had said, so bloody genteel. But it was slow going, and, at this moment, standing in the untidy bathroom with a wet towel in her hand, she looked so downcast, so uncertain, that Peggy said, as nicely as she could, "Hadn't you better go down and cope with Henry? He's out on the terrace having far too many drinks. Besides, Nigel bores him. It's better if one of us is there."

Nigel was Peggy's husband, a plump young man in a blazer.

It was offensive, being ordered about in one's own home this way, having Henry referred to as a grasping old man, almost a drunk. Once again, she failed to think of the correct crushing remark. Nor was there time to worry about it. Stella was anxious to get Henry alone, to place him on her side, if she could, in the tug of war with his daughter. She didn't want to turn him against his own flesh and blood; in Stella's world, that kind of action was said not to bring happiness. She simply wanted him to acknowledge her, in front of the others, mistress of the house and mother of the heir. It seemed simple enough; a casual word would do it, she thought—even a look of pride.

She sped down the stairs and found Henry alone on the dining-room terrace. He was drinking the whisky Nigel had brought from England and looking with admiration at the giant cacti in the garden. Stella wondered how he could bear to so much as glance in their direction. The garden was another of her grievances. Instead of grass, it grew gravel, raked into geometric patterns by the cook's son, who appeared to have no other occupation. There were the big cactus plants—on which tradesmen scratched their initials to while away the moments between the delivering of bread and the receiving of change—a few irises, and the inevitable geraniums. The first year of her marriage, Stella had rushed at the garden with enthusiasm. Part of her vision of herself as a bride, and a lady, had been in a floppy hat with cutting scissors and dewy, long-stemmed roses. She had planted seeds from England, and bedded out dozens of tender little plants, and buried dozens of bulbs. Nothing had come of it. The seeds rotted in the ground, the bulbs were devoured by rats, the little plants shriveled and died. She bought *Gardening in Happy Lands* and discovered that the palm trees were taking all the good from the soil. Cut the palms, she had ordered. She had not been married to Henry long enough then to be out of the notion of herself as a spoiled young thing, cherished and capricious. The cook's son, to whom she had given the order, went straight to Henry. Henry lost his temper. It appeared that the cutting down of a palm was such a complicated undertaking that only a half-wit would have considered it. The trunks would neither burn nor sink. It was illegal to throw them into the sea, because they floated among the fishing nets. They had to be sliced down into bits, hauled away, and dumped on a mountainside somewhere in the back country. It was all very expensive, too; that was the part that seemed to bother Henry most.

"I wanted to make a garden," Stella had said, too numb from his shouting to mention palms again. "Other people have gardens here." She had never been shouted at in her life. Her family, self-made, and with self-made rules of gentility, considered it impolite to call from room to room.

"Other people have gardeners," Henry had said, dropping his tone. "Or, they spend all their time and all of their income trying to create a bit of England on the Mediterranean. You must try to adapt, Stella dear."

She had adapted. *Gardening in Happy Lands* had been donated to the British Library, and nearly forgotten; but she still could not look at the gravel, or the palms, or the hideous cacti, without regret.

Nigel had gone to change, Henry said, but changing was only an excuse to go away and restore his shattered composure.

"I told him I'd made my will entirely in favor of the boy," he told Stella, chuckling. "Only there won't be anything to leave. They can worry and stew until I'm dead. Then they'll see the joke."

Henry had begun hinting at this, his latest piece of humor, a fortnight before, with the arrival of Peggy's letter announcing her visit. Relations between Henry and his daughter had been cool since his marriage. It was no secret that Peggy had never expected him to marry again. She had wanted to keep house for her father and live in Italy. Three months after Stella's wedding, Peggy had married Nigel. (No one ever said that Nigel had married her.) Henry had not been in the least sentimental about Peggy's letter, which Stella considered a proper gesture of reconciliation. Nigel and Peggy were coming about money, he said, cheerful. They wanted to find out about his will, and were hoping he would make over some of his capital to them now. Nigel was fed up with the English climate and with English taxation. However, if they were counting on him to settle their future, they had better forget it. Henry still had a few surprises up his sleeve.

"Thank God for my sense of humor," he said now.

"Henry," said Stella bravely, "I don't think this is funny, and I must know if it's really true."

"It's enormously true and enormously funny." He was tight and looked quite devilish, with his long face, and the thinning hair plastered flat on his skull.

"Not to me," said Stella. She tried again: "You might think of your own innocent child."

"She's quite old enough to think for herself," Henry said.

"Not that child—*my* child," Stella almost screamed.

"By the time he grows up, the State will be taking care of everyone," Henry said. "I intend to enjoy my old age. Those who come after me can bloody well cope. And stop shrieking. They'll hear."

"What does it matter if they hear?" said Stella. "They think I'm common, anyway. Peggy called me that at our very own wedding. My mother heard her. A common little baggage, my mother heard Peggy say."

Henry's answer was scarcely consoling. He said, "Peggy was drunk. She didn't draw a sober breath from the time I announced my intentions. She read the engagement notice in the *Times*, poor girl."

"Oh, why did you marry me?" Stella wailed.

Henry took her in his arms. That was why he had married her. It was all very well, but Stella hadn't married in order to be buried in an Italian seaside town. And now, having had a son, having put all their noses out of joint by producing an heir, to be told there was no money!

It had not been Stella's ambition to marry money. She had cherished a great reverence for family and background, and she believed, deeply, in happiness, comfort, and endless romance. In Henry she thought she had found all these things; middle-aged, father of a daughter Stella's age, he was still a catch. She hadn't married money; the trouble was that during their courtship Henry had seduced her with talk of money. He talked stocks, shares, and Rhodesian Electric. He talked South Africa, and how it was the only sound place left for investment in the world. He spoke of the family trust and of how he had broken it years before, and what a good life this had given him. Stella had turned to him her round kitten face, with the faintly stupid kitten eyes, and had listened entranced, picturing Henry with the trust in his hands, breaking it in two.

"I don't believe in all this living on tiny incomes, keeping things intact for the sake of grown children who can earn their own way," he had said. "The next generation won't have anything in any event, the way the world is heading. There won't be anything but drudgery and dreariness. I intend to enjoy myself now. I *have* enjoyed myself. I can seriously say that I do not regret one moment of my life."

Stella had found his predictions about the future only mildly alarming. He was clever and experienced, and such people often frighten one without meaning to. She was glad he intended to enjoy life, and she intended to enjoy it with him. She hadn't dreamed that it would come down to living in an unheated villa in the damp Italian winter. When he continued to speak contemptuously of the next generation and its wretched lot, she had taken it for granted that he meant Peggy, and Peggy's child—never her own.

Nigel and Peggy came onto the terrace, ostentatiously letting the dining-room door slam in order to announce their presence.

"How noisy you are," Henry said to Peggy. "But you always were. I remember—" He poured himself a drink, frowning, presumably remembering. "Stella, I fancy, was a quiet little girl." Something had put her frighteningly out of temper. She paced about the terrace pulling dead leaves off the potted geraniums.

"Oh, damn," she said suddenly, for no reason.

They dined on the terrace, under a light buried in moths.

"How delicious," Peggy said. "Look at the lights on the sea. Those are the fishing boats, Nigel. It's the first sign of good weather."

"I think it's much more comfortable to eat indoors, even if you don't see the boats," Stella said sadly. "Sometimes we sit out here bundled in our overcoats. Henry thinks we must eat out just because it's Italy. So we do it all winter. Then, when it gets warm, there are ants in the bread."

"I suppose there is some stage between too cold and too warm when you enjoy it," Peggy said.

Stella looked at the gravy congealing on her plate and said, "We adore Italy, of course. It's just the question of eating in or out."

"One dreams of it in England," said Nigel. It was the first time he had opened his mouth except to eat or drink. "We think of how lucky you are to be here."

"My people never went in for it at home," said Stella, suddenly broken under Henry's jokes, and homesickness. "Although we had a lovely garden. We had lovely things—grass. You can't grow grass here. I tried it. I tried primroses and things."

"This extraordinary habit the English have of taking bits of England everywhere they go," said Peggy, jabbing at her plate. Nigel started to say something—something nice, one felt by his expression—and Peggy said, "Shut up, Nigel."

Soon after dinner Stella disappeared. It was some time before any of them noticed, and then it was Peggy who went to look. Stella was in the garden, sitting on a bench between two tree-sized cacti.

"You're not crying, are you?"

"Yes, I am. At least, I was. I'm all right now. I wish I were going home instead of you," Stella said. "I'd give anything. Do you know that there are rats in the palms? Big ones. They jump from tree to tree. Sometimes at night I can even hear them on the roof."

Peggy sat down on a stone. The moon had risen and was so bright it threw their shadows. "They've gone indoors," she said. "Henry's quite tight. I suppose that's one of the problems."

Stella sniffled, hiccupping. "It isn't just that. It's that you don't like me."

"Don't be silly," Peggy said. "Anyway, why should you care? You've got what you wanted." Stella was silent. "I'm not angry with you," Peggy went on. "But I'm so angry with Henry that I can hardly speak to him. As for Nigel, he came upstairs in such a state that I thought we should have to take the next train home. We're furious with Henry and with his cheap, stupid little games. Henry's spent all his money. He spent his father's, my mother's, and mine. No one has complained and no one has minded. But why should he talk to Nigel of wills and of inheritance when we all know that he has nothing in the world but you?"

"Me?" said Stella. Astonishment dried her tears. She peered, puffy-eyed, through the moonlight. "I haven't anything."

"Then that was Henry's mistake," said Peggy calmly. "Or, perhaps it was your youth he wanted. As for you, what did you want, Stella? Did you think he was rich? Hadn't anyone else proposed to you—someone your own age?"

"There was a nice man in chemicals," said Stella. "We would have lived in Japan. There was another one, a boy in my father's business, a boy my father had trained."

"Why in the name of God didn't you choose one of them?"

Stella looked at her sodden handkerchief. "When Henry asked me to marry him, my mother said, 'It's better to be an old man's darling than a young man's slave.' And then, it seemed different. I thought it would be fun."

"Oh, Stella."

The lights of the fishing boats blinked and bobbed out at sea. They could hear the fishermen thumping the sides of the boats and shouting in order to wake up the fish.

"I should have been you, and you should have been me," Peggy said. "I love Italy, and I can cope with Henry. He was a good parent, before he went sour. You should have married Nigel—or *a* Nigel."

The crushing immorality of this blanked out Stella's power of speech. It had been suggested that she ought to marry her stepdaughter's husband—something like that. There was something good about being shocked. It placed her. It reaffirmed her sense of being morally right where Henry and his kind were morally wrong. She thought: I am Henry's wife, and I am the mistress of this house.

"I mean," said Peggy, "that sometimes people get dropped in the wrong pockets by mistake."

"Well," said Stella, "that is life. That's the way things are. You don't get dropped, you choose. And then you have to stick to it, that's all. At least, that's what I think."

"Poor little Stella," Peggy said.

PAOLA AND RENATA

DURING the weeks that preceded the engagement, Paola and Renata discovered new ways of combing their hair. Paola's was short and brushed forward in a style Renata's mother called "Charleston." Over the Charleston locks she tugged a bathing cap made up of yellow daisies. Renata's mother said that the sun and the lake water would turn Paola's lovely head to rust if she didn't take care now, while she was young. The older woman caressed Paola's hair—the dry crown and the silk wet fringe that had touched water—and said she wished her own daughter had thick curls and blackberry eyes; but that was polite hypocrisy and accepted as such. Renata was the one who was almost engaged. Her father was a corporation lawyer in Milan, and her mother could have provided Renata's dowry out of her own jewel box, if she had chosen to. Paola was the child of a widow. The father had died not quite two years ago, and there was a faint new difference between the girls, delicately felt, invisible still, like the turning of summer.

Renata could swim without wearing a cap—indeed, she was urged to do so, so that the sun and the water would bleach her hair to the washed-sand color for which her mother had another name: "Scandinavian." Renata idly swam on her back with her hair spread and floating, but she was not mad, not drowning, not Ophelia. She was making herself very beautiful for her engagement. Coming out of the water she was to Paola's sun-struck eyes a mythical girl. She raised her thin arms as if unconscious of them and pulled her Scandinavian hair back and held it taut with a curving tortoise-shell comb. Unknown bathers peered through the bamboo fence that hedged their private beach, but Renata was calm and scornful. The hair-style, like the disdainful look on her face, was copied from a magazine; but it was also true she did not yet know other people existed. She had still to learn the hard darting glance her mother and Paola's mother could send other women: the measuring regard that ascertained clothes, hands, and weight in carats. Renata was aware of herself. Floating on her back with her eyes shut to the sky, wishing herself alone on the lake in the circle of mountains, she saw the reflection of a girl, Renata, long, brown, her thin arms outspread, her hands and her feet like marine plants. She saw with her eyes shut her shadow on the bottom of the lake, a cloud transversed with small quick fish. Hers was the exquisite shadow of summer, the most memorable, the most precisely cast.

Paola and Renata and Paola's little sister Anna and the two mothers lived that holiday, their last together, in Paola's mother's house. It was the last of anything; the house was sold to a Swiss couple from Zurich, and in the autumn the furniture would be sold at auction or stored in Milan. If Paola's father had put the deed to the house in his wife's name, it would have been a kind and practical gesture, and saved on income tax; but he died with the house his, and taxes owing, and only his mistress provided for. A block of flats in San Remo was in her name. Everything was going, now, and the family done for, and the father had struck at them within his lifetime, secretly, perhaps thinking he would never die; but he must have expected to die. Otherwise, would he have thought of his mistress, and provided for her? Of all this Paola said nothing as she brushed her Charleston hair forward or threaded ribbon through the lace of Renata's peignoirs. She thought, but said nothing. Everything was going, done, except Paola's mother's dowry, which her father had always said was never quite enough. Paola heard her mother crying, but it was difficult to tell if she was grieving for her dead husband, or mourning his infidelity—exposed and dissected by lawsuits—or simply lamenting the disorder of his memory. It was almost as though he had wanted to be assured of survival, no matter how. "Dead and gone, and jealous of the living," cried Paola's mother, in a fit of hate for which she immediately begged forgiveness. Paola forgave. The father's photograph, kept so that Anna would know what he looked like, gave way to the specter of a stoutish man with a rather large head and a mistress on the Mediterranean coast.

It was the last of everything; this house was, it had been, the last

Italian villa. Everything else was German, Austrian, and German-Swiss. The campsites and hotels bore signs saying GERMAN SPOKEN, and GERMAN MANAGEMENT, the only Italians to be found were in the hotel kitchens, and one could walk miles without hearing a word in Italian: this the two mothers said with passion and spite. From their scrap of pebbly private beach, Paola and Renata watched with indifference shoals of floating inflated mattresses, each holding a Swiss, an Austrian, or a Bavarian, usually blistered red, but singing. The songs were melancholy and stirring, and although the words were in a foreign tongue the tunes were familiar. The girls could sing French and American songs, without understanding all the words. They were bored by the mothers' passions. They were as bored with them as with patriotism or tales of war. These were the only matters that bored them. No summer had ever been as distracting as this last summer on the lake with Renata about to become engaged.

The obstacle to the engagement was Renata's parents. The parents found nothing to criticize in Guilio's fortunes or his person, but they began as if it were a game with the premise that he was unfit and must be proved desirable. He was twenty-eight, eleven years older than Renata, and still had not passed his examinations. He was studying law. At the rate he failed his examinations he would be studying law at the age of forty. Renata's father—a lawyer—declared there were too many lawyers in Milan. Renata raged, Paola consoled. Up in Paola's room, which the girls shared, Renata lay prone on the marble floor, limp with tantrums, and cried, "They want me to be an old maid." "They don't, of course," said Paola sadly. Bereaved and mourning, undone by her father and the unknown San Remo whore, she wanted Renata to be engaged because that was the thing Renata wanted. Paola would always see a stout man with a large head signing papers, conspiring, casting his family on an ash-heap. Consoling her friend, she sat on the floor beside her and stroked her hair. Her hand was firm, and her voice warm and low and wise. "They don't want you to be an old maid. You know that." Renata knew that Paola was right.

Guilio had studied in Italy and Geneva and Heidelberg and now he wanted to go to the United States and study there for a time. Guilio's parents said that if Renata married him, and took over the moral responsibility for Guilio's life, they would send him to the United States or anywhere he liked; but Renata's father wanted Guilio to go away alone and come back for Renata when he had passed his examinations. The responsibility for Guilio was too great for a girl of seventeen. That was the story they told Renata. It might or might not be the truth.

That went on in July. In August Renata stopped raging and began to weep. She had to wear sunglasses at the dinner table to hide her bloated eyes. She scraped her increasingly Scandinavian looking hair away from her innocent forehead, and sat as though rebuffed, contemplating an untouched dinner, while the others talked at once. Paola tried to feel, We shall be somewhere else this time next year, but only this summer counted as a faithful season. A father died without warning. Without warning Renata would say, "I am engaged."

The two mothers were thin and hard. The new difference between them was physical. Paola's mother had stopped tinting her hair, as a sign of sorrow or of desperation. It was half mahogany, half dull gray. Renata's mother was blonded white, and her head sleek and neat as a boy's. Paola admired her large glossy red earrings and her brown shoulders and her quick tongue. She admired her rings and her sweet hypocrisy and her temper and her car. None of those attributes had come with marriage. She was born with some and inherited the means to have the rest. Renata's mother was kind to Paola—so obviously not a threat—and took no notice of her own grieving girl, except when the sunglasses and the accusation they concealed seemed a reproach too great to ignore. Then she lost her temper. Once she lost her temper seriously and knocked the bowl of water in which grapes were cooling, half silver coated, half submerged, on to Renata's lap. Renata jumped up, screaming, with her dress ice cold and pasted against her thighs. Her mother tried to hit her across the face with her napkin, but missed.

"There will be no engagement," her mother cried. "You impertinent monster! *There will be no engagement.*"

Paola was laughing so that she could scarcely understand Renata's hysterical answer (probably a suicide threat) from the stairs. Presently Renata returned in a starched peignoir, with a white ribbon around her hair, and they had their coffee in peace on the terrace, beneath the trellis of green grapes and black wisteria branches and white roses that suddenly dropped petals like secret letters. The two mothers played gin rummy under a light surrounded by moths, and the girls listened to records of Anthony Perkins singing in French. The songs did not disturb the mothers; no one cared about the people sleeping in hotels on either side of the house, and little Anna could slumber through earthquakes.

The only person distressed by the tears, the lamentations, and Anthony Perkins' voice was the frightened young Austrian girl who had been employed as Anna's nurse for the summer. She was spending the most miserable summer of her life. Not only did she hear Austrians insulted in this house from morning till night, but she was bitten and spat upon by little Anna. When Anna spat the girl asked, "Are you doing it on purpose?" and Anna said, "Yes." Anna's hair had to be brushed and fastened with an elastic in the morning before they went down to swim. Just when the nurse had the hair brushed and ready, and the elastic stretched on her outspread fingers, Anna would shake her head and send the pony-tail flying. The nurse would then have to roll the elastic back on her wrist, clutch Anna, and begin again. She needed several hands: one for Anna, one to hold the brush, one to grasp the pony-tail, and one for the elastic band. When Anna's mother came to see what was keeping them, Anna clasped her mother's knees and bent her head meekly, so that her mother could slide the band on without trouble.

The Austrian girl had tears in her eyes. "Anna has bitten me again," she said, and held out her hand with the small crescent.

"If I had known you did not like children I would never have brought you here," Anna's mother said.

"How I hate children," said Renata, lying on Paola's bed. It was a hot day and neither of them had dressed.

"Oh, so do I," said Paola, with something in her voice that resembled Renata's in a rage.

"That cow expression people have when they look at Anna. It makes me vomit."

"You will have children if you get married," Paola said.

"I know. I've thought about it. Guilio hates children too."

"There are things you can do so as not to have them."

"I know. But I don't know what they are."

Paola would have said, "Guilio knows," but that was going far, even between Paola and Renata.

Renata sighed, with her chin on her hands, and contemplated the pictures on the wall above the bed: Anthony Perkins, Yevtushenko, and Mrs. Kennedy. The fourth and most important picture lay beside her. It was a photograph of smiling Guilio, glassed over, surrounded by an imposing silver and leather frame. His name was signed obliquely across one corner. He lay smiling between the two girls. Renata had tried sleeping with the picture, but was afraid of rolling on it and smothering Guilio. Also, she shared Paola's bed, and Paola had not been hospitable. She did not object to Guilio, but to the heavy silver corners of the picture frame. She was not frightened of stifling Guilio, who was not a newly born kitten, but of hurting herself. Renata's engagement to Guilio had to do with the picture in its frame, with her red eyes and sunglasses, her scenes at dinner, and her remote hair drifting on the lake. There were also Guilio's letters.

Renata was permitted to write one letter to Guilio every week. This letter was read by her mother, who then took it to the post office and sent it by ordinary mail. Guilio was in Switzerland for the summer, quite close by, but a letter dispatched by ordinary mail took as long as four days to reach him.

Renata wrote to Guilio every morning. Paola carried the daily letter downstairs to Spirella, the cook, who gave it to the groom in one of the hotels next door. The letter went out with the hotel post, marked "Most Urgent," and was in Guilio's hands a morning later.

"Where are you going?" Paola's mother asked her.

"To the kitchen, to get lemonade." Renata's letter was in the pocket of her shorts.

"Don't keep running to the kitchen. Don't bother Spirella. Tell Spirella to bring lemonade out for all of us." These were the contradictory orders of a widow in distress. Paola's disobedience was of little importance. She had no dowry and no prospects and was not even nearly engaged.

Renata was watched more closely than Paola that summer because the talk of her engagement, even the assurance that it would never come to pass, made her important, tricky, and furtive. She was more important than she had ever been. She might be up to anything. Renata's mother looked as if she were trying to smuggle a forbidden object over a frontier. All summer she said, "Renata, where are you?" and "Where are you going?" and "Who was that on the telephone?" and "Wait for Paola," and "Wait for us."

Renata lay on the bed and looked at Guilio while Paola slipped down to the kitchen and gave the "Very Urgent" letter to the cook. Guilio's letters were sent to Spirella in care of the hotel next door, and came up in the morning with Renata's breakfast, under a napkin. "There is no law against posting letters," Spirella told Paola. Paola knew it was the cook's weapon against two mothers. What could the mothers do confronted with the smooth and guileless faces of Paola, Renata, Spirella, and the groom next door?

About once a week, a letter arrived for Renata, correctly addressed, in care of Paola's mother. Paola's mother gave it to Renata's mother, who read it in her room. In these official letters, Guilio doubted Renata's love, asked if she were reticent or simply pure, and insisted that he would marry her if she were penniless and in rags. Renata's mother sat on the edge of her bed with her legs crossed and the letter spread on one knee, and she bit the side of her thumb as she read. She kept the letter until evening so that she could read it over the telephone to her husband in Milan, who called every evening at eight o'clock. Renata was given the letter the next day. Weekends, when Renata's father arrived from Milan, he asked to see the letters and read them as if he had not understood his wife on the telephone. "There are no others?" he would ask. Renata looked at her hands, her mother shrugged.

The official letters, intended for parents, Renata read aloud to Paola in an affected voice. Paola, racked with laughter as if in pain, pressed her pillow to her face. Renata kissed the teeth on Guilio's smiling picture and put the picture away with the unofficial letters. His real, his clandestine letters, which she did not read aloud, were tied and hidden in Paola's old toy cupboard. There were perhaps twenty of them, less than half the number she had written him. They were ranged and marked in such a way that Renata would know instantly if anyone had touched them. Knowing that the packet of letters was full of snares, Paola let them be. Renata's mother, determined as the police, but less thorough and calm, ransacked the room but missed the cupboard of toys. Renata knew, or felt she knew, when her mother was up to a search, and it was her private pleasure to leave the cupboard door ajar, revealing stuffed animals and a wicker sewing basket. She imagined her mother, impatient and tough, banging the door shut, missing the treasure in her impatience to find it. The official letters were tied with ribbon and in a drawer. The mother untied the ribbon and counted the letters and flung them back between nightgowns. She said aloud, alone, that she wished God had never given her a daughter. Blessed was a mother with an only son!

Towards the end of August, Renata's father went to Geneva for his affairs, and called casually on Guilio's family in their Swiss summer home. A few mornings later Renata was summoned to her mother's room.

"I have a letter here from Guilio," her mother said. "How many letters have you had from him?"

"You should know."

"One came this morning, and not in the usual way." She kept the letter face down, with her hand over it. Renata's eyes met her mother's and held the gaze. Neither stared the other down, but each moved, slightly, to break the deadlock.

Renata had saved face. "May I have my letter?" she said.

"I haven't decided. You know what it will mean if you have had a secret correspondence."

Renata did not know, but a threat was a threat. "Guilio is honorable," she said. "So am I. You make me wonder what you were like when you were young."

She was braced for a slap, but her mother said only, "I promise not to tell your father if you give me the others."

"What others?"

"The letters, you impudent monkey. The other letters. There is no question of an engagement now. A man who would lie to his mother-in-law would lie to his wife. If you give me the letters I won't tell your father."

"I haven't had any letters except the letters you have seen," said Renata.

The mother was looking away, watching Renata in a mirror across the room. The girl sat quietly and emptied her expression of unhappiness or reproach. She was a novice supreme in her innocence and decision. From Paola's mother's sitting room came the sound of half a conversation: "A good girl, but without imagination, and too severe. My Anna has been a martyr to discipline all summer. Apart from that—yes, honest enough."

"Is the nurse leaving?" said Renata.

"How should I know?" said Renata's mother. "Who cares about her?"

Renata suddenly smiled. "I shall marry Guilio when I'm twenty-one. It's only four years."

"Four years ago you were a monster of thirteen," her mother screamed. "A horror! Skinny, tall! Why couldn't I have had a son? Why couldn't I have a daughter like Paola? I'm glad to be rid of you. There will be an engagement. Do you hear? There will be a wedding September twenty-seventh and Guilio is taking you with him to the United States. God help you, with a husband who tells lies and rushes the wedding. We have barely five weeks to get ready. We are leaving for Milan tomorrow. Now you know."

She crept into Paola's room and sat stiffly on the edge of the bed.

"I'm being married September twenty-seventh."

"You wanted to be engaged."

"Yes, but I'm not being engaged. I'm being married. There isn't a real engagement."

When she began to pack she said, "You can keep the letters."

"What do I want with Guilio's letters?" They were not friends as before.

After Renata and her mother had departed, distraught and waving scarves from the sky-blue Giulietta Sprint, Paola looked in the toy cupboard and found Guilio's picture and the secret letters. Renata had taken the official letters and would probably keep them and reread them all her life.

Paola unfolded one of the letters, but it was not a message of secret love; at least not as she had imagined it. It was about Guilio and water-skiing. She picked out another at random but it was about Guilio too. She tore the others up without reading them and got rid of them by swimming quite far out in the lake with scraps of paper in the top of her bikini. It was not as exciting as smuggling letters to the kitchen had been, but she relived the feeling of summer and secrecy, and the unrevealed act. She put the picture aside in case Renata should ask for the frame.

Paola and her mother were alone on the beach with Anna. The Austrian girl had left without regret, and it required both of them, Paola and her mother, to look after Anna. The mother said nothing about going back to the city, and there seemed to be nothing waiting there, except Renata's wedding. By the time all the letters had been torn up and dispersed, it was almost too cold for swimming. Paola shuddered and rubbed her arms and legs with a rough towel as soon as she came out of the water. In less than a week the climate changed. They dragged their towels and cushions away from the shade of the bamboo fence and followed the sun. When they sat on the beach—Paola, and her mother, and little Anna—Paola was conscious of them as a family without men. She did not miss Renata.

"I wish something would happen," she said.

"You'll be engaged later," said her mother. "Seventeen is too young."

"Can't anything happen without an engagement?"

"Don't be meaningless and clever," said her mother. "Don't be clever at all. Men don't like women who are too clever." She did not scream, like Renata's mother. Her voice was quiet. The girl shivered in the breeze from the lake as her mother said, "Renata would never have caught Guilio by being clever. Do you think it was her brains he admired? Her face? He was waiting for the marriage settlement. That was all."

Anna had taken off her bathing suit and was dancing in shallow water.

"Come here instantly," her mother said, without the hope of being obeyed. Anna splashed them. "Very well," said the mother. "Don't come. Break my heart. You'll regret it when I am dead." Anna took no notice, knowing perfectly well that nothing ever came of threats.

"I wish I were Anna," Paola said.

AN EMERGENCY CASE

ANY DAY now, the doctor had said, Oliver would be going home. Oliver had been sitting up for his meals and going down the hospital corridor to the bathroom for more than two weeks. Sometimes a nurse went with him, holding his hand. It wasn't really necessary, he was quite old enough to go alone, but he looked small and defenseless in the oversize bathrobe that didn't belong to him. His left arm was out of its plaster cast. The elbow hurt, and so did one foot, but it seemed to him that he had always been like this. He did not know that he was very pale and that his eyes looked bruised. When people passed him in the corridor and cried *"Pauvre petit!"* he scowled and shied away from their hands.

"C'est un petit Anglais," the nurse with him would say. Often she would add the rest of his story in a low voice. "It's all right," she would say. "He doesn't understand French. Besides, he knows. The doctor has explained."

The hospital was in Geneva; that much Oliver knew. He knew that he was in Geneva, and that he was nearly ready to go home to England, and that they were coming to fetch him any day. The car in which he had been driving with his parents had turned over twice. He knew that the way he knew he was in Geneva; he had heard a nurse telling a maid or someone in the corridor. He did not speak French, but he understood more than they thought he did. His doctor always spoke to him in English. In English he had told Oliver that Oliver's parents were now in Heaven; but Geneva, and going home soon, and the car's having turned over twice were the facts Oliver had retained.

"Your aunt is coming for you on Wednesday," the doctor said. He made his round in the morning and usually got to Oliver's room by ten o'clock. Oliver had no clock, and in any case he couldn't tell time, but he knew exactly when everything was going to happen—when they would come to wash him, when they would wheel in the cart with his lunch, and when they would bring the glass of milk after his afternoon sleep. His room was white and contained two beds, one of them empty and half hidden behind a white screen, and two colored photographs, one on each side of the door. The photographs showed cows at pasture in the Alps, standing in bluebells. On the back of one of the pictures was Oliver's temperature chart; whatever the nurse marked on the chart belonged to Oliver, and he was quite sure that the picture was his and that he would take it home. There was a glass door, hung with white gauze curtains, that opened out to a little balcony. There Oliver was sometimes taken, bundled in blankets, and left in a deck chair. Since there was nothing to see but a bare, sodden garden, he much preferred being inside, in the room he now accepted as home. He preferred it but never said so. He had never once asked for anything.

Oliver's room was called the emergency room; Mme. Beatrice, the most talkative of the nurses, had told him that. They kept it for people who came to the hospital unexpectedly, as Oliver had done, but they also used it for ordinary cases when the floors were crowded. Oliver's version of a crowded floor was a linoleum nursery floor covered with little tanks. He stared while Mme. Beatrice told him that he had stopped being an emergency case but was still in the emergency room because there was nowhere else for him to go. She said all this, and he seemed to understand. The truth was that he could not imagine anywhere else.

"Your aunt," the doctor said to Oliver. "Your charming aunt, Miss Redfern, will be here on Wednesday. Won't that be jolly?" The doctor was fat and wore horn-rimmed glasses. He was loud and cheerful and friendly and kept telling Oliver that he had two little boys of his own.

"That's not *my* aunt," Oliver said.

"Miss Redfern," the doctor said patiently. They had been repeating this dialogue for days. "Your charming aunt, who came to see you after your accident."

"Nobody came."

"Miss Redfern did. She is called Aunt Catherine."

"Oh, Auntie Cath," said Oliver indifferently. He bent over his drawing. There was a small painted table set over his knees, on which he played with the modeling clay they had given him, cut up magazines, and drew airplanes and cats. He drew cats in boots and pullovers, and he drew their toothbrushes and the tubs in which they were bathed at night. When the doctor, pointing to some clumsy, disjointed shape, asked "What is that?" Oliver covered his drawings with his hands. The doctor was curious about the drawings, because he had mistaken the cats' bathtub for a motorcar and thought that Oliver had been drawing the automobile in which his parents were killed.

He asked what kind of an automobile it was, and Oliver muttered something.

"What did you say?"

"I said," said Oliver, shouting, "we've got a bigger car than you have at home."

The doctor told the nurses to be watchful and to report anything Oliver said that might indicate he was unquiet or anxious. Oliver was unrewarding. He did not draw, or mention, accidents, his father, or his mother. He spoke of a place called Bedlington Gardens, where everything was bigger, better, and cost more than anything in the emergency room. In his personal reckoning, pennies equaled and perhaps surpassed pounds, but he liked the phrase "costs a lot more." The coming of Aunt Catherine did not excite him. "Is she bringing me a present?" he said. When the nurse replied that she didn't know, Oliver lost interest. He was sitting with the bed levered up and pillows at his back. He still had a pain in his back from some injections, but he was used to it. The doctor had come and gone, and had said this time that Aunt Catherine was coming tomorrow. Now that the doctor's visit was over, Oliver knew that nothing else would happen until lunch, and lunch would be vegetable broth and a bit of meat with two vegetables, kept hot over a dish of warm water. The only uncertainty was dessert, which might be pudding or fruit.

Shortly before lunch, the doors swung open—the padded-leather hall door and the white-painted inner door—and two nurses pushed in a rolling stretcher on which lay a sleeping woman. They pushed aside the screen that separated the two beds, and rolled the wagon up beside the empty bed. They tipped the stretcher, and the woman rolled neatly onto the bed. She wore a short white nightgown, and Oliver saw her legs were fat and white and streaked with iodine. She moaned, but the moans sounded as if they were coming from far away, so deeply was she in sleep.

The doors opened again, and an important-looking nurse, the one who wore a cone-shaped hat and always came around with the doctor, looked at the woman and felt the bed, and said something angry-sounding to the nurses. They had neglected to warm the bed. She spoke in French, but Oliver understood. Then the nurse looked over at him and, changing her manner to something more pleasant, said, in English, "So you are leaving us tomorrow?"

"I don't know." He kept on staring at the sleeping woman.

The nurse went out, and the others followed. Oliver sat up a little straighter, then found he could see better by getting up on his knees. The sleeping woman lay on her back, breathing noisily through her mouth. He watched her, motionless, and was still watching when they brought in his lunch.

"Oh!" The waitress seemed shocked, and she put the screen between the two beds, so that Oliver couldn't see.

"Did she have an accident?" he said, but the waitress spoke no English.

He ate his lunch. After a bit, a nurse came in and disappeared behind the screen. "Feeling better?" he heard her say, very loud.

The heavy breathing stopped, and a faraway voice said, "Yes, I'm all right."

He heard a rattling sound, then the nurse's voice again: "Do not swallow, please. Hold the water in your mouth and spit it out."

"Is that mine I hear crying?" said the voice, as if its owner were coming closer to the surface.

"You are hearing them all," said the nurse. "This room is over the nursery. I'm afraid it is the emergency room, and not very comfortable. We really were not expecting you just yet."

"Nearly had her on the plane," said the woman, and Oliver heard her laugh softly. He liked her voice, now that it sounded less buried.

"Did you have an accident?" he said loudly.

"There is a little boy in the room," the nurse said swiftly, "but he goes tomorrow." Her voice dropped and Oliver heard only certain words. He felt the tone, full of anxiety, and he felt the sensation in the room of shared secrets.

"Poor little thing," he heard. "Take the screen away. Can I sit up?"

"Not yet." The screen was folded back, and Oliver and the sick lady looked at each other. She had the expression he had seen on people in the corridor and on the faces of new nurses who had just had everything explained to them.

"So you speak English," she said, at last. "I'm so pleased. I shall have someone to talk to, at least until you go."

"Did you have an accident?" he said again.

The two women laughed together. "Mrs. Chapman found a baby in a cabbage in the garden," said the nurse.

Oliver did not reply.

They replaced the screen later in the day, and a nurse told Oliver to be very quiet so that Mrs. Chapman could sleep. He did not see her again until the next morning, after his bath. Then they took the screen away, because it was a sunny day and the screen hid the sun from his neighbor. She lay very flat, and Oliver had to kneel on his bed again in order to see her face. She was not young and not pretty.

"That was a nasty dream you had last night, Oliver," she said. "What was it all about?"

"Didn't dream."

"Don't you remember? I rang for the nurse. We put the light on. You spoke to us. Don't you remember at all?"

He said, "I didn't dream. Did finding the baby make you sick?"

She laughed and winced and said, "Don't make me laugh. It hurts. I didn't find the baby. I had it. But that's not what made me sick. I'll tell you all about it if— Can you get out of bed? Of course you can. I saw you trotting off earlier. And you're going home today. Well, then, get out of bed and come over here and find my purse in that drawer. Open the purse and you'll see a packet of cigarettes, and some matches in a little box. Take them out."

He was already across the room, in his white hospital jacket open down the back. The tiles of the floor were cold under his feet. He opened the bag with great care and found the cigarettes and the matches. "You've got money," he said, looking inside, "and a comb, and a dirty handkerchief."

"Don't be rude," said Mrs. Chapman. "Throw over the cigarettes. Can you find me an ashtray? What about the saucer under the drinking glass? That's it." He placed the saucer carefully on the white counterpane and stood waiting. She lit the cigarette and held her breath, and then blew out smoke. "Thank God for that," she said. "I enjoy cigarettes again. I never stopped smoking, but I just didn't enjoy it. Now, let me see. What did I start to tell you? Oh, yes. Well, after I had my baby—she's my fifth, so I can nearly think about something else at the same time—about two hours after, I had to have an operation. That's what made me sick. Understand?"

He nodded. "I had an accident," he said.

"I know."

Oliver stirred, waiting. "What else is there?" he said.

"You mean what else about me?"

He wasn't sure what he meant. He didn't want to get back into bed, and he liked watching her while she smoked.

"Do you want to know why I'm in Geneva?" she said. "Because my husband works here. Do you want to know where he is now? He's at a conference in Ceylon. That's so far away I won't even try to tell you about it. Do you want to know why I was on a plane? Because I had to go to England to see *my* mother. She was ill and in a nursing home just like this. Do you like all that?"

"Yes." They smiled comfortably at each other.

"I expect you ought to be in bed," Mrs. Chapman said.

"The doctor comes soon," Oliver said. "The doctor comes, and then lunch."

"You've got the timetable down perfectly," she said. "But I still think you'd better get back into bed."

"My Auntie Cath's coming," he said, lingering.

"She's taking you home, is she?"

"No," said Oliver scornfully, drawing it out. "She can't take me home. We don't even live in the same place."

He climbed back in his bed and watched the door. There was a curious air of change about the day. When the doctor came in, he scarcely looked at Oliver, except to say "Well, my brave little man," which was not his usual manner at all. The waitress who brought the comforting lunch of soup and meat and vegetables said, "*Au revoir, mon petit*," which was quite new. A maid came in and took away the modeling clay. It didn't belong to Oliver but to the hospital. Mrs. Chapman slept, not in the moaning way of the day before but quietly. She awoke suddenly and told Oliver that she felt very well indeed.

"Shall I get you a cigarette now?" he said. He had been waiting for this.

"I can reach them, thank you." She looked across at him and said, "You can't read yet, can you?"

"I've got books."

"I know. I mean, can you read writing? . . . I thought not. Don't be so offended. I'm going to write down my address and my name, and maybe your aunt will let you come and visit me. You could come in the summer."

"No," he said. "We go to Warbleswick."

"Where?"

He was pleased at remembering this, and thought it strange that she shouldn't know. "We go to Warbleswick," he repeated.

The afternoon nurse came in and began to gather up his toys. She put them in a cardboard box. "You must be washed now, to look nice for your aunt," she said, smiling at Oliver.

"I've had my bath." The nurse handed him his bathrobe and started to put slippers on his feet. He said, "I've *had* my bath," and when she persisted, grasping his foot, he kicked her with the foot that was free.

"How can you be so naughty when you're going home?" said the nurse. She turned to Mrs. Chapman, aggrieved. "He has always been so good. I think we have spoiled him. Did you see what he did? *Un coup de pied!*"

"I should leave him alone if I were you," Mrs. Chapman said.

Oliver had by now thrown bathrobe and slippers on the floor and retreated under the bedclothes.

"He's never been like this," the nurse kept saying, and Mrs. Chapman kept answering. "I'm sure it hasn't been properly explained."

It seemed to Oliver high time that they stopped all this, and high time that his mother came to fetch him away. If Auntie Cath took him, his mother wouldn't know where he was. The taking away of the toys, the unscheduled attempt to wash him suggested that something unusual was about to take place. It could only mean his mother. When the door opened and he heard the voice of Auntie Cath, he stiffened and held the bedclothes, prepared to resist.

BONAVENTURE

HE WAS besieged, he was invaded, by his mother's account of the day he was conceived; and his father confirmed her version of history, telling him *why*. He had never been able to fling in their faces "Why did you have me?" for they told him before he could reason, before he was ready to think. He was their marvel. Not only had he kept them together, he was a musical genius, the most gifted child any two people ever had, the most deserving of love. He began to doubt their legend when he discovered the casualness of sex, and understood that anyone who was not detached (which he believed his own talent would oblige him to be) could easily turn into parent and slave. He was not like his own father, who, as a parent, seemed a man who had been dying and all at once found himself in possession of a total life. His father never said this or anything like it, though he once committed himself dangerously in a letter. The father was more reticent than the mother; perhaps more Canadian. He could say what he thought, but not always what he felt. His memories, like the mother's, were silent, flickering areas of light, surrounded by buildings that no longer exist.

The son could not place himself in their epic story. They talked, but until the son became an eyewitness their lives were imaginary. Before he *was*—Douglas Ramsay—the world was covered with mist, palm fronds, and vegetarian reptiles. He said to his father, "The trouble is there are still too many people alive who remember all that." "All what?" "Oh, everything. The last war." He was trying to show the distance between them, yet he would have died for either one—perhaps the father first. That made him more violent toward them, and sometimes more indifferent. A year ago, when he was nineteen, he was awarded a fellowship that permitted him to study in Europe. He seldom wrote.

Sometimes he forgot all about them. Their existence was pale, their adventure niggling, compared to his own. Family feeling had never dominated his actions; never would. Nevertheless, he discovered this: when he was confused, misunderstood, or insufficiently appreciated, a picture of his father stood upright in his mind. His father's face, stoic and watchful, transferred from a wartime photograph taken before true history began, appeared when Ramsay's emotions were dispersed, and his intellect, on which he depended, reduced to water.

He was in Switzerland, it was a June day, he was recently twenty, and he had to get rid of chocolate wrappers. He had spent the morning in Montreux, and in the short train journey between Montreux and the stop nearest the chalet where he was a guest for the summer, Ramsay had eaten three quarter-pound bars of the sweet, mild chocolate only women are said to like. He could not abandon the wrappers on the impeccable train; he was suddenly daunted by Swiss neatness and the eyes of strangers. Hobbling up the path from the station, he concealed the papers under ferns and stones.

The chalet, set up on its shelf of lawn, seemed to be watching. It was like an animal, a bison, or a bear, hairy with vines and dark because of its balconies. Once he had got rid of the evidence, he stared boldly back. Parts of his body were unhinged; he was clamped together by invisible hooks that tore the fabric. His knees, his shoulders, his neck were wrenched loose, like the punishment of Judas in an engraving Katharine Moser had put in his room. He had been in a car accident two years before, and would never mend entirely. "Neither will my father," he said to himself. Their suffering—his own and his father's—burned the day black. The shrieking of birds, which Katharine Moser thought he ought to like because he was a musician, sank and lodged in every bone. He shut his eyes and stood still, and waited for the seizure to pass, for the muscles to unlock; then he opened his eyes and looked at the lawn. It had not been wrecked by a war or by a woman in temper but by something ordinary—a country storm. The grass was bestrewn with branches, bark, leaves, peony petals, chairs knocked sideways, a child's watercolors, a strand of dripping vine. A branch shivered and the drops that fell were colder than any water he had ever touched. He imagined Katharine Moser standing here and saying to Heaven, "How dare you do this to my lawn?" As he thought this, the sun came on in a burst of fire, and his face and hands were riddled by stinging light. He saw the mountains, whose names he was daily told and at once forgot, and he saw the burning color of houses that were miles away. This was the landscape that had belonged to Adrien Moser, the great conductor; it had no other reason to command his gaze.

The prospects Ramsay had known until this summer were of cities—Montreal, and then Berlin. They were the same to him, whether their ruins were dark and soft, abandoned to pigeons and wavy pieces of sky, or created and destroyed by one process, like the machine that consumes itself. The air he had breathed was filled with particles of brick dust. He accepted faces, not one of which he would put a name to, and knew the smell and touch of wet raincoats worn by people he would never meet. In the streets of one place, Berlin, he walked on the dead, but both cities were built over annihilated walls scarcely anyone could remember. He knew that a lake is a lake—that is, a place to swim—and that parks and trees are good for children, but he had never known the name of a leaf or a tree until Moser's widow began telling him, comparing one wild grass with another, picking a flower, showing its picture in a book. In the morning, standing beside him in the ravine on the far side of the house, she pointed to fields of white anemones that seemed covered with frost, and she gathered forget-me-nots, wild geranium, mauve and violet and pink, and valerian like lace, and mare's-tails with fronds of green string. "The first plant life on earth," said Katharine, bending down. For a reason he could not immediately interpret, the words, and the sight of the plant in Katharine's hand, rushed him back to his mother screaming, and the wartime photograph of his father, which, of course, was mute.

Wishing for life without its past, for immeasurable distance from the first life on earth, he groped to Sabine and Berlin instead of Katharine and now. In the short daydream, Sabine frowned and turned her head sharply, then felt among the clothes on the floor for a cigarette. She told Ramsay she had had one abortion and would probably never marry. Later, she said she would travel and try a different husband in every country. She was not the doting German girl his father's crowd talked about in their anecdotes of the war. Her flat was shut up tight except when the janitor's wife came to clean and flung the windows wide. The janitor's wife was not concerned about Ramsay (who had not spent an entire night with a girl before) or Sabine dressed in two towels. "I saw a wild beast in the courtyard with black eyes, like an Italian," she said, scrubbing the sink. This was the only house on the street older than Ramsay, and the courtyard was full of rats and secrets. When it rained the courtyard smelled of ashes. Laughing about the janitor's wife and the Italian rat, Sabine stood naked before her mirror and said, "Look at how brown I am." One of her admirers had given her a sunlamp.

The first plant life on earth was spongy and weak; and the sun, in and out of clouds, sucked up every trace of color from Katharine Moser's hair and hand and eyes. He had seen color paler than Katharine's hand on angles of brick—was it paint splashed? Car lights washing by? There were no fissures in the brick, no space for fronds and stems, no room for leftovers. Why is brick ugly? Who says it is? Ramsay's father knows how much gravel per cubic centimeter is needed for several different sorts of concrete; he wrote his thesis on this twenty years ago, when he came back from the war.

"In Berlin," Ramsay started to say—something about bright weeds growing—but Katharine saw a magpie. "This is their season," she said. "They prey on fledglings." She told of the shrike, the jay, but he was thinking about the black, red-brown, smoke-marked courtyard in Berlin, and Sabine, shivering because she was suddenly cold, tender when it was too late, when there was no need for tenderness, asking what she considered serious questions in her version of English: "Was that all? Worth it? All that important?" She was not looking into space but at a clock she could not bother winding that was stopped forever at six minutes to three.

He and Katharine walked back to the lawn and the breakfast table, and she tipped her head like Sabine's, though not in remembrance of pleasure, only because the sun was strong again. She spoke to the cook's little boy, in straw hat and red shorts, pretending to garden; he was at their feet. Then behind and above them a branch rocked. It was Katharine's cat attacking a nest. The fury of the battle could be measured by the leaves rustling and thrashing in the windless day. A cat face the size of the moon must be over the nest; the eyes and the paws—there was no help for it—came through sunny leaves. The sky was behind the head. "Stop him, stop him!" Ramsay screamed like a girl or like a child.

"Pip! Naughty Pip!" She clapped her hands. "He's got one, I'm afraid." She was not disturbed. Neither was the cook's little boy, though he sucked his lip and stared up at the tree a moment more. "It is the cat's nature," she said. "Some things die—look at the spruce." (To encourage him.) "We think it is dying, but those fresh bits are new." The trees were devoured by something he did not understand—a web, a tent of gray, a hideous veil. The shadows netted on the breakfast table, on cups and milk and crumpled napkins, seemed a web to catch anything—lovers, stretched fingers, claws. He tried to see through Katharine's eyes: the cat had its nature, and every living thing carried a name.

"Do you notice that scent, Douglas? Does it bother you? It is the acacia flowering down the valley. Some people mind it. It gives them headaches. Poor Moser," she said, of her late husband, the conductor, who had died at Christmas and would have been seventy-four this summer. "When he began having headaches he thought all trees were poisonous. He breathed through a scarf. That was the form his fears took."

"It's only natural to be scared if you're dying," said Ramsay. He supposed this; until this moment he had not given it a thought.

"Old people are afraid," she said, as if she and Douglas were alike, without a time gap. (He had reckoned the difference in their ages to be twenty-five years.) "Although we'll know one day," she said, as if they would arrive at old age together. Lowering her voice, in case her adolescent daughter was spying and listening, she told how Moser had made her stop smoking. He did not want her to make a widower of him. He had chosen to marry Katharine because she was young, and he wished to be outlived. He was afraid of being alone. She, a mere child then, a little American girl nearly thirty but simple for her age, untalented, could not even play the piano, had been chosen by the great old man. But he forgot about being alone in eternity. "I told him," she said, putting the wild flowers in a glass of water on the breakfast table. "Unless two people die at exactly the same moment, they can never meet again." With such considerations had she entertained the ill old man. He had clasped her hands, weeping. His headache marched from the roots of his hair to his eyebrows, down the temples, around the eyes.

Ramsay was careful how he picked his way through this. For all his early dash and promise he was as Canadian as his father, which is to say cautious and single-minded. He had a mother younger than Katharine, who began all her conversations on a deep and intimate level, as if coming up for air was a waste of time. That made him more prudent still. He said, "Those the acacias?"

"The plum trees? They can't be what you mean, surely. That's the cuckoo you're hearing, by the way. If you count the calls, you can tell how many years before you get married. Peggy and Anne count the whole day." He considered the lunatic cuckoo, but having before him infinite time, he let the count trail off. The cook's small boy, squatting over one mauled, exhausted, eternally transplanted geranium, heard Ramsay and Katharine, but they might have been cuckoos too for all he cared. The only English words he knew were "What's that for?," "Shut up," and "Idiot." This child, who was a pet of Katharine's, lunched with the family. Until Ramsay had come, a few days ago, the boy had been the only man in the house. He sat on a cushion, an atlas, and a history of nineteenth-century painting, so as to reach the table, and he bullied and had his way; he had been obeyed and cherished by Katharine Moser and her daughter Anne; by fat Peggy Boon, who was Anne's friend; and by Nanette Stein, who was Katharine's. Now Ramsay was here, tall as a tree to the stooping child. When Ramsay said something to him, in French, he did not look, he went deaf, he muttered and sang to himself; and Ramsay, who had offered dominoes, and would have let the boy win the game, limped on up to the house, feeling wasted.

Peggy Boon, fourteen, too plump and too boring to be a friend for Anne—unless Anne, already, chose her friends for contrast—had been mooning about the lawn ever since the storm ended, watching for Ramsay to come up the path. She let him look at the Mosers' view a full minute, and then stepped round from behind a tree. She had been making up a poem, she said flutily. No one made up poetry; Ramsay had never seen anyone making up poems. He glared over her head. She stood there, straight of hair, small of eye, fat arms across new breasts she was flattening at night with a silk scarf—this information from Katharine, by way of Anne. She was an English rose, she feared silence, and pronounced her own name "Piggy."

"Everyone's out," she said, coloring deeply for no reason he cared to know. "Anne is playing tennis. I'm not keen . . . so . . . Nanette, well, I don't know *where* she is. She didn't say. Mrs. Moser went to visit the bees in case the thunder frightened them. She tells them everything. When Mr. Moser died she told the bees. She told them you were coming, and she's told them she is moving your things out of the house and into Mr. Moser's garden pavilion, and that you are his . . . his . . ." Unfolding her arms, stooping, she clutched at grass, as though weeding; she straightened up, she took courage, and announced, "*You* are Mr. Moser's spiritual heir." He was not listening to her. "If you don't tell the bees everything, Mrs. Moser says, they go away. But my mother," she added urgently, "says this is nonsense."

Like all English voices, hers sounded to him underdeveloped. He stared down at the cardigan, drooping and empty-armed, at the tight belt and bulging seat of what he supposed was a dainty frock. He had avoided one sort of Canadian girl all his life, and here was the pure, the original mold. He asked, "Did you know Adrien Moser?" It seemed impossible.

"Oh goodness, yes. This is the fourth time I've been here." She was gasping, as if he had splashed her with seawater. "I've been here a summer, and a Christmas, and an Easter, and *this* summer. Of course, he's not here now, is he?" If only Ramsay would say, "He must have been charming"—something like that. She pretended he had: "Oh he *was* charming! He used to do so many kind things. Once he offered to buy me a bicycle. I refused, of course. But imagine! He'd hardly known me five minutes then." Chewing on grass, airy and worldly now, she said, "I've been wondering . . . No one's told me. Are you a composer?"

"I'm studying with Jekel in Berlin." And I am his best and strongest pupil, and if you knew anything you would know that, his mind continued. He had heard, for years, "Are you really only twelve?...only sixteen?" The voices had stopped; no one is ever likely to say, "Are you really only twenty?"

"Don't you want a chair?" said Peggy, wiping the seat of one with her cardigan sleeve. "You're not supposed to stand too long. I've heard ... there's something wrong."

"Nothing's *wrong*. I was in a smash-up about two years ago, that's all. This girl was driving," he said. "It wasn't even her own car. There was all hell with the insurance. No one was killed."

"Oh, *good*." Having offered Moser's kindness, and had news of Ramsay's health, Peggy said, "Do you like Switzerland?" But she had lost him. Katharine Moser, with her cat in attendance, came toward them, smiling. The shadows that bent over her hair were cast by trees whose bark was like the skin of a snake. He had imagined another face for her; until a few days ago, he had known her only in letters. He had given her soft hair streaked with white, and humorous, intelligent eyes. His idea of a great man's wife was very near a good hospital nurse. Even now, when he thought, I am in Moser's house, he was grateful to the intelligent hospital nurse, who did not exist; at least she was not Katharine. Her eyes were green, uptilted. The straight parting in her hair was coquetry, to show how perfectly proportioned was her face. The only flaws he had seen were the shape of her nose, slightly bulbous at the tip, and the too straight body, which was a column for the fine head. The bees' scent, which clung to her hands and dress, was like incense. She was impressive, beautiful, fragrant, and until she lifted her arm to point to the pavilion where he would now sleep, and saw the skin of the arm, palely freckled, spotted, slack, he almost accepted her own idea of herself, which was that she was guileless, a child bride, touchingly young.

"I wanted to know you before I put you in the pavilion. You do understand why? It mustn't be a museum, but I want it kept alive just by people he liked, or might have loved. It's furnished with— What is it, Peggy?" The smitten girl was following them across the grass. Katharine watched Peggy Boon skip off (pretending joy) and become excluded.

"That girl is having a rotten time. My daughter is so rude," she said, and sighed, and forgot all about it. "Now, Moser's bed and his tiled stove came from the curé's room in a château. I bought them at an auction."

He ducked his head to enter the pavilion. The first thing he saw was the piano, small and gaily colored, looking like the piano sometimes given a little girl for her first lessons. He could not see the name of the maker, which had been covered over with paint.

"Those engravings belonged to a fervent German monarchist who collected caricatures of the new rich, unaware that he was mocking himself. Moser liked objects that came from rich houses, providing they looked poor. He always thought he might die of hunger any day. He saved screws and tacks and elastic bands—you'll find boxes full of rubbish, all labeled. Moser told me that the walls of his family's house were covered with rugs they would not put on the floor, and that there were sheets over the rugs to protect them from light. I hope you will like your bed."

The bed was carved and bore a coat of arms and an angel's head. The angel had a squint; Ramsay could not tell if it was looking reproachfully to Heaven or out of the window. The pavilion had been prepared in secret, while Ramsay was down in Montreux at a movie. He saw roses, a reading lamp, and then he saw the last photograph of the old man. The old man sat on a bench, in sunlight, holding a scarf. Katharine stood with one hand on his shoulder. Moser's eyes were wild and fixed.

"This is a great picture," he said, taking it up. "It was in the papers when he died. Someone in Berlin said it looked like a famous picture of Freud going into exile."

"I don't know what you mean by that. Moser was never in exile. He died in his native country." She shifted ornaments on the washstand. A shell porcelain soap dish was moved from the extreme left to the far right. The vase of roses took its place. "Now, there are things you can look at, if you want to. Testimonials. All the obituaries. Boxes of caramels—I found them after his last stroke. He loved them, but wasn't allowed to have any. When we found the empty boxes I knew he'd been eating on the quiet. I've kept them—I don't know why. This one wasn't opened." When she spoke of something she touched it. When she finished speaking she touched Ramsay's arm.

"Here's what they'll find after me," he said, and tumbled out of his pockets the marbles, the Yo-yo, and the sponge ball that were part of the reeducation of his injured hands. He was arrogant, he never doubted; it was a joke only in part. When Douglas Ramsay died, his Yo-yo and the plastic marbles would be placed on a shelf and labeled and dated, and dusted every day. He had never had parents; there was nothing behind him, nothing to come; the first plant life on earth had never existed; the cities would be reduced to mossy boulders; he would never have children; he would be mourned nevertheless. The curé's bed, Moser's bed, was Ramsay's bed. "How did he sleep in it?" they would say. "He was so big, and the bed is so small!"

The first night Ramsay spent in the pavilion a large moth brushed against his face. He knew it would not bite or sting, but its touch was pure horror, and his reaction uncontrolled. The moth was paper-white until it blundered against the pillow, and then he saw it was cream. Indigo eyes were painted upon its wings. He shot XEX out of the blue can Katharine had left for mosquito-killing. The battle the moth put up for its life now frightened him witless. It flapped its way under the bed. The frantic wings were louder than his heart. During the fight, scores of incidental casualties—gnats, midges, spiders, flies—dropped from the ceiling. He was afraid to open the window or the glass doors in case any more creatures came in, and he lay in the poisoned room blowing his nose all night long. He was on a mattress of straw that was just slightly too short. He was covered with tons of eiderdown. In his mind he had an image of his mended bones beginning to slip. If he got up now, he would not be able to stand. He could see, in moonlight, the paved terrace and the chair that had been the old man's. The pavilion was like another beehive, and the old man had been sent here, with a curé's bed and a doll's piano, and told something: "You will be alone in eternity." "Don't eat sweets." "If you think you are dying, ring that bell."

At a quarter to six the sunlight on the wall made a stately shadow of the roses. The sun was smaller than a marble. Hills and trees received its light at an angle that made them a single spongy substance. Birds were shrieking. Ramsay pulled the eiderdown up to his eyes, which left his feet bare. When he woke up two hours after this, he took inventory of the roses; there were four yellow, two pale pink, and two garnet, which were dying. These were probably sensitive—like him—to XEX. He had nothing better to do than count by color; he was in the grip of believing that he would fail, that he was ungifted, that his crushed body would betray him, and that the years of his life—fifteen out of twenty—involved with music were a waste. He had a premonition that he would be the victim of an inherited fault. His father should help him now. His father had willed his existence: he existed in his father's mind from the moment his father knew he had survived the Dieppe raid in the last war. This extra time, when Ramsay existed in desire, gave him a margin of safety. He felt as if he had been given a present of time; no one else had this. He would outlive everyone. Moser had wanted to be outlived. His father was better than Moser. His father would never have whimpered and breathed through a scarf. His father had a calm, closed, gentle disposition. Patience and endurance distinguished his face, which otherwise might have seemed boyish. If only his father had not depended on love, or on an ideal of what a woman must mean in his life; if only he had not been implicitly certain he could expect only good of women, that love was the constant survivor; if only he had let his wife leave him when she wanted to—but then, what about Ramsay? After his accident, his father had put something in a letter that he was too reserved to say when he came to see Ramsay in the hospital. (Where had he written the letter, and how had he slipped it out to the mail? From his office, probably. Ramsay's mother, having once tried to cast his father away, was now devoutly jealous—a wastebasket hunter, letter filcher, telephone spy. She thought his father's pocket diary was written in code.) His father wrote, "I suppose two things have bedeviled our life. First, that I am hideously shy and totally lacking inwardly in any confidence. Second (and this is fact, not fiction), that I've puzzled and puzzled over what happened in 1942, over the hundred-million-to-one shot that landed me back among living people when I had joined the dead. The greatest denial of death is to love as I always shall love you and your mother." Ramsay was too weak and too ill when he read it. He began to cry. They kept feeding him answers when he hadn't asked for anything. He would never say (though he thought it), "You both make me sick." There was still the early admiration for his father—not only for his unfaltering conduct but because of a childhood illusion that his father could, for example, look at the engine of a car and see what was wrong with it. And there was more—the conspiracy of two quiet men living in the same house with an intolerant woman.

As the sun above the dying spruce expanded, rose, became too brilliant to see, Ramsay surveyed his father's life and found it simple. "I love you" or "I don't love you" seemed puerile. His father had never had to cope—as Ramsay was doing—with doubts and terror and the possibility of lapsed genius. He had not even had to cope with a lot of women—only that one.

Owing to an exchange concluded with the enemy, Ramsay's father came back to Montreal about a year before the end of the war. He was part of a contingent of sick, wounded, and tubercular prisoners taken at Dieppe. Bonaventure Station received him. This was a dusty building with, on both the front and the back, a wooden porch that is called, in Montreal, a gallery. The paint on the gallery was scrofulous and diseased, and the station itself was the dark dry red that deflates the soul. It was at the foot of a steep hill; streetcars stopped before it after an awkward turn. For a long time the station had been used only for freight traffic, and then the Army took it over entirely. The Army put up cardboard squares with the letters of the alphabet so the next of kin would know where to wait, and assigned dozens of men to make sure the next of kin did not trample one another to death. Ramsay's mother was twenty-one. She sat under R for Ramsay the better part of a day, with her hands in the pockets of her camel-hair coat and her bare brown-painted legs stuck out straight before her. Ramsay knew, because she had told him, that there were no nylon stockings in those days, and that she wore her coat on a blazing hot day because of a guilty and confused desire to cover up. The men came through a door at the far end of the station, one by one. His father appeared; swung his kit down from his shoulder; stared into the dark. It was like a monkey house by then, with the dirt of the place, and the stopped-up toilets, and the children frightened, and the women screaming. She pushed her way up to him and with her fists in her pockets said, "I don't want to live with you. I don't want to be married at all. I couldn't tell you while you were a prisoner. Anyway the censor might not have let it through." Some women took their husbands home and lay like corpses so the husbands could see for themselves the marriage was over, but Ramsay's mother wouldn't have that. She was fiercely honest and saw nothing the matter with manslaughter. In the slow-motion film of someone else's memory, Ramsay saw his father there, home, alive, yes, but in a sense never seen or heard of again. His father was Canadian-silent, Canadian-trained, and had to make an intellectual effort not to be proud. He struggled out of the station and walked up the hill beside his wife and sat down with her on a bench in Dominion Square. A Salvation Army band played "Lamb of God, Sheep of God," which was taken up by a drunk woman sharing their bench. His father was so stunned, so exhausted, he forgot his name. He forgot what he was doing here—forgot the name of his native city. His wife said he would be an invalid all his life. He heard her say she hated sick people, and had married too young. Yet at the end of the afternoon she led him home and turned out the girl whose apartment she shared. Why? Pity, she told Ramsay. No, said his father; it was justice, the power of love. Bonaventure Station was destroyed before Ramsay could see it. Most of the buildings his father and mother looked at when they were deciding his existence or nonexistence stand only on old postcards and in their account of that day. The bed belonged to the girl turned temporarily out of the flat, and no one knows what became of her. She married some man, said Ramsay's mother, and they left Montreal.

Katharine Moser, companion of genius, generator of talent, dispenser of comfort, and mind reader as well, said, without leading up to it, "I suppose you were close to your mother?" They were in the car, and she was driving him he did not know quite where—to fetch drinking water from a spring, she said.

"I was closer to my father, actually"—this reluctantly. He pinched his lips together, for he had in his pocket one of his mother's long, self-justifying letters, jumpy with dates: "In January 1946," "Just after the Korean War," "When we met at Bonaventure"—that was the important date, when he was not conceived, was not present, was not even deaf, blind, and upside down. She defeated him by making him present on that occasion. He was still her witness, as if she had wanted nothing more than a witness. He saw her belted coat, her curly hair brushing the collar, her straight bare legs. He was afraid of contamination; his father's sweetness, his gentleness were in the blood. He knew—because many times told—how she had been persuaded. Victory for the man! Yet it was she who stood up abruptly, slung her handbag over her shoulder, and took him home to bed.

"You are so quiet—you live in music, I can see that," said Katharine, driving. "Do you have"—she sounded eighty-five and senile to him now—"time for girls?"

He had slept badly, and his legs were too long for the Mini-Minor. He edged slowly around so that he was facing her profile and, after the second's reflection in which he decided not to say, "Mind your own damn business," he suddenly told her about Sabine. He handed over Sabine, the slut, the innocent, the admirer of her own body, the good-natured, the stupid, the avaricious, the maker and seeker of love. The first woman he had spent a whole night with became an anecdote. He said, "Finally, she met an Arab prince. I mean a real one, in skirts. Jeweled dagger. He gave her some crappy bracelets that probably came from Hong Kong. She was excited. Every time you'd see her she'd be trying to write him a letter. But she made an awful mistake. When he left Berlin she said, 'Well, *shalom*.' She thought it was a kind of Middle Eastern '*Ciao*.' You know what the Arab said? He said, 'That's not exactly us.'" Ramsay's laughter was loud.

"And that wiped her out as a wife for you? Her *bêtise*?"

"I'm not looking for a *wife*." He wondered if she knew he was twenty and would have to live for a long time on grants and on the allowance his father gave him.

"Creative men should marry young. It stabilizes them."

What was she getting at? He looked at her calm profile, at her competent hands. She had the habit of opening and closing her hands as she drove, and slightly lifting her foot, so that the car, for a fraction of time, had to drive itself—though never long enough to take them off the road. He muttered about affinities and someone whose interests, whose mind and background...

"That's not marriage," said Katharine impatiently. "You didn't sleep with Sabine for her mind and background. Moser did his best work after he married me. I brought him back to the country, where he belonged. I made his life calm and easy, and kept him close to nature."

Owing to a mistake in time, he was having a conversation with a very young girl who was somehow old enough to be his mother.

"I would have thought that anything Moser did was separated from nature," he said. "He would have been what he was in a hotel room. In jail."

"Without the wind in the trees and the larks?"

Ramsay reflected that these had probably been a nuisance. Katharine's letters had been intelligent; she had used another vocabulary. If she had talked about the wind and larks, he would never have come. "I've explained it all wrong," he said, though he thought he had not. "I mean that everything he did was intellectual. He was divorced from nature by intention. Now do you see?"

"Nothing can be divorced from nature and survive." She looked angry, creased suddenly. He saw how she would be fifteen years from now. "Look at what has happened to music. To painting. It is the fault of people like you."

He should have let it go, but he was angry too. Who was she to attack him? She had invited him here; he had not arrived like a baby on the doorstep. When the old man died, Ramsay had written a polite and thoughtful letter to his widow, in care of the Swiss nation, and had been surprised to receive a warm embrace of an answer, in English. *She* had kept on writing; *she* had—the fine, and humorous, and courageous hospital nurse. (He forgot how it had pleased him, for once in his life, to play up to a situation, to pretend it was not over his head, to show off his opinions, pretending all the while to be diffident—to gather favor, to charm.)

If, at this moment, she was thinking, You are not what I expected, she was to blame. She was ignorant of music. She was the persistent artists' friend who inspires nothing but a profound lack of gratitude. He was feeling it now. He said, "Painters learn to paint by looking at pictures, not at hills and valleys, and musicians listen to music, not the wind in the trees. Everything Moser said and wrote was unnatural. It was unnatural because he was sophisticated." Her head shot round, and to her blazing eyes he said, bewildered, "It is a compliment."

They drove on in a silence that presently became unbearable. "Very soon it's too late," his mother had remarked, of quarrels. Her staccato letter jumped through his mind: "I said if you can't take a holiday when I need one I had better go without you. I shall go where there are plenty of men, I promise you that. He said, Go where you like my darling. I said, A woman like me shouldn't travel alone. I must have bitched up my life. He had the gall to say, All right I agree you've bitched it up but it wasn't all my fault. I was driving and I felt his crippled existence beside me and I thought mine might not be better. The weather is beautiful as it always is in Montreal when he is being impossible. There must be more accidents more murders more nervous breakdowns more hell in October and June. Where was I? Oh yes. When I got out of the car I saw he was crying. Pity for himself? Guilt over me?"

All at once Katharine parked sharply. Reaching behind her for a basket of empty bottles that had been rattling on the floor, she said (smiling to show they were friends again), "Is it true you have never seen a spring?" In an evil grotto a trickle of water squeezed out of the rock. A mossy stone pipe rested on the edge of a very old bathtub and dispensed a stream that overflowed the tub and ran deviously along a bed of stones, under a stone bridge, and out of sight. They stood, she worshipping, he blinking merely, each crowned with a whirling wreath of gnats. "I *own* this source," she said, and to his horror she immersed the bottles one by one in the tub. She filled each with typhoid fever, conjunctivitis, amoebic dysentery, blood poisoning, and boils. She capped them, smiling all the while, and put them back dripping in the basket; the basket was packed in the car, and they drove away.

Night after night he fought flies, midges, mosquitoes, and moths, most of which expired on his pillow or on the white bedsheet. They seemed determined to perish upon a white expansion—some mountaintop of their own insect literature and mythology—instead of going and dying in a corner where Ramsay need never see them again. One night a dying fly got in his wastebasket and thrashed and buzzed. Every time he thought it had stopped it began again. At luncheon next day he told how it had kept him awake.

"All you had to do was squash it," said Anne. She was tall, and still growing. She looked at him intently. The others seemed to concur—piggy Peggy (whom he had just interrupted) and Katharine and her friend Nanette Stein.

"Shut up," said the cook's little boy, but they turned to English now, putting a stop to Peggy's recital, in creeping French, of a visit she had made three days before to the market at Vevey. She rushed into English too: "There was nothing Swiss in Vivey, you know, nothing but vigitables." They were all sick of her. She was Anne's guest, but Anne had left her once again for the whole morning. "Time went so fast when you were away," Peggy went on calmly. "Goodness, it was half past ten before I knew *when* it was. I washed my green woolly and I wrote Mummy and Phyllis and I went for a lovely walk." A barely perceptible collective sigh went round the table, a collective breath of boredom. "I went farther and farther, straight on and up and on. The road was so steep! I thought, What if I should slip and fall? What a long way it would be! And so I turned and came back. I saw a herd of lovely Jersey cows, each wearing a bill, and I thought, How lovely! The biggest cow had the biggest bill, and the smallest one had the smallest bill. They made heavenly music."

"Bell?" said Nanette.

"Yes, bill," said the crimson child. "I thought, Goodness, why haven't I got a camera here?"

"I would have lent you a camera," Nanette said. "For such an original photograph."

Peggy's flush now seemed merely gratitude that the subject had been taken up. "If they don't move the cows, I could find them again easily."

"Aren't you afraid, going out alone among a herd?" said Nanette. She seemed subordinate, playing up to the others, and Ramsay wondered exactly what her role had been when the old man was alive.

"Not of cows, no, but actually as I went up and up I was thinking of that English lady who was waylaid and killed on a lonely road in Switzerland. It was near here."

"Never in Switzerland," said Nanette.

"And then there was that other one, a younger one. I remember it. You know, knocked down and bashed about. I'm sure it was here. I thought, Well, there's no use hanging about here waiting for *that*."

"Men do attack girls," said Anne suddenly. The rest were uneasy, for now the ridiculous obsession had shifted from Peggy, who was a joke, to Anne, whom they were expected to take seriously. Peggy had touched an apprehension so deeply shared by the women that Ramsay felt himself in league with the cook's child, and suspected of something. For some reason, confirmation that she had been in danger made Peggy cheerful. She passed around a trunk key found on the road half an hour away from the house. No one claimed it, and so she dropped the key back in the pocket of her blazer and went skipping out of the house and across the lawn, fat and maddening, with Anne behind her. The others sat smoking, watching the pair through the dining-room window.

"I hope her holiday is a success this time," said Katharine gravely.

"It never will be," said Nanette. "This is as successful as life can ever be for that girl—going to stay with a friend and talking twaddle."

Katharine waited until she and Ramsay were alone. "I want to ask you something," she said. "A great favor. Would you be nice to Nanette? Pay attention to her? She's a lost, unhappy creature. She was a bright young pianist, though you wouldn't know it now. Moser encouraged her. Do you notice how Anne ignores her? About two years ago Nanette began writing to Anne, who wasn't quite thirteen. What could I do? Anne had often seen her here. But I didn't understand why Nanette should write every day to a child half her age." Moser was too old to be bothered. What Katharine had done, she said, was slip into her daughter's room and find Nanette's letters. Anne had gone out early. She found the letters easily; Anne had her father's Swiss neatness. She saved programs, menus, anything to do with herself. There was a narcissism about Anne . . .

"What happened?"

But Katharine would not be rushed. Her own upbringing, she said, had risen like a wave. She felt watched by her own mother, who would never have done such a thing. She almost put the letters back.

This, Ramsay thought, was a lie. Katharine had sat on her daughter's bed, like her mother before her, like his mother pursuing his father, and read methodically, smoothing the pages on her knee. What Katharine saw, she said (holding up thumb and finger joined, to show with what distaste she had invaded Anne's life, and how revolting the letters were), made her see that the correspondence must stop. She drove to Ascona to have a word with Nanette, who was discovered sharing a cottage with a gendarme Englishwoman. She described that too: the rage, the tears, the abject guilt. Katharine looked tolerant and sad.

"What's Nanette doing here now?"

"But she's a friend—an excellent person. Besides, Anne has outgrown her. I sent Anne to a school where her letters are surveyed. She needed English, and her manners wanted straightening out."

Reflecting on Anne's treatment of Peggy, he thought the school wanting. And he still did not see why Nanette should be here, in the house.

He started to write to someone back home, "Honest to God, the *radar* around here," but tossed it in his basket. When it disappeared from the basket, he remembered something his father had said about women's curiosity: "You can't leave a thing around. They *uncrumple* everything."

Nanette Stein was a slight woman of twenty-seven, with a small, squashed face and a fringe of curly hair that seemed to start up from the middle of her forehead. She watched Ramsay eating his breakfast, and asked fierce questions about the racial problem in America. She told him that when an African concert tour had been organized for her (and a lot of work it had been, Katharine put in, letting Ramsay know who had been the influence behind it), she had been asked to leave South Africa. She had been shunned by British women in Northern Rhodesia. She was proud of it. Music was a waste of time when you saw the condition of the world.

Katharine, shelling peas under a large hat, seemed grave and interested, and nodded without committing herself. Nanette had gone to Barcelona just to help a strike once. She had been arrested and conducted to the frontier. When she saw the mounted policemen, the horses, something in her, a revolt against injustice (she brought her fist down on the table, remembering), made her scream and curse and fling herself against them, pummeling the horses, swearing at the police.

"I know, they say you made a lot of noise," said Katharine mildly.

Ramsay's mind snapped off; he tuned them out. He could see how this would appeal to an extremely bright girl of twelve or thirteen. Katharine might have been wrong. Nanette had perhaps been proselytizing impersonally, politically.

"I decided never to touch a piano again," said Nanette.

No one touched a piano here. He had expected it to be the house of music, but he heard only the very light quarreling of women. The music room with its records and library of scores might have been surrounded with vines and brambles. Nothing had been added for years. When he asked Nanette to play for him one evening (his way of answering Katharine's request to be nice to her), she fetched a tape recorder and they sat in the garden listening to her repeating one movement of a Haydn concerto. When she stumbled she said "*Merde*," and that was the clearest part of the tape. He thanked her when she turned the machine off.

"It's about three years old," she said. "I was trying to make something decent for Katharine."

"Does she like music?"

Nanette looked completely scandalized, as if he had been angling for gossip. She scowled and said, "I don't know what either of them liked, finally. He was old when I met him. He came to a concert in Lausanne. It meant a lot to me. He never came out anymore. It was known he hated crowds and towns. If you wanted to play for him, you had to come up here, and then you might get a telegram at the last minute telling you not to come. He had something like asthma. Some days he lay gasping—there." She pointed to the chair where Ramsay sat. "He sat with a shawl over his knees, looking down at the lights of towns he never went to. I'd played the Prokofieff Second. I hardly dared ask what he thought. He said, 'Very pretty, my child, very pretty.' Pretty! It's so Swiss—everything is *joli*. But *she* fascinated me. She was in green, in a dress like a sari, with the black hair, and the eyes. I felt like a little provincial. She had so much more than anyone, and he was fine-looking, still. I never had seen a couple like them and never will again. And then she called me and said, 'We would like to see you again.' Oh, they were such a couple. People fell in love with them. And Moser—of course, he stopped doing anything here. All that wild grass was bad for his asthma. But *before*! He was a conductor and a teacher and ..."

"I know."

"Look at them now. Look at your hero, Jekel, in Berlin. What does he write? A ten-minute opus every other year."

"Not my hero—my teacher." Ramsay was secretly reassured. He admired his teacher but did not mind hearing him attacked.

"My mother thinks activity is genius," he said, and smiled.

"He was a bit dotty at the end," said Nanette, trusting Ramsay. She walked beside him with the docility of a little dog. As they passed the kitchen—Nanette staring straight before her and talking in a low voice—Ramsay turned and saw the face of the cook, which was frightened and haggard, and so exhausted that, although her eyes met Ramsay's, she did not see he was there. The kitchen was on the north side of the house, under a long balcony; a single light above the stove had already been turned on, and the cook moved toward it and became saffron-colored. "They dote on her little boy and spoil him," Ramsay said to himself, "but I have never even been told the cook's name."

"He was a bit touched, at the end," Nanette said. "He was fond of Peggy in a senile way, but she was so stupid she didn't seem to notice she was being pawed. He would offer to buy her presents, and she would simper and say no. Katharine was deathly afraid the child would tell her mother. That's why she's asked her back now; she wants to show it is a normal household."

"Did Moser like living here?"

"It was his house."

"You don't feel he lived here. That piano ..."

"He didn't need a piano. He used to go for walks and be lost or tired, and then he would get some farmer to ring her. She was always rushing off in the car to bring him home. She would find him sitting in a hot kitchen, and he would get in the car smelling of cabbages and cooked fat. His clothes reeked of farm kitchens, but that isn't to say he felt at home there either. He was never comfortable with country people. He would sit with his hands on his walking stick, waiting for Katharine. Katharine was foreign-looking, but she got to them. She would sit down, and she would just begin telling about herself and her bees, never asking questions. Why, I've seen farmers come to help her get a swarm back, and you know they don't bother about each other, let alone strangers. As for him, oh, presently he began to hate walking. And the doctor said he had to walk, he had so much wrong with him. She had to coax him out, bribe him with caramels—because he wasn't supposed to have them and they were a treat. 'Just one ten-minute walk,' I've heard her say, 'ten out, ten back, twenty minutes in all,' but he was too muddled to count. It was along here." She meant the path where stones were now hurting Ramsay's feet. He also was supposed to exercise, but he hated it. He trudged on with Nanette, counting ten out, ten back, twenty minutes in all. She plunged her hands in the pockets of her leather coat. Her Aberdeen Angus hair seemed to him touching. Old maid at twenty-seven, older than Katharine, she let her hands pull at the shape of her coat.

The old man was dragged for a walk along this road, Ramsay reflected, looking at the silken grasses he did not care to identify, though he knew they were not alike. Like Moser, he craved anything sweet. He would have gone to the village, but if he asked for the car, Katharine would know. She would have driven him, without reproach, but he did not want her to know. Ramsay saw the old man on a bench on this stony road with smuggled chocolate in his mouth. He broke off only one square and let it melt slowly. If the old man had chocolate, then he would look at anything she wanted—at fields and chalets catching the strong evening sunlight, and clouds going pink, and one cloud pressing like a headache on a peak. If he walked to the village—but that was impossible, he never would again, for it was thirty-five minutes down, even on the shortcut by the tracks, and nearly fifty back, because it was so steep. Perhaps she thought he was meditating here on the bench. He was huddled into his cape because the evening was suddenly cold. His intellect dissolved, his mind was like water, his powers centered only on the things to eat he was forbidden to have.

"This is where the picture was taken," Ramsay said, stopping before the bench. "The old man, with Katharine beside him. Now I know why he looked in exile. He had to go for walks, and he couldn't eat what he wanted. Like a kid."

Nanette looked at the bench too. "Everyone in music is childish," she said. "Our mothers stand beside us when we practice, from the age of four."

"Somebody has to."

"Musicians live between their mothers and their confessors, forever and ever. If they lose them, they find substitutes. They invent them. *Marry* them. They marry one or the other. Always two in their lives, you'll notice. The mother and the confessor."

"No, it is not childish," Ramsay was saying to himself. "I know that I am not childish, I am older than my parents, but sometimes, even when I am not hungry..." He stopped; it was too secret. Then, crossing his mind, unsummoned, came "cruelty." It was only a word, a tag on a tree; it was like Katharine's voice saying "larch," "spruce," "acacia."

"He should have been in a city," said Ramsay. "It's as simple as that. That mania he had for collecting, even. It's a clue. They are all things you use in cities—pieces of metal, paper clips."

"A simple case of thrift," said Nanette. "Very Swiss."

He looked down at her face. "Where's your home?" he said. "Where are you from?"

"I've told you. Ascona." Her face seemed smaller all at once. "All right. From Vienna. Before that, Poland. Now you know everything. If you want the whole truth, the real truth, he didn't like foreigners. He made horrible jokes about Jews in front of me, to see if I would laugh." All Nanette had done was apply a new name, just as Katharine had said grass was millet. Ramsay would see her now wearing a tag. They heard cowbells from the valley. "Katharine thinks they sound like Oriental music," she said, smiling miserably.

"Shows how much she knows about that."

But she would not follow up what she had been saying. Without meaning to, he had made her unhappy. She talked as if they had only just met, and began all over again about the racial question in the United States.

Ramsay had accepted the old man's bed, but the bath repelled him. He was glad when, one day, the taps ran nothing but rust and he was obliged to share one of the bathrooms in the house. He came into an early-morning house, with the cook stirring and the little boy eating bread on the stairs, and Nanette, encountered in the hall, wearing a striped bathrobe. Nanette had left the room full of steam and lavender. Wet washcloths festooned the tub. He removed a wire hanger holding six stockings, and, just before he turned the shower on, he listened to church bells and to thunder. Ten minutes later the lawn was obliterated by gray smoke. The tree where Pip had hunted was still. Over the thunderclap came more bells, as if to silence the sky. The wind rose all in a moment, and the first drops of rain were flung against the house. By the time he had finished shaving, soft silent rain fell from a bright sky. The air was cold. Birds sang, but the strongest sound was a brook. Now a voice covered it—Katharine's voice, complaining about last night's supper. "The soup was out of a can, the hamburger was cooked black, and I don't call half a slice of tinned pineapple on a bit of rusk a pudding. It really is unfair—I take the boy over entirely. I keep him out of the kitchen. You've got nothing to do but the meals. As for the salad, there was too much vinegar *and* too much oil. I don't know how you manage to have too much of both."

In the room where the young girls slept, light came through flimsy curtains. Ramsay, coming into the room, saw Peggy hunched, sheet up to her forehead, tufts of coarse fair hair showing like bristles. Her pillows were on the floor. Anne lay with a leg and an arm and a small breast outside the blanket. On the pillow a wreath of dead wild flowers was half crushed by her head. Her brown smooth face was lightly oiled. Watching the sleeping girl, he knew what he could be capable of, provided she loathed him, or was frightened of him. Better fear than hate. When he touched Anne her breathing changed; he thought he saw a gleam between her lashes. Watching, she made no move. She was waiting to see what could happen. Outside, Katharine called, "Pip, Pip!," beating her hands. Peggy awoke and, with a rapidity he would never have thought possible in the dull girl, sat up and looked. There they were, Anne cold and excited, her heart like a machine under his hand, and Ramsay the vivisectionist, and poor Peggy, who had been in love.

To amuse Ramsay, Katharine now organized excursions. She took them to restaurants where they lunched sitting on balconies brilliant with roses, where she ordered the food with frowning care, putting on her glasses to read the menu, suggesting and planning for them all. She had noticed that he was greedy. She watched him, sagely and fondly. She had wakened something—perhaps only a craving for strawberries and cream—she later intended to curb. Nanette looked at her, and at Ramsay, and began having headaches, and finally dropped out of their party altogether. She looked dark and wretched when she was left behind. "The truth is, she gets carsick," said Katharine, as if some other excuse had been offered and was a lie. The young girls looked through Ramsay and round him and not much at each other. They played an acquisitive game called Take It Home and fought over museums, ancient jewelry, ski lifts, whole restaurants, a view, a horse, other people's cars, but stopped short of people. Peggy was pink with joy at being included, but Ramsay knew that she, and not Anne, had been scared to death that morning in their bedroom.

After these excursions he was stiff and sore, and could hardly move his arms and legs at night or turn in bed. His memory of each day was of eating and drinking beer on blowy terraces and of parasols knocked down by wind. Katharine took him to see a famous church treasure, and to Zurchers for tea, where they sat next to Noël Coward, and to Lausanne for an exhibition of French sculpture and painting. She brought the cook's child this time, and the two girls went to a movie. Katharine wore her glasses, and looked at the catalogue in her hand before examining any of the paintings. The two men of the household walked one on each side of her. Ramsay, shut up in a series of large rooms full of paintings, rid of three out of four of the women, began to breathe.

"These Impressionists," he began. "They seem kind of tied to their wives, you know what I mean. They were limited to their wives' gardens. You feel they all had something wrong with them and that the wife was waiting with a cup of tea and some medicine." Katharine glanced at him. That had been her role, and she knew that he knew it.

"Sit down, Douglas," she said, suggesting the circular sofa in the middle of the room. "You must be tired, after all this walking around. There is nothing more tiring than looking at things that don't interest one."

Ramsay found himself sitting and looking at the headless statue of an adolescent girl. He looked at the small breasts, slightly down-pointed. The hips were wider than the chest, the legs columns. A piece of bronze, he told himself. No one had ever been like that. He put Anne's head on the bronze neck, and presently was conscious of being watched. It was the boy, who was running round and round the sofa. The little boy circled closer. He sat down, and Ramsay smiled into what seemed an open face. The child breathed something difficult to hear. He pointed at Ramsay (and he had to bring his hand all the way from a far place to do so; he liked great gestures). He breathed again—something that sounded like "Idiot."

"What?"

"Idiot," the child said. The index finger still pointed; the arm was a soft arc.

"Who?"

"*Vous.*"

Ramsay stared down at him in fury and outrage. "Idiot, am I? What do you think you are? You supposed to be clever?"

The child did not understand English, but he understood the tone. A mistake had been made; he had been bolder than he intended. "You, for instance," said Ramsay. "What are you supposed to be? *Tu n'es pas un peu idiot?*"

"*Moi, je suis gentil,*" said the child, sliding off the sofa and beginning to back away. His face trembled. He said "*zentil,*" but this evidence of his age—his inability to pronounce some letters—did not endear him to Ramsay, who rushed on, "You're a rude little bastard. *Gentil*! You're a little bastard, that's what you are."

From the safety of Katharine, the child looked boldly back. What a fool I've been, Ramsay thought. Of course the child had not remarked he was looking at the statue of an adolescent girl and thinking spell-bound thoughts about Anne.

"Peggy wants to go back to England," said Katharine, and sighed.

"But she hates her family," Nanette protested.

"She may not know she does."

"She's fourteen and old enough to admit that her father isn't a god and her mother an angel," said Nanette.

"That is true." Katharine bowed her head with simulated meekness.

Anne appeared, with wet hair plastered on her cheeks. She washed it daily. She was struggling with a pullover. "Are you talking about me?" she said as her head emerged. "I thought I heard my name. Peggy is packing, by the way." She plunged down on the grass at their feet and said, "We've decided she's leaving because I've been so awful to her."

"I shall speak to her," Katharine said, looking oddly like the woman Ramsay had imagined before he ever saw her.

"I have been awful to her," said Anne. "You won't make her change her mind."

"It is the same story every time she comes here," said Katharine. "That wretched girl always threatens to leave because of some nonsense she has imagined. It used to be—" Nanette stopped her. "Now it is Anne she complains of," Katharine said.

"I want to see you alone," said Anne to her mother casually, "when you've finished with Peggy."

Katharine was already walking across the lawn, in her striped dress, in an old, large straw hat, with all her bracelets rattling. Throughout this exchange Ramsay might as well have been invisible. The group was disintegrating. The cook's child no longer came to lunch. Ramsay could observe all he liked now, for there was no one to catch him at it. Even the old man's phantom had vanished. Ramsay no longer saw or felt him, demanding chocolate, querulous and lost, too cosseted, smothered, destroyed. "Yesterday," said Nanette's small radio, "was the hottest twenty-second of June since 1873." Ramsay isolated three birds by sound: one asking a question, one cackling derisively, one talking to itself in a conversational tone.

Picked out in the headlights, a badger crossed the road, steadily, like an enormous dachshund. It turned and looked into the lights, and Ramsay, sitting next to Katharine, experienced the revulsion he felt in the presence of animals and wild creatures in particular. They had taken Peggy to the airport at Geneva and there—as at the exhibition of French paintings—he had felt completely himself and at home.

Back at the chalet was the incomprehensible language of birds, and the cat with its savage nature, and the cannibal magpies, the cannibal jays.

"If we park here, the car will be in shade tomorrow," he said.

"No, the trees are on the wrong side," Katharine said.

"There must be some shade, no matter which side they're on."

"You would have thought that after years of this, they would either have enlarged the garage," Ramsay remarked to himself, "or built another, or figured out which side of the trees received the morning sun." The car lights were put out, and flashlights distributed. Larch branches pressed on the car windows, white in the night. Katharine sat as the others—Anne and Nanette—got out. Ramsay, holding the door for her, shone his flashlight on her face.

"Do you think much about that girl in Berlin?" she said.

No. He thought of his mother in a camel-hair coat, her legs thrust out, staring straight before her. He said, "Most of the time I never think about her."

"Anne had a conversation with me today," she said. His stomach contracted; his hands were without strength. He released the switch of the pocket light. "Never mind about it," said Katharine. "There's a moon. Anne wants to go to Ascona with Nanette this week. She wants to stay all July. She and Peggy have funny holidays—school in August."

"Are you letting her?"

"Why not?" she said, without looking at him. "She wants to get away from home, which is normal. I told her she could go wherever she liked. She is old enough. I can't..."

You can't read her mail forever, he thought.

"What are your plans, Douglas? You can stay as long as you like. I feel there have been too many people around. We've never had a real conversation, have we? I'm afraid you'll have to put up with my cooking in July. I've fired the cook."

The cuckoo, at daybreak, was an interruption to his sleep. He saw the notes—not as notes of music but as a new kind of shorthand. He did not know enough of the shorthand to read the notes, or enough of the new language to reply. He dreamed that everyone was skeletal, while he had got enormously fat. He got up and dressed—by flashlight, to avoid doing battle with insects—and packed, not caring much what he left behind, and stepped out into the garden. Across the front of the house was a carved inscription, naming the builder, and giving a date— 1780—and reminding Ramsay, or anyone who stopped to read it, that death waits for life. The motto did not belong to this chalet but came from another region. Katharine had bought it and put it there about a year before Moser's last stroke. The chalet—like a bison, like a bear— watched him slip and slide down the path with his two suitcases. He sat down in the station shelter in a state of such lunatic joy at his deliverance that presently he was close to tears.

At the *pension* he went to in Montreux, a tall, dignified woman wearing a white apron greeted Ramsay. His cases were put in an ice-cold room with a linoleum floor. He looked through the north window at another *pension*, then at the varnished bed, the eiderdown, the table, and the clean, unironed checked cloth. A small Buddha, the only ornament in the room, sat on the chest of drawers. Ramsay picked him up, but no matter how he tried he could not catch Buddha's eye.

"That was left behind," the woman said, "by a Professor Doctor. The meal hours are eight, twelve, and seven. Breakfast in your room will be fifty centimes more. With the prices we charge we cannot afford extras."

From the kitchen came a crash of plates and loud cursing. When that died away he heard the soft silent crunching, like silkworms feeding, that came from the dining room, where the others were all at breakfast.

The first thing he unpacked was the unopened box of caramels: Caramels à la crème de Gruyères. He tangled with the Scotch Tape and pulled the box open. It's only fudge, he thought. He did not know what he had been expecting. He ate half the box—Moser's legacy—and felt sick, and drank tap water. "Good thing I left," he told himself, realizing indignantly what he had been driven to. By now they would know he had gone. He had left them up there with the cat and the cannibals. He was down where there were signs of life and work. He found one of the signs in a drawer, left by the Professor Doctor—a drawing of a naked and faceless woman wearing a pearl necklace. At ten he went to a film and watched a pretty German girl mixed up with some man who looked like a toad. But they were all so comfortable and so well dressed, and their problems were real problems, such as money lost and found. He could not sit in the cinema forever, but first things first: his room in the students' residence in Berlin was taken by someone else until July. He said, "Look here, Katharine, I'm not interested in weather and the color of the sky. I hate knowing what the weather is. I don't know what you mean by having inner resources. Are you supposed to recite poems from memory while the whole world dissolves into fog, goes away, and stays gone?" He blinked at the sleepy noon streets, the petunias in tubs, the brown balconies with washing under the eaves. He bought a newspaper and saw a prime minister wearing a miner's helmet. In the middle of the front page, boxed to show its importance, was this:

LES PREMIÈRES FRAMBOISES
*Les premières framboises mûrissent
sur la rive droite de la vallée.*

He translated everything except "*mûrissent*," which he could have sworn he had never seen before. He substituted for it "have exploded," which gave the item some stature. He did not know what he was doing here, unless he was waiting for Katharine to come and find him. In the

pension dining room he was the victim of provincial staring, because
of his youth and his limp. There came the memory of the months he
had spent after his accident completely at the mercy of other people,
depending on nurses and resenting it. He had always been active, had
lived on decisions; he remembered how his parents had respected him,
let him make his own choices about what he would study and the life
he would lead. He ate steadily grated carrots, meat, potatoes, wet salad,
gray bread. A bowl of custard was placed beside him. He spooned some
of it onto his plate, where it ran everywhere. Since the orgy of caramels
sweets disgusted him. He dreaded the mattress in his room, but it was
only for a night. In the morning he would take the train to Zurich and
from there fly to Berlin. His room there was taken, and his girl had
vanished—she was too old for him anyway. "Listen, Sabine," he had
said, "is the guy really a prince?" "No, only his bodyguard. But I ruined
it anyway with '*shalom*.'" Ramsay laughed. "Is not funny," Sabine said.
She showed him what remained of the railway station where both her
parents were killed. "Who cares?" she said, meaning "Do you?"

Two days later he was still there. He looked at the sky, the blue on
the horizon, the gray, then the pink. When he entered his room, mist
arose outside the window as if it had been lying waiting for him to
approach. One night in the dining room he started up from the table,
thinking she had come. Katharine in her silk dress could save him from
everything mediocre, commonplace, vile, and poor. The room was
filled with solemn English couples; the women wore heavy white shoes
and yards of stoles. Katharine might enter this room, warm and inquisitive, as if it were a new experience. It was not new: "He used to go
for walks and be lost or tired, and then he would get some farmer to
ring her." In the *pension* dining room, television accompanied their
supper. Chairs were arranged so that everyone faced in the same direction. A girl who looked like Sabine lay on a piano and sang. Every few
seconds, though the song continued without interruption, the girl wore
different clothes. Now she stood with her hand on the pianist's shoulder; he looked up into her eyes, and the pair posed that way. The screen
went blank, but the sound continued. They listened to a chorus from
West Side Story, in a foreign language. Everyone looked at the empty,
glowing screen, across which sticks and marbles moved, ran together,

parted. Faces were lifted, for the set was high on a corner shelf. Again he thought Katharine had arrived. Nothing had happened. The screen had not changed, and the sound was nearly gone.

Early in July, in his old room in Berlin, Ramsay opened the letters that had been kept for his return. There was a letter from Katharine, written at the end of May, that must have arrived the day he departed for Switzerland. The great conductor's widow wrote that now the rain had stopped. She had seen young Italians in spotless shirts hanging about waiting for the cinemas to open—their Sundays were sad. On the promenades, by the lake, in the towns, couples are strolling. The sky changes color; the girls' white skirts are flattened against their legs. The lake is harsh-looking. The wind shakes the trees. Flower petals are strewn on the grass, and it is like the end of a season instead of the beginning. This was a letter written before she had ever met him. He felt buoyant and lightheaded tearing it to shreds. He was amazed at how simple it became. He was not sure if he had left Sabine, for example, or if she had rejected him. She had said, "Oh, I like you, but now is enough," spitting grape seed into her palm; but Ramsay had his ticket to Switzerland, bought that very day. What his father would like would be to start again, to arrive at Bonaventure, but how can he? The station is no longer there. "Lamb of God, Sheep of God," sings a woman, and the Sally Ann band is nearby. Very attractive, very nostalgic, he said to the remains of Katharine's letter, but what about the *pension* and the smell of mediocrity? What about your cook in the kitchen, with frightened eyes? We drove slowly, crawling, because Katharine had seen a white orchis somewhere. Did anyone dare say this was a waste of time? The orchis was a straggly poor thing with sparse anemic flowers . . . Surely he had passed a test safely and shown he was immune to the inherited blight?

Only afterward did he think that he might be mistaken, but that day, the day he arrived in Berlin, he was triumphant because he sat with his back to the window and did not know or care what the weather was like outside.

THE CIRCUS

UNLIKE its posters, which had promised a fight between a crocodile and a leopard, the circus, when it came to the village, had no animals save a few starving dogs. At the last minute, in time for the performance, a van that had been held up at Port Bou, on the frontier, arrived with a lion. Among the artistes were a clown, a stout woman who sang and danced, and a girl who climbed a rope and hung limply as if she did not know what to do next. The tourists and the summer people had the best seats in the tent; the villagers, chattering in Catalan, were perched on narrow benches high up and well behind the rest. Their faces in the weak, unsteady light were daubs of ivory paint.

Instead of watching the girl and the rope, Laurie looked back at them. "That would be something to paint," he said to his mother.

"Oh, Laurie, don't go around saying everything is something to paint. No one will ever take you seriously." He understood she might be afraid he would talk too much, like his father. The clicking of fans from the villagers' benches sounded like hail and nearly put him to sleep. The tourists clapped for the girl, who had finally come down to earth, but the Catalans felt she had not done enough, had not risked her life, and they shouted insults. The clown, who came next, rode his bicycle under an avalanche of scorn. Laurie hoped he would get down from the bicycle and walk away, but he carried on as if to applause. It reminded the boy of something he could not put a name to. He shut his eyes and tried to memorize the shapes of shadows, the ivory faces.

His mother did not laugh once, not even when the stout woman danced the Twist a few feet away from the lion. They were here at the circus because the money had come. They lived for the post that brought

the money, but as soon as it arrived, Ralph, Laurie's father, began seeing how it could be spent. It seemed to worry Ralph when there was
money; money was like a strange animal that had to be chased from
the house. He would pay a few of the debts in the village, at least in
part. He never cleared up a debt. Laurie's mother said it was like stopping a leak with putty. Sometimes less than a week after the money
had come the mother had to start asking for credit again, and watching
to see if the grocer and the charcoal vender were writing down the
correct amount in their books. After the money had gone, the father
would curse the village. He was stranded; he was enslaved by merchants
and shopkeepers; he would never get away. But when the money was
there and they could have got away, he spent it in the bar, and on
strangers, and on outings like the circus.

The mother sat, saying nothing, with a sleeping baby on her lap.
Ralph was talking to a stranger. He ignored her, disowning his family,
as he often did before people he did not know. He was deep in conversation with a grave elderly man wearing a dark suit. The man had put
on a suit to come to the circus on a stifling night, as though he were
attending a play or a concert in a large town.

The stranger said seriously, "It must be the last circus of its kind.
Look at the clown. He had real bones tied to his ears."

"I'm the last of my kind, too," said Ralph, laughing loudly. He was
always friendly, at first.

When they stood up to leave, the elderly man understood that Ralph
belonged with these three—the woman, the baby, and the boy. Ralph
stretched his arms. He was huge. He looked as if he could crush the
stranger with one blow of the hand.

"... married," Laurie heard the stranger say, as they filed out. Ralph
was greeting the villagers, kissing the old women and thumping the
men on the shoulders. He thought they loved him, because they laughed
and smiled; it seemed more important to him to be loved by foreign
peasants and fishermen than by his own family. Laurie, who played
with the village children, understood that there was a mockery in their
acceptance of Ralph, but it was not entirely clear to him and he could
not have put it in words. The clock on the village square gave the hour
as twenty past one, which meant it was even later. They followed Ralph,

headed toward the bar. He had not yet told them to get away from him, to go home and go to bed.

"Of course I'm married," said Ralph pleasantly. "I wouldn't live without a wife. I've had three, but this one is the best. I'd be a sodden, raddled, alcoholic wreck if I hadn't married Chris. Ask her. She'll tell you." The sarcasm was not for the stranger but for the family straggling behind, within earshot. Still charming, he introduced himself, put out his hand. He spoke his own name clearly—Ralph Jennings—and he waited for the other to show he had heard the name before. When there was no recognition, he shrugged. Never mind, he seemed to be telling himself.

"Hare," said the man. He announced it in a sharp way, as if he were really saying "here," to be followed by "sir," as Laurie had been made to speak at his old school, before they came to live in Spain. Ralph strode with his hands in his pockets. The man named Hare walked smartly at his side, keeping up with neat, even steps. Laurie and his mother fell back, and she said, "That's an Army walk, Laurie. He looks as though he'd always worn proper clothes in a hot climate to set an example, doesn't he?"

"Is that a good thing?" said Laurie, pretty certain that Ralph would have said it was not. He minded being back here with his mother and the baby. He would rather have been with the men.

Ralph sat down at a table in the bar and immediately seemed to be filling the room. Hare stood, waiting for Chris and the children. He held her chair. "I don't know about this modern stuff," he said to Ralph. "I saw some of Francis Bacon's pictures in the Sunday *Times*. To tell you the truth, I wouldn't have given a shilling for the lot."

"Have you ever given a shilling for any painting of any kind?" said Ralph. "If you have, it almost gives you the right to have an opinion."

He sounded violent, but Laurie sensed it was still all right. The proprietor of this bar knew that the money had come. He laughed, and shook hands, and brought a bottle of Fundador and four glasses to their table. He accepted Ralph's invitation to have a glass with them, and he left the bottle there. The mother called after him: Laurie would have a grenadine-and-soda, please. Calling, turning her head, she had drawn Ralph's attention. He sat back and stared, as if he had not noticed her until now. He was sick that Hare had not recognized his name, even though Hare knew about Francis Bacon only because he had seen him in the Sunday *Times*.

"What the bloody hell kind of top are you wearing?" he said to his wife.

She had made a blouse with two cotton scarves. The ends were tied round her neck and under her breasts. Her arms were bare. "It's new," she said, as confidently as if she were sure of praise.

"It is most attractive," said Hare.

"Who do you dress for here, anyway?" said Ralph. "The summer lot? Do you want the beach queers to say 'Darling, you look ravishing'?"

Laurie put his head down on the edge of the table and watched the grenadine curling in soda water like red mist. She never defended herself. It was maddening; it made him want to join the attack. Presently he felt his mother stroking his hair. It was an absentminded gesture. She was thinking of something else.

"I wish I had married," Laurie heard. "But, you see, seventeen years in the Singapore police . . . and we had ideals. Fifteen bachelors we were, all in our thirties, and none of us ever had a mistress. You see, it was all an ideal."

"Christ."

"Then I was sorry I hadn't married, but it was too late. I felt stranded. I can't think of another word. It was like being left behind. I knew it was too late. There was a nurse, an Army nurse, but I never dared ask. She would have refused."

Laurie moved his head, and his mother's hand slid away. He sat up, blinking, and was astonished to see the stranger more excited, more talkative even than Ralph.

"It must be hard to feel stranded," said Laurie's mother.

"Yes, we can't imagine that, can we?" said Ralph, looking at her with hate.

"I felt that if a woman came to me she would be giving up something more important than I could replace," said Hare. "How would you feel if someone took your wife away from you?"

"If someone did *what?* Why? Do you want her?"

"Don't," said his wife, and she looked at the other man, but he must have misunderstood her look, for he went on, making it worse: "A woman with a sense of duty."

"She's got that, all right. Would you go with him, Chris? Let's hear about your sense of duty. Would you go off with our new friend Hare if he asked you?"

"If he asked me to," she said, making a statement to herself. "If he asked me? I don't know."

Ralph put his great hands flat on the table, pushing glasses every way. He said, "Would you consider it? Would you think of going away?"

"If I went, I'd be going away," she said. She sounded reasonable.

"You wouldn't leave the children." Suddenly realizing that of course she would not, he cried, "I wouldn't give them to you! Try taking them. Just try!"

The stranger looked at her with fear and wonder, because she had not said no. He spoke as if out of a dream: "Would you leave? Would you come away if it meant giving up your children?"

"It's hard to say," said the mother. "I might. There's no telling."

"Could you do that?" said Hare, marveling.

"I've never had to decide."

Laurie said, "I don't feel well."

His mother did not move or speak or feel his forehead.

"The boy's ill," said Ralph. He looked at his wife and said, "Take me home."

Ralph was hurt; he said they had hurt him, all of them. Walking home, he held Laurie's hand, although Laurie was too old for that. Hare had gone down to the beach to see the sun rise. The sky was lightening, as if drawing away. Laurie had sometimes frightened himself with two ideas: his mother might take him away from Ralph (where to?) or else she never would. He had never supposed she could go away alone. She walked in silence, as she always did, but now it was the father and Laurie who lagged behind. She led the way home. Tears rolled down Ralph's cheeks. He said now that he was hurt because she had not liked the circus. What about the old lion who blinked and put out a paw? What about the clown?

"It was the last circus in the world," he said. "We shall never see anything like it again."

She had said she might go—at least that she could consider it—but she was still here. She was here, shifting the weight of the baby so that she could get the door key out of her purse and let them into the house.

"It was the last of its kind," said Ralph, who really seemed to have nothing but this to feel sorry about. "We shall never see anything like it again."

Laurie, who was watching his mother, squeezed his hand. "Please stop saying it," he said.

A QUESTION OF DISPOSAL

BELIEVING that she was dying, and certain she would die before the end of the year, Mrs. Glover told her son, Digby, to choose the place they—she and Digby and Janet, his fiancée—would go to for their holiday in June. Digby's and Janet's vacation problems were beyond her now; they would have to begin making plans of their own.

But all the decisions of Digby's life, save one, had been made by his mother. Greatly dismayed by the prospect of freedom, the cause of which he had not been informed, he carried a number of Royal Automobile Club maps into his mother's sitting room and spread them on the floor. Crouching, he stared at the black tracings—the winding highways, the names of strange towns. Here there would be mountains, he said to himself, and that was certainly the sea. It seemed to him that he and his mother and Janet had been to every possible country, and had started over from the beginning years before. His hands, shuffling the maps, were aimless and weather-burned; his shrug had something of the adolescent's "Leave me alone." Digby was thirty-four.

"There," he said, having made, he thought, a picture of Western Europe, with most of the pieces in place. He looked up, smiling, with one hand over Spain. He held a cigarette in the other hand, and tried to be careful about the ash; but he was not careful enough, and his mother watched without saying anything as it lengthened and fell.

Because Mrs. Glover never quite asked for anything she wanted, or said plainly what she would like, Digby could not know now that she did not wish to go abroad at all. If this was to be her last June, as the doctors had said it might be, she wanted to spend it in London, listing the furniture and the linen and preparing instructions about the change from summer to winter curtains. He felt the weight of an unexplained silence, and supposed that even though he had said nothing except "There," it had probably been the wrong thing. He returned his attention to the floor and its terrible possibilities. He could not understand these maps, which were so simple when he was driving somewhere and had been told where to go, and so muddy when they presented a conundrum, as they did today. He rocked on his toes, whistled, shifted his hand, saw where it had been resting. He said he expected they could go to Spain.

"You and Janet met in Spain," said Mrs. Glover. "Is that why you want to go back there now?"

Digby had forgotten about having ever met her anywhere. He did not say so. He could not always tell where his mother was leading him, and had learned to take care.

"Oh, Janet," he said; or it may have been "*Old* Janet." The tone suggested the second.

Looking down on Digby, Mrs. Glover remembered her death, with the satisfaction of someone whose mouth is obstinately closed on a secret. She knew that everyone, including old Janet, would be shocked and astonished when they heard of her long, concealed decline. She knew they would say that her death was a blessing for Digby and a release. Without his mother to thwart him, Digby would do whatever he liked. But Digby did not want to do anything. Crouched at his mother's feet, he seemed to her as incapable of deciding anything as the day he was born. Murmuring over his maps, burning holes in the carpet, he represented not so much a piece of her heart as one of her last commissions on earth. Mrs. Glover had lived for many years as though expecting to be run over by a bus; her affairs were in order. She believed she could have died in a minute, without a word of complaint, had there not remained two questions of disposal. One was this house in London, which she cherished; the other was Digby, her bachelor son.

The disposal of Digby caused her anxiety, but the fate of the house caused her pain. Digby, though puzzled, would not mourn her long. He would continue driving about in hairy pullovers and gym shoes, and reading publications about motoring, and he would go on contributing to one of them—mostly paragraphs about restaurants in which he had luckily not been swindled. He would say that his mother had gone to a better place, and that he was bound to turn up there, too, eventually. That was the total Digby, in his mother's eyes, except for one unexplained action. One night, seven years ago, in a village in Spain, Digby had become engaged to healthy Janet Crawley, who, with three other girls from her office, was staying at the Glovers' hotel. For a time, Mrs. Glover had feared he might actually marry Janet. She had no great fear of losing Digby but did not want to acquire Janet as well. She had feared he might marry Janet; now that she knew she was dying, she feared he never would.

Digby must marry Janet for the sake of the house. It was a narrow, three-storied house, to which she had given all the obsessive passion she had once felt for India. A perfectionist, she could not really love a human being. Human beings were imperfect, and resisted her. Something in the nature of people—even Digby's nature—said "Hands off." India had been a vast idea, and Indians dying were poetic; but then they tried to trade mystery for politics, and lost Mrs. Glover. But the house was herself. It had not opposed her, and was unlikely to disappoint her or develop a will of its own. She had it on a ninety-five-year leasehold, which was certainly longer than one could ever expect to keep a husband or a son. The lease would not expire until 2032; Digby would fill at least thirty years of the span—forty, if Janet looked after him—and then, unless poor Janet had waited too long to marry, there would be heirs. Until 2032, then, the house must stand. Mrs. Glover's shade would be there, but she could not depend on its powers. Her husband had died, her friends had vanished; she doubted the powers of ghosts.

Digby, still breathing heavily and talking to himself, traced the eastern coast of Spain with his thumb. "We could go where we went that other time," he said, pursuing his bright idea. "Where I met Janet, as you say."

"Did you like Spain?"

"You don't have to like a place just because you go there for holidays," he said.

"Tell me something else then. Think before you answer. Do you like this room?"

Digby looked around him and said, "It's not bad, but all that pale stuff gets dirty."

"What about Janet? Has Janet ever said anything about the room?"

"I don't know. She asked me if all the stuff was ours, once. I mean from our people. I told her no, from antique places and auctions. I told her it was something like Georgian and French. I suppose that was right."

"Would Janet mind about its being so pale if she lived here?"

"Janet probably has things fixed the way she wants them at home," he said reasonably. "Tell me if it's all right about Spain. I've got to fix it up with old Janet and fix up the tickets and all that."

It was Mrs. Glover's habit to allow Digby the last word. Looking contented—for he had silenced her, he thought—he rolled his maps and slid them into containers. She wondered what he would say if she were to tell him this was to be her last June, and consequently their last journey abroad. She had refused the operation the doctor had offered; it seemed to her that Digby should know without having been told. But, as always, Digby was unable to see into her mind. He might not have believed what he saw; he might have supposed, with reason, that anyone able to dwell on her own death with so much distance could not believe in it either. In truth, Mrs. Glover realized that she had not yet understood, and she did not believe for a moment that she would not be here, a year later, saying, "That was my last spring."

Toward the middle of June, when Janet's annual holiday began, Janet and Digby and Mrs. Glover flew from London to Barcelona. At Barcelona they crossed the city by taxi and got into a bus. Janet enthusiastically recognized it as the bus she had taken on her last trip to Spain, seven years before. Mrs. Glover could not remember anything about it. During the bus drive—ninety miles—Digby sat by himself. He believed himself to be desperately sick in anything moving unless he was at the wheel, and in the course of their long engagement Janet had learned not to argue. She sat beside Mrs. Glover and watched the backs of Digby's ears turn dead white. He would not take anything for his indisposition, would not even eat less than usual before a trip. He refused to roll down the window so as to have a little air. He told the two women to let him alone.

Janet plainly was feeling a little squeamish herself after the bumpy air trip, but she kept up a conversation with Mrs. Glover about the cycles of life. She was accustomed to thinking of older parties first, and feared that if she sat there saying nothing Mrs. Glover would think her impolite.

"Every seven years a new cycle of life begins," said Janet, talking with the clarity of extreme nausea. "It is exactly seven years since you and Digby and the girls and I all met in Spain."

"Digby is being sick," said Mrs. Glover.

They finished the journey in the last hour of the blazing afternoon. The heat inside the bus was stifling; the countryside was as unwelcoming as Mrs. Glover remembered it. At the hotel, they parted with the speechless animosity of people who have traveled badly.

When they all three met again for dinner, Janet carried an angora stole. She declared the holiday officially open. "Oh, lovely," she said, of nothing at all. Their table in the dark dining room had been spread with perspiring tomatoes and garlic sausages. There was a bottle of brackish water, and a lump of bread apiece. Janet smiled and sat down and said, "Yes, every seven years. Digby darling, take that little bit of pepper out of the sausage, it will give you the most frightful tummy ache, especially after what happened this afternoon on the bus. When I was seven, or something *like* seven, Hitler came to power. Digby was nearly seven when his father died."

"Why doesn't he bring us some wine?" said Digby, looking round.

"Don't bother," said Janet. "I'll catch his eye. When I was fourteen—another seven years, you see—I was confirmed. By a coincidence, that was the year the war broke out. There he is . . . *Vino, camarero, por favor.* Digby, I don't mind drinking that water, and I believe in drinking the water of a country, and smoking the cigarettes of a country, but I imagine your mother might want something better."

Mrs. Glover could not have said just what she had been doing here seven years before. She and Digby had come into a valley, she remembered, and seen a village of white paint and stone. There was a fair, and a grove of chestnut trees, and beyond that the umbrella pines that told them they were nearing the sea. They had driven from the treeless interior, and because of the trees and the anticipation of the sea Mrs. Glover had told Digby to stop. It was too late to drive on to Barcelona that night, she said, and the pleasure of waiting for the sea might be better than the truth of it, which was likely to be dirty and hot. Janet and her three office friends were in the hotel, as if waiting for Digby. They had been victims of a travel-bureau fraud. They had paid for an all-in holiday, had given up their travel allowances, and *look* at the place! Disaster made them bold enough to speak; Digby was tall and English and competent-looking. The four girls fell on his neck.

"... life," Mrs. Glover suddenly heard. "At twenty-one," said Janet, tearing bread, "I had a tragic experience."

They knew. Her first lover, recovering from a broken ankle, developed pneumonia and died in a day. Seven years later, still inconsolable because unclaimed, she met the Glovers here.

"And now we are all back again, and nothing has changed," said Janet, with a fall in her voice, as if the subject had finally ended. "Nothing has changed. That's what I mean to say about life."

Nothing had changed except Janet, Mrs. Glover thought. The dining room was unquestionably as it had been, and Digby was much as ever; he still fancied himself a sporting figure, in his Tyrolean pullovers. As for Mrs. Glover, her passion for furniture and arranging rooms had led her to resemble a piece of furniture—but had she not always? There were photographs of her taken thirty years before that a clever caricaturist could have turned into something stiff and unremarkable—a Parigiano ballroom chair.

"There is a fair, Digby," said Janet. "I saw it when we were coming into the village this afternoon. I think we might go and look at it."

Janet has changed, Mrs. Glover thought. She is the only one of us who has become someone else.

At twenty-eight, Janet had worshipped Digby across the table with a look that must have been, for him, a new kind of mirror. He stared back at this image, gave orders, and began showing off. Janet could stammer out only the barest facts about herself. She lived with her parents, who were vegetarians. Her father had been a clerk with a shipping line out in India. She had a job; she was not a typist or a secretary but something more important. She really ought to have been farther along than she was, she had told them, blushing steamily, but in her field all the opportunities went to men. To Mrs. Glover, who knew little about jobs of any kind, it sounded astonishing, gritty, and rather hot. She changed the topic and said that Digby, too, had been in India as a child.

"Ah, no, not really?" cried Janet, clasping her hands. Wasn't the world small? You met someone in Spain, in a forsaken village, and discovered you were both in India at the same time. Digby looked modest and felt praised. But Janet became silent when told that Digby's father had not been with the Army, or Shell, or anything like that, but had gone out there with his wife and son because he liked it. Liked doing what? said Janet. Why, nothing, Mrs. Glover said. They liked India; that was all.

Well, Janet had heard some funny things in her life, as they were often to hear her say, but when she heard about Digby's father and mother in India for no reason to speak of, she pursed her lips as if to whistle. It *was* odd. The three girls from Janet's office seemed to agree with her. They glanced at Digby's hands to see if he hadn't a touch of colored blood. Digby at that instant looked questioning, blunt, and plain, as if the most innocent elements of parental behavior had always been a mystery to him, too. To Digby, none of the reasons for choosing mattered; he had never heard of freedom. His mother had taken India up and put it down. She admired India, and then it fell from her personal tree and smashed to bits. Digby didn't care. What he wondered now was, what made people go to hot, dangerous places? Why should his father have died in Madras, where there was cholera, instead of dying in England, of some homely ailment, on a moist afternoon? Janet's expression gave the question form. That night, under the chestnut trees next to a fairground, Digby and Janet became engaged.

The morning after the engagement, Janet took Mrs. Glover for a walk and showed her the place where she and Digby had been sitting. She indicated a rock, but Mrs. Glover looked at the flattened grass beside it. "You had a pretty view," she said, pointing to the pine trees on the opposite bank. But Janet had lost her blush.

The mystery to Mrs. Glover was that Digby had ever got as far as that; he was such an uninspired boy. She wondered if he had followed seduction with remorse, and asked Janet to marry him on that account.

In any event, he had got no farther. Janet had brought to life, with one unbelieving expression, part of a total secret he had been wondering about for years, but he had no more questions to put; there was nothing for Janet to answer. They had never married. He lived at home with his mother, and Janet had her absorbing job. Except for one three-week holiday every summer, he and Janet seldom saw each other alone. There was no other way, was there? Not short of marriage. Janet lived with her family, Digby's mother seldom dined out, and women like Janet do not make love in doorways. It seemed to Mrs. Glover, at times, that Digby had a wife in London and that Janet was a girl he took abroad.

Actually, with her clamp hold on three weeks of his life every year, Janet was about as wifelike as anything Digby had imagined. One year, having become dazzled by another girl, a jolly girl who drove an Aston Martin, he tried to put off taking Janet abroad; he hinted. Janet instantly vanished from his life, and returned his ring by registered post. It was a small diamond-and-turquoise ring that had belonged to Mrs. Glover's girlhood, and she was pleased to see it again; all the same, she urged a reconciliation. She was quite certain that Janet and Digby would never marry, while the Aston Martin girl was far too lively to keep, and might be noisy about the house.

"You'd better ring Janet up, Digby," she had said.

"She doesn't expect it."

But in the end he gave in, his mother invented such a moving picture of Janet, puffy and swollen-eyed, not too far from the telephone, not too near: Janet, who had given him the best of her life, starting with twenty-eight. She described, so that it was too real to bear, Janet's mother washing the leaves of the plants with weak tea, while the father constructed a ship in a bottle. It was enough to get Digby to the telephone and urge Janet to come out of there, if only for an evening. Actually, he knew it wasn't as bad as all that; not entirely. The Crawleys lived in Putney, and ate rice, and had a garden and quite a lot of Oriental brass.

"I suppose," said Janet, with slightly more tension this time, "we might as well go to the fair." She looked meaningfully at Digby; he ought to be helping his poor old mother up the stairs, and suggesting tactfully that she go to bed. He did nothing of the kind. He sent a waiter for his mother's wrap, and they all three set out together, as they had often done the summer of the engagement.

"It's quite a climb," said Digby, looking up at the slope and the chestnut trees and the rising lights of the fair.

"What an extraordinary moon," said Janet. "You can see everything."

Mrs. Glover, possessed by pain that was now silvery and quick, now black and square, said, "Nonsense, Digby, it's no climb at all . . . Yes, Janet, that is a full moon." On this hill, Digby had proposed to Janet. The lovers passed the place without remembering it, but Mrs. Glover hesitated and saw the rock and remembered the grass. "But where are the pines?" she said. "Those beautiful pine trees." There was no answer; the others had gone on.

Upon a raised platform, couples from the village shuffled and stared. The orchestra consisted of one accordion, one drummer, one horn. Nearby was a life-size cardboard bull, before which one could be photographed. "Fancy," said Janet vaguely, as if she were trying to see herself and Digby and Mrs. Glover having their picture taken with the bull. Mrs. Glover imagined it clearly, and walked on. "Be careful, you two," said Janet, for her attention was held by the booths and the dancers, and she feared that the Glovers, without her constant solicitude, might come to grief.

Digby was increasingly fretful. In India, when he had been a funny, jaundiced-looking little boy, his mother had taken him to a fair in the hills where jewels were piled in sea shells; there had been shells of sapphires and emeralds and a large shell full of pearls. One pearl was like the moon. "I want that one," Digby said, and she had replied, "You shall have it," meaning that one got what one wanted out of life.

"Take care, you two," came Janet's voice. She had stopped now to examine the treasures offered in a stall—paperweight guitars, and sombrero ashtrays. She looked gravely at them, considering. Digby wore an expression Mrs. Glover remembered from his childhood. It meant "I am going to be very naughty now." Poor boy, thought Mrs. Glover, and she took his arm. I never understood that you meant what you said about the pearl, and I never said what I meant; is it any wonder you have grown puzzled?... She might have told him, "Digby, they say I am dying, and you must marry Janet for the sake of the house," and that would have been saying what she meant, for once, but just then she heard him mutter that it had been a mistake, coming here.

"You're tired," he said.

"I'm not!"

"Well, you're not enjoying it."

"Perhaps Janet is." She looked around, but Janet was lost. "Digby," she said, "see if you can find Janet. I shall be there," she said, pointing, "you see, between the fairground and those pine trees." For that hadn't been the rock, of course; she had been mistaken. The proposal had taken place on this side of the fairground. "I shall sit down on the first rock I come to, and I shall wait. Bring Janet when you find her, and we can all go back. I don't think we're liking Spain."

"You might be cold," he protested. Had he always been this concerned? She sat down, after he had left her, not far from the place where Janet had held out her hand and said "Digby asked me to marry him there." The fair and the chestnut trees were behind her; the pine trees held out their weighted branches on the opposite slope. They no longer gave their promise of the sea. She saw them in the summer moonlight, stripped to the bark, hung with thousands, no, millions, of white cocoons. There, she thought, as if it had never occurred to her until now; everything dies.

That night she dreamed the dream that was becoming a common landscape now. It was a long Galsworthy- or Walpole-like family tale, in which Mrs. Glover was not herself at all but a thin, dark-haired girl named Amabel. As Amabel, she journeyed with a young mother, four or five sisters, a governess, and a butler to spend long, sunny holidays beside the sea. She saw the bright rooms of the house, breathed the sea air, touched cups and curtains sticky with it, shook jellyfish out of her bathing costume, saw the morning sun in squares on the bedroom walls, smelled her dream sisters' salty young hair on the pillows. And she knew, waking, that she was being drugged and softened and prepared by this dream so that she would go, without fighting, into oblivion, and she knew that, one night, on a journey as Amabel, with the mother and the pastel sisters and a charming young butler, she would die in her sleep.

Ah, but she had no desire to die that way; not, at least, until she was forearmed. The pleasure of the repeated dream must be stopped; for supposing she did dissolve into Amabel, and then from Amabel into someone else? She would no longer remember the worry of having once been Mrs. Glover, but that still left Digby and the unsolved problem of the house. Those promises from beyond the grave, she thought, the world was full of them: small, tinny reverberations, the only immortality one could trust.

When she descended in the morning, she found Janet in the dining room. Janet said she had hardly slept a wink. She was hot-eyed but calm. Digby had not returned to her at the fair. He had vanished among the dancers. Janet had finally come home alone, and then sat and waited in her room, where she had eventually fallen asleep in a chair. Now she had been sitting hours in the hot, fly-buzzing dining room, drinking foul coffee and making inquiries. She learned that Digby had come in at four o'clock this morning dragging a cardboard bull. The bull was there, behind them; the waiters pointed to it. Instead of looking, Janet took on the high voice of command and ordered Mrs. Glover's breakfast. Protein makes up for lost sleep; she sent up a second breakfast for Digby, with plenty of bacon and a soft-boiled egg.

"Janet, my dear, I'm afraid I lost you, too. I spent some time looking for the pine trees, and then when I saw them they were dead."

"I know," said Janet. "I saw them, too." She leaned her head against her hand, in a pose of classical melancholy. She said, in a tired voice, "They are something called processional caterpillars. They kill everything, but I don't believe they ever become anything much—just a little browny sort of moth. I have to know a little bit about that. You know, it's my job." As though something of the most excruciating intimacy had been said, she turned red—the blush she had lost with her long engagement.

No, Mrs. Glover did not know; but she knew there is control from beyond the grave, if one is careful to establish it in time. Janet must marry Digby because Digby was unfit to stay alone, and because Janet must learn to take care of the house, the pictures, the rugs, the tables, the knives and the forks, the glasses and chairs. Mrs. Glover's unwelcome death must be provided for; Janet must be given time to learn.

"Digby is restless," said Mrs. Glover.

This was the first time they had ever mentioned Digby in his absence, and Janet sat quite still. She looked at the stains on the tablecloth and the flies devouring crumbs. She said, "I'm devoted to Digby, of course."

"Devoted" was as much as Mrs. Glover was likely to get. Janet might adore her own mother, or a fine day, or a pretty tune, but she would never be more than devoted to a lover. Mrs. Glover understood it, and was grateful. Understatement made it possible to be both sensible and cruel, and since living often obliged one to be both, it gave the assurance that no one would be harmed too deeply. She was grateful to Janet for being devoted and nothing more.

"I am devoted to Digby," Janet went on, playing with crumbs, "but last night has changed things. If he's going to be that sort, coming in drunk and that, I don't want him."

Mrs. Glover wasted no time thinking this was not true. She saw the tight lines around Janet's mouth; the wretched woman was hopelessly moral where marriage was concerned. She would trail on in an endless engagement as long as Digby wanted, probably accepting some peevish story of mother love, only man of the family, mother would perish; but she would not marry a man who could desert his mother and his betrothed at a public fair in a foreign country and come in at four o'clock in the morning with a cardboard bull. That was the lucky thing about a long engagement, she could almost hear Janet say—it gave you time to find every possibility out.

"Digby is slightly restless, and marriage would settle him," said Mrs. Glover, pitying Digby, who now joined the company of men whose fate had been settled by a pair of women over empty cups.

"It's changed things," said Janet again. "I shall have to think about it now."

"Perhaps there isn't much time," said Mrs. Glover.

"Oh, there's plenty of that," said Janet sadly, as though nothing but time were left.

VACANCES PAX

MIDSUMMER night has always been a pagan festival, and the Christians did not change its nature by naming the day for St. John the Baptist. In Scandinavian countries the sun does not set and people behave immorally. In villages in France and Germany, the same pagan fires are still burned, but they are called "*les feux de la St.-Jean*" or "*Johannisfeuer*," and engaged couples jump over the embers hand in hand and are blessed by the priest.

According to tradition as well as that year's lunar calendar, the twenty-fourth of June should have been dry and clear but turned out to be steamy and hot. Stuart Fenwick had persuaded a tall fat girl named Valerie to come and see the trench where he had planted peanuts. (It took Fenwick to consider this a form of courtship.) Valerie walked before him, on the trodden path between holiday bungalows. She had what seemed to his besotted eyes a Tudor bearing, and was majestic in flowered slacks. She carried a dirty fine-toothed comb.

Two and even three times a day, sitting cross-legged on a plastic raincoat on a terrace she thought was private, she clutched strands of ginger hair with her left hand and combed the wrong way, from the ends to the roots. A matchbox transistor strapped to her wrist relayed Radio Monte-Carlo close to her ear as she combed. Fenwick imagined the horrible music as a sort of elastic, now plump, now taut. He was supposed to be going about his business, which was the running of a holiday colony called Vacances Pax, but he parted the cypress hedge to look down on the combing without guilt or haste. It seemed to him a gentle and virginal rite, like weaving. When Valerie gathered the locks that framed her brow, made a fan of them, and placed them tenderly over the rest, allowing no stragglers, no nonsense, it was the final gesture, like biting off a thread.

The vacation colony was a collection of little prefab bungalows going down the terraced side of an arid Maritime Alp just behind Grasse. It dated from the early nineteen-fifties, when the "One Europe" idea had enormous emotional appeal, and it was thought that all national differences would be dispersed and all prejudices effaced if a few people believing this could be so were to spend their holidays together, talking and exchanging ideas and being decent and kind. Every bungalow flew a different flag, and meals were taken together—the whole colony. On fine days they ate out-of-doors, and when it rained too hard for the cane trellis and grapevines that were supposed to protect them, they moved into a large bare bungalow used constantly in the old days for meetings and discussions—now only sometimes, if a vacationer wanted to show slides or his own movies. It was a long way from the kitchen, and there were many days of rain.

It had not been easy to get Valerie to come and look at the peanut trench. She was down here in the South of France to rest and recover from an appendectomy—so she said. Far from being the one never to ask questions, Fenwick asked a great many. Her Tudor headdress covered fragile or perhaps selective eardrums. She took no notice of his questions.

"Now, that is interesting." She meant a drum-shaped yellow metal box, bearing KLM tags and PERISHABLE—KEEP COOL in large letters. Several of the Dutch members of the vacation colony were standing in a circle around it. The drum contained herring, which, all chipping in, they had ordered from home as a treat. Whoever brought it here had deposited it in the middle of greenery that he perhaps took to be weeds but that happened to be Fenwick's moss campion, transplanted with devotion from Alpine distance. They were all included—the Dutch, and Fenwick, and Valerie, and Tom Waterford, who had strolled up after them.

"You'll want a tin opener, to start with," Fenwick said.

It turned out that somebody had one. Until now, they had simply been admiring the box. No one was pushy; no one wanted to be first.

Valerie gave the youngest adult a grave nod, as if to say, "I understand and approve." This man, wearing a neat mustache, and with a shirt lightly laid over his sunburn, then crouched down with the tin opener and in a minute bent back the lid. From the metal drum the smell of fish spread out in widening rings.

"Ah, herring," he said, and sighed, and they all looked with solemn pleasure at the dark brine.

"Now, that *is* interesting," said Valerie, perhaps to Fenwick. "Because every herring is the same size, and I think there must be layers."

"A plank!" said the man who had done the opening. He should have been a naval officer. Instead, he was dedicated, by his own choice, to Shell Oil for ever and ever. He eyed Valerie, but received no more encouragement. She had already told Fenwick she came abroad to be not entertained but informed, and Fenwick was beginning to see what she meant. A four-year-old boy ran and fetched the wrong thing, but finally a large, clean plank was found. The man with Shell Oil, whom Fenwick now hated (he also hated the shape of the drum, thinking Valerie might compare it with his), cleaned several of the fish and cut them into fillets. The first went to a little girl. She tipped back her head, held the fillet between two fingers, and swallowed like a seal. Then everyone had some, as fast as the young man could clean them. Presently, their tongues swollen and thick, the Dutch members apologized to Valerie—the herring was too green. They fetched thick slices of fresh bread from the kitchen and made sandwiches, and when that palled, they cut up onions and added those to the bread. At half past twelve, when the gong sounded, the drum was nearly empty, ants were forming battalions to carry off the debris, and the Dutch dispersed to get ready for lunch.

The extraordinary thing was, to Fenwick, that they would eat; they would all of them eat as if they had never seen food in their lives. They came here because it was cheap, because they went everywhere, and they came with no provision for their ferocious sunburns. Their presence in great numbers meant a large meal at noon with boiled potatoes. Afterward, they would drink coffee with milk. No good cook would stay. Fenwick should have presided over this meal, if only to register the complaints, but there were days when he could not watch one more fork break open one more potato, or see how the men loosened their belts or pushed back from the table with a groan. Valerie, reduced to one meal a day because of her figure, accepted the tribute of a sandwich without onions and walked on, Fenwick after her. He had never had Valerie alone, free of Shell Oil, or Tom Waterford, or the children who placed an ear to the wristwatch radio, their faces rapt.

"In the old days," he said, desiring not only her company but her attention, "Vacances Pax was a noble try. One Europe, no frontiers." He was sorry he had started this; it made him sound ancient. What if he were to say to that tower of red hair, "This is the twenty-fourth of June, and tonight I am going to build a bonfire"? Then, to see if she was listening, "And burn Tom Waterford as an offering to the gods." No, she might choose that moment to hear, and then tell it. They plodded on, slightly out of breath because they were going uphill.

"Do you know what I think?" said Valerie, stopping and stunning him with her full consideration and her soft brown eyes. "I think it was kind of those people to share their fish with us. I can think of a lot of English who wouldn't share"—she hesitated as if consulting a guide for some national dish—"their chocolates."

"You would, though," he said dotingly.

"I never eat anything fattening," she said, with regret, and there was nothing to do but walk on, for he could not see how to move on through this conversation, which seemed enclosed by some special Valerie-minded fence. To court a woman properly, you had to understand not only her feelings, which were less tender than he had been led to think in his youth, but also her mind. Speculations about Valerie's mind occupied him agreeably until they climbed the last steep path and stood before the peanut trench. From below, a man's voice said, "I think I'll skip lunch," and then a crystalline female English voice said, "It's filthy." It sounded like Tom Waterford's wife. Valerie had reached the edge of the trench and was gazing down, waiting to be informed. Fenwick took a step nearer. He began to speak distinctly but with haste, for one of the things he did not know about Valerie's mind was its limit of concentration. "First I had the idea," Fenwick said, "and then, you see, I just started to dig the trench."

Appearing at the herring festival at the last minute, just before the tin was opened, Tom Waterford was given a sandwich and wandered away.

He was being especially polite, for the day before he had overheard an extremely unpleasant thing said about him and it had changed his feelings toward the Dutch, who until then had seemed so jolly. He, of the light-blue eyes and hair going gray, had heard, "Good-looking in a conventional English way. Yes, they look as if they might be intelligent, but it is only an appearance, almost a joke." This is what he had heard from the next terrace, and of course knew he was not meant to overhear; if his critics were speaking English it was only because it was the common language of this place and season. The cross-section of Europe he and his wife had been promised had turned out to be English-German-Dutch. What an impostor Fenwick was! What a poseur! Of all the false prophets, those who mixed brotherhood and politics were the worst...Waterford was for one or the other, each in its place. Coming here had been an idea of his wife's. They tried something new every year. The "European cross-section" had one thing in common: they were all taking a June holiday to escape the summer rush. That put everyone in one basket. But there was a drawback, for it meant having small children about, under school age—the Waterfords had expected none at all. At times, the place was no better than a public nursery. If Tom hated luncheon it was because of the babies, sitting on their mothers' laps, pawing the food on their mothers' plates. The guests ate at trestle tables—another of Fenwick's ideas. His notions of One Europe all seemed to be connected with food—everyone eating the same thing, everyone chewing. Meg Waterford did not mind the trestle tables; what she minded was the absence of nannies. She did hate chaos so. She could not hide her feelings. When she talked about juvenile delinquency, her face went dry as paper. Everything retreated—all the humanity, all the blood—and only something that looked like paper was left. They ought to be birched, flogged, she said.

"Tell us about your dogs that bite everybody," said one of the children at the lunch table. That had to be translated, of course.

Meg smiled, and repeated with clarity, as if asking directions in a foreign capital, "Our—dogs—bite—strangers."

"But only strangers who come to the back door," finished the child. No one minded translating. Perhaps everyone, even the grown people, wanted to hear it. Another subject they liked was Tom, who was a magistrate and could send people to prison for up to six months. Really, Meg was tired of explaining what it was that a man with no legal training had this power. To say "no knowledge of law," as Fenwick once had, was a bit thick, for being a magistrate implied knowing something; you acquired knowledge with the first case that came before you, and from there on it was common sense.

Tom drew near now, sandwich in hand. He was wearing a red-and-white striped shirt and, she thought, a quite astonishing burgundy scarf. He had said something about driving down to Grasse to get something for the twenty-fourth of June bonfire. Matches? What else could it be? She looked once more at this scarf, and went back to what she was saying. She had never in her life remarked on anyone's clothes. She did not know what her husband owned. From time to time a tie or a handkerchief astonished her, that was all.

Tom heard Meg speaking about "Nennie." It was "Nannie," but that was the way Meg spoke. He always had trouble adjusting his ears to a woman's voice, even his wife's, as if to a dialect. He never had that trouble with men. "How she would slap our hands!" said Meg joyously, and imitated the gesture, saying "Slep, slep." Nannie was an ignorant, an uneducated woman—Meg thought it only fair to describe her entirely—now in retirement. She spent her time making shoetrees and coat hangers for her former charges. "I save up bits of satin and velvet for her," said Meg, with a tight smile.

When Tom was speaking about Meg, he often said, "She's worth ten of me."

"I think I'll skip lunch," he said now.

"I don't blame you," she chanted, loud and icelike. "It's filthy."

Valerie, Tudor-headed, looked down at the peanut trench. In wet ground, ordinary unroasted peanuts (kind bachelor Fenwick explained) would and did produce roots that were a mass of dry threads, and dark-green leaves that spread like clover. If Valerie liked instructive conversation as much as she said she did, Fenwick was serving it up on a plate. He had now given up the hopes and dreams of years ago, he said, and had schemes that he thought of as vengefully selfish—a grapefruit monopoly, for instance, or the first pineapple plantation in Europe, or a thriving market in avocados. His earlier hopes had failed because they had not sprung from a motive sufficiently sordid; venality equals reality. And so now he raised spindly avocado plants to a height of at least sixteen inches before they died.

"One could make a fortune in limes, too," he said. "Limes grown in Europe."

"Money can't buy love," Valerie remarked, quoting her wrist radio. If she was stating a profound conviction, then Fenwick was on the wrong track. Someone—a singer—had got to her first, and told her that love was to be praised and money decried. What if before that she had heard a song called "Love Can't Buy Money"?

He was about to propose it, when Valerie said placidly, "I don't think the food here is filthy. I think there's just too much of it."

Either her mind spread and darted and flew, too fast for him to follow, or it tucked its head under its wing and slept. He told her, nevertheless, how in the old days they had all come here for One Europe and had eaten the hated garlic in a spirit approaching good will. There had been peaceful demonstrations. Once, the French-Italian frontier between Menton and Ventimiglia was left open for a few hours, and the whole Pax colony packed up and drove those bumpy miles in the midget rattly cars people had driven when Valerie was a little girl, with "Holland Believes in Europe" streaming from some, and any number of Scandinavian flags. That demonstration, legendary now, was confirmed in photos Fenwick kept in his bungalow. They showed the customs men grinning and waving while all the French sped into Italy to load up on cheap petrol and the Italians swarmed the other way, to get at Fenwick knew not what—perfume and bananas, it turned out. Nobody believed in anything now, he said. The poxplague of Mediterranean restaurants had their food sent, frozen, from distant parts. You could buy the same salad bowl from San Remo to Marseille. Fenwick received all-Europe products, such as washing powder, with instructions in four languages, and in each of the four languages there would be mistakes in spelling and grammar. They held the universe lightly; it was not Fenwick's fault.

He perceived that he had talked too much; he seldom saw girls anymore, except for the inevitable English pair, one a case of sunstroke and one of food poisoning, and no longer knew how to talk to them. And here, this June, was his regal Valerie, burned to a bright pink but not complaining.

She waved her herring sandwich, having stood through this monologue, and perhaps even listened. "What's that thing?"

"A datura."

"Oh." Munching and staring.

"Not a date palm. Nothing to do with dates."

"I know. I've seen a whole forest of date palms in Spain. I've forgotten where. I did see it, though, on a tour."

"If you sleep under a datura tree," said Fenwick, proceeding with his idea of courtship, "you might die."

"Who has? Anyone?"

"Just don't do it."

She threw the rest of the sandwich away and licked her fingers. She said, "If anyone's going down to Grasse or Cannes, I need some things for my transistor."

"I'll take you down a bit later," said Fenwick, staring at her arms. "I've been drying wood for the bonfire. I want to look at it first."

The peanut trench was a gathering place, a watering hole, for now Tom Waterford bobbed up and said, "I'll take you," and the last Fenwick saw of his Tudor queen was her flowered stretch pants as she climbed into the Waterfords' Mini-Minor, head first.

Fenwick was in time to join his guests for coffee. Between the straw mat and the edge of the table a strip of hot metal, a forgotten spoon, stung his wrist. Meg Waterford was talking about animals. "I love wild animals—tigers," she said, as if she had often been contradicted, as if all wild animals were to be taken away from her. A German told of having seen on television tons of strawberries ruined by hail somewhere, and farmers crying. Telling it, he could not keep his voice steady. Fenwick, mourning his beloved, left them—they were all getting on so well. They sounded like the ingenious all-Europe programs in which the best drummer from Denmark performs from a studio in Copenhagen, along with a trumpet from Stuttgart, an electric guitar from Milan, and France's finest clarinet. No musician can hear or see the others, for each is in his home city, but owing to the competence of sound technicians, they can be heard all playing "Dinah" at the same time.

Fenwick began to gather together wood and the dried herbs and plants for tonight's fire; he could still believe in magic. He needed seven elements to make the fire succeed, but they were woods found in the North. He would have to settle for rosemary, broom—whatever was sweet-smelling and would burn. Valerie might be induced to leap over the ashes. A fertility rite, but Fenwick would tell her it was for peace, harmony—anything that might appeal to her sleeping or soaring mind. The thought of great Valerie leaping cheered him.

"I do believe you are some sort of Druid," Meg called to him from the table.

"No, no," said Fenwick, "only a bard."

He began piling the dried herbs with some perception of happiness, all the while listening to Meg telling the others that she had lost, somewhere, once, long ago, in a place she could not remember, a really valuable ring.

GOOD DEED

HOUSES of widows on the French Riviera have in common the out-size pattern of flowers on the chintzes; there is too much furniture everywhere, most of it larger than life. The visitor feels, as he is intended to, very small. These are child's-view houses, though real children may feel oppressed in them, and are not often welcome to stay. The photographs jostling each other on the tables are of grown, formidable people—sepia-tinted parents in profile, brothers dressed for old wars. All are dead now. The most recent pictures are likely to be of animals; inquiring, the visitor learns they have died too. In the kitchen, where a slut in felt slippers has been taught to make treacle pudding, the food on the shelves gratifies, at last, a nursery craving for sweets. There is jam and honey and golden syrup, and condensed milk that can be poured over or stirred into nearly everything. Left to herself, with the possibility of having life as she now wants it, the solitary old woman recovers a child's dream diet, a child's pet animals; she furnishes a vast drawing room intended for giants, and creates her mother's bedroom, as she remembers it—bright and secret, with smooth curtains, and cats all over the bed.

The room in which Olivia now waited for her guest to arrive contained, along with a tribe of animals, a moth-eaten shako hung on a nail, a regimental drum, a parrot cage with nothing inside it, and the picture of a baby boy or girl, perfectly bald, upon a cushion. Although she was naturally idle, waiting for anyone tried her nerves. She began, in her mind, a letter saying, "My dear Hugo, It is three o'clock, and there is no sign of your secretary. I am afraid the poor creature has perished. The plane that was bringing her from London was seen punctually descending upon Nice Airport, when suddenly it exploded and shot, flaming, into the sea. Old Joseph, who was standing beside his taxi holding a cardboard sign with Miss Freeman's name printed on it, heard the screams of young women (your secretary's certainly among them) above the roar and hiss of the flames as the plane met the waves. I am most frightfully sorry about your having lost Miss Freeman, and do hope you find another secretary soon."

In reality it was only half past two, which still left a margin of time for Miss Freeman's destruction. Olivia now began to revise the instructions she had drawn up for the disposal of her own body after her death. She wished to be cremated, which would cause one great and final inconvenience. She was certain to die where she lived, on the coast below Nice; which meant that the person chosen by Olivia would be obliged to accompany her coffin to Marseille and, as recommended by a curious French law, identify her once before she was rendered unrecognizable. She thought of every grotesque possibility, including that of a real mistake, and added to the list of victims the name of Hugo Mellett. Hugo was quite far down on the list. First (and he would certainly be the first refusal) came her brother-in-law, who was a Greek living in Athens, and who had never been able to bear the sight of Olivia in life. Next came old Joseph, who had once been her chauffeur, and now drove a taxi. A habit of slavishness might bind Joseph to commands from beyond the grave; he was dutiful in his behavior but stealthy with regard to his own feelings. Olivia had called him a coolie to his face, and his face had not changed. For many years she had been trying to give old Joseph a shock; she could think of no greater shock for him than the sight of his former employer going up in flames. She added to her instructions, "I want this treated as a pagan ceremony," for Joseph was an unquestioning Roman Catholic.

Just after three o'clock she heard his old green Daimler creeping along the drive. Miss Freeman had evidently caught the right plane, which was clever of someone who had been described to Olivia as not quite right in the head. Olivia then heard the bell, the door, the car starting up again, and finally a sound that was still absolutely excruciating to her, though she had left Ireland some sixty years before: an English female voice. The pitch of Miss Freeman's voice was an octave higher than it need have been, as if a penny whistle were lodged in her throat. The clock in Olivia's room chimed the quarter hour, which made Olivia grumble, "What a lot of noise, and she's only just got here."

Miss Freeman had been admitted by Olivia's latest kitchen slattern, who climbed the stairs silently to announce the guest. Olivia placed a long finger against her lips. The cook shrugged; she was here only because she would put up with the cats, and understood English. Madame was resting but would shortly put her clothes on, Miss Freeman was told. An hour later the cook came up again and stood looking at Olivia. "What am I to say to her now?" she said. "That Madame is fully dressed and playing with her cats?"

"Give the creature tea."

"She prefers to wait for Madame."

"Isn't there a newspaper she can read? She could go for a good walk. That's it—tell her to go for a walk."

There were no walks—none, at least, Miss Freeman could know about. Olivia's house backed on a highway clogged with cars. Moreover, if what Olivia had heard of Miss Freeman was true, she would never be brave enough to venture out alone in a strange place.

Miss Freeman belonged to Hugo Mellett; Olivia imagined her made up from one of Hugo's ribs. Hugo and Olivia maintained a light ironic correspondence, in which Hugo revealed a good deal of himself. He trusted Olivia completely. He had not seen her for twenty years now, but she remained in his mind as the beautiful elderly widow who had once shown him uncommon understanding.

"Wendy Freeman is a first-rate secretary," he had written. "Try to find out what has gone wrong. It might be overwork, but this office is better designed and infinitely more pleasant than her own home. As her breakdown was set off by the sight of an electronic machine, I should keep all mechanical objects out of her way. It happened when she saw a computer. What do you imagine the poor child had expected to see?"

"Now, *that* is a *brain*," Hugo had said of the computer.

"It is larger than I had thought," Wendy Freeman had remarked. "But it can't be a brain, because it has nothing but memory. It has no feelings. It can't even change its mind."

"That is the best part about it," Hugo had replied. "It can do a job without steaming up the atmosphere." It was known to Hugo that computers were capable of violent and unreasonable behavior, of hysteria even, but he did not tell his secretary this, for he did not wish her to follow suit. She had been tearful and jumpy recently, and this visit to a display of electronic machines was Hugo's attempt to distract and cheer her up. He was an architectural engineer consulted on large housing projects. He had worked in Zurich in the nineteen-thirties, and in Milan after the last war. He knew to the cubic centimeter the amount of space into which a family may be compressed without incidence of paranoia; he knew when to allow half an inch lift to a ceiling and when to be firm.

"What an ass you are," Wendy said, staring at the computer. He pretended not to hear. Breakdowns in machines and in persons seldom occur without warning. He felt responsible.

"I should like to send you to an old friend of mine in a warm climate," he said. "She is a marvelous person." Wendy's eyelids turned pink. He pretended not to see.

"You are generous," she said, a week later, as he drove her to a place unpropitious to outbursts of any kind—the London airport. He was not unaware of Wendy, and, as he was something of a hypochondriac, often wished he had someone to look after him; but he thought he was too old for Wendy, and he had been married twice.

"I expect I *am* generous," he said.

"And kind," Wendy went on bitterly.

"That too." He did not think of it as flattery on her part, or conceit on his own. Who should know Hugo better than these two, his secretary and himself?

If he had known at this moment how Wendy was cooling her heels in a decayed drawing room, sitting on the edge of an armchair that had been clawed by cats, staring, terrified, at the monstrous cat on the mantelpiece that seemed about to spring at her face, he would not have thought Olivia rude. Olivia, when younger, had kept people waiting for hours, and they had always come back. The attraction women exert lies often in what has been said about them. Her lovers were a legend, her women friends faithful, and her husband had worshipped her. Hugo had heard him described as a funny, ugly little Greek. The Greek admired her because she was blue-eyed and fair, and he thought her an intellectual—something he would not have tolerated in a woman from his own country. It was true that she had a reputation for cleverness. She had, at the age of twenty, written a spiteful novel about her Irish relations, cutting herself off from them forever but gaining a lively existence based on a rumor of past performances; for no one remembered exactly what it was she had done. The Greek died, before the clumsy villas they had lived in along the coast became old-fashioned and were torn down. The books he had amassed for his wife, thinking she read them, became speckled and brown. After his death Olivia discovered he considered her cold and brainless and a fraud. She was shown a copy of a letter he had sent his brother in Athens. "They love and pursue her *because* she is made of marble," he said. "If I live long enough, I may understand." He made his brother his heir, which was, she thought, a trivial way of showing dissatisfaction. This house, which was Olivia's for her lifetime, reverted to the brother-in-law at her death. He was eighty-one, but he wished to outlive her so that he could demolish the villa and put up a garage and filling station in its place; he had said so.

Hugo came to Olivia at a time of great crisis in his life. He sat at her feet, wondered if he was in love with her, and unburdened himself of secrets that were no one's business but his. It was, for him, unforgettable; he supposed he and Olivia were now tied for life. She was old enough to be his mother; would she claim him forever? It turned out that she did not want to. For years, remembering her, he praised her composure and her disinterested replies. She never judged me, he believed. But her calmness was only because she had heard anguish before. Questions such as "What am I to do? What will become of me?," which one might hear in the course of a close friendship, in an atmosphere of stress, were Olivia's small talk. As her husband had observed, her fascination resided in her failings. People were drawn by her cynicism and selfishness; by her known preference for animals over people; by her cruel theories about her friends and her indifference to their fate. She heard, with self-possession, the usual questions: "Where did I go wrong? Was there one first mistake? Am I repeating a pattern? Is the failure in my character, or have I been unlucky?" She sat, hands folded, only the pressure of one thumb on the other betraying a brief impatience.

Hugo had thought, She despises everyone except me. He had not sought a warm listener, for warm people are not exclusive: they are kind about everything. He had looked for, and found, the concentration that could be obtained only from someone entirely idle, with a shrewd eye, a selective ear, and a spirit of flint.

"There is nothing whatever the matter," Olivia had said, slowly. "You are thoroughly selfish, Hugo, and that's all. You've got enough to live on?" It was the only problem she took to heart—that and one's health. ("A pain? Where, right side or left? Before or after your food? I have seen people carried off in twenty-four hours.") She had no qualms about saying it, and no one had ever minded being told. Hugo was relieved; believing himself exploited and indecisive, it was a deliverance to be thought selfish and headstrong. The threat of a fatal illness froze his terrors into a single shape. He was completely demented when he left her, but cured of his immediate torments. This was more than twenty years in the past, and blurred at the edges. He said to Wendy, "I am sending you to someone very kind."

Olivia did not come down; Wendy was summoned upstairs. She found her hostess wearing a crêpe de Chine dress that reminded Wendy of old films in which the heroine has curly blond hair. Wendy still wore the clothes she had put on that morning. Hugo and the airport seemed weeks ago. She felt in exile. The cook had lied about having offered tea; and no one had asked her if she wanted to wash her hands. She sat on the edge of Olivia's bed and became homesick.

Olivia's first question was "How did you like old Joseph? I am speaking of your taxi-driver."

"He had a sign with my name," said Wendy. "I thought that was intelligent of him. We didn't speak much, though he does know English."

"Hugo said it was best not to have you paged at the airport," said Olivia. "A mechanical system."

Wendy did not respond; she seemed in fact puzzled.

"Hugo thinks you are overworked," Olivia continued.

Wendy submissively stroked the cat that was trying to take possession of her part of the bed. Her obsession was Hugo Mellett. She was putting her faith once and for all in Hugo's magic friend. She would have lighted a candle before Olivia's effigy if she had thought it would do any good. She was an eager but careful girl; she felt she had been too careful until now. She did not mind how many times he had been married. She saw Olivia's long hands, and wild white hair. Wendy believed in the solidarity of women and thought her youth would render her appealing to Olivia. She looked straight into the old woman's eyes, in the mirror.

Olivia had fallen asleep; she often slept with her eyes open now. In a brief dream she saw old Joseph, who, after having been chauffeur to this lady and that, had kept the habit of driving at thirty miles an hour in the stately car someone had let him buy on easy terms after sixteen years of service. It still resembled a private car, with fresh flowers in containers, and the folded rug on the seat. No one had ever been so docile; as pleased with little. Olivia awoke and began rattling rings and pins in a china dish on her dressing table. "Sapphires would look well on you," she said, as though there had never been an interruption. How long had Wendy been in her room—hours? Days? "They are mine, but promised to my niece, who is a fat bore." She spoke rapidly and did not address her remarks to Wendy. "Are you superstitious? Some women are, about opals. These would suit you, but they belonged to Nicky's mother and must go to his brother in Athens after I die. He is dull, and so is his wife. Most people are dull dogs, when it comes to that. I feel it most keenly about the Greeks, though I have never set foot in the country. When my sister-in-law came here from Athens on a visit, she put on sparklers every night, but I made her sit down to a poached egg on toast. 'That is my supper,' I told her. 'Cutlet or egg, and that is that.' If I went to Athens I would eat slops without complaining. I told her that too."

"What a dear little girl," said Wendy, of the bald baby. She had not been able to follow anything of Olivia's explanation. "Is it you?"

"My son," said Olivia. "Just as he was becoming interesting to me he had a sort of fit and died. If he were still living, he would be older than Hugo."

Wendy, watching closely to see that Olivia was not looking at her, put down the cat. She had been prepared to accept everything about

Hugo, and had swallowed whole the assumption that understatement was the mark of a delicate mind. Hugo might have said exactly the same thing, in the same negligent tone: "had a sort of fit and died." She was determined to save Hugo, and hoped she had not been born too late.

Wendy was not forthcoming about her problems, and before the end of her stay, which was seven days long, Olivia was sick of having her about. The girl's eager face when she came down to lunch put her off for the rest of the day. "You don't want to talk to an old thing like me," she said, knocking the cane on the floor to summon the cats for their meal. She made as much noise as she could.

"Oh but I do," said Wendy. "Because that's what I'm here for."

Exasperated, Olivia suddenly leaned on the cane. She seemed so disjointed and helpless that Wendy rushed forward, thinking Olivia had doubled over and could not straighten up—which was in fact what had happened.

"I am all right," said Olivia. "I find the position restful. My dear, why don't you marry some young man instead of wasting your time with old people? You have cried every night—your eyelids are like fuchsias."

"I am in love with someone who never looks at me," Wendy muttered. That was her secret, her neurotic confession. Olivia, having straightened up without help, was tempted to slap her. She thought, with nostalgia, of the old days, when one could get rid of a dull guest by sending him down the coast to Rapallo with a letter of introduction, or up the other way to Mr. Maugham. How dare Hugo send me this, she thought.

Wendy repeated her charge that some man or other never looked at her.

"Forget about him. Marry someone."

"I can't. I see him every day. He is the one I love."

"Love?" said Olivia. "What you need is eighteen months' travel and some decent dresses."

"You must have loved your husband," said Wendy, controlling

herself. She knew, and minded, about her eyelids coloring. Her sandy lashes darkened after only a few tears.

"I don't know about that," said Olivia. "I wanted to get out of Ireland. Has Hugo ever tried to make love to you?"

"No," said Wendy. "No, he has not."

Olivia, having cut her poached egg up with a spoon, put the plate on the floor for one of the cats. "Are you sure he likes it?" Wendy had asked the first time she saw this. "No, he never touches it," Olivia replied. "But, you see, he is so terribly fond of me." With a little shudder, Wendy now averted her eyes. Not knowing what Olivia was talking about was no help at all; it simply made her feel she had been put down a well.

Olivia said, "Secretaries know everything about the men who employ them, isn't that so? Hugo was a dedicated homosexual until the age of twenty-seven, when he married a woman for her money. Ianthe was her name. She died of drink in a hotel room in Geneva, and he then married a crony of hers, whose hair was purple and who wore garnets on a dried or nonexisting bosom. They paraded their squalid alliance up and down this very coast, and then she died. He neglected her shamefully in her last illness, and after a short period of neutrality began having—as a sort of pre-senility, I suppose—affairs with young females."

Wendy listened with her head bent and her lips apart. Then she said, "I doubt if he has lived on anyone's money. He has practiced his profession all his life. I once had to catalogue his published articles—I don't know of any gaps. I don't gossip or listen to gossip." She had been quite brave, but now she choked.

To stop any sign of tears, which she could not countenance, Olivia produced one of her eternity games, with which she had often sent her true neurotics home for a sleepless night. She omitted the simplest question, "Would you prefer, for eternity, to be shut up in a cloistered nunnery or an Oriental bordel?," knowing the innocent and devoted girl would jump at the bordel, thinking that that was where she could do the most good. "I wonder... I know so little about young people now," Olivia said. "Which would you choose for eternity? Now, do think carefully. A cell crowded with filthy and ignorant prisoners, or a charming house and garden provided with every mortal comfort except a human presence?"

"Why, the cell full of people, of course," said Wendy. She spoke with composure, and even some surprise.

"It is forever," said Olivia. "And their habits are disgusting."

"So are people's minds," said Wendy. "Even when their manners seem perfect. Habits can be broken."

"They are unteachable. You would never have a second's privacy again."

"I wouldn't try to teach them all. I would take one, and teach him. The only privacy you can have in real life is invented anyway." She had just experienced the greatest fright she had ever thought possible: she had seen an infinity of silence and light, millions of silent perfect meals, silent aimless walks in a garden where the sky was a witness but would never speak.

"You say 'him' as if he existed," Olivia said. "You are not playing the game. He would never understand a word you were saying. He would laugh at you."

Wendy did look then, not at Olivia but at the door left open for the cats. "I wonder if in eternity there would be no such thing as corruption anymore. How do we know there aren't planets where everything we think right is forbidden, and what seems decent to us revolting to them?"

Olivia said, to the girl who had broken down over an electronic machine, "You aren't afraid of dying, then?" Wendy did not reply, and presently Olivia went on, "I think Hugo ought to marry you."

"Why?" said Wendy. "He won't think of it, and if he asked me now I would refuse. I'm speaking the truth." She felt baited beyond endurance, and could only lie with all her heart. "If he asked me, I would say no."

Eternity has done it, Olivia decided. She will see everything as solitude or a cell.

She wrote that day to her old friend, "You must ask this girl to marry you. She could be your salvation. She is quite sensible, but madly in love with you, and would accept in a minute. Tell her it is forever—that you have thought it over carefully." Believing that both his previous wives must have proposed to him, she added, "Take her out and feed her and get a very good bottle of wine." She had a shadowy desire to punish Hugo for having foisted on her this dull girl, but there was a nagging irritation too. For twenty years, and without her ever having to see him, she had remained the only woman in his life. He had never bothered about the health or the feelings of anyone, until Wendy. If he believed her letter but did not wish to marry Wendy—if, indeed, the very idea was abominable to him—he would feel uncomfortable keeping Wendy in his office. If she refused him, he would be humiliated. If she accepted, he would soon learn he was in a cell with an ardent educator, and fly to Olivia for counsel.

After posting the letter, Olivia accompanied Wendy to the airport. She could scarcely conceal her excitement that the girl was leaving.

"Joseph was the best chauffeur on the coast years ago," she said, loudly, as she sat in the back of his car with Wendy. "But he drove terrible women...Joseph! Who was it wouldn't let anyone eat oranges because if she smelled oranges she would be sure they had been stolen from her trees?"

"Mrs. Willcox, Madame," he said, without turning.

"And smoking—who wouldn't allow the smell of it anywhere?"

"Many ladies, Madame. Nearly every one."

Wendy said only, "There is nothing like that now."

Olivia smiled. "Who was the one with the riding crop, Joseph?" she called again.

His eyes, seen in the mirror, did not change. They crept along the Corniche road with a streamer of cars behind. He seemed to be considering something outside himself. "Madame is thinking of my next-to-last employer," he said.

"So I am! She had a riding crop or a little belt—am I right, Joseph?— and when he drove too fast or too slowly or hadn't stopped where she wanted because of some silly rule, she would beat him about the shoulders. She was a sight! He put up with it. It might have been a fly. Oh, he was used to it, of course." And so she saw Wendy off.

Hugo's telegram arrived seven days later. It said, DONE AND DONE A THOUSAND THANKS. Wendy had accepted! If Olivia had stopped to think of the sound of "a thousand thanks," she would have been struck by its finality. A language softer than English might leave room for an answer, but the double "th" was barbed wire. *Done, a thousand thanks*...Why, she thought, it was the lightest kind of gratitude. It applied to a pleasant luncheon party or a box of *marrons glacés* or a month-old copy of the *Observer* containing some outrage. Hugo might have wired exactly the same message if she had advised him to have a tooth pulled and supplied the name of her dentist. She wrote, "Hugo, do not marry this girl. We are both mistaken about her, you in thinking she was insane, and I in believing she was too innocent. She is a liar, and as hard as nails. *Do* consider this letter, for I think the warning I am sending you may be my one good deed. Miss Freeman butters her bread and cuts it into little squares. She spends half the day looking for her comb. She only pretends to listen. She will drive you mad."

They came south for their honeymoon, and on their way home stopped overnight at a hotel near Olivia's house. The bride had brought a tin of Jackson's Earl Grey tea for Olivia, and a family of rubber mice for the cats. They did not call on Olivia but asked her to come and see them. She was so astonished at being summoned that she went. She was kept waiting in their sitting room. She sat fully six minutes, depositing cat hair on a blue velvet *bergère*. Wendy came in, blooming, in command, and looking some fifteen years older. Her hair was cut straight across her brow, and she had added a false chignon.

"I think Hugo may have had a mild form of sunstroke," said Wendy in a low voice. "You will see that one of his eyes is quite bloodshot."

"It was always his weak point," said Olivia. "Reckless exposure. What is that sound?"

"Hugo's electric razor."

"Poor man!" said Olivia, meaning how unfortunate, what a comedown, what a miserable link with the world of ordinary men. Hugo *was* bloodshot, but younger. The two had conspired, in a short time, to arrive at an average age of about thirty-seven.

"Come along, Hugo," said Olivia. "I'm giving you lunch. No intellectual conversation, now. I want to hear something interesting."

Hugo replied, "What's the food going to be like?"

Wendy said patiently, "It's too late for lunch, darling. It's nearly suppertime, and we shall have that on the train."

"We were remembering Olivia's famous luncheons," he said, and turned slightly away from her, as if he did not wish to be overtaken by the memory.

"They really consisted of bringing together people who could not possibly like one another, and letting them try to get the better in conversation until the wine made them all too stupid to talk," said Olivia. "But sometimes I took my party to a restaurant. I would decide the menu for everyone in advance. I took it for granted they all went out to be nourished. Would a sane person desert his own table for any other reason?"

Hugo looked confused, as if time were tangled in his mind, and Wendy said, "I'm afraid he must rest until train time. By the way, do you think Joseph would drive us?"

"A good deed in a naughty world, or something of the kind," said Olivia, rising. But Hugo seemed to have forgotten what she meant.

They strolled, following the porter, up to the end of the platform. When the train swept in, she remembered having read in her girlhood a warning that the vacuum created when air was displaced by an on-rushing express, or even the giddiness caused by the sight of the wheels, could make one lose consciousness. In her mind was a traveler, sur-rounded by alps of luggage, including a bird in a cage; the traveler stepped back from the train, an example of prudence. She stepped back and nearly fell. Wendy was reading the numbers on the carriages as the express slowed.

"Seven, that's ours." With dumb show she indicated the carriage to the porter. Seeing his wife walking away with the porter, Hugo rose from the bench where he had been resting. He trusted Wendy to attend to everything, and to come back for him. The porter was handing their luggage in through the window to the sleeping-car attendant. Wendy, having set this in motion, took his arm. "The train only stops a minute," she threw over her shoulder. Olivia, who had established long ago that she disliked being kissed, wondered why neither of them kissed her. From the window of their compartment they looked down—first Wendy, who said something and smiled and urged Hugo to stand up and say a word to his old friend, who was on the platform.

"Hugo," Olivia said loudly, leaning on her cane and looking up at him. "I am very ill." His eyes expressed mild distress, perhaps about the train, which had begun to roll slowly. They were borne apart. She felt as if she were sliding and unable to stop herself. She said, over considerable noise, "Pain in my ribs, just below the shoulder, on the left side." Hugo smiled anxiously. "My brother-in-law is going to sell my house. Do you hear me? It is in his name. He can do whatever he likes with it. What shall I do? When they visited me from Greece"—her voice rose—"my sister-in-law tried to throw me down the stairs. The cats have taken over the house. I am afraid of them. Someone ought to protect me from the cats. One sits on my chest in the night, and when I try to move . . ."

"Goodbye, Olivia," said her old friend. She saw the words take form and float. He leaned out of the window. Beyond the station the train bent round a curve, and now a hand with a fluttering handkerchief replaced Hugo's bowing form.

Hugo is deaf as a post, Olivia decided, walking away. I hope he will not send me any more of his friends.

"Joseph!" she said. "What would you do if I were to die? Would you look after my funeral?"

She sat in the middle of the back seat, and Joseph drove at a snail's pace, taking no notice of the furious drivers behind. "Answer me!" she said. "Would you adopt all my cats?" His head, his neck, his hands on the wheel seemed acquiescent. What a coolie he was! He had the soul of a carpet. "Why don't you answer?" she said. "I know *you* aren't deaf."

"I would do whatever was correct," he said. That was all.

If she had had a riding crop, a belt with a buckle, she would have struck him. His head turned an inch, then another; for a second his eyes left the road, but his expression was as she had always known it.

What a terrible face he must have when he is not with me, she thought. "Joseph!" she said. "Do you think I am dangerous and old?"

THE SUNDAY AFTER CHRISTMAS

AT A QUARTER to four the sun moved behind a mountain. The valley below us went dark, as if an enormous bird had just spread its wings. For a moment I understood what my mother means when she complains I give her the feeling of being outside life. The two of us, and the American girl my mother had picked up, were still on the terrace between the ski-lift and a restaurant. I saw, as the lights of the restaurant welled up, how the girl looked quickly, wistfully almost, at the steamed windows and the hissing coffee machine.

"Don't you want to go in?" said my mother's new friend. "It's kind of cold now the sun's gone."

My mother made a wild, gay movement of turning to me, as if this were only one of a hundred light-hearted decisions we made together. It is extraordinary how, in Italy, she becomes the eccentric English-woman—hair flying, sunglasses askew, too friendly with the waiter at breakfast, but unexpectedly waspish if a child brushes against her chair: "Harold, didn't you notice? The little brute deliberately barged into me!" An hour later she will be ready to tell the little brute my life's story and what I was like when I was his age. Her greed for people makes her want to seem attractive to almost anyone—a child, or a waiter, or this girl, whose absence of charm and mystery made her seem, to me, something like a large colored poster. My mother dreads being alone with me. In the last of the afternoon, when she suddenly says, "You must be cold," meaning that she is, and we gather everything together and start the slow progression back to the hotel, I sense her panic. The dark minutes between afternoon and night creep by; she looks surreptitiously at her watch; she imagines she has been walking beside me down a twilit street for years on end. To engage and hold my attention on the way home she will comment on everything she sees—the patches of snow so curiously preserved on a shutter, the late skiers in the distance like matchstick figures, the expressiveness of those matchsticks. "Look," she says, at red berries, green moss, beeches, a juniper, reeds frozen in a black stream, the plumed grasses above the snow. I am not an old man in a fur-lined pelisse; she is not pushing me along in a wheelchair (I may, in fact, be carrying her skis); I am not snow-blind. I must be all those things in her eyes. I am crippled, aged, in the dark, an old man she diverts with the crumbs of life because part of him is dying, and even a partial death is like her own. "Why don't you talk to me?" she used to say. She is past that kind of pleading now. She knows that I can hear her thinking, so that speech isn't needed. To answer the silent sentences in her mind, I answer, "Yes, but if that little old man died, you would at least be free, wouldn't you?"

"Oh, Harold," she replies. "Your father *is* dead, darling, and he was never old."

It had rained until shortly before Christmas. There was deep snow only on the upper slopes, which were marked "*difficile*" on the map in our hotel. We took the chair-lift to the very top every day and came down at four o'clock. I heard her telling her newest American friend how she used to come to this village years ago, with my father, without me. She could remember electric cars shaped like the swan boats she used to be taken for rides in when she was a child. She would have liked to ski all the way down to the village, but hardly anyone did. The runs were too short, broken by stone walls and the boundaries of close-set trees, and lower down no snow at all except on a mule path, which was hard and icy and followed the course of a mountain stream. She would have tried it, she said, had there been anyone to go with. She was not confident enough alone. Suppose she were to fracture a leg and lie for hours without help? At fifty a break is a serious matter; she might never walk without limping again. Her hands shook as she lighted the girl's cigarette and then her own.

"Harold sits for hours, as long as there's sun," she said. "He doesn't feel heat or cold. He wanted marvelous equipment; now he won't use it. I don't insist."

The new girl, who had said her name was Sylvia, pulled off her knitted cap. Her hair, dark, fell over the shoulders of a white sweater. An exchange of intimate gossip, my mother's alternative to friendship, was under way. The girl said quite easily, "There doesn't seem to be any friction between you two, but my mother never lets me alone. I've traveled with her sometimes and it's no joke. She drinks too much and she gets loud. She'll have her breakfast in the bar and ask the bartender a whole lot of questions—things she wouldn't do at home."

"I think I'm always the same," my mother cried—like something screamed at a party.

"I am sorry for her," the girl went on. "She needs all of somebody's life and she hasn't ever had that."

"Not even your father's?"

"He looked after her, but he didn't give her all his life. No one has the right to a whole extra life." Her pure, humorless regard rested on each of us. Her look preached to us; one of us was being warned. "I lived with her for a year after my father died. I've got to leave her now. I came all this way just so as not to spend Christmas at home. She's got to get used to it. It's a sort of shock treatment."

"Well, that's very strong of you," said my mother. "Isn't that so, Harold? But are you really leaving so soon? Can't you stay until after New Year's Eve? You may never be here again."

I could hear her thinking, *Don't go. Stay. Are two or three days so much to give me? You gave your mother a year.*

I love my mother and I don't care two pins about you, I heard the girl answer.

She said, "No, I've got to get back."

I looked at the lights strung along the street, and the lights slowly moving out of the car park at the foot of the lift. I saw the girl shiver, as if she felt that great wing rushing over the valley.

"I can't go down," I said.

"Of course you can't," said my mother. Her little apricot face looked cheerful. "We're going down in the lift."

I said, "I can't go down in the chair either. I can't go down at all."

"It's mountain sickness," said my mother, making roundabout movements with her cigarette, as if to show what vertigo means. "It will be over in a minute. It just means a wait. What a bother for you!" She was taking it for granted, of course, that the girl would not feel free to leave us there.

"Shouldn't we go in?" said the girl, again attracted by the warm light.

"He'll want to stay out, I'm afraid."

"Oh. Well, we can have coffee, anyway," said the girl. "We're all freezing." She went into the restaurant and I saw her leaning on the counter, fingering chocolate bars, wishing she had never talked to us. A ski club from Turin filled the place. They were noisy as monkeys, ordering hot drinks and food and combing their hair before a little mirror. I saw the girl smiling at them, waiting for the coffee, but they were too full of themselves to notice a stranger.

"I don't believe this," my mother said to me. "There's nothing wrong with you today. You're perfectly well. You're shamming, shamming." Her voice broke on her habit of repeating the same word twice. She was as disappointed as a child over the girl. I tried to reason with her: Was Sylvia her real name? It did not seem an American name to me; it was, in fact, the name of one of my aunts. But by now my mother had left me and joined the girl. I could see her back, and the girl's face. On the counter was a tray and three cups. My mother was telling her about me: "He had an unusual experience, you know," she was saying. "He was one of a group of university students visiting a large hospital. While they were waiting for their conducted tour, a nurse told Harold that the place was run by a most eccentric doctor who did experiments on children and on young people, and that Harold and his friends were the new victims. The patients, when they survived, were so changed in character that they were no longer fit for life in the outside world. 'Didn't you notice the scars on the necks of the little boys playing football outside?' the nurse said. She advised him not to fight, as there was nothing he could do. Harold argued for his freedom. His argument centered on two things—that he was young and had a right to live, and that he still hadn't decided what he wanted to do, and needed time to find out. It seemed impossible to him that she shouldn't understand this. She was a serious person—a nice girl. They went outside and sat discussing his life on a bench overlooking the playing field. Suddenly, in a second, it was clear that the nurse had been convinced by Harold's arguments and had purposely brought him out-of-doors, and, just as he understood, she said, 'Run for it.' His reflexes are very slow, but he must have pulled himself together, and he did run, through the players, to liberty, and the road outside, and to his own home—safe, safe."

She bobbed her head as she repeated the last word. I did not think, or guess, or imagine what she was saying; I *knew*. She must have then said, "Pretend it is funny," because the girl laughed, and was still remembering her laughter as she picked up the tray and brought it out to me.

My mother said, "I was telling Sylvia about that midnight Mass where they had the live animals, and how the priest said the goat was an incarnation of the Devil and had to be taken out, and then the goat broke loose, and all the villagers said later they had seen the Devil, really seen him, with his flaming eyes."

"I wish I had seen that," said the girl, with a lift to the sentence, as if it were half a question, as if giving me a reason to speak. I was already thinking about the trip down, and the slight sighing of the cable.

"He's fine now," my mother said.

Below, because it was Sunday, everyone except the visitors looked awkward and solemn. It seemed an unnatural day, that had to be lived through in formal, festive clothes. The men wore thick mustaches turned up at the ends, and black felt hats, and knee breeches. They looked distinguished and calm, and not like any idea the girl had ever had about Italians, I heard her say. She drew near my mother. She repeated that she had not known before coming here that Italians could be patient, or naturally elegant, any more than she had known they possessed an educated middle class. In her mind (she had not really given it thought) she had been coming to a Rossellini, a De Sica country.

While she was saying this, she was also saying to me, *Was it a dream?*

Did you really have an experience like that? If it was a dream, why didn't she say so?

I answered, "It was a long experience, lasting well over a year."

"Harold, Harold!" my mother said, looking not at me but at the girl. We had reached the girl's hotel, and the long goodbye my mother would now insist upon would be, in her eyes, one minute's friendship more. "Are you leaving because there isn't enough snow?" she said. "There will be a Mass for snow on New Year's Eve. All the hotel owners and all the shopkeepers are contributing, they say." In my mother's poor, immediate vision of future events (never more than three or four days in span), she and her new friend walked in moonlight. Vega was bright and blue as a diamond; their shadows were hard and black as if cut out with knives.

"The goat, of course, the goat," I said. "'Don't move,' I said to Mother. 'When he sees the Cross he's sure to panic.'"

"I never move anyway," said my mother to Sylvia, to prolong the goodbye. "Nothing makes *me* move." She smiled, and even when the girl had turned aside forever, kept the smile alive.

STORIES OF PARIS AND BEYOND

VIRUS X

I

A BUNCH of holly hanging upside down at the entrance to her hotel was the first thing Lottie Benz saw in all of Paris that seemed right to her. Even a word like "hotel" was subject to suspicion, since it was attached to a black façade in no way distinguished from the rest of the street. The people walking on the street did not look as if they had sisters or brothers or childhood friends, and their clothes and haircuts in no manner indicated to her a station in life. The New Look had spread from this place, but none of the women appeared to have given it a thought. As for the men, alike in their gray raincoats, only their self-absorbed but inquisitive faces kept them from seeming unemployed. Lottie, whose mother had made the dress she was wearing from a *Vogue* pattern, could have filled the back seat of her taxi with polka dots, the skirt was so wide. Stepping down, she shook order into the polka dots and her mother's ankle-length Persian-lamb coat, lent for the voyage. That was when she saw the holly. Even as the taxi-driver plucked every bit of change from her outstretched hand, she turned to this one familiar thing. A city that knew about holly would know about Christmas, true winter, everything.

That day, which was Tuesday, December 9, 1952, was laid on with a light brush. The street had been cut out of charcoal-colored paper with extremely fine scissors. Lottie had come here out of a tempest of snow. She drew a breath of air that seemed mild—her first breath of Paris. It swept into her lungs and was immediately converted into iron. She withdrew her hand, relieved of its francs, and pressed it against her chest.

Two boys passed her, walking in step, without a glance at Lottie stranded, the taxi grinding out and away, or the bags the driver had dumped upon the curb. One boy said to the other, in an American accent, "If people depress you, why do you bother seeing them?" The iron weight shifted as she bent to pick up her suitcases. An old man in porter's uniform watched Lottie through the frosted glass door. His eye appeared as part of the pattern of lilies etched on the glass, and then his nose. He consented to hold open the door. Lottie offered him a tip, which he pocketed. She had been advised to tip for consideration, however slight, no matter how discourteously shown. In a place where Americans were said to be hated because of the Korean War, she intended to put up a show for her own country, which was Canada. She smiled. The hotel, or France, personified by the woman at the desk with frizzy red hair, did not care. Lottie conveyed with a second smile that it was of no importance.

For the first time in her life she was compelled to put her name to a police questionnaire. Bending over the form, she wrote "Charlotte Maria," and wanted to put "Lottie" in brackets, but there was no room. Her home address—the Princess Pat Apartments, in Winnipeg—also seemed to want explaining. She could have written reams of explanation about everything, had there been space. She imagined a policeman reading her answers attentively. Next to "Profession" she wrote "none yet." The woman with frizzy hair made her cross this out and write "student" in its place. Lottie gave up the questionnaire, and with it her new blue passport.

Three messages awaited her. First, a letter from her mother, written four days before Lottie left home. Though sent with loving intention, so that Lottie would have news the instant she arrived, it contained no news. As for Kevin, he had cabled, MISS YOU ALREADY LOVE, a few hours after her plane took off. Supposing he discovered twenty hours later that he did not miss her at all? She examined the cable gravely. The last message was from a girl named Vera Rodna. It welcomed Lottie to Paris, and gave a telephone number. Upstairs, in her ice-cold, beige-colored hotel room, Lottie tore all three messages across, then found there was no wastebasket.

A sunbeam revealed dust on the window and dust on the floor but, curiously, none in the air. (Perhaps in this place they deliberately allowed dust to settle. Was this better? Better for Lottie—for her asthma, her chronic bronchitis, her fragile lungs?) The bed, the cupboard containing a washbasin, the wardrobe that contained one bent wire hanger were all clean. There were no pillows, window shades, towels, or drinking glass. There were any number of mirrors, however, evenly shaded with dust, and velvet curtains that she accepted as luxurious.

Wondering why she was noticing so much, checking herself lest she become introspective or moody, she remembered that this was the first time she had ever been anywhere alone. The notes she was taking mentally were for future letters—the first to Dr. Keller, her thesis director, the second most likely for Kevin. She unpacked her new cake of Palmolive, her toothbrush, her unworn dressing gown with rose-pink petal neckline. A hot bath, she learned, from a notice posted on the back of the door, would cost three hundred and sixty francs, which was more than a dollar. Lottie was to live on a Royal Society scholarship, supplied out of Canadian funds frozen abroad. Any baths from now on would be considered pampering. She intended to profit from this winter of opportunities, and was grateful to her country for having provided it, but in no sense did she desire to change or begin a new life.

By Sunday the weather in the street was the weather of spring. The iron of the first breath had disintegrated, vaporized. At the bottom of her lungs was a pool of mist. She reminded herself that back home the day had not begun. The city she had left was under snow, ransacked by wind, and on the dark side of the globe. She was not homesick.

Vera Rodna, whose message had so quickly been turned into paper scrap, came to the hotel one day when Lottie was visiting the *Mona Lisa*. She left a new letter, this time asking Lottie to come to lunch, and she indicated the restaurant with a great X on a map. "*Une jeune fille très élégante*," the frizzy redhead down at the desk remarked. Lottie had to smile at that. No one here could know that Vera was only a girl from Winnipeg who had flunked out of high school and, on a suspicion of pregnancy, been shipped abroad to an exile without glamour. Some of the men in her family called themselves Rodney, and at least one was in politics. End syllables had been dropped from the name in any case, to make it less specifically Ukrainian. Vera had big hands and feet, a slouching walk, a head of blond steel wool. The nose was large, the eyes green and small. She played rough basketball, but also used to be seen downtown, Sunday-dressed, wearing ankle-strap shoes. Vera had made falsies out of a bra and gym socks—there were boys could vouch for it. In cooking class it turned out that she thought creamed carrots were made with real cream. She didn't know what white sauce was because they had never eaten it at home. That spoke volumes for the sort of home it must be.

Lottie accepted Vera's invitation, though there was no real reason for them to meet. Having been raised in the same city did not give them a common past. Attempting to impose a past, beginning with a meal in a restaurant, Vera would not establish herself as a friend from home, if that was what she was trying to do. But Vera, being Ukrainian, and probably no moron in spite of her scholastic and morals records, would have enough sense to know this.

The restaurant was an Italian place on the Rue Bonaparte. Wavy, sooty dust masked the wall paintings except for a corner where someone had been at work with a sponge. There Vera waited, backed up by frothing geraniums and blue-as-laundry-bluing seas. Ashes, Sunday papers, spilled cigarettes, and bread crumbs gave her table the look of an unswept floor. Vera's eyes tore over Lottie, head to foot, gardenia hat to plastic overshoes. She said, in a full voice that all at once became familiar and a second later had never been forgotten, "Well, this is great. Sit down."

"This is very nice," said Lottie neutrally.

"It's not bad. I've tried most of them."

Lottie had not meant the restaurant but the occasion of their meeting. Vera began to wave at a waiter and also to talk. She sloshed wine from a bottle that was nearly empty into a glass that seemed none too clean, and pushed this at Lottie. "Some rich bastard's Chambertin," she said. "Might as well lap up the dregs."

Lottie lifted the glass and sipped, and put it down forever, having shown she was game. She said, "How did you know I was in Paris, Vera?"

"My mother, from my sister Frannie. Fran's in your father's math-and-Latin. She's smart—makes up for me."

The name Frannie Rodna conveyed nothing, and Lottie accepted with some pride and some melancholy that she was now part of an older crowd.

"By the way, what are you doing here, exactly?" Vera asked. She was dressed in a black-and-brown checked cape, and a wool hat pulled straight down to her eyebrows. She may have been quite smart by local standards, which undoubtedly she knew about by now, but Lottie could not help thinking how hunkie she looked. Vera's crocheted gloves fell off the table. Her hands looked as if they could easily deal with the oilier parts of a motorbike. "Whadja say?" said Vera, after fishing round for her gloves.

"I *said*, Vera, that my *professor*, Dr. *Keller*, is *from* Alsace, and that's the reason I'm going there. My thesis is about the integration of minority groups without a loss of ethnic characteristics."

"Come again?" Vera's elbows were planted in ashes and crumbs. She turned from Lottie to deal with the waiter, and ordered an unknown something on Lottie's behalf.

"Like at home," Lottie said, when the waiter had left. "Vera, you do know. That's the strength of Canada, that it hasn't been a melting pot. Everybody knows that. The point is, I'm taking it as a good thing. Alsace is an example in an older civilization. With Dr. Keller's contacts in Strasbourg... Vera, don't stare just on purpose; I do find it unpleasant. I'll give you a simple example. Take the Poles." Delicacy with regard to Vera's possible feelings prevented her saying Ukrainians. "The Poles paint traditional Easter eggs. Right? They stop doing it in the States after one generation, two at most. In Canada they never stop. Now do you see?"

Vera was listening to this open-mouthed. Lottie felt she had sounded stupid, yet the idea, a favorite of Dr. Keller's, was not stupid at all. She knew it was a theory, but she was taking it for granted that it could be applied. If it could not, let Vera prove it. Vera closed her mouth, drew her lips in between her teeth, let go her breath, and when all that was accomplished said, "You crazy or something?"

"Think whatever you like."

"Do you even know what a minority is?"

"I ought to," said Lottie, and she took the bread and began peeling off the crust, after cracking its surface with her nails.

"You don't. It was always right to be what *you* are."

"Oh, was it, now?"

An explanation for Lottie's foolishness suddenly brightened Vera's face. She clasped her hands, her big mechanic's hands, and cried, "Keller's in love with you! He's meeting you in Alsace."

"He's got a wife and everything. Children, I mean. Honestly, Vera!"

"I think everybody's in love," said Vera, and indeed looked as if she thought so. "Who is it, then? Still Kevin?"

"Yes, still."

"You're going to be away, in Alsace or someplace? That's taking a chance." She seemed to be fumbling over something in her mind, perhaps a memory of Kevin. "I guess you needn't worry," she said. "You've kept him on the string since you were sixteen. You'll bring it off."

"What do you mean, Vera, 'bring it off'?"

Vera looked as if Lottie should know what she meant. A platter of something strange was placed between them. Vera dug into a bone full of marrow, extricated the marrow, and spread it over a mound of rice. It might have been dog food.

"Delicious," said Vera with her mouth full. "Know one thing I remember, Lottie? You used to choose the meals at home, and your brothers had to eat whatever you happened to like. That's what they told around, anyway."

Lottie, surprised at Vera's knowing about this, said, "Everybody favors girls."

"Boy, my father didn't," said Vera. "He kind of respects me now, though. Your father used to scare me even more than my own. His voice was just a squeak when he got mad. You could hear every word, but the voice was up around the ceiling. When he told my father I wasn't college material, and not even high-school material, his voice sounded artificial. You take after him a little, but your voice just gets slower and slower. Your father was a fine man, all the same. Old Captain Hook."

Mr. Benz had been called Captain Hook by his pupils, but there was a further matter, which Vera did not mention—Captain von Hook. That was an old wartime joke. You would have thought the mean backwash of war could never have reached them there, in the middle of another country.

Lottie said with slow care, "How is your brother, Vera, the one who went into politics? Wasn't there some kind of row about him? Honest Stan Rodney?"

"Honest slob. Listen, what are you doing over Christmas? I'm going to Rome. I've got this friend there. He's from home, but you don't know him. He's a Pole. Far as I know, he doesn't paint any Easter eggs. I used to think he was a spy, but he turned out to be a teacher. Slav lit. *When* he's working. Boy, the trouble *he* gets into." Vera's admiration for the trouble made her go limp. "Do you want to do something in Paris before I go? See a play or something? You've been up the Eiffel Tower, I suppose. I like going up and looking down. You see this shadow like a kind of basket, when there's any sun. There's Versailles and that. Euh, Fontainebleau ... boring. Katherine Mansfield's grave, how about that? Remember Miss Pink? She fed us old Mansfield till it ran out of our ears. She's buried around Fontainebleau. Mansfield is, not Miss Pink." Vera laughed with her mouth wide.

"She was my favorite author until I specialized," said Lottie primly. "Then, I'm sorry to say, I had to restrict my reading."

Vera dug into her rice as if looking for treasure. "Right," she said. "We'll go out to the grave." Lottie consented to nothing of the kind.

Vera must have mistaken Lottie's silent refusal, for the next Saturday, at half past ten, she turned up while Lottie was still in bed.

Lottie had been out with a cousin of Kevin's, who worked at the Embassy. He had made her pay for her own drinks, as if they were still students having cafeteria coffee. Lottie was puzzled by the bar he took her to, full of youngish American men, and even more by the hateful, bitter singer at the piano. Kevin's cousin seemed to feel that she had no right to criticize anything, having only just arrived, though he himself never stopped complaining. His landlord was swindling him; he was sick of dark rooms and gas heaters. He blamed Paris for its size. Until now he had lived in a house, never in a flat. His accent shot from one extreme of broad vowels to the opposite. He did not want to sound

American but looked it. In the bar full of crew cuts, he matched any one of them except in assurance. Toward the end of the night, he began bemoaning his own Canadian problems of national identity, which Lottie thought a sign of weakness in a man. Moreover, she learned nothing new. What he was telling her was part of Dr. Keller's course in Winnipeg Culture Patterns. She had wasted the government's money and her own time.

Vera said she was leaving for Rome, which she called Roma, any minute. Slumped over an ashtray on the foot of Lottie's bed, she urged an excursion to Fontainebleau. It was a lovely sunny day—just the weather for visiting graveyards. Sleepy and pale, caught with curlers in her hair, Lottie rose and dressed, turning her back. Vera scarcely allowed her time to brush her teeth. They were doomed to catch, and they caught, the Lyon noon express. The train was filled with *hommes d'affaires*, who had all the seats. Lottie stood crushed against a window, looking at the backs of towns. She was cold, and speechless with hunger. After Melun she began to feel calmer, and less hungry and unwashed. Trees such as she had never seen before, and dense with ivy, met and glided apart in the winter light. Touching the window, she felt a thin cool film of sunlight. The ivy shone and suddenly darkened, as if a shutter had been swung to. Lottie forgot she had asthma, chronic colds, low blood pressure, and that Vera would regret this.

"I always thought I was going to die at the same age as Mansfield," she remarked to Vera. "I may still."

"Not the same way."

"At my age, you already know what you're going to die of." Lottie was thirteen months older than Vera, who would be twenty-one in February. Unspecified illnesses of a bronchial nature had kept Lottie out of school for months on end. A summer grippe only last August had prevented her coming over here in September.

"You used to wear those hand-smocked dresses," Vera suddenly chose to recall.

"A friend of Mother's made them," said Lottie, and closed a door on that with her tone of voice. Though ignominiously clothed then, she had been small for her age, and almost unnoticeable in the classes of children younger than herself. She skipped grades, catching up, passing, but no one praised her. They said Captain Hook had helped.

Vera explained her commitment to Mansfield, which was an old crush on Miss Pink. It had led Vera to read this one writer when she never read anything else, or wanted to. Now that she was away from the Miss Pinks of this world, she read all the time.

Lottie's transparent reflection was ivy green. "Do you think I look weak?" she asked, meaning that she wanted her health kept in mind.

Vera, who was tall, caught Lottie's face at an angle Lottie had never seen. "Weak, in a way," she said, "but not frail." Lottie's reflection went smug. Vera, squinting down and sideways, looked as if she thought weakness could not account for everything.

When they alighted at the station, Vera consulted a taxi-driver, whose head was a turtle's between muffler and cap. Showing off in French, she seemed to think the driver would think she was French and take them to a gem of a restaurant. Lottie felt cold and proud. She would not mention her low blood pressure. Actually, she was supposed to drink tea or coffee almost the minute she wakened; her mother usually brought it to her in bed. She had never fainted, but that was not to say she never would. Their driver rushed them up a dirt road and abandoned them before a billboard upon which was painted in orange RESTAURANT—BAR—DOLLARS ACCEPTED—PARKING.

"We aren't going to like it," said Vera. "He took you for an American." Nevertheless, she rushed Lottie onward, through a room where an American soldier slept in a leather armchair, past a bar where more soldiers sat as if Saturday drinking were a cheerless command, and into a totally empty dining room that smelled of eggs frying. Not empty: out of the dim corner where he was counting empty bottles came the proprietor of the place, unshaven, clad in an American gabardine. His thick eyelids drooped; he had already seen enough of Vera and Lottie. Vera was tossing her scarf and her cape and saying chummily, "Just an omelette, really—we aren't at all hungry," and then they were in a small room, and the door to the room shut behind them. Here ashes and orange peel spilled out of a cold grate. Three tables pushed against the wall were barricaded behind armchairs, an upright piano, dining chairs, and a cheval glass. The two girls pulled a table and chairs clear and sat down. Lottie had a view of a red clay tennis court strung with Christmas lights. She turned to see what Vera was staring at. Another table was taken, but the noise and confusion coming from it at first seemed part of the chaos in the room. Lottie now saw two American soldiers and two adolescent girls who might be their wives. One of the girls, the prettier of the two, cried out, "But tell me now, am I talking loud? Because I sound to myself like I am talking loud." The laughter from the others was a kettledrum, and Lottie and Vera displayed their first pathetic complicity: "We aren't Yanks," said the look they exchanged.

Dissociating herself and perhaps Lottie from the noisy four, Vera gave their waitress a great smile and a skyrocket of French. *"On n'a que ça, les Americains,"* said the waitress, shrugging. Vera's flashy French, her flashy good will did not endear her. Lottie watched the waitress's face and understood: she didn't like them, either. When Vera praised the small neat lighter she kept in her apron pocket, the waitress said, *"C'est un briquet, tout simplement."* She served a tepid omelette on cold plates and disappeared into a more interesting region, whence came the sound of men's voices. Lottie and Vera sat on, forgotten.

Vera said, "There should be a thing on the table you could hit that would go cling, cling."

"A bell," said Lottie, taken in. "The thing is a bell."

"I know. I was showing you how Al talks." Smoking, Vera told about walks in Roma and meals when she and her Polish friend from home had nothing to eat but hard-as-a-rock cheese. Once, he gave his share to a dog.

"Are you hard up for money, Vera?" Lottie did not mean by this she had any to lend.

"No, not really. But I sort of am when I'm with him. I pretend not to have any at all and live the way he does." Vera was bored; she was always quickly bored. Blowing smoke all over Lottie, she began defending the four Americans. "You've never seen how abominable Canadians can be."

Americans could be trained to set an example, Lottie insisted. They should be loved. Who was to blame if they were not?

Vera mashed her cigarette out on her plate. "D'you know how Canadian soldiers used to cut the Germans' throats?" she said. "Al showed me. You push the helmet like this," and she reached across quick as a snake and pressed the long helmet Lottie Benz would have been wearing had she been a soldier into the nape of her neck and drew her forefinger under Lottie's chin.

Lottie understood that an attempt had been made against her life and that she was safe. She said, "I love my country, Vera, and even if I didn't I wouldn't run it down."

"I'm not running it down. I'm telling you stories."

The bill was nineteen hundred francs. Vera said it was grossly excessive. "They took you for an American," she said. "It's those damned overshoes."

The air outside smelled of earth and eternally wet leaves, as though this place were unmindful of seasons. At the end of a walled lane the walled graveyard was a box. The sky (the sun was covered up now) was the lid. Lottie was still disturbed by Vera's attack. She knew if you show nothing, eventually you feel nothing; presently, feeling nothing, she was just herself, a visitor here—not a guest, because she was paying her way. She walked a pace or two behind Vera, who had taken on a serious and rather reproachful air, sniffing at rusty iron crosses, shaking her head beside a fresh grave covered over with planks. At the only plot of grass in the cemetery, she stopped and announced that this was it. A brownish shrub had been clipped so that it neatly surrounded a stone bench. Someone—now, in December—had planted a border of yellow pansies. Vera, stalking dramatically in her cape, left Lottie to think her thoughts. A restless pilgrim, she slashed at weeds with her handbag and all at once called, "It's not where you are, Lottie. It's over here." Lottie rose slowly from the bench, where she had not been thinking about Katherine Mansfield but simply nursing her several reasons for not feeling well. Where Vera stood, a block of polished granite weighed upon a block still larger. The base was cemented to the ground.

"'Katherine Mansfield,'" Vera droned. "'Wife of John Middleton Murry. 1888-1923. But I tell you, my lord fool, out of this nettle, danger, we pluck this flower, safety.' Well, I don't know what *that* means. Another thing I wish you'd tell me—what is that awful china rose doing there instead of real flowers? It's so puritan. You can't just aban-don people that way, under all that granite. It's less than love. It's just considering your own taste."

"She is not abandoned, Vera; she is buried."

The orator heard only herself. "The stone is even moss-resistant," she said. But no, for the first wash of green crept up the granite step and touched a capital "M."

Lottie, whose ears might have been deaf to everything but Vera until now, heard other sounds—a rooster crowing, a sudden rush of motors somewhere, a metallic clanging that certainly had to do with troops. Vera planted one foot upon the step and with more effort than seemed needed removed the rose. She tossed it aside; it landed in the tall grass of another grave. Then she picked a handful of yellow pansies and strewed them where the rose had been. Like all gestures, it seemed to Lottie suspect.

Lottie need never have seen Vera again after this. Vera departed for Rome, having first turned out her bureau drawers and left at Lottie's hotel a number of things she did not require. Lottie still had not looked up all the people to whom she had been given introductions. She woke up early each day wondering whom she would be seeing that night. Despite Vera's remark about overshoes, she went on wearing hers, and she wore her hats—the gardenia bandeau, the feather toque with veil, the suède beret—even though people turned and smiled and stared. Lottie told her new acquaintances that she had only just arrived and was eager to get to Strasbourg, where the university library contained everything she wanted; but she made no move to go. One mild rainy night, like a night in April displaced, a couple she had talked to on the plane from Canada invited her to the Comédie-Caumartin to see Danièle Delorme in an Ibsen revival. The theater reminded Lottie of Vera, although she could not think why. It was stuffy and hot, and had been redecorated, and it smelled of paint. "We may get a headache from this," Lottie warned. The new friends, whose name was Morrow, thought she had said something remarkable about the play. The Morrows were dressed as if they had not planned to spend the evening together—he in tweeds and flannel, she in a sleeveless black dress with layers of silk fringe overlapping down the skirt. The bracelets on her arm jangled. Her hair was short (it had been long on the plane) and pushed behind the ears. They had both changed since the journey, but nothing about them seemed definite. Lottie thought they were not wearing their clothes from home but new outfits they were trying for effect.

Soon after the lights went down, a quarrel began in the audience. Groans and hisses and shouts of "*Mal élevé!*" covered the actors' voices, and the curtains had to be drawn. The actors tried again, and got on safely until one of them said how hot it was, upon which the audience began to laugh, a spectator shouted "*Oui, en effet!*" and threats were exchanged, though no one was struck. Baited by the public, the actors seemed to Lottie too intimate, too involved. She lost the thread of the story and became self-conscious, as though *she* were on the stage.

Languidly, the Morrows glanced about as if they knew people, or expected to know them soon. "I can't imagine why she revived it," Mrs. Morrow said during the interval.

"The sets are dull," said the husband. "The rest of the cast is weak."

Lottie said, "We had better stuff than this in Winnipeg; we had these really good actors from England, and the audience knows how to behave." Why should that make the Morrows so distant, all at once?

The husband was the first to unbend. Forgiving Lottie for her provincialism, he described the play he was over here to write—a murder, and several people who are really all one person. The several persons are either the victim, or the murderer, or a single witness. It was all the same thing.

"What will you be doing apart from that?" said Lottie.

"Nothing. That is what I *am* doing."

There was something fishy about him. He was too old to be a student, yet clearly wasn't working. Did he have money, or what?

"What do you think Ibsen did apart from that?" said the wife, turning her big black-rimmed eyes on Lottie. She held her elbow in one hand and a cigarette holder in the other.

"Nobody knows," said Lottie. "Anyway, goodness, we're none of us Ibsen."

When Lottie called the Morrows at their hotel a day later, Mrs.

Morrow said that Lottie was not to take this personally but she and her husband were working hard—she was typing for him—and her husband did not want to spend too much time with Canadians over here. Lottie was not offended. It confirmed her suspicion of fishiness. Nevertheless, she did want to be with someone familiar at Christmas, and so was not displeased when she found a telegram from Vera. The telegram said, MEET YOU ALSACE SEE LETTER. The letter came two days later. Pages long, it told where and how they were to meet, although not why.

2

Vera was dressed this time in a purple skirt and sweater she said had come from a five-and-ten in Rome. She stood idly, hand on one hip, in the lobby of their hotel while Lottie filled out a questionnaire for the police of Colmar. If her answers varied by so much as a spelling mistake from the answers she had given in Paris, she was sure she would be summoned for an explanation. Vera's hair was thick and straight and blonder than it had been. "Didn't I have a good idea about Christmas?" she said.

"It seemed like a good idea," said Lottie, in the tone of one only prudently ready for anything.

"You couldn't of done any work over Christmas anyway."

"But why Colmar, Vera?"

"You'll see enough of Strasbourg. You might as well look at something else." Lottie let Vera link an arm through hers and guide her out of the hotel into a light-blue evening. The shape of what seemed to be a street of very old houses was outlined in colored lights. Near a church someone had propped a ladder and climbed into a spruce tree to hang tinsel balls. The spire of the church had been lighted as well, but half-heartedly, as if the electrician in charge had run out of light bulbs. Lottie thought, I have not sent Kevin a cable for Christmas.

In the restaurant Vera chose for their dinner that night, she was loud and too confident, and Lottie felt undervalued. She had submitted to a wearing journey from Paris, with a change of trains at

Strasbourg. From Strasbourg to Colmar she stood, her luggage in everyone's way, until she saw a city in a plain as flat as home, and understood this to be her destination. This much she let Vera know. What she did not say was how she had without a trace of fatigue left her luggage in the station at Strasbourg and gone out to find the cathedral. It was an important element of her thesis, for both Catholic and Protestant services were held inside; also, Dr. Keller had said something about an astronomical clock he admired. Flocks of bicycles swooped at Lottie, more unnerving than the screaming cabs of Paris. She heard German. Once, she was unable to get directions in French. When the first words of German crossed her lips, she thought they would remain, engraven, to condemn her. Speaking the secret language, she spoke in the name of unknown Grandmother Benz, whom she was said to resemble. The cathedral seemed to right itself before her—frosty, chalky, pink and trembling in the snowy air. A brown swift river divided that part of the city from the station. True Christmas was praised in shopwindows, with wine and nuts and candied peel. A gingerbread angel with painted paper face and paper wings cried of home—not of Winnipeg but of a vestigial ceremony, never mentioned as German, never confirmed as Canadian. The Paris promise of Christmas had been nonsense—all but the holly outside the hotel, and one night someone stole even that. The cold air and certain warm memories tinged her cheeks pink. She saw herself without disapproval in a glass. Sometimes strangers smiled. They were not smiling meanly at her overshoes or her hat. None of this was Vera's business.

Vera chewed on a drumstick, and told what had happened in Rome. She had found her friend Al Wiczinski living with a French family in a crummy unheated palazzo. He was adored by the daughter of the family, aged seventeen, and also by her father. Al was just too nice to people. But he was coming to Alsace. ("Coincidence, eh, Lottie?") A college had been opened for refugees in Strasbourg, and Al had been offered a teaching job. Politics, in a way, said Vera, but mostly the culture racket. After all, teaching Slav lit to a bunch of Slavs was what, culture or politics? Radio Free Europe was running the place. Lottie had never heard of it. Vera glanced at her oddly. Al had been told that he could obtain the visa he needed in Colmar more easily than in

Strasbourg, and had sent Vera on to see what she could do. In theory, Al was not allowed to live along any frontier, especially this one.

"Why not?"

"Don't ask me. Ask the police."

"I don't see why a Canadian should have any trouble," said Lottie.

"He's only sort of Canadian," said Vera. "If you ask me, I don't think he should have a passport. I mean, he sort of picks on the place."

"You can't be sort of Canadian. If he is, he doesn't have to be in trouble anywhere."

"Oh, come off it, Lottie," said Vera, smiling at her. "Suppose you had to explain what you were doing here this very minute, what would you say?"

Lottie gave up. Sulking and pale, she let Vera glance at her several times but would not say what the matter was. She thought she had been taken in.

After dinner they walked beside a black gelatinous canal in which stood, upside down, a row of crooked houses. Lottie said, "Sometimes I think I've got no brains."

"You've got brains, all right," said Vera.

"No." Out of the protective dark she spoke to upside-down houses. "I've got a good memory. I can remember anything. But I've never worked on my own."

Lottchen. When she stuffed her mouth full of candy, her mother knew it had been taken without permission, but the boys were scolded instead of the little girl. Why? Oh, yes—they had put her up to it. Captain von Hook told them what he thought of it, in a high and frightening voice. He was meant to be principal of his school, but after 1939 his career was blocked.

The promenade along the canal ended Lottie's first evening in Alsace. She and Vera parted in the hotel lobby—Vera was going to stay and converse with total strangers in the bar—and without waiting to see if this was all right with Lottie she kissed her good night.

On the morning of Christmas Eve, Vera rose at seven and, after shaking Lottie awake, dragged her—cold, stunned, already weary—into streets where pale lamps flickered and aboard a bus filled with pale people asleep. They rolled into dark hills, which, as the day lightened, became blotter green. Lottie was not yet accustomed to steep hills and valleys; she wanted them to be more beautiful than they were. Desolate, she shut her eyes, believing herself close to a dead faint. She heard a girl cry "*C'est épouvantable*," but it was only because an elderly Alsatian peasant could not speak French. In the town of Munster, they descended before a shuttered hotel. The dining room was closed, glacial—Lottie had a glimpse of stacked chairs. In the kitchen a maid was ironing sheets, while another fed two little boys bread in the shape of men with pointed heads and feet. Vera ordered red wine and cheese for breakfast, and asked the price of rooms. Lottie wondered why. The wine stung and burned, the cheese made her lips swell. One day she would tell Vera about her low blood pressure, and how her temperature was often lower than normal, too, and she would let Vera understand how selfish and thoughtless she had been. On their way out through the courtyard, Vera banged on a door marked PISSOIR. Lottie walked on. "You'll have to get over being fussy," Vera remarked. Lottie affected not to hear. She concentrated on the view of Munster, smoke and blue in a hollow. Above the town a blue gap broke open the metal sky. They set off downhill over wet earth and melting snow. Lottie walked easily in her comic overshoes, but Vera was pitched forward by the heels on her Italian shoes. They saw no one except a troop of little boys in sabots and square blue caps who engulfed them, fell silent, giggled after they had gone by. A snowball struck the back of Vera's cape. The boy who had thrown it wore rimless glasses and was absolutely cross-eyed. "Brat," said Lottie, who did not care for children. But Vera laughed back at him and put out her tongue.

They missed the bus they ought to have taken back to Colmar and had a three-hour wait. Vera pretended it had been planned that way. Tugging at Lottie, she made for a café. Here a Christmas tree gave off fragrance in waves, like a hyacinth. Radio Stuttgart offered them carols. Vera ate a mountain of sauerkraut and ham and sausage and drank a bottle of white wine. "Poor old Al, he's got no one but me, and here it is Christmas Eve!" she said gaily.

Elbows on table, head in her hands, Lottie read a newspaper. "Pinay has resigned," she said.

"No skin off my nose," said Vera.

"It'll skin theirs. He was keeping the franc up." Hearing the carols on the radio, Lottie wished she were religious. It might take her mind off such things as high finance, her own health, and scholarship.

"You know about exchange and all that," said Vera. "I just know when I can't afford to do what I want."

"May I ask, Vera, what you live on?"

"My family, for the moment. But Frannie and my brother Joe will both be in college in about a year and then I'll have to be on my own. The family can't keep all three of us."

"It's good of them to keep you now," said Lottie. "You don't work or anything."

"They get me instead of a holiday in California. I'm their luxury."

"Don't they think you should work?"

"They haven't said," said Vera, grinning. "I'm waiting for the right suggestion. You know where I was this time last year? In Rome. I'd just met Al."

"You've been away a long time," Lottie said. "I could never stay away that long."

"Who wants you to?"

The trouble with Vera was that she was indifferent. She had made Lottie come all the way to Colmar, with a complicated change of trains, and had tramped her up and down the rainy slopes on Christmas Eve, just so that she, Vera, would not feel lonely. Vera whistled with the radio, stopped, and said, "I had a little girl."

"I don't understand you. Oh, I'm sorry. I do."

"She's been adopted."

Lottie said stiffly, "I'm sure she's in a good home."

"I dream she's following me. In the dream I'm not like me. I look like Michèle Morgan. I dream I'm leading her through woods and holding branches so they won't snap back in her face. She could be dead. When it's raining like it was this afternoon, she could be outside, with nobody looking after her."

The only protection Lottie had received until now in her native country was an implicit promise that no one would ever talk this way.

"The family were over here a couple of times. Nothing's changed. They still say, 'Why don't you do something about your hair?' They don't seem to think I'll ever come back, or want to. The doctor who looked after the adoption kept writing to them, *'Il faut lui trouver un bon mari.'* Instead of doing that, they put me in a sort of convent school, and I nearly died. You don't know how it was over here four, five years ago. Now they let me do what I like. I'll find a *mari* if I feel like it. If I don't, too bad for them." Vera at this moment looked despairingly plain.

"It's a sad sort of life for you, Vera. You've been on your own since you were what—seventeen?"

"You feeling sorry for me?"

Feeling sorry had not occurred to Lottie; she was astonished that Vera would think it possible. Feeling sorry would have meant she was not minding her own business. Vera had certainly been away a long time. Otherwise she would never have supposed such a thing.

The next morning at breakfast, in a coffee shop Vera liked because the *croissants* were stuffed with almond paste, Lottie gave Vera her Christmas present—a leather case that would hold a pack of Gauloises. Vera had nothing for Lottie. She turned the case over in her hand, as if wondering what the occasion was. Lottie, slightly embarrassed, picked up from the leather seat beside her a folded, harsh-looking tract. She spread it on the glass-topped table. It was cheaply printed. In German, it informed its finder that "in the mountains" a Separatist movement that seemed to have died had only been sleeping. Recent injustices had warmed it to life.

"I know all about this," said Vera importantly, snatching it away. Her political eye looked for the printer, and she was triumphant pointing out that the name was absent, which proved that the tract was from a clandestine press.

"Of course," said Lottie, puzzled. "Who else would print it? That's what it's about, a clandestine movement. What I don't understand is, what do they want to separate from?"

"France, you dope," said Vera.

"I know all that," said Lottie, in her slowest voice. "I'm only trying to say that if there are people here who don't want to belong to France, then my proposition doesn't hold water. The idea is, these people are supposed to be loyal but still keep their national characteristics."

"There aren't many. Just a couple of nuts."

"There mustn't even be one."

"It's your own fault for inventing something and then trying to stick people in it." Vera talked, or, rather, rambled on, until the arrival of hot chocolate and *croissants*, when she began to stuff her mouth. Lottie folded the tract with care. A few minutes later she was once more rattling around inside a bus, headed now for Kaysersberg. "Good place for Christmas," Vera decreed, consulting but not sharing a green guide-book she kept in the pocket of her cape.

"You said Colmar was a good place for Christmas!" Lottie said. Vera took no notice of this.

Kaysersberg might have been chewed by rats. The passage of armies seven years ago still littered the streets. They walked away from here and over fields toward another town Vera said would be better. The sun was warm on Lottie's back, and her mother's Persian-lamb coat was a suit of armor. Beside the narrow road, vines tied to sticks seemed to be sliding uphill. It was a trick of the eye. Another illusion was the way the mountains moved: they rose and collapsed, soft-looking, green, purple, charcoal, deserting Lottie when she turned her head. All at once a vineyard fell away, and there for one minute, spread before her, was the plain of the Rhine, strung with glistening villages, and a church steeple here and there poking through the mist. Across the river were dark clouds or dark hills. She could not see where they joined the horizon or where they rose from the plain. So this was the place she loathed and craved, and never mentioned. It was the place where her mother and father had been born, and which they seemed unable to imagine, forgive, or describe.

"Well, that's Germany," said Vera. "I'll have to go over one of these days and get my passport stamped. They didn't stamp it when I came in from Italy, and it has to be done every three months."

Lottie wished she were looking at a picture and not a real place. She wished she were a child and could *pretend* it was a picture. "I'll never go there!" she said.

They walked on and entered Riquewihr in a soft wash of mud that came over the tops of Vera's shoes. "Three stars in the book," said Vera, not even trying to be jaunty anymore. "God, what a tomb! You expect people here to come crawling out of their huts covered with moss and weeds."

"But you've been here, Vera? You said you had been all over."

"I haven't been exactly here. I thought it would be nice for you for Christmas."

Lottie considered briefly the preposterous thought that Vera had not been trying to wear her out but to entertain her. Suddenly, as if it were Lottie's fault, Vera began to complain about the way streets had been in Winnipeg when Vera's mother was a girl. Where Vera's mother had lived, there hadn't been any sidewalks; there were wooden planks. If Vera's mother stepped off a plank, she was likely to lose her overshoe in the gumbo mud. In the good part of town, on Wellington Crescent, there were no pavements either, but for a different reason. When Ukrainian children were taken across the city on digestive airings, after Sunday lunch, to look at Wellington Crescent houses—when their parents had at last lost the Old Country habit of congregating in public parks and learned the New World custom of admiring the houses of people more fortunate than they were—the children, wondering at the absence of sidewalks, were told that people here had always had carriages and then motorcars and had never needed to walk.

Vera was passionate over a past she knew nothing about. It was just her mother's folklore. Vera's mother, Lottie now learned, had washed in snow water. Vera herself could remember snow carried into the house and melted on the kitchen stove.

"Well, then, your father moved the whole family, I suppose," said Lottie, remembering Winnipeg Culture Patterns with Dr. Keller.

"That's right," said Vera, without inflection. "To your part of town."

Lottie had still not sent the Christmas cable to Kevin. Could she send it from here? It was early morning in Winnipeg—scarcely dawn.

Lottie intended to set off for Strasbourg the instant Christmas was over, but Vera gained another day. In the morning they went to see a movie called *Das Herz Einer Frau*, subtitled *Ich Suche Eine Mutti*—an incredibly sad story about a laundress and her little boy. Lottie, exasperated, turned to say something but saw that Vera was wiping tears. Later, she and Vera boldly entered a police station, where Vera asked questions on Al's behalf. Lottie sat staring at a sign: *C'est* CHIC *de parler Français!* "*Chic*" was in red.

It was plain that Vera's plans had gone wrong; Al's arrival should have coincided with Lottie's going. Vera did not want to go off to Strasbourg in case he came here, and she did not want Lottie to desert her. She coaxed from Lottie one more excursion, this time not far away. After a mercifully short bus trip, they walked under pines. In these woods, so tame, so gardened, that Lottie did not know what to call them, they stumbled on a ruin covered with moss and ivy. "It is part of the Maginot Line, I think," said Vera.

Lottie, frantic with being where she did not want to be, turned from her and cried, "Is that what it is? The Maginot Line? No wonder they lost the war."

"Is that what Dr. Keller taught you? Why do you think one piece is all of everything?"

"What else can you do?" said Lottie. The mist carried in her lungs since Paris darkened and filled her chest. "You don't understand, Vera. I'm not strong physically. That's what I meant that day on the train, when you said 'weak, not frail.' I *am* frail, and I have to do this thesis on my own. I have to choose my own books and work with people I've never met before. I've never used a strange library. You've made me walk a lot. I've got this very low blood pressure. One day my heart might just stop."

"Yes, well, it was a mistake," said Vera. She folded her arms under her cape and kicked at the Maginot Line instead of kicking herself, or Al, or Lottie.

3

The advantage of Strasbourg over any other place was that Lottie here had a warm room. In a hotel on the Quai des Bateliers, discovered by Vera, she unpacked the notes and files. She could see the spire of the cathedral, encased in scaffolding, rosy and buoyed up on plain air. Chimes and bells evenly punctuated her days and nights. Every night, at a dark foggy hour, she heard strange tunes—tunes that seemed to be trying to escape from between two close parallel lines. The sound came from a shack full of Arabs, across from the hotel, on the bank of a canal. In the next room but one, Lottie had a neighbor, a man who typed. The empty room between them was a sounding box. She heard him talking to himself sometimes and walking about. His step was quick. Vera was also on this floor, at the end of a corridor papered with lettuce-sized roses. Her room gave onto nothing of interest, and her window sill was already a repository for bread, butter, dime-store knives, and old newspapers.

On January 9th, a month to the day after her arrival in France, Lottie wrote her first long letter to Kevin. The postcards she had sent from Paris and Colmar said, "I am working hard," which was not so, and "It is terribly cold," and "I'm saving it up to tell you when I get back." Her real letters to him were those she composed in her head and was too shy to write. She could imagine him listening to anything she had to tell him but not reading what she wrote. "I went to the opening of the European Assembly in a new prefab building that already looks like a shack, looks left over from the war," she wrote, hoping that this would be a letter of such historical importance he would keep it in a folder. "A sign said that anyone showing approval *or* disapproval would be thrown out. There were hardly any visitors, and I did not have the feeling that history was being made. It was all dry and dull. I listened to the translators through the headphones, but it was more of a strain than just hearing an unknown language. Sort of English-English and bored French. M. Spaak was not there, because he had rheumatism (at least that's what I understood) and just when this was announced I felt the start of a chill and had to rush out and home in a cab. I was shaking so much in my fur coat that Vera was frightened. It's not serious"— she felt her beginning going off the rails—"but I've got a chill and a fever and a bad cough and a pain in my chest and a sore throat. Vera has bought me some pills full of codeine. Vera believes in sweat. A dog that belongs to this hotel, name of Bonzo, came in to see me. I gave him a piece of stale bread and he took it under the bed, with his legs and tail sticking out flat. It suddenly occurred to me today that there is no such thing as sociology. When you are a sociologist, all you can do is teach more of the same, and every professor has his own idea about what it is. Vera says that if I were studying the integration of Indians, which never happened anyway, it would not be called sociology. Vera will take this out to mail."

Lottie could eat nothing until the next day, when, mostly to pacify Vera, she picked at a helping of macaroni and gravy. Vera sat at Lottie's clean table and proceeded to make a mess of it. She drank beer out of a bottle and, when she had drunk all she wanted, poured the rest in the washbasin. "Do you mind the smell?" she asked, too late, peering down. Vera was already on a first-name basis with the whole hotel, and particularly friendly with the man who typed. He was an elderly madman, who had only a week before been released from the mental ward of a military hospital.

"What do you type?" Vera had asked him.

"Poems," he replied, looking at her with one eye. (The other was glass.)

Vera read aloud from *France-Soir* to Lottie, who disliked being read to. "*Le trentième anniversaire de la mort de Katherine Mansfield est célébré aujourd'hui à Avon.*"

"They'll see I got rid of that china rose," said Vera, very pleased.

In the night, Lottie spat blood. It looked bright and pure, like a chip of jewel. She had coughed enough to rupture a small blood vessel. Out of childhood came recollections of monumental nosebleeds, and of the whole family worried. As if to confirm the memory, Vera came bustling in, for all the world like Lottie's mother. She found Lottie lying across the bed with her head hanging back. She closed the window, then covered Lottie with the eiderdown. Lottie was irritated. "I need lots and lots of air," she said. Being irritated brought on an attack of coughing and pain. Vera began opening and closing windows again.

Lottie wanted to write to Kevin, "My coldness to Vera frightens me. She came in again now and was sweet and kind, and I thought I would scream. She smelled of the bar downstairs in the hotel where she likes to hang out eating stale chips and talking to men. She sat on the bed and stroked my pillow saying, 'Isn't there anything I can do for you?' She seems lost and lonely because Al hasn't turned up. She offers all the kindness she can in exchange for something I don't want to give because I can't spare it. A grain of love? Maybe the Pole, Al, is hell. It is not my fault. I shrank into myself, cold, cold. We are all like that. So are you, Kevin. Finally I said, 'Vera, would you mind awfully opening the window?' and she aired the room (she likes doing that) and held her cape so as to protect me from the draft. She looked around for something else to do. 'I'll go and complain about that washbasin,' she said. 'Yes, do go,' I said. I wanted to be left alone. She felt it, and went away looking as if she would never understand why."

This composed, but not written, Lottie dragged herself from her bed and down the rose-papered hall to Vera's room, on an impulse, to say something like "You were kind," but Vera's door was locked. She thought she heard Vera whispering to someone—or else she heard the curtains moving, or the rustle of the papers Vera kept on her window sill.

"Even when I am nice to Vera," she finished the letter, "it doesn't mean anything, because I don't honestly like her."

Vera had complained about the washbasin and then proceeded to the post office to collect her mail. She and Lottie were both using poste restante, because they thought the Quai des Bateliers was temporary. Lottie wanted to get into a students' residence where she would meet interesting people, and Vera was waiting for Al. Vera came back from the post office with a picture of Al. He was in Paris now—he seemed to be approaching in stages and halts, like a traveler in an earlier century—and had sent, along with his photograph, a letter full of requests and instructions. Lottie looked at a round face and enormous dark eyes with fixed, staring pupils. He seemed drugged or startled. "His eyes are blue," said Vera. "They look dark with that fancy lighting. I've been out to the refugee college, asking around. He's got it all wrong. It's only a dorm. They go to the university for classes. It sounded funny in the first place, teaching Slav lit to Slavs. Maybe he's found something else to do. Or not to do, more like it. He's got in with some Poles who live outside Paris and do weaving. They may also have prayer and patriotic evenings. Right Wing Bohemia," said Vera, looking down her large nose, "lives in the country and weaves its own skirts. *You* know."

Over Lottie's cringing mind crept the fear that Vera might be some sort of radical. Ukrainians were extreme one way or another. You would have to know which of the Uke papers Vera's parents subscribed to, and even that wouldn't help unless you could read the language. "Get this," said Vera, and, adopting a manner Lottie assumed must be Al's, she read aloud, "'You cannot imagine what a change it is for me—yesterday *le grand luxe* in Roma, today here. But I must say, even though I have the palate of a gourmet, I find nothing wrong with the cooking.'"

"He just doesn't sound Canadian," Lottie said.

"In the evening the old man came to my room," composed Lottie, introducing the old man to Kevin without warning. "He stood in the doorway, with his battered face and his one eye, and said, 'I am going to write a poem about Canada in honor of you and your friend Mademoiselle Vera. In which city is there a street called Saint-Jean-Louis?'"

"In the first place," Lottie had said earnestly, "is there any such saint?"

"Could it be in Winnipeg?" the old man said.

"No, Quebec." She recalled crooked streets, and one street where the houses were frozen and old; over the top of a stone wall had bloomed a cold spring tree . . . But I was never in Quebec, she remembered next.

There was no transition from day to night. She heard him typing, like someone dropping china beads one by one. She coughed, and put the pillow over her face. If he comes in and talks about the poem again, she thought, it might make me homesick. If something made me homesick I might cry, and that could break the fever. If something could make me homesick, I would go home and not wait for someone to come and fetch me. But when she wanted to think of home, she thought of a church in Quebec, and a dark recess where the skull of General Montcalm, preserved by Ursuline nuns, and exposed by them, rested in a gold-and-glass cage. But I have never seen it—someone described it to me. It has nothing to do with home. Her eyes filled with tears, but not of homesickness.

A mounting litter of paper handkerchiefs and empty yogurt jars spilled out of the paper carton Vera had put beside Lottie's bed. "*À quoi bon?*" said the hotel maid when Lottie asked her to empty the box. The maid was not obliged to clean a room unless the tenant went out. It was a rule. Bribed, she said she would see about the washbasin but nothing more.

Lottie wanted to give the old man something better than an imaginary street for his poem, but now the idea of a city she had not seen obscured her memory. "What, do you mean you were never there?" he might ask if she told him she had never been to Quebec. "It was a tremendous excursion," she would have to say. "Nobody over here knows how far it was, or how much it would have cost," and tears of self-pity followed the others.

Bonzo, the hotel dog, stole under the bed and tore to pieces a box of matches. Lottie had lost her voice. She whispered, "Bad dog!" and "You'll make yourself very sick!" and on her hands and knees retrieved a slimy piece of wood. She had a high fever now. She knew it by the trouble she had getting back into bed—she could not judge its height—and she saw it reflected on the face of the nurse who had been summoned by Vera. The nurse, a peasant girl in a soiled head scarf, twin sister to the maid in appearance, told Lottie what her temperature was, in a disapproving voice. It was in centigrade and meant nothing.

"*Ma voisine!*" cried the old man, standing in the hall. "It is very warm outside, so warm that one can go out without a coat."

"Good," whispered Lottie. She heard him go out into the bitter day, perhaps without a coat.

She felt well enough to go on with her letter to Kevin: "My neighbor does exercises in the doorway to show me how spry he is. At the end of each one he hops up and stands at attention, giving just one small disciplined bound in place. He is like someone who has done these things for years in a row with other men—in a jail, or a military hospital, or a prison camp, or the Army, or a mental home. In any one, or two, or three..."

Lottie and the old man shared a view. At night they heard the iron chimes of the cathedral. At dawn they could see the pink spire briefly red. Inside the cathedral, Death struck the hours in Dr. Keller's clock, and at noon Our Lord blessed in turn each of the Apostles. Every noon—or, rather, at half past twelve, for the clock was half an hour off—the betrayal was announced by a mechanical cock flapping stiff wings. One night the neighbor typed all night, and, talking loudly to himself, went to bed before six, the hour at which the whole clumsy performance of the clock—chariots, pagan deities, signs of the zodiac, days of the week, Christ and the Apostles, the betrayal—finished its round. Lottie understood that night and day were done for before time from home could overtake them. She was dislocated, perhaps forever, like the clock.

The nurse returned next day with a doctor, who said, "It is a little fever."

"What kind?" Lottie asked. Her teeth were chattering. "What about my nosebleeds?"

"A little simple cough. You take yourself too seriously." He wrote out a prescription for three kinds of remedy, which were all patent medicines. Two of the three Vera had already bought. Lottie composed for Kevin: "I imagined—because with a fever you don't know where imagination begins and a dream leaves off—that my mad neighbor had to repaint the outside of the high school. I said, 'Can't the parishioners afford to hire someone?' Isn't it funny, my thinking it was a church?"

Her health improved; she got dressed and walked along the river, with Vera beside her. At the post office was a letter from Kevin, and for Vera a receipt from American Express in Rome for five hundred lire she had left as a deposit for forwarding her mail. This Vera misread as five hundred dollars she had received from home, and even when Lottie pointed out the error she continued to prattle on about what she was going to do with the money. She would take Lottie south! They would visit Al Wiczinski in Paris! Laughing, she picked up a glove someone had dropped on the pavement and put it in her pocket. Lottie was suddenly wildly angry about the glove, as if all the causes Vera had ever given for anger were pale compared with this particular offense. She walked back to the hotel, trembling with weakness and fury, and plotting some sort of obscure revenge.

The letter she had from Kevin began, "I'm fine. Sorry you aren't feeling well." She put it away with the Separatist tract found in the coffee shop. They were documents to be analyzed.

Vera said, "Listen, Lottie, I'm hard up for the moment. No, don't look scared. I'll just pawn something. If you've got anything you could lend me to pawn, that would be great."

"Kevin," Lottie thought she would write, "this morning I bundled all my trinkets into a scarf of Vera's—Granny's pearl and sapphire earrings I can't wear because my ears aren't pierced, and my cameo, which turned out to be worth nothing—and I went with Vera, who was whistling and singing and not worried at all. I had to leave my passport, because they said they were giving me a lot of money—fifteen thousand francs, which I handed to Vera, who took it as if it were a gift. She paid her hotel bill. In the afternoon, she forgot where the money came from and what it was for, and she invited me with a grand air to the Kléber, a big café like a railway station. We drank three thousand and fifty francs' worth of kümmel. Vera also invited the mad party from down the hall. He said he could read English and had been reading the love letters of Mark Twain. The band wore red coats and played 'L'Amour Est un Bouquet de Violettes.' Everywhere you go, you hear that played. The waiters were reading newspapers; there were high ceilings and trays of beer and enormous pretzels. Vera sang with the band. I wonder if I shall ever get my passport back."

Whatever Lottie's fever had been, it had worn itself down to bouts of coughing. Her head was stuffed with felt. When she looked at her old notes or tried to read anything, her eyes shut of their own accord. Without her passport she could not collect her mail. Why had Vera not given up her own? Because, said Vera, astonished at the question, then she would not have been able to get *her* mail, and, as she was expecting money from home, she needed it.

Lottie began to be worried about money. She had spent more than ever planned for on medicines, on the doctor and nurse, on the Christmas holiday in Colmar, which now seemed wild, wine-drenched.

On a cold, foggy winter Saturday, when she could hope for nothing in the post, and could not shake off her cough or rid herself of her pallor, the newspapers finally mentioned an epidemic of grippe that was sweeping through Europe. The symptoms resembled those of pneumonia. The popular name for it was Virus X. There had been two new deaths in Clermont-Ferrand. "Why do they always tell about what happens in Clermont-Ferrand?" said Vera.

She had received three hundred dollars from home. Without making a particular point of it, or showing any gratitude, she returned the fifteen thousand francs. "What I never did understand," she said, as if discussing ancient history, "was why you didn't just take your own money and unpawn your stuff and get your passport back."

Lottie could not make sense of that. The passport had been tied up by Vera, and only Vera could undo the knot.

Vera had also received a birthday box from her sister-in-law, the wife of Honest Stan. It contained aspirin, Life Savers, two cards of snap fasteners, colored ribbon, needles, thread, a bottle of vitamin pills, Band-Aids, and Ivory soap. One aspirin was missing in each tin. "She sends me old clothes sometimes," said Vera, groping at the bottom of the box. "She's from a good old United Empire Loyalist family, true-blue Tory, one-hundred-per-cent Anglo-Saxon taste in clothes." Lottie felt obscurely offended, as if her own taste had been impugned. Kevin was probably Irish, but, being Protestant, he counted as English. Remembering that Vera was a nut who collected lost gloves, Lottie ranged herself and Kevin on the side of Honest Stan's wife. "There," said Vera, with satisfaction, and pulled out a summer frock of blue voile sprigged with roses. It had puffed sleeves and reached midway between Vera's hip and knee. Vera opened the window, shook out the dress, and sent it off. The dress, picked up by the wind, rose and then floated down. The Arab music had begun—it accompanied a certain dark hour of the day—and Vera said the dress was dancing to it.

On Sunday, when the sky was full of bells, and the snow along the canals a blue that was nearly white, Lottie walked with Vera, believing that this was spring. Upon the water was the swift circle of a flight of birds. When the girls looked up from the reflection, the birds were white dots in the sky. Bridges, bare trees, and cobbles passed them, and Lottie, walking on a treadmill, was all at once drenched in sweat, and trembling, and had to lean on Vera's arm. Put to bed, she lay limp, mute, her mouth dry, her hands burning. There was a new electric pain in her lungs. In her mind she wrote to Kevin, "My thesis is a mess. I haven't done any work, and here it is past the middle of January. Most of the things Keller let me think weren't true..."

The firemen's band marching beneath the window played a fat, German-sounding military air. She was like a wooden toy apart at the joints, scattered to the four corners of the room. Each of the pieces was marred. Yet by evening she was suddenly better. She got up again and walked with Vera in the cold, snowy night, dragging Bonzo on the end of a rope. She thought, but did not say, that it was the most beautiful night she had ever seen. She admired, in silence, the lamps in the brown canals and in the icy branches above. Suddenly Vera snatched Bonzo's rope and, cape flying, ran like a streak. Vera could be perfectly happy with or without Al, probably with or without Lottie. The important thing was feeling free, and never being alone.

Only one letter was waiting at the post office when Lottie turned up, passport in hand. Kevin wrote, "A funny-looking girl called Rose Perry has been around this winter. Some friend of yours introduces us saying we have a lot in common because she is a sociologist, like you, and also High Anglican, though I don't know why that gives us something in common. She's around thirty, red hair, funny-looking—I already said that. She's from England, either taking some other degree or just picking up material on the white-collar class in the prairie provinces for her own fun. Now, why couldn't you have done just that and never left home? Rose says the integration idea isn't new. She's been having a hungry winter. Her scholarship isn't a hell of a lot, and it's in pounds, not dollars. We've had her over to the house."

He likes her, and I know why, Lottie thought. Because she is English. His family will look after her, feed her, find her a place to stay. If I were having a hungry winter, I would be the immigrants' child who hadn't made it. I wouldn't dare have a hungry winter.

The sun shone—a pale sunlight, the first of 1953. Vera climbed up the spire of the cathedral while Lottie waited below—two hundred-odd steps of winding stone to a snowy platform where pigeons hopped on the ledge, and where eighteenth-century tourists had carved the record of their climb. Up there, Vera heard the piercing screams of a schoolyard full of children. She went up a smaller and older-seeming spiral to the very top, above the cathedral bells, which she could see through windows carved in stone. Ice formed on the soles of her shoes. She was mystically moved, she declared, by the appearance of the bells, which seemed to hang over infinite space.

Walking in Vera's shadow, Lottie thought, I should never have seen her after that trip to Fontainebleau.

The days were lighter and longer. The rivers and canals became bottle green, and the delicate trees beside them were detached from fog. Vera and Lottie went often to the Grande Taverne de Kléber. When Lottie had enough kümmel to drink, Vera made sense. On one brilliantly sunny day, two girls came into the Kléber laughing the indomitable laughter of girls proving they can be friends, and Lottie said, "Look, Vera, that is like you and me." Presently they got up and changed cafés, moving by this means four streets nearer the hotel. The table here was covered with someone's cigarette ash—someone who had been here for a long time. There was in the air, with the smell of beer and fresh coffee, a substance made up of old conversations. The windows were black and streaked with melted snow. Each rivulet reflected the neon inside.

"Let's go over to Germany," Vera said for the second time. "It's nothing—just another bus ride. Maybe a train this time. All I have to do is get my passport stamped and come right back. It's just like crossing a road."

"Not for me it isn't."

Falling asleep that night, Lottie heard, pounding outside her window, a steam-driven machine the Arab workers had somehow got their hands on but could not operate. They sounded as if they were cursing each other. The sounds of Strasbourg were hard and ugly sometimes: trams and traffic, and in the night drunken people shouting the thick dialect.

"Lottie, wake up," Vera said.

Lottie thought she was in a café and that the waitress had said, "If you fall asleep here, I shall call the police." The room was full of white snow light, and Lottie was still clothed, under the eiderdown. Someone had taken off her shoes. She saw a bunch of anemones, red and blue, in a glass on the edge of the hopelessly plugged washbasin. "The nut next door brought us each a bunch of them," said Vera. She was bright and dressed, wearing tangerine lipstick that made her mouth twice as big as it should have been. "You know what time it is? One o'clock. Boy, do you look terrible! Al's just called from Paris. I wonder who paid for *that*? I thought he was calling because it's my twenty-first birthday, but he's just lonely. He wants me to come. I said, 'Why are we always doing something for *your* good? You've already left me stranded in Alsace.' I don't think he ever intended to come. He said, 'You know I need you, but I leave it up to you.' It's this moral-pressure business. Would it work with you?"

"Yes," said Lottie. She lay with her eyes open, imagining Strasbourg empty. How would she go alone to the post office?

"I hate letting him down. He's been through a lot."

"Then go."

"I don't think I should leave you. You look worse than when you had Virus X."

"We'll go out and drink to your birthday," Lottie said. "I'll look better then."

Walking again, crossing rivers and canals, they saw a man in a canoe. The water was green and thick and still. Along the banks the trees seemed bedded out, like the pansies in the graveyard. How rough and shaggy woods at home seemed now! Nothing there was ever dry underfoot until high summer, and then in a short time the ground was boggy again.

"I always felt I had less right to be Canadian than you, even though we've been there longer," Vera said. "I've never understood that coldness. I know you aren't English, but it's all the same. You can be a piece of ice when you want to. When you walked into the restaurant that day in Paris, I felt cold to the bone."

The canoe moved without a sound.

In a *brasserie* opposite the cathedral, where they celebrated Vera's coming of age, smoke lay midway between floor and ceiling, a motionless layer of blue. "I only want one thing for my birthday and there it is," said Vera, pointing to a player piano. Rolls were fed to the piano ("Poet and Peasant," the overture to "William Tell," "Vienna Blood") and not only did the piano keys rise and fall but the circle of violins, upside down, as if reflected, revolved and ground out spirited melodies.

Two little lamps with spangled shades decorated the instrument, which the waitress said was German and very old. That reminded Lottie, and she said, "I'll go with you tomorrow, if you want to, to get your passport stamped."

"It's not Moscow, for God's sake," said Vera. "It's only over there."

They stayed after everyone else had gone, and the smoke and the smell of pork and cabbage grew cold. They drank kümmel and made perfect sense.

"But Vera"—Lottie tried to be serious—"what are you going to *do* now that you are twenty-one?"

"I don't know. Find out why one aspirin was missing from each tin."

When they reached the hotel, drunk on friendship and with nothing to worry about but what to do with the rest of the day, Kevin was there. He sat with his habitual patience, in the hotel lobby, wearing his overcoat, reading a stained, plastic-covered, and over-confident bar list—the hotel served only coffee and chips and beer. He was examining the German and French columns of the menu with equal forbearance; he understood neither, and probably had no desires.

One day, she would become accustomed to Kevin, Lottie said to herself; stop seeing him, as she had nearly grown used to mountains. She thought, crazily, that if it had been Dr. Keller or any other man here to take her away, she would have clung to his hands and wept all over them. He looked so reassuring. She thought, A conservative Canadian type, and the words made her want to marry him. The confidence he assumed for them both let her know that if she had not worked on her thesis it was Dr. Keller's fault; he had prepared her badly. If she had been taken ill, it was because of a virus no one had ever heard of at home. When she saw the shapeless overcoat and the rubbers over his shoes that would make people laugh in Paris, she did not care, and she was happy because he could not read anything but English. That was the way he had to be.

"We can't talk here," she said. "Come upstairs."

"Is it all right?"

"Oh, *they* don't care."

He followed her up the stairs. He was ill at ease. He was worried about the hotel detectives.

"It's a lovely room, Kevin. Wait till you see the view, like a Flemish painting. And so warm. They leave the heat on all night. In Paris..."

From the doorway, looking around, he took in the half-drained basin with its greasy rim, the carton she used as a wastebasket, her underthings drying on a wire hanger, the table covered with a wine-stained cloth, the unmade bed. Lottie thought he was admiring her anemones. "My crazy neighbor gave them to me," she said. "The old boy from the military hospital. The one who's been writing the poem for Vera and me."

"No," said Kevin. "You never mentioned him. You mentioned this Vera just once. Then you stopped writing."

"I wrote all the time."

"I never got the letters. One of mine was returned. I guess the mail system here isn't exactly up to date."

"It must have been returned when I was too sick to go to the post office. You have to show your passport."

"I know, but I got just this one letter. If Vera hadn't been writing and telling your mother not to worry, I'd have been over before. It was a long time of nothing—not even a card for Christmas. Vera said how hard you were working, how busy." He left the door ajar but consented to sit on the unmade bed. "So, when I got the chance of a free hop to Zurich, a press flight..." He looked as if he would never grow old. The lines in his face might deepen, that was all. "I knew you'd had this flu. That can take a lot out of you."

"Yes. It was good of you to come and see how I was. How long can you stay?"

"One, two days. I don't want to interfere with your work."

Vera had said, "You've kept him on the string since you were sixteen. You'll bring it off." Ah, but it was one thing to be sixteen, pretty but modest, brilliant but unassuming. Her frail health had been slightly in her favor then. She had made the mistake of going away, and she had let Kevin discover he could get on without her. She held his hands and pretended to be as conscious as he was of the half-open door. They had never been as alone as at this moment and might never be again. They were almost dangerously on the side of friendship. If she began explaining everything that had taken place, from the moment she saw the holly in Paris and filled out her first police questionnaire, then they might become very good friends indeed, but would probably never marry.

"What I would like, Kevin—I don't know if you'll think it's a good idea—would be to go back with you. If I stay here, I'll get pneumonia. It's a good thing you came. Vera was killing me."

"Her letters didn't sound like it. Who is she, anyway?"

"A girl from home. A Ukrainian. She got in trouble, and they sent her away. Forget Vera."

"They could have just sent her to Minneapolis," said Kevin.

"Too close," said Lottie. "She might have slipped back."

"I guess you'll be glad to get out of here," said Kevin, as the bells struck the hour. He left her and returned to the hotel near the station, where he had taken a room. He could not rid himself of the fear that there might be detectives.

As she had promised, Lottie accompanied Vera to Germany. Kevin was with them. Once her passport was stamped, Vera thought she would go to Paris and help Al out of whatever predicament he was in, perhaps for the last time. "I liked it in Rome, where it was sort of crazy, but Paris is cold and dirty, and now he's twenty-six," said Vera.

"You mean, he should settle down," said Kevin, not making of it a question, and without asking what Vera imagined her help to Al could consist of.

Vera was hypocritically meek with Kevin, though she smiled when he said "Ukarainian," in five syllables. Lottie saw that if Vera had for one moment wavered, if she had considered going home because Lottie was leaving, the voice from home saying "Ukarainian" had reminded her of what the return would be. That was Vera's labyrinth. Lottie was on her way out. Kevin held Lottie's hand when Vera wasn't looking. He was friendly toward Vera, but protective of Lottie, which was the right imbalance. Lottie guessed he had made up his mind.

They walked on a coating of slush and ice—they had left the sun and the rivers on the other side.

In a totally gray village nothing stirred. Beyond it, on the dirty, icy highway by some railway tracks, they came upon a knot of orphans and a clergyman. The two groups passed each other without a glance. In a moment the children were out of sight. Answering a remark of Kevin's, Vera said they were ten or eleven years old, and unlikely to remember the air raids eight years ago. The sky was low and looked unwashed. On the horizon the dark blue mountains were so near now that Lottie saw where they rose from the plain. "Appenweier"—that was the name of the place. It was like those mysterious childhood railway journeys that begin and end in darkness.

"Are you girls by any chance going anyplace in particular?" said Kevin.

They turned and looked at him. No, they were just walking. Vera was not even leading the way.

"Well, I'm sorry then," said Kevin, "but as the saying goes, I've had it," and he marched them to the bombed station, and onto a train, and so back to France.

If that was Germany, there was nothing to wait for, expect, or return to. She had not crossed a frontier but come up to another limit.

Vera packed some things and left some, and departed for Paris. She and Lottie did not kiss, and Vera left the hotel without looking back. Her room—because it was cheaper—was instantly taken over by the mad neighbor. Kevin spent the evening, supperless, and part of the night with Lottie. Vera also must have been an inhibiting factor for him, Lottie decided—not just the phantom detectives. He might have taken Lottie to his hotel, which was more comfortable, but he thought it would look funny. They had given Vera a day's start. Kevin and Lottie were leaving for Zurich in the morning, and from Zurich flying home. Lottie did not think this night would give her a claim on Kevin, but when she woke, at an hour she could not place—woke because the Arabs were quarreling outside the window, got up to shut the window and, in the dark, comb her hair—she thought that a memory of it could. Vera had left a parcel of food. If she had not been afraid of disturbing Kevin, she would have spread it on the table and eaten a meal—salami, pickles, butter, and bread, half a bottle of Sylvaner.

Kevin now rose, obsessed by what the people who owned the hotel might be supposing. He smoked a cigarette, refused the wine, and put

450 · MAVIS GALLANT

on his clothes. He and Lottie were to meet next morning at the station; there was some confusion about the time. Kevin remarked, with a certain pride, that as far as he was concerned it was now around seven at night. He had brought a traveling clock to lend to Lottie so that she could wake up in plenty of time to pack. He set it for six, and placed the clock where she could reach it.

Lottie made a list not of what she was taking but of what she was leaving behind: food, wilted anemones, medicine, all Vera's residue as well as her own. The hotel maid would have a full day of it, and could not get away with saying "À quoi bon?" Lottie could not make herself believe that someone else would be sleeping in this room and that there would be no trace of Lottie and Vera anywhere. She rose before the alarm rang, and stood at the window with the curtain in her hand. She composed, "Last night, just at the end of the night, the sky and the air were white as milk. Snow had fallen and a thick low fog lay in the streets and on the water, filling every crack between the houses. The cathedral bells were iron and muffled in snow. I heard drunks up and down the sidewalk most of the night."

This could not be a letter to Kevin; he was there, across the city, and had never received any of the others. It was not a letter to anyone. There was no sense to what she was doing. She would never do it again. That was the first of many changes.

THE STATUES TAKEN DOWN

CRAWLEY turned his two younger children loose day after day in the Palais-Royal gardens, because he thought it would keep them amused, but they were not brought up to spend a whole afternoon sitting on iron chairs. They had not, as Crawley imagined children must have, any kind of secret language or code. It was convenient for him to imagine they were close and inviolate and that he, as an adult, was excluded, but all Hal and Dorothy had in common was their coloring, which was fair, and houses lived in—they lived with their grandmother in Dutchess County, or in New York City with their mother when she could have them—and journeys shared, and the American tongue. Their accent made them sound alien, for Crawley's older children, by another wife, were English, like their father.

"The first time I met your mother," said Crawley, as if speaking to children who had no connection with that particular person, "I was flat on my back in the American Hospital and she very efficiently and almost patiently—you know how nurses are always in a hurry—drew quite a lot of blood from my arm, perhaps to measure the degree of alcohol. I had been brought in after a fistfight. She looked like the Holbein portrait of Lady Parker, with that sweet mouth and almost lashless blue eyes, and the hair parted in the center, and a flat coif around the back of the head, and I had not yet heard her speak. I said, 'I love you, and will you marry me?' She smiled and went away, and the next day she came again, and I said, 'My name is George Crawley, I love you, will you marry me?' She smiled, and measured the blood she had taken against the light, but still did not speak. I said, 'I am divorced, but even if you are a Catholic there is no impediment, for I was never married in church.' She said then, in a soft voice, 'I am almost engaged to the doctor I've been working with in Malaya.' 'Is he still in the East?' said I. 'No,' she said, 'I am talking about the American doctor in *Malaya*.' And what do you think she was saying?" He looked from one face to the other and was looking not at his own children but at images of Victorian children in repose, between reprimands, safely over whatever they had been deprived of that morning in the way of food or comfort and considering the safest way of avoiding an unknown offense. They were Victorian in expression, in watchful calm. The girl's rather thin blond hair was held by a red band. The boy wore a shirt with a big sign of the zodiac printed on it. "What she was saying," Crawley rushed on, aware now that he was telling these children about their mother, "was 'the doctor in my lab.'" He hurried the end, though it was a story that had made many other people laugh. The children thought it was a reasonable mistake for George to have made, for he was slightly hard of hearing.

Crawley spoke a peculiar sort of English, full of idioms translated literally from French—he had lived in France such a long time. He said of a lodger now staying in his flat, "I took him on as a favor to a friend. Actually, I don't like his head," meaning "There is something about him I dislike." He did not know how funny he sounded. He had a nose broken like a boxer's, and a head of thick, curly gray hair. He did not look like their last memory of him, which was three years old, or their mother's description, which was not physical but only that he was a poet. He did not resemble his pictures. He seemed heavier, softer. He said he hoped the lodger would find another place to stay. He said this quite loudly, but without petulance. He might go on saying it the whole summer long. As for the lodger, he closed doors silently and laid the telephone back on its cradle as if it might explode. The trace of his presence was humble, such as a nylon shirt dripping at the kitchen window, or a hairbrush he kept (it seemed its permanent abode) on the edge of the tub. This brush, backed by some transparent and thumb-printed plastic material, its jagged and gleaming bristles faintly coated with oil and a web of fine hair, told Dorothy, the elder of the children, that George suffered from a kind of blindness. He saw only what he wanted to; otherwise, he would surely have told the lodger to keep his personal stuff in a drawer. The children believed that the lodger did not like them. This was of no consequence. They were not dependent on their charm, and understood claims of a practical nature, outside the domain of love. The lodger was only a pale eye, a hostile and melancholy nose glimpsed when he opened his door an inch or two—it sometimes happened that he was wanted on the telephone. He seemed a failed adult, therefore a kind of weed. Had he been where nature meant him to be, growing in plant form, by a dusty path, and not here, where he was not desired and not expected—had he been, say, a dandelion clock, the girl's summer skirt could have brushed off his head and she would never have noticed the harm.

Dorothy could remember three summers in Paris, Hal only two. This year, so as to have room for them, their father had sublet a sunless, high-ceilinged place that smelled like a pet shop. The lodger, in some complicated way, had come with the flat, which, in turn, was the property of a girl named Natasha. At first it was cold—so cold that Dorothy wore a sweater under a raincoat and Hal walked with his head pulled down, as if the act of shortening his neck would keep him warm. The blooming of the city, of the chestnut trees in particular, was four to six weeks late. They saw the legendary trees, round as sponges, covered with little green lettuce leaves. A frost, said Hal, would finish them off. Then all at once it was a true summer, with a wilderness of leaves, and that was something Dorothy remembered. She confused plane and linden and chestnut, though one of them had flowers, for she did not know trees at home, except for birches and elms. Dust blew up in their faces when they entered the closed park of the Palais-Royal. It was smaller than the space retained in their minds. It would continue to shrink; perhaps they would come back grown and find it the size of a drying sheet. A red chestnut tree, as they approached it, became pink; from underneath, the flowers were pink as floss. They trod on fallen petals, which from a distance were again red. Venturing out and farther, they saw great flapping flags on high, cold, imposing standards.

"Those are for some Negro king," said Dorothy, the elder, the informed. "Father told me."

"Which king?" said the boy, not wishing to say he had never seen one. He invented eyes, robes, a coronet, and sticking-out ears.

"It means an important visitor," said Dorothy. "When they have an important visitor here, they call him a Negro king." She smoothed her hair as she explained, developing conscious, feminine conceit. Had she been older, she would have asked now for a cigarette and held it just so for the flame. She did not know whether she ought to say "Father told me" or "George" or something more foreign-sounding. "George" thought he was the center of the universe and that the planets, highly polished and lighted from within, circled round him, chanting his praises. But "your father" was also generous and impulsive and unreliable and famous—this last they had only recently been told, by their mother. If true, then why the lodger? Why no cleaning woman, and why furniture sagging or cigarette-burned or mended with glue? Some piece of information about him had been overlooked or misunderstood. Quite often they were handed information they could not use and did not understand. For example, their grandmother kept geraniums in her kitchen in large Crisco tins, and said it was because the depression had marked her.

In the Palais-Royal, Hal played soccer with an unknown boy until a guard put a stop to it. He bought ice cream on a stick, an egg puzzle of polished wood that came apart and could not be put together, comic books he could not enjoy because they were in French, and a bracelet of make-believe jade for his mother. And then he kicked Dorothy's chair and said, "What'll we do?" Dorothy read a green-backed pornographic novel she had found on the bathroom window sill. It was smug and precise, and full of what she took to be the wrong information. She knew and had known for some years that you do not have babies by kissing, but the private anarchy here described could not be truthful, either. When she saw couples kissing perfectly still, pressed together under the late-blooming trees, she reverted to an earlier, childish belief, and thought they were in danger.

The Palais-Royal became too small; she moved with Hal to the Tuileries, and there, for the first time, she read her father's poems. One of them told how a swallow in a narrow street, skimming too low, migrating, was caught in a net. Crawley, when he saw Dorothy carrying the book, and opened it to that page, was heedless or unknowing enough to say, "That was your mother." If Dorothy had seen swallows, she had not recognized them; she could not imagine a street so narrow that a net would reach across it, or a bird too clumsy to fly up and away.

A pigeon, perhaps, if it had been wounded first. Even the pigeons—she saw many of them here—could scatter like gunfire. Her mother was not a bird that waddled or went off in some foolish direction. If she had been a bird, she would have walked on long legs, though she was not like a picture of a stork, or bright as a postcard flamingo. The pigeons' neck feathers were iridescent, their square tail feathers like lopped-off fans...

Hal said, "What'll we do, Dottie? Are we just going to hang around here?" If you sat on an iron chair, you had to pay for it. She found a cinema for him, a place that showed nothing but horror movies. The sign outside said FESTIVAL DU VAMPIRE and also that no one under sixteen would be admitted, but this rule did not appear to be enforced. She abandoned him there; he was to meet her later in the park. Hours later she was shocked—drawn awake, in a sense—by a darkening across the sky, as if black wool were being combed out in great streaks. It coincided with the rushing movement she had already observed at a certain hour, when people fled home. They did not get up and go quietly, they ran away. She looked at lovers again, and then at entwined statues. (Hal was seeing the vampire festival the third time through, eating chocolate in the dark to give him energy so that he could bear his emotions.) The intimation of danger here, in the park, the sudden rush of the clouds, made her think sentimentally of her father, alone and possibly lonely. The wind, rising, was heavy and hot. She was fed up with Hal, with his weight as a brother. He would have to find his own way home.

Closing her book, she saw that the lovers and the children around her had been replaced by idle men, and that she was watched from benches and chairs and from behind trees. Her spine was stiff from the iron chair. The lovers, the children, the mothers, the grandmothers had disappeared, leaving the entwined and emotional statues and these silent men. It was as though animals had crept out of their cages and were afraid to do more than stare. It was not yet night. With theatrical precision, thunder shuddered in the air. She got up and walked away, the last girl in the park. Hal, in communion with American vampires, was certainly safe. He might be on his way home, or here, hoping to find her.

Nothing she wanted to know, either about her sudden fear or her sudden cruelty—the way she wanted to be rid of Hal—had been explained in her father's poems. The sound of the lodger stealthily closing doors, the dwindling thunder, the whisper of traffic as she approached the Rue de Rivoli—these indications that she could at least *hear*—were no help to her; they were fugitive, suggestive sounds, like the clues to her father's past. They were as close, and as evocative, and as general as his early life with their mother, or his life with someone else. Other people moved behind walls of gossip. Dorothy could look at pictures; she could read George's diaries, for he had let them be printed. It was hard to believe he had ever had a secret. He told of lying in bed with a sister-in-law while his wife lay with a newly born son in a nursing home not far away. Dorothy could have questioned anyone, even the lodger; George would never have thought it a betrayal. He lied only sometimes, suiting a fancy.

Because she knew that Hal trusted her and that she had left the park on a pretext of fear—no, perhaps she had been frightened; but when she paused, deciding this, it was too late to go back—she seemed to herself inferior and unworthy of the poet's past. He was said to have been courageous. The women he had known had been brave, too, though some had been other things—beautiful, multilingual, insane, alcoholic, notorious, discussed. All but her own mother, the one he had called Lady Someone in a picture, and a swallow in a poem. She had been the most useful wife, because she had nursed him. But when George talked about women he said, "That was a real woman," as though anyone else was only pretending. He said "Natasha," or "Portia," or "Felicia"—real women had names that ended in "a." The names evoked, for his daughter, their large breasts and abundant hair, their repeated pregnancies, and their chain-smoking. They had been photographed when the camera was askew or the light bleak, when their hair was lank after rain, when their babies half slipped off their corduroy laps like parcels on a bus. She imagined them not as they had sat for false cameras but as they must have been in life. She was from a thinner generation, a generation of stick figures. Figures from his time seemed twice the size of life. "Is it true," her father asked, as if she should know, "that they are taking down the statues in the Tuileries and replacing them with Maillols?" She did not know, and he did not bestir himself to see. "They were wild and romantic," he said, "and the Maillols are going to look damned silly with pigeons on their heads."

The children met Natasha close to the end of their stay. Her arms were thin as a starved child's. Her black sweater and checked skirt, her black stockings and pixie shoes made her seem a child from an institution. She had invented her own uniform. She removed the cotton scarf that protected her from the driving August rain, and a great puff of dyed hair rose like a fan. Penciled brows arched, clownlike, on a high, bald brow. She had somehow found a puddle to walk in—around her shoes water collected. Elf-sized lakes were created, and then, because of the inclination of the ancient floor, a pair of rivers. She had not come to stay but only to visit. The lodger had departed under circumstances that had been kept from Hal until now, and from Dorothy until yesterday: he had shot himself in the courtyard of the Palais de Justice and, still alive, had been taken to a hospital.

"Two forces hung over him for most of his childhood," said Natasha.

"His mother and father, like everyone," said George.

"No, George. Hitler and Stalin." Then she said, staring, "Oh, these are the *nurse's* children," and George stared, too, as if children, unless legends, with warm, wild, and legendary mothers, confounded him. He lit his pipe with watery old-man sounds.

"Don't exaggerate," he said to Natasha. "Don't exaggerate." This was new, this repeating everything as if other people were slightly deaf. Natasha sat in her chair and seemed to be cowering. He had said of her, to Dorothy, "She is a remarkable woman, with considerable charm. She has a rackety sort of life." The story had been notorious once: George had persuaded Natasha to elope from Moscow, and then he had left her and gone to live with the Austrian translator of his poems. He blurred the story in the telling, having perhaps forgotten much of it. Dorothy knew one thing—the swallow had rushed away from him. That put her outside the legend and outside his generation, in a way. When he talked of his generation, he said it was well tempered, and Dorothy thought, Kind, he means—they were kind. He confused the living and the dead, or seemed to. When Dorothy started saying "generation," he stopped her and said, "You have none. We were a well-tempered crowd."

Speaking of the lodger, Natasha said, "He knows he is dying. He knows I have called his father in Moscow. He knows his father cannot get a visa. Well, this has been the worst day of my life. I feel close to death."

"You aren't," said George. "He is."

"He cannot lift his head from the pillow. If you would help me, George, if you would accept some of the responsibility."

"Accept!" cried the man, and with a blunt gesture took in the boy and the girl. "I ask for it, I *assume* it, when it is mine. *You* brought him out of Russia."

"Well, the only thing to be done ... I suppose I should take him some soap."

"Yes, yes, take him some soap," said George, but without vehemence now. He looked at Dorothy as if he had her between himself and death in a public hospital. He mentioned the things his loyal daughter would bring him when the time came: "Soap, a razor, rubbing alcohol, and a toothbrush."

"That is what I decided," said Natasha. "That was what I had decided before I came to see you. I thought it was the only thing to do—take him some soap."

"You shouldn't forget this," said the children's father. "It is more important than you think." Dorothy, playing at being mistress of the house, emptied Natasha's ashtray. Hal stolidly tried to put together the egg puzzle he had bought in the early days, at the Palais-Royal. He had all the pieces, nothing was missing, but still could not make it whole. Dorothy pulled everything she knew apart and started from the beginning. My mother looked like Lady Something in a Holbein. George was a swallow. My mother was the net.

THE HUNTER'S WAKING
THOUGHTS

Between Friday night and Saturday noon, the courtyard filled with cars and station wagons, lined up like animals feeding along the wall of the hunting lodge. The license plates were mostly 75s, from Paris, but some of the numbers meant Lyon and one was as far away from Sologne as Avignon. Across the court, under the oak trees, the dogs, each chained to his kennel, barked insanely. Only two of the shooting party had brought dogs; the twelve chained dogs belonged to M. Maitrepierre, who had let the shooting rights to his estate for the season. Walking under the oak trees to have a better look at the dogs, the men in their boots trod on acorns and snails. The men were stout and middle-aged but dressed like the slimmer, handsomer models in *Adam*. A recent issue of *Adam*, advising a wardrobe for the hunting season, was on the window sill of the dining room reserved for the party. There was also *Entreprise*, a business journal, and several copies of *Tintin*.

The hunters slammed doors the whole morning and carried bushels of equipment from the cars to the lodge. M. Scapa, a repatriated pied-noir from Algiers, had brought a chauffeur to look after his guns, his own case of whisky, and his plaid-covered ice bucket. The lodge was ugly and awkward and had been built two hundred years after the other buildings on the estate. The big house was sold. M. Maitrepierre reserved for himself, his wife, and his married daughter and her family a cottage separated from the lodge by a locked gate and a wall. The shooting rights, which were high, were not his only source of income; he ran a sheep farm and half a dozen of the secret French economic tangles that come to light during family squabbles or taxation lawsuits. He built blocks of flats in Paris, sold a hotel in Normandy, bought part of a clothing factory in Lille. He kept his family tamed by the threat that they were doomed and bankrupt and on the verge of singing for their supper on some rainy street.

The shooting season had been open for over a month, but game was still so plentiful here in Sologne that pheasants, with their suicidal curiosity about automobiles, stood along the roads. Small hunter-colored couples, they were parodies of hunters. Anyone gathering mushrooms or chestnuts raised pheasant and quail. In pastures the hind legs of hares were glimpsed in the long grass. Saturdays and Sundays the farmers tied their dogs and kept the children inside, for the men who arrived in the big cars with the smart equipment shot without aiming; they shot at anything. A man wearing a suede jacket had been mistaken for a deer and wounded in the shoulder. There were any number of shot cats, turkeys, and ducks. Every season someone told of a punctured sheep. Casual poachers who left their cars drawn up on the edge of the highway came back to find a hole in the windshield and a web of cracked glass.

This was flat country in a season of rich colors—brown, dark red, gold.

Colin Graves, who was in love with M. Maitrepierre's married daughter, Nathalie, and younger than she was by nine years, had been put in the lodge. The lodge smelled like a school. Colin had not come to shoot but to be near Nathalie. Now that he was here, and saw that he was to sleep in the lodge, and that Nathalie's husband had arrived, he wondered if there had been a mistake—if he had turned up on the wrong weekend. The hunters strode and stamped, carrying whisky glasses. The wooden stairs shook under their boots. Some went out on Saturday afternoon, but most of the party waited for Sunday morning. They ate enormous meals. They neither washed nor shaved. It was part of the ritual of being away from their women.

Colin had been given a room with a camp bed and a lamp and a ewer of cold water, and a bucket with an enamel cover. Nathalie showed him the room and let him start to undress on the bed before changing her mind. She worried about what the family would think—so she said—and she left him there, furious and demented. Was it because of the husband? No, she swore the husband had nothing to do with it. She talked rapidly, fastening her cardigan. Nothing went on between

Nathalie and the husband. It had gone wrong years ago. Well, one year ago, at least. The husband's room in the lodge was next to Colin's. Nathalie was to spend the night in her own girlhood bed, in her father's house. What other evidence did Colin want?

He was the only foreigner here. He was a bad shot, and loathed killing. He supposed that everyone looked at him and guessed his situation. Why was he here? She had invited him; but she had not told him her husband was coming, too, or that she would be sleeping in another house. They were an odd couple. Colin was slight and fair. He was in Paris, translating Jules Renard's letters. He had met Nathalie because it was through one of her father's multitudinous enterprises he had found a place to live. Nathalie was Spanish-looking, and rather fat since the birth of her second daughter. Colin loved her beyond reason and cherished dreams in which the husband, the two little girls, and Nathalie's own common sense about money were somehow mislaid.

On Sunday morning, he walked with a party of women. There were three: Nathalie, her mother, and Nathalie's closest woman friend. If he included Nathalie's little girls, he had five females in all. The lover trailed behind the women, peevish as a child. They were walking far from the shooting party, on the shore of a shallow pond. Along the path he saw a snail and trod on it, afterward wiping his shoe on fallen leaves. Most galling to him was the way the women admired Nathalie; there was no mistaking the admiration in their eyes. She was bringing off a situation they could only applaud; she was getting away with murder. She had put her husband and her lover in adjacent rooms while she slept in calm privacy in her father's house. Now here she was, fat and placid, with the lover tagging like a spaniel. What was the good of keeping slim, starving oneself, paying out fortunes to be smart, when fat Nathalie could keep two men on the string without half trying? Colin saw this in the other women's eyes.

He knew they thought she was his mother; but the maternal part of her life disgusted him. The idea of her having ever been a mother— the confirmation, the two girls, ran along before the women (Colin was like one of the women now!)—made him sick. Early that morning, Nathalie's father had taken Colin on a tour of the sheep farm, and at the sight of a lambing chart on the wall of a pen—a pen called le nursery—Colin had been puzzled by the diagram of a lamb blind and doubled up in a kind of labyrinth. His mind first told him, "Surrealistic drawing"; then he realized what it was and was revolted. The thought of Nathalie on a level with animals—ewes, bitches, mares—was unbearable. He could not decide if he wanted her as a woman or a goddess. When he returned from the sheep pens, he found that Nathalie, meanwhile, had been attending to her husband—unpacking for him, and giving him breakfast.

The children, the women, and Colin walked along the edge of the pond, and separated the strands of barbed wire that marked someone else's property. Before them, at the end of a long terrace, among oak and acacia trees, rose a shuttered house. It was an ugly and pretentious house, built fifty years ago, imitating without grace a deeper past. He saw the women admiring it, and Nathalie yearning for it—for a large, shuttered, empty, pretentious house. Nathalie was already seeing what she would "do" to the place. She described the tubs of hydrangeas along the façade and wrought-iron baskets dripping with geraniums. He pressed her arm as if afraid. What will become of us? What will happen if we quarrel?

The two women, Nathalie's mother and Nathalie's best friend, were as kind to Colin as if he were a dog. He felt the justice of it. He had the dog's fear of being left behind. He was like the dog shut up in the automobile who has no means of knowing his owner will ever return. He had seen dog's eyes yellow with anxiety... The most abject of lovers can be saved by pride. He dropped her arm, made her sense he was moving away. It was no accident he had chosen as a subject of work conceited Jules Renard. The hideous house belonged to a broker who had fumbled or gone crooked on a speculation, but (explained Nathalie) luckily had this place to fall back on. He seldom lived in the house, but he owned it. It was his; it was real. He knew it was there. Nathalie could admire storybook castles, but she never wanted them. Storybook castles were what Colin wanted her to want, because they were all he could give her. He hadn't a penny. She was waiting for an inheritance from her father, and another from her mother. Her husband hadn't quite gone through her marriage settlement; not yet.

Nathalie stuffed her pockets with acorns and cracked them with her teeth. She was always making motions of eating, of biting. She bit acorns, chestnuts, twigs. She was solid as this house, and solidity was what she wanted; something safe, something she could fall back on. She spat a chewed acorn out of her mouth into her palm. "You're too young to remember the war, Colin," she said, smiling at him. "We used to make coffee out of these filthy things."

Sunday night the bag was divided, the courtyard slowly rid of its cars. Colin, earlier, had walked around the tableau de chasse, the still-life spread on the ground, pretending admiration. He saw hares so riddled they would never be clean of shot. He was sick for the larks. He was to spend Sunday night at the cottage, with Nathalie's father and mother. Her father would drive him up to Paris on Monday morning. He was to sleep in Nathalie's girlhood bed. His sheets had been thriftily moved from the lodge and carried the smell of the unwashed house. Nathalie's husband all at once wanted to be in Paris. He wanted to pack the car and leave now. The weekend was over; there was no reason to remain another second. Fat and placid Nathalie screamed at him, "You have imposed a dinner party on me for tomorrow night. Now, take your choice. We leave now, this minute, and you take tomorrow's guests to a restaurant. Or you wait until the game is divided and we have a hare." The family were not entitled to any of the game, except by courtesy. Nathalie's husband had gone out with the shooting party, but he had not paid his share of the shooting rights on his father-in-law's property; he had no claim to so much as a dead thrush.

"You can't cook a freshly killed hare," said Nathalie's mother. Everyone else kept out of it.

"He knows the butchers are closed on Mondays, and he knows I have an incompetent Spanish maid, and thrusts a Monday-night dinner party on me," cried Nathalie. The husband, black with temper, read *Tintin*. The little girls played dominoes on a corner of a table. Colin watched Nathalie without being noticed. If he had laid a hand on her now, she might have hit him.

She left, at last, with the token hare in a basket. Nathalie's mother's voice wailed after the car, "Nathalie! Nathalie! The hare should marinate at least twelve days!" She returned to the cottage and saw her daughter's guest, the lover, standing in the middle of the room. "My son-in-law is indescribable," she said. "My daughter is a saint. Have you enjoyed the weekend, Colin? Do you like the country, or do you like cities better? Would you like a drink?"

Her husband, Nathalie's father, had gone, flashlight in hand, to the hunting lodge, to recover anything left by the party: dregs of whisky in open bottles, half-crumbled chocolate bars.

"How sensible you are not to marry," said Nathalie's mother, sitting down. "The world would be simpler if women lived with women and men with men. I don't mean anything perverse. But look at how peaceful we were without the men today." They had their drinks, and Colin crawled into his sheets, in his mistress's girlhood bed. It was then he started to wonder if he shouldn't look for someone to marry after all.

CARELESS TALK

THEIR language—English—drew them together. So did their condition in a world they believed intended for men. They were Iris Drouin, the London girl inexplicably married to a French farmer (inexplicably only because other people's desires are so strange), and Mary Olcott, her summer neighbor and friend. On a June night Mary had suddenly appeared in the Drouins' kitchen doorway while the family were at their meal. She was Irish and twenty-seven, with the manner of a Frenchwoman of forty—foxy and Parisian in her country clothes. She was a shade too sure of herself; it went down badly in this corner of Burgundy, where summer visitors were disliked. Lounging in the doorway, letting in mosquitoes and moths, Mary addressed the men—Iris's young husband and her old father-in-law—but her wide smile was for Iris as well. The two men went on shoveling boiled beef.

"Please don't get up," said Mary—as if they meant to! "I am Mme. Olcott, your new neighbor. I've rented the pink house—I'm sure you know. News travels so fast in these places. I should like to buy my milk and eggs from you now."

She had created the Drouins Providers by Appointment, but the men's faces said she had something to learn. Mary was a woman; it was up to another woman to put her down. And so Iris, the Cockney stray, sick with shyness, hugely pregnant with her first child, had to answer, "We don't sell in small quantities. Everything goes to the cooperative. You can buy your milk in the village."

When Iris talked French her mouth was full of iron filings; that was how it sounded and felt. Mary caught the accent and cried in English, "Oh, how marvelous! Even if you won't sell me milk, let me come over and talk to you sometimes. I miss English." Her hand in the pocket of her suede coat might have held a stone. Iris had a queer reaction of fright. She looked first at the two men, as if seeking permission, then back at Mary. Their eyes met, as women's seldom do at a first encounter.

Mary won, of course. From that evening on she bought milk, eggs, butter, honey, and cheese at the farm. She came and went like a chatelaine, and nothing heralded her approach; not the bell at the gate, not even the dogs. Iris thought sometimes that Mary had power over animals but was not aware of it, and did not know she was almost a witch.

"The first time I saw you, you were like a character in 'Goupi-Mains Rouges,'" Mary said to Iris about a year later. "None of you spoke. I remember the bare petrol lamp on the table. The stars were so thick I could see the dogs sleeping when I crossed the courtyard. In the kitchen, you looked evil and wicked, as if you were hiding a bag of gold or a corpse. Suddenly there *you* were, an honest London sparrow chirping away."

Iris had thought, She's like the queen of spades.

Since her marriage, Iris had lived where nothing changed except the weather, yet everything seemed out of joint. No homely object was like any she had seen; a chair was not a chair now, because it was *une chaise*. This was particular, personal; no one could know what it was like. She sensed at the beginning that her stylish new neighbor would never mind her own business. Most Frenchwomen minded that above everything else. Then Mary said something in English, and was therefore safe. Iris had married into a life she had not expected, and safety came down to language now. French was quicksand and English the rock.

She went into friendship without caution, without posting mutual bail. Mary gave her something she missed to the point of illness: a language that made sense. During the winter, when Mary's pink house was shuttered and Mary's existence assured by the rolled-up English papers she posted from Paris—papers that Iris hadn't time to open, let alone read—Iris lived on stored talk. She heard Mary's voice, and she thought she heard her own. The topics never varied; there wasn't a second to spare for casual chatter. Iris had work to do, and Mary was pulled by a private life. Iris talked about time, and how time changed your view, like a turn in the road. She talked about money; surely money was freedom? She talked about women's lives. Women's lives could be bent like wire in the hands of men. Iris didn't care what was said about modern women in a modern world; she had seen her mother's life and now she was living her own.

Mary agreed about time, which was abstract, and was vague about money; she had nearly all she needed of both. But men, now! "Ah, don't get me started," she would beg, and sometimes Iris was sorry she had started, for her friend became a bird in a room, blundering against the walls, too frantic to see the door. Not that Mary Olcott was a bird; she was dark, with a legend of dark women behind her. She had the whole village in her pocket from the first summer on. Iris was a little jealous of that. From her height Mary looked down on lesser lives, giving bad marks or, worse, none at all. Marcel, Iris's husband, fled like a hare at the sight of Mary. From a distance he said, "*Très américaine.*" In the village they said, "*Très anglaise.*" She was neither; her parents had come over from Ireland in the early twenties, and Mary was born some ten years later. It was the only fact she ever told. Iris thought that even if she were to live in the pink brick house with Mary, listen to her telephone conversations, look at the postmarks on her envelopes, she would still never know more.

For two summers Mary Olcott rented the house next to the Drouins' farm, and the third summer bought it. In the village it was said that a married lawyer, Parisian, had made her a present of it. Iris never listened to gossip. It was enough, for her, to have Mary nearby from June to October. The pink house was in sight of Iris's bedroom. Pinning back her hair at dawn (she never had time for a mirror), Iris saw the shaded windows and the west lawn, with the rose garden still asleep. The house was surrounded by the Drouins' fields on three sides. The Drouin men knew to a centimeter where the boundaries stopped, and they encroached upon Mary, inch by inch, every season. The two houses were six miles from the village, which was as far as Iris traveled, and about two and a half hours from Paris—on weekdays an easy drive.

Mary went up to Paris often. She seemed to like the country as a setting, but the threat of rain was enough to chase her away. Now, three years after the first meeting in the Drouins' kitchen, this is how matters were. Mary was Iris's only friend, and Iris was Mary's when Mary happened to be down at the country place.

Mary Olcott's pleasure was collecting confidences, not giving them out. She had a talent for friendship, or, rather, for taming people. The more shy and resistant they seemed, the more she displayed her charm, her strength, and her sense of timing. She hunted the cautious person whose sudden unguarded word or gesture gave a secret away. Dozens of women had said to her, "You are my only friend." She had exclusive friendship for each of them. She played simultaneous chess games, ten at a time. The conquest of Iris (and the collateral defeat of two men, Drouin father and son, who had tried to refuse to sell Mary eggs and milk) had not been as complete as it appeared. During the winter, when Mary was away, she forgot what Iris was like. She had any number of Irises to take up her time. She sent magazines and papers because she hated throwing anything away. At their first meeting, until Iris spoke, Mary had thought, She could be the old man's wife. Then Iris's dreadful accent gave the question depth, like more and more gauze curtains going up. Mary found hardest to place, in the first minute, Iris's wizened dowdiness, as if it were a disease that must inevitably follow first youth. Later, Mary changed her mind a hundred times. Iris was simple, yes, but not so simple as all that. She clung to Mary as though she were sinking, but sometimes of her own accord Iris let go the boat, and Mary never knew why. Iris was cold; she cried and laughed like a Latin. She worked. She was disorganized, lazy, slack. Here Mary thought a word she had not used for years—"slack." Iris's teeth were going. One day soon, she would have no age at all; but she was younger than Mary by three or four years. She wept for English, but when her two babies were born she talked to them in French. Marcel did not want his children to be strangers—that was the reason Iris gave. Iris had always felt like Iris, never doubted what being Iris meant, until now, talking French to her own children.

"He only suggested it, but it was really an order. Sometimes I don't feel like myself at all."

Iris could say this to Mary without a preliminary statement, picking up an idea dropped last Wednesday, Thursday, any day. She could say anything. Iris and Mary were an island, an English fortress, here in hostile France. She said anything to Mary without wondering how far it would go. It was a triumph for Mary, but she had to remember never to be too sure of herself; she never knew when Iris would open her hands and let go the boat.

This was Friday morning and Mary's next-to-last weekend for the season. She stood in the kitchen doorway with a heavy gray sky behind her. An Italian basket dangled from her hand; she had come for the eggs or cheese for that day's lunch. Really, she had come to talk to Iris. Iris's babies played on the stone floor, among piles of dirty clothes sorted for the wash. They saw the visitor, but Iris didn't. The kitchen was full of steam and noise. Because the second child was a son, Marcel had brought electricity into the kitchen and made his wife a present of a water heater and a second-hand washing machine. The machine was a tub on stilt legs. It made a sound like a battering-ram and in motion rocked the house. Iris sensed her visitor, felt the presence in the doorway, and turned off the machine. The noise died, and she held out her hands, smiling, happy to see her friend.

"Mary, look at my hands," she said. "Just look at them. They look like boiled lobster. Do you know, my mother made my bed and darned for me and washed my things until the day I was married? My mother said, 'Have a good time while you can.' She said, 'When a man gets hold of you, you'll work enough for him.'"

"True," said Mary Olcott, who had never worked for anybody. "But you must have wanted this life. Otherwise you wouldn't have chosen Marcel."

She's in *that* mood, Iris thought.

Mary's profile was cold, her black hair drawn back over her ears. She was too strong; no one could live up to the standards she set for her friends. No wonder she frightened Marcel! In the silence of the kitchen Iris thought, She doesn't frighten me.

Curled by the steam in the room, Iris's thin hair looked sculptured. The curl had been induced by a packaged home perm her mother sent from England. Relief parcels kept Iris in touch; her frocks and the children's toy were Marks & Spencer. Her wedding picture—an English bride in a chromium frame—stood on a shelf above the washing machine. Marcel had been made to go to England for his wedding, but it was his only trip abroad. On his sole seaside holiday he had met Iris, and his marriage involved a journey, too. He did not see why he should go beyond the village again.

"*Bonjour*," said Mary gravely to the blond dirty babies, aged two and one. The second was her godson.

"I mind mostly that they'll never have English nursery rhymes and English songs," said Iris. "They'll never know my rhymes."

"That was the sacrifice you made when you married a stranger," Mary said.

"It wasn't a sacrifice," Iris said passionately, pleading for justice.

"You weren't a girl of seventeen."

"No, but I was so ignorant. I thought I knew it all, but I was ignorant."

This great confidence Mary accepted as her due. She was the rock on which weaker natures broke. She saw their hopes and failings turned back like waves. Hard, lucid, tirelessly inquisitive, her eyes looked beyond Iris, measuring Iris. She seemed totally just.

"You can be mistaken about a kind of life without being mistaken about the person you marry," Iris said. She turned on the washing machine so that the noise put an end to that kind of talk, for the moment. She did not look at her babies; they were too beautiful, too personal, too betrayed by what she had revealed to Mary. Whatever happened, *they* must never be shared. Even looking at the children now with Mary in the doorway would have been sharing.

"My friend has arrived," Mary said.

"I saw the car."

"I said, my friend is here."

"I *know*."

They were shouting over the battering-ram of the machine. Their voices came back from the walls. The stones of the house understood nothing but French; they could shout all they liked. The mud in the courtyard was French, soaked in French. Mary said something in a normal tone, unheard. Iris switched off the machine.

"...over seventy. She's marvelous. She's brought a Dominican with her. He drove her up from Bordeaux. She never goes out of the house, but when she decides to, she cruises around the country in an old, old Mercedes. With a Dominican."

"Oh. Well, very interesting, I'm sure." Iris was a Catholic convert. She had become a Catholic when she married Marcel. First she wanted to please him; then, because she brought her Protestant self along, as an act of faith she became wholly Catholic and a bigot. Mary Olcott was Catholic, but sloppy about it. She had what Iris called "views." Moreover, Iris was suspicious of the French, the social part of Mary's life—her traffic with the enemy, as it were.

Iris's "I'm sure" was quite sarcastic, but Mary missed the change in tone and went on, "She's marvelous, old Mademoiselle. Everyone in her family calls her 'Mademoiselle,' even her family—even her doddering old brothers. It's teasing, but it's a kind of homage, too. She's such an old *girl*—such a maiden. She should have been a nun at Port Royal. I can see her there, defying everyone—defying the King. She never looks at a newspaper. She doesn't know a thing about the Algerian war, except when one of her great-nephews is called up. But she reads Greek, and she taught herself Russian when she was sixty, because she wanted to read Pushkin. She's priest-ridden, though. She always has some decayed old padre around. But this one isn't old. This one is young and modern."

Iris stood, frowning, with her hand on the switch of the washing machine.

"A young Dominican," said Mary. "You'll meet him. You'll bring the children to tea this afternoon—please. *He's* staying the night; then he goes to Paris. He is a psychologist," said Mary with light scorn. "Confessor to society women. Confessor to débutantes. 'Tell me all about it. I understand the world.' Well, I must think about their lunch. I'll have eggs, Iris, and cream if you can spare any. If you have any of your soft white cheese, I'll take a pound or so."

She's in that mood, Iris thought. She's in that mood again. She doesn't frighten me.

"We stopped in the village," said the old Frenchwoman, in her asthmatic voice. Her hair was chopped straight at the tip of the ear. She was wearing what must have been plush curtains once. "We stopped to ask directions, and also because we were early and feared it would be a bother for you, dear Mary, if we arrived before you were expecting us. We sat in a café named Chez Mémé and saw the news on television. The news is the same as when I last looked at it. Men are being chased by other men holding sticks. This salmon is perfect. I've had nothing like it in twenty years."

Mary Olcott instantly forgot she had been irritated because her friend Mademoiselle and Mademoiselle's new friend, Father Eugène, had stopped in *her* village. They had stopped so that Mademoiselle could gather gossip. The mention of perfect salmon restored her.

The young Dominican, at the head of the long table, with a woman at either hand, was clearly enjoying his lunch, but his mind was elsewhere—not far: on himself. Both Mary's guests were talkative, and each voice had a peculiarity. The old woman's was gaspy, the priest's rapid and faint. Both talked with their mouths full. Mary let them talk to each other. She fixed her attention on the yellow dahlias that were almost all that remained of the autumn garden. The hazelnut tree was dying a mysterious lingering death. The hazelnut and the dahlias were all she could see of the east lawn. The immortal acacia, which she loved superstitiously, under which they would presently meet Iris and her babies for tea, was on the west side. There, if the sun broke through as Mary wanted, they would sit and drink their tea and admire Mary's roses. Beyond the garden, surrounding Mary's house on three sides, were the Drouins' fields.

A Drouin tractor moved toward the dining room and the east lawn; it stopped, backed, turned, a few feet from the dying hazelnut tree. Perched on the tractor, dressed in boots and working clothes, was the village priest.

The young Dominican in his creamy robes said, "In Professor Thibeault's group I wore lay clothes and did not say I was a priest. I was afraid it would make the patients afraid."

"You were spying," gasped Mademoiselle.

"I was learning. Group therapy."

"Spying," the old woman said.

"In that group was a teacher of mathematics, a Stendhal expert, a

Jew, and two homosexuals," said Father Eugène. "After four sessions they discovered I was a priest and were dismayed. I spoke about troubles of my own, so that they would go on. Otherwise they would have frozen. They would have frozen first of all because I am a priest, and secondly," said the young man, with composure, "because I am not a neurotic."

At every wicked word the old woman looked briefly at the ceiling. It just might fall.

"But you *were* spying," said Mary, who always ate less than anyone else and had time to listen, elbows on the table, her chin in her hands. "You were a spy and the psychiatrist was your accomplice. Isn't that so?"

Father Eugène stared through horn-rimmed spectacles as round as his boyish face. He laid his knife and fork down with care. He had not suppressed his personality but could behave as if he had. "I was studying, and had been sent there for that purpose," he said. He was accustomed to arousing spitefulness and even hate in some women, just as he accepted being fawned upon by others. Unless the reaction was deeply interesting and unexpected, he did not pursue the cause. Father Eugène and Mary Olcott had no time for each other. Whatever she had to tell she would not say to him; and he would most certainly not confide in her. They were rival talkers; more important, and fatal for the harmony of the party, they were also rival listeners.

"You have no right to have any problems," the old woman told him. "I don't see what problems you can have. You are fed and clothed. Everyone admires and respects you. Nothing costs you a speck of dust in love or duty, because your life is a sacrifice and you wanted it that way. If I had a son, I would want him to be exactly like you. As for *our* so-called problems, or the problems of those unfortunate maniacs, who seem to talk such a lot, they are *not* your affair. You are the director of my conscience, but you have no right to search my mind. It is undignified and unfair."

"But that isn't fair, either," said Mary eagerly. "You can't just say what you want to say and leave the rest dark. There is more to confession than sin. If you won't give up voluntarily, it is his right to search."

He glanced at her. So you are on our side, are you?

Oh, no, she stared at him. Make no mistake about me. I am not.

"Our Father in Heaven knows what He wants," said Mademoiselle, suddenly very coy. "So did my father. What a tyrant! And so Father Eugène must know what he is doing, too." And she gave him a look as coy as a little girl's. She had remembered that he was a representative of her father, or her Father, and she was as silly as a girl. Mary had never seen her silly. She had seen Mademoiselle with tatty hangdog priests she could bully; but Father Eugène, who could have been her grandchild, was promoted several generations on. How can she be such a ninny, Mary wondered. Mademoiselle had a brain; she read Greek and learned Russian, alone, when she was past sixty. Her books were sent to her from Russia—a Tolstoy fantasy country that had nothing to do with the real world. She had not looked at a newspaper for years. Yet she was quick when it came to saving money; she soon found out that Russian books cost less if they came straight from Russia. She knew all about filling in forms, and the name of the export office in Moscow. The books, the beautiful alphabet on harsh paper, sternly bound, came from a soft-focus grassy place where young girls wearing exquisite frocks played croquet.

Mademoiselle wore old plush curtains and kept scraps of cloth—scarves, of a sort—to spread on her head when she felt a draft. She could feel a window open in a pantry when she sat knitting five rooms away. When she was not reading, she knitted. In the old days, her knitting had gone straight to Africa. Now it appeared that the Africans were getting their hot clothing somewhere else. There was no longer the same demand. The nuns had told her so, without explaining why. She sent bundles of garments to her young friend Mary Olcott, begging her to distribute them among the poor. Every so often Mary undid a parcel from Mademoiselle and found a pullover for a swan, a bathing suit for an octopus. The knitting was large and loose as a child's, full of knots.

Mademoiselle was coy with the young priest, promoting him to superpaternity, but she had the last word. After lunch, when he blessed the women, she barely let him finish before saying, "You may direct my conscience, but it stops there. Don't you dare pry into my mind."

Late in the afternoon, the neighboring farmer's children were brought to tea. The Drouin babies were like *putti* and a local sight, outdoing the oak tree, said to be a thousand years old, near the village. The sun had come out, as Mary expected. They sat on the west lawn. The old closed-in courtyard had been here when the house was a farm. Now the outbuildings were torn down and replaced by low soft-pink brick walls. There was Mary's acacia and the rose garden, and a view of the Drouin fields. The brown, green, blue, and pink of medieval miniatures were perfectly proportioned here, although the blue of the real sky was on top instead of the rose of heaven—Mary pointed this out.

"Earth, water, fire, and air are the only Christian symbols I need," said Mary, settling her guests in basket chairs. "And the acacia, because it never dies. This is why I wanted the house." A slight insistence on "wanted" did not escape one of the guests, and implied that the house had, perhaps, been a present.

Mademoiselle had slept for two hours and was knitting now, drawing up an endless thread of ugly yellow from a basket at her feet. To the two French visitors, the west lawn was a wretched room without a ceiling. The autumn sun was cold. They would have appreciated the rose garden just as well framed by curtains and cut up in squares.

Iris, in a sleeveless English print dress, sat on the grass, with her babies nearby. They were washed and pink, and their hair was like silk. Mademoiselle looked at them and said, "They are beautiful children," and "They look foreign," as if each remark were of equal value, and worth about a glass of water. She pointed her needle and the flag of knitting to the field where a tractor came and went. The tractor had followed Mary's party; it had threatened the dining room, and now rattled and roared on the west side of the house. "I understand the village priest works for you," said Mademoiselle.

"He's our best worker," said Iris.

"Aren't you impressed, having your curé on the tractor?"

"Glad, not impressed," said the English girl. "He's the best worker we have."

"I should be intimidated," said the old woman.

The English girl flushed and raised her voice. "Why? He likes the work. He's a farmer, the son of a farmer." She broke off, as if she had discussed all this before. She went on in a lower tone. "He's obliged to work, and that's all wrong. You should see the collection at church.

Centimes. People have the nerve to leave centimes. Rich Parisians here for the summer. Summer people with big cars. They ought to be ashamed."

"The farmers are discontented," said the old woman placidly. "It was explained on the television Chez Mémé this morning. Also, Father Eugène and I read their propaganda posters along the roads."

"Do you think it's right that a bottle of mineral water costs more than a bottle of milk?" said Iris, looking up, grass in her hand pulled by the roots. "All they have to do with water is put it in bottles. For milk you need cows and what every cow represents as an investment— you don't know what it represents."

"It is absolutely incorrect—" began Father Eugène, but he never finished; they never knew whose side he was on. The women gave him a look of bitter surprise. He kept his social comment to himself. Undisturbed, he watched the receding tractor. The acacia seemed a poverty-stricken tree, and, despite his hostess's medieval faith, its mortality was proven. He was spending the night and going on to Paris in the morning, leaving Mademoiselle, who had nagged him. The countryside was outside his province; it was neither a complex personality nor a work of art.

"How did you know the curé was on the tractor?" said Mary. "What a lot of information you picked up on the television Chez Mémé!" She wanted Iris to know she had not been tattling about the village priest. But she had talked, more than a little, about Iris's curious marriage: how lost the London girl was here, how her father-in-law bullied her. She had told it as an interesting story, but now the story had substance, because Iris was here.

Iris pulled grass as if it were enemy hair. Mary must have made a good thing of the parish priest working for Marcel, but Mary was betraying her in any case, just by having these strange friends and speaking perfect French to them. Because they were foreigners, Iris did not grade them on the English staircase. They were all dangerous and all the same. Mary had no class awareness, but that seemed to Iris a handicap, like an inability to tell the time. Mary ought to have been born a snob, and her not seeming one made Iris uneasy. Yes, thought Iris, she has the farmer's wife to tea, and I sit on the grass; but she would think it normal to have me or that old lady or the Dominican washing up afterward in the kitchen, and that is where Mary makes one unsteady... And so Iris seemed anxious, suddenly; looked to see where the babies had got to—they were not far. She remembered how much she loved them, and that none of these three had children—not Mary, who would not say what she had done with her husband or who had given her the house; or the old woman; or the clever priest. The old woman went on knitting, as if to prove she could do one thing women usually did well.

Iris got up, abruptly, and shook hands all round, as she had learned to do over here. The Dominican laid his hand in hers as if confiding it.

"I must see Marcel," said Iris. "He might want something. He might be hungry."

"It's not his suppertime," said Mary idly. "Can't he wait?"

"Why should he? Besides, I've scarcely seen him the whole day."

The look on her listeners' faces was fleeting but odd. What had Mary told them, Iris wondered. As rudely as possible, she turned and walked away.

Father Eugène and Mademoiselle saw no reason to remain outside a second longer. They returned to the house and sat down on each side of an empty fireplace. Mary saw Iris as far as the road. Iris's face was stubborn and closed. She had dropped away; she would sink and drown, but she would not be cheated. No use asking her what had gone wrong, for the moment. Mary wondered if something careless had been said.

In the house, she found Mademoiselle beside the cold hearth and was told that Father Eugène had gone up to his room. He had had enough of them, too, Mary supposed. Perhaps Iris had bored him. Why read too much into it? He might have wanted to write a letter or say a prayer. She sat in his chair. She looked cold and pure and was wildly worried. Judgment Day had not been this afternoon, but it was always closer.

"What a nice girl that farmer's wife seems to be," said Mademoiselle, knitting violently. "In the village, they say she is a convert and exceptionally devout."

"Converts have it soft," said Mary. "They come to it late, without ever having had the Devil under the bed. They sail in and admire the stained-glass windows. All the dirty work has been done."

"You don't like converts, and I see you don't care for Father Eugène." Mademoiselle employed a tone suitable for an underpaid, overworked, and complaining servant. "The Church is the Church. You are always free to go."

"You know I am not."

Mademoiselle put a scarf on her head and wound the ends around her throat, but still Mary did nothing about the fire.

"I shall have nightmares tonight," said Mary. "I think it was all his talk at lunch. The mad Stendhal expert—can you see him? You may be right . . . I don't like them, not really. They put our dogs down a well."

"Who?"

"Young seminarists. In Ireland. Over politics. Our two spaniels. Just for the pleasure of watching them struggle and drown. Clawing the sides."

"You saw this?"

"No, it was years before I was born. I heard the story so often."

"You must never imagine things you've never seen. It is far worse to imagine cruelty than watch it. It seems to me wicked to fill your mind with horrible things you never saw. The dogs may not have scratched the sides of the well at all. They may have gone down like stones. Like the sad dog in one of my dear Turgenev's stories. You are imagining cruelty. I must say, I am surprised in a woman as charitable as you."

"I don't trust any of them," said Mary. "That's the truth. Men in skirts."

"What about men in aprons? Freemasons! A skirt has more dignity. Besides, Father Eugène would never drown a dog. He doesn't notice animals."

"I don't trust any of them." It took in a wider clan than priests.

"Life is so different now," said the old lady. "All this constant talk. 'That's what I don't like,' Oblomov said. 'Everyone talking.'" With the unpredictable jumps of the aged, she said, "When I was a child I never looked into a mirror. We were four sisters and none of us ever looked at her own face. We weren't taught it was wrong, but simply unworthy. Coquetry was beneath us. Nowadays, my nieces and their daughters . . ."

Mary Olcott must often look in the mirror. The perfectly smooth and glossy hair required staring—concentrated staring.

"I shall have nightmares," said Mary. "I'm sure of it. The mad Stendhal expert! But Father Eugène will sleep."

"Why shouldn't he?" said the old lady. "He is a healthy young man. Let me tell you something. Men sleep. Women float on the surface, but men go down without fear. How many men have been murdered in their sleep? How many could be? Men sleep in trust; women float."

If this was the reflection of something seen, then it was the most incredible confidence Mary had ever been given—the climax of a career of hunting and waiting. Unfortunately, she did not take it in. She was thinking about Iris and wondering what had gone wrong, why the afternoon had failed, why Iris had gone down the road with a closed face.

Mary was leaving the next weekend, and by next summer the afternoon of betrayal would be forgotten, but Mary daren't wait. It was too risky. Tomorrow she would call on Iris and get the chess game moving again. She could never play fewer than ten games at a time. When she had only nine she thought she had none.

LARRY

SOME MEN give their children sound advice about property and investment. The elder Pugh had the nerve to give advice about marriage—this to the son of a wife he had deserted. He was in Paris on a visit and had come round to see what Larry was up to. It was during the hot, quiet summer of 1954.

Larry was caretaking for July and August. He had the run of sixteen dust-sheeted rooms, some overlooking the Parc de Monceau, some looking straight onto the shuttered windows of other stone houses. Twice a week a woman arrived to clean and, Larry supposed, to make sure he hadn't stolen anything.

He was not a thief—only a planner. His plans required the knowledge of where things were kept and what they amounted to. After a false start as a sculptor he was trying to find an open road. He went through the drawers and closets left unlocked and came across a number of towels and bathmats and blankets stolen from hotels; pilfering of that sort was one of the perks of the rich. A stack of hotel writing paper gave him a new idea for teasing Maggie, his half sister, who also lived in Paris—near the Trocadéro, about eight Métro stops away.

The distance between Larry and Maggie was greater than any stretch of city blocks. He saw it as a treeless plain. It was she who kept the terrain bare, so that she could see Larry coming. He had to surmise, because it would be senseless to do anything else, that Maggie failed to trust him. He wondered why. Total strangers, with even more reason to feel suspicious, gave him the keys to their house. When he looked in a mirror, he felt he could trust himself. A French law obliges children to support indigent parents and, in one or two rare cases Larry had heard of, siblings—a sister or brother. Maggie probably lived with the fear of seeing Larry shuffling up to the front door, palm up. Or carrying a briefcase stuffed with claims and final warnings. Or ringing the bell, in a tearing hurry, with a lawyer waiting in a taxi. Or that she would be called to his bedside at the American Hospital in Neuilly, with an itemized statement for intensive care prepared at checkout. She might even be afraid she would have to bury him, in the unlikely event of his dying first. Maggie's mother, but not Larry's, had been crowningly rich. Larry's generation would have said that he and Maggie had different genes; Maggie's would have taken it for granted they had different prospects.

Fiddling around with the hotel stationery, he sent Maggie letters from Le Palais in Biarritz, the Hôtel de Paris in Monte Carlo, Le Royal at Évian-les-Bains, Le Golf at Deauville. Some carried the terrifying P.S. "See you soon!" From the Paris Ritz he counseled her not to mind the number of bills he was having referred to her from Biarritz and those other places: he had made a killing in Portuguese oysters and would settle up with her before long.

He wondered if the tease had worked, and if she had bothered to look at the postmarks. He had sent all the letters from the same post office, on Boulevard Malesherbes. The postmarks should have shown Maggie that it was just a prank, not an operation. But then she probably thought him too old for practical jokes and wholly unsuited for operations. A true trickster needed to have the elder Pugh's clear conscience—his perfect innocence.

Paris was hushed, eerie, Larry's father said. That was what he noticed after so many years. He'd gone back to America long before the war. For some time now Maggie had been paying him an allowance to keep away. She lived in Paris because she always had; it did not mean that she kept open house. Larry was here for a different reason: he had been at the Beaux Arts for as long as he could stretch the G.I. Bill. He was just wavering at present: stay or go.

He told his father why Paris was silent. There was a new law about traffic horns. His father said he didn't believe it.

Here, near the park, in midsummer, there was no traffic to speak of. In the still of the afternoon they heard the braking of a bus across the empty streets. Shutters were bolted, curtains drawn on the streets with art names: Murillo, Rembrandt, Van Dyck.

Larry's father said, "I suppose you found out there wasn't much to art in the long run." From anyone else it would have been wounding. His father meant only that there were better things in life, not that anyone had failed him.

Larry took the dust sheets off an inlaid table and two pink easy chairs. The liquor cabinet was easy to pry open; he managed with a fork and spoon. They pushed their chairs over to a window. It was curious, his father remarked, how the French never wanted to look *out*. Notice the way salon furniture is placed—those stiff little circles. People always sat as if they weren't sure what to do with their ankles and knees.

The drawing room was pale in color, and yet it soaked up the light. Larry was about to ask if his father had ever seen a total eclipse, when the old man said, "Who lives around here? It was a good address before the war."

Before the other war, he meant—before 1914. He was fine-looking—high-bridged nose, only slightly veined; tough, kindly blue eyes. He seemed brainless to Larry, like Maggie, but a stranger might not have noticed. His gaze was alert as a wren's, his expression one of narrow sincerity. If there were such a thing as artistic truth, his face would have been more ingratiating; about half his plots and schemes had always died on the branch. He must have seen the other half as enough. Unlike most con men, Larry's father acted on sudden inclinations. It was a wonder anything bloomed at all.

Larry did not think of himself as brainless. He did not even consider himself unlucky, which proved he was smart. He was not sure whether his face said anything useful. It was almost too late to decide. He had stopped being young.

His father had no real age; certainly none in his own mind. He sat, comfortable and alert, drinking Larry's patron's best Scotch, telling Larry about a wonderful young woman who was dying to marry him. But, he said, probably having quite correctly guessed that Maggie would cut his funds at the very glimmer of a new wedding, he thought he'd keep the dew on the rose; stick to untrammeled romance; maintain the constant delight and astonishment reserved for unattached lovers. She was attractive, warmhearted, and intelligent; made all her own clothes.

Larry refrained from asking questions, partly out of loyalty to his late, put-upon mother. Dead or alive, she had heard enough.

"Marriage is sex," said his father. "But money is not necessarily anything along that line." In spite of his wish not to be drawn, Larry could not help mulling this over. His father was always at his most dangerous, morally speaking, when he made no sense. "The richer she is, the lower the class of her lovers. If you marry a rich woman, keep an eye on the chauffeur. Watch out for unemployed actors, sailors, tailors. *Customs officers*," he said, as though suddenly remembering. He may have been recalling Maggie's mother. He sighed, though not out of discontent or sorrow, and lifted his firm blue gaze to an oil portrait of a woman wearing pearls Maggie's mother would have swum the Amazon for. "I was never really excited by rich women," he said calmly. "Actually, I think only homosexuals are. Well, it is all a part of God's good plan, laid out for our pleasure, like the flower beds down there in the park."

Larry's father was a pagan who regularly prayed for guidance. He thought nothing of summoning God to smile on His unenlightened creations. Maggie, another object of close celestial attention, believed something should be done about the nature of the universe—some tidying-up job. She was ready to take it on and was only waiting to be asked. Larry lived at about eye level. He tried the Catholics, who said, "What would you like? Jam for breakfast? Eternal life? They're yours, but there's a catch." The Protestants greeted his return with "Shut up. Sit down. Think it over." It was like swimming back and forth between two crowded rafts.

"I met *your* mother just before I lost most of my money," his father said, which was a whitewashed way of explaining he had been involved in a mining-stock scandal of great proportions. "Never make the mistake of imagining a dumb woman is going to be more restful than a smart one. Most men crack up on that. They think 'dumb' means 'silent.' They think it's going to be like the baaing of a lamb and the cooing of a dove, and they won't need to answer. But soon it's 'Do you still love me?,' and that can't be left in the air. Then it turns into 'Did you love me when we got married? Did you love me when I was pregnant? Did you love me last week? Do you love me now?'"

Larry said, "I saw Maggie about a year ago. She says she's leaving everything to an arts foundation."

"She can't," said his father.

"She thinks she can, and she's got lawyers. It's her way of wanting to be remembered. But it's the wrong way. The French never remember anything except their own wars. She won't even have her name on a birdbath."

"Now, that's where you're wrong," his father said. "There'll be a memorial birdbath and Maggie's name—which, incidentally is yours and mine; I'm leaving you both a good name—and in the bowl of the birdbath there'll be the Stars and Stripes in red-white-and-blue mosaic. That is exactly what they'll give Maggie's memory. Where they will choose to put the monument I can't predict. No sane man wants to survive his own children, so I won't say I'd like to see the inaugural ceremony. You'll be there, though—well dressed and smiling. Life has been good to me. I hope it's just as good to you."

It was true that life had treated the old man gently; it had kept him out of jail and in cheerful company.

"I haven't made a formal will yet," he said, quite as though he had anything to leave. "But there's one particular thing I want *you* to have. It's a painting of me. I sat for it here, in Paris, before the war. Around 1912. I don't remember the artist's name, but he was big in those days. If you ever have a son, I want him to have the picture. Promise me you'll come and get it no matter where you happen to be when I go."

He helped himself to a drink and, as though no answer from Larry were needed, began to talk about something else he owned—an ancient hookah, a museum piece. Maggie would appreciate having it, he thought.

Larry noticed that their drinks were leaving rings on the inlaid table. He rubbed them with a corner of a dust sheet, but it was too late.

The next day, while he was trying to sandpaper the stains, Larry remembered the portrait. It showed his father wearing a hat at a jaunty angle, his hands clasped on a walking stick. He appeared to be elegant and reliable, the way things and people are always said to have been when one looks back at them across a war.

When Larry's father left Larry and his mother, he took the portrait with him. It must have been hanging in a dining room, because Larry saw him taking it down, and then tossing a bundle of money, cash, on a polished table. His mother sat in profile, turned away, arms folded. She looked toward, but not at, the little glass shelves at the window, where she kept her collection of miniature cacti in pottery dishes. She wore the look of dark grieving no child can enter. When he saw that she was not going to turn back his way or say something to him, Larry's father secured the portrait under his arm and walked out. There was a blank place on the wall, and on the table, deeply reflected, a packet of bills that seemed a lot but that never was or could be enough.

Over the next few days and until the end of August, when it was time for Larry to move on, he continued to work on the inlaid table, repeating the operation of sandpaper and wax until the rings showed but palely, and only under direct, strong light. Except for those faint circles, and a few sheets of hotel stationery and a few ounces of whiskey gone, he left no other trace behind him of loss or mischief.

A REPORT

"THE BOOTS are not authentic," says M. Monnerot. "Authentic boots must exist somewhere, but I have never found them—at least not in my size. Everything else seems real."

He stands with his hands on his hips, scowling at himself in the glass. He wears the uniform of a Waffen S.S. superior officer, but the effect is patchy, and for a good reason—the components of the uniform were bought separately. Willi has no emotional feeling about the uniform whatsoever, but his sense of order is offended by the decorations. No soldier could possibly have been simultaneously on so many fronts, and if you look closely you can see that some of the ribbons are not even German. M. Monnerot is an impostor, though he looks impressive. Next to him, a man in civilian clothes appears ridiculous. Willi, the civilian, looks as if he exercised some marginal trade, such as photographing tourists as they come out of the Louvre, or asking thirty selected families how often they clean their shoes; but he is a translator, entrusted with difficult and often secret texts, at the rate of eleven centimes a word.

M. Monnerot is small of eye; he pulls the cap sideways and down so that his gaze is shadowed. According to one of the detectives who have been following him (his wife is trying to obtain evidence for a divorce), he is handsomer in uniform than Himmler, whose picture hangs on the wall, but not nearly so effective as Heydrich, who strides beside Himmler. Heydrich's greatcoat swirls, his arm swings; the whole sense of the picture seems to be menace and movement. He wears a sword. M. Monnerot is on the look-out for one like it. Swords are easy enough to find, but every time he buys one he compares it with the photograph and some detail seems at fault. Could it be that Heydrich had a sword specially made for himself? Willi, questioned, shakes his head. It could be true; it seems to him that during his childhood in Germany he heard opposing opinions—for instance, his mother believed that very high-up Party members spent rather a lot on their own adornment, but his father knew better, and maintained that every pfennig of tax collected was somehow or other returned to the people.

Upon M. Monnerot's table, folded, are two red, black and white flags. One came from the Flea Market, where several merchants now make a specialty of Nazi souvenirs, and is said to have flown high in Kiev. There is no way of proving it, but as it may have come such a long way, he paid more for it than he would have for any of the others.

He turns to Willi and says, "I am not blaming you, but I don't think the flag *you* sold me is authentic."

Of course it is not. When Willi was asked for a flag he said they only existed in films; and when M. Monnerot insisted, first wheedling, then raising his price to three hundred francs, Willi went to the Bon Marché department store and bought red, black and white bunting and made a passable flag. His first try was nearly a failure—he had his swastika running counter-clockwise. He had to unstitch it and sew it twice. He soaked the flag in salt water and let it dry, then dipped the flag, folded, into a solution of Javelle water. Thus, battle-marked and travel-marked, the flag was welcomed by M. Monnerot, and envied by some of his friends, who are also collectors.

"The size of the swastika seems wrong," M. Monnerot now complains. "I don't know why, but when you compare it with some others—a friend of mine pointed it out to me."

Willi says solemnly, "The Kiev flag must have been made after 1942. In 1942 the size was standardized. Now you have one of each."

"You are right," says M. Monnerot. "I have one of each."

Willi would like to share this joke with someone, but with whom? He is in the confidence of M. Monnerot's wife, and knows she is having her husband followed. She is hoping to catch him at something, but so far he has been careful: he has never stayed out overnight, and never brought a woman into his house—he knows better. "I respect my wife," he has often told Willi, "and her part of my life is sacred." Willi knows that although Mme. Monnerot might enjoy the story about the flag she could make trouble for Willi later on. She might be so enraged to think of her husband spending money foolishly that she could not resist telling him. Willi knows, from experience, that mortal enemies often end up in each other's arms. Also, if M. Monnerot keeps his mistress out of his home, it is simply because she has a place of her own, rue du Commerce. Part of the detective's report describes how M. Monnerot has to fight for parking space on that busy street—how he tries to intimidate his opponent without actually coming to blows. He becomes so red in the face that the author of the report thinks he might die of a stroke one of these days. Willi knows more than the detective, but he keeps his information to himself. Perhaps he could sell what he knows—but no; the truth is, he doesn't trust any of these people an inch.

He has seen the latest report, which begins, "The situation has not changed. M. Monnerot leaves his office on the stroke of twelve and, after fetching his car in the garage behind the Madeleine, drives in the thick of midday traffic to the corner of the avenue Émile Zola and the rue du Commerce. As he can never find a place along the curb, he leaves his Ariane double- and even triple-parked while he buys two small filet steaks, or one lean entrecôte. At the greengrocer he buys two apples or two bananas. Occasionally he omits the fruit and walks half a block to buy two vanilla yogurts. He pays cash everywhere and is not known to have any debts. Recently he obtained control of a dry-cleaning establishment, rue du Commerce, which he wanted to name Mon Pressing. However as there are four establishments by that name in the telephone book he has changed his mind, and the sign now reads PRESSING BRIGITTE. M. Monnerot has a valid reason for his daily trips to the Émile Zola-rue du Commerce area of the city."

Willi could add that the apartment on the rue du Commerce where M. Monnerot has his share of the steak, fruit, or yogurt was occupied from May to July by Fräulein Ilse (Bobbie) Bauer, born of a French corporal with the Army of Occupation and a seventeen-year-old German bilingual stenographer, in Coblenz, May 5th, 1947. Before taking up residence in the rue du Commerce, Bobbie was *au pair* cook, housemaid, laundress and governess in the home of M. and Mme. Laurent, their daughters Chantal and Eliane, baby Charles, and gray poodle Tisane. Bobbie had a room on the sixth floor of the apartment building, along with the servants working for other families, and students to whom the rooms were rented at two hundred francs a month. Some rooms contained clandestine Spanish families, one member of which—wife, sister, fiancée—was employed as a maid, and who, by means of mattresses piled in the daytime and distributed on the floor at night, was able to house four or five persons in a room already filled by a single bed, a chair, and a wardrobe. The students have their meals at the university restaurants, and the space taken in the Spanish rooms by alcohol stoves and saucepans is devoted, in their chambers, to a record-player and the records of Jacques Brel, Georges Brassens, Barbara, Guy Béart, and Bob Dylan.

Although she was nauseated by the smell of cooking oil from the Spanish quarters, and disturbed by the records in the students' rooms, Bobbie spent her evenings upstairs. The Laurents had never invited her to share their television. Because her mother had borne her at the age of seventeen, Bobbie was afraid to go out alone until after her eighteenth birthday. Once another girl took her to the Select, in Montparnasse, where she met Willi. She told him about the Laurents, and that on the sixth floor there was one toilet, Turkish style, without a lock, and one basin with a cold-water tap, and that her favorite poet was Lamartine. Willi advised her to go home to Coblenz. She said she could not until she had learned enough French to become a bilingual stenographer; her mother had married a man who was interested in Bobbie, and (showing off her French) she was *de trop* at home.

On her eighteenth birthday, her French hosts invited her to watch a film on television. The program was already under way when she arrived. She slipped into a chair. Eliane and Chantal sat cross-legged on the floor, rapt, though the white wobbling square on the lower left-hand corner of the screen was an official warning that the program was not recommended for children. M. and Mme. Laurent did not turn their heads when Bobbie entered the room. Bobbie was extremely puzzled and depressed by the film, which had no action whatever, but showed ugly, unkempt, naked women standing in a field of tall grass, in a disorderly queue. She believed it at first to be a film about prehistoric people; she thought it could be some lost tribe in a jungle, perhaps in South America. The jumpy light and abrupt camera movements suggested the scene had been filmed from the wrong distance, and by an amateur. Presently the image changed to an abstract design of white faintly striated in gray, which, when the picture became sharper, was seen to be a pile of bodies. As Bobbie half rose from her chair, M. and Mme. Laurent swung away from the screen. She saw their profiles, then their faces. Mme. Laurent said bitterly, "*You* did this," and her husband said, "If it wasn't you, it was your father."

Bobbie left the room, ran down the stairs and walked in the spring night as far as the Trocadéro. The fountains were playing. A number of tourists took pictures of the Eiffel Tower and the lighted water. M. Monnerot, who was on his way to dine with a friend from out of town at Le Petit Marguery, and had stopped at the Trocadéro to admire the view, discovered Bobbie without her purse, without her coat, without her identity card or passport, and without a key to get back into the Laurents' apartment house. She was weeping bitterly. After a short conversation during which she shook her head several times, she joined the two men for dinner.

The apartment on the rue du Commerce—as Mme. Monnerot knows—was bought, as an investment, by M. Monnerot's unmarried sister, who lives in Lyon and never goes near the place. Nevertheless, the telephone is in her name, and the gas, light, and water (though the bills are paid by successive tenants) are in her name, too. No tenant has ever been given a lease to sign, and the concierge is bribed. Bobbie moved in as one more incarnation of M. Monnerot's sister. The arrangement lasted less than two months. Fräulein Bauer was frightened by M. Monnerot—no one knows why. She made the mistake of calling M. Monnerot at his office, and the greater mistake of calling him at his home. That telephone call was, in fact, the beginning of Mme. Monnerot's suspicions, and the reason she began receiving detectives' reports. By the time the detectives began working, however, Bobbie had disappeared. Someone told Willi she was seen with a suitcase around the Gare de l'Est. Perhaps she followed his advice and went home. The official report knows only this: "M. Monnerot's sister's apartment is occupied by Mlle. Brigitte Vanderplank, who is a French citizen. Mlle. Vanderplank works for a wholesale dress firm as hostess and model when coats and dresses are shown to buyers in Belgium, Luxembourg, Holland, and Switzerland. She is twenty-four, and speaks French, Flemish, and several German dialects. It is to her apartment that M. Monnerot takes his daily steak et cetera. Sometimes he and Mlle. Vanderplank meet and shop together. In that case she chooses the food and he pays. He sometimes allows her to drive. When the car is parked to his satisfaction he rushes to open the door for Mlle. Vanderplank, helps her out and kisses her hand. M. Monnerot has told a few friends that he is on close terms with a young countess who belongs to a family from the northern part of France. Mlle. Vanderplank wears an apple-green suit and white shoes. She carries a white purse with a gold chain. She has been described variously as 'exquisite,' 'undernourished,' 'common,' 'distinguished,' but all are agreed that she has blond hair. M. Monnerot has told Mlle. Vanderplank that he was a secret agent in the last war, and also with the paratroops. Mlle. Vanderplank has been heard to say that her landlady's brother (as she correctly describes him) is a decent citizen; his patriotism is unquestioned; he believes in republican institutions; he detests the Americans, the British, the Russians, the Chinese, and he despises the Germans for having been defeated in the last war. Some time ago Mlle. Vanderplank asked for a lease 'to show her parents,' who, she said, were concerned about her housing arrangements. M. Monnerot drew up a lease, and filled out several 'receipts' for the monthly rent. Mlle. Vanderplank had the lease and receipts photocopied in the presence of two trusted friends, one of them a solicitor, and returned the originals to M. Monnerot, who tore them up."

"What do you think?" said Mme. Monnerot when Willi had read the report. Willi seems to her the very bastion of common sense. He may be ready to sacrifice his principles, but no one can say what his principles are. He does not appear venal. He is extremely discreet, and no trouble to women.

Willi sticks to the information in the report. He speaks like a rational machine. He tells her that, one, M. Monnerot has not committed an offenses that can be proved. Two, she has no grounds for a divorce. Three, Mlle. Vanderplank is the legal tenant of the apartment (though the landlady's brother has yet to discover this) and has photocopies of receipts.

"Is there anything you know and are not telling me?" she pleads.

"No," says Willi. "All I have is an enlarged photograph of an officer's sword, which he said he wanted."

"Then nothing can ever change," says Mme. Monnerot.

"No, nothing," says Willi, which might be the expression of a more general belief.

"He is odious," she says. "Why do you waste time doing favors for him?"

"Oh—you know," says Willi vaguely.

He thinks to himself, One, I need the money. Two, it stops him from nagging. Three, I am not sure; I must be expecting something.

Expecting what? He sees the faked flag, the dead decorations, the symbols counter-clockwise, and feels bewildered, as if he had been given permission to laugh. "Tell him," he says, and breaks down. He cannot stop laughing. It is disgraceful; he sees Mme. Monnerot is offended. He cannot stop, and begins to weep. "Tell him," he says, when he can draw breath, "tell him I'll look for the boots."

THE OLD FRIENDS

PART OF the plot of their friendship, the reason for it, is that the police commissioner has become an old bachelor now, and his life rests upon other lives. He rests upon people for whom he is not really responsible. Helena is by far the most important. She is important quite in herself, because anyone with television in this part of Germany knows her by sight. The waitress, just now, blushed with excitement when she recognized her, and ran to the kitchen to tell the others.

The commissioner and Helena have been friends forever. He cannot remember when or how they met, but if he were asked he would certainly say, "I have *always* known her." It must be true: look at how charming she is today—how she laughs and smiles, and gives him her time; oh, scarcely any, if the minutes are counted, but as much as he needs, enough. She is younger than the commissioner, but if she were to turn away, dismiss him, withdraw her life, he would be the orphan. Yes, he would be an orphan of fifty-three. It is the greatest possible anxiety he can imagine. But why should she? There is no quarrel between them. If ever there was, he has forgotten it. It was never put into words. He is like any policeman; he knows one meaning for every word. When, sometimes, he seems to have transgressed a private rule of hers, it is outside the limits of the words he knows, and he simply cannot see what he has done. She retreats. In a second, the friendship dissolves, and, without understanding why he deserves it, he is orphaned and alone.

When the weather suits her and she has nothing urgent to do, she lets him drive her to a garden restaurant on a height of land above Frankfurt. It is in a suburb of quiet houses—"like being in the mountains," he says. He sniffs the air, to demonstrate how pure it is. "But you really should come here at night," he says; for then the swimming pool in each of the gardens is lighted blue, green, ultramarine. The commissioner flew over in a helicopter once, and it looked . . . it was . . . it should have been photographed . . . or painted . . . if it had been painted . . . described by *Goethe*, he cries, it could not have been more . . .

"Tell us about Goethe," Helena interrupts, laughing.

She has brought her little boy along. The three of them sit at a table spread with a clean pink cloth. On a silver dish, and on still another pink cloth, this one embroidered, are wedges of chocolate cake, and mocha butter cakes, and Linzer torte, and meringue shells filled with whipped cream, sprinkled with pink, green, yellow sugar. The champagne in the silver bucket is for the commissioner and Helena.

There is no view from here, not even of swimming pools. They are walled in by flowering shrubs. It is a pity, he says, for if they could only see . . .

"Tell the child what all these flowers are called," Helena interrupts. But the commissioner does not know their names. He knows what roses or tulips are, but most flowers have names he has never *needed* to know. Flowers are pale mauve or yellow in spring, blue or yellow as summer wears on, and in the autumn orange, yellow, and red. On a hot autumn day, the garden seems picked out in bright wool, like a new carpet. The wine, the cakes, the thin silver vase of bitter-smelling blooms ("Nasturtiums," he suddenly cries out, slapping the table, remembering) attract all the wasps in the neighborhood. He is afraid for Helena—imagine a sting on that white skin! He tries to cut a wasp in two with a knife, misses, captures another in the child's empty glass.

"The child needs men, you see," Helena goes on. "He needs men to tell him what things are. He is always with women."

Somewhere in her career she acquired this little boy. She does not say who the father is, but even when she was pregnant, enormous, the commissioner never asked. He treated the situation with great tact, as if she had a hideous allergy. It would have been a violation of their friendship to have pried. The rumor is that the father was an American, but not a common drunken one, an Occupation leftover—no, it was someone highly placed, worthy of her. The child is a good little boy, never troublesome. He eats his cakes with a teaspoon, and it is a wobbly performance. His fingers come into it sometimes; then he licks them. He scrapes up all the chocolate on his plate, because his mother dislikes the sight of wasted food.

"I mean it. Talk to him," Helena says. She may be teasing; but she could be serious, too.

"Child," says the obedient commissioner. "Do you know why champagne overflows when the cork is taken out of the bottle?"

"No, why?" says Helena, answering for her son.

The commissioner reflects, then says, "Because air got in the bottle."

"You see?" she tells the boy. "This is why you need men."

She is laughing, so she must be pleased. She is giving the commissioner her attention. On crumbs like these, her laughter, her attention, he thinks he can live forever. Even when she was no one, when she was a little actress who would travel miles by train, sitting up all night, for some minor, poorly paid job, he could live on what she gave him. She can be so amusing when she wants to be. She is from—he thinks— Silesia, but she can speak in any dialect, from any region. She recites for him now, for him alone, as if he mattered, Schiller's "The Glove"— first in Bavarian, then in Low Berlin, then like an East German at a radio audition, then in a Hessian accent like his own. He hears himself in her voice, and she gets no farther than *"Und wie er winkt mit dem Finger,"* because he is laughing so that he has a pain; he weeps with it. He has to cross his arms over his chest to contain the pain of his laughter. And all the while he knows she is entertaining *him*—as if he were paying her! He wipes his eyes, picks up his fork, and just as he is trying to describe the quality of the laughter ("like pleurisy, like a heart attack, like indigestion"), she says, "I can do a Yiddish accent from Silesia. I try to imagine my grandmother's voice. I must have heard it before she was killed."

She has left him; he is alone in the garden. He does not know the word for anything anymore. He has forgotten how one says "hedge" or "wasp" or "nasturtium." He does not know the reason for the transparent yellow light in his glass. Everything assembled to please her has been a mistake: the flowers on the table smell too strong; the ice in the bucket is melting because the sun, too hot, is straight upon it; and the bottle of champagne, half empty, tipped to one side, afloat, is inadequate and vulgar. He looks at the red trace of the raspberry cake he had only just started to eat, at the small two-pronged fork, at the child's round chin—he daren't look at Helena. He discovers a crumb in his throat. He will choke to death, perhaps, but he is afraid to pick up his glass. Here he is now, a man in his fifties, "a serious person," he reminds himself, in a bright garden, unable to swallow a crumb.

She sits smoking, telling herself she doesn't need him—that is what he imagines. The commissioner is nothing to her, a waste of time. It is a wonder she sees him at all. He feels the garden going round and round, like the restaurant in Frankfurt that revolves on its hub. He would have taken her there often if she allowed it. He likes spending money on her, being reckless; and also, when he gives his card, the headwaiter and all the waiters know the commissioner and Helena are friends. But the restaurant is too high up; it makes her ill and giddy just to look out the window. And anyway she has enough publicity; she doesn't need to have a waiter bow and stare. What can he do for her? Nothing, and that is what makes her so careless—why she said the wounding thing just now that made him feel left out and alone.

Oh, that grandmother! That mother! She has a father somewhere, alive, but she shrugs when she mentions him, as if the living were of no use to her. The commissioner knows nothing about the mother and grandmother. He never met them. But he knows that where Helena was concerned a serious injustice was committed, a mistake; for, when she was scarcely older than the child at this table, she was dragged through transit camps on the fringes of Germany, without—thank God—arriving at her destination. He has gone over it so many times that her dossier is stamped on his mind, as if he had seen it, typed and signed, on cheap brownish wartime paper, in a folder tied with ribbon tape. To the dossier he adds: (One) She should never have been arrested. She was only a child. (Two) She is partly Jewish, but how much and which part—her fingers? Her hair? (Three) She should never have been sent out of the country to mingle with Poles, Slovaks, and so on. Anything might have happened to her. This was an error so grave that if the functionary who committed it were ever found and tried, the commissioner would testify against him. Yes, he would risk everything—his career, his pension, anonymous letters, just to say what he thinks: "A serious mistake was made." Meanwhile, she sits and smokes, thinking she doesn't need him, ready at any second to give him up.

The proportion of Jews in the population of West Germany is .04, and Helena, being something of a fraction herself (her fingers? her hair?), is popular, much loved, and greatly solicited. She is the pet, the kitten —*ours*. She wasted her lunchtime today on an interview for an English paper, for a special series on Jews in Germany. Through an interpreter (insisted upon by Helena; having everything said twice gives her time) she told a story that has long ago ceased to be personal, and then the gaunt female reporter turned her head and said, filtering her question through a microphone, "And was the child?...in these camps?... sexually?...molested?"

Rape is so important to these people, Helena has learned; it is the worst humiliation, the most hideous ordeal the Englishwoman can imagine. She is thinking of maniacs in parks, little children attacked on their way to the swimming pool. "Destruction" is meaningless, and in any case Helena is here, alive, with her hair brushed, and blue on her eyelids—not destroyed. But if the child was sexually molested, then we all know where we are. We will know that a camp was a terrible place to be, and that there are things Helena can never bring herself to tell.

Helena said, "It was forbidden."

The interviewer looked at her. Do you call that a bad experience, she seemed to be thinking. She turned off the tape recorder.

"Rape would have meant one was a person," Helena might have gone on to say. Or, "There wasn't that sort of contact." She has been wondering for years now exactly what it is they all want to hear. They want to know that it could not have been worse, but somehow it never seems bad enough. Only her friend, the commissioner, accepts at once that it was beyond his imagination, and that the knowledge can produce nothing more than a pain like the suffering of laughter—like pleurisy, like indigestion. He would like it to have been, somehow, not German. When she says that she was moved through transit camps on the edge of the old Germany, then he can say, "So, most of it was on foreign soil!" He wants to hear how hated the guards were when they were Slovak, or Ukrainian. The vast complex of camps in Silesia is on land that has become Polish now, so it is as if those camps had never been German at all. Each time she says a foreign place-name, he is forgiven, absolved. What does it matter to her? Reality was confounded long ago. She even invents her dreams. When she says she dreams of a camp exactly reproduced, no one ever says, "Are you sure?" Her true dream is of purification, of the river never profaned, from which she wakes astonished—for the real error was not that she was sent away but that she is here, in a garden, alive.

His failing, as a friend, is his memory. He thinks she has three birthdays a year, and that he has known her forever. They met on a train, in Austria, between Vienna and Salzburg. He thinks she was always famous, but he has forgotten that she was just beginning, barely known, so anxiously dressed that sometimes people thought she was a prostitute. They were alone in a compartment. He sat with his hands on his knees, and she remembers his large cufflinks and his large square ring. He was like the economic miracle not yet at its climax of fat. Or he had been obese a long time ago—she saw, around him, the ghost of a padded man. He talked very seriously about the economic life of every town they passed, as if he knew about it, but the one thing she could recognize, whatever its disguise, was a policeman.

It makes her laugh now to think of the assurance with which he asked his first questions: Are you married? What do you do? Why were you in Vienna? She had been recording a play for a broadcast. She was just beginning, and would travel anywhere, overnight, never first class. She thought he had recognized her—that he had seen her, somewhere, once. The card she gave him, with her name engraved, was new. He studied the card for minutes, and ran his thumb over it absently.

"And in Salzburg you will be . . . ?"

"A tourist." To make the conversation move faster, and to tease, to invent, to build a situation and bring it crashing down, she said, "No one is expecting me."

"Are you expected anywhere?"

"Not until Monday. I live in Frankfurt."

He looked out the window for some time. He put the card in his pocket and sat with the tips of his fingers pressed together. "If no one is waiting for you," he said finally, "you could skip Salzburg and come on to Munich with me. I have some business there, so I would be busy part of the day. But I am free in the evening, and it is a very lively place. We could go to a night club. There is one like a stable; you drink in the horses' stalls. In the daytime, you could go to a museum. There is a very good museum where you can see ancient boats made out of hide, and you can see the oars. There are guided tours . . . The guide is excellent! And the station hotel is very good. If you don't want to, you needn't leave the station at all. Then we could both be in Frankfurt on Monday. I live there too. No one is meeting me. It wouldn't even matter if we were seen getting off the train together."

"What would happen if I went to Munich?" she said. "Would you give me money?"

"I? No."

"Well, no money, no Munich."

What went over his face was, Let me straighten this out. I thought you were one sort of person, but it seems you are another. What can this mean?

"Before I get down at Salzburg, I just have time to tell you a funny story," she said. "It is about paying for things. I heard it when I was a child, in a concentration camp." How tense they become, she thought. Just say two words and they stiffen, as if they had been touched with the point of a pin. "This is my story. A poor old Jew who was eating his lunch out of a piece of newspaper happened to be sitting opposite a Prussian officer in a train. The train was going to . . . to Breslau. After a time the officer said, 'Excuse me, but I want to ask you a question. What makes you Jews so clever, so that you always have the advantage over us?' 'Why, it is because we eat carp heads,' said the old man. 'And as I happen to have one here, I can sell it to you for thirty marks.' The officer paid for the fish head, and ate it with some disgust. After a time he said, 'But I have paid you thirty marks for something a fishmonger would have given me for nothing!' 'There, you see?' said the old man. 'It's working!'"

Her innocent eyes never left his face. He looked at her, so bewildered, so perplexed. What went wrong in our conversation, he seemed to be saying. Where was my mistake? Why are you telling me this old story? What have I done? He was red when he began to speak. His throat unlocked, and he said, "I never thought I should offer you money, Miss Helena. Excuse me. If I should have, then I apologize. You seem . . . a woman like you . . . so educated, so delicate . . . so refined, like a . . . *Holbein*." All this in his Hessian accent, which she was already recording, in her mind, for her own use.

If she were to remind him now about that man on the train, the commissioner would say, "What a fool! He could have been arrested." She imagines the commissioner arrested, still on the train, both hands against the pane and his face looking out between them—the anguish, the shock, as the train slid off and he wondered what he had done. "Now do you see?" she would say to him. "Now do you see what they are about—all those misunderstandings? You are that man too." But he would only know that another injustice had been committed; another terrible mistake.

In their conversations there is only one context. No remark is ever out of the blue. And so, when she leans forward, putting her cigarette out, at the table spread with a pink cloth, and says, "I was never raped," he does not look surprised. He says, "When you were in those places?"

"Yes. Rape did not occur. It was, in fact, utterly forbidden."

Putting out the cigarette she seems to lean on it. He knows only one thing, that the crisis is over. He has come through, without being wounded. Whatever the quarrel was, he is forgiven. They are here, with the child, in the garden restaurant, with the flowers like colored wool. He is still the old bachelor in part of her life. Now he begins to understand what she has just said—the meaning of it. He would like to stand up and announce it, tap his fork on the wineglass and when he had everyone's attention say loudly, so that he could be heard all over the gardens and swimming pools, "Nothing like that happened—nothing at all. It was strictly, utterly forbidden!" He finds he can swallow—nothing, at first; just a contraction of the throat. Then he swallows a sip of his drink. He picks up his fork, bites a piece of raspberry cake, swallows. Tears stand in his eyes. She is the best friend he could ever have imagined. She has, again, brought him out of anxiety and confusion; he is not an orphan. When she lets the wasp escape from the glass he says nothing. He knows that a little later she will tell him why.

POOR FRANZI

"SO HERE you are," said Franzi Ebendorf's grandmother. She held out her sunburned hand to Elizabeth Dunn, but her eyes were on her grandson. They settled down to the table she had saved on the crowded hotel terrace, its floating white cover anchored in the wind by a jar of flowers. She might have been waiting some time: bees swooped familiarly at the jam, pollen had shaken down to the empty plates. She had eaten nothing. The bread overlapped in its basket, brown on white, and the cake was wrapped in linen, like a well-made bed. She glanced at the table, and then clapped her hands for the coffee.

The sound of it gave the people at the next table an excuse to turn. Their name was Wright, they were from Baltimore, and they had been limp with curiosity ever since Franzi's ramshackle roadster had turned off the winding mountain road. Stranded in the Austrian mountains by the hay fever of one of their party, they were spending a hot and empty fortnight, with little to say. Spinning out the event of their afternoon coffee, they had watched Baronin Ebendorf climbing up from the valley on foot, her rings blinking in the sun a quarter mile to the hotel terrace.

"Well, look at that," young Coralie Wright had said to her mother. "And we send *them* money!" This was not a serious remark; it was intended only to tease and annoy an English Miss Mewling to whom Coralie's brother, Charlie, had unaccountably attached himself, and who now shared their table and much of their day. Miss Mewling, wearing the local costume worked in cross-stitch, sat up straighter and remarked:

"It is possible that none of your country's money reaches the Baronin. She is a very poor old lady who lives in a farmhouse in the valley.

She lost everything in the war, and all but two of her family. One of them lives in Salzburg, a grandson, a thoroughly useless person. She waits for him here every Sunday and he never comes."

"Maybe he doesn't have the bus fare," said Coralie.

"He is engaged to an American," said Miss Mewling, in the treble tones of a member of the Royal Family delivering an address over the air. "His young friend, although I can't say that I know her, must be very foolish."

"It's easy for young girls to be carried away," said Mrs. Wright, whose main difficulties on the journey had been with Coralie and her sister Joan.

"And young men," said Coralie, looking hard at Charlie. It had been Coralie's and her sister's wish to spend the summer alone in Europe, and it was no fault of theirs that the party included their mother, a brother, and an elderly cousin who had to lie down every day. "Miss Mewling should be careful, too."

"I traveled with my father until his death," said Miss Mewling, placid. "He was an excellent judge of character."

"I'm sure he was," said Mrs. Wright, now interested only in Baronin Ebendorf, who had placed herself at the next table, her cane resting on the bench beside her. "Just the same, I tell the girls, you have to be careful. Nowadays, they all want to marry Americans, just to get into the country. It's worse than the old fortune hunters. Someone in Paris even asked Coralie to have a *mariage blanc*, and promised to pay afterward for the divorce."

"She thought it meant being married in a church," Charlie said.

"I see," said Miss Mewling, who was not listening but frowning into the sun behind him. "That's him, the grandson," she said. "That's his car, the old thing that looks held together with string. That must be the girl with him."

"Are you sure?" Coralie said. "He's terribly good-looking. He looks sort of Danish. The girl looks like nothing." She sounded wistful and her mother glanced at her sharply.

"Most certainly not Danish," said Miss Mewling. "They all have a little Czech, although they deny it. And he has no manners." Pressed by Coralie, she admitted that although she and Franzi had been twice introduced, he never spoke. "He wouldn't behave that way if one cared, or took pains," said Miss Mewling. "But nowadays, who can afford that kind of nonsense?"

In a moment they were able to turn and stare at Elizabeth Dunn, who, evidently, could. Elizabeth was studying Franzi's grandmother and wondering what it would be like to take her to America and send her to live with her own parents up in Brewster. She tried to imagine the sunburned old creature with her ringed stubby hands reclining in a garden chair while her mother talked about the rose cuttings. She smiled quickly at Franzi, as if they were sharing the joke, but he had rolled a ladybug on its back and was passively watching its struggles. She looked at the two, Franzi and his grandmother, searching for physical likeness and finding only the same measure of blandness and good manners and something evasive that might be panic. She often did this, weighing her marriage as if she had shopped out of season for a costly and perishable fruit.

She had not chosen to fall in love any more than one would choose the measles over a simple cold; but, as she had written her worried parents, there it was. Happy, she glanced around the sunny terrace, although her shortsighted gaze could carry her no more than a few feet. Mistaking for hostility the intent stare of myopia, the Wrights and Miss Mewling, turned all at once like a coy chorus, were swept back to their coffee cups, indignant.

"She's twenty-eight, at least," said Coralie. "At least that." For some reason this pleased the table, and Miss Mewling confided that to her certain knowledge, Franzi was no more than twenty-three.

"I am very happy today," the Baronin was saying. "I am so glad you like your ring. I gave it to Franzi for you, but I was afraid you would find it old-fashioned."

"I love it," said Elizabeth. "I didn't know it was yours. Franzi didn't say."

"I forgot," said Franzi, and smiled the smile, bemused and distant, that caused people to call him at once by his Christian name, and a diminutive at that. Elizabeth said nothing: she had already decided that his motives were none of her affair, that they must not at any cost embark on an agglutinative relationship of sharing every thought. She could not complain about Franzi. He showed no desire to share her thoughts.

They finished their coffee and Franzi made the first move to go. While his grandmother paid, fishing for coins in a deep linen handbag, he released the ladybug and sent it through space, clinging to a leaf. Elizabeth frowned and pressed his feet under the table, meaning that perhaps he ought to pay. Misunderstanding the pressure, and the look, he stared across at her, taking notice for the first time. Sometimes she seemed to swim deliberately into the focus of his attention and he would look, eyes wide, as if perplexed at their being together. Elizabeth, who had read a great deal about love but was ignorant of its processes, found the look adorable. As they left the terrace she slipped her hand into his, which was observed by everyone but Coralie, who, when it was told to her, accidentally bit her tongue.

The three drove away in Franzi's rattling car and dropped the Baronin at the farmhouse where she boarded. "How nice it is," said Elizabeth, looking at the white-painted house with its broad carved balcony and flowering vines. "It must be quite old."

"Yes, old," said the Baronin, mistaking this for insult. Being old, the house was damp; the leaded vine-encumbered windows admitted chinks of greenish light. Winters, in the rainy season, the old woman remained in bed for days on end.

"We'll come again, whenever you like," Elizabeth promised. "And you must come into town, too, and let us take you to dinner." She kissed the Baronin, who, alarmed at the familiarity, glanced helplessly at Franzi. He bent down, permitting his grandmother to kiss him on the forehead, and then waited until she was indoors before driving away.

"She's wonderful," Elizabeth said into his ear, over the sound of the motor. "We should visit her often."

"She doesn't expect it," Franzi said.

It was one week after this, on a hot July evening, that Franzi learned of his grandmother's death. It had been painless, and nearly quick. She had died on Sunday morning, of a cerebral hemorrhage, at the hour when Franzi and Elizabeth were driving to St. Gilgen to swim. Her death was a mercy, the doctor said, for she might have lingered for years, blurred in speech and totally paralyzed. Franzi drove out to the farmhouse on Monday evening, after his grandmother had been removed, and sorted over her few belongings. There was a little money, and the deed to an old property near Mistelbach, in the Russian zone. He had already decided that in order to survive he must not encumber himself, and he kindled a small fire in the stove that stood against the wall and committed the paper to it.

There was little else to salvage: the good pieces of jewelry had been sold, and there were only useless stones left, in old-fashioned settings. He gathered them into a handkerchief and put the handkerchief in his pocket. There were photographs of his grandparents, of his father, of his sister Adelaide and himself as children in the garden at Landeck, before the house that had received a direct bomb hit while his father and mother sat in the dining room, with nothing to eat. His sister had married and gone to Australia, and she had not written to anyone for three years. Her husband farmed, her children were called Ian and Doreen, and she would have left them all in a minute had there been anywhere else to go.

After he had burned the pictures, and a package of letters he did not trouble to read, he found a photograph in a silver frame of his grandmother's sister as a girl. She sat in a high-backed chair, dressed in a striped taffeta frock that stopped short of her buttoned boots. Her hair was held back by a ribbon as big as her head, and she clasped her hands palm upward, as if she expected something to fall into them. He struggled with the picture for a while, but it was held fast, and he finally carried it away as it was.

He was on his way out when the farmer's wife, Frau Stangl, with whom his grandmother had lived, stopped him and mentioned the funeral. It was to be on Wednesday; she and her husband had made all the arrangements, even to remembering that the Baronin was Protestant, and she hoped he was pleased with what they had done. Franzi assured her that whatever she had planned was quite all right. Frau Stangl twisted her apron in her hands like a child and whispered that there had been expenses. Considering, Franzi selected from the handkerchief a garnet brooch and a pair of earrings and said he expected that would cover everything. At this Frau Stangl began to cry.

"I'll keep them," she said. "I couldn't sell them. It wouldn't be right."

"As you like," said Franzi, and hurried away.

He drove straight to Elizabeth, who expressed concern, sympathy, and even cried a little when he gave her a ring and a locket and the picture of his great-aunt. She looked at the picture and said: "You have no one now in the world but me." She asked about the funeral and then, to spare him, said no more.

The two spent their working hours on opposite sides of Salzburg. Elizabeth, who had a temporary job with the American occupation forces, sat under a tiring light in one of the gray buildings ringing the Mozartplatz. Franzi was connected in the loosest imaginable manner with a firm that sold electrical comforts in the bombed vicinity of the railway station. The firm was in chronic difficulties, what with Austrian factories producing too little, and American things costing too much, and no one in Austria being able to afford thirty-part vacuum cleaners or caring much for jump-up toasters.

"It's different for you," Franzi's partner, Herr Rattner, often said, mournful. "By Christmas you'll be in America." Fortunately, that week someone was coming in to see about electric heaters for a hospital and Franzi's name, usually of no more utility than Schneider or Schmidt, might be helpful. "You talk to them," Herr Rattner said. "I am ill." He went into his office and arranged himself tenderly on a couch. He admired American business practices and copied behavior he had seen in films: he would have liked a switchboard and a girl like Betty Grable in *Rosies Skandalchronik*, but there was only Franzi.

Elizabeth chose that moment to ring up. She seldom did this from her office, for her alliance was not approved of, and more than one person of authority had taken her to lunch and counseled second thoughts.

"I've arranged for time off this afternoon," she said to Franzi. "I'd like to go to the funeral with you, if I may."

He was about to ask, "What funeral?" but then he remembered and said, "It's terrible, but I can't go."

"Is anything wrong?"

"No." With his free hand he worked open a package of American cigarettes and pulled one out. "No. I just can't get away."

"I've never heard of such a thing. Did you explain to Mr. Rattner?"

"Yes. Are you laughing at something?"

"No," said Elizabeth, shocked. "Although I was thinking... it's a joke, in English I mean, about going to one's grandmother's funeral."

"I see," said Franzi. Not seeing, he nonetheless smiled politely.

"I can't understand Mr. Rattner," Elizabeth said. Out of the misty workings of the firm, she had somehow identified their relationship as employer and employee. "Look, where is the funeral?"

"Just a moment," Franzi said. "Someone came in." He put down the telephone and crossed to the office where Herr Rattner was lying down. He leaned into the room. "Where is my grandmother's funeral?"

"Your what?" They regarded each other soberly.

"She lived near Elsbethen," Franzi said.

"Then she'll be buried there. You're not leaving me today, are you?"

"No." He closed the door quietly and picked up the telephone. "Elsbethen," he said. "It's a little old church. We've passed it in the car."

"Yes. I think I know." Embarrassed, she paused, and said, "If you can't go, perhaps I ought to. I mean, I'd like to."

"That would be nice of you."

"Unless you'd rather I didn't." It had occurred to her that he might not want strangers about: all morning she had thought about the world that separated them and how his family, all of them, had moved into an increasingly desolate landscape, saying that things were changing, until there was only Franzi left to know that now things had changed. "My poor Franzi," she said.

He had been looking for a match and now found one in a desk drawer. "It would be nice if you could go," he repeated. He was suddenly conscious that the day was hot, and that he had had no lunch: counting his money that morning, he had been able to put together only enough to take Elizabeth to dinner. He was about to add that she might enjoy the funeral, for he often committed these absurdities in conversation, following only the rhythm of the sentences and thinking all the while of something else. He was at that moment looking at a sample electric heater that stood on his desk, and thinking, to no purpose, that the rate of exchange between the dollar and the schilling was thirty-three at the hotel down the street, and that the Jews before the bombed-out church gave only thirty.

"Well," said Elizabeth, still hesitating, not wishing to be tactless, "I'll call you again when I get back. Are you sure you don't mind? It's just that I think that someone, that one of us . . ." Feeling foolish, she at last said goodbye.

Up at the hotel, the Wrights and Miss Mewling had decided to attend the funeral of Baronin Ebendorf. Their visit nearly at an end, they were badly on each other's nerves and it seemed a neutral enough excursion. They were not exactly strangers to the Ebendorfs for, as Miss Mewling once more pointed out, she and Franzi had been twice introduced.

The hotel was full of gossip about Franzi, how his grandmother had lain speechless and unmoving for two days, looking at the door through which he might, but did not, appear: how he had stolen her jewelry and burned her will. Conscience-stricken, he had given the Stangls, who had cared for the old lady until her death, a trinket of no value. One could only guess what the vanished testament had willed to them.

All of this had been passed up the mountain to the chambermaids and on to the Wrights. "Can you imagine?" they asked one another. "He hasn't done one solitary thing about the funeral, hasn't sent flowers, just left everything to those poor peasants!" They wondered how he would behave, and Coralie, in fancy, exchanged with him a long look of understanding over the open grave. "It's a good thing we're going," Coralie said. "The hotelier said he was *glad* we were going because they have no family here." Starting down the mountain, each of them saw the abandoned churchyard and the minister at his lonely task, reading prayers with no one to hear.

This thought, and this curiosity, drew together in the cemetery more than a dozen persons, among them Elizabeth. Her arrival caused a disturbed murmur, for the Stangls, who were providing the funeral, stood a little forward of the rest, replacing next of kin. They wondered if they should move away for Elizabeth: they had paid for the funeral out of helplessness and decency, and they felt, momentarily, cheated of their small acquittance. Nervous, they faced the coffin that lay on the path before the church, the flames of the candles at its four corners stretching and diminishing in the wind. Elizabeth unwittingly settled the matter by stepping behind them in order to remove herself from the Wrights, whose milky looks of kindness displeased and confused her. Frau Stangl, vindicated, smoothed her black cotton gloves.

A Protestant, the Baronin could not be buried from the church: her coffin lay on the ground covered with a lacy shawl, marked with the wax of other candles and other deaths. The Lutheran minister, who had been fetched from another town, droned unfamiliar words in German. "*Du, Augusta Adelaide*," he said coldly, looking over his prayer book to the coffin. Frau Stangl stared around the churchyard, at the decorated wrought-iron crosses, and began to cry.

So that was her name, Elizabeth thought. Ever since Franzi had given her the picture of his great-aunt, without troubling to identify it, she had struggled to connect the clear-eyed girl in the taffeta dress with Baronin Ebendorf pouring coffee, her rings crammed together as if she dared leave nothing in her room. What had happened between, thickened the eyelids, thinned the mouth, she could not have said: age, of course, and trouble, and fear. Of these Franzi had had his share, all but the age. She thought of the sister who never wrote, and the solitariness that had separated him even from his grandmother; nothing else must ever happen to him, now that he has me, she told herself. On the wall of the church, beside which they stood, evergreen wreaths hung on pegs, stirring in the wind. They looked like Christmas garlands, inwoven with berries; she guessed that the local people had made them and she wondered which of them Franzi had sent.

The row of mourners stirred. Coralie tied the streamers of her lacy black hat and prodded Joanie, who wore dark glasses, as if she had been crying hard. They looked at Elizabeth who had not seen the four pall bearers pick up the coffin and, as the little procession circled once around the churchyard, found herself crowded into the Stangls. The procession was trailed by fair-haired school children, pious frauds, who had passed the cemetery on an errand and seen something of interest going on. They ringed the grave, and Elizabeth, peering blindly, decided that the Baronin had had strange friends: peasants and school children and well-dressed Americans.

The coffin was lowered. One by one the mourners shook earth on it from a shovel, shuddering at the noise it made. Coralie Wright wiped her eyes: they were going to Italy in two days and then home, and she had had no fun at all. "We might as well be dead," she said to her sister.

Miss Mewling, who had disapproved of the proceedings from start to end, looked coldly at Coralie and said aloud, "She was the end of a good line. We have buried a way of life."

"Oh, Miss *Mew*ling," said Mrs. Wright, distressed. She had seen in the funeral a morbid foretaste of her own. Only Charlie, who had stopped speaking to his family because of Miss Mewling, had nothing to say. They filed by the Stangls, who shook everyone's hand, as if they were guests leaving a party. Elizabeth said soberly, "You have been very kind." She felt nearly as if she ought to make some excuse for Franzi. Frau Stangl, wearing the garnet brooch, brimmed over and sobbed. "Such a sweet little churchyard! She would have loved it!"

"I know, I know," said Elizabeth, not understanding. They must have loved her very much, she thought.

She could not wait the twenty minutes that separated her from Salzburg to speak to Franzi, and she called him from the inn that was also a bus stop. The telephone rang a long time and then it was answered by Herr Rattner. "Moment," he said. As a door was opened and shut she heard a burst of laughter: Herr Rattner's cinematic business methods were in full flower and glasses clinked and the man who had come to see about electric heaters was telling them a funny story.

"Franzi!" Elizabeth cried. It surprised her a little that he sounded so cheerful.

"I can't hear you," he said. "You sound queer."

She had wanted to say: I'm sorry that your grandmother did not inherit the earth, as had been arranged, but was buried instead by a few peasants and some tourists. But an American sergeant stood shuffling behind her, waiting to use the telephone, and she said instead, "I'm not going back to work. Meet me at the terminal by the railway station and we'll go somewhere and talk. It's right near your office."

"But I can't leave today," he said. "I told you, remember?"

"I wish you could meet me for a few minutes," she said. "The funeral upset me a little. About you, I mean."

"About me?" Then he said, "Oh, the funeral! So you went! Well, my little conscience."

"I wanted to go," she said. Her voice rose.

"You mustn't be upset," he said. There were voices behind him, and she finally said quickly:

"It's all right. I'll see you when you're free."

After she had put up the telephone she walked out to the highway to wait for her bus. The Wrights sat together at a round painted table, drinking apple juice. They were waiting for a taxi: although it would be expensive, they were unable to find their way about on foot, even with Miss Mewling to guide them. "Blind as a bat," said Coralie, as Elizabeth walked straight past them.

She was frowning. It had not been her intention to be the little conscience of anyone, and only her pity for Franzi excused her from being angry or even hurt. Did he not want me to go? she wondered. Far down the road she heard the rattle of the ancient bus and she looked around the country, at the hazy summer mountains, as if she had been told she was never to see them again. Behind the solid peaks were softer shapes, shifting and elusive: she could not have said if they were clouds or mountains. But then, she thought, no one can, unless they have better eyes than mine, and know the country very well. She settled into the bus and closed her eyes. What will happen to me if I marry him? she wondered; and what would become of Franzi if she were to leave him? Now, as she had fifty times in her own room at Salzburg, she eliminated one by one a parade of hazards and arrived, restored, to the place where he would not be waiting.

"You should have heard the way she talked to him on the phone." said Coralie. "I was right near, trying to get cigarettes. She was practically ordering him, on the day of his grandmother's funeral. Poor Franzi."

"Poor both of them," said Mrs. Wright, and she looked at the dust where Elizabeth had vanished, at the sheltering haze, and the landscape that none of them knew.

HIS MOTHER

HIS MOTHER had come of age in a war and then seemed to live a long grayness like a spun-out November. "Are you all right?" she used to ask him at breakfast. What she really meant was: Ask me how I am, but she was his mother and so he would not. He leaned two fists against his temples and read a book about photography, waiting for her to cut bread and put it on a plate for him. He seldom looked up, never truly saw her—a stately, careless widow with unbrushed red hair, wearing an old fur coat over her nightgown; her last dressing gown had been worn to ribbons and she said she had no money for another. It seemed that nothing could stop her from telling him how she felt or from pestering him with questions. She muttered and smoked and drank such a lot of strong coffee that it made her bilious, and then she would moan, "God, God, my liver! My poor head!" In those days in Budapest you had to know the black market to find the sort of coffee she drank, and of course she would not have any but the finest smuggled Virginia cigarettes. "Quality," she said to him—or to his profile, rather. "Remember after I have died that quality was important to me. I held out for the best."

She had known what it was to take excellence for granted. That was the difference between them. Out of her youth she could not recall a door slammed or a voice raised except in laughter. People had floated like golden dust; whole streets of people buoyed up by optimism, a feeling for life.

He sat reading, waiting for her to serve him. He was a stone out of a stony generation. Talking to him was like lifting a stone out of water. He never resisted, but if you let go for even a second he sank and came to rest on a dark sea floor. More than one of her soft-tempered lovers had tried to make a friend of him, but they had always given up, as they did with everything. How could she give up? She loved him. She felt shamed because it had not been in her to control armies, history, his stony watery world. From the moment he appeared in the kitchen doorway, passive, vacant, starting to live again only because this was morning, she began all over: "Don't you feel well?" "Are you all right?" "Why can't you smile?"—though the loudest sentence was in silence: Ask me how I am.

After he left Budapest (got his first passport, flew to Glasgow with a soccer team, never came back) she became another sort of person, an émigré's mother. She shed the last of her unimportant lovers and with the money her son was soon able to send she bought a white blouse, combs that would pin her hair away from her face, and a blue kimono. She remembered long, tender conversations they had had together, and she got up early in the morning to see if a letter had come from him and then to write one of her own describing everything she thought and did. His letters to his mother said, Tell me about your headaches, are you still drinking too strong coffee, tell me the weather, the names of streets, if you still bake poppy-seed cakes.

She had never been any sort of a cook, but it seemed to her that, yes, she had baked for him, perhaps in their early years together, which she looked back upon as golden, and lighter than thistledown.

On Saturday afternoons she put on a hat and soft gray gloves and went to the Vörösmarty Café. It had once had a French name, Gerbeaud, and the circle of émigrés' mothers who met to exchange news and pictures of grandchildren still called it that. "Gerbeaud" was a sign of caste and the mark of a generation, too. Like herself, the women wore hats and sometimes scarves of fur, and each carried a stuffed handbag she would not have left behind on a tabletop for even a second. Their sons' letters looked overstamped, like those he sent her now. She had not been so certain of her rank before, or felt so quietly sure, so well thought of. A social order prevailed, as it does everywhere. The aristocrats were those whose children had never left Europe; the poorest of the poor were not likely ever to see their sons again, for they had gone to Chile and South Africa. Switzerland was superior to California. A city earned more points than a town. There was no mistaking her precedence here; she was a grand duchess. If Glasgow was unfamiliar, the very sound of it somehow rang with merit. She always had a new letter to show, which was another symbol of one's station, and they were warm messages, concerned about her health, praising her remembered skill with pies and cakes. Some mothers were condemned to a lowly status only because their children forgot to write. Others had to be satisfied with notes from foreign daughters-in-law, which were often sent from table to table before an adequate reading could be obtained. Here again she was in demand, for she read three foreign languages, which suggested a background of governesses and careful schools. She might have left it at that, but her trump credentials were in plain sight. These were the gifts he bestowed—the scarves and pastel sweaters, the earrings and gloves.

What she could not do was bring the émigré ritual to its final celebration; it required a passport, a plane ticket, and a visit to the absent son. She would never deliver into his hands the three immutable presents, which were family jewelry, family photographs, and a cake. Any mother traveling to within even a few miles of another woman's son was commissioned to take all three. The cake was a bother to carry, for the traveler usually had one of her own, but who could say no? They all knew the cake's true value. Look at the way her own son claimed his share of nourishment from a mother whose cooking had always been a joke.

No one had ever been close to Scotland, and if she had not applied for her own passport or looked up flight schedules it was for a good reason: her son had never suggested she come. And yet, denied even the bliss of sewing a garnet clip into a brassière to be smuggled to an unknown daughter-in-law, she still knew she was blessed. Other women were dismissed, forgotten. More than one had confided, "My son might as well be dead." She did not think of him as dead—how could she?—but as a coin that had dropped unheard, had rolled crazily, lay still. She knew the name of his car, of his street, she had seen pictures of them, but what did she know?

After he disappeared, as soon as she had made certain he was safe and alive, she rented his room to a student, who stayed with her for three

years in conditions of some discomfort, for she had refused, at first, to
remove anything belonging to her son. His books were sacred. His
records were not to be played. The records had been quite valuable at
one time; they were early American rock slipped in by way of Vienna
and sold at a murderous rate of exchange. These collected dust now,
like his albums of pictures—like the tenant student's things too, for
although she pinned her hair up with combs and wore a spotless blouse,
she was still no better a housekeeper. Her tenant studied forestry. He
was a bumpkin, and somewhat afraid of her. She could never have
mistaken him for a son. He crept in and out and brought her flowers.
One day she played a record for him, to which he listened with defer-
ence rather than interest, and she remembered herself, at eighteen,
hearing with the same anxious boredom a warped scene from "Die
Walküre," both singers now long dead. Having a student in the flat
did not make her feel she was in touch with her son, or even with his
generation. His room changed meanwhile; even its smell was no longer
the same. She began to wonder what his voice had been like. She could
see him, she dreamed of him often, but her dreams and memories were
like films with the sound track removed.

The bumpkin departed, and she took in his place a future art historian—the regime produced these in awesome numbers now—who
gave way, in turn, to the neurasthenic widow of a poet. The poet's
widow was taken over in time by her children, and replaced by a couple
of young librarians. And then came two persons not quite chosen by
herself. She could have refused them, but thought it wiser not to. They
were an old man and his pregnant granddaughter. They seemed to be
brokenly poor; the granddaughter almost to the end of her term worked
long hours in a plasma laboratory. And yet they appeared endowed
with dark, important connections: no sooner were they installed than
she was granted a telephone, which her tenants never used without
asking, and only for laconic messages—the grandfather to state that
his granddaughter was not yet at home, or the girl to take down the
day and hour of a meeting somewhere. After the granddaughter had
her baby they became four in a flat that had barely been comfortable
for two. She cleared out the last of her son's records and his remaining
books (the rest had long ago been sold or stolen), and she tried to es-

tablish a set of rules. For one, she made it a point to remain in the kitchen when her tenants took their meals. This was her home; it was not strictly a shared and still less a communal Russian apartment. But she could go only so far: it was at Gerbeaud's that she ranked as a grand duchess. These people reckoned differently, and on their terms she was, if not at the foot of the ladder, then dangerously to one side of it; she had an émigré son, she received gifts and money from abroad, and she led in terms of the common good a parasitic existence. They were careful, even polite, but they were installed. She was inhabited by them, as by an illness one must learn to endure.

It was around this time—when her careless, undusted, but somehow pure rooms became a slum, festooned with washing, reeking of boiling milk, where she was seldom alone or quiet—that she began to drift away from an idea she had held about her age and time. Where, exactly, was the youth she recalled as happy? What had been its shape, its color? All that golden dust had not belonged to her—it had been part of her mother. It was her mother who had floated like thistledown, smiled, lived with three servants on call, stood with a false charming gaucherie, an arm behind her, an elbow grasped. That simulated awkwardness took suppleness and training; it required something her generation had not been granted, which was time. Her mother had let her coat fall on the floor because coats were replaceable then, not only because there had been someone to pick it up. She had carried a little curling iron in her handbag. When she quarreled with her husband, she went to the station and climbed into a train marked "Budapest-Vienna-Rome," and her husband had thought it no more than amusing to have to fetch her back. Slowly, as "eighteen" came to mean an age much younger than her son's, as he grew older in Scotland, married, had a child, began slipping English words into his letters, went on about fictitious apple or poppy-seed cakes, she parted without pain from a soft, troubled memory, from an old gray film about porters wheeling steamer trunks, white fur wraps, bunches of violets, champagne. It was gone: it had never been. She and her son were both mistaken, and yet they had never been closer. Now that she had the telephone, he called her on Easter Sunday, and on Christmas Eve, and on her birthday. His wife had spoken to her in English:

"It's snowing here. Is it snowing in Budapest?"

"It quite often snows."

"I hope we can meet soon."

"That would be pleasant."

His wife's parents sent her Christmas greetings with stern Biblical messages, as if they judged her, by way of her son, to be frivolous, without a proper God. At least they knew now that she spoke correct English; on the other hand, perhaps they were simple souls unable to imagine that anything but English could ever be.

They were not out of touch; nor did he neglect her. No one could say that he had. He had never missed a monthly transfer of money, he was faithful about sending his overstamped letters and the colored snapshots of his wife, his child, their Christmas tree, and his wife's parents side by side upon a modern-looking sofa. One unposed picture had him up a ladder pasting sheets of plastic tiles on a kitchen wall. She could not understand the meaning of this photograph, in which he wore jeans and a sweater that might have been knitted by an untalented child. His hair had grown long, it straggled in brown mouse-tails over the collar of the lamentable pullover. He stood in profile, so that she could see just half of a new and abundant mustache. Also—and this might have been owing to the way he stood, because he had to sway to hold his balance—he looked as if he might have become, well, a trifle stout. This was a picture she never showed anyone at Vörösmarty Place, though she examined it often, by several kinds of light. What did it mean, what was its secret expression? She looked for the invisible ink that might describe her son as a husband and father. He was twenty-eight, he had a mustache, he worked in his own home as a common laborer.

She said to herself, I never let him lift a finger. I waited on him from the time he opened his eyes.

In response to the ladder picture she employed a photographer, a former schoolfriend of her son's, to take a fiercely lighted portrait of her sitting on her divan-bed with a volume of Impressionist reproductions opened on her lap. She wore a string of garnets and turned her head proudly, without gaping or grinning. From the background wall she had removed a picture of clouds taken by her son, then a talented amateur, and hung in its stead a framed parchment that proved her mother's family had been ennobled. Actually a whole town had been ennobled at a stroke, but the parchment was legal and real. Normally it would not have been in her to display the skin of the dog, as these things were named, but perhaps her son's wife, looking at the new proud picture of his mother, might inquire, "What is that, there on the wall?"

She wrote him almost every morning—she had for years, now. At night her thoughts were morbid, unchecked, and she might have been likely to tell about her dreams or to describe the insignificant sadness of a lifetime, or to recall the mornings when he had eaten breakfast in silence, when talking to him had been like lifting a stone. Her letters held none of those things. She wrote wearing her blue, clean, now elderly kimono, sitting at the end of her kitchen table, while her tenants ate and quarreled endlessly.

She had a long back-slanting hand she had once been told was the hand of a liar. Upside down the letter looked like a shower of rain. It was strange, mysterious, she wrote, to be here in the kitchen with the winter sun on the sparkling window (it was grimy, in fact; but she was seeing quite another window as she wrote) and the tenant granddaughter, whose name was Ilona, home late on a weekday. Ilona and the baby and the grandfather were all three going to a funeral this morning. It seemed a joyous sort of excursion because someone was fetching them by car; that in itself was an indication of their somber connections. It explained, in shorthand, why she had not squarely refused to take them in. She wrote that the neighbors' radios could be heard faintly like the sounds of life breaking into a fever, and about Ilona preparing a boiled egg for the baby, drawing a face on the shell to make it interesting, and the baby opening his mouth, patting the table in a broken rhythm, patting crumbs with a spread-out hand. Here in the old kitchen she shared a wintry, secret, morning life with strangers.

Grandfather wore a hearing aid, but he had taken it apart, and it lay now on the table like parts of a doll's skull. Wearing it at breakfast kept him from enjoying his food. Spectacles bothered him, too. He made a noise eating, because he could not hear himself; nor did he see the mess around his cup and plate.

"Worse than an infant!" his granddaughter cried. She had a cross-looking little Tartar face. She tore squares of newspaper, one to go on the floor, another for underneath his plate. He scattered sugar and pipe ash and crusts and the pieces of his hearing aid. At the same time he was trying to attend to a crossword puzzle, which he looked at with a magnifying glass. But he still would not put his spectacles on, because they interfered with his food. Being deaf, he traveled alone in his memories and sometimes came out with just anything. His mind plodded back and forth. Looking up from the puzzle he said loudly, "My granddaughter has a diploma. Indeed she has. She worked in a hospital. Yes, she did. Some people think too much of themselves when they have a diploma. They begin to speak pure Hungarian. They try to speak like educated people. Not Ilona! You will never hear one word of good Hungarian from *her*."

His granddaughter had just untied a towel she used as a bib for the child. She grimaced and buried her Tartar's grimace in the towel. Only her brown hair was seen, and her shaking shoulders. She might have been laughing. Her grandfather wore a benign and rather a foolish smile until she looked up and screamed, "I hate you." She reminded him of all that she had done to make him happy. She described the last place they'd lived in, the water gurgling in the pipes, the smell of bedbugs. She had found this splendid apartment; she was paying their rent. His little pension scarcely covered the coffee he drank. "You thought your son was too good for my mother," she said. "You made her miserable, too."

The old man could not hear any of this. His shaking freckled hands had been assembling the hearing aid. He adjusted it in time to hear Ilona say, "It is hard to be given lessons in correct speech by someone who eats like a pig."

He sighed and said only, "Children," as one might sound resigned to any natural enemy.

The émigré's mother, their landlady, had stopped writing. She looked up, not at them, but of course they believed they could be seen. They began to talk about their past family history, as they did when they became tense and excited, and it all went into the letter. Ilona had lost her father, her mother, and her little sister in a road accident when, with Grandfather, they had been on their way to a funeral in the suburbs in a bus.

Funerals seemed to be the only outing they ever enjoyed. The old man listened to Ilona telling it again, but presently he got up and left them, as if the death of his son allowed him no relief even so many years later. When he came back he had his hat and coat on. For some reason, he had misunderstood and thought they had to leave at once for the new excursion. He took his landlady's hand and pumped it up and down, saying, "From the bottom of my heart . . . ," though all he was leading up to was "Goodbye." He did not let her hand go until he inadvertently brought it down hard on a thick cup.

"He has always embarrassed us in public," said Ilona, clearing away. "What could we do? He was my father's father."

That other time, said the old man—calmed now, sitting down in his overcoat—the day of the *fatal* funeral, there had been time to spare, out in a suburb, where they had to change from one bus to another. They had walked once around a frozen duckpond. He had been amazed, the old man remembered, at how many people were free on a working weekday. His son carried one of the children; little Ilona walked.

"Of course I walked! I was twelve!" she screamed from the sink.

He had been afraid that Ilona would never learn to speak, because her mother said everything for her. When Ilona pointed with her woolly fist, her mother crooned, "Skaters." Or else she announced, "You are cold," and pulled a scarf up over Ilona's apple cheeks.

"That was my sister," Ilona said. "I was twelve."

"Now, a governess might have made the child speak, say words correctly," said the old man. "Mothers are helpless. They can only say yes, yes, and try to repeat what the child seems to be thinking."

"He has always embarrassed us," Ilona said. "My mother hated going anywhere in his company."

Once around the duckpond, and then an old bus rattled up and they got in. The driver was late, and to make up for time he drove fast. At the bottom of a hill, on a wide sheet of black ice, the bus turned like a balky horse, rocked, steadied, and the driver threw himself over the wheel as if to protect it. An army lorry came down the hill, the first of two. Ilona's mother pulled the baby against her and pulled Ilona's head on her lap.

"Eight killed, including the two drivers," Ilona said.

Here was their folklore, their richness; how many persons have lost their families on a bus and survived to describe the holocaust? No wonder she and Grandfather were still together. If she had not married her child's father, it was because he had not wanted Grandfather to live with them. "You, yes," he had said to Ilona. "Relatives, no." Grandfather nodded, for he was used to hearing this. Her cold sacrifice always came on top of his disapproval.

Well, that was not quite the truth of it, the émigré's mother went on writing. The man who had interceded for them, whom she had felt it was wiser not to refuse, who might be the child's father, had been married for quite a long time.

The old man looked blank and strained. His eyes had become small. He looked Chinese. "Where we lived then was a good place to live with children," he said, perhaps speaking of a quarter fading like the edge of a watercolor into gray apartment blocks. Something had frightened him. He took out a clean pocket handkerchief and held it to his lips.

"Another army lorry took us to the hospital," said Ilona. "Do you know what you were saying?"

He remembered an ambulance. He and his grandchild had been wrapped in blankets, had lain on two stretchers, side by side, fingers locked together. That was what he remembered.

"You said, '*My mother, my mother,*'" she told him.

"I don't think I said that."

Now they are having their usual disagreement, she wrote her son. Lorry or ambulance?

"I heard," said Ilona. "I was conscious."

"I had no reason. If I said, 'My mother,' I was thinking, 'My children.'"

The rainstorm would cover pages more. Her letter had veered off and resembled her thoughts at night. She began to tell him she had trouble sleeping. She had been given a wonderful new drug, but unfortunately it was habit-forming and the doctor would not renew it.

The drug gave her a deep sleep, from which she emerged fresh and enlivened, as if she had been swimming. During the sleep she was allowed
exact and colored dreams in which she was a young girl again and men
long dead came to visit. They sat amiably discussing their deaths. Her
first fiancé, killed in 1943, opened his shirt to show the chest wound.
He apologized for having died without warning. He did not know that
less than a year later she had married another man. The dead had no
knowledge of love beyond the span of their own lives. The next night,
she found herself with her son's father. They were standing together
buying tickets for a play when she realized he was dead. He stood in
his postwar shabbiness, discreet, hidden mind, camouflaged face, and
he had ceased to be with the living. Her grief was so cruel that, lest she
perish in sleep from the shock of it, someone unseen but conciliating
suggested that she trade any person she knew in order to keep him with
her. He would never have the misery of knowing that he was dead.

What would her son say to all this? My mother is now at an age
when women dream of dead men, he might tell himself; when they
begin to choose quite carelessly between the dead and the living. Women
are crafty even in their sleep. They know they will survive. Why weep?
Why discuss? Why let things annoy you? For a long time she believed
he had left because he could not look at her life. Perhaps his going had
been as artless, as simple, as he still insisted: he had got his first passport,
flown out with a football team, never come back. He was between the
dead and the living, a voice on the telephone, an affectionate letter full
of English words, a coin rolled and lying somewhere in secret. And she,
she was the revered and respected mother of a generous, an attentive,
a camouflaged stranger.

Tell me the weather, he still wrote. Tell me the names of streets. She
began a new page: Vörösmarty Place, if you remember, is at the beginning of Váci Street, the oldest street in the Old City. In the middle of
the Place stands a little park. Our great poet, for whom the Place is
named, sits carved in marble. Sculptured figures look gratefully up to
him. They are grateful because he is the author of the national anthem.
There are plane trees full of sparrows, and there are bus stops, and even
a little Métro, the oldest in Europe, perhaps old-fashioned, but practical—it goes to the Zoo, the Fine Arts Museum, the Museum of Dec-

orative Art, the Academy of Music, and the Opera. The old redoubt is there, too, at least one wall of it, backed up to a new building where you go to book seats for concerts. The real face of the redoubt has been in ruins since the end of the war. It used to be Moorish-romantic. The old part, which gave on the Danube, had in her day—no, in her mother's day—been a large concert hall, the reconstruction of which created grave problems because of modern acoustics. At Gerbeaud's the pastries are still the best in Europe, she wrote, and so are the prices. There are five or six little rooms, little marble tables, comfortable chairs. Between the stiff lace curtains and the windowpanes are quite valuable pieces of china. In summer one can sit on the pavement. There is enough space between the plane trees, and the ladies with their elegant hats are not in too much danger from the sparrows. If you come there, you will see younger people, too, and foreigners, and women who wait for foreigners, but most of the customers, yes, most, belong to the magic circle of mothers whose children have gone away. The café opens at ten and closes at nine. It is always crowded. "You can often find me there," she went on, "and without fail every Saturday," as if she might look up and see him draw near, transformed, amnesiac, not knowing her. I hope that I am not in your dreams, she said, because dreams are populated by the silent and the dead, and I still speak, I am alive. I wear a hat with a brim and soft gray gloves. I read their letters in three foreign languages. Thanks to you, I can order an endless succession of little cakes, I can even sip cognac. Will you still know me? I was your mother.

AN AUTOBIOGRAPHY

I

I teach elementary botany to girls in a village half a day's journey by train from Montreux. Season by season our landscape is black on white, or green and blue, or, at the end of summer, olive and brown, with traces of snow on the mountains like scrubbed-out paint. The village is made up of concentric rings: a ring of hotels, a ring of chalets, another of private schools. Through the circles one straight street carries the tearooms and the sawmill and the stuccoed cinema with the minute screen on which they try to show things like *Ben-Hur*. Some of my pupils seem interested in what I have to say, but the most curious and alert are usually showing off. The dull girls, with their slow but capacious memories, are often a solace, a source of hope. Very often, after I have been on time for children raised to be unpunctual, or have counseled prudence, in vain, to these babies of heedless parents, I remind myself that they have not been sent here to listen to me. I must learn to become the substance their parents have paid for—a component of scenery, like a tree or a patch of grass. I must stop battering at the sand castles their parents have built. I might swear, at certain moments, that all the girls from Western Germany are lulled and spoiled, and all the French calculating, and the Italians insincere, and the English impermeable, and so on, and on; but that would be at the end of a winter's day when they have worn me out.

At the start of the new term, two girls from Frankfurt came to me. They giggled and pushed up the sleeves of their sweaters so that I could see the reddish bruises. "Tomorrow is medical inspection," said Liselotte. "What can we say?" They should have been in tears, but they were biting their lips to keep from laughing too much, wondering what my reaction would be. They said they had been pinching each other to see who could stand the most pain. There are no demerits in our school; if there were, every girl would be removed at once. We are expected to create reserves of memory. The girls must remember their teachers as they remembered hot chocolate and after-skiing, all in the same warm fog. I disguised the bruises with iodine, and said that girls sometimes slipped and fell during my outdoor classes and sometimes scratched their arms. "*Merci, Mademoiselle*," said the two sillies. They could have said "*Fräulein*" and been both accurate and understood, but they are also here because of the French. Their parents certainly speak English, because it was needed a few years ago in Frankfurt, but the children may not remember. They are ignorant and new. Everything they see and touch at home is new. Home is built on the top layer of Ur. It is no good excavating; the fragments would be without meaning. Everything within the walls was inlaid or woven or cast or put together fifteen years ago at the very earliest. Every house is like the house of newly wed couples who have been disinherited or say they scorn their families' taste. It is easy to put an X over half your life (I am thinking about the parents now) when you have nothing out of the past before your eyes; when the egg spoon is plastic and the coffee cup newly fired porcelain; when the books have been lost and the silver, if salvaged, sold a long time ago. There are no dregs, except perhaps a carefully sorted collection of snapshots. You have survived and the food you eat is new—even that. There are bananas and avocado pears and plenty of butter. Not even an unpleasant taste in the mouth will remind you.

I have light hair, without a trace of gray, and hazel eyes. I am not fat, because, unlike my colleagues, I do not hide pastry and *petits fours* in my room to eat before breakfast. My calves, I think, are overdeveloped from years of walking and climbing in low-heeled shoes. I am a bit sensitive about it, and wear my tweed skirts longer than the fashion. Because I take my gloves off in all weather, my hands are rough; their untended appearance makes the French and Italian parents think I am not gently bred. I use the scents and creams my pupils present me with at Christmas. I have few likes and dislikes, but have lost the habit of eating whatever is put before me. I do not mind accepting gifts.

Everyone's father where I come from was a physician or a professor. You will never hear of a father who rinsed beer glasses in a hotel for his keep, or called at houses with a bottle of shampoo and a portable hair-drying machine. Such fathers may have existed, but we do not know about them. My father was a professor of Medieval German. He was an amateur botanist and taught me the names of flowers before I could write. He went from Munich to the university at Debrecen, in the Protestant part of Hungary, when I was nine. He did not care for contemporary history and took no notice of passing events. His objection to Munich was to its prevailing church, and the amount of noise in the streets. The year was 1937. In Debrecen, on a Protestant islet, he was higher and stonier and more Lutheran than anyone else, or thought so. Among the very few relics I have is *Wild Flowers of Germany: One Hundred Pictures Taken from Nature*. The cover shows a spray of Solomon's-seal—five white bells on a curving stem. It seems to have been taken against the night. Under each of the hundred pictures is the place and time we identified the flower. The plants are common, but I was allowed to think them rare. Beneath a photograph of lady's-slipper my father wrote, "By the large wood on the road going toward the vineyard at Durlach July 11 1936," in the same amount of space I needed to record, under snowdrops, "In the Black Forest last Sunday."

I have often wondered whether tears should rise as I leaf through the book; but no—it has nothing to do with me, or with anyone now. It would be a poor gesture to throw it away, an act of harshness or impiety, but if it were lost or stolen I would not complain.

I recall, in calm woods, my eyes on the ground, searching for poisonous mushrooms. He knocked them out of the soft ground with his walking stick, and I conscientiously trod them to pulp. I teach my pupils to do the same, explaining that they may in this way save countless lives; but while I am still talking the girls have wandered away along the sandy paths, chattering, collecting acorns. "Beware of mushrooms that grow around birch trees," I warn. It is part of the lesson.

I can teach in Hungarian, German, French, English, or Italian. I am grateful to Switzerland, where language is a matter of locality, not an imposition, and existence a question of choice. It is better to avoid dying unless the circumstances are clear. If I fall, by accident, out of the funicular tomorrow, it will only prove once again that the suicide rate is high in a peaceful society. In any case, I will see the shadow of the cable car sliding over trees. In a clearing, a woman sorting apples for cider will not look up, although her children may wave. There I shall be, gazing down in order to frighten my vertigo away (I have been trying this for years), in the cable car of my own will, hoping I shall not open the door without meaning to and fall out and become a reproach to a country that has been more than kind. Imagine gliding— floating down to them! Think of the silence, the turning trees! Sometimes I have thought of adopting a strict religion and living by codes and signs, but as I observe my pupils at their absent-minded rites I find they are all too lax and uncertain. These spoiled girls do not care whether they eat roast veal or fish in parsley sauce on Fridays—it is all the same monotonous meal. Some say they have never been sure what they may eat Fridays, where the limits are. My father was a non-believer, and my mother followed, but without conviction. He led her into the desert. She died of tuberculosis, not daring to speak of God for fear of displeasing her husband. He never carried a house key, because he wanted his wife to answer the door whatever the hour; that is what he was like. My only living relation now is my mother's sister, who has disinherited me because I remind her of my father. She fetched me to Paris to tell me so—that old, fussy, artificial creature in a flat stuffed with showy trifles. "Proust's maternal grandfather lived on this street," she said severely. What of it? What am I supposed to make of that? She gave me a stiff dark photograph of my mother at her confirmation. My mother clasps her Bible to her breast and stares as if the camera were a house on fire.

What I wanted to comment on was children—children in Switzerland. I rent a large room in a chalet seven minutes from my school. Downstairs is the boisterous Canadian who married her ski instructor when she was a pupil here eleven years ago. She has a loud laugh and veined cheeks. He had to resign his post, and now works in the place near the sawmill where they make hand-carved picture frames. The house is full of animals. On rainy days their dining room smells of old clothes and boiled liver. When I am invited to tea (in mugs, without saucers) and sit in one of the armchairs covered with shredded chintz and scraps of blanket, I am obliged to borrow the vacuum cleaner later so as to get the animal hairs out of my skirt. One room is kept free for lodgers —skiers in winter, tourists in summer. In August there were five people in the room—a family of middle-aged parents, two boys, and a baby girl. Because of the rain the boys were restless and the baby screamed with anger and frustration. I took them all to the woods to gather mushrooms.

"If a mushroom has been eaten by a snail, that means it is not poisonous," said the father. Rain dripped through the pine trees. We wore boots and heavy coats. The mother was carrying the bad-tempered baby and could not bend down and search, but now and then she would call, "Here's one that must be safe, because it has been nibbled."

"How do you know the snail is not lying dead somewhere?" I asked.

"You must not make the boys lose confidence in their father," the mother said, trying to laugh, but really a little worried.

"Even if it kills them?" I wanted to say, but it would have spoiled the outing.

My mother said once, "You can tell when mushrooms are safe, because when you stir them the spoon won't tarnish. Poisonous mushrooms turn the spoon black."

"How do you know everyone has a silver spoon?" said my father. He looked at her seriously, with his light eyes. They were like the eyes of birds when he was putting a question. He was not trying to catch her out; he was simply putting the question. That was what I was trying to do. You can warn until your voice is extinguished, and still these people will pick anything and take it home and put their fingers in their mouths.

In Switzerland parents visit their children sometimes, but are always trying to get away. I would say that all parents of all children here are trying to get away. The baby girl, the screamer, was left for most of a day. The child of aging parents, she had their worried look, as if brooding on the lessons of the past. She was twenty-six months old. My landlady, who offered to keep her amused so that the parents and the two boys could go off on their own for once, had cause to regret it.

They tricked the baby cruelly, taking her out to feed melon rinds to Coco, the donkey, in his enclosure at the bottom of the garden. When she came back, clutching the empty basket, her family had disappeared. The baby said something that sounded like "Mama-come-auto" and, writhing like a fish when she was held, slipped away and crawled up the stairs. She called upstairs and down, and the former ski instructor and his wife cried, "Yes, that's it! Mama-come-auto!" She reached overhead to door handles, but the rooms were empty. At noon they tried to make her eat the disgusting purée of carrots and potatoes the mother had left behind. "What if we spanked her?" said the former ski instructor, wiping purée from his sleeve. "Who, you?" shouted his wife. "You wouldn't have nerve enough to brain a mad dog." That shows how tough they thought the baby was. Sometimes during that year-long day, she forgot and let us distract her. We let her turn out our desks and pull our letters to bits. Then she would remember suddenly and look about her with elderly despair, and implore our help, in words no one understood. The weeping grew less frightened and more broken-hearted toward the end of the afternoon. It must have been plain to her then that they would never return. Downstairs they told each other that if she had not been lied to and deceived, then the mother would never have had a day's rest; she had been shut up in the rain in a chalet with this absolute tyrant of a child. The tyrant lay sleeping on the floor. The house was still except for her shuddering breath. Waking, she spoke unintelligible words. They had decided downstairs to pretend not to know; that is, they would not say "Yes, Mama-come-auto" or anything else. We must all three behave as if she had been living here forever and had never known anyone but us. How much memory can be stored in a mind that has not even been developed? What she understood was that we were too deaf to hear her cries and too blind to see her distress. She took the hand of the former ski instructor and dragged it to her face so that he could feel her tears. She was still and slightly feverish when the guilty parents and uneasy boys returned. Her curls were wet through and lay flat on her head. "She was perfect," the landlady said. "Just one little burst of tears after you left. She ate up all her lunch." The mother smiled and nodded, as if giving thanks. "Children are always better away from their parents," she said, with regret. Later, the landlady repeated, to me, as if I had not been there, a strange but believable version of that day, in which the baby cried only once.

That was an exceptional case, where everyone behaved with the best intentions; but what I have wanted to say from the beginning is, do not confide your children to strangers. Watch the way the stranger holds a child by the wrist instead of by the hand, even when a hand has been offered. I am thinking of Véronique, running after the stranger she thought was making off with the imitation-leather bag that held her cardigan, mustard, salt, pepper, a postcard of the Pont-Neuf, a pink handkerchief, a peppermint, and a French centime. This was at the air terminal at Geneva. I thought I might help—interpret between generations, between the mute and the deaf, so to speak—but at that moment the woman rushing away with the bag stopped, shifted it from right hand to left, and grasped Véronique by the wrist.

I had just been disinherited by my aunt, and was extremely sensitive to all forms of injustice. I thought that Véronique's father and mother, because they were not here at the exact moment she feared her bag was being stolen, had lost all claim to her, and had I been dispensing justice, would have said so. It was late in June. My ancient aunt had made me a present of a Geneva—Paris round-trip tourist-class ticket for the purpose of telling me to my face why she had cut me out of her will: I resembled my father, and had somehow disappointed her. I needed a lesson. She did not say what the lesson would be, but spoke in the name of Life, saying that Life would teach me. She was my only relative, that old woman, my mother's eldest sister, who had had the foresight to marry a French officer in 1919 and spend the next forty years and more saying "Fie." She was never obliged to choose between duty and self-preservation, or somehow hope the two would coincide. He was a French officer and she made his sense of honor hers. He doted on her. She was one of the lucky women.

Véronique was brought aboard at Orly Airport after everyone else in the Caravelle had settled down. She was led by a pretty stewardess, who seemed bothered by her charge. "Do you mind having her beside you?" she asked. I at first did not see Véronique, who was behind the stewardess, held by the wrist. I placed her where she could look out, and the stewardess disappeared. This would be of more interest if Véronique were now revealed to be a baby ape or a tamed and lovable bear, but she was a child. The journey is a short one—fifty minutes. Some of the small girls in my school arrive alone from Tcheran and Mexico City and are none the worse for the adventure. Mishaps occur when they think that pillows or blankets lent them were really presents, but any firm official can deal with that. The child is tossed from home to school, or from one acrobat parent to the other, and knows where it will land. I am frightened when I imagine the bright arc through space, the trusting flight without wings. Reflect on that slow drop from the cable car down the side of the mountain into the trees. The trees will not necessarily catch you like a net.

I fastened her seat belt, and she looked up at me to see what was going to happen next. She had been dressed for the trip in a blue-and-white cotton frock, white socks, and black shoes with a buttoned strap. Her hair was parted in the middle and contained countless shades of light brown, like a handful of autumn grass. There was a slight cast in one eye, but the gaze was steady. The buckle of the seat belt slid down and rested on one knee. She held on to a large bucket bag—held it tightly by its red handle. In the back of the seat before her, along with a map of the region over which we were to fly, were her return ticket and her luggage tags, and a letter that turned out to be a letter of instructions. She was to be met by a Mme. Bataille, who would accompany her to a *colonie de vacances* at Gsteig. I read the letter toward the end of the trip, when I realized that the air hostess had forgotten all about Véronique. I am against prying into children's affairs—even "How do you like your school?" is more inquisitive than one has a right to be. However, the important facts about Mme. Bataille and Gsteig were the only ones Véronique was unable to supply. She talked about herself and her family, in fits and starts, as if unaware of the limits of time—less than an hour, after all—and totally indifferent to the fact that she was unlikely ever to see me again. The place she had come from was "Orly," her destination was called "the mountains," and the person meeting her would be either "Béatrice" or "Catherine" or both. That came later; the first information she sweetly and generously offered was that she had twice been given injections in her right arm. I told her my name, profession, and the name of the village where I taught school. She said she was four but "not yet four and a half." She had been visiting, in Versailles, her mother and a baby brother, whose name she affected not to know—an admirable piece of dignified lying. After a sojourn in the mountains she would be met at Orly Airport by her father and taken to the sea. When would that be? "Tomorrow." On the promise of tomorrow, either he or the mother of the nameless brother had got her aboard the plane. The Île-de-France receded and spread. She sucked her mint sweet, and accepted mine, wrapped, and was overjoyed when I said she might put it in her bag, as if a puzzle about the bag had now been solved. The stewardess snapped our trays into place and gave us identical meals of cold sausage, Russian salad in glue, savory pastry, canned pears, and tinned mineral water. Véronique gazed onto a plateau of food nearly at shoulder level, and picked up a knife and fork the size of gardening tools. "I can cut my meat," she said, meaning to say she could not. The voice that had welcomed us in Paris and had implored Véronique and me to put out our cigarettes now emerged, preceded by crackling sounds, as if the air were full of invisible fissures: "If you look to your right, you will see the city of Dijon." Véronique quite properly took no notice. "I am cold," she stated, knowing that an announcement of one's condition immediately brings on a change for the better. I opened the plastic bag and found a cardigan—hand-knit, light blue, with pearl buttons. I wondered when the change-over would come, when she would have to stop saying "I am cold" in order to grow up without being the kind of person who lets you know that there is a draft in the room, or the beach is too crowded, or the service in the restaurant has gone off. I have pupils who still cannot find their own cardigans, and my old aunt is something of a complainer, as her sister never was. Despite my disinheritance, I was carrying two relics—a compote spoon whose bowl was in the form of a strawberry leaf, and the confirmation photograph of my mother. They weighed heavily in my hand luggage. The weight of the picture was beyond description. I knew that they would be too heavy, yet I held out my hand greedily for more of the past; but my aunt's ration stopped there.

The well-mannered French girl beside me would not drink the water I had poured into her glass until advised she could. She held the glass in both hands and got it back in its slot without help. Specks of parsley now floated on the water. I said she might leave the remains of the cold sausage, which she was chewing courageously. Giddy with indiscipline, she had some of the salad and all of the pear, and asked, indicating the savory pastry, "Is that something to eat?"

"You can, but it's boring." She had never heard food referred to in that way, and hesitated. As I had left mine, she did not know what the correct attitude ought to be, and after one bite put her spoon down. I think she liked it but, not having understood "boring," was anxious to do the right thing. With her delicate fingers she touched the miniature salt and pepper containers and the doll's tube of mustard, asking what they were for. I remembered that some of the small girls in the school saved them as tokens of travel, and I said, "They are for children to keep."

"Why?"

"I don't know. Some children keep them."

I wondered if this was a mistake, and if she would begin taking things that did not belong to her. She curled her hand around the little mustard tube and said she would keep it for Maman. Now that she was wearing the cardigan, her purse was empty save for a mint sweet. I told her that a bag was to put things in, and she said she knew, looking comically worldly. I gave her a centime, a handkerchief, a postcard—searching my own purse to see what could be spared. The stewardess let us descend the ramp from the plane as if she had never seen Véronique before, and no one claimed her. I had great difficulty finding anyone at the terminal who knew anything about Mme. Bataille. When I caught sight of Véronique, later, hurrying desperately after a uniformed woman who did not slow her pace for a second, I feared that *was* Mme. Bataille; but fifteen minutes after that I saw Véronique in the bus that was to take us to the railway station. She was next to a mild, thin, harassed-looking person, who seemed exhausted at the thought of the journey to come.

Now, mark the change in Véronique: She shook out her hair and made it untidy, and stood on the seat and jumped up and down.

"You are a very lucky little girl, going to the mountains *and* the sea," said Mme. Bataille, in something of a whine. Véronique took no more notice of this than she had of Dijon, except to remark that she was going to the seashore tomorrow.

"Not tomorrow. You've only just arrived."

"Tomorrow!" The voice rose and trembled dangerously. "Papa is meeting me at Orly."

"Yes," said the stupid woman soothingly, "but not tomorrow. In August. This is June."

The seats between us were now filled. When I next heard Véronique, the corruption of memory had set in.

"It was the stewardess who cut up your meat," said Mme. Bataille.

"No, a lady."

"A lady in a uniform. The lady you were with when I met you."

"*No.*"

The reason I could hear them was that they were nearly shouting.

Presently, all but giving in, Mme. Bataille said, "Well, she was nice, the lady. I mean, the stewardess."

Two ideas collided: Véronique remembered the woman fairly well, even though the flight no longer existed, but Mme. Bataille knew it was the stewardess.

"I came all alone," said Véronique.

"Who cut your meat, then?"

"I did," said Véronique, and there was no shaking her.

2

Even if Peter Dobay had not instantly recognized me and called my name, my attention would have been drawn by the way he and his wife looked at the station of our village. They got out of the train from Montreux and stood as if dazed. One imagined them blinking behind their sunglasses. At that time of year, we saw only excursion parties— stout women with gray curls, or serious hikers who would stamp from the station through the village and up the slopes. Peter wore a dark suit and black shoes, his wife a black-and-white silk dress, a black silk coat, and fragile open sandals. Her blond hair had been waved that day. I wondered how she would walk in the village streets on her thin high heels.

When we were face to face, Peter and I said together, "What are *you* doing here?"

"I live here—I teach," I said.

"No!" Turning to his wife, he said excitedly, "You know who this is, don't you? It's Erika." Then, back to me, "We've come up to see my wife's twins. They're in a summer school here."

"Better than dragging them round with us," said his wife, in a low-pitched, foggy voice. "They're better off in the fresh air." She touched my arm as if she had always known me and said, "I just can't believe I've finally seen you. Poodlie, it's like a *dream*."

I was faced with two pandas—those glasses! Who was Poodlie? Peter, evidently, yet he called her "Poodlie," too: "Poodlie, it's wonderful," he said, as if she were denying it. His wife? Her voice was twenty years older than his.

He went off to see to their luggage and she stopped seeing me, abruptly, as if now that he was gone nothing was needed. She looked at the village—as much as she could see, which was the central street and the station and the shutters of the station buffet. All I could see was her mouth and the tight pinpoint muscles around it, and the flour dusting of face powder.

"Well?" she said when Peter returned.

"I can't believe it," he said to me, and laughed. "*Here!* What are you doing *here*?"

"I teach," I began again.

"No, here at the station, now, on Sunday."

"Oh, that. I was waiting for the train with the Sunday papers."

"I told you," he cried to his wife. "Remember it was one of the things I said. Even if Erika was starving, she'd buy newspapers. I never knew anyone to read so many papers."

"I haven't had to choose between starving and reading," I said, which was a lie. I watched with regret the bale of papers carted off to the kiosk. In half an hour, those I wanted would be gone.

"*We're* starving," he said. "You'll have lunch with us, won't you? Now?"

"It's early," I said, glancing at his wife.

"Call it breakfast, then." He began guiding us both toward the buffet, his arms around our shoulders in a peasant-like bonhomie that was not like anything I remembered of him.

"The luggage, Poodlie," said his wife.

"He'll take it to the hotel."

"What hotel?"

"The biggest."

"Then it's there," I said, and pointed to an Alpine fortified castle, circa 1912, of yellowish stone, propped behind the street as if on a ledge.

"Good," he said. "Now our lunch."

That was how, on a cool bright day, just before the start of term, I saw Peter again.

In the dark buffet, Peter and his wife kept their glasses on. It seemed part of their personal decorum. Although the clock had only just struck twelve, the restaurant was nearly filled, and we were given a table between the serving pantry and the door. I understood that this was Peter, even though he didn't look at all like the man I had known, and that I was sharing his table. I avoided looking at him. Across the room, over an ocean of heads, was an open window, geraniums, the mountains, and the sky.

"You have beautiful eyes," said Peter's wife. Her voice, like a ventriloquist's, seemed to come from the wrong place—from behind her sunglasses. "Poodlie never told me that. They look like topazes or something like that."

"Yes," said Peter. "Semiprecious stones from the snow-capped mountains of South America."

He sounded like a pompous old man. His English was smooth as cream now, and better than mine. I spoke it with too many people who had accents. Answering a question of his wife's, I heard myself making something thick and endless out of the letter "t": "It is crowded because it is Sunday. Tourists come for miles around. The food in the buffet is celebrated."

"We'll see," said Peter, and took the long plastic-covered menu with rather an air.

His wife was attentive to me. Parents of pupils always try to make me eat more than I care to, perhaps thinking that I would be less intractable if I were less thin. "Your daughter is not only a genius but will make a brilliant marriage," I am supposed to say over caramel cake. I let myself be coaxed by Peter's wife into having a speciality of the place—something monstrous, with boiled meat and dumplings that swam in broth. Having arranged this, she settled down to her tea and toast. As for Peter—well, what a performance! First he read the whole menu aloud and grimaced at everything; then he asked for a raw onion and a bunch of radishes and two pots of yogurt, and cut up the onions and radishes in the yogurt and ate the whole mess with a spoon. It was like the frantic exhibition of a child who has been made uneasy.

"He isn't well," said his wife, quite as though he weren't there. "He treats it like a joke, but you know, he was in jail after the Budapest uprising, and he was so badly treated that it ruined his stomach. He'll never be the same again."

He did not look up or kick me under the table or in any manner ask me not to betray him. It occurred to me he had forgotten I knew. I felt my face flushing, as if I had been boiled in the same water as the beef and dumplings. I thought I would choke. I looked, this time with real longing, at the mountain peaks. They seem so near in the clear weather that sometimes innocent foot travelers set off thinking they will be there in three-quarters of an hour. The pockets of snow looked as if they could have been scooped up with a coffee spoon. The cows on the lower slopes were the size of thimbles.

"Do you ski at this time of year?" said Peter's wife, without turning to see what I was staring at.

"One can, but I don't go up anymore. There's an hour-and-a-half walk to the middle station, and the road isn't pleasant. It's all slush and mud." I thought they would ask what "the middle station" meant, but they didn't, which meant they weren't really listening.

When I refused a pudding, Peter said, with his old teasing, "I told you she was frugal. Her father was a German professor at Debrecen, the Protestant university."

"So was yours," said his wife sharply, as though reminding him of a truth he forgot from time to time.

"It never affected me," said Peter, smiling.

"That's where you met, then," said his wife, taking her eyes from me at last.

"No," said Peter. "We were only children then. We met when we were grown up, at the University of Lausanne. It was a coincidence, like meeting today. Erika and I will probably meet— I don't know where. On the moon."

It is difficult enough to listen to someone lying without looking shocked, but imagine what it might be to be part of the fantasy; his lies were a whirlwind, and I was at the core, trying to recognize something familiar. We met in Lausanne; that was true. We met on a bench in the public gardens. I told him I had lived in Hungary and could speak a few sentences of Hungarian still. He was four years younger than I. I told him about my father in Debrecen, and that we were Germans, and that my father had been shot by a Russian soldier. I said I was grateful for Switzerland. He told me he was a half Jew from Budapest and had been ill-used. His life had been saved in some remarkable way by a neutral embassy. He was grateful, too.

He was the first person to whom I had ever spoken spontaneously and without reserve. We met every day for ten days, and when he wanted to leave Switzerland because he thought it would be better somewhere else and would not go without me, I did not think twice. The evening lamps went on in the park where we were sitting, and I thought that if I did not go with him I would suffer every evening for the rest of my life, every time the lamps were lit. To avoid suffering, I went with him. Yet when I told my father's old friends, the people who had taken me in and welcomed me and kept me from starving, I said it was my duty. I said it was Peter who could not live without me. It is true I would never have gone out of Switzerland, out to the wilderness, but for him. My father had friends at the University of Lausanne, and although after the war some were afraid, because the wind had shifted, others took me in when I was seventeen and homeless and looked after me until I could work. I was afraid of telling about Peter. In the end, I had to. I quoted something my father had once said about duty, and no one could contradict that.

It lasted only a short time, the adventure, and can be briefly and accurately remembered. Quickly, then: He had heard there was a special university for refugees in a city on the Rhine, and thought they might admit him. We lived in a hotel over a café, and discovered we were living in a brothel. The university existed, but its quota was full. We were starving to death. We were so attractive a couple, so sympathetic-looking, that people dulled with eating looked at us fondly. We strolled along the Rhine and looked at excursion boats. "Your duty is always before you, plain as that," my father had said, pointing with his walking stick to some vista or tree or cloud. I do not know what he was pointing at—something in his mind.

Because of Peter I was on a sea without hope of landing anywhere. It grew on me that he had been jealous of my safety and had dragged me beyond my depth. There had been floods—I think in Holland—and money was being collected for the victims. Newspapers spoke of "Rhine solidarity," and I was envious, for I had solidarity with no one now. It took me time to think things out, for I had no illusions about my intelligence, and I wondered finally why I did not feel any solidarity with Peter. I loved him, but together we would starve or drown.

"You can't stay here," said the owner of the hotel one day. "It isn't safe for refugees. We have the police in too often."

"We can't move," said Peter. "My wife is ill." But that did not give me a feeling of solidarity, for I was not his wife, and he was a person who would keep moving from one place to another.

He never told the same story twice, except for some details. He said he was picked up and deported when he was ten or twelve. He was able to describe the Swiss or Swedish consulate where they tried to save him. In his memories, the person who hid him was always different. Sometimes he said it was a peasant, sometimes a fat woman who shut him in a cupboard. The forced march must have been true. Someone— he did not say who—was working on his behalf. He hinted he was illegitimate, and that a person of noble birth, who did not wish to be known, was his protector. It is true that sometimes in the marches from Budapest to the border one person in the column was saved, if the order came through in time. It was often at night. The column stopped by the side of the road, and the torches, hooded because of the air raids, moved from face to face. One night, the light picked out an old man who would have died soon in any case, and Peter. He could not see his deliverers—he saw the light moving from face to face. The light was lowered. He tried to hide, but they spoke his name. He thought the light meant an execution. He was taken away in a car, back to Budapest, and in the car was comforted with chocolates. These were the details he repeated: the light on his face, the voice saying his name, and the chocolates. Sometimes, being boastful, he said he was active in the Arrow Cross Party; but he was a victim, and a child. Once, he said he was poor and had sold papers in the street to pay for his shoes. But he was such a liar. He may have been poor, or he may have been from a solid family who lost him along the way; but it was not a Protestant family, and his father was not a professor at Debrecen. Also, he was not in Budapest during the uprising in 1956. He was in a city on the Rhine, starving, with me.

We stood at the foot of the cathedral in this city one day. We had nothing to eat and nothing to do. I could not understand why Peter had brought me here or what he wanted now. He urged me to write my father's old friends in Lausanne, or to my aunt in Paris, but I was proud, and ashamed that he would ask such a thing. I think he believed I was a magic solution just in myself. He lived in a fantasy of false names, false fortunes, false parents, and here was a reality of expired visas and dry bread he could not explain away.

"Goethe climbed to the top of this cathedral to cure himself of vertigo. You should try it," Peter said.

"Oh, Goethe would," I said, and that was the only thing that autumn that made Peter laugh. We climbed and climbed, and looked down at matchbox cars. I felt vertigo, and was surprised he did not. I held out my arms to receive him if he fainted—I was so sure he would not stand this—but he stood smiling down with no intention of toppling over. Below was the sweet nursery world, nursery-sized, with toy trams and toy people. It smiled back at him; he was its lord, at least from up here. My world was my size, and often bigger. I was afraid of the shrunken world as he saw it; he made me unsteady. I left him that day. He went alone to the post office to see if there were phantom letters from ghost friends, and I made myself as tidy as I could and went to my own consulate with a plausible story. And that was the last Peter saw of me, until Peter, or Poodlie, called my name at the station.

I don't know what he remembered. He had taken my family as his, and expected me to smile. Actually, I did. I made him a present of my family. But by now he must have believed that whatever came into his head was true, for he did not thank me—neither then nor later. I leaned over the table and said, "I see what is making the difference. It is the dark glasses." He immediately took them off, but I saw that I still did not recognize him.

An excursion party now trooped into the buffet. Their accents were, I think, industrial England over, I think, Viennese. One of the women smeared thick white cream on her sunburned arms. "Let's finish and pay and get out of here," said Peter's wife, sharply. I stared at him then, but his face showed nothing. He did not add or contribute. It might have had nothing to do with him. She slipped him folded money so that he could pay the bill. I tried to think, but they had stuffed me with food. I clung to one idea: no one would get me out of Switzerland again, as he once had to a city on the Rhine, as my old aunt had got me to Paris. Each time I returned I was wounded, or had failed. Outside the station, I stopped at the kiosk, but of course my newspapers were gone.

The next afternoon, I sat in the lobby of their hotel. His wife now looked through the windows to the station, as if afraid of missing the train out. She poured tea from a leaky pot, and passed chocolate biscuits, shell-shaped, in a thin coating of sugar. They were Poodlie's favorites; she was sorry he wasn't here. She poured with a tense, strong hand—I admired the long fingers, and the short nails, on which the red was thickly spread. Absently but politely, she asked about my work, as if she were a headmistress interviewing me for a post.

I described flowers next to snow, and plants so perfect and minute, rooted on stone, that they must be like the algae on Mars.

"Oh, yes, edelweiss," she said.

He was a parcel posted without an address, and he had come to her.

Now I heard her inviting me to join them. I heard the words "The twins would adore you, and he is a different person when you're there. I've never seen him so gay and happy as he was yesterday at lunch." He had put her up to it, and now he was out, walking around in the village, waiting for the barter to be completed. "He has talked about you such a lot," she said.

"What did he tell you?"

"Why, that you were a wonderful person. He said you had been so kind to him."

That part of it ended there. She explained that Peter was walking, not in the village, as I had supposed, but somewhere up a mountain. He had gone up in a cable car. "I didn't bring the right clothes," she said. "We could drive somewhere, but we never do." It was the only sign of her discontent. The person she had gone to consult when she contemplated this marriage—a rapid psychotherapy, she explained—had warned her not to take over too many head-of-the-family functions from a young husband. That meant, among other things, that she was never to drive the car. But Poodlie was too wild to drive. She gave him cars, but could not trust him to drive them. I thought of him wandering along a steep, windy slope now, not knowing how to keep a foothold in his slippery shoes. He was up above the village in his dark suit and dark glasses and shoes. How could she let him go that way—as if he were lost or had strayed from the towns? He was alone, shivering (no one had told him how cold it would be), dreaming and inventing things to be remembered.

I did not meet her children, but I saw her with them in a tearoom: two plump girls of about fourteen, in clay-colored tights and long pullovers that covered their sturdy hips. They were not girls I had ever seen before. They looked sullen there in the dark shop, which was suffocating with the smell of chocolate. They were choosing éclairs, pointing, discontented and curt. Their school had not yet taught them manners, and their mother, with a stiff smile on her lips and her sunglasses hiding her opinion, could see only the distance between what they were and what they ought to be. She was not an educator. The girls' clumsiness was a twist of the spirit, a sprain. She watched them choose and eat, and I thought how much time she spent watching people choose and eat their food. She removed the glasses and rubbed the space between her eyes. She saw me, and her glance meeting mine almost begged something. Information? Advice? She had the psychotherapy for advice, and she had Peter to tell her stories. Perhaps she wanted me to change my mind about going with them. He must have asked for me, as he asked for cars she would not let him drive because he broke them.

It would have been easy for her to make me believe my choices were wrong, but it would have been another matter to make me change my mind. Once when she was busy with the twins, he came to me. He looked at the saucer full of moss and Alpine plants; and the shelf with tea and hard biscuits and cereal and powdered milk; and at my bed with its shabby cushions; and my walls decorated with photographs of snow and skiers—searching for something. He twitched a curtain as if it hid a view he liked and said, "It's all dirty green, like a customs inspector's uniform."

But I had traveled nearly as much as Peter, and over some of the same frontiers. He could not impress me. I think (like the remark about semiprecious stones and snow-capped mountains) it was a way of talking he had developed because it amused his wife. He knew it was no good talking about the past, because we were certain to remember it differently. He daren't be nostalgic about anything, because of his inventions. He would never be certain if the memory he was feeling tender about was true.

I watched him at the window—the town lad, hating the quiet. "What is that racket?" he said angrily. It was the stream running outside through the garden. There was also Coco, the donkey, braying in his enclosure. He would have preferred a deafening, continued, city noise. I remembered him on streets full of trams and traffic; I remembered the quick turn of his head. When I remembered the horror of the room over the café, I thought it had been the horror of living on a street.

The view here, after the long garden, was of the roof of the chalet farther down the slope. A crash: my bookshelf, containing *Wild Flowers of Germany*, fell from the wall. The house shook.

He looked at the perpendicular, windless rain that had begun to fall. He turned back to the room; he was still searching. "You used to read," he said, still in pursuit of something. I pointed to the floor. "Didn't you hear them fall?" He made a silly remark—I remember the sense of it, not the words. He could not trust me, because I had once run away, vanished, but as he had long ago fabricated something else, he could not remember why he could not trust me. The room grew dark. I served coffee in cups with *Liberté* and *Patrie* and a green-and-white shield of the Vaud on them. The parents of a pupil had bought them in Montreux for me once. He held his cup close to his eyes and read the words, and put it down without saying anything.

I said to myself that he was only a man about whom I had known a great deal and it was so long ago that much of it might have been told to me by someone else. Nostalgia is a weakness; he would be the one to indulge in it, if he dared. I had not gone to him out of duty and had not left him out of self-preservation. It was not that simple. I would have talked, for I knew he was waiting for me to scrape away the dreams and begin again with the truth, but I thought, I shall write him a letter. That will be easier. I shall write about everything, all of the truth.

They came up by train and they left by train—the little red train that has its start among the hotels and swimming pools along the lake. As neither of them could drive the other, they had to take the train. They were leaving the twins behind. The twins were happy, and the fresh air was doing them good. They were enrolled for the autumn term.

The first-class carriages of those trains look as if they had been built for miniature royal tours. There are oval satinwood panels and Art Nouveau iron roses. Some of the roses had iron worms eating their hearts. I imagine the artist meant something beautiful and did not know it was hideous. As you can imagine, the trains are beautifully polished. The panels gleam, and dust is not allowed to accumulate in the rose petals. The windows are clear for a view of cows and valleys, the ashtrays are emptied and polished, and the floors are swept. I like best the deep-rose velvet, with its pattern of brown leaves and ferns, that covers the seats. It wears slowly; in some very worn places the color is light apricot and the palest lemon, and the pattern can scarcely be seen. Somewhere in storage, preserved from dust and the weather, are bales of the same velvet, and when a seat becomes too worn they simply patch it up again.

He would have stayed if I had wanted. Yes, Poodlie would have left Poodlie. He knew I would never go with them. I might have been for sale, but not to her. At a word of truth he would have stayed, if only to hear the rest. He would have made furious plans, and left such an imprint on this place that after his departure I could not have lived here anymore. Or perhaps this time one of us would have stayed forever. These are the indecisions that rot the fabric, if you let them. The shutter slams to in the wind and sways back; the rain begins to slant as the wind increases. This is the season for mountain storms. The wind rises, the season turns; no autumn is quite like another. The autumn children pour out of the train, and the clouds descend the mountain slopes, and there we are with walls and a ceiling to the village. Here is the pattern on the carpet where he walked, and the cup he drank from. I have learned to be provident. I do not waste a sheet of writing paper, or a postage stamp, or a tear. The stream outside the window, deep with rain, receives rolled in a pellet the letter to Peter. Actually, it is a blank sheet on which I intended to write a long letter about everything—about Véronique. I have wasted the sheet of paper. There has been such a waste of everything; such a waste.

DÉDÉ

PASCAL Brouet is fourteen now. He used to attend a lycée, but after his parents found out about the dealers in the street, outside the gates, they changed him to a private school. Here the situation is about the same, but he hasn't said so; he does not want to be removed again, this time perhaps to a boarding establishment, away from Paris, with nothing decent to eat and lights-out at ten. He would not describe himself as contriving or secretive. He tries to avoid drawing attention to the Responsibility clause in the treaty that governs peace between generations.

Like his father, the magistrate, he will offer neutrality before launching into dissent. "I'm ready to admit," he will begin, or "I don't want to take over the whole conversation ..." Sometimes the sentence comes to nothing. Like his father, he lets his eyelids droop, tries to speak lightly and slowly. The magistrate is famous for fading out of a discussion by slow degrees. At one time he was said to be the youngest magistrate ever to fall asleep in court: he would black out when he thought he wasn't needed and snap to just as the case turned around. Apparently, he never missed a turning. He has described his own mind to Pascal: it is like a superlatively smooth car with an invisible driver in control. The driver is the magistrate's unconscious will.

To Pascal a mind is a door, ajar or shut. His grades are good, but this side of brilliant. He has a natural gift—a precise, perfectly etched memory. How will he use it? He thinks he could as easily become an actor as a lawyer. When he tells his parents so, they seem not to mind. He could turn into an actor-manager, with a private theater of his own, or the director of one of the great national theaters, commissioning new work, refurbishing the classics, settling questions at issue with a word or two.

The Brouets are tolerant parents, ready for anything. They met for the first time in May of 1968, a few yards away from a barricade of burning cars. She had a stone in her hand; when she saw him looking at her, she put it down. They walked up the Boulevard Saint-Michel together, and he told her his plan for reforming the judiciary. He was a bit older, about twenty-six. Answering his question, she said she was from Alsace. He reminded her how the poet Paul Éluard had picked up his future wife in the street, on a rainy evening. She was from Alsace, too, and starving, and in a desperate, muddled, amateurish way pretending to be a prostitute.

Well, this was not quite the same story. In 1968 the future Mme. Brouet was studying to be an analyst of handwriting, with employment to follow—so she had been promised—in the personnel section of a large department store. In the meantime, she was staying with a Protestant Reformed Church pastor and his family in Rue Fustel-de-Coulanges. She had been on her way home to dinner when she stopped to pick up the stone. She had a mother in Alsace, and a little brother, Amedée—"Dédé."

"Sylvie and I have known both sides of the barricades," the magistrate likes to say, now. What he means is that they cannot be crowded into a political corner. The stone in the hand has made her a rebel, at least in his recollections. She never looks at a newspaper, because of her reputation for being against absolutely everything. So he says, but perhaps it isn't exact: she looks at the pages marked "Culture," to see what is on at the galleries. He reads three morning papers at breakfast and, if he has time, last evening's *Le Monde*. Reading, he narrows his eyes. Sometimes he looks as though everything he thinks and believes had been translated into a foreign language and, suddenly, back again.

When Pascal was about nine, his father said, "What do you suppose you will do, one day?"

They were at breakfast. Pascal's Uncle Amedée was there. Like everyone else, Pascal called him Dédé. Pascal looked across at him and said, "I want to be a bachelor, like Dédé."

His mother moaned, "Oh, no!" and covered her face. The magistrate waited until she had recovered before speaking. She looked up, smiling, a bit embarrassed. Then he explained, slowly and carefully, that Dédé was too young to be considered a bachelor. He was a student, a youth. "A student, a student," he repeated, thinking perhaps that if he kept saying it Dédé would study hard.

Dédé had a button of a nose that looked ridiculous on someone so tall, and a mass of curly fair hair. Because of the hair, the magistrate could not take him seriously; his private name for Dédé was "Harpo."

That period of Pascal's life, nine rounding to ten, was also the autumn before an important election year. The elections were five months off, but already people argued over dinner and Sunday lunch. One Sunday in October, the table was attacked by wasps, drawn in from the garden by a dish of sliced melon—the last of the season, particularly fragrant and sweet. The French doors to the garden stood open. Sunlight entered and struck through the wine decanters and dissolved in the waxed tabletop in pale red and gold. From his place, Pascal could see the enclosed garden, the apartment blocks behind it, a golden poplar tree, and the wicker chairs where the guests, earlier, had sat with their drinks.

There were two couples: the Turbins, older than Pascal's parents, and the Chevallier-Crochets, who had not been married long. Mme. Chevallier-Crochet attended an art-history course with Pascal's mother, on Thursday afternoons. They had never been here before, and were astonished to discover a secret garden in Paris with chairs, grass, a garden rake, a tree. Just as their expression of amazement was starting to run thin and patches of silence appeared, Abelarda, newly come from Cádiz, appeared at the door and called them to lunch. She said, "It's ready," though that was not what Mme. Brouet had asked her to say; at least, not that way. The guests got up, without haste. They were probably as hungry as Pascal but didn't want it to show. Abelarda went on standing, staring at the topmost leaves of the poplar, trying to remember what she ought to have said.

A few minutes later, just as they were starting to eat their melon, wasps came thudding against the table, like pebbles thrown. The adults froze, as though someone had drawn a gun. Pascal knew that sitting still was a good way to be stung. If you waved your napkin, shouted orders, the wasps might fly away. But he was not expected to give instructions; he was here, with adults, to discover how conversation is put together, how to sound interesting without being forward, amusing without seeming familiar. At that moment, Dédé did an unprecedented and courageous thing: he picked up the platter of melon, crawling with wasps, and took it outside, as far as the foot of the tree. And came back to applause: at least, his sister clapped, and young Mme. Chevallier-Crochet cried, "Bravo! Bravo!"

Dédé smiled, but, then, he was always smiling. His sister wished he wouldn't; the smile gave his brother-in-law another reason for calling him Harpo. Sitting down, he seemed to become entwined with his chair. He was too tall ever to be comfortable. He needed larger chairs, tables that were both higher and wider, so that he would not bump his knees, or put his feet on the shoes of the lady sitting opposite.

Pascal's father just said, "So, no more melon." It was something he particularly liked, and there might be none now until next summer. If Dédé had asked his opinion instead of jumping up so impulsively, he might have said, "Just leave it," and taken a chance on getting stung.

Well; no more for anyone. The guests sat a little straighter, waiting for the next course: beef, veal, or mutton, or the possibility of duck. Pascal's mother asked him to shut the French doors. She did not expect another wasp invasion, but there might be strays. Mme. Chevallier-Crochet remarked that Pascal was tall for his age, then asked what his age was. "He is almost ten," said Mme. Brouet, looking at her son with some wonder. "I can hardly believe it. I don't understand time."

Mme. Turbin said she did not have to consult a watch to know the exact time. It must be a quarter to two now. If it was, her daughter Brigitte had just landed in Salonika. Whenever her daughter boarded a plane, Mme. Turbin accompanied her in her mind, minute by minute.

"Thessalonika," M. Turbin explained.

The Chevallier-Crochets had spent their honeymoon in Sicily. If they had it to do over again, they said, they would change their minds and go to Greece.

Mme. Brouet said they would find it very different from Sicily. Her mind was on something else entirely: Abelarda. Probably Abelarda had expected them to linger over a second helping of melon. Perhaps she was sitting in the kitchen with nothing to do, listening to a program of Spanish music on the radio. Mme. Brouet caught a wide-awake glance from her husband, interpreted it correctly, and went out to the kitchen to see.

One of the men turned to M. Brouet, wondering if he could throw some light on the election candidates: unfortunate stories were making the rounds. Pascal's father was often asked for information. He had connections in Paris, like stout ropes attached to the upper civil service and to politics. One sister was married to a Cabinet minister's chief of staff. Her children were taken to school in a car with a red-white-and-blue emblem. The driver could park wherever he liked. The magistrate's grandfather had begun as a lieutenant in the cavalry and died of a heart attack the day he was appointed head of a committee to oversee war graves. His portrait, as a child on a pony, hung in the dining room. The artist was said to have copied a photograph; that was why the pony looked so stiff and the colors were wrong. The room Pascal slept in had been that child's summer bedroom; the house had once been a suburban, almost a country dwelling. Now the road outside was like a highway; even with the doors shut they could hear Sunday traffic pouring across an intersection, on the way to Boulogne and the Saint-Cloud bridge.

The magistrate replied that he did not want to take over the whole conversation but he did feel safe in saying this: Several men, none of whom he had any use for, were now standing face to face. Sometimes he felt like washing his hands of the future. (Saying this, he slid his hands together.) However, before his guests could show shock or disappointment, he added, "But one cannot remain indifferent. This is an old country, an ancient civilization." Here his voice faded out. "We owe...One has to...A certain unbreakable loyalty..." And he placed his hands on the table, calmly, one on each side of his plate.

At that moment Mme. Brouet returned, her cheeks and forehead pink, as if she had got too close to a hot oven. Abelarda came along next, to change the plates. She was pink in the face, too.

Pascal saw the candidates lined up like rugby teams. He was allowed to watch rugby on television. His parents did not care for soccer: the players showed off, received absurd amounts of money just for kicking a ball, and there was something the matter with their shorts. "With all that money, they could buy clothes that fit," Pascal's mother had said. Rugby players were different. They were the embodiment of action and its outcome, in an ideal form. They got muddied for love of sport. France had won the Five Nations tournament, beating even the dreaded Welsh, whose fans always set up such eerie wailing in the stands. Actually, they were trying to sing. It must have been the way the early Celts joined in song before the Roman conquest, the magistrate had told Pascal.

No one at table could have made a rugby team. They were too thin. Dédé was a broomstick. Of course, Pascal played soccer at school, in a small cement courtyard. The smaller boys, aged six, seven, tried to imitate Michel Platini, but they got everything wrong. They would throw the ball high in the air and kick at nothing, leg crossed over the chest, arms spread.

The magistrate kept an eye on the dish Abelarda was now handing around: partridges in a nest of shredded cabbage—an entire surprise. Pascal looked over at Dédé, who sat smiling to himself, for no good reason. (If Pascal had continued to follow his father's gaze he might be told gently, later, that one does not stare at food.)

There was no more conversation to be had from M. Brouet, for the moment. Helping themselves to partridge, the guests told one another stories everybody knew. All the candidates were in a declining state of health and morality. One had to be given injections of ground-up Japanese seaweed; otherwise he lost consciousness, sometimes in the midst of a sentence. Others kept going on a mixture of cocaine and Vitamin C. Their private means had been acquired by investing in gay bars and foreign wars, and evicting the poor. Only the Ministry of the Interior knew the nature and extent of their undercover financial dealings. And yet some of these men had to be found better than others, if democracy was not to come to a standstill. As M. Brouet had pointed out, one cannot wash one's hands of the future.

The magistrate had begun to breathe evenly and deeply. Perhaps the sunlight beating on the panes of the shut doors made him feel drowsy.

"Étienne is never quite awake or asleep," said his wife, meaning it as a compliment.

She was proud of everyone related to her, even by marriage, and took pride in her father, who had run away from home and family to live in New Caledonia. He had shown spirit and a sense of initiative, like Dédé with the wasps. (Now that Pascal is fourteen, he has heard this often.) But pride is not the same as helpless love. The person she loved best, in that particular way, was Dédé.

Dédé had come to stay with the Brouets because his mother, Pascal's grandmother, no longer knew what to do with him. He was never loud or abrupt, never forced an opinion on anyone, but he could not be left without guidance—even though he could vote, and was old enough to do some of the things he did, such as sign his mother's name to a check. (Admittedly, only once.) This was his second visit; the first, last spring, had not sharpened his character, in spite of his brother-in-law's conversation, his sister's tender anxiety, the sense of purpose to be gained by walking his little nephew to school. Sent home to Colmar (firm handshake with the magistrate at the Gare de l'Est, tears and chocolates from his sister, presentation of an original drawing from Pascal), he had accidentally set fire to his mother's kitchen, then to his own bedclothes. Accidents, the insurance people had finally agreed, but they were not too pleased. His mother was at the present time under treatment for exhaustion, with a private nurse to whom she made expensive presents. She had about as much money sense as Harpo, the magistrate said. (Without lifting his head from his homework, Pascal could take in nearly everything uttered in the hall, on the stairs, and in two adjacent rooms.)

When they were all four at breakfast Mme. Brouet repeated her brother's name in every second sentence: wondering if Dédé wanted more toast, if someone would please pass him the strawberry jam, if he had enough blankets on his bed, if he needed an extra key. (He was a great loser of keys.) The magistrate examined his three morning papers. He did not want to have to pass anything to Harpo. Mme. Brouet was really just speaking to herself.

That autumn, Dédé worked at a correspondence course, in preparation for a competitive civil-service examination. If he was among the first dozen, eliminating perhaps hundreds of clever young men and women, he would be eligible for a post in the nation's railway system. His work would be indoors, of course; no one expected him to be out in all weathers, trudging alongside the tracks, looking for something to repair. Great artists, leaders of honor and reputation, had got their start at a desk in a railway office. Pascal's mother, whenever she said this, had to pause, as she searched her mind for their names. The railway had always been a seedbed of outstanding careers, she would continue. She would then point out to Dédé that their father had been a supervisor of public works.

After breakfast Dédé wound a long scarf around his neck and walked Pascal to school. He had invented an apartment with movable walls. Everything one needed could be got within reach by pulling a few levers or pressing a button. You could spend your life in the middle of a room without having to stir. He and Pascal refined the invention; that was what they talked about, on the way to Pascal's school. Then Dédé came home and studied until lunchtime. In the afternoon he drew new designs of his idea. Perhaps he was lonely. The doctor looking after his mother had asked him not to call or write, for the moment.

Pascal's mother believed Dédé needed a woman friend, even though he was not ready to get married. Pascal heard her say, "Art and science, architecture, culture." These were the factors that could change Dédé's life, and to which he would find access through the right kind of woman. Mme. Brouet had someone in mind—Mlle. Turbin, who held a position of some responsibility in a travel agency. She was often sent abroad to rescue visitors or check their complaints. Today's lunch had been planned around her, but at the last minute she had been called to Greece, where a tourist, bitten by a dog, had received an emergency specific for rabies, and believed the Greeks were trying to kill him.

Her parents had come, nevertheless. It was a privilege to meet the magistrate and to visit a rare old house, one of the last of its kind still in private hands. Before lunch Mme. Turbin had asked to be shown around. Mme. Brouet conducted a tour for the women, taking care not to open the door to Dédé's room: there had been a fire in a waste-paper basket only a few hours before, and everything in there was charred or singed or soaked.

At lunch, breaking out of politics, M. Turbin described the treatment the tourist in Salonika had most probably received: it was the same the world over, and incurred the use of a long needle. He held out his knife, to show the approximate length.

"Stop!" cried Mme. Chevallier-Crochet. She put her napkin over her nose and mouth; all they could see was her wild eyes. Everyone stopped eating, forks suspended—all but the magistrate, who was pushing aside shreds of cabbage to get at the last of the partridge.

M. Chevallier-Crochet explained that his wife was afraid of needles. He could not account for it; he had not known her as a child. It seemed to be a singular fear, one that set her apart. Meantime, his wife closed her eyes; opened them, though not as wide as before; placed her napkin neatly across her lap; and swallowed a piece of bread.

M. Turbin said he was sorry. He had taken it for granted that any compatriot of the great Louis Pasteur must have seen a needle or two. Needles were only a means to an end.

Mme. Brouet glanced at her husband, pleading for help, but he had just put a bite of food into his mouth. He was always last to be served when there were guests, and everything got to him cold. That was probably why he ate in such a hurry. He shrugged, meaning, Change the subject.

"Pascal," she said, turning to him. At last, she thought of something to say: "Do you remember Mlle. Turbin? Charlotte Turbin?"

"Brigitte?" said Pascal.

"I'm sure you remember," she said, not listening at all. "In the travel agency, on Rue Caumartin?"

"She gave me the corrida poster," said Pascal, wondering how this had slipped her mind.

"We went to see her, you and I, the time we wanted to go to Egypt? Now do you remember?"

"We never went to Egypt."

"No. Papa couldn't get away just then, so we finally went back to

Deauville, where Papa has so many cousins. So you do remember Mlle. Turbin, with the pretty auburn hair?"

"Chestnut," said the two Turbins, together.

"My sister," said Dédé, all of a sudden, indicating her with his left hand, the right clutching a wineglass. "Before she got married, my mother told me..." The story, whatever it was, engulfed him in laughter. "A dog tried to bite her," he managed to say.

"You can tell us about it another time," said his sister.

He continued to laugh, softly, just to himself, while Abelarda changed the plates again.

The magistrate examined his clean new plate. No immediate surprises: salad, another plate, cheese, a dessert plate. His wife had given up on Mlle. Turbin. Really, it was his turn now, her silence said.

"I may have mentioned this before," said the magistrate. "And I would not wish to keep saying the same things over and over. But I wonder if you agree that the pivot of French politics today is no longer in France."

"The Middle East," said M. Turbin, nodding his head.

"Washington," said M. Chevallier-Crochet. "Washington calls Paris every morning and says, Do this, Do that."

"The Middle East and the Soviet Union," said M. Turbin.

"There," said M. Brouet. "We are all in agreement."

Many of the magistrate's relatives and friends thought he should be closer to government, to power. But his wife wanted him to stay where he was and get his pension. After he retired, when Pascal was grown, they would visit Tibet and the north of China, and winter in Kashmir.

"You know, this morning?" said Dédé, getting on with something that was on his mind.

"Another time," said his sister. "Never mind about this morning. It is all forgotten. Étienne is speaking, now."

This morning! The guests had no idea, couldn't begin to imagine what had taken place, here, in the dining room, at this very table. Dédé had announced, overjoyed, "I've got my degree." For Dédé was taking a correspondence course that could not lead to a degree of any kind. It must have been just his way of trying to stop studying so that he could go home.

"Degree?" The magistrate folded yesterday's *Le Monde* carefully before putting it down. "What do you mean, degree?"

Pascal's mother got up to make fresh coffee. "I'm glad to hear it, Dédé," she said.

"A degree in what?" said the magistrate.

Dédé shrugged, as if no one had bothered to tell him. "It came just the other day," he said. "I've got my degree, and now I can go home."

"Is there something you could show us?"

"There was just a letter, and I lost it," said Dédé. "A real diploma costs two thousand francs. I don't know where I'd find the money."

The magistrate did not seem to disbelieve; that was because of his training. But then he said, "You began your course about a month ago?"

"I had been thinking about it for a long time," said Dédé.

"And now they have awarded you a degree. You are perfectly right— it's time you went home. You can take the train tonight. I'll call your mother."

Pascal's mother returned, carrying a large white coffeepot. "I wonder where your first job will be," she said.

Why were she and her brother so remote from things as they are? Perhaps because of their mother, the grandmother in Colmar. Once, she had taken Pascal by the chin and tried to force him to look her in the eye. She had done it to her children. Pascal knows, now, that you cannot have your chin held in a vise and undividedly meet a blue stare. Somewhere at the back of the mind is a second self with eyes tight shut. Dédé and his sister could seem to meet any glance, even the magistrate's when he was being most nearly wide awake. They seemed to be listening, but the person he thought he was talking to, trying to reach the heart of, was deaf and blind. Pascal's mother listens when she needs to know what might happen next.

All Pascal understood, for the moment, was that when Dédé had mentioned taking a degree, he was saying something he merely wished were true.

"We'll probably never see you, once you start to work," said Pascal's mother, pouring Dédé's coffee.

The magistrate looked as if such great good luck was not to be expected. Abelarda, who had gone upstairs to make the beds, screamed from the head of the staircase that Dédé's room was full of smoke.

Abelarda moved slowly around the table carrying a plum tart, purple and gold, caramelized all over its surface, and a bowl of cream. Mme. Turbin glanced at the tart and shook her head no: M. Turbin was not allowed sugar now, and she had got out of the habit of eating desserts. It seemed unfair to tempt him.

It was true, her husband said. She had even given up making sweets, on his account. He described her past achievements—her famous chocolate mousse with candied bitter orange peel, her celebrated pineapple flan.

"My semolina crown mold with apricot sauce," she said. "I must have given the recipe away a hundred times."

Mme. Chevallier-Crochet wondered if she could have a slice half the size of the wedge Abelarda had already prepared. Abelarda put down the bowl of cream and divided the wedge in half. The half piece was still too much; Abelarda said it could not be cut again without breaking into a mess of crumbs. M. Chevallier-Crochet said to his wife, "For God's sake, just take it and leave what you can't eat." Mme. Chevallier-Crochet replied that everything she said and did seemed to be wrong, she had better just sit here and say and do nothing. Abelarda, crooning encouragement, pushed onto her plate a fragment of pastry and one plum.

"No cream," she said, too late.

Mme. Brouet looked at the portrait of her husband's grandfather, then at her son, perhaps seeking a likeness. Sophie Chevallier-Crochet had seemed lively and intelligent at their history-of-art class. Mme. Brouet had never met the husband before, and was unlikely ever to lay eyes on him again. She accepted large portions of tart and cream, to set an example, in case the other two ladies had inhibited the men.

M. Turbin, after having made certain that no extra sugar had been stirred into the cream, took more cream than tart. His wife, watching him closely, sipped water over her empty plate. "It's only fruit," he said.

The magistrate helped himself to all the crumbs and fragments of burnt sugar on the dish. He rattled the spoon in the bowl of cream, scraping the sides; there was nearly none left. It was the fault of M. Chevallier-Crochet, who had gone on filling his plate, as though in a dream, until Abelarda moved the bowl away.

The guests finished drinking their coffee at half past four, and left at a quarter to five. When they had gone, Mme. Brouet lay down—not on a couch or a settee but on the living-room floor. She stared at the ceiling and told Pascal to leave her alone. Abelarda, Dédé, and the magistrate were up in Dédé's room. Abelarda helped him pack. Late that night, the magistrate drove him to the Gare de l'Est.

Dédé came back to Paris about a year ago. He is said to be different now. He has a part-time job with a television polling service: every day he is given a list of telephone numbers in the Paris area and he calls them to see what people were watching the night before and which program they wish they had watched instead. His mother has bought him a one-room place overlooking Parc de Montsouris. The Brouets have never tried to get in touch with him or invited him to a meal. Dédé's Paris—unknown, foreign almost—lies at an unmapped distance from Pascal's house.

One night, not long ago, when they all three were having dinner, Pascal said, "What if Dédé just came to the door?" He meant the front door, of course, but his parents glanced at the glass doors and the lamps reflected in the dark panes, so that night was screened from sight. Pascal imagined Dédé standing outside, watching and smiling, with that great mop of hair.

He is almost as tall as Dédé, now. Perhaps his father had not really taken notice of his height—it came about so gradually—but when Pascal got up to draw a curtain across the doors that night at dinner, his father looked at him as if he were suddenly setting a value on the kind of man he might become. It was a steady look, neither hot nor cold. For a moment Pascal said to himself, He will never fall asleep again. As for his mother, she sat smiling and dreaming, still hoping for some reason to start loving Dédé once more.

THE ASSEMBLY

M. ALEXANDRE CAISSE, civil servant, employed at the Ministry of Agriculture, bachelor, thanked the seven persons sitting in his living room for having responded to his mimeographed invitation. Actually, he had set chairs out for fifteen.

General Portoret, ret., widower, said half the tenants of the building had already left for their summer holiday.

Mme. Berthe Fourneau, widow, no profession, said Parisians spent more time on vacation than at work. She could remember when two weeks in Brittany seemed quite enough.

M. Louis Labarrière, author and historian, wife taking the cure at Vichy, said that during the Middle Ages Paris had celebrated 230 religious holidays a year.

M. Alberto Minazzoli, industrialist, wife thought to be living in Rome with an actor, said that in his factories strikes had replaced religious feasts. (All smiled.)

Dr. Edmond Volle, dental surgeon, married, said he had not taken a day off in seven years.

Mme. Volle said she believed a wife should never forsake her husband. As a result, she never had a holiday either.

Mlle. de Renard's aunt said it depended on the husband. Some could be left alone for months on end. Others could not. (No one knew Mlle. de Renard's aunt's name.)

M. Alexandre Caisse said they had all been sorry to hear Mlle. de Renard was not feeling well enough to join them.

Mlle. de Renard's aunt said her niece was at this moment under sedation, in a shuttered room, with cotton stuffed in her ears. The slightest sound made her jump and scream with fright.

General Portoret said he was sure a brave woman like Mlle. de Renard would soon be on her feet again.

Mme. Berthe Fourneau said it was probably not easy to forget after one had been intimately molested by a stranger.

Mlle. de Renard's aunt said her niece had been molested, but not raped. There was an unpleasant story going around.

M. Labarrière had heard screaming, but had supposed it was someone's radio.

M. Minazzoli had heard the man running down five flights of stairs. He thought it was a child playing tag.

Mme. Volle had been the first to arrive on the scene; she had found Mlle. de Renard, collapsed, on the fifth-floor landing, her purse lying beside her. The man had not been after money. The stranger, described by his victim as French, fair, and blue-eyed, had obviously crept in from the street and waited for Mlle. de Renard to come home from vesper service.

General Portoret wondered why Mlle. de Renard had not run away the minute she saw him.

Mlle. de Renard's aunt said her niece had been taken by surprise. The man looked respectable. His expression was sympathetic. She thought he had come to the wrong floor.

Mme. Berthe Fourneau said the man must have known his victim's habits.

Dr. Volle said it was simply the cunning of the insane.

M. Labarrière reminded them that the assault of Mlle. de Renard had been the third in a series: there had been the pots of ivy pilfered from the courtyard, the tramp found asleep in the basement behind the hot-water boiler, and now this.

Mme. Berthe Fourneau said no one was safe.

Mme. Volle had a chain-bolt on her door. She kept a can of insect spray conveniently placed for counteraggression.

M. Alexandre Caisse had a bronze reproduction of *The Dying Gaul* on a table behind the door. He never answered the door without first getting a good grip around the statue's waist.

Mlle. de Renard's aunt said her niece had been too trusting, even as a child.

M. Minazzoli said his door was fully armored. However, the time had come to do something about the door at the entrance to the building. He hoped they would decide, now, once and for all, about putting in an electronic code-lock system.

M. Alexandre Caisse said they were here to discuss, not to decide. The law of July 10, 1965, regulating the administration of cooperatively owned multiple dwellings, was especially strict on the subject of meetings. This was an assembly.

M. Minazzoli said one could arrive at a decision at an assembly as well as at a meeting.

M. Alexandre Caisse said anyone could get the full text of the law from the building manager, now enjoying a photo safari in Kenya. (Having said this, M. Caisse closed his eyes.)

Mlle. de Renard's aunt said she wanted one matter cleared up, and only one: her niece had been molested. She had not been raped.

Mme. Berthe Fourneau wondered how much Mlle. de Renard could actually recall.

Mlle. de Renard's aunt said her niece had given a coherent account from the beginning, an account from which she had never wavered. The man had thrown her against the wall and perpetrated something she called "an embrace." Her handbag had fallen during the struggle. He had run away without stopping to pick it up.

Dr. Volle said it proved the building was open to madmen.

M. Alexandre Caisse asked if anyone would like refreshments. He could offer the ladies a choice of tonic water or bottled lemon soda. The gentlemen might like something stronger. (All thanked him, but refused.)

M. Minazzoli supposed everyone knew how the electronic code system worked and what it would cost.

Mme. Berthe Fourneau asked if it would keep peddlers out. The place was infested with them. Some offered exotic soaps, others ivory trinkets. The peddlers had one thing in common—curly black hair.

M. Labarrière said the tide of color was rising in Paris. He wondered if anyone had noticed it in the Métro. Even in the first-class section you could count the white faces on one hand.

Mme. Volle said it showed the kind of money being made, and by whom.

Black, brown, and yellow, said M. Labarrière. He felt like a stranger in his own country.

Dr. Volle said France was now a doormat for the riffraff of five continents.

M. Alexandre Caisse said the first thing foreigners did was find out how much they could get for free. Then they sent for their families.

General Portoret had been told by a nurse that the hospitals were crammed with Africans and Arabs getting free operations. If you had the bad luck to be white and French you could sit in the waiting room while your appendix burst.

M. Minazzoli said he had flown his mother to Paris for a serious operation. He had paid every centime himself. His mother had needed to have all her adrenaline taken out.

Mme. Volle said when something like that happened there was no such thing as French or foreign—there was just grief and expense.

M. Alexandre Caisse said it was unlikely that a relative of M. Minazzoli would burden the taxpaying community. M. Minazzoli probably knew something about paying taxes, when it came to that. (All laughed gently.)

Mlle. de Renard's aunt said all foreigners were not alike.

General Portoret had commanded a regiment of Montagnards forty years before. They had been spunky little chaps, loyal to France.

M. Labarrière could not understand why Mlle. de Renard had said her attacker was blue-eyed and fair. Most molested women spoke of "the Mediterranean type."

General Portoret wondered if his Montagnards had kept up their French culture. They had enjoyed the marching songs, swinging along happily to "Sambre et Meuse."

M. Minazzoli said in case anyone did not understand the code-lock system, it was something like a small oblong keyboard. This keyboard, affixed to the entrance of the building just below the buzzer one pressed in order to release the door catch, contained the house code.

Mme. Berthe Fourneau asked how the postman was supposed to get in.

M. Labarrière knew it was old-fashioned of him, but he thought a house phone would be better. It was somehow more dignified than all these codes and keyboards.

M. Minazzoli said the code system was cheaper and very safe. The door could not be opened unless the caller knew what the code was, say, J-8264.

Mme. Berthe Fourneau hoped for something easier to remember—something like A-1111.

M. Labarrière said the Montagnards had undoubtedly lost all trace of French culture. French culture was dying everywhere. By 2500 it would be extinct.

M. Minazzoli said the Lycée Chateaubriand was still flourishing in Rome, attended by sons and daughters of the nobility.

Mme. Volle had been told that the Lycée Français in London accepted just anyone now.

Mme. Berthe Fourneau's daughter had spent an anxious *au pair* season with an English family in the 1950s. They had the curious habit of taking showers together to save hot water.

M. Alexandre Caisse said the hot-water meters in the building needed to be checked. His share of costs last year had been enough to cover all the laundry in Paris.

Mme. Berthe Fourneau said a washing machine just above her living room made a rocking sound.

Mme. Volle never ran the machine before nine or after five.

Mme. Berthe Fourneau had been prevented at nine o'clock at night from hearing the President of the Republic's television interview about the domestic fuel shortage.

M. Minazzoli said he hoped all understood that the security code was not to be mislaid or left around or shared except with a trusted person. No one knew nowadays who might turn out to be a thief. Not one's friends, certainly, but one knew so little about their children.

Mlle. de Renard's aunt wondered if anyone recalled the old days, when the concierge stayed in her quarters night and day like a watchdog. It had been better than a code.

M. Labarrière could remember how when one came in late at night one would call out one's name.

General Portoret, as a young man—a young lieutenant, actually—had given his name as "Jack the Ripper." The concierge had made a droll reply.

M. Alexandre Caisse believed people laughed more easily then.

General Portoret said that the next day the concierge had complained to his mother.

Dr. Volle envied General Portoret's generation. Their pleasures had been of a simple nature. They had not required today's thrills and animation.

M. Labarrière knew he was being old-fashioned, but he did object to the modern inaccurate use of animation. Publications from the mayor's office spoke of "animating" the city.

M. Minazzoli could not help asking himself who was paying for these glossy full-color handouts.

Dr. Volle thought the mayor was doing a good job. He particularly enjoyed the fireworks. As he never took a holiday the fireworks were about all he had by way of entertainment.

M. Labarrière could recall when the statue of the lion in the middle of Place Denfert-Rochereau had been painted the wrong shade. Everyone had protested.

Mlle. de Renard's aunt had seen it—brilliant iridescent coppery paint.

M. Labarrière said no, a dull brown.

Dr. Volle said that had been under a different administration.

General Portoret's mother had cried when she was told that he had said "Jack the Ripper."

Mlle. de Renard's aunt did not understand why the cost of the electronic code system was to be shared out equally. Large families were more likely to wear out the buttons than a lady living alone.

M. Alexandre Caisse said this was an assembly, not a meeting. They were all waiting for the building manager to return from Kenya. The first thing M. Caisse intended to have taken up was the cost of hot water.

Mlle. de Renard's aunt reminded M. Caisse that it was her grandfather, founder of a large Right Bank department store, who had built this house in 1899.

M. Labarrière said there had been a seventeenth-century convent on the site. Tearing it down in 1899 had been an act of vandalism that would not be tolerated today.

General Portoret's parents had been among the first tenants. When he was a boy there had been a great flood of water in the basement. When the waters abated the graves of nuns were revealed.

Mlle. de Renard's aunt said she often wished she were a nun. Peace was all she wanted. (She looked around threateningly as she said this.)

General Portoret said the bones had been put in large canvas bags and stored in the concierge's kitchen until a hallowed resting place could be found.

M. Labarrière said it was hard not to yearn for the past they were describing. That was because he had no feeling for the future. The final French catastrophe would be about 2080.

General Portoret said he hoped that the last Frenchman to die would not die in vain.

M. Alexandre Caisse looked at his watch and said he imagined no one wanted to miss the film on the Third Channel, an early Fernandel.

General Portoret asked if it was the one where Fernandel was a private who kept doing all the wrong things.

Mme. Volle wondered if her husband's patients would let him get away for a few days this year. There was always someone to break a front tooth at the last moment.

General Portoret was going to Montreux. He had been going to the same *pension* for twelve years, ever since his wife died.

M. Alexandre Caisse said the film would be starting in six minutes. It was not the one about the army; it was the one where Fernandel played a ladies' hairdresser.

Mlle. de Renard's aunt planned to take her niece on a cruise to Egypt when she felt strong enough.

Mme. Berthe Fourneau and her daughter were traveling to Poland in the footsteps of the Pope.

M. Labarrière knew it was dull and old-fashioned of him, but he loved his country and refused to spend any money outside France.

M. Minazzoli was taking a close friend to Greece and Yugoslavia. He believed in Europe.

M. Alexandre Caisse said sometimes it was hard to get a clear image on the Third Channel. He hoped there would be no interference with the Fernandel, which must be just about starting.

Dr. Volle said he was not likely to see that or any other film. He went to bed every night before ten. He rose every morning before six.

M. Alexandre Caisse said he thought they would all be quite safe if they left, now, together, in a group. (He held the door open.)

Mlle. de Renard's aunt said she thought the assembly had been useful. Her niece would feel reassured.

Mme. Berthe Fourneau said perhaps she would no longer feel impelled to open and close her bedroom shutters the whole time.

Mlle. de Renard's aunt said her niece slept all day.

Mme. Berthe Fourneau said yes, but not all night.

General Portoret said, After you.

M. Labarrière said, Ladies first.

(All said goodbye.)

APPENDIX

Three Early Stories

GOOD MORNING AND GOODBYE

HE OPENED his eyes that morning, and remembered first that he was sad, and then why. He turned his head on the pillow and saw the sun and the green leaves at the window, and the transparent shadow of one leaf above another. The trees moved in the wind and the shadow moved to the edge of the leaf and back again.

He lay there and looked at the leaves and the crooked pieces of blue between them and thought, *I, Paul, am going away again*. He had changed his name to Paul because the other sounded too German, and every morning for a long time he had said, "I, Paul, today will do thus and so." In this way he had become one with the name. It had finally divided him into two separate people: one here, and one almost lost, on the other side of an ocean.

He could hear the hum and clatter of Sunday morning breakfast downstairs, and the drone of the radio, and the rattle of voices. Always, in this house, the voices. He got up quickly and stood on the bumpy hooked rug. Mrs. Trennan had packed everything except the clothes he needed to wear that day, on the train. One day he had overheard her telling someone that he had no initiative and never did anything for himself. *I would if she would let me*, he thought, and was angry because she had packed his clothes. Then he remembered that there was no need to be angry anymore. He thought of his first months in this house, and of how his shyness had been a physical agony. He would catch his breath and tremble if he dropped a book on the floor, or ran the bath water too loudly. Now he knew that these things were not important to the Trennans. Not half as important as the ability to express oneself in words, loudly and often.

It talked, this family. Even when the house was empty, the rooms were articulate. There was always some piece of unfinished business in each room, some thing half done, that said the family would be back soon to attend to it. They said everything and kept nothing back. They scraped the day of its doing every night at the dinner table. At breakfast, they discussed their dreams and each told how he had slept. Every headache, each anger, every reaction, was broken down into words and phrases and exclamations.

In the beginning, Paul understood nothing. He could say yes and no, please and thank you. They talked to him and at him and about him, but all he could do for answers was smile. Twice, he had tried to speak of himself. The first time was the most important. He told them that he had changed his name. "Paul, now," he said. It had taken all his strength and courage. Then he had spoken once more because he wanted to share and explain a great burden that was so overwhelmingly his own. He showed them his passport. There was a large red "J" stamped on each page.

"This is in my life, a certain thing..." he began, and then the groped-for clumsy English words receded again, and he faltered. It was because he could see they thought he was ashamed of it, and he did not know how to go on. The family stopped what it was doing and listened, but there was a tension in the listening that confused him, because they wanted to hurry on to something else, and so he could not speak. Gradually, he sank into a well of silence, understanding little, saying nothing, eating stiffly, moving awkwardly from room to room.

These were the people who had done everything for him. They had helped him cross the ocean. They had sent him to school. Now that that was finished, they had written to people, and the sum of their writing was the list of addresses in his wallet. Someone to see about a job. Someone to see about a room. Somehow, fumblingly, he had fitted into their pattern and it had grown around him. Now he must change again.

He had learned in his life of many changes never to say, "This is the last time I walk down these stairs to breakfast" or "This is the last time I say good morning." But it was there, the sense of ending, and the slipping into the vacuum that lies between the patterns in a life.

Everyone was considerate that morning. The boys grinned, and even attempted a little casual horseplay. The girl realized suddenly that he was leaving, and that he was, after all, male, and not a brother. She poured his coffee and wished he were more attractive. Mr. Trennan, wearing a sweater because it was Sunday, said something forced and jovial. Paul looked at Mrs. Trennan and they both smiled. She had never made the futile attempt to cross the gap between them, but they accepted each other in a way that needed no explaining. He knew that he would think of her often.

Mr. Trennan said, "Bags all packed?" And Paul nodded. He saw that the car was already backed out of the garage into the driveway.

"We'll all go to the station," the girl said, but Mrs. Trennan said quickly, "No, just Father and myself."

The boys carried his suitcases out to the car, and he could hear their voices and the thick slam of the car door. Mrs. Trennan had the keys in her hand, and there was an envelope for Paul "in case there's no time at the station, or in case I should forget." He felt, again, the choked embarrassment of acceptance with thanks. Then he said goodbye and shook hands with the boys, who had never tried to like him, and he shook hands with the girl, who was just becoming aware of him. They wished him luck, and then came and stood in the driveway to watch the car start, and he had to keep smiling out the window at them. Then the car started and they turned out of the driveway onto the road, and he waved, and they waved, and everyone was relieved.

Mr. Trennan was driving and smoking at the same time. The ashes from his cigarette blew past the window of the back seat, where Paul was looking out. Mrs. Trennan turned sideways in the front so that she could talk to him.

"The city is really exciting, and you won't be lonesome once you get settled. You can come up for weekends, and we'll come down and see you."

Paul knew that he would never come back, and she knew it too. Then why did she bother saying things? Even in his final association with this family he must be made aware of their waste of words.

Mrs. Trennan waved to someone as the car pulled into the station yard. It turned out to be Mrs. Jackson, and another woman. She said hello to Paul, and "Well, you're finally off to the big city." And to the

Trennans "Guess you're sorry to lose your big boy." She went on again, quickly, because everyone looked so embarrassed. "They say it's hot in town." She indicated her guest, who was wearing high heels and a white hat and dress. After that no one said anything.

Then they heard the train coming around the bend, and they could see the smoke. Mrs. Trennan said, "Wait a minute, Mrs. Jackson, we'll drop you off on the way home." For the Trennans, it was still possible to interlock events. The train ran in front of them, loudly and dustily. They said goodbye, goodbye, take care of yourself, write and let us know. Mrs. Trennan suddenly looked frightened. Paul was climbing the steps and carrying his bags and indicating a confused farewell. He was the only passenger at that station.

He almost fell when the train started. He scrambled his bags into a seat and took a long time getting organized for the journey, so that he would not see the Trennans in case they were still on the station platform, waving.

When the hills and houses grew unfamiliar and finally completely strange, he knew that he was free. He found himself thinking in English and was surprised. He noticed, then, that for the first time in two years, he was not braced against the sound of a voice, speaking to him and expecting an answer. He noticed something else, too, and smiled. The only words he had spoken aloud that day since waking were good morning and goodbye.

THREE BRICK WALLS

THE BOY was a stranger in the city, and his room faced a brick wall. There was a narrow street between the window and the wall, and a lamp post, and a small twisted tree.

It was his first night in the room. The key to the front door lay slantwise on the bureau, but he was not yet aware that it belonged to him and could be used. The paper on the wall was blurred and brown. There was a single bed with a green-and-white striped seersucker bedspread, and a chair wedged between the foot of the bed and the window. The bureau was painted green. The drawers were lined with brown paper and there were crumbs in the corners under the paper. The boy, Paul, had some money in an envelope and more money folded in his wallet. Part of it was supposed to be emergency money, to be set aside, but he carried both packets. Had it been possible, he would have carried everything he owned. He loved whatever was his. He had given the Irish lady downstairs four dollars and fifty cents for the room, and he felt very proud and free, and conscious that the room belonged to him. He took the envelope out again and looked at it. He could do anything. He could go to a restaurant. He could go to the movies. He was free. He was absolutely completely unrestrained and free. He took the key from the bureau and went out the door, down the steps, into the street.

It was half past six, a gray evening in a gray city. The street was no longer than one block and bounded on three sides by brick. Beyond the walls, you could sense the life and movement of the rest of the neighborhood. You could hear trolleys and taxis, and see a haze of smoke, and a reflection of light. On this street, there were no children. The people who poked repetitive keys into the doorways and climbed the stairs inside were those who have nothing of themselves outside lying around loose. They went downtown to work in the morning and ate their meals at tile counters. Sometimes they went to the movies. Sometimes they came in early and lay across their beds, smoking and staring at the ceiling. They had names, but they were no one.

The boy, Paul, felt the anonymity of the street, but felt secure because of it. The three brick walls stood for shelter.

He turned the corner and walked across to where there were lights and sound. There was a lunchroom across the street, with apples and oranges stacked in pyramids in the window, and colored posters advertising soft drinks. One sign said MILKSHAKES, ALL FLAVORS. Another listed different kinds of sandwiches with their prices. He went inside, where it was dark and the smell was moist, of milk and water. The man at the soda fountain was reading a newspaper. There was a ring of dark hair around the back of his head, ending in two little tufts, like rosettes behind the ears. The top of the head was bare and shiny. Paul felt silly and awkward, walking across the long stretch of restaurant, past the empty booths with the man watching his approach. Finally they stood facing each other, and the man didn't smile, but stood with his hands spread on the newspaper across the counter. Paul had thought vaguely and pleasantly of eating good things, sweet things, the sorts of things one didn't get at home.

Instead, he found himself reading the signs above the rows of coca-cola bottles and overcome with the same desperate tension he felt when people were waiting for him to say something, and all he could think was *I know what I mean but can't say it.* He had developed within himself a mechanical system of questioning and answering, the questions terse and the answers formal.

Is this important enough to say aloud?
No, nothing I think is important.
Then let us say no more about it.

The man said, "Sandwiches, peanut butter, Western, tomato. No ice cream. No ice cream till the first of the month."

"Tomato," he said—and knew he didn't want it.

The man nodded and put two slices of grayish bread side by side.

He covered the middle of one with butter and sliced half a tomato thickly on the other. Then he scooped some mayonnaise into a small oiled paper dish, put it all together on a plate, and pushed it across to Paul. He turned back to his newspaper, and looked up long enough to say, "Anything to drink? Tea?"

After Paul had said yes, he began to question himself again.

Why did I say I wanted it?

Because the man suggested it. If he had not mentioned it I could have refused, and finished the sandwich, and left.

It is not important. I am still free.

Yes, I am still free.

The man groped under the counter and pulled out a thick white cup and saucer. He put a tea bag attached to a string in the cup, and holding the string on the edge with his finger, filled the cup with hot water. He said, "That'll be thirty cents."

He took the two coins from the counter and did not look up again, not even as Paul slid down from the round stool and walked away.

The boy moved down the street, aimlessly. He thought of the man in the restaurant and felt a great fear that very soon he would discover that the city was composed of groups and units, and that he would be forced to make a contact with them. He wanted to be part of a crowd. He would be forced to speak, and worse, to listen. He would not lose himself. He would not be free.

He stopped in front of a theater, which was set back somewhat from the line of the street. The entrance was wide and bright, and the ticket office was squarely in the center. It looked very open and very vulnerable.

He thought of how satisfactory it would be if the ticket office were to one side, and there were great crowds of people, coming from one direction only, and of how easy it would be then to be part of something. Instead, there were two or three people looking at the display cards, one man shaking change out in his hand while the girl with him waited to one side, and a woman in a polo coat talking to the girl at the ticket office. This infuriated him, because people who sold tickets, and with whom he was forced to make a contact, should be inanimate and not flaunting their friends before him. "Contact" was a word he had learned at home. "You'll never get anywhere unless you make contacts." Always contacts, never friends.

He turned away and walked back to his street, to his room. Papers and dust blew up from the gutters. *If people see me hurrying along alone*, he thought, "they will think it is to escape the rain." When he turned the corner and saw the house he lived in, he almost ran. Just as he closed the door of his room, the rain began to fall against the window. He bent his arms and leaned on the shutters, trembling with a sweet loneliness which required no people. The slow rain passed like a curtain through the arc of the street lamp, and the street was dark and wet. Beyond the walls, there was the city, and from the ledge of the window, he could slide back to the thought that it was a mass of people, a safe mass, without form.

He pressed his forehead against the damp glass, and felt himself falling into sleep.

Whatever happens, he thought, *I am still free.*

Yes, I am still free.

A WONDERFUL COUNTRY

I CALLED him the Hungarian because I couldn't pronounce his name. If he had a name for me, I never heard it. We weren't what you'd call chummy.

It was early in the war then, when there were still houses to rent, and apartment hunters who could afford to be choosy. I was junior assistant in a real estate office, making next to nothing and chasing every cent. That was how we met.

If it had been any other way, we might have become friends because we were both so lonely in Montreal. But as it was, he needed a furnished house, and I needed the commission, so I never bothered to ask if he liked Canada or anything else. I just waved street maps and leases and talked fast.

He didn't know very much about this side of the world and I was too busy to help him. He lived alone in a hotel, waiting for his family and seldom going even to the Hungarian club. All he could say was "Yess?" or "Please?" or "No, no, no," all of which meant "I don't understand."

It was hot that summer. I rang sticky doorbells and talked to cross, perspiring people all over the city trying to find a Hungarian a house. It had to be furnished. It had to have a yard, and a nice room for his little girl. I'd like to see him try that these days. Even then, with places available, it wasn't easy.

Then a phone call came in one afternoon with something that sounded just about right. I didn't put it on the office list. I just picked him up at his hotel and started explaining in a taxi.

"It's suburban," I said, trying to make it sound all right. "A little far, a little quiet. Not too original, but good for the children."

He smiled amiably.

579

"I wouldn't want it for myself," I said impetuously, then stopped at once. "You'll like it," I went on firmly. "And besides they're leaving all the linen and dishes for you."

"Yess?" he said.

As I said before, we had few conversations. Talking to him was like being lost in the bush. You could either sit down and give up, or just keep stumbling ahead hoping to come to something familiar.

"Linen," I repeated. "Towels, blankets, sheets. Pillow cases, bath mats, table cloths. Glasses, cups, soup plates."

"Please," he said.

I gave up.

The taxi stopped in front of a small brick duplex on one of those semi-suburban streets. There was a small lawn, yellow from the August sun, and a bicycle leaning against the porch. All the shades were down, as though the tenants had left for the summer. The street was still and flat, edged with telephone poles.

I turned and said quickly, "After all, it's the inside that matters," but he was smiling, and bending his smooth gray head toward the window.

"So," he said with a certain finality, and marched up the cement walk. The couple who answered the door were alike as two pink junkets. The woman looked a bit sharper, as I remember her now, and rather sick. Her husband, whom she called Frank, was taller, but with the same pale eyes and thin fair hair. They didn't look at each other. Sometimes, by accident, their glances crossed, and it was like two express trains passing at full speed.

She did all the talking. Once in a while she would turn to him with a quick "Isn't that right Frank," then pick up the conversation again before he could answer.

She had made duplicate lists of every item in the house, she told us, and wanted them all checked. My Hungarian went on smiling, and sometimes made small chirping sounds under the current of her words. Frank looked bored and sleepy.

I just stared at the brown wall paper and wondered if she wore hair nets to bed and hoover aprons in the morning. It was all beyond me. I couldn't imagine why she was moving out or why he was moving in. I didn't know any of them.

"I suppose you want to look the place over," she finally offered.

"No," said the Hungarian. "No, no, no."

"Come on," I said impatiently. "He'll stand there all day saying that. He doesn't know what you're talking about. Show him the living room."

The woman looked a little amused and turned her shrewd small face to a curtained arch.

"In there," she said.

We moved past her and plunged at once into a lifeless room so like a convent that I expected to hear a bell or see a plaster saint in one corner. You could smell wax and lemon oil and sense a faint layer of dust. But you couldn't see very much because the air was dark green, from years of being strained through window shades.

It was ugly. I remember, out of that clutter of plush and seashells only one beautiful object: something made of tortoiseshell, like a piece of fair freckled skin.

The woman circled the room, droning the items from her list and touching each thing as she mentioned it.

"One large radio," she read. "One radio lamp. One lace cover on radio. One small mat under radio. One squirrel on swing."

She hadn't gone mad. The squirrel was two inches high and made of felt. He had probably come from a sale at the IODE. His place was on the radio, and as far as she was concerned, he was going to stay there, no matter who took over the house.

That was the astounding part of it. Not only had she taken the trouble to collect the room's ugly contents, but she had confirmed their existence by writing them in a list, one under the other. Now she was double-checking their identity by taking us on a tour and pointing out each plaque and dolly as if it were a museum piece.

The Hungarian looked a little puzzled, but his smile was amiable as ever. I wished for the first time that I had made more effort to know him. The four of us were so disorganized in that room, it would have been nice to have felt some unity.

The dining room took less time to examine. The woman ticked off the furniture quickly and was starting in on the china cabinet when I cut in with:

"Let's look at the kitchen."

I felt that I couldn't bear twenty minutes of "One china girl holding vinegar bottle, one small mustard pot marked Brantford, Ont."

There ought to be a law against people who paint their kitchens buff, and have strange gray cloths hanging from the pipes under the sink. It isn't that the kitchens aren't clean. It's just that all you can imagine coming out of them are puddings and cold cuts. But the kitchen was the last room in the house, so I smiled reassuringly at the Hungarian.

He was watching the woman as she opened a drawer in the table and emptied it on the enamel top.

"One paring knife," she began. "One egg beater."

The Hungarian picked up the egg beater. He twirled the handle.

"What," he announced.

"Eggs," I said. "You beat them, see, like this."

Frank looked a bit indignant, but his wife actually broke an egg into a bowl and showed how it was done. The Hungarian loved it. He was particularly enchanted with the little top which fitted around the beater so it wouldn't splash. He beat the egg into a great lemon froth. Then lovingly and reluctantly, he put the bowl down.

"Madam," he said. "What a wonderful country."

It was the longest English sentence I had ever heard him speak. His cadence was that of child's sing-songing, something like "BEES are there, BIRDS are there, BUTterflies, IN the air..."

The woman stopped reading from her list and just watched him. His enthusiasm was wonderful. He exclaimed over everything, the string-bean cutter, the cherry pitter, the breadknife with the measuring gadget, even the dish strainer.

I couldn't believe he had never seen these things before. I thought he had come to life in this room because, bleak as it was, it was the only living part of the house. It was here that you could sense the thousands of oranges cut for breakfast, the hundreds of dish towels put to soak, the stacks of empty cereal boxes, the rubbers and overshoes draining by the back door, the toast crumbs, the coffee grounds, the potato peels, the shreds of pie crust. Nowhere else was there debris of living, or any explanation for the couple's years together.

But I was wrong. When the Hungarian spent ten minutes playing with the automatic foot pedal on the garbage can, I knew it was all genuine. For the first time, I saw the couple exchange a direct look. They thought he was foreign and ridiculous, and it was in his strangeness that they could find something in common.

"He's worth ten of them," I thought, though I scarcely knew him better. It was just that it annoyed me to see them standing in the doorway together, looking smug and secure.

"Let's look at the linen," I said, "and leave him here. He's perfectly happy."

The woman looked at her husband once more, and led the way to a cupboard in the hall.

"You'll find it all here, I think," she said vaguely, then turned and said so low I could hardly hear, "I'm going into the hospital and my husband's taking a furnished room. My little girl has gone to Toronto to stay with my mother. Fifty-fifty chance."

It was a moment or two before I realized what she meant.

"Fifty-fifty," I repeated stupidly, then realized she meant her chances in the hospital. I said something idiotic like "Oh, you'll be all right," but she was back counting the linen again.

I wanted to shake her. It was like my neighbor whose son was killed at sea saying, "I suppose you heard about the laddie," then rushing on to some inanity about gas rationing. "If you feel awful," I wondered, "why don't you scream and cry?" But there was no point to saying it.

When we went back to the kitchen, I tried to let the Hungarian know that the people weren't bad, that they were in as much of a spot as he was. But I knew this was no time to start explaining them to him, or him to them. The interplay was all their own and I had better leave them to it.

We turned down the hall together and the woman held the front door open for us. I couldn't look at her. Just as we were starting down the steps, he turned suddenly and caught her hand.

"Madam," he said earnestly, "believe me, a wonderful country."

"Well," she said without expression. "I guess you could call it that."

We didn't hear the door slam till we were half way down the walk. He was still chattering to himself about the wonderful country. I have often wondered how long the egg beater kept him happy.

SOURCES

Banks, Russell. "Introduction." *Varieties of Exile*. New York: NYRB Classics, 2003. vii–xiii.

Besner, Neil Kalman. "Mavis Gallant's Short Fiction: History and Memory in the Light of Imagination." Diss. U of British Columbia, 1983.

Boyce, Pleuke. "Image and Memory." *Books in Canada*. Jan/Feb. 1990: 29–31.

Bureau, Stéphan. "An Interview with Mavis Gallant." Trans. Wyley Powell. *The New Brick Reader*. Toronto: Anansi, 2013. 208–233.

Chambrun, Jacques. Editorial correspondence, 1951–1952. *The New Yorker* Records. New York Public Library.

Coe, Jonathan. "The Life of Henri Grippes." *London Review of Books*. Sept. 18, 1997: 13.

The Complete New Yorker. DVD-ROM. New York: The New Yorker, 2005.

Dvorak, Marta. "When Language Is a Delicate Timepiece: Mavis Gallant in Conversation with Marta Dvorak." *Journal of Commonwealth Literature*. Vol. 44, Issue 3 (2009): 3–22.

Evian, Christine. *Douglas Gibson Unedited*. Brussels: Peter Lang, 2007.

Fabre, Michel. "An Interview with Mavis Gallant." *Commonwealth* (Dijon). Vol. 11, Issue 2 (Spring 1989): 95-103.

"The Four Seasons of Mavis Gallant." *Ideas*. Prod. Megan Williams. CBC radio. Feb. 15, 2012.

Gallant, Mavis. "The Art of Fiction No. 160." [Interview with Daphne Kaloty]. *The Paris Review*. Issue 153 (Winter 1999): 192–211.

——— "Between Zero and One." *Home Truths*. Toronto: McClelland & Stewart, 2001. 273–298.

——— "Bonaventure." Ibid.: 156–198

———"Dédé." *The New Yorker.* January 5, 1987: 28–34.

———"Diary." *Slate.* Aug. 12, 1997. Accessed at <slate.com/human-interest/1997/08/mavis-gallant-6.html>

———"The Doctor." *Home Truths* (2001): 338–362.

———Editorial correspondence, 1949–1984. *The New Yorker* Records, ca. 1924–1984. New York Public Library.

———"The Flowers of Spring." *Northern Review,* June-July 1950, 31–39.

———"The Hunger Diaries." *The New Yorker.* July 9 & 16, 2012. Accessed at <www.newyorker.com/magazine/2012/07/09/the-hunger-diaries>

———"Introduction." *Home Truths.* Toronto: Macmillan, 1982. xi–xxii.

———"In Youth Is Pleasure." *Home Truths* (2001): 251–272.

———"Its Image on the Mirror." *My Heart is Broken.* New York: Penguin, 1991: 100–155.

———"The Life of the Writer." Reprinted in *A Writer's Life: The Margaret Laurence Lectures.* Tortonto: McClelland & Stewart, 2011. 23–51.

———"The Old Place." *The Texas Quarterly.* Spring 1958: 66–80.

———"Paris Diary (1992)." *The New Yorker.* December 24 & 31, 2001. 102–103

———*Paris Notebooks: Essays & Reviews.* Boston: Godine, 2023.

———"Preface." *The Collected Stories of Mavis Gallant.* New York: Random House, 1996. ix–xix

———"Sartre Tells of Philosophy on Visit Here." *The Standard,* March 16, 1946.

———"Thank You for the Lovely Tea." *Home Truths* (2001): 3–19.

———"Varieties of Exile." Ibid.: 299–322.

———"Voices Lost in Snow." Ibid.: 323–337.

———"With a Capital T." Ibid.: 363–378.

Gallant, Mavis and Jhumpa Lahiri. "Useless Chaos Is What Fiction Is About." *Granta* 106 (2009): 102–155.

Gibson, Douglas. "Editor's Note." *Going Ashore.* Mavis Gallant. Toronto: McClelland & Stewart, 2009. xv–xvi.

Hancock, Geoff. "Interview with Mavis Gallant." *Canadian Writers at Work: Interviews with Geoff Hancock.* Toronto: Oxford U.P., 1987. 79–126. [originally in *Canadian Fiction Magazine,* 1978.]

Harriott, Esther. "Mavis Gallant." *Writers and Age: Essays on and Interviews with Five Authors.* Jefferson, NC: McFarland & Company, 2015. 134–148.

Lahiri, Jhumpa. "Introduction." *The Cost of Living: Early and Uncollected Stories.* Mavis Gallant. New York: NYRB Classics, 2009. vii–xxii.

——"Mavis Gallant's Choice." *The New Yorker: Page-Turner* [blog.] Feb. 20, 2014. <www.newyorker.com/page-turner/mavis-gallants-choice>

Lawrence, Karen. "From the Other Paris: interview with Mavis Gallant." *Branching Out.* February/March 1976: 18–19.

Leith, Linda. "Remembering Montreal in the 1940s: A Conversation with Mavis Gallant." *Border/Lines* 13 (Fall 1988): 4–5.

Manera Sambuy, Livia. "I've Lived Very Freely." *The Paris Review Daily.* March 14, 2014. www.theparisreview.org/blog/2014/3/14/ive-lived-very-freely

Manguel, Alberto. "Introduction." *Going Ashore.* Mavis Gallant. Toronto: McClelland & Stewart, 2009. xi–xiv.

Martens, Debra. "Mavis Gallant." *So to Speak: Interviews with Contemporary Canadian Writers.* Montreal: Véhicule Press, 1987. 250–282.

Mount, Nick. *Arrival: The Story of CanLit.* Toronto: Anansi, 2017.

——"Nick Mount on Mavis Gallant." Rec. Innis Town Hall, University of Toronto, Sept. 25, 2017. Accessed at <youtube.com/watch?v=p-jFd4zYSDo>

Mulhallen, Karen. "A Sense of Human Folly: An Interview With Mavis Gallant." *Numéro Cinq.* Sept. 5, 2014. <numerocinqmagazine.com/2014/09/05/a-sense-of-human-folly-interview-with-mavis-gallant-karen-mulhallen/>

Ondaatje, Michael. "Introduction: A Handful of Small Shipwrecks." *Varieties of Exile.* New York: NYRB Classics, 2002. vii–xii.

The Paris Dispatch. Directed by Wes Anderson, performances by Frances McDormand, Timothée Chalmet, Bill Murray, and others, Searchlight Films, 2021.

"The Pilot Light: A Conversation Between Wes Anderson and Susan Morrison." *An Editor's Burial: Journals and Journalism from The*

New Yorker and Other Magazines. Ed. David Brendel. London: Pushkin Press, 2021. 7–24.

Prose, Francine. "Introduction." *The Collected Stories of Mavis Gallant.* New York: Everyman's Library, 2016. xi–xx.

Richler, Mordecai. "Afterword." *The Moslem Wife and Other Stories.* Mavis Gallant. Toronto: McClelland & Stewart, 1994. 247–252.

Royer, Jean. "Mavis Gallant." *Interviews to Literature.* Toronto: Guernica, 1996. 71–77. [originally in *Le Devoir*, May 21, 1983]

Samway, Patrick H. "An Interview with Mavis Gallant." *America.* June 13, 1987: 485–487.

Somacarrera Iñigo, Pilar. *Atlantis.* Vol. 22, Issue 1 (June 2000): 205–214.

Triesman, Deborah, host. "Ann Beattie Reads Mavis Gallant." *The New Yorker Fiction Podcast*, December 1, 2019. Accessed at <www.newyorker.com/podcast/fiction/ann-beattie-reads-mavis-gallant>

Twigg, Alan. "Mavis Gallant." *Strong Voices: Conversations with Fifty Canadian Authors.* Madeira Park, British Columbia: Harbour Publishing, 1988. 102–7.

Updike, John. "Imperishable Maxwell." *Higher Gossip.* New York: Knopf, 2011. 121–133.

Wachtel, Eleanor. "Mavis Gallant." *The Best of Writers & Co: Interviews with 15 of the World's Greatest Authors.* Windsor, Ont.: Biblioasis, 2016. 307–321.

Weintraub, William. *Getting Started: A Memoir of the 1950s.* Toronto: McClelland & Stewart, 2001.

Williams, Kathy. "Genesis of a Story: Mavis Gallant Describes the Creative Process Behind Her Award-winning Stories." *Aurora.* Issue 1988 (July 1, 1988). Accessed at <web.archive.org/web/20200713072742/http://aurora.icaap.org/index.php/aurora/article/view/48/61>

Yagoda, Ben, *About Town: The New Yorker and the World It Made.* Da Capo: 2000.

OTHER NEW YORK REVIEW CLASSICS

For a complete list of titles, visit www.nyrb.com.